THE ARMSTRONG TRILOGY

From the Heat of the Day
One Generation
Genetha

Roy Heath

Persea Books
New York

Persea Books, Inc.
60 Madison Avenue
New York, New York 10010

Library of Congress Cataloging-in-Publication Data

Heath, Roy A. K.
      The Armstrong trilogy / Roy Heath.
            p.   cm.
      Contents: From the heat of the day — One generation — Genetha.
      ISBN 0-89255-199-2 (pbk.) : $15.00
            1. Marriage—Guyana—Georgetown—Fiction.
      2. Family—Guyana—Georgetown—Fiction.
      3. Georgetown (Guyana)—Fiction. I. Title.
      PR9320.9.H4A89   1994
      813—dc20   93-46461

Manufactured in the United States of America
First Edition

Contents

From the Heat of the Day

For De W

I

Pain was in the wind
Before it descended
Into the heart.

1

The Courtship of Gladys

It was February 1922, the year Georgetown witnessed the rise of a brilliant young newspaper columnist writing under the name of Uncle Stapie.

"Georgetonians," he wrote in one Sunday article, "are of two kinds: those who live in Queenstown and their unfortunate neighbours who inhabit the remaining part of our garden city."

From that Sunday the circulation of *The Argosy* — Uncle Stapie's paper — shot up, while that of its rival *The Daily Chronicle* fell.

The Davis family lived in Queenstown, in a recently built cottage at the corner of Irving and Laluni Streets. And it was in that house that Armstrong courted Gladys, the youngest Davis daughter, for six months, during which time they never once went out alone. He came three nights a week to her there and she looked forward to his coming. Her two sisters made disparaging remarks about his manners and his dress, but Gladys explained to them that he was a bohemian who cared little for these things. He was writing a book which would make him famous and they would be able to boast that he used to visit their house. They laughed at her and begged her to remember them when they came as beggars to the door of the famous author. Gladys Davis, too refined to accuse her sisters of jealousy, wished ardently that they would like him; but if they could not she would take their sneers without reproach.

"I bet he used to run about naked-skin in a village when he was a boy," teased her elder sister mercilessly, "and he doesn't say 'stick', but 'jook'. Are you sure he can read? He's probably like the milkman, who puts his tongue out when he wants to write, and lifts one foot up on the chair."

Their laugher was like barbed wire drawn across her skin; and when he came the following night she asked him to copy for her a recipe from a magazine, while she went on with her crocheting. Vastly relieved to see that he did not put his tongue out or raise one foot on to the chair, Gladys took the sheet of paper to her sisters, triumphantly pointing out the fluent, attractive handrwriting of her intended. But to her disappointment the paper did not prove to be the vindication she had expected.

"Well, can you find one good thing about him?" asked Gladys. "Is he good-looking then? Well, tell me; is he?"

Her two sisters looked at each other and then one of them said, "He's got nice eyes."

Gladys had never noticed his eyes. And in truth, she reflected when she was with him again, "He's got nice eyes. And when he puts his hands akimbo there's an air of authority about him."

When it rained and he was late she would sit at the window, pretending to be on the look-out for the occasional carriage or motor car. The moment she caught sight of his bicycle lamp bobbing up and down as it turned the corner from Anira Street she felt a sudden tugging in her throat. Then, affecting not to notice him, she would only wave when he waved first. Her cool welcome never failed to surprise him and he sometimes wondered whether she loved him and if there was any point in coming to visit her every night when he might be playing billiards with his friends. He wondered, but he came, drawn by the phantom of an eventual conquest.

Her eldest sister's favourite way of teasing her about Armstrong was to say that Gladys liked him for his patent-leather shoes, just because she had remarked years ago, as a young girl, that she would only marry a man who wore patent-leather shoes. After one of her sisters laughingly told Armstrong of this youthful vow he tried to take liberties with Gladys while they were sitting alone in the gallery. She got angry and quarrelled with him so violently he was obliged to leave earlier than usual. The next night he again took liberties with her, but this time she did not protest. Once the barrier of her upbringing had fallen she found herself defenceless in the face of Armstrong's passion. All his ruses succeeded, and had it not been for the proximity of her sisters, who were in the drawing-room, he would have attained his ultimate goal.

But on the whole Armstrong never felt happy in Gladys's

10

house. The piano-playing, the embroidery, the sketching, the genteel talk made him feel an intruder in a world to which he could never belong. Deborah, the eldest sister, had once asked him what he thought of a piece of music she had just played. It sounded pleasant enough, but he did not think anything about it. The piece had been composed by Mendelssohn, she informed him, as if she were talking about a friend round the corner. When the sisters invited him to breakfast he agreed to come, but later sent a message saying that he had fallen ill. He had had no intention of going from the start, knowing full well that at their table he would be on test. The mention of forks and fish knives, napkins and serviettes would put him in a panic and he would probably fart as he got up from the table and belch as he tried to excuse himself.

Eventually Armstrong wrote to Gladys's father formally asking for her hand in marriage; and the following night he arrived at the house to find all the lights blazing and the family assembled in the gallery to greet him.

"Congratulations, my son!" exclaimed Mr Davis, shaking Armstrong's hand vigorously and patting him on his back with his left hand at the same time. "Nice to have you as one of the family."

Mrs Davis then stepped forward and shook his hand in turn, while Gladys's sisters looked on mockingly.

To Armstrong's dismay Gladys, her sisters and mother retired without bothering to sit down, leaving him alone with Mr Davis, who offered him a chair ceremoniously and then himself took the seat opposite.

"Things change, don't they?" remarked Mr Davis, shaking his head and smiling affably. "When I was a young man the girls had to get married in order of seniority. Deborah would have had to go first. But now. . . . Foolish custom, though, don't you think?"

Armstrong nodded, desperately wishing not to let this man down.

"And your people? Still alive?" Mr Davis enquired, changing the subject abruptly.

"My father is. My mother died some years ago."

"Sorry to hear that. Any . . . ?"

"Yes. I have a sister who lives on the East Coast."

"Family," said Mr Davis reflectively. "The root of everything, I always say. On good terms with her, I hope?"

But Mr Davis did not wait for an answer, perhaps sensing Armstrong's embarrassment. "We have to treat the women right," he pursued at once. "Anyway, that's the sort of advice you don't need, I can sense."

And so the conversation went, Mr Davis trying his best to draw Armstrong out, but with little success.

Then Mr Davis began to speak of his own courting days and of the 'nineties, when "teachers did not even have a pension when they retired. Only Civil Servants did; and they were mostly white. And look at the aboriginal Indians! You have to be careful not to call them 'bucks' nowadays, and the law doesn't permit you touch their women."

Then without warning he said to Armstrong, looking him straight in the eye: "You intend to get a servant, I suppose."

Taken completely by surprise, Armstrong could only murmur incomprehensibly.

"What's that?" Mr Davis persisted.

"When the first child comes along," declared Armstrong, an unmistakable note of irritation in his voice.

"Oh, well," said Mr Davis, stretching his legs in the pretence that they had gone to sleep.

The gesture was not lost on Armstrong. Mr Davis, who had always treated him with deference, had shown his hand. You only had to cross these people, thought Armstrong, and they expressed disapproval. Let him come straight out with it if it hurt him so. Out with it! *He* was in the lion's den and he would fight. A quick submission for the sake of peace, followed by a lifetime of misery? Oh, no! *He* was not going to run his home in consultation with a father-in-law.

But by the time Armstrong got up to leave, Mr Davis's talk had set his mind completely at rest.

Their wedding was a modest affair, attended by the friends and relations of the bride; and that night the couple went by carriage to their new rented house in Agricola, a village on the East Bank, where Gladys duly delivered up her virginity on the tray of propriety, the consummation of a blameless girlhood.

2

A Buried Time

The better Gladys got to know her husband the more she missed the repressive days of her youth and the company of her sisters. The trench that ran along their street, with its green moss-like growth and stagnant water where on May nights the stars bloomed in fiery clusters, drew forth tears of longing for a buried time.

When, in the second year of their marriage, she was expecting her first child, she took on a young woman from the village, a frail but independent creature who worked for two meals a day and returned to her hovel at eight in the evening, even when there was nothing more to be done in the house. Gladys, appalled to discover that her servant had no change of clothing, ran up a dress and petticoat on the sewing-machine for her using discarded garments from the bottom of the chest-of-drawers.

Genetha was born. She was a good baby, everyone said, who dropped off as soon as she was laid in her cradle, never failed to sleep through the quiet village night and smiled at strangers who came to the house and fondled her.

The young woman, unhappy about the extra work that came with the infant, complained incessantly and often reminded Mrs Armstrong that the women of Agricola disliked doing such a menial job.

Then one morning while Gladys was pregnant with a second child, her destitute servant failed to turn up for work. Later in the day her common-law husband, a cane-cutter who worked the East Bank estates during the short cane-cutting season, came to explain why his lady could no longer continue in Gladys's employment. He came when ash from the burning canefields was fluttering down over the village.

"She couldn't come no more, miss," he said, baring his head in respect. "She couldn't come 'cause she too delicate. Everybody say that she too delicate."

14

"She's slim, Mr Charles," Mrs Armstrong told him, "but not delicate. In the year she's been with me she put on a lot of weight. You must've seen that yourself."

"I not complaining, miss. You treat her good; but she was always sickly. On her mother's side they does die like flies when the sick season come."

Mrs Armstrong asked Mr Charles if he knew a girl who would be willing to take her place.

"A lot of them, miss," he said, and offered to make enquiries at Diamond, where he would be cutting cane during the following weeks.

Mr Charles was as good as his word. Three weeks later he brought a message from a man living at Little Diamond that his twelve-year-old daughter would come to work for her. And it was thanks to the disappointment at losing her first servant that Gladys Armstrong came to take on Esther, whom she herself fetched from Little Diamond on that fateful afternoon. The grave child came to live in, bringing as her only possessions two dresses and a comb. Armstrong took one look at her and decided that she was reliable, even though she did not look you in the eye.

Rohan was born two years after Genetha's birth and came to carry the fond name of Boyie. And Mrs Armstrong's involvement with her children and household robbed her of the joys of recollection; and only occasionally some incident, some object, recalled a childhood experience. She would then smile and forget almost at once.

After Boyie's birth she was ordered by the midwife to remain in bed for a couple of weeks. Armstrong suggested that Deborah, her eldest sister, might stay with them for a while, to which Gladys agreed.

With Deborah came a world of scent, doilies and twice daily showers. At meal times she insisted that Genetha washed her hands before and after eating, to the dismay of Esther, the servant, who resented the new authority. Deborah even made observations on the cooking and suggestions as to how Esther might improve it.

Armstrong, as it turned out, enjoyed Deborah's presence in his home. On leaving for work in the morning he invariably

15

asked her if he might bring something home for her from town, although these little gifts cost him money he could ill afford. Once he bought two avocado pears, and after learning that they were her favourite fruit he felt obliged to buy them as often as he could. But in the end he had to confess that they were too expensive for him; and even though she said she did not mind he was humiliated.

Despite these attentions, Deborah kept her distance. Whenever he wanted to stay and chat at table after a meal, she found some excuse to get up and busy herself with some trivial task. And gradually it dawned on Armstrong that his sister-in-law did not care much for him. He tried to put the matter out of his mind, telling himself that she would be in his house for no more than a week or so longer. In any case, what was the point in making an issue of her conduct when Gladys was still confined to her bed?

One night when he came home from work, however, the storm broke. Deborah complained that Esther was encouraging Genetha to stay up late: she should have been in bed at six o'clock. Armstrong replied that six o'clock was an absurd time for a child to go to bed and that he agreed with the servant. Deborah, hurt at the rebuff in front of Esther and the two-year-old Genetha, replied that in every civilised household children went to bed at six o'clock.

"When you get your own you can give them orders," thundered Armstrong, "but in my house the servants and children obey me!"

From the bedroom Gladys could hear the vexed voices of her husband and sister.

"Deborah!" she called out.

Her sister came to see what she wanted.

The kerosene lamp was burning low on the table at the foot of the bed and the excessive tidiness of the room bore the unmistakable mark of Deborah's influence.

"You and Sonny'll wake the baby," she said, nodding in the direction of the sleeping infant, who was lying on the bed beside her.

"Your husband insulted me," complained Deborah.

Gladys looked at her and answered nothing.

16

"Don't quarrel with Sonny; he likes you," Gladys then said, after a short silence.

"He does, does he?"

"Why don't you ever call him by his first name?" Gladys asked testily.

"I can't," replied Deborah.

"What's he ever done you?"

"He hasn't infected you with his persecution mania, has he?"

"Since you arrived you've never stopped criticising," Gladys observed, roused by her sister's uncompromising attitude. "You find fault with everything he does and says, even—"

"Have I ever said so?" asked Deborah.

"No. But it's in your eyes . . . and your silence whenever he speaks or I speak of him."

"Look, Gladys," Deborah said haughtily, "I won't have you talking to me like that. Your relations with Armstrong—"

"Sonny's his name!" Gladys shouted at her.

The baby began crying and Armstrong came hurrying into the room. Deborah bent down to pick up the infant as she often did during the day, but Gladys took up the child before her sister could get to it. Deborah drew back, her face contorted with disbelief and pain, while the infant's arms thrashed the air and it screamed in protest.

Armstrong gently lifted the child from his wife's arms and, to hide his embarrassment, left the room, while Deborah, in her anger, was unable to move away from her sister's bedside. But she felt equally incapable of remaining. When, finally, Gladys spoke to her, she summoned up what little dignity she had left and walked out of the room without minding to answer.

The next morning Armstrong got up at five o'clock to feed the fowls. After they had eaten the mixture of rice and corn, he caught the hens one by one and thrust a finger into their backsides to check which of them would lay that day. That done, he filled the goblet with rain water from the vat and began to climb the stairs with it.

When Armstrong was halfway up the stairs, the back door opened and Deborah appeared, carrying her suitcase.

17

"You're not going?" Armstrong asked, putting down the goblet.

"Yes. It's best for all concerned," she answered.

"Don't you ever quarrel in your home?"

"No.'

"Ah."

He put out his hand and shook hers.

"Would you like me to carry your grip for you?" he offered.

"Thanks, no. It's not heavy. Goodbye."

"Goodbye, then," Armstrong returned.

He went to the gate and watched her out of sight. From the cab driver's yard came the tinkle of harness as he prepared to go out on his daily search for fares. The fresh morning breeze rustled the cherry tree over the fence and brought the smell of the river to Armstrong's yard. A cock crowed from a yard deeper in the village, and its voice reverberated on the air, heady with the smell of vegetation and dew and horse dung. The cab driver had pulled out his cab on to the road, where it stood with its shafts dug into the ground. In a moment he would be hitching his horse to it and he would be off. It occurred to Armstrong that it was too early for a tram and that his sister-in-law would be standing on the Public Road for a good hour.

"Fool!" he muttered.

Armstrong drew satisfaction from the thought of her spindly legs supporting her overweight body for sixty minutes in front of the rum shop, while the village awakened. He went back to his goblet, which he took upstairs and placed on the dresser. It was going to be a hot day and Esther would probably need to fill it again.

What hurt Deborah especially was that she was obliged to carry her own suitcase to the Public Road. She had put it down several times before reaching the point where she was to wait for the tram. As she stood and re-enacted in her mind the quarrel of the evening before, the feeling gradually overcame her that yesterday was probably the beginning of a permanent estrangement between herself and her sister.

Before she came to Agricola her father had warned her

against interfering in the way of life of the household. As things turned out this was impossible. She had taken over many of the duties of her convalescing sister and it was not practicable to enquire in detail as to how they should be done. But yesterday's scene need never have occurred. She had underestimated Armstrong, who the day before had been friendly enough. What had been responsible for his fit of temper? Her attitude towards him had been consistent and she had always made sure that Esther had a hot cup of chocolate ready for him when he came home in the evenings. What's done is done! He lacked breeding, and there was nothing she could do about that.

"Do you know the time?" she enquired of a barefooted East Indian couple who were about to cross the Public Road.

"Me in' know no time, missie. But if you waiting 'pon the tram he in' going come till sun come up good."

"Thanks," she answered.

The couple crossed the road, the woman treading in the man's footsteps.

"What did I do to offend him?" the question kept coming back to her.

And at one point Deborah felt like returning to ask Armstrong why his attitude towards her had altered.

"It would've been a place to come for a change," the thought occurred to her. And Genetha had grown fond of her. She could tell.

"But the servant needs her wings clipping. She thinks she owns the place."

An orange glow which had appeared in the sky ridged the houses in Agricola with a line of light. When the tram appeared suddenly, long before the couple said it would, Deborah just had time to wave it to a stop. She climbed in and sat next to a woman who was apparently going to market and had contrived to heap on her lap a basket of vegetables, a bunch of plantains and a live chicken. Deborah was obviously destined to travel to Georgetown with a plantain in one ear and a cock threatening to descend on her head with every jolt of the tram. The ride was not conducive to reflection and she passed the time listening to the conversation round her.

19

Back home she told her parents and her sister her version of what had occurred.

"I always said he was an odd sort," Mr Davis observed, sucking at his empty pipe. "Poor Gladys! And with two children on her hands. . . . Great pity she didn't marry someone with backbone — and background. Without background you're nowhere."

His wife shook her head in harmony, as always, with her husband.

"God knows best," she muttered.

"You ever heard them quarrelling?" Gladys's other sister asked.

"No. But you can feel there's something. As soon as my back was turned I'm sure it came out again."

"Poor Gladys!" repeated Mr Davis, shaking his head knowingly.

After Deborah left, Armstrong fell into a surly mood. The sight of his wife, healthy looking and in good appetite, immobile while he had to be up early, annoyed him. The midwife had prescribed two weeks' rest; but a week ago she was ill. Now she was as fit as he was. She said so herself.

When Armstrong remarked to Gladys that she was well enough to get up she said she ought to do as the midwife said, but would get up if he wished it.

"No," he rejoined magnanimously.

But the same night, on returning home after a drinking bout with his friends, he shouted at her for lying in bed like a "fat sow".

"Now you taste a couple of weeks in bed, you don't want to lef' it, eh?"

Whenever he was drunk he threw away the grammar he so sedulously cultivated in the presence of educated people.

"You lazy, good-for-nothing!" he shouted at the top of his voice. "Get your tail up an' earn you keep. You can begin by making me something fo' eat. I don't want this tripe that Esther did make here. You want to turn me into one of these aunty-men who kian' even tell whether he coming or going? Is me who got for turn out early in the morning to work for

20

you and your children. You sister come here and behave as if she own the village. One week and she cause confusion! It's all this piano-playing and embroidery. If you pass you childhood tinkling away 'pon a piano and pushing a needle you in' going be good for nothing. You kian' even cook cook-up rice. It's a disgrace! If I sit down home and don't work your father would soon be round here telling me I married an' got to support his daughter. Make no bones about it! He would come round here and like all you family he would start laying down the law. I know your people, girl. They had you on the shelf an' was so anxious to get you off it they accept any Tom, Dick and Harry. But when things not going right they want the man to account to them."

He was breathing heavily and stood by the bed-post with a finger pointing down at her face.

"I can't talk to you when you're in this condition," she protested.

"Why the hell I din' marry a woman from my own village I don't know. One of them big-batty women with powerful build who kian' tell a piano from a violin. At least she would'a been up the day after she deliver she child, and I wouldn't have she father sitting on the sidelines judging me."

Genetha, who had come into the room unnoticed, began to bawl, and immediately afterwards the infant began to cry as well.

"You see!" continued Armstrong. "He begin again. The child begin again. I kian' even talk in my own house any more."

Gladys hurriedly picked up the baby, alarmed at his menacing attitude. Armstrong screamed for Esther, who hurried into the room.

"Take this child out'f here!" he bellowed.

Then, suddenly, he sat down on the bed and covered his head with his hands.

"Oh, God, I dunno," he muttered.

He wanted to throw himself at his wife's feet and say he was sorry. How could he explain that he did not mean a single word he had spoken and that all he wanted was to provide a happy home for his family? What force within him drove him to do the very thing he did not want to do?

21

The infant's wailing became a whimper and in the end gave way to sleep.

Armstrong got up and went into the drawing-room, where the light from the oil lamp failed to reach the corners. He sat down in a chair by the ornamental pedestal, in the most obscure part of the room. From where he sat he could see Esther ironing. She had given the infant back to its mother and was now tackling a pile of clothes on the dining table. From the top of the heap she took a garment to be pressed as soon as she had laid a finished one on the chair. He saw his wife go into the kitchen to prepare the meal he had asked for, but did not really want and from time to time Esther would slip off to change irons and blow the embers of the burning charcoal. Genetha, cowed and silent, was sitting in a chair at the table where Esther was ironing, her thumb in her mouth.

After putting her husband's meal on the table Mrs Armstrong signalled to Genetha to go inside and wait for her. She walked around as in a dream, wiping her hand on the corner of her dress as some people wash their hands, without any reason, except to relieve the tension in their minds. If her husband had been out she would have taken over the ironing from Esther, just to give her hands something to do for a few hours. The washing-up was not absorbing enough; embroidery was not possible in the half-light. Tonight she would find it impossible to sleep, but he would sleep like a log. He always did, no matter how badly they quarrelled. Whenever he got up to drink a glass of water or to urinate and found her sitting at the open window, he became angry and asked her if she was studying the stars. Only people with bad consciences could not sleep at night. She would then go back to bed to please him and in a short while he would be snoring again.

Armstrong ate his meal, picked his teeth with his fingers and then got up from the table to go into the kitchen. The fire was going out, but instead of speaking sharply to Esther about it he put some new charcoal on the coal-pot and replaced the irons on top. He could see the two huge pots with their blood-leafed croton plants in the back yard. Filling an enamel basin with water he went downstairs to water the shrubs and pick off the dead leaves. He heard the noise of the iron as Esther brought it down on the table and thought that he must get new lime for the latrine in the yard and send for Baboo to cut the grass, which had grown right up to the foot of the back stairs. In the end he had to go back upstairs and face the silence, broken only by the pounding of Esther's ironing.

Soon Armstrong could hear his wife speaking softly to Genetha, The gentle voice soothed his agitation. like cochineal on a burning head. When they were just married he used to play ducks and drakes in the trench at the back of the yard, where he revelled in his ability to make a mango seed skid on the surface of the water. In those days he was less irritable. It was as if a cancer were growing in his body and gaining control so effectively that he was no longer master of his own actions. He knew how to achieve peace in his house, but as soon as things were going well, as soon as Gladys began to talk a little the cancer would grope into the part of his brain that ordered his actions and would dictate an outburst without cause, when she was smiling or offering to do something that might please him. And he knew that with every outburst, with every quarrel, her silences lasted longer, so that the time might come when the gulf between them became so great that no penitence, no sustained act of indulgence could bridge it. Was it true what her family thought of him? That he was coarse? Was it really his fault that Deborah had left, without even saying goodbye to her sister? Was he wrong about her and her arrogance? He puzzled over these questions until the dull noise from the iron stopped.

3

Rohan

Unlike his sister, who as an infant slept long and fed readily at the breast, the boy-child spent several minutes adjusting his mouth to the nipple, only to suck fitfully when he had it firmly in his mouth. His sleep was as restless as his feeding, so much so that his father deserted the conjugal room in order to make certain of a full night's rest. He exchanged sleeping quarters with Esther, who had to get up whenever the baby cried and try to soothe him to sleep.

At first Armstrong made much of his son and he bought him a little shak-shak made of celluloid to amuse him during his waking hours. His favourite game with the infant consisted of picking him up in such a way that he gripped his fingers, demonstrating to his wife and anyone who cared to watch that infants had a powerful grasp at an early age.

Armstrong, deciding that the christening of his boy-child should be celebrated, invited his friends and those he knew tolerably well in the village. His in-laws were invited by letter, as a formality only, since he was certain that they would not come. But, to Gladys's delight, they came. She took advantage of the occasion to become reconciled with Deborah, who promised that she would return to stay with them another time, without having the slightest intention of keeping her promise. Alice, the second sister, admired the baby, not failing to observe that it bore a strong resemblance to its father.

Armstrong took Alice downstairs to show her the crotons and the pineapple bed by the trench. It was dark, and the rustling of a salipenta in the long grass startled her. She had never seen a lizard as large as that before and remarked that if she lived there she would make sure that the grass was kept short. They went back upstairs when the music began.

Mrs Davis wanted to see the yard as well and the fruit trees at the back, but her daughter warned her against going down, on account of the salipentas.

Alice pitied her sister because there was no indoor toilet; and when, in the kitchen, she discovered that there was no running water either, she asked Gladys:

"How d'you manage?" puckering her brows in an expression of concern.

"Sonny brings up water from the vat before he goes to work."

"Oh," Alice said, relieved.

A young man came to invite Alice to dance and the couple danced off, maintaining a distance of at least two feet from each other.

One of Armstrong's friends pretended to give the infant a schnapp-glass of rum, and though Gladys's parents were shocked by such ribaldry they were obliged to laugh.

"He just like his father, you know," remarked the friend, to Armstrong's annoyance. "He know how much liquor he can take."

Gladys's parents looked at each other, an exchange of glances that did not escape the infant's mother, whose only wish was that the evening would pass without incident. Each of Armstrong's friends danced with Alice in turn, pushing and dragging her round the drawing-room at a furious pace, in the manner of the new dance step which Alice had never dared practise at home.

Armstrong's friends teased him, saying that he was more interested in his sister-in-law than in his wife, which gave rise to a discussion about Alice's figure. Her breasts were firm, for some, but on the small side, they agreed. Her backside was too large for some, but just right for others. There was no disagreement, however, on the fact that her mouth was formed to be kissed. One of them observed that he preferred the mother, at which they all burst out laughing. They then turned to the other women in the drawing-room, rejecting some as hopeless specimens and admitting others as a fit subject for discussion.

From time to time Armstrong went over to his wife, who was sitting in a corner with the infant on her lap, apparently unmindful of the noise around him.

At ten o'clock the table on which the cake stood was dragged to the centre of the room, where everyone gathered round it. Armstrong's father-in-law, who was adjudged the most educated man present, was asked to make the speech. He cleared his throat, paused for a suitable length of time and then began. A child was born into the world, he said. The next few years would probably be his happiest, when all the best things would come to him at no cost in money or anxiety. (At this point there was a groan of approval from the women present.) Later, he went on, when he started to earn his living, when he married and had to maintain a household, perhaps two — and here there was a roar of laughter from the men and scowls from the women — he would come to know the other side of life, the uncertainties, the wanting, the pain of unfulfilled hopes.

"And it all comes down to one thing," remarked Mr Davis, "money."

There were clapping and shouts of approval at the manner in which Mr Davis had expressed himself, and at the speed with which he had come to the heart of the matter.

"And it is money I ask you to give this child, my friends, so that his future can be assured, to the extent of what you bestow on him."

One of Armstrong's friends stepped forward and placed a dollar note on the table. Others followed until a pile of notes and coins formed a little mountain beside the iced cake.

Armstrong was impressed by his father-in-law's eloquence. He had never got to know him well and regretted it. He spoke as Armstrong always dreamed of speaking. He was, in short, master of the word, of that powerful element which was in the beginning.

When Mrs Armstrong came forward with her husband to cut the cake, her eyes were moist.

One of the women remarked, "When I see two people happy like that it brings tears to my eyes."

The young people were anxious to get on with the dancing and while the table was being pushed back into the corner there were murmurs of approval from them. Two of them had had too much to drink and were sitting on the chairs against the wall, their heads bowed.

Alice had enjoyed the company of one young man, but did

26

not know what to do to attract him back to her, without endangering her reputation. She suddenly wished that her parents were not there so that for once she could act as she wished. The two shots of rum she had drunk, against the express strictures of her father, had brought a warmth to her whole body, a warmth she had never before experienced.

Over by the wall a girl was sitting on a young man's lap and the mere sight of such a commonplace scene filled her with the strangest desires. She went out on the porch and waited, for what she was unable to say; then a few minutes later she went downstairs and waited, but no one came and nothing happened, except that, when the music stopped someone started calling her name from the landing. It was her mother. She quickly turned and went back upstairs.

"What were you doing there?" her mother asked reproachfully.

"I was looking at the crotons," Alice said limply, feeling slightly sick at the effect of the alcohol.

People began to drift away at about midnight until, by two o'clock, only a few were talking in the drawing-room. The floor was strewn with cigarette ends trodden flat and pieces of paper and matches. The Davis family had departed before the musicians, and when Armstrong made a little joke about hearing a cock crow, those remaining took the hint and said goodbye.

Esther, who was sleeping in her mistress's bed with the baby at her side, had to be awakened to make something for the Armstrongs and to give the infant its final feed before morning.

Alone in the kitchen she took it into her head to play mothers with the infant and undid the buttons of the cast-off garment she wore as a nightdress. She placed his mouth against her small breast; but the offering gave him no satisfaction, and after a few vain and increasingly frenzied attempts to secure a grip on it he gave up in a fit of yelling. Esther then hurriedly took him up into her arms, while his milk bottle, newly filled from the thermos flask, cooled sufficiently to start feeding him.

4

Seaweed and Bitterness

As the months went by, Armstrong seemed to lose interest in the boy. He no longer romped with him on the floor or took him on his lap. To Gladys's remark about his neglect he objected that he found Boyie as engaging as ever, but that he was waiting until he was old enough to run about and play a game of cricket. He would buy a real bat for him and they would then play out in the street with his friends.

"That'll be the day," his wife remarked cynically.

Armstrong's father died a few months after the christening, and left his son his two cottages; but to his daughter he left his thriving wheelwright business.

Bitter at the inequitable distribution of the estate, Armstrong found little consolation in his promotion to Postmaster of a Georgetown post office. With his father's business he could have retired and lived as he had always dreamed. Of what use was the money to his sister, ugly and unmarried at thirty-two? How could his father, who treated her like a slave during his lifetime and never let her out of his sight, leave her a business about which she understood nothing?

Gladys took her sister-in-law's part. Armstrong's sister was alone and the business would give her something to occupy herself with. If her sister-in-law understood nothing about it, neither did her husband. Armstrong, blind with rage at her disloyalty, called her a "blasted cunt", but her only reaction was to look at him with mute satisfaction.

The following week Armstrong was sent away to help organise new post offices in various parts of the country, and it was only six months later that he came back to a home where he felt himself a stranger. However, his wife, whose bed had been cold for so long, welcomed him ardently. Gladys's changed attitude softened his manner towards her somewhat, but his feelings for her had cooled even before he had gone away, so that now he began to look around for a mistress with whom he could spend the evening hours.

At times he and Gladys talked until late at night. She agreed that it was unjust that his sister should have come into the bulk of his father's inheritance. With the income from the business Boyie could be given a university education.

At odd moments when they were just sitting on the porch he would catch her looking at him intently and, flattered by her affection, he began courting her again. But at other times they sat and listened to the sounds at night, the bull-frogs croaking and the dogs barking, and watched the lights in the house opposite.

Once, when she heard him tapping his feet to a tune he was humming in a low voice, she believed that they had begun again from the beginning, after he first came to her house in Queenstown and was obsessed by her ankles. They were married despite her sisters and were embarking on a life-journey. She had longed for him when he was away, recalling the sweetness of copulation, which became for her the heart of their marriage, so that she visualised his return as the start of an endless coupling of ineffable satisfaction, in which her anxieties would dissolve like salt in a cup of tepid water.

In the middle of a conversation he would go over to her and kiss her on the cheek and then on her mouth, and while undoing her bodice he would gently pull her into the bedroom and on to the connubial bed where, amidst the bedclothes, he would rediscover the passion of their first days together.

When Gladys told her husband that she was expecting her third child his happiness was complete. In a burst of activity he had the roof reshingled and the house repainted, and hung two maidenhair ferns in baskets in the gallery. He informed his friends of the impending birth and began making plans for the child's education. He even visited his wife's family in town, whom he professed to dislike, to tell them the good news.

On leaving, he thanked his mother-in-law.

"Thanks for what?" she asked, taking him by the arm.

"Just thanks," he answered, feeling his chest swell with goodwill towards all his wife's family.

29

"What a funny chap!" his mother-in-law remarked to her husband when he had gone away.

"He's never got a crease in his trousers, you noticed?" Mr Davis observed.

"D'you think they're going to be happy?"

"Never can tell with these people," declared Mr Davis thoughtfully. "So many of them're getting jumped up these days. Types like him will be working in the Civil Service soon, mark my words."

"Well," put in his wife, "the better he gets on the better it'll be for Gladys. She hasn't got the grit the other two have. If things go wrong she mightn't be up to it."

The child was born a weakling and died in its third month. And for some strange reason Gladys Armstrong found herself weeping months after the infant's death, as if it had been her first-born. Armstrong, mystified, made vain efforts to console her, assuring her that she would have others who would grow up as healthy as Rohan and Genetha.

"I know," she said. "It's not that I don't know. . . . What it is I can't tell. The tears just come . . . by themselves."

However, the weeping stopped after the dead infant appeared to her in a dream and spoke like a wise old man. He was happy where he now was, but if his mother continued to weep as she did she would make him unhappy and afraid.

And after that Mrs Armstrong was wont to tell Esther and the neighbour who lived opposite that her dead child had only come visiting, as if that remark explained her grief and its vanishing.

Then in the following months a rift again appeared in the marriage. Armstrong invariably interrupted her attempts at conversation by reminding her that he was reading and had to give back the book by a certain day, or by watching her blankly and then asking, when she had finished, what it was she had been talking about.

In time they found little to say to each other and Armstrong became so irritable that Gladys got into the habit of speaking to him through Esther. On the slightest pretext he went out and often returned home in the early hours of the morning; and if she enquired where he had been he would reply that he was with friends who frequented a cake shop in Georgetown where they played draughts.

One Saturday night he took her for a carriage ride to the sea-wall on the edge of Georgetown. The children waved excitedly to their parents while the cab driver waited patiently, as listless as his horse; and after Gladys and her husband had climbed in, a flick of his whip was sufficient to start the animal trotting down the unlit road. The children were so carried away that Esther was obliged to restrain them lest they fell out of the window.

Gladys Armstrong's heart was pounding at the thought of the drive past the big sugar estate just outside Georgetown and the railway crossing at Lamaha Street. Perhaps they might come back by way of Camp Street where the tall tamarind tree was. Lower down, there were the black-pudding and souse stalls and the peanut sellers. They conjured up the time when she was free and went walking with her sisters and parents in Regent Street on Saturday nights, and she stole glances at the boys when under her father's watchful eye. More than once she fell head-over-heels in love with a young man she saw for the first time among the crowds in Regent Street, and swore she would marry no one else. A chance meeting would bring them together again at some time in the future and then she would introduce him to her parents. She would sit at her window every afternoon, scanning the faces of the young men who passed by, in the hope of catching sight of the object of her secret passion.

"I asked if the shaking of the carriage's worrying you," Armstrong enquired, annoyed that he had to repeat his question.

"No, I don't feel anything."

Satisfied that nothing was wrong he fell back into his silence.

They reached Upper Camp Street, where the absence of shops and the cool breeze contrasted with the hurly-burly of Camp Street and Regent Street. At last the carriage drew up alongside the band-stand and the couple got out. They climbed the flight of stairs leading to the embankment and took another flight of stairs down to the beach. The tide was far out and the sand glistened wanly in the moonlight as they stopped by a tuft of dead grass which rose out of the beach where it was overlaid by mud.

Suddenly Armstrong found himself struggling with a wave of irritability that seemed to have no cause. The presence of his wife, the strong wind, the noise of the surf, like the breathing of some leviathan, the money spent on the journey, everything seemed designed to put him out of sorts. She was walking beside him, stubbornly silent; yet, he knew that if she spoke her words would only contrive to deepen the sense of futility he felt. Why could he not accept things as they were, recognise the failure of their marriage and settle for a guarded peace? After all, it might be a good idea to permit her to go home to her parents from time to time. But he would never do that; it would only make things worse.

Her thighs were becoming thick and her breasts flabby. Yet whenever he thought of taking a mistress his conscience reproached him. It was damned absurd. Everybody did it and even boasted of it. Since his promotion and the acquisition of the two cottages there was no longer the excuse that he could not afford it.

Every time he broached the subject of his cottages and the difference the money was going to make to their lives she went into her shell, as if there was something unhealthy about their ownership. Why not divorce her? And start the whole business over again? The choosing of a partner was no different from being blindfolded and picking the first girl you touched. Besides, he would miss the children, and it was doubtful if he could keep the servant when they separated. There must be some way. . . . His weakness was showing such concern for their relationship. He needed only go on as if he were happy at the way things were. She would be the sufferer, since he went out and met people and saw his friends in the evening when he needed a game of draughts or a few schnapps of rum.

At this point in his reflections Gladys tripped over a stick camouflaged by a mass of seaweed, and involuntarily she held on to his arm for support. The slender thread of his composure snapped and, turning round, he walked briskly towards the sea-wall.

"Where're you going?" she called out.

"Home!" he replied brutally, leaving her standing, a solitary figure on the beach.

"Sonny!" she called to him by his fond name; but he kept on across the sand, then climbed the stairs and disappeared over the wall.

She was left alone on the beach, standing as if rooted to the spot. She looked out to sea and for the first time the idea of suicide came to her. It was said that the sea claimed at least seven victims a year, as of right, fishermen mostly, who robbed it inconsiderately. From Gladys's old home in Queenstown the incessant roaring of the waves at flood-tide could be heard at the dead of night, like a jaguar on the prowl. No one in her house spoke of it, in a tacit denial of its very existence, though the wall along the coast was proof of an obsession. The sea and those birds with curved beaks that hovered on the edge of her youthful dreams, limpid-eyed and expressionless. Then, after dwelling on the possibility of suicide for a while, she began to make her way to the sea-wall.

A couple were going by, arm in arm. She was slim and her skin was tight. The young woman's backside curved as Gladys's had before she had children. As she approached the couple she noticed that they were not in fact arm in arm; rather, the woman was holding the man's arm as if grappling for dear life, or out of fear that he might run away.

Armstrong sat waiting for her in the carriage; and when she appeared and opened the carriage door she saw him looking out of the window in the other direction.

The carriage drove off to the sound of the clop-clopping of the horse while someone on the sea-wall laughed aloud, as if mocking her. And the rolling of the carriage gave her bad feelings and her back no longer seemed to be supported by her spine, so that she closed her eyes in an attempt to forget where she was.

"What've I done?" she asked quietly.

"It's not I who'm sending you 'to your father's house', as you call it," he declared.

This was a reference to a remark she had made the day before when they had been quarelling.

"You know that even if I wanted to go home my father would drive me out," she observed.

"Home?" he shouted. "You still consider there home? When the hell are you going to wake up to the fact that you're married? Home!" he exclaimed scornfully. "You and your sisters went out once a week and you didn't know what went on in the rest of the world. I came from my father's house and my father's house was as good as your father's house. If I didn't talk about it, it's because I've grown up. You all cringed before your father and had to ask his permission even to open the window. The only difference between our fathers was that mine punished me with the belt while yours punished you by not talking to you for days. And you threaten me with going back to your father's house. . . ."

"I wasn't threatening you. I was just saying—"

"What's the kiss-me-ass difference?" he sneered.

She tried to say something else, but he uttered a sound of impatience which brooked no further talk. The carriage rolled along Main Street, under the flamboyant trees, the amber-tinted street lamps and past the mansions of the rich. The flamboyants were in bloom and the pedestrian walk that divided the two arms of the road resembled some covered garden where couples strolled hand in hand under the flowering trees. The rhythmic sound of the horse's hoofs on the pitch echoed down the side strets, giving Armstrong a reassurance he sought in his frustration.

"Probably it was not like that at all," he thought. "Maybe she loves me and talked of her father's house because I'm always in a bad mood. But if I was bad-tempered yesterday was she not the cause? Oh, God! If only I knew." The best thing to do was to allow her to go and see her people, to go home as she called it.

"Home!" he thought, roused to anger again. "But home is my house!"

The carriage went past La Penitence Market and crossed the bridge into the suburbs.

When they reached home, Armstrong's anger had abated. He helped his wife down from the carriage and paid off the cabbie; then the cab turned round ponderously and drove the fifty yards

34

home. Armstrong followed his wife up the stairs and thought, as he gripped the balustrade, that it was in need of repair.

5

The Servants

Esther had come to work for the Armstrongs when Mrs Armstrong was carrying Rohan. The arrival of the carriage in Little Diamond had caused a stir, except, as Esther remembered, to her own family who had been expecting the woman from Agricola the day before.

After much talking between her parents and the brown-skinned lady, she remembered leaving the hut and walking down the village street between her mother and younger sister, in the footsteps of Mrs Armstrong, who was lifting her dress slightly in order to protect it from the mud of the dirt road. And even then, at the beginning of their acquaintanceship, she was striving to copy Mrs Armstrong's walk, as later she was to imitate her speech and her gestures.

It was only months later, when recollections of Little Diamond came to her without her seeking them, that Esther consciously looked back at her childhood and youth, at her parents, her brothers and sisters and a house of endless births.

The night Esther's father went out in search of her eldest brother with her two maternal uncles was a landmark in her life. They found him drunk on the Public Road and brought him home. He was only sixteen, but responsible for organising the family's work in the fields. Her two uncles stripped him and held him down in the yard while her father flogged him with the cow-whip until blood came and the neighbour's wife shouted out in protest. The power of those men — in a village where there were women bringing up a family single-handed — the helplessness of her mother, revolted her. And from then on she dreamt of going away from the village, her hut and the cloying stench of asafoetida.

On learning of the woman's coming visit and her wish to have one of the girl children, Esther prayed that she would be chosen, in preference to her sister who was nine, three years younger than she.

In the carriage, while they were on their way to Agricola, Mrs Armstrong spoke to her for the first time.

"I'm expecting. Do you know what that means?"

"Yes, miss. You belly goin' get big," came the prompt reply.

"You must say," corrected Mrs Armstrong, " 'You are expecting a child'."

"I understand, miss," said Esther.

And those simple words contained the message of her inordinate ambition. Esther understood. And, like a sponge, her understanding sucked up all she saw and heard, all the things that separated her from the Armstrongs, the brass that had to be cleaned on Sundays, the daily dusting of furniture, leather-bound books, vast umbrellas, shoes, elegant lacquered boxes and the repose of flowers in vases with flaring tops.

There grew in Esther a fierce attachment for the Armstrong children. She took them to church, even after Mrs Armstrong no longer went, and was once entrusted with Genetha on a trip to Georgetown — Rohan was too young to accompany them — where they went to see the ocean-going ships rising above immense wharves, and the barnacles that clung to their hulls. Genetha marvelled at the ebb-tide and the driftwood from up-river, and at the shining bodies of the stevedores.

Back home Esther felt betrayed when Genetha ran and threw her arms round her mother.

"The neighbour said you were a capable girl, Esther," Mrs Armstrong remarked, pleased at the success of the outing.

"Thank you, mistress," replied Esther.

"I can't understand how you learn so fast. It's uncanny. Some people take weeks to learn to do a simple stitch; but you. . . . Are you happy?"

"Yes, mistress."

"Don't you miss your family?" pursued Mrs Armstrong, who lived in fear of Esther's mother taking her away when she discovered how accomplished she had become.

"I'm sure I do, mistress."

"You're sure you do?" enquired Mrs Armstrong, not knowing what to make of the girl's answer.

"Yes, mistress."

"Would you want to go away if your mother came for you?"

"I don't think so, mistress."

"You're not sure, then," remarked Mrs Armstrong, attempting to conceal the anxiety she felt.

"I am sure, mistress."

Mrs Armstrong smiled. The girl would never express herself with less equivocal words. She was like that. If she were a boy, people would say that he was destined to become a lawyer.

And this disinclination to give a direct answer exasperated Mrs Armstrong in the end. It was impossible to get near the girl. Should she ask her opinion about the meal for a particular day or enquire about a neighbour, Esther would answer so deferentially and give so little away that her words amounted to a prevarication. She resented this girl from Little Diamond, who was nevertheless indispensable to her way of life.

Mrs Armstrong gave up her attempts to get close to Esther, and the latter felt more at ease with a distance between them.

The arrival of Marion, the new servant, more than four years after Esther herself came to live with the Armstrongs, brought Esther close to panic, for the girl, a good year younger, would surely compete with her for the children's affection and her mistress's trust.

One night she dreamt that the Armstrongs went to Georgetown, taking the children and Marion, and left her behind to look after the house. She pretended not to mind, but secretly hated Marion for it. The next morning when she found she had only been dreaming she was all the more incensed.

The feeling of foreboding Marion's presence aroused in her dogged her for weeks and it was only grudgingly she showed the new girl how to set the table and do the hundred other chores of the household.

Esther often lay awake at night, mulling over her anxieties, when the silence was only broken by the barking of a dog. Beside her, on the floor, was Marion, her mouth open and breathing deeply, while a few feet away lay the two children, prostrate on their iron frame bed.

Yet, as time passed, Esther lost her mistrust of the younger servant and even came to regard her as a friend. One night when the family were out they decided to raid Mr Armstrong's rum bottle. It was Esther's idea. She knew where the rum was kept, under his bed. She poured out the cane spirit into two cups and made some lemonade, which she mixed with the rum in the cups, replacing the missing spirit with water from the goblet. The two girls were soon giddy and giggled long and senselessly, and went to the window from time to time to see if the family were coming back. Then Marion wanted to take some more rum, but Esther was afraid.

Emboldened by her euphoria, Marion showed her friend how they danced in Mocha. She writhed and wined violently, urging Esther to imitate her, but she could only flail her arms and throw her body around like someone who had never danced before. Marion laughed so much that tears came to her eyes. She held Esther by the waist and tried to demonstrate the rhythm by pushing her to the right and to the left, but to no avail. Esther pulled herself away and began to dance after her own fashion.

When, on going to the window, Marion saw the family coming up the street, the two girls rushed down the stairs and ran to the back of the yard, where they hid behind the latrine. No one called them and Esther suggested that they wash out their mouths with trench-water. Then they crept along the ground in the tall grass until they reached the trench. There they lay on their bellies and rinsed out their mouths with the brackish water.

Once, when Armstrong was not at home, Marion had a long conversation with her mistress.

"You're happy, Marion?" Mrs Armstrong asked her, putting the same question to her that she had asked Esther.

Mrs Armstrong, elegant in her mollee and simple frock, had large eyes set in a dark brown face.

"Yes, mistress."

"You miss Mocha?"

"Yes, mistress," she answered, intimidated by Mrs Armstrong's cordiality.

"Agricola is bigger than Mocha, though, and there's the police horse on Saturday night. Once one of the boys in the village pulled a hair from its tail. You can imagine the commotion. . . . You think I'm good-looking, girl?" she asked out of the blue.

Marion, open-mouthed, stared at her.

"Well, answer," Mrs Armstrong ordered. "Don't be afraid. Speak the truth."

"You nice, mistress. Even with you grey hair you nice."

Mrs Armstrong bit her lip and stared hard at the girl.

"Tell me something, Marion. Do you really like me?"

When she saw that the girl was once more thrown into a state of confusion she went on without waiting for an answer.

"I wasn't vain when I was young, but now I'm getting older I spend hours before the mirror. I cut a bit of hair off at the temple and wish I could put it back again. I've got some of my hair from when I was eighteen years. Wait, I'll show you."

She went to the chest-of-drawers, rummaged in it for a while and then took out a box covered with faded blue paper. Opening it carefully, she showed Marion the strands of jet black hair, neatly held in place by a thin length of wire tightly wound round it. The girl could only see it as hair with no significance except that it was a different colour from the hair Mrs Armstrong now had.

"You see . . . don't touch it! Just look," Mrs Armstrong urged.

She placed the wound hair against her own and went up to the mirror of her chest-of-drawers. With a brusque movement she put the memento back into the box, which she hastened to replace in the drawer.

"If only you could see people behind closed doors. . . . I don't know why I'm telling you all this. Promise not to repeat a word to Esther."

Marion shook her head.

"No, mistress."

"Do you like Esther?"

"Yes," Marion answered at once.

"The children like her," said Mrs Armstrong, "I don't know why. There's something disturbing about Esther. More than once I've caught her watching me as if she knew something. I don't know what there is to know. The hurtful thing is that she can run the house single-handed. She knows how to save

40

money and how to spend it. When there's no money left it's then she cooks the things to make your mouth water. She picks callaloo in the back-dam and breadfruit from the churchyard. And then with bird-pepper and pigeon peas from the yard she does the rest. You see, I haven't anyone to talk to. . . . You know all of this already. Are you tired of listening?"

"No, mistress! " exclaimed Marion.

"You had a boy friend in Mocha?"

Marion bowed her head and said, "No," softly.

"Look out of the window and see what the noise is."

Marion went to the window. "It's a man selling something on a cart," she said.

"Doesn't matter; I haven't got any money."

There was a short silence.

"Esther doesn't talk much," Mrs Armstrong continued. "But she watches and stores up in her mind what she sees. Do you like people who see and pretend they don't see? But I'm a Christian so I'm bound to like Esther. Look, Esther talks to you. You're the only person she's taken to — no, it's true. She's taken to you. I can tell. You must come and tell me everything she says. Promise. Promise?" she asked eagerly.

Automatically Marion nodded.

"You're lucky, Marion. Everyone likes you. You're fresh and you laugh from here." And saying so Mrs Armstrong put her hand on her chest.

"When I was your age," she continued, "everyone used to say, 'She's nice-looking, she's beautiful,' and they would walk away, just as I wanted to say something."

Her voice faltered as if she had been hurt by a recollection.

"If only I lived in Georgetown," Mrs Armstrong went on, "I could at least sit by the window and watch the people go by."

There was a pause, painful for Marion, who attempted to get up.

"No, don't go yet. I'm dying to give you advice. But it would be useless in any case, because you wouldn't take it. And if you did you'd regret not having had your own way."

She paused again and looked at Marion fixedly.

"Marion, do you dream?" Mrs Armstrong asked, emphasising these words in a remarkable way.

"Sometimes, mistress."

"Do you ever have wild dreams about strange men crushing you and biting your face and beating you to the ground?"

Her eyes were staring; then catching sight of Marion's expression she added quickly, "I don't have that kind of dream, but one of my servants used to. She was before Esther's time, you understand. Go on with your work now," she ordered, looking at the girl from the corner of her eye.

Marion was to remember that conversation for a long time afterwards, as if she had engaged her mistress in a contest and had got the better of her. Some of the awe with which Mrs Armstrong had inspired the girl had disappeared, lost in that inexplicable influence of words. Mrs Armstrong must have felt the loss, for immediately after the conversation she treated Marion with unwonted harshness, while showing Esther a deference that surprised the older servant.

6

Season of Galoshes

In Agricola, Gladys Armstrong was regarded as being mad. People said she only wore black at home and fed the bats that hung from the eaves. It was her husband who drove her mad, they said, for he had nothing more to do with her.

Gossip also had it that she was afraid of her own small son. One of the servants had confided in the grocer that Mrs Armstrong would sometimes hold him and stare into his eyes and then push him away from her, saying, "Go away. You resemble your father too much."

Her guitar had aroused curiosity from the time she and Armstrong came to live in the village. She had bought the instrument as a substitute for the piano she could not have after she married.

"Who ever heard of a woman playing the guitar? I bet he drag she from Panama or somewhere like that. You only got to look at she face," one woman opined.

But it was only since Marion came and she was completely freed from the housework that anyone had heard her play. When on a warm night the sound of her playing drifted away into the darkness the neighbour with the cherry tree in his yard would say to his wife, "You hear that? She alone again. He tell she more than once he gwine tek it away if she play it. You wait!"

And the sound of the playing and the noise of the night insects would accompany one another.

She taught Marion a few chords on the instrument and the girl, in time, became a better performer than she was. When, once, she heard her playing for Esther a new calypso called "If you can't stand the digging, give me back me shilling" she took the guitar away and forbade her to play it for a week.

"I think Mr Armstrong's got a lot of money in the bank, Marion," Mrs Armstrong once said to the younger servant.

43

"You don' know?" Marion asked.

"He hides his bank book," replied Mrs Armstrong. "But he left a letter lying about telling him to send it in for the interest to be recorded. You know, I've only been to see his house once. He doesn't talk about them," Mrs Armstrong went on.

"He don't talk at all," Marion declared.

"He talks when he's with his friends. I know. . . . Can you smell something burning?"

"Is Esther," Marion reassured. "She make a fire in the yard with the grass that Baboo cut."

"He even gets the grass cut every month."

"I going go an' help Esther with the burning," Marion declared.

She was dying to tell Esther about Mr Armstrong's money in the bank.

"No, stay here with me."

"You should get a friend in the village," Marion suggested.

"The midwife used to come and see me; but somebody told her I said things about her that weren't true and she never came back. Me! Say things about her! Whom do I talk to? And who talks to me? I talk to myself half of the time."

"I know. I hear you."

"Well, don't tell anybody," Mrs Armstrong warned. "You know what they say about people who talk to themselves. What can I do if no one's there to talk to? In the night when you're all sleeping I listen to the radio and pretend it's all happening in the drawing-room. . . . I just had an idea."

"What?" Marion asked.

"I'll ask Mr Armstrong to buy a newspaper every day."

"You think he'll do it?"

"I think so."

"But I kian' read good enough to read a paper," Marion protested.

"Esther can read for you."

"I suppose so. But she in' going always be in the mood," Marion said.

"Nonsense! She'll like showing off."

Gladys Armstrong placed her hands between her head and

44

the back of the chair, leaned back against them and closed her eyes. Marion, thinking that she had fallen asleep, got up and tiptoed out of the room.

After she had gone Gladys opened her eyes and thought for a moment of going to fetch the children from school. She did not like them lingering in the road, and besides, the walk would do her good.

Why was Marion not as ambitious as Esther? She seemed content to speak as she did, to let others read for her. Her only goal appeared to be to get married and to bring children into the world. Was that really all there was to life for women? To breed children and obey their husbands? And there was little doubt that Marion would grow up to be more contented than Esther. Was little Genetha's life to be a repetition of her own? What would be her lot if she braved her father and married the man she loved? What would she do when he said, "Obey or get out"? Would she dare get out? Could she afford to?

The smell of burning grass and the sound of laughter rose from the yard and Gladys Armstrong sighed and began to get dressed.

Children were running along the road on the way home, while others were standing in knots in front of the school. A boy bolted out of the school yard into the street. It was Boyie, she thought; but when he turned round she recognised him as a boy living across the public road in Jonestown.

"I don't like you coming to meet me. I'm not a baby."

The voice came from behind her. Boyie had been speaking to a friend who lived opposite the school and on catching sight of his mother waiting for him he left the boy to come over and protest.

"I didn't come for you. I came for Genetha," she lied.

"Oh," he muttered, disappointed.

Instead of going back to his friend he began to kick the ground with the tip of his right shoe. A minute later Genetha appeared in the company of another girl who shyly smiled and walked away. Gladys and the children started off home when, suddenly, Boyie said that he did not want to go home right away.

"Why?" Genetha asked.

"Is none of your business," he said sharply.

"Don't forget to be home for tea," his mother reminded him. He did not answer, but darted away.

"What did you do at school today?" she asked Genetha.

"Nothing."

"All day?"

"Well, a little of everything. I came second in spelling."

"Who beat you?" asked her mother.

"Mavis. She always guesses the right answers."

Mrs Armstrong smiled and remembered her own school days. Boyie never spoke about what went on in school. In fact, he resented being asked. If she tried to enquire from his teacher how he was getting on he would never forgive her. So she was left in the dark as to his progress.

"Mrs Strachan said she's going to lend me a book to take home and read," said Genetha, "and Joy said she could read better than me and she should have the book to take home. And Mrs Strachan said Joy was rude and she had a big head and was not the best in reading. I know she's the best in reading and I don't know why Mrs Strachan said she wasn't and Joy won't talk to me and she said she wasn't my friend any more and she wanted her skipping-rope back. And I said I didn't have her skipping-rope and that I'd given it back to her and she said that I wasn't to play with her any more."

All of this came tumbling out like the contents of a bag that was turned over in one movement.

"You like school?" Mrs Armstrong asked.

"Only when I come first," Genetha answered.

"Does Joy like school?"

"I don' know. She says she does, but she says one thing one day and something else another."

They continued to walk while Genetha skipped for a few yards and walked a few more.

"Is Boyie good at school work?"

"Don't know," replied Genetha.

46

Mrs Armstrong then asked her daughter if she wanted any sweets.

"Yes. A nut-cake."

On the way to the shop she skipped so much that Gladys let go of her and allowed her to skip ahead. She bought two nut-cakes for a cent each and kept one for Boyie.

"That's the bigger one you're keeping for Boyie," protested Genetha.

"No, it isn't. Now stop that," her mother reproached.

Genetha sulked for a while, but was soon herself again.

"Joy's mother buys her the nut-cakes for a penny."

"Some children never eat nut-cakes in their whole lives," Mrs Armstrong told her daughter.

"Is Joy's mother rich?" Genetha asked.

"I don't know," her mother replied.

"She must be," said Genetha after a moment's reflection, "to buy Joy nut-cakes for a penny. A whole penny!"

"A whole penny!" her mother mocked her.

That night Gladys Armstrong sat looking out into a street where no one passed by and nothing ever happened. It was ten o'clock by the ponderous grandfather-clock that stood on the floor against the partition. The street was unlit and the bushes by the paling and the gutter could barely be made out in the shadows. If she stayed up long enough she would see the cab driver come home. He would get down from his seat, unhitch the horse and lead it across the bridge and under his house. He would then reappear a few minutes later to lower the hood of the carriage. Then, lifting the two shafts he would pull the carriage over the bridge and under the house where it remained until morning. The routine was invariable, but it was something to look forward to. The sound of chains, the two lamps lighting up the street, the jaded horse standing mutely between the shafts, ensured a certain poetry. Sometimes Armstrong came home before the cabman, at other times after him. She had taken to rushing to bed and pretending to be asleep whenever she saw him coming, as she was unwilling to face him when he might be bad-tempered or drunk.

And so the months passed. The rainy season gave way to the

dry and the dry season to the floods of January. The bridge was under water and the children caught the red, plump shrimp that came in from the canal simply by placing two baskets across the gutter. Then, the night air was heavy with moisture and there was an infinite sadness about this season of raincoats and galoshes, about a cabman who never uttered a single word, and a grandfather clock that ticked away one's life with a reassuring sound, resembling nothing else on earth.

7

The Arrangement

Armstrong told his wife that there were rumours of the sugar market collapsing. The country depended on sugar, he told her, and God knew what would happen if they could not sell the year's crop.

The foreboding in the air about sugar's future was echoed by the newspapers. The *Daily Argosy* warned against the dangers of panic and when, the same day, it was announced over the radio that sugar sales on many foreign markets were suspended those who held sugar shares tried to sell them at whatever price they could get. There was talk of suicides and a rumour that there would be a budget deficit. Several sugar estates were in danger of closing down and the government had drawn up plans for retrenchment and suspended recruitment to the Civil Service.

Gladys followed the crisis in the newspaper her husband brought home every day now. The gloomy forecasts all seemed to be correct and the news, followed over the radio and in the newspapers, filled people with dismay. Prayers were said in the churches for the recovery of the economy, the poor state of which was attributed by many ministers of the church to the wickedness the people of the country had courted in a time of plenty.

One of these men of God, the Reverend McCormick, gave sermons that attracted considerable attention. They were dubbed by the newspapers "The Doom Sermons", for reasons evident in an extract from one of them:

"Like Sodom and Gomorrah you sow what you reap and like Sodom and Gomorrah your harvest will be destruction. When the fire falls from the sky and you can hear the sword being fashioned by the smith it will be too late, you generation of lechers. From this very pulpit I warned you time and time again, when you were fattening yourselves and your children, when you were wearing bright clothing and be-

49

decking yourselves with jewellery; but you turned away like disobedient sheep. And now you come whining to me. This church has never been so full, not only with your sinful bodies, but with your fears. Look at you down there, your frightened faces gazing upwards as if I can help you. Only He can help you, provided you can rouse his compassion and trust. I tremble to think that you have fathered children, you who are incapable of guiding yourselves. You trust no one, not even your employers or your ministers. Take the strike that was called at the sugar estate last week: was it necessary? Haven't your employers looked after you like a father his children? Turn away, turn away from the path that led the Gadarene swine to their destruction and follow the way of the Lord."

The sermon was published in full by one newspaper, which also ran an editorial gleefully approving it and calling for an end to wage rises. The interests of employers and employees were identical, it said; if the one suffered so did the others.

One night, on returning home, Armstrong found Gladys entertaining his sister.

"Well, is what bring you to look me up?" he greeted her. "One thing I know, you didn't drop in on your way to the poor-house."

There was no reaction from the visitor, who avoided her brother's eyes. Gladys made a sign to him to desist.

Looking from the one to the other Armstrong waited for an explanation.

"She's got something to tell you," Gladys almost whispered as she got up from her chair and left the drawing-room.

"Ask Esther to light the other lamp and bring it," he called to Gladys as he went towards the kitchen.

"I know what you think of Father and me, Sonny. But you've got to help me!" his sister blurted out.

He stared at her, his face masking a feeling of satisfaction.

"I've lost a lot of money. I had twelve hundred dollars in sugar shares. . . . You know I don't know much about these things."

Armstrong's eyes opened wide.

"Twelve hundred dollars!" he exclaimed, his words followed

by a high-pitched whistle. "Where you get all that money?"

His sister put her hand to her mouth and coughed. She looked up and faced him, as if imploring him for something.

"Father left it for me," she answered reluctantly.

"With the business?" he asked.

"It was part of the cash that went with the business."

Armstrong got up from his seat, his hands thrust in his pockets. At that moment Esther appeared with the lamp, which she placed on the dining-table.

"Haven't I told you a hundred times not to put a lamp on that table?" Armstrong said irritably.

He took the lamp from her as she lifted it up from the table. After looking for a suitable place to put it, and finding none, he laid it on the floor near to his sister, so that it lit up her face in a grotesque fashion. His wife came back into the room.

"It sounds like a lot of money," his sister said, "but it only brought me in eight dollars a month. With the rent I get from a house I bought I could just make ends meet."

"And Father didn't even say a word to me about what he was leaving," observed Armstrong. "I always wondered why there wasn't any cash. But you were always sly. Even when he was dying, even then you made him believe he was going to live. Well, I couldn't stand his eau-de-cologne, his white kerchiefs and—"

"I know you had a hard time," she began.

"A hard time!" Armstrong exclaimed. "A hard time! He was always saying he'd be glad to see the back of me, yet if I wasn't in by a certain time he'd curse and shout."

Armstrong was almost frothing at the mouth with rage.

"Oh, Christ! I wonder why I did stick it so long," he went on. "Anyway he died like an animal. When his friends saw that he wasn't getting up any more they didn't bother to stick around. And those friends who took out his coffin took him out head first, not caring how he went. If he'd only seen how few people came to his funeral!"

He sat down, hardly able to contain his anger.

"But you," he continued after a while, "you played your part to the end. He and his kerchiefs."

51

"I did love Father," she said quietly, but defiantly. "And you don't have any right to talk about him like that."

Armstrong stood up again and looked down at his sister's frail figure; her expensive clothes annoyed him immeasurably.

Months ago he confided in a friend that he had forgotten about his family. His father was dead and there was no point in holding anything against him. He no longer held it against his sister for receiving the bulk of the inheritance. Now, as all the old hatreds that lay dormant in him were flaring up, he took in his sister's pointed shoes, her watch and shiny handbag. One more provocative word out of her and he would chase her out of his house.

Armstrong got up and began pacing up and down the room. He had not yet taken off his bicycle clips, which gripped the bottom of his trousers in such a way that, in normal circumstances, he would have appeared a figure of fun. Gladys was frightened and sorry for him, but she could not keep her eyes off his sister, whom she had imagined as a large imposing woman, a female version of Sonny Armstrong. Every time Armstrong spoke she seemed to shrink in her chair, like a nail in a hole, under the blows of a hammer.

If only Armstrong realised what a lonely woman his sister was, and that, with tactful handling, she would have been willing, on their father's death, to accede to any reasonable arrangement regarding the property that he might have suggested, his manner would have softened towards her. It was his stubbornness and his uncompromising attitude that had come between them, more than any selfishness on her part.

She had come to ask him to help her sell the wheelwright business at a good price. In the end, he said that he did not know if he was prepared to help, but that if he changed his mind he would come and see her.

Gladys accompanied her to the Public Road and saw her on a tram.

When Gladys returned home she found Armstrong sitting at the table. He had taken up the lamp from the floor and had put it in the middle of the table, precisely what he had forbidden the servant to do an hour ago. In his excitement he called her "Glad girl".

52

"What d'you think of that, eh, Glad girl? We'll see. We'll see. But you noticed how, though she came to beg, she still wore her fancy shoes? They come from New York, you know. You could see New York written all over them. Oh, yes! You got to hand it to her. She can dress."

When he was sixteen he used to stand in front of his sister's petticoat and stroke it and then, once he had looked round to make certain that no one was watching him, he would bend down and look under it. That petticoat folded over the clothes' horse had cost him many a sleepless night.

"Yes, she can dress," he repeated. "Now let's see: a thousand dollars, less advertising and lawyers' fees. That would make about nine hundred and fifty dollars. I could even buy the business from her myself."

He mused over the possibility of acquiring his sister's business, and as he flirted with the idea he began to think seriously of the obstacles in his way. It occurred to him that while he was at it he might suggest selling her house as well.

The very next day he made enquiries as to the money the business and property would fetch and he was advised to "Sell now!" The bottom would *soon* fall out of the property market as was happening with the other markets.

The very next day he went to see his sister and told her the bottom had already fallen out of the property market and that she would have to sell at once at a give-away price. He, however, anxious to become reconciled, would buy the property at a reasonable price she herself would fix. She agreed to sell for four hundred and fifty dollars and thanked him for the trouble he had taken, and for his generosity.

Three months later the Armstrongs moved into the Foreshaw Street property in Georgetown. The bottom-house room was reserved for his sister, to whom he let it below the price a similar room would fetch.

Gladys suspected what was going on, but dared not ask him. Besides, the dream of living in Georgetown again was realised when it seemed for certain that she would be buried in Agricola for the rest of her life. The fact that the house was in Foreshaw Street, not far from her parents' home, was of little importance. They were to live in Georgetown; and even if it had to be in a range-yard she would have been content.

8

The Move

Armstrong decided to move house at night. Like that he needed to hire no more than a dray-cart, for the darkness would effectively hide his possessions.

The children and Mrs Armstrong took the cab to town, while Armstrong himself accompanied the dray-cart and its driver. At first he tried to ride beside them, but found the pace so slow, he was forced to dismount and make the journey on foot, pushing his bicycle all the way.

A smoking kerosene lamp swung beneath the rickety cart, while Armstrong's own bicycle lamp cast a faint ray on the furniture, piled precariously behind the ass. The metal casing of the wheels made a grinding noise on the gravel and rattled over the bridges spanning the canals and trenches while, from time to time, a late vehicle went by in a cloud of dust.

On the outskirts of Georgetown, where the sugar-cane was in flower and all the frogs of the cane fields seemed to be croaking, Armstrong was anxious that his household goods, held in place by a deftly tied rope, should not fall off the cart. Occasionally he made the cartman stop, so that he could adjust a chair or retie the rope to ensure that it was firmly secured. This concern was greeted by a succession of suck-teeths and glances of scorn from the cartman, who would not waste any words on his hirer and his wretched possessions.

A strike of municipal cleaners had just come to an end, but the men in their carts had not yet had time to clean up the vegetable peel and rotting fruit lying around the vast wrought-iron market place in Bourda. The stench in Orange Walk, over which the cart was now making its way, was overpowering, and even the cartman, accustomed to daily excursions to wharves and the incinerator, was obliged to press his nostrils together.

Then, a few hundred yards further on, all was clean in residential Queenstown, the unblemished district, with its tall houses and blossoms on year end, and painted palings like flattened spears embracing yards darkened by thick branches of fruit trees.

Gladys was waiting at the window of the empty house for her husband.

Armstrong wanted to take in a mattress first, so that the children could sleep on the floor; but Gladys thought that in the excitement they would be unable to fall asleep anyway, and so they remained up to wander round the house and watch the bedsteads, commodes and other heavy pieces moved in.

A group of children gathered round the cart and amid the clatter of kitchen utensils one of them shouted out, "Look the po!"

They all exploded in a volley of laughter at the sight of the enamel chamber-pot. Armstrong pretended to reach for a gun in his breast pocket and at this the group dispersed immediately, frightened and delighted at the same time. But they continued to watch from afar in little groups, approaching a bit closer as each piece of furniture came off the cart.

"Is what that t'ing, man?" one of the children asked. "You ever see a t'ing like that?"

This remark was prompted by the appearance of the ornamental pedestal.

"Is what that for, man? Fo' put the po 'pon?" the wit persisted.

The groups of children burst out laughing again.

"You stupid or what, man?" another boy asked. "You can't sit 'pon a po on top o' that thing. You want to shite you'self with fright?"

Another roar of laughter followed this, for by now the youngsters, who were again close to the cart, were prepared to laugh at anything.

"I bet they come all the way from the bush. I bet that furniture an' all full-full o' snake."

Armstrong, afraid of making a fool of himself, pretended he had not heard these observations.

"Them not bush people, man. Them is a special people they call 'po' people."

The laughter that followed this was almost unbearable and

Armstrong decided to go inside and remain there for a while. But the observations and laughter continued unabated. And when the commode appeared and its lid flew open, revealing the tell-tale hole, the hilarity became an uproar.

"Look at that thing wit' the hole in the middle. Is wha' you put in that hole, mister?" the wit asked the imperturbable cartman.

"You batty!" exclaimed another boy, pre-empting the cartman.

Two women passing by could not resist chuckling.

"The po first, then you batty; else you might as well do it 'pon the floor."

"Look the racking-chair. Me gran'mother got a racking-chair," put in a very small boy who had until then not spoken.

"He grandmother got everything," a voice said scornfully.

"But I bet she in' got the t'ing with the hole in the middle, though."

"Shut you mouth!" the youngster spoke up boldly. "You never even been in me gran'mother house."

"You call that t'ing she living in a house? Is a fowl coop, man."

But before the boy could defend his grandmother, someone noticed the guitar, which the cartman was holding in his left hand, while in his right he held two upright chairs.

"Look that violin. I wonder which o' them does play the violin?"

"I bet is the man. When he sitting 'pon that high thing shitting in the po he does play the violin."

"That's what you call making loud music."

The other laughed but not as heartily as when Armstrong was there.

Someone shouted out in the direction of the house:

"Mister, come down quick, you furnitures falling to pieces."

But, unable to tempt Armstrong back out, the groups began to disperse, until only two barefoot boys of about four or five years old were left to see the rest of the possessions in.

Inside the house Gladys kept threatening the children with bed if they were not quiet. She was preoccupied with thoughts about the neighbours. Were they friendly? Did they have difficult children? Did they have dogs? Through the window she could see the well-lit street, the verandas of the houses opposite and the people who occasionally passed by on the road. Even the dingy cake shop they saw on the way seemed different from the shops in Agricola. It seemed to beckon you in.

Although much had not changed since she was married and went away, she felt like a stranger rather than someone who was coming back to the district in which she was born and spent her youth.

In the end all the furniture, utensils and boxes filled with goods were piled pell-mell in the drawing-room. Armstrong paid off the cartman, who disappeared round the corner in his empty cart, as slowly as he had come when it was full.

The night was damp, with rain threatening every moment, and only the odd passer-by could be seen hurrying home on foot or on his bicycle. A drizzle began to fall, noiselessly spattering the window-panes in fits. The children bedded down on the mattress, the iron members of the bed having been placed on the floor of the small bedroom, to be set up the following day.

And after the children and servants were asleep, the Armstrongs found themselves talking to each other. Gladys was sitting on a straight-backed chair, while Armstrong was squatting on a box, opposite her. The uncertainties that plague those who move into a new house and a new district had brought them together.

Armstrong looked straight at his wife, as in the old days, but she avoided his eyes.

"I used to go to that school, at the corner of Albert Street," she told him. "I think it's Albert Street. And the shop at the corner used to be owned by a man called Bertram. We used to buy shave-ice there on Saturday nights. There's a baker somewhere round the corner too. Funny how you forget things like that."

She kept avoiding his eyes, and he, noticing that she was trembling, went over to her. He kissed her on the mouth while stroking her breast with his right hand, and she whimpered like a puppy in pain. Armstrong lifted her off the chair on to the floor and bared her legs, pulling her drawers halfway down. Then, a few feet away from the sleeping children they made love on the floor, for the first time for three long months, so that she shuddered violently and hoped that he would not tire.

In the adjoining room Esther and Marion were lying near each other. Esther, who had not yet fallen asleep, reflected that she was the only one who saw the move as a change for the worse. While Marion was encouraging the children in their excited chatter during the drive to Georgetown, behaving like a "never-see-come-fo'-see", and Mrs Armstrong kept leaning forward to take in all the sights, restraining her own excitement under her dignified behaviour, Esther alone remained unmoved. After all, it was in the house in Agricola that she had started a new life and, like many people who look back on their first job with an inexplicable feeling of nostalgia, she held fast to the memories of those early days, like Boyie's birth and the discovery of books not meant for school.

Only a week ago she heard a school teacher, who had recently retired, talking to Mr Armstrong about the first class he had ever had.

"I can remember all the names on the register," he had said, "just as if it was today."

And he proceeded to reel off the names of the children in alphabetical order.

That was how Esther felt. And because she felt that way she was unable to understand the feelings of the children, of Marion and of Mrs Armstrong.

The drizzle had become a downpour under which the leaves of the trees in the back yard swished and sighed, and the rain pounded the shingle roof where the water poured into the gutters and into the large rain-water vat in the back yard.

When the rain stopped the street was asleep, while gusts of wind shook the trees, which gave up their water. The street lamp clattered in the wind, and above, the angry-looking clouds massed and fled, exposing for a brief minute a bright, full moon.

9

Dismissal

Marion and her mistress had become all but close friends and, unknown to Mr Armstrong or Esther, the servant was given a little allowance. The two women were often closeted for long periods, to the chagrin of Esther, who had to be satisfied with the children's affection as wages for her devotion.

"I hear Esther telling somebody she don't get pay," Marion told Mrs Armstrong one day. "And this person tell her she should make you pay her, 'cause all the servants in Georgetown does get pay. But don't tell her I tell you."

"The ungrateful girl. After all I've done for her," Mrs Armstrong rejoined. "Who was she talking to?"

"I don't know the woman," Marion replied.

"But you heard it yourself?"

"Yes. I hear it myself. But don't tell her I tell you," Marion urged anxiously.

"What did she say exactly?" Mrs Armstrong pressed her.

"She say a lot of things. She say you and Mr Armstrong don't hardly talk to one another. And she say you don't like her although she work her finger to the bone for you. I kian' remember all she say."

That same night Gladys asked Esther if she had been talking about what went on in the home, suspecting nothing of Marion's malice. Esther denied that she had. When asked whether she had told anyone that she was not paid, Esther admitted having been asked by the woman at the bakery if she was paid and telling her that she was not. It was not she who had brought up the subject. Mrs Armstrong made it plain that she did not believe her, but Esther insisted that she was not lying and said that she was prepared to face whoever gave her the information. However, Mrs Armstrong replied that that would not be necessary.

Afraid of the consequences of Marion learning that she had not kept her word, Gladys Armstrong wanted to tell Esther not to say anything to the younger servant; but she could not bring herself to ask her this favour and risk that haughty nod of the head that irritated her so much.

That night Gladys decided to tell her husband about Esther's conduct, but he came home gloomy and uncommunicative. She let him be and was glad when he went into the gallery, away from the rest of the household.

Following on rumours of dismissals — as part of the government retrenchment measures — Armstrong and a number of postmasters had received an official letter marked "O.H.M.S." that morning. With trembling hands he had opened his, to find that his salary had been reduced by a quarter. He nearly wept with relief. But as the hours passed his relief was replaced by resentment at the cuts that would have to be made in his spending. He had paid for his sister's property with money borrowed from the bank in anticipation of the sale of the Agricola home, which, however, realised much less than he expected. Consequently he was obliged to raise a mortgage on the Georgetown house in order to pay the difference. He was no better off than he had been in Agricola, what with the new mortgage and the considerably higher rates and taxes. Besides he was obliged to let the houses at a low rent, for gradually, as a result of the recession, boards advertising houses "To Let" had sprung up all over town.

Late that night when Gladys came out to bid him good night he told her of his salary cut.

"One of the servants will have to go," he said. "I just can't afford to feed so many mouths."

She was in favour of dismissing Esther, but Armstrong thought that Marion should leave as she had been with them a shorter time and was the less responsible of the two.

"What you got against Esther?" he asked her. "She worships the ground your children walk on."

"That's one side," replied Mrs Armstrong. "I can't trust her."

And in answer he made a gesture of impatience.

"Just because she doesn't like listening to your endless complaints!"

Armstrong's remark had struck home.

"Marion listens to me, yes. After all, I don't have anybody to talk to."

Armstrong, touched by the confession of what he had known all along, capitulated. Esther would go.

"Only, don't tell her when I'm at home," he said to his wife.

And the next day Gladys Armstrong told Esther that her husband said that he could not afford to keep her.

"You can always come and visit the children whenever you want," she added, in a sudden access of sympathy for the young woman.

Esther had suspected that something was in the air. Since she had been questioned about what had happened in the bakery she could not suppress a feeling of uneasiness. But the sudden blow left her speechless and she kept looking at Mrs Armstrong as if the older woman had struck her.

"It's not the end of the world," Gladys Armstrong remarked, unable to find suitable words of reassurance.

"Where'm I to go?"

"Why, to Little Diamond, back to your people," advised Mrs Armstrong.

"What am I going to do in Diamond? You came for me and took me away — but I can't go back. You took me away and now you're sending me back. . . ."

Mrs Armstrong, disarmed by Esther's helplessness, was tempted to change her mind; but her fear of offending Marion was enough to make her stick to her decision.

"I'm sorry, Esther."

"Marion won't take care of the children, you'll see," Esther warned.

Gladys Armstrong did not reply and Esther stood there, looking at her as if there were another solution which depended only on her. Then, irked by the servant's unwillingness to take no for an answer, she said:

"Haven't I given you everything I've given my children? Didn't you read whatever I was reading and put on what I wore? Compare yourself with any other girl in your position. Compare the way you talk now and the way you used to talk. My God! You even talk better than Mr Armstrong."

"I'm only a servant and can't do anything else," observed Esther.

"I'll give you a testimonial; and the way you talk you won't find any difficulty in finding a job in one of the big houses."

A wave of desolation overcame the young woman. The day after they moved to the new house Mrs Armstrong sent her back to Agricola to look for some brass, which was missing when the things were unpacked. When Esther stood in the drawing-room of the empty house, surrounded by space where once were chairs and lamps, brackets, a pedestal, window blinds and all the bric-à-brac that go to make a house's soul, she closed her eyes and listened to the silence. There she had become a woman, shedding the garments of her girlhood in the corner of the bedroom, alone and untutored. She remembered how she had lain on the floor, afraid that something terrible had happened to her; she was being punished for some wrong she had forgotten. She prayed that the fault in her body would be healed and wished desperately to confide in Mrs Armstrong. But she found her own solutions and later discovered that Nature had not dealt with her in a singular fashion.

A cup still lay on the kitchen dresser, where it had been left by Marion, who had been responsible for collecting up the crockery. The vat tap was dripping; it was she herself who had neglected to switch it off properly. In the morning heat a number of marabuntas were circling languidly under the mango tree, heavy with unpicked orange-coloured fruit. She sat down on the lowest step of the back stairs. On the paling which divided the yard from the neighbour's a lizard was scurrying, pursued by another, each appearing and disappearing in turn behind the staves until they went out of sight for good, hidden by the concrete pillar of the empty house. Had they really left this place for ever? She heard a child's voice coming from the direction of the Decembers' house across the trench. . . .

On the way back to town she was unable to get the house out of her mind. She would return, she thought to herself, and then remembered that the next time someone else would be living there. The furniture would be different and the blinds

63

would be a different colour, and the sounds issuing from it would be different.

"Can I stay here until I find another place?" Esther asked Mrs Armstroig.

"Of course, Esther. As long as you like."

That night, when everyone else was asleep, Esther sat at the window looking on to the back yard. In the dark she could see nothing except the outlines of the houses. She went out front and sat by a casement window, through which shone the garish light from the street lamp. In town the people seemed tight-lipped, unfriendly and intimidating, she mused. Then her thoughts turned to Marion. From the first moment she set eyes on her she knew that the younger girl would contrive her fall. Never before nor since had she had such a presentiment. . . . Where would she work? In a mansion or in a cottage like the Armstrongs'? How was she to start looking for work? Ought she to go from house to house? She knew no one in town, unlike Marion, who had already made friends with a young woman who worked for a lawyer in New Garden Street. She was also on speaking terms with the grocer, who gave her credit without demanding to see her mistress. She got the best pig-tails from him and free salt; and he even introduced her to his wife, saying how nice the servant was. Esther detested Marion from the bottom of her heart.

"They'll see how much she cares about the children!" she found herself saying aloud, as if she were speaking to someone in the yard.

After Esther had gone, Gladys Armstrong experienced bitter pangs of regret. The young woman had been with the family for eleven years and had left her imprint on their way of life. Boyie adored her. She used to read him stories from the news-papers and magazines and feed his taste for fantasy with talk of Masacurraman, Old Higue and other lore figures. She loved him as if he were her own, and believed that his rebelliousness was not unnatural, but something to be appeased, a form of energy to be transformed into something constructive. When he made a sling-shot to shoot birds she showed him how to trap them with bird lime, and then took the sling-shot away.

Mrs Armstrong had admired her way with her son and had wished that she would never get married before Boyie was off their hands.

It was impossible to tell if she missed Esther because of their long association or on account of her fears for the effect of her absence on Boyie.

10

Confessions

Since the move to Georgetown, Armstrong's estrangement from his wife seemed to take a decisive turn. He even neglected to observe the formalities of polite conversation he had maintained for the children's benefit. And in proportion to the couple's drawing apart from each other, the friendship between Gladys Armstrong and Marion developed, so that she became more a companion than a servant. She began to have a hand in spending the household money Armstrong gave Gladys; and when Genetha misbehaved she would slap her in her mother's presence; and Gladys, afraid of offending Marion, would say, "Do as Marion says, darling."

Sometimes, when Marion came back from market Mrs Armstrong found that she had bought ground provisions to make a breakfast different from the one she had planned. Once the servant came home with a string of crabs, which Gladys detested; but when she objected Marion sharply reminded her that she could not always please herself.

At other times Marion played the servant perfectly. She would massage Gladys's shoulders with soft, firm strokes of her fingers, till she groaned with pleasure. They would disclose to each other their innermost thoughts, as if their friendship was reinforced by the very difference in their social positions.

"Mr Armstrong hasn't been with me for over a year," Gladys once confessed. "Sometimes I get terrible headaches, but the doctor says it's because I don't get sufficient exercise. I know what it is, but I still go to the doctor. Over the past year I've taken more medicine than over the rest of my whole life."

One morning, just after Armstrong had gone to work, Genetha did something wrong and refused to apologise to Marion.

"I'm not apologising."

"Why?" asked Marion.

"I'm not telling you."

"You better!" Marion threatened.

66

"No!"

Marion raised her hand, but Genetha stared at her without flinching.

"Go on, hit me! I dare you to hit me. I'm not Mother, I don't care."

"You li'l bastard!" shouted Marion. "You watch! You going end up a street woman. You goin' see where them fine airs going get you."

From behind the door Gladys was listening, more embarrassed than hurt; and by the afternoon she and Marion were as thick as ever.

"I had a dream last night," Gladys told her during one of their lengthy conversations, "about Boyie. I was calling him by his right name, Rohan. He kept ignoring me whenever I asked him anything. I was getting all worked up, but I tried to control myself. Then all of a sudden he turned to me and said, 'Father doesn't like you any more.' I don't know what got into me, but I kept seeing little lights in front of me and it was as if I was floating, above and away, over the houses, away from Boyie and his father and everything."

Gladys's eyes were glazed, as if she had got up suddenly in the middle of the night and did not realise where she was.

"What happen then?" asked Marion.

But Mrs Armstrong did not reply to the question.

"It's Esther," she said vaguely. "I'm sure she'll do something to Boyie."

"But she gone," Marion said.

"My mother used to say," pursued Mrs Armstrong, "that some people pray for you and then something is bound to happen to you. They go to church and kneel down in a pew and pray and pray and pray until they know the prayer'll be answered. You can pray for somebody to get well, but you can also pray for them to get sick and waste away slowly and then die. And you know how Esther likes going to church."

"You got her on your mind," Marion remarked. "Tobesides, a dream in' got nothing to do with praying for you. If you ask me, Boyie not going to come to no good. I mean, they kian' even handle him in school. Look at the marks on his backside. Every day he get more and he don't care."

"I don't know, but I've never dreamt so much in my life as since I've come to live here. I'm always dreaming of Agricola, and yet I couldn't stand it there. The other night I dreamt of the cab man."

"Oh, him!" Marion said scornfully at the thought of the scruffy cab-driver. "What you dream then?"

"I'm not sure," Mrs Armstrong replied. "Everything was so confusing. I can't remember."

"Sometimes you frighten me the way you talk," Marion said.

"Don't you dream?" Gladys asked.

"Sometimes," replied Marion. "But not like that. In Agricola . . . you not goin' laugh if I tell you?"

"No," Gladys promised.

"Well, in Agricola I used to dream of the minister."

"Who? The young one?" Gladys asked.

"Yes."

"And what you dreamt about him?"

"You going to laugh," Marion protested.

"No, I promise," Gladys said, impatient to hear what her servant had dreamt of the personable minister of the village church.

"Well, I dream that one day he chase me down the yard and I fall under the jamoon tree. He then fall 'pon me — and it happen."

"What?"

"You know," Marion said with a giggle.

"What? In daylight?"

"Yes. What's the difference?"

"A dream's a dream," observed Gladys.

"Well, it wasn't exactly a dream," Marion ventured.

"You mean it really happened?"

"Yes. But not with him."

Gladys put her face near to Marion's and whispered.

"With who, then?"

"With the man next door. He was coming from he field and he give me two banana. He poke his finger in my stomach and say I was getting fat. Then he pretend to chase me and I begin to run. And when he did ketch me he put his hand round my

68

waist and burst out laughing. I start to feel all funny inside. . . ."

"Here?" Gladys suggested, pointing to the pit of her own stomach.

"Yes, there," Marion agreed. "But really all over. And then he begin chasing me again and when he ketch me he did throw me down in the grass and ask me what I got in here."

She pointed to her bodice.

"And I say to him, 'Why you don't look?' And he laugh and put his hand in my bodice and start talking to me. And he say he going to cover my face with my dress, and he lift it up and cover my face . . . and then it happen."

Gladys felt strangely excited and wanted to be alone. Marion, thinking that she disapproved of her story, said, "If you want me to stop."

"No," replied Gladys.

Marion looked down at the floor, waiting to see if Gladys was willing to pursue the conversation.

"When I was a girl I never went out alone," Gladys said after a while.

"In Mocha," Marion said in turn, "the boys were always hanging round you, you know."

"I don't know, Marion. We used to watch the boys from the window and think about them, that's all."

"Well, as I say, in Mocha the boys was always hanging round you. But the one I did like never take hold of me and never ask me for anything, like the neighbour."

"Did it happen again? With the neighbour?" Gladys enquired.

"The next day I go to the house, when his wife out. He ask me what I did want, as if he never see me before. He so vex he tell me to get out of the house. 'You want to get me in trouble?' he shout. 'If me wife see you here she going kill me.' And when I stay by the door he fly at me and tell me to go away or he'd call the police. After that he never talk to me again."

Gladys looked back on the days in Agricola and tried to recall the neighbour and to connect him with Marion. He had a pinched face and his breath always smelt of alcohol. Suddenly Marion disgusted her. She was getting too full of herself. Her mother had always said you had to keep servants at arm's length, otherwise they became too familiar.

"We're going to the gardens today?" Marion asked.

"No, you've got the brass to do," Gladys said bluntly.

She intended to stop the rot, keep the girl in her place. Gladys Armstrong stood by her resolution for a few days, no longer helping her with the cooking nor accompanying her to the market in the morning, and if ever she ate alone she left the things on the table to be cleared by Marion. She even got her husband to speak to her about the way she swept the house, and when the young woman protested to Gladys about Armstrong's treatment she spoke to her sharply, reminding her that Mr Armstrong was her employer.

But with the passing days Gladys's loneliness overcame her pride and, as suddenly as she had rejected Marion's companionship, just as suddenly she took her to her bosom again, showering her with kindness. Gladys asked Marion to forgive her, while Marion denied that she had suffered any cruelty at Gladys's or her husband's hands.

And Gladys, as proof of her gratitude to Marion, made a confession she had been on the point of making more than once.

"People look at you and say, 'How you're lucky! See what you've got! You talk so nice!' And they fail to understand how pathetic and vulnerable you are. . . . I dread meeting people I used to know, because I've forgotten how to make conversation and would only make a fool of myself. And just the thought. . . . . I need my husband more than ever, but he spurns me as if I'm a leper. Yet in the old days when he came courting he was circumspect and kind and kept this side of him hidden from me. How people change! And now I've come back to live near my family it's too late because we hardly know one another any more."

Mrs Armstrong covered her eyes with her forearm, in the way young children attempt to hide from adults, without even turning their heads — a gesture that cut Marion's heart more than tears could.

At a loss for words Marion was about to say the first thing

70

that came into her head when Mrs Armstrong spoke once more, her head slightly bowed and her right hand still over her eyes.

"I protected him from my family, quarrelled with my sister on account of him. Could I do any less? He's the father of my children. For more than a year he hasn't caressed me and I've lost all confidence in myself. After Boyie was born he wouldn't touch me, as if having a child was a crime. I waited and waited, but he offered no explanation, not even after I said I needed him to sleep by me. I begged him, practically went on my knees and told him I'd do *anything* he wanted, provided he lay by me. God is my witness I was driven to it. It isn't as if I think of nothing else but that. Then when— Then he started taking an interest in me again and the third child came along. But it died soon afterwards, before it could be christened, before it had a name. Its tiny body withered and died, its tiny hands and feet and its tiny head withered and died. Mr Armstrong took the coffin under his arm and laid it in the hearse where it was lost among the white flowers and taken to St Sidwell's cemetery. And for weeks afterwards I would start crying, in the street, at table, on going to bed, and for no reason . . . as if all my children had died. . . ."

"My little brother and sister," broke in Marion, "dead before they was a year old too. And my aunt child—"

"You don't understand, Marion," Mrs Armstrong said gently, turning to face her. "Above all I cried because I knew that the child's death meant the end between Mr Armstrong and myself. He went further and further away from me, like a flock of dark birds. Throughout the world there are women who abort their children, millions of tiny aborted bodies are flushed away every year, some of them whimpering and screaming. . . . How innocent you are! But, you see, Nature does it without wincing. . . . I've never been able to understand my husband's bitterness. In my family we accept things as they are. Anyway, one day we'll all have to account before our maker for our deeds and our thoughts. Oh, yes! And our deeds. Do you know why I got rid of Esther?"

"No."

"She was in love with Mr Armstrong," Gladys went on.

"He did know?" asked Marion.

"I don't know. But I couldn't bear it. Since she came to live in Agricola with her girlish body, without breasts, she was in love with my husband. All these years I suffered the mortification of watching her love for him grow. Now you see why she was never interested in men?"

Then Mrs Armstrong fell silent, foundering in the exposure of her pain. She waved to Marion, who then left the room. And she shook her head, recalling her courting days and the days before, when she and her sisters would walk on the beach in a line, like country women, and edge round the little lakes of grey water that dotted the sand where the tide had washed the beach a few hours ago.

II

Our furtive conversations
Were like lightning at evening
But your prints in the wet leaves
Where you stood
And your ringless fingers
Are all that I remember now.

11

The Epileptic Whore

Armstrong reduced his wife's allowance when his own salary was cut. Boyie's shoes were taken away from him when he came home from school in order to spare them, while Genetha's dress had to last all week. Gladys herself wore clothes at home that she would have cast off and given to the servant while they were in Agricola. The butter, which previously had been kept on the table and used at will, was now carefully rationed. Even Marion's white headdress, insignia of her status as servant, was not replaced when it began to suffer from constant laundering, so that the last evidence of rank that distinguished her from her employer was removed.

Armstrong was the only one to dress as well and eat as well as he had always done. He could not walk into his post office looking like a pork-knocker, he declared; and it was in the interest of the whole family that he should be well fed. In these days, when there were six men breathing down your neck, ready to step into your shoes when you went down with ague, it was no good saving on food. Look at Stuart, one of the best postmasters in Demerara. After four months on sick pay they retired him on a pension that could not feed an estate mule, and appointed a new man to Providence Post Office.

Yet, he could not ignore the dark rings under his wife's eyes.

"You should go to sleep earlier, like in Agricola," he advised her. "You used to go to sleep early there. Mind you, who can sleep through the night with all these stray dogs roaming the street and keeping up that racket. You pay your rates and taxes to run a city pound that doesn't even do its job."

"I sleep longer than you," she retorted. "In fact I spend half my life in bed."

Armstrong, despite his preoccupation with money matters, was happier that he had ever been. If in Agricola he sometimes came home at ten or eleven at night, he now did so regularly; and on Fridays he invariably crossed his bridge at midnight,

75

tottering uncertainly as he put away his bicycle under the house.

He and his friends frequented a cake shop in a Kitty back street. After work, he used to ride the two miles or thereabouts from his post office in Lombard Street to see a school teacher friend who lived a stone's throw from the cake shop. At Doc's home another friend called for them and the three went off to play dominoes and drink beer until the shop closed.

On Saturday nights the friends were in the habit of going "on the binge", as they liked to say. Occasionally they walked to the red-light district in and around Water Street, where they drank with the whores.

On these excursions Armstrong at first felt like an adventurer in uncharted country; but in time, when he got to know the girls' names and developed a predilection for the smoke and liquor-scented rooms and the sound of the strident music, he looked on these sorties into depravity as outings into some forbidden but beautiful well of sin.

Sonny Armstrong was particularly taken by a whore named Lesney. While his two friends talked to the people round them he liked watching Lesney dance, mesmerised by the way she threw out her right foot. She danced with little effort, in comparison with the others; and her limbs, frail and supple, suggested a vague promise of repose. No one else seemed to share his high opinion of her good looks and, in fact, Doc thought her plain. Armstrong was afraid to dance with her, lest he made a fool of himself, so he confined his attentions to speaking to her. But her reticence made him so nervous he found himself taking twice as many pulls on his cigarette as he normally did, and, no sooner had he finished one than he lit another, a practice he abhorred in others.

Their conversations went like this:

"Thank God it's stopped raining," he would say. "Want a cigarette?"

She would then show him the cigarette she was smoking. After tapping with his fingers on the table and pulling up his socks, which were well secured by suspenders, he would then move his shoulders to the music.

"Want to dance?" he would ask.

Then, as she got up he would say, "We better wait for a slow piece. I like slow pieces."

At that point someone might come up to her and invite her to dance, thus saving him from further torture.

One Saturday night, inflamed by the skin exposed by her deeply-cut dress, he invited her to dance, throwing caution to the winds. He held her close, so that he could feel her small, firm bubbies against his body.

"Your place far from here?" he asked, emboldened by the effect of the rum he had drunk.

"Robb Street," she answered laconically.

"What about leaving now?"

"If you want to," she agreed, snuffing out her cigarette on the floor.

Armstrong bade his friends goodbye and left with the girl. She had put on a thin jumper against the cool night air. Once outside he was tongue-tied and they walked silently along the wet pavement, glistening from a recent downpour. He made up his mind to put his arm round her waist when they got to the next street lamp, and then, in full glare of the electric light he thrust his hand under her jumper and round her waist.

On reaching the building where she had a room she pushed the door open. Armstrong followed her along the corridor and up the stairs. On the landing she rummaged in her handbag for a key.

Inside the room she took off her jumper, then her shoes, before she sat down on the bed, her hands on her lap.

Armstrong went and stood by the window, from where he surveyed the meagre furnishings in the room, the chest-of-drawers on which stood a basin with a jug rising from its deep recess, painted with a floral design. A clean white towel hung over the lip of the jug and rested for part of its length on the chest-of-drawers.

Armstrong's eyes wandered towards the girl's naked feet, the toes of which were warped into the shape of the shoes she wore.

He turned to look out of the window. Below it lay the yard of a Chinese restaurant, over which was stretched a line strung up with dozens of thin-skinned, pink sausages. Vague outlines of kitchen workers seen through the back window of the res-

taurant were moving about like puppets behind a translucent
screen.

Armstrong pretended to be interested in what he could see
through the window, while in reality he was wondering how he
should set about seducing the girl.

"It's her business. She does it for money," he kept telling
himself. But whenever he turned round to look at her, at her
dress, her unshod feet, he took fright at his intentions and
clung to his post at the window. The shadows behind the
restaurant window came and went at irregular intervals, pro-
viding a kind of accompanying suspense to his indecision.

Armstrong found himself looking through the window as well
as at it, for imprinted on the glass was Lesney's reflection,
immobile, slightly hunched. He saw her turn for a moment, no
doubt to see what he was up to, only to turn back again to
face the door. Then he saw her light a cigarette and exhale a
horizontal column of smoke, which gathered in an irregular
mass before rising slowly above her head.

"You don't ever talk?" Armstrong asked, joining Lesney on
the bed.

"Yes."

"Why you so shy?"

"I not shy," she replied.

"You like dancing, eh?"

"Yes."

"What else you like?" he enquired in an attempt to get the
conversation going.

But her only answer was to shrug her shoulders and then
to reach out for the packet of cigarettes which she had placed
on the wash stand.

"You like me?" Armstrong went on.

"You all right," she answered.

Hell, he thought, *I can't just throw myself on her like an
animal.*

"You're comfortable?" he asked.

"Yes."

"You like me?"

"I say yes," she replied impatiently.

If it were not for her little bubbies, Armstrong would have

78

got up and gone home. He sat down beside her on the bed and drew her towards him, frail and unresisting. Her hair was parted down the middle and the two plaits joined in an upward sweep.

"You're so frail!" he whispered.

But she gave no answer.

He then opened her blouse, exposing her chest, and felt a strong urge to smother her in kisses. He felt her heart hardly beating and the apparent indifference only served to fire his passion.

"Open my trousers, ne?" Armstrong told her, while guiding her hand.

But, instead of responding, she slipped out of his arms and fell to the floor. He watched the contortions of her attractive face as the convulsions of an epileptic fit began to shake her whole body.

In an attempt to flee Armstrong opened the door, not understanding at first what had come over her. But at the head of the stairs he turned round and noticed a light under the door of the room adjoining the girl's. He knocked softly on the strange door and a gruff voice called out, "Is who?"

"Me," Armstrong answered.

"Me who?"

He knocked again without answering and waited until a middle-aged woman opened.

"Is who?" she asked pugnaciously.

"A girl in the next room. . . . I brought her home. She's got fits."

"Oh, Lesney," said the woman, her harsh expression vanishing with the words.

Turning round, she addressed an unseen companion.

"Is Lesney," she said, "she got a attack."

Brushing past Armstrong she hurried into Lesney's room. Then almost immediately she reappeared and went back into her own room, from which she emerged once more with a spoon in her hand.

"Gi'e me the pillow on the bed," she ordered Armstrong without looking at him.

Armstrong complied and the woman placed the pillow under

Lesney's head. Then, with Armstrong standing above her she watched Lesney through a succession of fits.

Some time later there was a knock on the wall.

"Stay with she; if I don't go now—" began the woman. But before she could finish a voice bellowed through the partition.

"How long you gwine keep me waiting, ne?"

The woman departed without more, leaving Armstrong to stay with Lesney who was lying flat on her back, legs apart and arms stretched out, away from her body. In between periods of calm her legs and arms would retract and then fly out violently and her head shift from side to side with each spasmodic movement. And Armstrong knelt by her, dreading an unexpected intrusion. Then the attacks ceased altogether and he was conscious of an unearthly silence round him and wondered how the young woman could stand it in that house on her own.

Before going away he placed a dollar note on the piece of furniture that passed for a dressing-table and went out into the night. His handkerchief was wet with the sweat he had wiped from the young woman's forehead.

When he got home he turned on the light in the dining-room, and noticing that the door of the kitchen where Marion slept was ajar, he went in and found her sprawled in the middle of the floor, her naked thighs exposed from turning in her sleep. Armstrong threw himself on her and satisfied his thwarted passion, while Marion made no effort to resist him.

The next night Armstrong sought out the prostitute again, partly because he could not get her out of his mind and partly to see if she had recovered. He took her back to her room, this time avoiding the well-lit streets.

"You're sure you're all right now?" he asked her.

"Yes."

He was put out by her inability to make small-talk; and to keep the conversation going he was soon telling her of his past and his dead parents.

He knew where his umbilical cord was buried, in the yard of the house where he was born. The tree that was planted over it must be quite large now, he told her. But Lesney was born in Georgetown and had never met anyone who set any store by that sort of thing. Nor did his disclosure that his

80

father used to exercise with dumb-bells interest her either. But when he mentioned his mother she seemed to pay attention.

"A man used to come home every Thursday night to talk to her about controlling her life," Armstrong told Lesney. "And he taught her how to let her spirit leave her body and wander about the village."

"You believe in that?" Lesney asked.

"I don't, but she did. There are things you can't account for . . . like why I can't keep my eyes off you."

Then he began to speak of how he came to be attracted to Queenstown and everything connected with it, even the men who went round the well-maintained alleyways with cisterns of oil which they sprayed on the gutter-water to kill the larvae of mosquitoes that carried malaria.

"Something did draw me to those houses in Queenstown," he continued. "In the village I come from, with pigs rooting for food in the mud, lived a woman from town. I used to read the Bible to her because she had cataracts on her eyes and couldn't read for herself. Whenever she invited me into her house I used to tremble with excitement. Everything there was from a different world — the furniture, the window blinds, the lamps, the bed — everything. Her house was always quiet and sometimes my own voice frightened me when I was reading. At times I used to go up the back stairs and slip through the open door, but her ears were sharp and she almost always heard. 'Is it you, Armstrong?' she used to say. She never once called me by my first name. My wife talks like her and, even though she does everything I say, has got the same superior manner, as if you could never hurt her. . . . At times I wish for something to happen so that I can show my wife how much I care for her, that everything I do is because of this unutterable love. And yet I treat her worse than a dog sometimes. If I did tell you the things I did and especially the things I'd like to do to her, the humiliation I'd like to heap on her. . . ."

Then, with unexpected violence he remarked:

"I don't know why her family does give themselves such airs! None of my people even went to a card-cutter by night to find out if they'd ever get married."

Lesney, whose interest in what Armstrong was saying had

81

waned, asked: "You mean you wife sister been to one of them women to find out if she going get married?"

"Yes."

"I didn't know people like you ever do things like that," the prostitute remarked.

"Ha!" Armstrong exclaimed bitterly. "They do it secretly, at the dead of night. They only go up the back stairs; and when they reach home they prostrate themselves on a bed and inhale smelling-salts."

Armstrong waited for the young woman to pursue the questioning, but she remained silent. Then he began talking again, harping on his inadequate background, his in-laws' aloofness and matters that cut deep into his heart. He talked late into the night, of the isolation in marriage that breeds unhappiness, and of the guilt he felt on account of the lack of contact with his children.

"What you thinking about?" he asked Lesney unexpectedly.

She answered without hesitation. "I thinking 'bout how much you going pay me."

Armstrong, annoyed at the girl's lack of sensitivity, fell silent. Through the open window came the muffled sound of footfalls on the pavement and the occasional noise of horses' hoofs as a late cab rolled by. He recalled the night he took Gladys out for a carriage ride and his unkindness when she seemed receptive to his efforts at reconciliation. The wounds they had inflicted on each other were now beyond healing. What he had told Lesney seemed now untrue: he no longer loved her. And this knowledge came to him like a thunderbolt and with it a sense of relief, as if a knot in his heart had loosened.

Armstrong got up, rummaged in his pocket and took out a couple of bank notes, which he handed the girl.

"You not doing it?" she asked, a little surprised.

"No."

"Please you'self. Is because o' yesterday?" she enquired, with a sudden show of concern.

"The fits? No! I'll come another time, you'll see," he assured her.

Once on the pavement he walked briskly away from the house in the direction of his home.

12

Friends

The next day, a Sunday, Gladys Armstrong, the children and Marion went to church and joined with the congregation in celebrating Harvest and the reaping that comes as the reward of man's labour.

On the following evening Armstrong went to look up his school-teacher friend, after he had made sure that everything at the post office was in order.

Doc was about forty and lived alone. His skill at dominoes and card games had earned him the name "Doc" among his cronies. Dark, with fine striking features, he was critical about everything and everyone around him. Anyone who caught the two men in conversation would have marvelled at the way Armstrong listened to his friend's interminable monologues, with that patience that springs from affection or great admiration.

Armstrong, out of pride, had carefully concealed from his friend the true state of his marriage. Doc, on the other hand, seemed to take pleasure in recounting his failures.

"I want to talk to you before B.A. comes," Armstrong told him. B.A. was their other friend.

"You're not in trouble?"

"No, no, it's not trouble," Armstrong replied.

The two men sat down, but immediately Armstrong got up. He then told his friend about what had happened after he left him on the night of Lesney's attack. He modified the story here and there, neglecting, for instance, to say that he had wanted to run away and leave the girl. Doc listened intently, thinking that the story had an exciting end. Armstrong confessed that he was afraid of the consequences of the incident, but did not tell of his return to the prostitute's room.

"But what could happen?" Doc asked. "You think that because the girl had a fit you'll end up in prison? My father used to have his bouts regularly, and when he fell down in

the house and started frothing at the mouth no one took the
slightest notice of him. He'd be twitching on the floor and we'd
be passing up and down like at the railway station. Sometimes
they used to last half an hour. Man,.if that's all you've got to
worry about you're on easy street."

Then, drawing his chair closer and casting a glance sideways
as if someone might be listening, he began to tell a story
Armstrong had heard a number of times.

"Ha! You talk about trouble! When my wife and I were
engaged she promised me milk and honey and everything you
can think of. Anyway, that's neither here nor there. The point
is you're happy. I'm not. I was after a headship some time ago;
and some fellow whispered into the ear of a natural superior
that I was an immoral man, because I'm separated from my
wife. I mean, you're allowed to be an immoral headmaster,
have your women on the side, drown yourself in liquor; but as
a headmaster, not as an aspirant to a headship. Why I separated, eh? I separated because my mother-in-law was always in
my house. Now, any self-respecting man would've shown her
the door, and that would've been that. But where the women're
concerned I'm no self-respecting man. I've never been at ease
with them. It's not that I'm afraid, mind you; you might call
it anxiety. With men it's different. I'm never at a loss for
words, but when there're women about my tongue grows fat
and I start grinning without knowing why. My legs start turning
to water and my nose needs blowing; and every action you
can perform with your hands I perform. Man, it's so stupid!
Whenever my wife said to me she was expecting someone,
I always wanted to run out of the house quick, before the lady
even got to the gate. But I was no coward. Oh, no! I used to
stand my ground. I mean, it was my house and my wife and my
time. I used to go into the back room and practise: 'Howdye
do,' I'd say. That was a mistake to begin with, saying howdye
do to a woman. Anyway I'd say to the mirror, 'Howdyedo? Do
come in!' And I used to work myself up into a state welcoming
this woman. Oh, yes, I used to stand my ground and wait for
her. But as soon as the bridge creaked I'd go lame.

"Anyway, as I was saying, my mother-in-law took it into her
head to start coming to look after the baby. She changed it,

85

cleaned it up, put it to bed and so on. She saved my wife a lot of work. But she was a pest, a menace on two feet. That woman intimidated me so much I was glad to get out in the mornings to school so I could push the children about and take it out on them. Especially the little girls who looked as if they would grow up to resemble my mother-in-law. The children used to call me the 'Hangman'. But it came to the point where I couldn't stick it any longer and I asked for a transfer to a Georgetown school. But they could only get me one in Truly Island. It was far enough and one Saturday I strolled down to Suddie Stelling as if I was going down to the sea for a walk. That was that. Freedom and eternal peace. And five years later I got my transfer to Georgetown."

"And what about the child?" Armstrong asked.

"What about my wife? What about my mother-in-law? God rest her pestilential soul!"

"You're not frightened somebody'll meet you?" asked Armstrong.

"I used to be," admitted Doc. "But you can't stay frightened all the time. Yes, man, you're lucky. . . . Sometimes I wonder if I did the right thing when I beat it. I hate the school I'm in. The teachers are afraid of the headmaster, who's afraid of the inspector, who probably pees himself when he's talking to the Director of Education. One day—"

Just then there was a whistle outside. Doc peered through the window and saw B.A. riding down the street.

"B.A.," he called out. But his friend did not hear him.

"He must've been whistling some time and we didn't hear him," Armstrong said, peeved that he might be missing his game of dominoes.

"Let's go down to the cake shop, ne?" Armstrong suggested.

"No!" Doc said, rejecting the idea. "He'll come back when he sees we aren't there. Then we'll all go down to the shop and play."

He went inside and came back with a big bottle of rum, already broached, but almost full. He had lit a cigarette, which was gripped firmly between his lips as he tried to pull the cork from the bottle. Armstrong helped himself to the rum, pouring the amber liquid into the glass his friend had brought him.

"As I was saying," pursued Doc. "'One day the headmaster asked me to take a letter to the Director of Education himself. Man! When I got there even the gravel in the drive was out of this world. The front door was open and I went in. The hall alone at the foot of the staircase was twice the size of this room. It was painted white and carpeted, and at the top of it was a climbing plant. As I went upstairs I could hear someone playing the piano; not your little tinkle-tinkle, bang-bang. No, the genuine sound like you hear over the radio at night, when the street is silent and it's the hour for listening. Oh, man, my skin did begin to crawl at that surge of music, and I thought to myself that of a sudden all the petty things in the world were blown away."

His face was transfigured as he relived the experience.

"Man," he continued, "I don't know anything about music. I can't tell anybody's major from his minor; but in all that sumptuousness, with that climbing plant and the scent of flowers from the garden, the new paint, that piano sounded rich and arresting. When I got to the top of the staircase I saw a man playing the piano, a big grand-piano, on which two men could lie down full length. He saw me and stopped playing. And then you know what he did? You know what he said? What Mr Bain-Gray said to me?"

His face was twisted in anger and he looked at Armstrong as if the latter had abused him.

"What'd he say?" Armstrong asked, eager to hear the story's end.

"He looked at me and in his educated, cultured voice, he said, 'Are you the new gardener?' You ever felt like spitting in someone's face? And yet, and yet this is probably the worst of it. When I said I wasn't the gardener and showed him the letter he said he was sorry, in his suave, persuasive voice; and I then regretted that I had felt like spitting at him. I told myself that I was too suspicious and violent. But whenever I look back on that visit I squirm, because I was right to feel as I did at first."

"Why?" asked Armstrong.

"While he wrote the note he wanted me to take back he didn't even ask me to sit down. There were chairs all over the place, straight-backed chairs, easy chairs, wicker chairs, enough

87

for a whole regiment. But I stood among those chairs and waited. What's a chair for, eh? For sitting on? For leaning on? To rest your feet on? To copulate?"

His voice was becoming shriller and shriller, and at this point he got up and thrust his hands in his pockets, a gloomy expression on his face.

Armstrong could not understand his friend's excitement. A show of obsequiousness in the presence of his superiors was as natural as expanding and contracting his chest. Besides, from the story Doc told this Bain-Gray man was a pleasant fellow. But there was no crossing his friend when he was like this. In order not to commit himself he leaned forward and poured some rum into his glass.

Doc sat down again, took his cigarette from the ash tray, but did not put it into his mouth. A long cylinder of ash was about to break off and fall to the floor.

Armstrong felt uncomfortable, for he wanted to talk about Lesney. This always happened with Doc. You'd start out by telling him your troubles and just when you were getting into things he would recount a period of his life or an incident that bore no relation to what you were saying.

"The function of conversation," he once said, "is not to exchange views, but to relieve yourself."

The trouble was, he seemed to be continually relieving himself instead of giving his companion a chance.

A whistle from outside broke his train of thought. Armstrong looked out of the window and saw B.A. dismounting from his cycle. Doc called him up.

B.A. was indignant that Armstrong and Doc had let him go down to the cake shop without telling him that they were there. But a couple of shots of rum appeased him and in a short time he was shrugging his shoulders to no purpose, a sure sign that he was relaxed and felt at home. This curious tic had got worse since he lost his job as a book-keeper a few months back.

"In America they eating out of dustbins," B.A. said. "I tell you I prefer to be in this old country than America, 'cause you'll never starve. You can always go down by the dam and pick a mango or catch a few cuirass and eat them."

"But who want to eat cuirass?" Armstrong objected, revolted at the idea of consuming the notorious shit-eating skin-fish.

"You don't eat cuirass 'cause you still got a steady job!" B.A. rejoined hotly. "I talking 'bout people that in' got a job."

"In any case," Doc butted in, "in America there're employment benefits."

B.A. laughed scornfully.

"I wonder when they draw these benefits? Before they rummage in the dustbins or after?"

This remark annoyed Doc. Armstrong wanted to listen to the radio, so as to ensure that the evening would end peacefully, but Doc wanted to talk.

In spite of B.A.'s thin skin, his two friends missed him when he was not there. They missed his poor logic, his obsessive concern with neatness and above all the fact that he never complained. Armstrong's money troubles did not seem serious when B.A. was around, neither did the indignities Doc suffered at the hands of his headmaster. In fact, it was only in his sour presence that they could laugh often and heartily. But lately Doc and Armstrong noticed that a change had come over him. Where before he had smiled occasionally, now he seemed incapable of any display of mirth.

The three friends left soon afterwards for the cake shop in Kitty. But while playing dominoes a particularly violent argument broke out, during which Doc tactlessly made a remark about B.A.'s immaturity.

"Jesus!" exclaimed B.A., "look who talking! You think that by talking you can find a substitute for something. You're the biggest coward in the country," B.A. flung at him.

The shop-keeper was sleeping like a child, his body heaped in his rickety chair under the overhead bulb, which bathed his head and shoulders in a pale light.

Doc, stung by B.A.'s malicious remark, looked at him long and silently.

"Come, let's play," suggested Armstrong, making a show of shuffling the dominoes.

"You two make me sick," B.A. said in a voice throbbing with violence.

Doc lit a cigarette ostentatiously, inhaled deeply and then

exhaled a great deal of smoke, while Armstrong looked from the one to the other, desperately hoping that some unforseen remark, some unlikely occurrence would save the situation.

"What's eating you, B.A.?" Armstrong asked.

"So it's my fault, eh? Jesus in heaven!" B.A. exclaimed, at the end of his patience.

"I didn't say was your fault, but lately you're flying off the handle for nothing," Armstrong said in a conciliatory tone.

"I can't talk to people like you," declared B.A. "You hear the man insult me and you tell me I'm flying off the handle. All right, I flying off the handle, but I don't got to stay here with the two of you," B.A. retorted.

Doc and Armstrong listened to him crossing the shop bridge. Stunned by his behaviour they sat without knowing what to say to each other. It was Armstrong who spoke first.

"It's this damn trouble he's having with his son. If I was in his place I'd tell him to go and find somewhere else to live."

"You're sure that's what's eating him?" Doc asked.

"There's been talk."

Doc slowly replaced the dominoes in their box. B.A. seemed to have something against him, he reflected, for Armstrong always came off more lightly than he did whenever he attacked them. What if he stayed away for good? No, that was impossible.

"Let's go to Water Street," suggested Armstrong.

"On a weekday?" Doc asked, surprised at the suggestion.

"Why not? The girls're there every day."

"I don't have money for drinks. It's near month-end," Doc said.

"I'll pay," Armstrong offered.

Then, as they were leaving the shop he added, "He does worship his wife's memory," referring to B.A.

"The woman's dead and gone a long time; what sort of nonsense is that?" Doc said irritably.

When they got to Doc's house he went upstairs for his bicycle, which he hoisted on his shoulders and brought down the high staircase into the yard, damp from the continuous drizzle. They then rode to Armstrong's house where he went in for his raincoat. The two friends then rode off in the direc-

tion of Water Street to the whore-house they frequented on
Saturday nights.

13

Jealousy

Since B.A.'s quarrel with Doc and himself, Armstrong resorted to spending more time at home. On Wednesdays he and Doc met at the latter's house to drink and talk, while Saturday was their night out in Water Street, where they had become regular clients. But the rest of the week found him stranded, as it were and sometimes, the mere sight of his house drove him to turn round and go to a rum shop before he returned home from work.

The first experience in Marion's arms had excited him, but with time he found her less and less desirable, knowing that everything she had to offer was his for the asking.

It was one day, months later, that he chanced to see her talking earnestly to a young man in front of the house. And from then on the young man and she met every night at the corner, under the street lamp.

One night when Armstrong went into the children's bedroom — where she sometimes slept — and attempted to caress her she repulsed him. The times when she had returned his embrace came back to him as he listened to her soft breathing. He recalled the surging of her body, and her even breathing now offended him.

Getting up slowly he left the room, not quite able to comprehend the finality of Marion's rebuff.

Marion was very circumspect, but this unwonted respect only riled him all the more; and deciding that it would be best to ignore her, for two days he feigned complete indifference. He addressed her in an off-hand way and when he settled in a chair by the window he would suddenly change his mind and go out for a walk instead.

On the second day, back from a walk he had not wanted to take Armstrong met Marion and her young man chatting at the gate. He stormed into the house and slammed the front door after him.

"The slut!" he exclaimed, half-aloud.

His wife came from the kitchen at that moment.

"What did you say?" she asked him.

"Nothing. I was talking to myself."

"Why did you come back so quickly?"

He gave her a murderous look. When he was alone again an irresistible force drew him to the shuttered window, which he flung open with such force that it rebounded into place with a clatter. Armstrong went to the door, opened it and closed it again, then he went back to the window and looked through the blind at the couple. Unable to restrain himself any longer he shouted out at the servant:

"Marion! Come in here!"

Marion addressed a few more words to her young man and then came upstairs.

"Where d'you think you are? In the back-dam in the country or something? You stand outside my house with a man friend as if you own the place. You're a servant in my house, remember that. And you'll damn well behave like one."

The children, who were playing under the house, crept up the back stairs and listened from the kitchen, while the mother and son who lived next door listened eagerly, having taken up a position at an open window without bothering to conceal themselves.

"Who's this man anyway?" Armstrong asked.

"Just a friend, Mr Armstrong," Marion answered.

"But who the devil is he?"

"Is the carpenter that working for Mr Dean."

"Well, let me tell you something. If I find you gallivanting with every Tom, Dick and Harry you meet you'll be back in Mocha in no time."

When it was all over the children ran downstairs, giggling and nudging each other. That same day Armstrong had abused one of the telegram boys for copying a message incorrectly, but when the youngster failed to defend himself he was overcome with regret and later gave him four cents. And that evening he was to be beset by a similar feeling for the way he shouted at Marion, mingled with shame at the way he had exposed his jealousy of her.

Gladys Armstrong, who had listened to her husband from

93

the bedroom, reflected that now everybody in the neighbourhood would suspect what his relationship with Marion was. On first making the discovery some time ago she felt so humiliated she believed herself incapable of living any longer; but with time she accepted it as she accepted everything else. What else could she do, she thought, when she relied entirely on her husband for support. She listened to Marion's confidences as before, but she herself could no longer confide in her, nor hold any lengthy conversation with her. Whenever the girl caught her looking at her they were both embarrassed, but pretended that nothing was amiss.

She turned to Armstrong's sister for consolation and received it in good measure. What did Gladys expect? It was a man's world. Women were not in a position to change it and were therefore obliged to accept it. The two women began to spend a lot of time together, Gladys preferring to go downstairs to her sister-in-law's room than to have her upstairs, an arrangement that her sister-in-law approved of, as she wanted to do nothing that might offend her brother.

Armstrong's sister found a malicious pleasure in consoling Gladys. She resented her dependence on her brother and had come to feel that his motives in helping her to sell the business some years ago had not been as altruistic as he had then pretended. She watched the progressive decline in the family's living standards with satisfaction, taking note of the loose paling-staves, the condition of the children's clothes and the departure of Esther.

Gladys, for her part, envied her her friends, who visited her regularly and at whose houses she often slept. It was they who had awakened her to the possibility that her brother might have swindled her.

As time went by she found it impossible to confine her resentment to her brother. She even came to dislike the children, and more especially Boyie, whose boisterousness appalled her. If her parents had been alive they would be sickened at the behaviour of their grand-children.

Armstrong began to follow Marion greedily with his eyes. He no longer went for walks at night, nor did he turn back at the gate to go to the rum shop for a quick schnapp. Now that he was no longer able to have her, Marion's tantalising gait seemed even more provocative, as did the manner in which she combed her hair, while she sat in front of the looking-glass dressed only in her petticoat.

He invented excuses to send her to the shops, found fault with her dusting and the way she washed the shirts. All this Marion bore without a word of protest, until the night Armstrong's wife told him that the young woman wanted to be paid a wage.

"What?" Armstrong said, not believing his ears.

"She says that the other servants in Georgetown get paid."

"To think she had nothing when she did come to us! Where's she now?" he asked.

"Somewhere at the back of the house," Gladys said. "I'll go and get her; you'll only wake Boyie."

She came back a few moments later with Marion.

"Mistress told me you want money for your work," he said angrily.

"Is my sweetheart tell me that all the servants in town get pay," Marion spoke up boldly.

There was a certain insolence in her voice that aroused Armstrong, as if she were challenging him to refuse her request for a wage.

"You know you're ungrateful, eh? We bring you up in Georgetown and everything . . . but I suppose you're right. I'll make it fifty cents a month, but if you're not satisfied it's back to the village."

Gladys could hardly believe her ears, for she thought her husband would stand his ground. Marion went back to the kitchen, disappointed that she had not got a dollar, but willing to stay on for what was offered her.

That Saturday, when Mrs Armstrong and the two children went for a stroll on the sea-wall Armstrong, who was cutting firewood under the house, came upstairs, a pile of wood on his arm. He heard the shower and noticed the open bathroom door through which, under the streaming water, Marion was rubbing herself. She saw Armstrong stop at the open door, but made no effort to close it. He put the pile of wood down on the floor, stretched out his hand and turned off the water. Then, taking the towel, which was hanging on a nail, he started to wipe down his servant, gently at first and then more briskly, until he was embracing her and smothering her with kisses.

Armstrong was the happiest of men. At the end of the month he paid Marion her wage as he had promised and, in a fit of generosity, bought his wife a new pair of shoes. The children were given a cent each to spend and at their bed-time Armstrong told them a long story and made extravagant promises about the future.

14

From the Beginning of the World

It was a Sunday morning and Gladys Armstrong lay awake in her bed beside her husband, who was still asleep. The house was unusually quiet. From the widow's cottage next door the sound of hymn singing could be heard, accompanied by occasional hammering from under her house. Marion ought to be up, she thought, but there was no noise from the kitchen, nor from the yard nor the children's bedroom. She could tell it was going to be a sunny day from the keskidee calls and the quality of the light.

Gladys was beset by a nameless unease. Her husband had not increased her house allowance for a long time and to make ends meet she had taken to using salt instead of tooth-powder and to cutting down to the bare minimum the food she herself ate.

Yet, something else was bothering her. She got up and went into the kitchen, but Marion was not there. The young woman was taking liberties, sleeping at that hour of the morning, she thought. But Marion was not in the bedroom either and the bedclothes on which she slept had been carefully piled in a corner. Puzzling over the girl's absence she went back into the kitchen and lit the coal-pot.

It was when she took down the pan from the dresser that she found the note, which read: "My swetheart aks me to come and live with him. I love him. Say goodbye to Boyie for me. Tell Genetha I going give her the mony I say I giving her."

Mrs Armstrong went and sat down on the top of the back stairs, the note in her hand. She had been a fool to be cold to the girl after she found out about her and Armstrong. What did it matter? After all, Marion was taking nothing away from her.

She had never confided in anyone as she had in Marion. The nights they sat by the window talking and laughing and making remarks about the men that went by! Sometimes they counted the drunkards that passed the house, after the rum-shops had closed, and speculated about what went on in these dens that reeked of liquor, out of which shouting and laughter came like belching from the belly of a contented diner. Were there any untoward goings-on? Did they ever talk about women? Marion did not think that they talked about women as much as women discussed men. Women did not play dominoes or cards or billiards or decide to go for a walk on the spur of the moment.

Gladys had often come near to telling the girl other things. When she was married she felt ashamed and inadequate, as if there had been some important lack in her upbringing. Had Marion stayed they would no doubt have become reconciled as they always had. Armstrong's sister could never share her secret life. Besides, how could she tell her things that would be, at the same time, a confession of her cerebral infidelity? Her sympathies would be with her brother, who neglected her and gave her only just enough money to live on.

"You know, sometimes I feel like giving myself to the ugliest man that passed by," she once said to Marion. "I mean I could choose the ugliest from the first twenty and invite him into the house and cook for him and then allow him to do with me whatever he wanted."

Marion had looked at her in astonishment, unable by any stretch of the imagination to share her mistress's feelings.

"I like good-looking boys," Marion rejoined, "with a moustache and a Buddy Jackson haircut. I couldn't stand a ugly man."

"I'd like him to hurt me," Gladys went on, as if Marion had not spoken, "as much as I could stand; and then, afterwards, punish me by going away without even thanking me. . . . Sometimes I believe I'm sick. Nobody's got these funny things coursing through them."

"You right. People don't think like that," Marion had said.

"One Christmas," she had told Marion on another occasion, "when I was about sixteen, my best school friend was staying with us; she drank too much of something . . . I can't remember what. Anyway, I liked this girl a lot and wanted her to come and live with us. She wore expensive clothes and talked about her aunt in the States and I admired her so much it was almost painful. Anyway, she wanted to throw up after drinking a lot of something or other. As she leaned out of the window I begged her to vomit over my hand. And in the end it came out. When I was washing my hands under the kitchen tap I was glad and thought I'd never forget that day as long as I lived."

Marion was watching her, an expression of disgust on her face.

"You shouldn't talk like that after eating black pudding and souse, you know," Marion told her.

One day Mrs Armstrong confessed that she had dreamt she did not like her children. Then, after a moment's reflection she said, "How can I care about my children when my husband doesn't care for me?"

"You love Boyie, though," observed Marion. "You kian' hide it."

"Boyie'll marry some long-suffering woman who thinks it's her mission in life to be his carpet. The more he maltreats her the more she'll love him."

"They in' got many of them women round nowadays," Marion observed.

"You don't know anything about life, girl," Mrs Armstrong remarked absently.

"No man goin' take advantage of me, I can tell you," Marion said defiantly.

Now Marion had gone and she was left alone. In her parents' home everything had seemed so easy. The women obeyed and loved; the man dispensed security and affection. Had she married the wrong man or was there a deeper reason for the failure of her marriage? Her father used to say that happiness in the home depended on the woman, but she had given everything there was to give, forgiven when there was no need to forgive. Was her father wrong? Had he and her mother been really happy? But this was manifest. At night they took walks, arm in arm, down Vlissingen Road, made observations on the changes in the district and climbed the stairs with that leisure that spells contentment.

Gladys got up and re-lit the fire that had gone out and set about preparing the morning meal; but the smell of the toast

99

made her feel sick. She leaned against the wall on her raised arms and began to cry bitterly as the rays of the sun filled the room. Next door somebody began to play a mouth-organ softly, but the tune glistened only briefly, then vanished like the ruby she once sold in haste. Gladys could not stop herself, even when she heard stirring in the bedroom and knew that one of the children had got up.

"Is what wrong, Mother?" Boyie asked, as he appeared in the doorway rubbing his eyes.

"Nothing. I don't feel well, that's all."

"Why not take some of Father's medicine?"

"I'll be all right."

"You burned the toast," he observed.

She took the hot, blackened bread and threw it on the table.

"I'm hungry."

"I'm going to be ready in a minute, Boyie. Why not go inside and lie down again?"

"I'm hungry," he repeated.

"All right."

The Sunday unfolded as if nothing had happened. The keskidees gave out their shrill calls, the ice-cart passed at ten o'clock, the church bells rang and fell silent when the faithful were all gathered in; and there was discretion in the air. The hours were long and heavy, the hot afternoon following the hot morning and the warm night growing soft with shadows.

Gladys went to church for the first time since Esther had gone away, putting on the black dress she had had made seven years ago and leaving the house when the bells began to ring.

She sat at the back of the church and waited, like the others, for the verger to distribute the hymn books. The solemnity of the occasion brought back to her the passion she once had for church going, when in her early teens. And with that came fleeting memories of her passion for her husband — which used to flare up at the slightest manifestation of interest on his part. They came and went like those glimpses of colour in running water that vanish the moment they are perceived. But stronger were the recollections of communal singing and the mysterious power of the verger, with his long black coat, his deep stoop and fervent eyes.

Looking at those round her she had the impression that she was only part of a vast whole, that her own spirit had flown away, leaving her stranded with urges from another time. As a child she would — often without success — make a great effort to suppress her desire to show off, especially when a male came visiting. In some odd way she had lapsed into that childhood state, a prey to urges that came from deep within her, too deep for her to exercise over them the rigorous control she had been taught was necessary. Marion had provided her with the opportunity to behave absurdly at times, and so made it easier to accept the mask she wore in the presence of others. Now that Marion had gone she was continually haunted by the possibility of a loss of control. And yet, more powerful than the desire to escape death, deeper than the longing for happiness, was the longing to be herself, but in being herself to lose nothing; to wear the clothes of her choice, make friends with anyone who happened to be passing, and thereby discover her own true desires, her own morality.

Gladys had no idea why she had to come to church, like someone who walks along a once familiar path only to realise that it had been taken without any apparent reason.

"You're going to church? Why?" Armstrong had enquired. And there she stood, lost for an answer.

When the congregation rose to its feet Gladys rose with them. Having missed the announcement of the hymn she had to wait until the organ began playing the opening bars of the tune, which she recognised at once; and with just enough time to find the page in the thick, hard-bound hymn-book, she began singing with those around her:

"Thou shepherd of Zion and mine,
The joy and desire of my heart,
For closer communion I pine,
I long to reside where thou art.
The pastures I languish to find
Where all who their shepherd obey
And feed on thy bosom reclined
Are screened from the heat of the day."

Neither Zion nor Babylon had any meaning for her now; yet on hearing the start of the second verse, "'Tis there I would

101

always abide", the urge to throw her hands above her head and shout her affliction for all to hear almost overwhelmed her. Twice she had visited a Pentecostal church in Agricola with Marion, and on both occasions the fervour of the congregation and the extraordinary effect produced on them by the hymn "The Lord's my shepherd, I'll not want" had frightened her. And the collapse of a young woman at the climax of the hymn,

"For thine is the Kingdom
And the power
And the glory . . ."

brought home to her the gulf between her own world and that of Marion and Esther. Now, however, it was among that congregation that her spirit wandered, in search of that closer communion of which the first hymn had spoken.

An old woman next to her was singing lustily, as if her life depended on it. At the end of the service she asked Gladys if she was coming next Sunday.

"I think so."

"I come," declared the old woman, "when my feet can stand the walking."

The two walked for a while and then the old woman said, "I did know a woman who did look just like you, you know, years ago."

"Oh, yes?" asked Gladys.

"She din' last long though. Funny how people come and go, eh? She used to sit just where you is now. They bury her some time ago. I 'member the funeral good, you know. My memory in' gone yet. Not like some old people. It's the memory that give them trouble first. Eh, heh! Is the memory. But wha' fo' do? When is we time and the maker call us, that's it. Sometimes I wonder if we in' better off up there than down here, you know? Since my husband gone to his long home is only the church I got left. The children got they own troubles and you feel you in the way. Eh, heh! Is so. Eh, heh! You turning up this street? Me too. Is nice to meet people, you know, especially when they not stuck up. Like you, you not stuck up. I mean my husband was a fine, decent man and his grandfather was a teacher, you know. Mm hm! He come from a decent family, but they did come down in the world. But he was a

102

good man. Nowadays things different and people in' got so much time. Years ago people used to share whatever they had, but now everybody want to keep what they got for themselves. Is so, you know. But He don't change up there. He's the same now as he was a hundred years ago, and according to the Bible from the beginning of the world. You turning down here? All right. I goin' see you then. Walk good! Try and come next Sunday. Mm hm! All right. I walking down this road here."

That monologue did wonders for Gladys and when she got home she started to plan for the next day, the first when she would have to work as every range-yard woman was obliged to work. Only the washing would be given out, unless her husband objected, which was unthinkable.

After cutting up the wood into varying thicknesses and laying it beside the coalpot, Gladys swept the kitchen floor, filled the goblets with water, cleaned the children's shoes and washed the plates. She then put on the radio and sat down at the window. There she fell asleep and as her head nodded against her chest, woke up with a start.

The wind was rushing down the street, blowing bits of paper and shaking the trees violently. She looked up in anticipation of the storm, which broke a few minutes later, in a fury of rain and wind. Getting up she made certain that she had locked the back door; then she went back to bed, where she listened to the rain on the roof and the wind shaking the panes.

15

The Quarrel

When Armstrong discovered that Marion had left he abused his wife.

"I told you! I told you! You showed Esther the door and kept that whore. Now you know what retribution is. If you hadn't treated this girl like an equal, then she'd never have dared to give notice like that. Notice? She didn't even give notice, did she? My God! She even used to wear your clothes. Who ever heard of a servant wearing your clothes before you discarded them? In every house they eat in the kitchen after everybody else finished. But not your Marion! she owned the house and wanted wages and days off like these Georgetown fancy servants. She wanted to be treated like one of the family. If I'd have followed my mind you would've beaten her and sent her back to where she came from. What in God's name got into you? You didn't see your mother treating her servants like that, eh? And I bet they weren't bumptious with her!"

"No, they weren't," retorted Gladys.

"And you've become so damned submissive. As soon as I open my mouth you agree with me. You haven't got a mind of your own? I'll tell you this much, you're not having another servant. I can't afford to pay anybody. I don't know what's wrong with you. If you ask me you belong in an asylum."

"You're right, my friend," said Gladys wearily. "I belong there. You think I didn't know how you used to carry on with Marion at night? And in the same room as the children?"

"You're talking damn nonsense," replied Armstrong heatedly. "You see, you've even become suspicious. I told you you're going off. Go and ask your doctor. It's one of the signs of madness."

"It's your fault," she said quietly.

Armstrong lost his temper at the accusation and, with a swift movement of his arm, struck her a blow across the face.

"You can't hurt me any more," declared Gladys, "because I don't love you any more."

Armstrong, in order to hide his consternation and dismay at this unexpected disclosure, shouted at his wife:

"You're raving. You don't know even what you're saying any more."

Genetha had come upstairs for a saucer to put her mud cakes in. She went into the bedroom when she heard her parents quarrelling.

"If it wasn't for the children," said Armstrong, "I'd be out of here like a shot, you know," he said, doing his utmost to hurt her as much as he was able.

"I would stay with you always, my friend, because it's my duty."

Gladys's words, delivered with an apparent calm, cut deep into his vanity.

On hearing this exchange Genetha covered her head with the pillow and lay down on the bed.

"All right," said Armstrong vengefully, "I used to go with Marion. What did you expect? What sort of company're you? According to Marion you can't even stand your own children. Don't go pointing your finger at me, my girl! How can a man respect a wife who can't stand her own children, the children she brought into the world? I know your kind," he went on, in an attempt to cover up his shame at his own confession, "under your fine ways you're more brutal than the people who end up in prison. I mean, what sort of conversation I've had with you these last few years? If I shout at you you sulk for a week and when I try to be kind you reject me for it."

"God is my witness that I've been a good wife," she declared feelingly.

"God!" he shrieked. "God! Do you know about the minister and his wife? He's a man of God! He practically lives in God's house, as you call it. But it's common knowledge that he hasn't spoken to her for years."

"Who do you want me to call to witness, then?" asked Gladys. "I don't know anyone. If I haven't gone mad yet it's because I pray every day for your salvation and mine. Probably I could've been a better wife, but whenever I was ready to forgive you I couldn't bring myself to say what I wanted to say."

"Ready to forgive me for what?" enquired Armstrong. "There're men who drive their wives like slaves, that test the furniture with their finger to see if it's got dust on it; and ask them to account for the way they spend the money. Did I ever go poking into your purse or ask you how much a pair of shoes cost?"

Then, all of a sudden, his anger subsided and compassion for this woman, his wife for more than a dozen years, took its place. She was still attractive and gentle, the qualities that set her apart from her sisters. Why could they not start from the beginning, at least for the children's sake?

He looked at her from the corner of his eye and for the first time he thought he could detect a look of hatred in her eyes. And his resentment at this discovery was so strong that all the violence began to well up in his chest once more. He always complained that she was too submissive, but any display of independence or hostility put him into an indescribable fury.

Armstrong's denial that his wife was a desirable companion had injured her pride. Frightened at first by his angry outburst, Gladys was now prepared to face up to him. She looked him straight in the eye, while he made a heroic effort to restrain himself from saying all the things he knew would offend her.

"We've got two children and a home," she said, "and you've got a job when a lot of men haven't worked for months. Can't you try and make a go of things?"

He attempted to interrupt her, but she insisted.

"Let me talk, for God's sake! When you leave the house you don't tell me where you're going, and if anything happens to you I won't be able to say where you've been. And another thing: at least you could sit and talk to the children. The only thing you ever say to Boyie is to threaten him if he does badly at school and to flog him when he does something wrong."

Armstrong could contain himself no longer.

"Look who's talking about the children! At least I love my children."

"And do you think I don't!" she exclaimed.

Meanwhile Genetha had gone downstairs to tell Boyie that their parents were quarrelling. He was playing in the yard of

106

a friend who lived a few houses away. Disturbed at the news he came with her. When, on reaching the gate, he heard the shouting he turned to his sister and struck her on the back, angry that the news she had brought was correct.

Genetha seized the opportunity to intervene in the quarrel. Rushing up the stairs, she shouted, "Boyie cuffed me!"

Hearing this, Armstrong summoned Boyie from the yard, dragged him into the children's bedroom and thrashed him on his bare backside.

These events, which occurred in the space of a few minutes, filled Armstrong with great sadness. He brooded over his wife's words and wondered if it was in his power to put into practice her admonitions. How could he come close to his children when he did not know what to do? Could he stroke Genetha's head? When? On what pretext? The child would run away if he tried to be gentle with her. And Boyie? He was so proud and sensitive; could anyone imagine him responding to a stroking hand, except to bite it? If he were to take them out where would they go? Then he remembered a conversation between his wife's father and a friend.

"All fathers are repressors, like teachers," his father-in-law had said.

The recollection of this judgement comforted him somewhat. And, in fact, when he thought of his teachers and his own father, the objects he connected most readily with them were the cane and the belt.

Armstrong's wife had uncovered in her husband a host of guilty feelings whose existence he had never before suspected. The intemperate punishment of Boyie for a minor misdeed was evidence of a brutality that had nothing to do with his own nature. Yet, at the time, he felt he could not act otherwise. His friends and acquaintances knew him as a restrained person who never raised his voice, and the harlots he met in the Water Street brothel saw in him a considerate type, a gentleman. It was as if, at home, he was urged by some private devil to bare his teeth and snarl like a fierce dog.

16

Baby

Armstrong found it impossible to stay home for the remainder of the day. He took a shower and passed his cut-throat razor superficially over his face. When he was about to leave the house he went up to his wife in order to kiss her on the cheek by way of atonement, but at the last moment changed his mind, and simply bade her goodbye.

He set out on the long ride to Plaisance, where he knew that Doc spent his Sundays with his mother. Once in the village he had little difficulty in finding the house in which Doc's mother was supposed to live, behind the jamoon tree by the trench which rose above the vegetation like a sentinel. Armstrong had to leave his bicycle leaning against the tree and cross the plank over the trench on foot.

After knocking on the door it occurred to him that it was foolish to ride all the way from Georgetown to Plaisance in the hot sun to see someone who might be somewhere else. Even if Doc were in Plaisance he was likely to be at a friend's house or to have gone visiting in the next village.

The door opened without the warning sound of footsteps and Armstrong found himself face to face with a wizened old lady. Without waiting to hear whom Armstrong had come to see she turned her head and shouted.

"Teacher! Is fo' you."

In saying this the old woman chuckled to herself, as if the visit were a joke.

A few moments later Doc appeared in pyjamas from the back of the two-roomed house, and when he saw Armstrong in the doorway he blinked in disbelief.

"Is you?"

Armstrong anwered with a gesture of embarrassment and stepped in from the sunlight.

"Man, you're the last person I expected to see down here," declared Doc. "I—I thought you were with your family, you

108

know. I thought at this time you'd all be dressed up and visiting with the family. . . ."

At this point the sound of female voices came from inside. Doc looked at Armstrong and smiled weakly and showed his friend the rocking-chair in the corner.

After Doc had disappeared inside, Armstrong sat alone in the drawing-room, surveying the walls, which were bare, except for photographs of married couples and little children. The two shutters were closed against the sun, streaming in through a chink between the window and the wall.

Armstrong felt as if he were sitting for ages, when out of the back came a striking looking woman in her twenties. She placed a bottle of rum and a glass in his hand and then drew up a straight-backed chair from the other side of the room on which to rest the rum bottle. She did not smile, but at the same time seemed quite friendly.

As the young woman disappeared into the back, Armstrong took the top off the bottle and poured himself a shot. He must have been alone for about half an hour by the time Doc reappeared. And despite the latter's neglect he was glad to be there. The strains of East Indian music came through the open door, the endless meanderings of a monotonous voice singing in Hindi. Occasionally people passed by on the village road, not caring to look through the open door. A dog was lying under a tree in the yard, sleeping with its legs in the air, stiff and twisted, as if it had died in that position. The vegetation growing beside the trench on the other side of the road was lush and deep green, dominated by a profusion of wild eddoe, and from time to time a light breeze sprang up and the leaves of the tree and the growth beside the trench would shudder and sway.

Doc returned clean-shaven and dressed in a sharkskin suit, and his hair was so liberally pomaded with Vaseline that he looked like a sweet man on a Saturday night.

If there had been a back door to the house Doc would have made the young woman leave when Armstrong arrived, for he could not entertain his friend out front while she stayed in the back all afternoon. However, now that the existence of his woman had been disclosed, Doc felt flattered that she was so attractive. The puritanical strain in his character had made him conceal the truth about his Sundays in Plaisance, but his man-of-the-world inclinations prevented him from going to any great lengths to keep his secret.

"To hell with it," he thought, "I'm not the only man in the country who's left his wife and is living with another woman."

In fact, Doc had been living a double life, teaching in Georgetown during the week, while spending his Sundays in Plaisance with a mistress he had known for three years. He was continually haunted by the thought of losing his livelihood if the Education Department or the manager of his school became aware of the facts of his private life. The manager of his school, a Methodist minister, considered him a fine man, whose only defect was the neglect of his soul. Furthermore, his wife in Berbice might get wind of his affair and she was not the sort to let sleeping dogs lie. It would be bad enough if she got hold of his address!

These thoughts only came to him when he was alone; but in the company of Baby and *mother*, far from the hurly-burly of Georgetown and the pressures of school life, he had learned to relax, walk around without a shirt and listen to conversations he would consider petty elsewhere. Often, in the late afternoon he, the old woman and Baby would sit on the steps without exchanging a word and the silence would be broken only by the greeting of a passer-by.

Baby was powerfully built. Her hips were round and her breasts full. She was barely literate and so ignorant that Doc's attempts at imparting to her an elementary knowledge of world affairs proved vain. In the presence of educated people Doc would rather she displayed her attractions with her mouth closed.

When Baby heard that someone had come to see Doc she felt a certain trepidation.

"Is what he want?" she had asked, as he came back into the bedroom.

"It's a friend of mine," he said, reassuring her.

He lifted up her dress and stroked her between the legs to show her that she was still his main preoccupation. And she watched him change, still harbouring the unease in her.

"Hey, take the big bottle and a cup for him. That's a good girl," he said, dispatching her with a slap on her buttocks.

Although she already disliked this man whom she had not yet seen properly she gave her hair a few strokes with a brush and smoothed her dress; and this concern for her appearance did not escape Doc, who, when she next addressed him, answered irritably. Their Sunday had already been spoiled by this man from town, she thought.

Doc went out to see Armstrong, clean-shaven and dressed in his usual immaculate way, and they got down to the business of consuming the obscure brand of rum.

On Saturday nights the friends drank only Russian Bear Black Label, smooth and rich. This cheap stuff had to be chased with soda water to put out the fires it kindled in a man's throat.

As they drank the two friends wondered what to say to each other.

"Rass!" thought Doc, "he didn't have to look for me down here."

Meanwhile, Armstrong was thinking that Doc was on to the sort of thing he had been after for years.

"He must be mad to ride all this way in the sun," thought Doc.

"My conscience would make me sick with worry, though," Armstrong reflected.

"Shit!" Doc said to himself, "we haven't even done it yet. If he doesn't go before seven o'clock that would be that, and I'd have to wait until next week again. A whole blasted week!"

"Doc, man, you're a first-class liar!" said Armstrong finally.

"I didn't lie, I just didn't mention her. I bet there's a lot you don't tell me. I bet you've got some little thing in Albouys-town."

Armstrong was offended at the mention of Albouystown, the worst slum quarter in Georgetown. If he had a mistress she would certainly not be living in Albouystown.

"In fact," Doc continued, "you didn't tell B.A. and me anything, except that you're married and got two children. And your wife? What's she look like? I mean, you're damned secretive. You and B.A. know a lot about me. You know about my wife and my mother-in-law — may her soul rot in Hell.

You've been in my house, you know about my work and the people I work with. Now you know Baby, the ignorant bastard."

"Is that her name?" asked Armstrong.

Doc nodded. "When I'm sick it's Baby who's going to look after me, not the woman I went up to the altar with."

"If I was you I'd hurry up and get sick," quipped Armstrong.

The two friends laughed, Armstrong with his deep guffaw and Doc with his high-pitched, contagious laugh.

The women, encouraged by their laughter, came out and joined them, and as Armstrong and Doc occupied the only chairs they sat down on the top of the stairs. The sun was still hot, but the steps were in shadow and Baby and the old woman leaned on their elbows and looked across the trench, where a woman squatting by the water was beating her washing with regular strokes. Overhead, a carrion crow wheeled lazily under the steel-blue sky.

After the bottle had been drunk Doc pretended that there was no more left. He was at his most talkative and opened his heart to Armstrong.

"See that old hag on the steps. She's the one to watch. She's always egging Baby on to squeeze me. Thinks I've got a lot of money. The other day she was telling her that teachers get a lot of money, and now she's got Baby believing I'm rich. You've got to hand it to her, she can make money go far. But she's always complaining she's sick and she needs to go to the doctor. And if I open a bottle of rum I might as well finish it, 'cause she drinks it and on Sunday when I come she tells me some cock-and-bull story about leaving the bottle open and the rum evaporating. Would you believe it?"

Doc leaned forward and looked through the door.

"I'm telling my friend what you do with my rum," he called out.

Her only answer was to give him a suck-teeth, long and eloquent. And Armstrong listened, the smile on his face concealing his envy. He could tell from the way Doc was talking that he liked the old lady.

"He gat another battle in there," the old woman said, letting the cat out of the bag by way of revenge.

Doc, caught out, made the best of the situation.

"Why didn't you tell me?" he asked. "Well, go and get it, ne?"

Baby got up languidly and went inside to fetch the bottle of rum.

"You stingy bad, you know," the old woman said.

"You think I'm a money tree?" Doc defended himself.

Baby brought out the rum and broached it for the two men.

"I'm warning you," said Doc, "we'll have to drink the whole bottle now, 'cause she'll only finish it."

And in saying this he nodded in the old woman's direction.

"Don't bother with him, mister, I don' drink. I does drink, Baby?"

But Baby, as if struck dumb by the heat, did not answer, and the old woman delivered herself of another long suckteeth.

"One Saturday," said Doc, "I came and found her sitting on the steps, smoking her clay pipe and drinking rum and ginger."

And then, addressing the old woman again, he said: "I thought you didn't drink!"

But she stood on her dignity and did not reply.

"She'd drink you and me under the table, I tell you," Doc pursued.

Doc had already forgotten that Armstrong had intruded in his Sunday nest and that he and Baby had not had time to make love. Indeed, what with the rum and the sun, he was glad that his friend had come to visit him, and hoped that he would stay till well into the night.

"A few months ago," he continued, "I bought Baby a second-hand machine, as an investment, mind you. She and the old hag fondled the thing and stroked it, but neither of the two knew how to use it. Baby promised to learn, but she still hasn't done anything about it. D'you know what the old lady wanted to do with the machine? Sell it! And she'd have sold it for more than I paid for it, I can tell you. She'd sell anything."

He laughed his uproarious laugh, then took out his handkerchief and wiped his eyes.

"And if you're not careful," he continued, "and you stand too long in one place, she'd sell you too, the old hag."

And at this observation he broke out into such a fit of laughter that he was obliged to hold his sides.

"Oh, God!" he exclaimed. "I laugh so much my sides hurting me."

He stopped talking in order to recover his breath and ease the pain in his sides. Armstrong refilled his glass and drank deeply from it.

In all his life he had never experienced such envy. He was jealous of Doc's association with Baby, of his relationship with the old woman, of his house in Plaisance. He felt that under the influence of the cane spirit he might commit an indiscretion. But he could not know that Doc's vanity had already interpreted his silence as envy, although he took care to pretend that he was not aware of it.

"Sometimes," said Doc, "I imagine myself with Baby in a boat on the river, with a bottle of rum in one hand and a book of poetry in the other. What does it matter if she understands what I'm reading or not, so long as she sits opposite me without talking, her legs slightly parted. Just slightly, so's not to spoil things. It's the suggestion, the promise. It's the difference between getting drunk on Russian Bear Black Label and on cheap rum like this. . . . I'm a *bad* man, I tell you, a *bad* man."

And he chuckled at his own words and the more refined implication of the word "bad".

"Beloved," he went on, "I shall love you like the wind and the sun and the driving rain. . . . Ah," he said, emptying his glass, "give me Baby any day for ten of your town women."

Armstrong felt a sudden urge to confess his unhappiness to his garrulous friend.

"You know," he said, "it was a mistake getting married. I'm not complaining, mind you, but it was a damned mistake."

He had blurted out the words, letting them go without really wanting to.

"You're not talking about yourself," said Doc, his display of merriment cut short by his friend's unexpected confession. "Look, you needn't. . . ."

And then, with a very serious air, he asked, "You're not in earnest?"

"I damn well am," replied Armstrong.

"What?"

"The thought of marrying into a Queenstown family, you know, when I was younger. What a mistake it is, marrying out of your class."

"She isn't unfaithful?" enquired Doc.

"No, nothing like that. Its just that I can't stand being home."

"Why?"

"The servant's gone," replied Armstrong, "and we can't afford anybody else. The boy's running wild and the wife's sick with worry. . . . The fact is, it's been always like that, since when we were living in Agricola."

Suddenly, he regretted having bared his soul to his friend, and Doc, sensing his embarrassment, started talking again, about something entirely different.

"It's a funny thing with some people, how they like talking about their small days. Old Schwarz at my school's a quiet sort of fellow. He'll sit with you all night drinking and hardly say a word. He'll listen and drink, listen and drink, as if it was a crime to mix in the conversation. But there's always one way to get Schwarz to talk. Let somebody mention small days and he'll smile and swallow the liquor as if it made out of water; and when he gets a chance he'll start off about his small days. And you'd think he was happy! Nothing of the sort. He used to live with his mother and father sometimes and at other times with his grandmother. When he was at his grandmother he used to pine away and think of home and when he was at home he used to threaten to run away to his grand-mother. But you should hear this man talking about the jamoon trees by Clay and the bananas he and his brother used to steal from the farmer, and the days when the trench-water used to overflow into Capitol Cinema and they used to sit in the pit with their feet in water. And when he was done he would take a long drink and fall silent for the rest of the night."

Doc emptied his glass and called out to Baby.

"Girl, get us another bottle. There's two more under the

115

bed, unless the old woman did drink them already, the sly, old hag."

"I thought you din' had any more," grunted the old woman. "You tell the man you din' got any more and now you talking 'bout the two under the bed. You see how he is, mister? He so stingy he would make monkey look like a wastrel. What about a new dress, ne?"

She got up and lifted up her dress to the knees.

"Look at this thing! Call this a dress? You in' shame to bring a stranger here when I look like this?"

"We see it, we see them," Doc said, with a look of disgust.

Her shrivelled legs were so skinny Doc was moved to remark, "That's the two wonders of the world. How those legs manage to hold up that body no man'll ever know."

Baby came back out with the rum and placed the bottle on the table. She then went inside once more for a kerosene lamp, which she hung on a nail, by the door.

"That's all right?" she asked.

"That's all right, girl," Doc answered.

Armstrong noticed the glint in her eye and felt the jealousy welling up in him once more.

"She's nice, eh?" Doc remarked. "You want a go?" he then asked mischievously.

Armstrong lowered his eyes and did not reply, although the suggestion made the blood rush to his face. If Doc had not really meant it he would look like a fool if he took him seriously. It was best to say nothing, he thought. And Doc did not fail to notice that his friend was following the girl with his eyes whenever she came in and left the room; he was such a fool, he thought.

"Nobody understands himself or his own troubles," Doc continued. "Everybody's making frantic efforts to get out of some deep pit. If it's not a husband or a wife or a mother-in-law behind them it's a boss or a neighbour or a father or son. There's always a tormentor kicking you back into the pit. From Monday to Friday I'm alone. I haven't got anyone in this bastard world but Baby. Well, it's the kiss-me-ass truth. If my radio breaks down I feel as if I'm going mad. I've got to get it repaired right away so's not to have to spend the nights alone. There's nothing worse than having to drink in a rum shop. It's not that I don't understand you, but I'll tell you, it's better to be unhappily married than to be single."

Doc felt that he had spoken the truth, but at the same time he was convinced that his weekends with Baby and his outings with Armstrong were ample compensation for his bachelor existence. He was the sort of man who could strike up an acquaintanceship in a cake shop or find someone to replace Baby if the need arose. He was in love with her and believed her indispensable to his way of life; but, in truth, he was persuaded that she would suffer more in the event of an estrangement than he.

"Light the lamp, ne?" Doc called out to Baby, who had joined the old woman on the step.

"Leave the child!" exclaimed the old woman. "You only showing off in front of you friend."

But Baby got up from the step and lit the lamp, which she replaced on the nail.

It had become dark and the lamp did little except cast shadows round it. The frogs had meanwhile started up a chorus of incessant croaking from the trench, choked with algae and wild hyacinth; and the evening was as warm as the day had been so that the women, sitting on the stairs, did not think it necessary to come inside. All the hens and the solitary cock which had been pecking about the yard all afternoon had disappeared into the back yard, where they had no doubt found some place to roost for the night. The East Indian music which came from deeper in the village took on a more ample sound in the waxing night, and, with the frogs, accompanied the conversation of the two men. Both had no more thought for time, and even Doc, annoyed at first that his love-making might have been spoiled by Armstrong's visit, was only concerned at keeping his friend with him as long as possible. In any case he was in no condition to do justice to his manhood in bed.

"He goin' be so drunk you goin' to put he in bed. I telling you!" said the old woman, addressing no one in particular.

"He might as well stay the night," Baby said.

"You can talk!" exclaimed the old woman, sucking her teeth so loudly that the men heard her.

"What's eating you now?" asked Doc. "If you're hungry why don't you go down and buy something from Fung-kee-Fung, ne?"

And saying this Doc took out a dollar note from his pocket and tended it to her.

"You know he shut now," she said.

"Knock on his back door, then," Doc suggested pretending to be exasperated with her.

The old woman got up slowly, trying to hide her pleasure at the windfall. She might as well spend the whole dollar note while he was drunk, she thought. And she left immediately for the shop, barefooted.

Armstrong heaved a deep sigh.

"You want some liqour, girl?" he asked Baby.

"No, I in' eat yet. After I eat."

"Come here let Armstrong feel your batty," Doc told her, stretching out his hand.

Pouting with displeasure she came over to Doc, who stroked her backside theatrically.

"Feel it, man. Come on!" he urged Armstrong.

Doc's guest allowed his hand to be guided by his host and to explore the contours of Baby's backside.

"That's a batty and a half and a piece 'pon top, eh?" Doc asked.

"You friend shy," Baby ventured.

"You see that?" Doc said, laughing heartily.

But despite his laughter Doc was not pleased at Baby's compliance.

"It's time you think about going home, man," he told Armstrong. "What's your wife going to say?"

Then to Baby he said, "You know these married men. After a bit on the side they rush home to their wives with black pudding and nut cake."

Baby smiled as if she understood and Armstrong got up, wavered on his feet and fell back into the chair.

"Come on, come on, you got to get going," Doc encouraged him.

He and Baby helped him down the stairs. Then Doc took his bicycle to the public road, while Baby held his arm. And

Armstrong, despite his condition, was aware of her body rubbing against his arm and wanted to go back to the house.

"We can't go back?" he asked her.

"Is what your wife goin' say?" she asked in return.

They skirted the trench, crossed the railway line and at last reached the Public Road, where Armstrong and Doc went behind some trees to relieve themselves.

"That was good," Doc said, as he shook his penis behind his tree.

Baby heard them laughing and wondered what they were laughing about. When they emerged from the darkness they were both buttoning their trousers, oblivious of their lack of propriety in the young woman's presence.

Doc and Baby waved to Armstrong as he mounted his bicycle and rode off in the direction of town.

"Once he mounts that bicycle he's all right. He can even sleep on it," Doc told her.

"You going have to stay the night," Baby told him, with obvious satisfaction.

"I know, girl. I'm going to drink a cup of cocoa and go to bed."

And the two walked back to the house, hand in hand, like young lovers.

Doc lay on the bed, listening to the women talk about goings on in the village. Bagwadeen's baby was sick with thrush and the nurse had promised to come, but had not turned up. Ramoo's wife had run away. Her father pleaded with her husband to go and look for her, but he refused and swore that if she did not return the following day he would have back the cow he gave him before the wedding. Doc soon fell asleep, bemused by the rum and indistinct memories of the session he had just shared with his friend.

17

A Malignant Growth

Armstrong heard from an acquaintance that B.A. had been taken to hospital with a malignant growth. He rode off to see Doc in Kitty that very afternoon to tell him what he had learnt and they went to the hospital at once.

B.A. was in the paupers' ward on the first floor of the immense complex of wooden buildings. Dressed like the other pauper ward inmates in a white garment that came down to his ankles, he was standing next to his narrow bed, as if awaiting some kind of inspection.

"Somebody tell me someone been enquiring for me," B.A. said cordially, but without smiling.

He got back into bed once the formalities were over.

"Now you know why I was always so irritable," he said apologetically.

"What is it exactly?" Doc asked, putting his arm round his sick drinking companion.

"Cancer. You didn't hear? They call it a malignant growth. Same thing. . . ."

"I don't know what to say, old war horse," Armstrong remarked, trying to hide his emotion.

"Don't say anything," B.A. ordered.

And then, to break the silence, he recalled how he was attacked by the masked masqueraders on Christmas Eve night some years before.

"They attacked the right one," he said jokingly. "I didn't have a cent on me."

Visitors were sitting on chairs and on the beds or were standing at the patient's bedsides, while the nurses — even without their uniforms — would have been conspicuous by their purposeful walk. There was the scent of sweet oranges in the air, and on looking round him Armstrong saw the fruit laid in twos and three on the beds of a number of patients. Some of the visitors were poised for flight — or so it seemed to Armstrong. Perhaps it was his own sense of discomfort he could read on their faces; but the fact was that a number of them were standing beside empty chairs.

Armstrong considered his neglect of B.A. in the past and his unconcealed preference for Doc. If he saw his own son behaving in a similar way he would speak to him of the need to consider the feelings of others. But he had behaved like that, without thinking.

The sight of B.A., dressed in a neutral garment of white, surrounded by innumerable beds in a vast ward like rafts on a windless sea, distressed him even more than his fatal illness.

"There's a man in here," said B.A., "who hops around. I mean it. He doesn't walk, he hops!"

"Hops?" asked Doc eagerly, anxious to make up for his part in the quarrel at the cake shop in Kitty.

"He puts his legs together," explained B.A. "and hops about. Somebody says that's how he used to get about even before he came into hospital; and the traffic had to stop to wait for him to cross the road. One of the doctors says he's got a castration fear. Hm! Or, he said, it could be he want to draw people's attention to his troubles. But you know what I think? I think he does hop about because he likes hopping about."

Both Doc and Armstrong smiled.

"If you wait," said B.A. "you'll see him come into the ward and cause confusion. But the nurses let him have his way."

Doc and Armstrong exchanged glances.

"I don't like this promiscuity," remarked B.A. emphatically. "Just 'cause I don't have a family they don't have to put me—"

"What about your son?" asked Doc, deliberately interrupting him.

B.A. did not answer at once.

"I hear his woman's already moved in," he said after a while, "in the three days I've been in here. . . . Sensible when you come to think of it, with the housing shortage being what it is. But they could've waited a li'l space of time, a decent space of time. After all, my smell must still be clinging to the walls and the bedclothes. . . . There's an Amerindian in here, from the bush, with a broken back. He comes from Paramakatoi. Every morning before anybody's up he plays his flute, three notes, just three notes haunting the place . . . bringing all that bush sadness into the hospital as if we don't got enough of it in town. And you know the nurses don't stop him either. They allow the patients to do as they like. It won't surprise me to wake up one morning and find them running the hospital."

Armstrong and Doc could not know that B.A. was acutely put out by their visit. He detested their show of sympathy and would have preferred them to stay away. Besides, contrary to the impression he gave, he had already made friends with one of the patients and was not certain that he did not prefer it to his freedom. He talked to hide his embarrassment and his resentment at the way Doc had treated him the last time they met. He resented their good health and the fact that when visiting time came to an end they would be able to get up and leave with the army of visitors.

"We came empty-handed," observed Armstrong. "You see? Everybody brought something, but we came empty-handed. Next time we'll bring a whole basket of oranges."

"I can't stand them," declared B.A. gruffly.

And wounded by the unexpected rebuff Armstrong did not pursue the matter.

The hum of voices emphasised the silence between the friends, and Doc, affecting an interest in the activity around him, glanced at the clock on the wall.

Finally, it was time to go when, amid the goodbyes and the voices of nurses calling out the time, there was a loud "Ha, ha!" from the other side of the hall. In the doorway stood a man, stock-still, his hands raised high above his head and his gaze directed at his feet. Then, when all eyes were on him, he started off across the hall in little, careful hops, his legs together. He made his way between the beds and among the visitors, who stood watching him as if he were on a stage.

"All right, all right!" a young nurse called out. "Time to go. It's time."

And the visitors only went reluctantly, most of them turning at the doorway to look back at the progress of the man across the room, who stopped occasionally so as to recover his balance.

122

"And when you think," said B.A. bitterly, "that he's going nowhere!"

"We'll come and see you tomorrow," promised Doc. "And we'll bring the oranges all the same, because we know you like them."

"See you then," said B.A., who stood up and shook their hands in turn, just as if Doc and Armstrong were strangers to him.

"Hey," B.A. shouted after them when they were already at the top of the staircase, "those men in the masks who attacked me — the masqueraders — they had your build . . . and the one who shouted at me sounded just like you, Doc."

But they both pretended not to hear the insult hurled after them.

"I think we should go round to his house and talk to his son," suggested Armstrong. "All he needs is a visit from him."

"Have you ever spoken to him?" Doc asked.

"No."

"If you had you wouldn't have made the suggestion. He's the nastiest young person you'll probably ever meet, you've got my word for it."

That settled the matter.

Walking slowly the two men set off for their cake shop in Kitty, as if by a prearranged agreement. Ahead of them the electric lamp posts stretched, with their outgrowth of metal lamps connected by black wires that dipped at mid-point and rose again towards the lamp-post further on.

It was an evening like so many others, darkness falling rapidly and the houses by the roadside competing with the street lamps to lighten the gloom. Passing cars blew their horns indiscriminately and the occasional bus trundled by, brilliantly lit up, like a ponderous intruder of the night, giving an unimpeded view of its passengers.

Armstrong reflected that his friendship with Doc and B.A., imperfect as it was and marred by frequent quarrels, was the constant source of pleasure in his life. It was precisely the element that was lacking in his wife's, however; and if, while they were living in Agricola, he could pretend that the lack was the fault of their isolation, that excuse was no longer tenable, for he actively discouraged the association with his sister, who, living just under them, might have turned out to be her constant and good companion.

They were walking past a photographer's parlour and the pictures displayed in the window recalled the afternoon of their marriage, when he managed to get hold of one of the new motor cars to take them to the street photographer. She and he stood side by side as a knot of passers-by looked on. How proud he had been to be seen in her company! She was his possession and would spend a lifetime serving him, attending to his needs, anticipating his wishes. Everyone looking on must know that. He could not complain that she had let him down in any way. Indeed it was her mute resignation that took the taste out of their marriage.

"Did you hear what he said?" asked Doc, interrupting Armstrong's reflections.

"B.A.?"

"Yes."

"When?" asked Armstrong.

"As we were going down the stairs," Doc replied.

"I heard him shout," said Armstrong, not wishing to admit that he had heard B.A.'s insult.

"He said something like, 'he sounded just like you, Doc!'"

"You think we should have gone back?" Armstrong asked.

"He sounded vexed to me. Not to you?"

"You're sure he said 'Doc'?" enquired Armstrong. "He might've been shouting at somebody else."

"I heard the word 'Doc' distinctly," said Doc. "And you saw how he reacted when you offered to bring him oranges."

"For God's sake, don't let him drag you down with him," said Armstrong impatiently.

They walked on until they reached the street in which Doc lived.

"I think I'll have an early night," Doc said.

"You're going to see him tomorrow?"

"Why not?" Doc said. "Words never killed anybody."

The two friends separated; and Armstrong, finding himself

124

alone in the street, so many streets from home, was taken with a sudden desire to go and see Lesney.

He set off quickly, walking faster and faster, then breaking into a trot a hundred yards on. In the end he was running as fast as he could along the pavement, his loose jacket flapping at the sides. From time to time he came onto the road to avoid colliding with someone, but quickly regained the safety of the pavement, so as to get out of the way of a carriage or of the odd bus. Then, seized with a sudden shame, he slowed down to a walk.

"What in the name of God is wrong with me?" he thought. "If *she* knew! A father and husband!"

And his conduct seemed so absurd he turned up a side street to hide from anyone who might read his thoughts.

Wasn't everything absurd? he reflected. The work others did he was incapable of doing, just as his occupation was a mystery to others. He did not choose to be born, just as he was unable to choose the moment he was going to die. The things he wanted most were beyond his grasp and whatever was within his reach appeared pale and insignificant. He was despised by his son and had just been cursed by his sick friend. Tomorrow would be a day of gestures like the days before, and some night he would weaken and sink back into the earth without the consolation of gratitude from his children, whose affection suddenly appeared infinitely desirable.

And there appeared to Armstrong a vision of himself lying on a bed, arms crossed on his chest, being stared at by his wife's relations, his father-in-law and mother-in-law, and his two sisters-in-law who were grinning down at him. Without warning they both bent over and placed flowers on his eyes, on his cheeks and on his mouth, yellow daisies that grew in profusion by the roadside. And the elder of the two opened the buttons of his trousers and started to fondle him, smiling all the while and reassuring him. She kept whispering words to him, unintelligible at first, but becoming more and more distinct.

"It was the same in Agricola, when you brought me the pears," she kept repeating to him. "Try and remember. It'll be so beautiful, just as it was then."

125

And he closed his eyes and felt her warm hand round his ungodly erection.

"So you cared in Agricola?" he asked her, rising from his bed.

"Just sleep," she answered softly.

And in an explosion of stars he fell back and found himself alone in the dark room.

Armstrong was roused by the sound of an approaching carriage, but the unwonted weakness in his knees caused him to lean against the balustrade of the stone culvert.

Hoping that no one would pass he tried to pull himself together. It would not do to be taken home by strangers, as if he were drunk and helpless: that sort of thing never failed to reach the ears of one's superiors.

He was not sure what had happened to him, but he had had a similar *experience* when he was a youth and, fatigued and hungry, he arrived home to find that all the family were out.

And he remembered a curious conversation between his father and a fisherman friend, who took his boat out every night in search of queriman and snapper, and whose eternal complaint was that the fishermen had to go out further and further to obtain a worthwhile haul. One afternoon he overheard him telling his father that people who went out on the sea were not as certain of things as others were.

"Nothing's certain out there," the man had said. "Sometimes the trade winds that supposed to blow in one direction all the time does swing round, without no storm, nothing. And one night we haul up the net and what you think we find inside? Something looking just like a man, but with webbed feet."

Those words had aroused something slumbering deep within Armstrong, which he could share with no one else. It was as if someone inside him had spoken, uttering hidden feelings. And this second experience, the one he had just had, far from frightening him, had comforted him, reassuring him, as it were, of the continued existence of an inward companion, who was still capable of asserting his presence.

At last he was on his way home, certain that no one had been watching him. The streets appeared new and clothed in a wondrous, diaphanous material; and if the familiar houses had suddenly burst into fruit he would not have been astonished. And if the young woman coming towards him had stopped and spoken to him familiarly or embraced him he would not have thought that out of the way either.

Armstrong was convinced that the experience by the culvert had dissipated the uncertainties about relations with his family. From now on he would march through life with firm steps, confident of his strength and of his companion's within him.

18

Retrenchment

The wind of fear was blowing through the post office and government departments. One morning Armstrong received a letter informing him that one of the employees was to be pensioned off. The man, Armstrong's closest associate, was usually left in charge of the post office whenever Armstrong was away.

He thrust the letter in his pocket and that night lay awake thinking how he could help his deputy. And the next day the deputy, who had that morning received his letter confirming the information already communicated to Armstrong, came to him, dumbfounded by the news. He promised to get in touch with the Postmaster General, knowing full well that the decision would not be reversed.

Armstrong did as he had promised. He telephoned the Postmaster General's office and had to endure a rebuff. His deputy's dismissal was none of his business.

Armtrong's own dismissal occurred three months later, being communicated to him by a similar letter to the one his deputy had received. Retrenchment was in full swing.

That night he told Gladys and they sat in the gallery, reflecting on the news.

"Where're you going?" he asked wearily, as Gladys got up.

"To warm up your dinner," she replied.

"I wonder if you know what's going to happen?" he asked.

"We'll manage somehow. There's some good news. I was keeping it as a surprise."

"What?"

"Boyie's won a scholarship," she said.

"To where?"

"Progressive High School."

"They must be crazy," declared Armstrong. "He's never had a good report in his life, except the last one, and that wasn't particularly good."

"Look. If things get too bad we can always send Genetha to learn to sew and buy a sewing-machine out of your savings."

"A sewing-machine?" he repeated, chuckling to himself, recalling Doc's remarks about the machine he had bought for Baby.

"What's funny about that?" Gladys asked him.

"Nothing," Armstrong said, "it's just that we sold the one we had in Agricola," and his face fell. Then, bitterly, he exclaimed, "A sewing-machine!"

"Anyway," said Gladys, "the scholarship's a big problem out of the way."

And, for the first time in months Armstrong lost his temper.

"What's the point of getting a scholarship if you're starving?" he asked.

Gladys felt for him in a way she no longer thought possible. He seemed much older and more vulnerable.

"It's not the end of the world, you know," she said, trying to comfort him.

He would have to sell the two houses, he thought. Now he was in the position his sister found herself some time back, without an adequate income and only a little capital with which to eke out a meagre existence.

Armstrong, like most men, had no idea to what extent he was dependent on his work. His colleagues, the routine, even the scent of ink were as indispensable to him as the oxygen he breathed. He had often cursed the regular hours he was obliged to keep and persuaded himself that this, together with the routine, had thwarted his initiative and robbed him of his imagination. Yet, at the moment, he was as frightened of being cut off from his post office as he was of losing his salary. To get up early in the morning when the rain was pelting down and to don raincoat and galoshes, muttering all the while under his breath, was, after all, a sweet experience. Discrepancies in accounts, lost telegrams, letters of reproof from above, all these were the pinpricks that rendered life all the more attractive.

Furthermore, he believed he was indispensable to the proper functioning of his post office. There were things a new man could never understand. Nothing was more complex, nothing demanded a cooler head than the successful running of a post office, especially with the calibre of youngsters being recruited these days. And even if a man were educated, he might be dishonest. The country must be going to the dogs if people like himself were not to be allowed to continue in their jobs. The trouble with those in authority was that they never knew what was happening anywhere else except at the top. They sat on their fat tails and gave orders without any idea of the consequences that might follow.

Suddenly he was stricken with a fierce jealousy of his friend Doc. The worst that could happen to teachers was a cut in salary. Living alone, with few responsibilities, he could indulge his lecherousness as long as his body permitted. He, Armstrong, could not even afford to spend an hour with Lesney now.

Armstrong and his wife ate late that night. She watched him holding his head in his hands, bent over the steaming plate of pepperpot which, in Doc's words, was the queen of dishes, the one justification for imprisoning women in the home.

"Damn him! Damn him!" he exclaimed in an outburst incomprehensible to his wife.

They sat for hours in silence, until Boyie shouted out in his sleep, when his mother remarked with a touch of pride in her voice, "That boy!"

In the end Armstrong got up and went inside, leaving his wife to ponder over their future.

Everybody was surprised that Boyie had won a scholarship. Boyie, however, knew exactly why he had won it, and the moment that, a year ago, he had set out to be first in his class. It was the occasion of somebody's jubilee, when pencils were being shared out to the top half of the class; and when he received a pencil there was an outcry from the other children.

"Boyie work not good, miss," one child remarked.

Miss Caleb looked over to the seat where he was sitting and declared amidst silence, "Boyie got a pencil because I like him."

It was as if a thunderbolt had struck Boyie. This, for him, was a declaration of love from his teacher, an open announcement of favouritism. He therefore returned this passion with commendable swiftness. From that day onwards school was a beautiful place, and Arithmetic, the mysteries of long division and area, furnished the excuse to take his work to be marked. He asked his mother to test him on his tables, to give him subjects for composition which he might write out with a pencil on Saturday nights. And his progress was so striking that Miss Caleb took his work to the headmaster as proof of her teaching ability; for poor, pock-marked Miss Caleb did not realise that she haunted Boyie's dreams and fired his enthusiasm during his waking hours.

One afternoon, on the way home from school he told his best friend, Ashmore, of his love for Miss Caleb.

"But she ugly!" he remarked.

Boyie stopped, a pained expression on his face. He looked at Ashmore as if he had said something disparaging about his, Boyie's mother.

"What wrong with you?" Ashmore asked, puzzled.

And in answer Boyie gave him a blow on the chin with a violent swing of his right fist. Ashmore lost his balance and fell on the wet pavement, astonished at his friend's behaviour. Boyie was aggressive, but until then, he and Ashmore had always fought on the same side; attacking each other was unthinkable. Ashmore grabbed Boyie's legs and pulled him to the ground and the two friends rolled into the gutter, belabouring each other.

A crowd of school children and a few adults gathered round them, the children shouting encouragement to both boys.

"Get he, boy; get he!"

"Tek he by he foot!"

"Put you foot round he neck an' bruck he neck!"

"Cuff he in he belly!"

"That's right, Ashmore, squeeze he eye out!"

"Stan' up and fight, man, like Tom Keene!" said a grown man, an admirer of the film star.

"Grab he by he balls!" one big boy shouted ecstatically.

Ashmore must have followed this last bit of advice, for at that moment Boyie let out a shriek which attracted even more passers-by. One burly man took the two boys by the scruff

131

of their necks and lifted them up bodily. He then let go and shouted, "Police!" and the crowd vanished like water down a sink, with Boyie and Ashmore hard behind those fleeing down Regent Street. The burly man grinned broadly and went on his way.

Boyie had fought for Miss Caleb and had had his balls squeezed for Miss Caleb. He was now ready to lay down his life for her and, while waiting for the call, he slaved away for her.

If Boyie had worked with such application from his Infant School days onwards he would have run away with the Primary School scholarship. Instead, his energies and anxieties had been channelled into mischief, into making life unpleasant for his mother at weekends.

He often wished his father would take him out kite-flying or to cock fights, as his friends' fathers did. He was hardly at home to witness the trouble Boyie caused his mother. A word from his father and he would have shown all those clowns in his class what it meant to be bright. None of them could beat him at marbles and most of them could not even hold a cricket bat properly, while he played in the fields with boys from secondary schools and could late cut a good length ball. None of them even knew what a good length ball was. Did they really think there was much difference between school work and cricket? Only teachers did, and they had as much sense as a stinking toe. Except Miss Caleb, of course. He decided to get to the top of his class and win the Primary scholarship for her.

The last day of term Boyie met Miss Caleb in front of the school and put her hand on his head.

"I'll miss you," she said, then turned away and left him standing alone by the wall.

And standing there he burst into tears, all of a sudden, without knowing why.

That night while he lay in bed he experienced the most shameful fantasies about Miss Caleb. As he ran his hand through her hair she covered his face with kisses, gathered him up in her arms and pressed him to her.

Boyie woke up and found his mother bending over him.

132

"Son, you're all right?"

"Yes, Mother," he answered.

"You've been muttering to yourself."

"It's nothing."

"You were dreaming?"

"I suppose so."

"You want me to stay with you?" his mother asked.

"No," he answered hurriedly.

She bent down to kiss him good night, but he quickly turned his head away.

His mother left the room and Boyie recalled the night when he saw his father and Marion embracing in the dark. He had never told anyone; he had never felt like telling anyone. But the secret was painful, and early the next morning, when everyone was asleep, he got up and searched for Marion's dress in the dark. He tried to rip a hole in it, but could not manage to undo the seam. And while he was looking round for something else of hers to destroy she woke up and asked him what he was doing.

"Is none of your business," he answered.

From then on he went to any lengths to inconvenience and annoy her, and he once told a boy at school that he wanted to die because he did not like their servant.

St Barnabas school, with its dingy walls and anxious teachers, had no idea what an impression it had made on young Armstrong who often had been condemned as a delinquent and caned as a rebellious spirit; who, except in his last year, possessed not even the saving grace of an agile mind; St Barnabas, where the powerful symbols of the cross and the cane nudged each other intimately. Yet Boyie, whenever he recalled St Barnabas, saw neither the cross nor the cane, but a dark hand on his forehead.

19

A Visit

If Gladys Armstrong had pretended not to be unduly worried about the future, in order to assuage her husband's fears, she was none the less as frightened as he was. What sort of pension would he receive? The proceeds of the sale of the houses would not last long and Armstrong would be too proud to take a menial job. As things were they were finding it difficult to make ends meet and she dreaded the thought that one of them might fall ill and end up in the paupers' ward of the Public Hospital. Perhaps one of the children could go and live with her parents; but she knew that her husband would never allow it. She herself could turn her hand to nothing, since her only talent was doing intricate embroidery, and playing the piano; and Armstrong had never thought it necessary to buy a piano. With the money from the houses they could well open a shop of some description; but she shuddered at the idea of standing behind a counter, dispensing wares to customers.

Armstrong would suffer most of all. He would have to forego the new clothes he liked so much and, at table, he would have to be content with what everyone else was eating. If Esther were still with them she would find some way of bringing money into the home. A business would flourish under her skilled guidance and the problem of who would sell behind the counter would be solved as well. But how was Esther to be found in a big town like Georgetown?

When Armstrong came home that afternoon she told him what she had in mind, but to her surprise he threw cold water on the plan at once.

"What you know about business?" he asked. "You know as much as me."

"Why not give it a chance, Sonny? Do you know of anyone who started a business and ended up poor?"

"Who you mean? Most of them are poor, these shop-keepers," Armstrong replied, but was interrupted by his wife.

134

"It doesn't have to be a cake shop," countered Gladys.

"Tcha! You don't even know what you're talking about."

Gladys gave up, bewildered by his lack of enterprise. Above all she was thinking of Boyie and the possibility of his education being cut short because they could not afford to keep him in shoes and shirts.

"I know it's Boyie you're worried about," Armstrong told her. "But the scholarship will pay for his school fees and if we can't buy books he can always sponge on his friends. I can tell you, that's the least of my worries."

"And what about Genetha?" Gladys asked.

"She's a girl," he said with a deprecating gesture, "and besides, you yourself said we can buy a machine for her and let her do sewing."

"And you'll buy the machine?"

Armstrong hesitated. "I'll have to wait and see. When you come to think of it a machine is expensive. I mean it's no use buying her one of these cheap second-hand things."

"Why not?" Gladys asked.

"For a start it won't last."

And in a desperate attempt to make her husband see reason Gladys went to look up her father and ask him to speak with Armstrong.

The old man pretended to drop in one night to find out how the family were getting on, and feigned surprise when he was told by Armstrong that he would be soon on pension. These were hard days and only a lucky few were in jobs that paid them a full salary. What would Armstrong do?

Flattered by his father-in-law's concern he disclosed that he would be selling his houses to tide them over the next two years until something turned up.

That was risky, thought Gladys's father, since all the experts thought that the recession would be a long one. Could he not buy a business?

Armstrong at once understood what had happened. He looked at his wife, who pretended to be absorbed in her darning.

"Business isn't for me," he told his father-in-law. "I'd only make a mess of it."

The older man realised that he could not mention Esther

135

without letting the cat out of the bag, so used other arguments to persuade Armstrong that business was the only way to beat the depression.

"You could even end up a rich," the older man remarked half jokingly.

When Gladys's father was ready to go, Armstrong said that he would accompany him home. But he declined his invitation to go into his house which looked no different from the way it did nearly fifteen years ago, except that it needed painting.

Slowly he made his way back down New Garden Street, looking up at the fine houses and admiring the large gardens in front of them, in which flourished roses and dahlias, their stalks maintained by a staff to which they were tied. In the midst of misery this was how some people lived, he thought. It could not be right. In front of one house several cars were parked and he could hear the hum of conversation coming from the well-lit gallery, where people were standing with glasses in their hands. He stood in front of this house, which was decorated with fixed jalousies and a wrought-iron grill below a line of windows. If he invested in a business would all this be within his grasp? Many businesses had had small beginnings. Suppose he were to lose everything? The thought kept recurring to dampen his aspirations and he could only see the obstacles, the hard work and the pains he would have to take to make the venture a success.

And Armstrong decided once and for all that business was not for him.

20

Age and Remorse

One evening Doc and Armstrong decided, after another visit to the paupers' ward, to leave their houses early the next morning and go to the groin for an early morning swim. Doc was agreeably surprised when Armstrong suggested he should pick him up at the house.

It was the start of the Christmas school holidays, a lonely season for him, and the invitation was like an unexpected gift. Armstrong had never before invited him in and had only once spoken about his family, on that afternoon in Plaisance when he was not entirely responsible for what he said.

As Doc knocked on Armstrong's door he tried to visualise the features and build of his wife, for he assumed that it was she who would open for him. But when the door opened it was Armstrong who stood in the doorway.

"Come in and meet my wife," he suggested.

Doc took a seat and waited for his friend to come back, marvelling all the while at the silence in the house, for he himself would have called out for his wife if it had been his home.

The drawing-room had a faded elegance and its wicker chairs and easy chairs were decorated with coloured cushions. Its walls were almost bare, except for a large sepia photograph of Armstrong that dominated the partition dividing it from a bedroom. A handsome oil-lamp capped by a decorated, opaque globe recalled the twenties, a decade ago, when many of the houses had yet to be provided with electricity.

The thought occurred to Doc that in that kind of house and with that sort of woman, who was capable of maintaining such a home, his ambitions in the teaching profession would surely have been realised.

Accompanied by an almost inaudible rustling of cloth Gladys Armstrong was suddenly upon him, smiling and hand outstretched.

"I've heard so much about you," she said. "Why didn't you come before?"

And Doc jumped up to take her hand.

"Oh," he stuttered, not knowing what to say.

She sat down opposite him.

"Sonny said you're swimming this morning. Perhaps you'd like to have breakfast with us afterwards."

"I'd very much like to," Doc said, "but it'll have to be another time. I'm going to Plaisance after the swim . . . to look up some people."

"What a pity," she said, with such sincerity that Doc was touched.

Armstrong came out once more, carrying a bag with his swim suit and a towel.

Gladys got up and followed them on to the porch, where she stayed to wave after them. And Doc, as he turned away from the house, would have liked to go back and tell her how he appreciated the way he was received.

"Well, I never!" was all he could manage to say as he walked by Armstrong's side along the road.

"How d'you mean?" asked Armstrong.

"You don't deserve a woman like that, that's all."

Armstrong made no reply but was none the less flattered, for his vanity prevented him from grasping the full import of Doc's remark.

Doc reflected that there was more that Armstrong could have told him about his wife. She seemed ill to him. But maybe she was the type, fleshless, but full of vitality.

And Armstrong's friend's observation about Gladys's appearance had not missed the mark. For several days she had been suffering from dizzy spells, but had said nothing, for fear of alarming her husband.

It was December. The rains had come soon and fell so vehemently Gladys had the feeling that she was living in a drum. To her dismay a leak appeared in the bedroom, over the bed in which she and Armstrong slept, so she moved it and put down a bucket to catch the water.

She had just finished the sweeping and had not yet begun

138

to cook the midday meal. The woman who did the washing had been up to ask if she could hang the clothes to dry under the house, for the rain prevented her from hanging them out in the range-yard where she lived. Gladys agreed, though she suspected that not only her clothes would be hung up, but the clothes of other families for whom the woman washed. Armstrong would almost certainly be angry when he found out; but the washerwoman was one of the most capable in the area and the clothes were always delivered on time, clean and bug-free. They were neither over-starched nor under-starched, and one had the impression that the Chinese laundry could not provide a better service.

What with such problems and the endless housework Gladys began to long for a protracted sleep, free of worry. Where could her husband find a man to repair the roof at little cost? This was the first month of his retirement and the washerwoman would have to be paid out of their savings. There was no doubt now but Genetha would have to leave school and relieve her mother of some of the housework. These thoughts scurried through her mind as she washed and picked the rice. Neither she nor Genetha could bend over a tub all day, scrubbing the nails from their fingers. God forbid that it should come to that!

Some time ago Armstrong's conduct had improved dramatically, for no apparent reason: he was more attentive and above all more patient. At first she was on her guard, expecting an outburst at any moment. But with the months she regained her confidence and sometimes even ventured to initiate a conversation on a subject about which she knew they had divergent views. Then came the news of his dismissal and a rapid deterioration in their relationship.

Gladys contemplated the bowl of rice in her hand, wondering at each grain, each a different shape, a different size and even a different hue, yet pressed together against one another in a bowlful. Then suddenly her hand lost its grip and the bowl fell to the ground and broke, scattering the grains across the floor. Instead of picking up the rice and the broken pieces she went into the children's bedroom and sank down on to their bed. She was feeling so badly that she lay on her side and experienced an almost irrepressible desire to shout for help. The thumping of her heart against her chest got worse, so she lay on her chest.

When she finally recovered she got the smelling salts bottle and applied it carefully to her nostrils. Who could live on twenty dollars a month? Was it possible that she was reduced to this? Long ago she took a cab whenever she went out, and in Agricola people called her "the lady". As she stepped out of her house, her parasol over her elegant molleed head they would look after her admiringly. Before she had married she wanted to have six children so that her house would be filled with light and laughter. Now she dared not look at herself in the looking-glass, lest the wreck with the rings round its eyes stare back at her. As girls she and her sisters loved to look through their father's binoculars, and their mother, irritated by their habit of holding the eye-piece at their eyes for long periods, often warned them: "You're going to get rings round your eyes you won't get rid of."

What if she took Boyie and Genetha and went home to her parents, at least for a few months? There they would eat well, there would be no housework, nor worry about leaking roofs, for her father, now manager of a large department store, seemed to be doing well.

But she could not entertain the dream for long; separation from Armstrong was unthinkable, and when he fell into the abyss the chain that bound their lives would drag her with him. She searched for a reason for this terrible liaison, but could not find one. Things were just so. There was a sky and an earth; there was the wind and the sun; and there was marriage.

She decided to get up and clean the kitchen floor, but found that she was unable to support herself. The giddiness and the heavy thumping returned, and as she tried to lift the smelling salts to her nostrils, the bottle fell out of her hand.

"Boyie!" she muttered, lowering her head gently on to the floor.

Doc paid for two lockers at the baths, changed and went outside to wait for Armstrong, who liked to spend a couple of minutes in the shower before going into the sea. He might have saved himself the trouble for rain had begun to fall and obscured the sea which was only about fifty yards away.

Turning round, Doc kept an eye on the single doorway of the long hutment from which bathers were emerging singly and in twos. Mostly teachers, he thought, believing he could recognise them "by the cut of their jib".

Odd that people seeing him and Armstrong in each other's company considered them close friends, Doc thought. Their heads were always together, yes, and their words exchanged in the certainty that they would be understood. But Armstrong had no idea how many things Doc hid from him, just as he discovered, with the opening of a single door that morning, a half of Armstrong he had heard speak of but had never seen, and whose dignity left him abashed.

Doc had never talked of the aboriginal Indian woman he had kept while teaching in the country and who had been the real cause of his banishment from the village and the threat of dismissal. That was the reason for his obsession with dismissal and his anxiety about his job. The aboriginal men isolated their women in huts for seven days of the month while they bled. Doc, who had been at that time associating with a charcoal burner, was introduced by him to one of them, a young, sidiom-skinned woman with feline eyes and a provocative gait, who did not mind lying naked in front of the hut while he gloated at her. He took her away to live with him in the village, parading her, scantily dressed, in the street under the hot sun. But his dream of living by instinct was cut short by a peremptory summons to visit the school manager's house.

Armstrong could not be relied on to accept this side of him, Doc thought. Therefore, he had told him about his wife, his *discipline*, as he described her, and with whom he could never achieve that roaring erection Taina called forth with a glance. Had it not been for Taina he would still have been yoked to his *discipline*.

Armstrong appeared at the door of the hutment, wearing one of the new short trunks fashionable among youthful bathers, an obscene invention that left little to the imagination, Doc reflected.

On seeing him Doc turned and made for the groin and

Armstrong promptly took off in pursuit, running into the wind with the exhilaration of friendship and the discovery, through his companion, of his good fortune in being married to Gladys.

They dived into the water, one followed by the other, and were soon swimming towards the open sea with the leisurely stroke of a crawl. Out they swam, in the wake of four-eyed shoals and the shrieking of shadowy gulls, smothered by the rain, till they had left the other swimmers behind and were alone among the grey, thundering waves.

The two men swam as in an effort to reach the limits of their understanding of each other, the secret behind their gestures, their affected carriage and guarded words. And the cruel thought occurred to Armstrong that B.A.'s fatal illness was the start of a deeper satisfaction in his relations with Doc. It was, as it seemed, the blood sacrifice essential to the flowering of a profounder frindship. When B.A. called out to them at the hospital that the two masked men who attacked him were of his and Doc's build, was he not right, in a way? Had not the same plan lurked in his, Armstrong's mind, taking care to clothe itself in moodiness when B.A. was late or made some untoward remark that bled his pride?

"I think we'd better go back," shouted Armstrong above the sound of the waves.

"Right," Doc answered.

And the two men turned and struck out towards the groin, barely visible in the rain.

Suddenly there was a piercing shriek and both men looked up to see a solitary gull wheeling in the rain. No other gull was in sight, while before scores had been diving and wheeling above them.

Armstrong was filled with foreboding. The single cry of the gull making wide circles in the rain, its head moving independently of its flight while it surveyed him and his companion, contained some momentous message, he was certain.

"You heard that?" he enquired of Doc.

"What? The bird?"

"Yes . . . hear how it screamed?"

"And what?" asked Doc.

142

Armstrong neglected to take the obligatory shower after leaving the salt, sea water. As Doc was going straight home anyway he bade him goodbye and hurried down the road, cursing himself for having come on foot.

He went past the slaughter house with its familiar sight of a line of black vultures perched on its roof and the reek of blood. And as he got further from the sea the wind fell, so that the rain no longer lashed his face.

Shoppers and others caught in the rain were sheltering under the corrugated iron awnings, like birds at roost. Every now and then Armstrong passed a carriage drawn by a pale brown horse with bedraggled head seeking the asphalt sheen and unmindful of its dejected master, whose whip was put away beside him.

"Damn it!" he thought, looking back at the carriage he had just passed. "I could have taken that one."

And now that he had resolved to hail a carriage the few that went by were occupied. There was no point in walking back to the cab-stand by the insurance company, for the distance home was now less than half a mile.

Anxiously he looked up to check the names of the streets he crossed, judging with each how far he must be from his house. Yet certain things came to his notice, the brick culvert and the only brick gutter he had ever seen in the town, and the brick pillars of a low-pitched house. And the observations of constructions in such an unusual material reinforced his foreboding.

Just before eleven, Armstrong returned home to find his wife on the floor, her face ashen grey and her hands dry as tinder. He knelt down and took her in his arms.

"Gladys, O my God! You're not going to leave me?"

But she could barely manage to ask to be taken inside. And holding her under her armpits he dragged her to the bed he had soiled more than once in sleeping with Marion.

Gladys could only mutter that she was feeling weak; but at his suggestion that he would fetch the doctor she grasped his hand and did not let go, muttering all the while that he must not.

143

"But your hands're so dry. . . . All right. When the children come home."

And when Boyie was heard chasing Genetha up the stairs, continuing a game begun in the street, Armstrong went out and told them to be quiet. He ordered Genetha to make her mother a cup of lemon grass tea and reminded her to be quiet when he was away in quest of the doctor.

The doctor, a pleasant old man who had forgotten most of his medical theory in the early years of his practice and had learned nothing new in the following years, professed to be perplexed. And on being asked by Armstrong what was wrong he said, "I'm not sure. I'll get a second opinion. Keep her warm and darken the room."

Armstrong gave the children bread and butter and cocoa and sent them out to play as soon as their meal was over, explaining that their mother was not well and needed all the sleep she could get.

In the afternoon the doctor came back with a colleague, who admitted to being as perplexed as he was.

And that night while the children were sleeping, Gladys Armstrong died. Armstrong, refusing to believe that his wife was no longer living, sat staring at the corpse.

After the rain, which had stopped falling about an hour ago, a profound silence had settled on the town, accentuated by the incessant dripping of water from roof gutters. Armstrong took his wife's hand in his. It was not possible that this hand that had grabbed his arm in the passion of their young love could feel like a dessicated leaf. Why had he not noticed before how pinched her face had become? Recalling the doctor's expression when he first examined her, Armstrong was ashamed that the signs of malnutrition should be so evident on her too-soon worn face.

No one could say that he had denied his wife and children food. With him his family had always come first. God was his witness! There were men who ate like hogs and let their people starve. That was not his way!

He got up and fumbled in the chest-of-drawers until he found an old photograph of himself and Gladys, taken soon after their marriage. He had his hands thrust in his pockets

144

while she was holding on to his left arm and smiling in that way he would always remember her.

If only a man could see in the future and understand! She had never laughed at him when her sisters did, nor spoken to him with that suggestion of patronage that was her father's way. There had never been a suspicion of infidelity, no tantrums. . . . She had given him two healthy children. Was it possible that the same body that had urged him to face up to his responsibilities a short while ago should be but a shell? All the days and nights, the conversations by the window in Agricola, the carriage drives, the glances exchanged come to nothing! And the horn of his days was filled with dust! The children meant nothing to him, except as an expression of her life and of her presence.

Armstrong drew up a chair and sat down by the door of the room in which his wife lay, too bewildered to take any action.

The children would grow up and he would grow old, he reflected, and it was inconceivable that such momentous developments could occur without her, who gave birth to them, who had anchored him as a family man, supported him through the anguish of his dismissal and presented to him the mirror in which he discovered himself so painfully. Below him his sister was sleeping, no doubt deeply, unaware of the stilled voice. She was his blood, but he would have seen her die a thousand times than let his life's companion steal away, from him, from her children, from her possessions. . . . How strange! How strange life was! Around him was so much that was inanimate and so little that throbbed with life, only his children and himself, fluttering from day to day. And so much pain, as if pain was in the wind before it descended into the heart. Surely with a few more years his voyage of self-knowledge would have been complete and he would have been able to take her out into the bright afternoon sunlight of their declining years, arm in arm, to know again the happiness of their courting days. And over and over his thoughts travelled the same round of his past mistakes, as if by recalling them he could bring his wife back to life.

Despite the animosity between Gladys and himself over the years they had grown into each other like the hundred-year-

145

old trees in the back yard, irrevocably entwined, and a matter of wonder to anyone who came visiting.

All of a sudden the thought occurred to Armstrong that his wife might not be dead at all. He dashed out of the house and ran all the way to the doctor's home, where he knocked hard on the door. The medical man, refusing to be hurried, walked with measured steps, Armstrong at his side.

After a cursory examination he pronounced Gladys dead and undertook to inform Mr Bastiani the undertaker.

"Pull yourself together. Think of the children!" he enjoined, annoyed that he had been dragged out of bed.

The next morning Armstrong's sister came upstairs to make the morning meal and to see that the children were prepared to go visiting, insisting that it was the best thing in the circumstances. Standing around the house would only distress them more.

"Do whatever you think necessary," Armstrong told Bastiani. "Give her a decent burial, but I leave the details to you."

Mr Bastiani was familiar with this attitude. Later on, when the realities of day-to-day living overcame the worst pangs of grief, the client would protest and make a show of refusing to pay. But they would see about that later. The problem now was to do the necessary for the corpse. A coffin of polished cedar, square glass panel above the head, purple lining, ornate metal handles and so on. . . . He would put Gittens on the job. Thank God death had come in the night! Convenient . . . very convenient, for that gave them time to work all morning. Pity everyone was not as considerate as that.

"Well, mustn't be too morbid," he thought, a smile lighting up his gaunt face.

Armstrong turned the pictures in the house towards the wall, as was the custom when there was a death in the house. He shut all the windows and the front door to keep out sympathisers, remaining in his bedroom for the rest of the day to brood on his bereavement; and only late that afternoon when the mourners' carriage arrived did he emerge from the house alone, forbidding the children to attend the funeral.

Alone in the carriage, which was moving at an unusually quick pace, recollections pressed on him, recollections of his children, his friends and of Lesney's dancing, as if thinking of his dead wife were unseemly. But as the carriage passed a gathering at a street corner — no doubt a religious meeting — his mind went back to the evening when, dressed in his best suit, he had stood on the edge of a crowd of people who were taking part in a Salvation Army meeting in Bourda. Carried away by the infectious singing and the sound of tambourines he forgot for a while that he was waiting to make his first visit to Gladys's house in Queenstown. He had set out too early and was obliged to wander around until he heard the music in the distance. No, her family would not have approved of tambourines or singing at street corners. Yet, such things stirred his heart. And these very things that separated them, these impulses, he suppressed for her sake, or perhaps for his own, believing that they were the signs of a defective upbringing.

The carriage turned right and, for the first time during the journey, he saw the undertaker's assistant on his cycle, leading the procession on a trip he made every afternoon. And behind him was the hearse pulled by a pale horse with strangely glowing mane.

From that evening with its resounding voices to this moment . . . a hearse with a gilded door, from the youth of her well-formed body to the emaciated remains there had been vouchsafed him a unique opportunity to raise a family successfully and die with dignity. For was not the family everything? Should he not have heeded the warning when he cursed his own father?

When the last spadeful of earth was thrown upon the grave he turned away and walked hastily up the path to the waiting carriage, along the avenue of eucalyptus trees that bordered the graves. He saw a group standing where two paths met and from among them emerged his father-in-law, who came up to him and pressed his hand in sympathy.

"Good luck!"

And as the old man walked away down the path Armstrong muttered, "Bugger you!"

The crowd of people went back to their carriages and cars, many of them glancing at him as they passed by the mourners' carriage, and his grief was replaced by a wave of anger at the sight of the well-dressed, well-spoken people, who had come to see his wife buried, but ignored his existence. It seemed to him that for them, it was as if Gladys had been married to a phantom which had managed to dress itself in mourning clothes for her committal to the other world.

And that same night, after the funeral, Armstrong stood by his wife's bedside. He must have loved her after all, for how else could he explain the feeling of desloation in his breast? Up to the day before, there had always been the certainty that she would be home when he came back home; that she would place before him the food he liked; that when he was in a bad mood she would tell the children to be quiet. In the presence of strangers she had been specially obliging and considerate. And what sort of life had he offered her? A wilderness of pain and anxiety.

He flayed himself with his remorse, and, in a fit of despair, began to weep silently. For a long time he kept his fingers over his eyes, as if he were being watched by onlookers before whom he was ashamed to display his grief. And the tears trickled through his fingers, down his chin to fall on to his shirt.

If only he knew how often she had sat in that self-same corner of their bed and wept as bitterly as he was doing. Boyie had more than once come over from the children's bedroom to ask her why she was crying.

Armstrong was roused by the water dripping into the bucket. He got up and went into the gallery to close the windows against the rain that had begun to fall again. The lamp post was gleaming under the light in the deserted street and the gate hung upon its single hinge, making a curious, short cry as it moved back and forth in the wind. The water, which had risen above the top of the street gutter, was rushing away noiselessly, covered with innumerable dots where the rain drops fell into it.

As Armstrong was about to close the Demerara window there appeared, in the middle of the street, a vision of a couple walking hand in hand. Her head rested on his shoulders as they ambled along, unmindful of the rain.

148

"I bet they're engaged," he thought.

As they approached he strained his eyes to see if the woman was wearing a marriage ring, and when they were quite near he bent forward to look at her left hand, which, however, bore no trace of a ring. He peered more closely to see their faces and shrank back in horror, for the man's face was deeply lined while she was equally aged, with soft, dark eyes. He recognised the two as himself and his dead wife and tried to grab the apparitions by the shoulder, only to see them vanish in the rain. Armstrong sank into a chair, trembling like a leaf.

The following day Armstrong's father-in-law came to see him and offered to take Genetha home for a few weeks or to keep her permanently with them, if Armstrong agreed. He consented to Genetha's stay for a few weeks, but no longer.

"Genetha!" Armstrong called out. "Come and talk to your grandfather. Ask him why he never came to see you all these years."

Genetha emerged from the back of the house and kissed her grandfather on the cheek. He had not seen the children at the funeral and wondered why they had not come; but this was not the time to ask.

"Where's your brother, Genetha?"

"He's probably playing at school," she answered, a little frightened of her grandfather.

"Don't you go with him to play?"

"No, I'm not allowed."

"Oh!" he exclaimed, not knowing what next to say to her. "Do you like school?"

"Yes," she replied untruthfully.

"Even when you have homework?" her grandfather asked, hoping that she would spin out her answers.

"No."

"What's one and one?"

"Two," she replied.

"Mm!" he exclaimed with feigned satisfaction.

She smiled and looked deep into his eyes.

"Are you good at your school work?"

"Only at English."

149

"All right, Genetha," he father broke in, "go inside and get ready."

Genetha dutifully asked to be excused and went inside, and when she came back her grandfather got up and took her by the hand.

"Call me 'Dad', like your aunts," he said, pinching her cheek between his thumb and first finger.

"Your tea's on the table, Father," she said.

Armstrong nodded, but made no effort to say goodbye to his daughter.

"I'll come again," declared his father-in-law, shaking his hand.

Armstrong got up and saw them both out, then went down the stairs and stood looking at them walk down the road hand in hand.

On the edge of a darkening sky were indigo islands, ablaze in the wake of a fallen sun.

Epilogue

It was I, it was I who killed him,
The serpent of Boropa
It was I who killed.
Then I was a child
All covered with buttons.
When the little girl sleeps
She puts her hand on her heart.

Brazilian song

Armstrong heard a noise on the bridge, got up and looked down through the jalousie. Catching sight of Doc he just had time to hurry into the bedroom without being seen. It was about eleven o'clock and he had already secured the windows for the night, but by some curious neglect had sat down before going to bed without having bolted the door. It was quite possible that Doc would take it into his head to open it and come searching for him.

The knocking was firm and when there was no answer came as near to pounding as a man's knuckles could make it.

"Armstrong! You're there?"

"If he wakes Boyie I'll have to open up for him," thought Armstrong.

"It's me! Doc!"

The knocking recommenced. But just as Armstrong was about to give in he heard the retreating footsteps on the stairs, then the footfalls up the deserted road.

Armstrong returned to his chair after bolting the door. He had not wanted Doc to find him in the mood he had been in all day, distraught and without counsel. When he recovered he would himself seek Doc out to find again those brighter days. And he would refrain from judging him, only remembering the need for companionship and hours of laughter. In the aftermath of his wife's death, black nights and mornings pale as clama-cherries, a kind of indefinable void. Only the day before, on his way to the market, hearing a burst of laughter behind him he turned round to discover who it was, but could see no one. A pale sun was shining from a sky scarred with clouds, and the ancient trees cast shadows across the canal dividing the two roads opposite the red-painted market. Once more the shrill outburst made him turn round. No living thing was there, not even a stray dog. There were no birds, no movement except the shuddering leaves of the giant trees. Then a man dressed in khaki shorts turned the corner from Orange Walk, ahead of Armstrong, who hurried onwards to seek the protection of his presence. On the way back home he took another road. As a boy he had heard his father say that he would never use a certain street; and, like everything else he said, it had seemed perverse to Armstrong at the time.

153

Armstrong wondered if his friend still went to Plaisance on Sundays, whether he would welcome an unexpected visit there as in the old days. He recalled that brilliant afternoon, his cantankerous "mother" and Baby, with her languid carriage. How long ago it seemed! How well-behaved everyone was then. In the last couple of years things seemed to have changed suddenly, and now you were liable to be knocked off the pavement by a youth learning to skate and be insulted into the bargain if you attempted to teach him a lesson for his brashness.

He went to bed with his thoughts and fell asleep to the high-pitched whirring of the cicadas.

The following afternoon Armstrong got dressed with the intention of visiting his in-laws. It was a few days after the New Year, the season of reconciliation. He put on his serge suit and black tie and at the last moment pinned on the black mourning-band to please Gladys's parents. The gesture would be lost on her eldest sister, but he was certain that her father would appreciate it.

There had been rumours that a new leader in Germany was seeking a war in Europe and this would provide a subject for conversation, which could occupy himself and his father-in-law for some time. He would not take his bicycle, which, for want of repair, was no longer suitable for a decent man.

Armstrong was adjusting his tie in front of the mirror when the front door closed noisily.

"The damn boy! He didn't even tell me he was going out; and his food's ready and all."

But the thought of seeing Genetha soon drove his son's unruliness out of his mind. Indeed, it was the idea that he and his daughter might grow away from each other that prompted him to make the visit. He suppressed his old rage against Gladys's family in the interest of his children, who should cleave to their grandparents and aunts, as was the case in most families.

Suddenly Armstrong was taken by a nameless anxiety. His blue serge suit, several years old but immaculate, appeared drab to him; his tie was the wrong colour and he found it difficult to align the mourning-band properly. Some indefinable

154

fear had scattered his thoughts so that he sat down on the bed and passed his hand over his face.

"What's wrong?" he asked himself aloud. "Dammit all! I only want to go and see my daughter. She is my daughter!"

He sprang up, tugged the mourning-band off his jacket and threw it on the bed. Without taking another look at his face in the looking-glass he strode out of the room and into the gallery, where he bolted the front door. After closing the back door — he left it unlocked in case Boyie should come home while he was out — he turned to descend the stairs. But he tripped on the second tread and fell forward. Desperately he grabbed the banisters of the back stairs and only just managed to hold on, his body stretched almost full-length across the treads of the steep staircase.

Badly shaken, Armstrong re-entered his house, seeing the accident as an omen. He went in search of a brush to clean his right shoe, which had scraped against the edge of one of the stair treads.

An indescribable weight seemed to bear down on him, causing his shoulders to droop and his defiant expression to vanish. Something was wrong, he reflected. But what? A mood? All of a sudden? From experience such moods disappeared once he ate something. Yet he had eaten only half an hour ago.

Gladys never approved of his superstitiousness, and he used to take care not to mention any such preoccupation to her. But the servants knew — and understood. God! After all he was from the country. And inevitably his thoughts turned to the gulf between himself and her family, an unbridgeable void that yawned between one way of life and another, like those mighty rivers that divide Amerindian tribes throughout the continent, as effectively as a high wall, and give rise to their own terrors. Armstrong recalled his father-in-law's manner when he asked Genetha in his presence why she thought he had not visited them all these years. He did not smile, did not seem put out in the least, did not even offer any reason for the neglect of his daughter or grandchildren. Could he not at least have said, "I thought that you disliked us, so we didn't come"? Nothing, not the slightest twitching in his features. And the renewed proof of his superciliousness, that certainty of status that was capable of overcoming even a crippled body or a devastating stammer, had driven Armstrong to distraction.

He decided against visiting, but visualised his arrival at the house in Irving Street, by way of Anira Street, just as at the time of his courting fourteen years before. There was the gate — the entrance — half-concealed beneath a growth of shrubs and flowers through which he used to pass in a kind of delirium. He always stopped under the house to take off his bicycle clips and adjust his jacket, to look around at the well-kept yard and marvel at the corrugated water-closet, one of the first to be built at the time of introduction of the sewage system in the early twenties.

Armstrong shook his head involuntarily and started undressing, when he suddenly called to mind his sister. A week ago he had found out where she was staying. If he were kind to her she would in all likelihood agree to come and live with them. Her last refusal had been made in a spirit of vengeance, and her character did not permit her to harbour a grudge.

Wasting no time he changed into more modest clothes, suitable for his mission.

She herself opened the door to him.

"It's you!"

"Yes. Do the people mind?"

"No, of course not. Sit down, ne. I'll just go in and tell them it's for me."

She looked well, he thought, disappointed that she was not as vulnerable as he had expected.

"You're all right here?" he asked, when she came out again.

"Yes. What about you and the children?"

"They're all right. Genetha is with her grandparents for a few weeks."

"And Boyie?"

"He's all right too. Looks as if he's enjoying secondary school."

"These people," he continued, "you know them well?"

"Oh, like that. Acquaintances more than friends."

"And they don't work you too hard?"

156

"No! I just have to be there and keep an eye on things when they're out. Do I look hard-pressed?"

"I didn't say so."

"Well, then," she said, lowering her voice to a whisper. "We can't always choose what we want. And as long as . . . as long as you're not unhappy."

"Did I say you were unhappy? You look well. And contented. Very contented. In fact when I came in I couldn't help noticing how contented you looked."

They talked of this and that, and all the while she wore a peculiar smile on her lips.

Judging that the right moment had come, he searched for something to say that might please her, but could find nothing.

"I want you to come and live with us . . . for my sake and the children's . . . and yours."

"I'm treated well here, Sonny. I want nothing," she answered, trying to hide her agitation.

"Do it for me then, and the children."

She reflected awhile.

"Will you give me Gladys's jewellery?" she asked, avoiding his eyes.

"There's nothing left," Armstrong answered. "Just a bangle."

"Only that?"

"We pawned everything."

"Give me the bangle then."

"If you want."

"And a share in your house?"

Armstrong cleared his throat and looked away. "All right; a share in the house too. Will you come?"

"No," replied his sister.

"But I thought," he protested.

"I'm not yet bitter," she said, as imperturbably as when the conversation began. "I'm still a young woman. D'you remember when I came for help in Agricola? Gladys was kinder than you. *She* became bitter."

"I forbid you to speak of Gladys!" Armstrong exclaimed angrily.

"Would you like a soft drink? The people I live with are very generous."

157

Someone turned on an electric bulb in one of the bedrooms and the light from it spilled over the low partition.

"So you won't help," he said, ignoring her offer of refreshment.

"I wish I could talk to you, Sonny. But you don't listen. I'm happy here, that's all."

"You keep on repeating that the people're generous and that you're happy," he said in exasperation. "But they're not family!"

The smile disappeared from her face and she looked at him unswervingly. She had died in puberty and then in her early thirties when it was certain that she would never marry. All her youth had been spent ministering to her father, whose death had brought Armstrong his freedom, but her a kind of enslavement to his memory. And now he, who had stolen her inheritance, came pleading with his two-mouthed words and talk of "family".

Armstrong's sister started to laugh softly. She sank her head in her right hand and laughed, laughed until no sound came. Her shoulders rose and fell convulsively and Armstrong, offended by her behaviour, got up from his seat and declared that he was going.

"Please don't come back," she said gently.

He left, angry, but aware of the danger of committing his past mistakes again. And as he went down the staircase, flanked by the painted balustrades, his sister looked up. Unknown to Armstrong she had been sobbing, above all because she had to dwell among strangers and depend on their hospitality. Yet, there was some satisfaction in living in a household in which the wife held sway and the husband knew his place.

Armstrong went in search of Esther in the main streets and by-ways. He even went up to Little Diamond, but her relatives knew nothing of her whereabouts. A shopkeeper suggested that he should insert an advertisement in the papers, which was bound to be spotted by one of her acquaintances. But the two pieces he paid for in the *Argosy* and *Daily Chronicle* brought no results. Odd it was that more than once he and the children had spotted Marion in town, threading her way between the stalls or standing in a cinema queue. But never Esther, as if she shunned public places.

So Armstrong came to terms with his life as it was. He was to bring up his children single-handed, having done what he could to enlist the assistance of someone close to the family. He had tried to visit his in-laws and could not get beyond his door-mouth. He had looked for Esther and was unable to find her. So he set out in quest of his wife under the eucalyptus trees that scattered raindrops like swarming butterflies, and stood in the thickening dusk watching the blown leaves and the pillow-stone. And looking down at her resting-place he meditated on his marriage and a child-big woman, on Doc and B.A. the seldom-pleasured friend, and on the years that spanned the twenties, a time, it seemed in retrospect, of plenty, when there was a rum-shop at every corner, and even immorality bore its flowers.

And Armstrong was overcome by a great calm that stilled the fears of Genetha growing away from him and his inability to handle his son. Then at the shout that the gates were closing he turned and left under a sky lit up at intervals by flashes of sheet-lightning, that announced the fullness of the rainy season.

One Generation

I have been one,
With voices gone.
(Amold Itwaru, Guyanese poet)

Mosquitoes swarming—
Is it memories of the seasons
Of the seasons
That make the mind swoon?
(*Eskimo Poems*)

1

The Consultation

Armstrong was sitting in a rum shop at the corner of Princess and Lombard Streets. A grey, three-day stubble grew from his chin and, in parts, from his face, which had been only partly shaven that day. He had quarrelled with his barber in the American barber shop and had walked out without waiting to have the job finished.

"Hey, Armstrong, buy me somet'ing, ne? Even if is a lemonade."

Armstrong looked at the drunk contemptuously, but did not answer.

"Some people does play great 'cause they got a private income," said the drunk as he walked back to the bar.

Armstrong was no better dressed than the drunk. The lining of his jacket hung down from the back, his trousers were darned at the knees and his shirt was filthy. His shoes were done up with string and the shoe of the left foot had a perfectly round hole in the sole. The children paid for his food, but insisted that he clothe himself from his pension. Since, apparently, Armstrong's pension went as soon as he drew it to pay off his rum shop account and the barber's bill, he had not been able to buy himself any garment for a long time.

"You only dress like that to spite me and Boyie. You're a disgrace," Genetha once told him, "and tobesides the rum's going to kill you."

"I suppose you even want me to stop cutting my hair," he replied sarcastically.

Unconcerned about his general appearance, he never failed to have his hair cut once a week. Genetha felt that Rohan could persuade him to spend some of his money on clothes and take some pride in his appearance, but Armstrong's son did nothing to hide the disgust his father aroused in him.

There was a permanent reek of liquor about Armstrong's person, and here, in the rum shop, he made certain that sobriety would never overcome him again.

He kept looking round at the door, as if expecting someone; and, in fact, it was not long before he was joined by a man in his sixties. The stranger sat next to him without a word. Armstrong got up, went to the counter and came back with a half bottle of rum.

"Why did I have to meet you here?" asked the stranger. "It's much better in a cake shop."

"Here, a cake shop, what does it matter?" asked Armstrong, pretending to be surprised at the question.

"If you boy see you in here, what you t'ink he'd say?"

"Don't talk to me about my boy," Armstrong replied hotly. "I don't want to hear his name."

"I din' call his name," the stranger said facetiously.

"They make a big song and dance about feeding me, but they're living in my house rent-free. Why I put up with it I don't know."

"I know, I know," Armstrong's acquaintance said. "We all got a cross to bear."

His mocking tone did not please Armstrong.

"I used to know you father," the man continued, almost absently.

"Every time you meet me you tell me you used to know my father," Armstrong protested.

"He had a lot of dignity."

"A wheelwright with dignity!"

"You're still a young man. . . ."

Armstrong looked at him in surprise. "I'm forty-five."

"Anyway, why did you want to see me?"

"I want—" Armstrong began, but his acquaintance interrupted him.

"Let's get up from here. Every time the door open there's a draught."

They both got up and settled at another table on the other side of the shop.

"I want to sue my boy," Armstrong told him after they had sat down.

"Sue him? You mean take him to court?"

"Yes."

"Sue him for what?"

"For support!"

"For supporting you?" the stranger asked disbelievingly.

"Yes, who else? All you keep doing is asking me questions."

"But you can't make a child support you."

Armstrong looked at him as if he had been responsible for the law. "What kind of law forces a man to support his children but says that a child don't have to support his parents?"

"I can only tell you what the law say."

"Drink up your glass and go," Armstrong said.

"What you getting worked up at me for? I din' make the laws."

There was a long silence between the two men.

"You know," the stranger said eventually, "I can't understan' you. You live on one side of the town and cut your hair and drink on the other." He took out a packet of Lighthouse cigarettes and offered one to Armstrong, who declined to take it.

"I drink where I like and cut my hair where I like. You can't forget the days when you were a lawyer's clerk and used to wear a suit and thief people's money."

"I in't do you anything," rejoined the stranger. "Why you cursing me and 'busing me?"

"That's not the real reason I wanted to see you." Armstrong emptied his glass and refilled it. "I want you to go and see a friend for me," he continued. "He's a teacher and lives in Kitty."

"Why you don't go yourself?"

"Looking like this?" he asked, surveying his clothes briefly.

"What you want me to tell him?"

"It's probably better not to go," Armstrong said hastily.

"Well, what you did want from him?"

"Forget it," Armstrong insisted.

"You ask me to come to meet you and you tell me to forget it?"

"Yes," Armstrong rejoined, looking straight at him.

His acquaintance turned round and shivered. "How they can build a rum shop next to a trench I don't know. The place cold like hell. Come le' we go. I'll buy you a meal at one of them places down the road."

Armstrong jumped at the offer. He would be able to go home and say that he was not eating his children's food.

"Good, good," Armstrong said, already up.

"Don't forget the bottle."

After walking several hundred yards the two men turned into a side street, where Armstrong's companion picked his way over a rickety wooden bridge leading into a cook-shop. Inside, two benches were ranged on either side of a long table in the centre of the room. Before they had taken their places, a voice from the back shouted out, "Is fish today!"

"Wha' kind?" Armstrong's companion enquired.

"Wha' you t'ink this is, Betty Brown?" the voice asked.

Armstrong looked round the dingy room with its unpainted walls and wrinkled his nose.

"The place got atmosphere. You could feel it," he said, carried away. And in truth it was his companion's chief haunt. Here you could talk freely, slip in and out without being scrutinised, bring a half bottle of rum and spend most of the day.

"You bring the rum?" he asked Armstrong, who took the bottle out of his pocket and uncorked it. Each of them then drank a swig straight from the green, narrow-mouthed bottle.

"What's this business with your boy, man?" the companion asked.

"When I think of the trouble he used to give his mother when she was alive! Now he's taking it out on me. He doesn't even want me to call him Boyie anymore."

"Why you don' put 'im out?"

Armstrong did not answer. Then, as if irritated by something he remembered, he burst out, "Can't you talk proper English? You talk like somebody from a village."

"I talk good English when I got to talk it. Why you don' answer me question?"

"I don't 'put 'im out', as you put it, because he's my son."

"Yet you want to sue 'im," the companion said sarcastically.

"O Christ! It's impossible to talk to you. How you work with lawyers I'll never understand."

The companion, in turn, began to show signs of irritation. "We discussin' you sordid domestic affairs, not my past," he said.

"Now I'm getting your blood up, eh?" Armstrong remarked. He grabbed the rum bottle by its neck and took another swig, but his companion was too annoyed to follow suit. Then a sour-faced woman brought in two plates stacked high with rice and curried fish. The two men fell to without a word and only began talking when they were halfway through their meal.

"You're a real lawyer," Armstrong said. "When I'm talking to you I get the feeling you're cross-examining me. I get the feeling you don't believe me."

"Your father was a gentleman."

"I don't give a damn what my father was," Armstrong said. "I'm sick and tired of being treated like a dog in my own house. When that boy comes home in the afternoon he doesn't say a word of greeting. He just does go to the table and eat. Then a quick shower and he's gone, without a word again, till about eleven o'clock, as if it's a boarding-house. You think that's normal?"

He looked at his companion fiercely, daring him to disagree, but the latter said not a word. Armstrong reflected for a while and then asked, "You think you can love somebody and treat him like dirt?"

"I can understand it, but I couldn't do it."

Armstrong kept shaking his head and his companion, more out of pity than a desire to receive an answer, enquired, "What you really wanted to see me for?"

"I don't know. Can you lend me two dollars? Till the end of the month."

"I don' got two dollars," the companion said and belched mightily.

"Where you come from, eh?" Armstrong asked him. "You don't go round belching like a fermenting barrel. I mean you couldn't belch while you were talking to a client, eh? I mean you'd lose people. You'd become known as the belching lawyer. What kind of reputation that would be? I mean, control yourself, man!"

The companion took out a two-shilling piece and knocked on the table with it. The woman who had served them came out, pocketed the coin and gave him change in return. Then, without a word he got up and walked out of the cook-shop. As he went through the door Armstrong shouted after him:

"You don't know anything about the law — why don't you admit it?"

167

Armstrong seemed quite content to be left alone and shifted to the end of the bench, where he leaned against the wall and became lost in his reflections. Much had changed in his family. Rohan, his son, now eighteen, worked over the river at the Commissary Office in Poudroyen, while Genetha was a shorthand typist in an office in Water Street. His sister, who once lived in the room under the house, had moved out soon after his wife's death, and the room had remained empty ever since.

When night fell suddenly, the woman turned on the light over the long table. Soon the night insects were swarming round the bulb, flying in endless circles and dropping one by one on to the table with exhaustion. Armstrong and another customer, who had fallen asleep, were joined by a young couple, who ordered their food and ate it silently. Finally they paid and left. It occurred to Armstrong that in those dingy cook-shops only the older people lingered on after eating, as if there was nowhere for them to go. In the end he, too, got up and went out into the night.

In Water Street and Regent Street there were a number of American airmen who had come down from the air base to eat at Brown Betty's and then go over to Mamus and the other brothels in the area. Since their money had begun circulating the whore-houses had doubled their business and the quarter had taken on the bright, brash appearance of a thriving red-light district. Armstrong hurried along the pavement, not wishing to recall the years when he, Doc and B.A. used to go there on Saturday nights and return home in the early hours of the morning. Everything was changing. Apart from the Americans the people who now frequented the area appeared to be younger than in days gone by. Young men, no more than boys, could be seen leaning against the shop fronts, talking to the street girls. Was this where Boyie came on Saturday nights with his friends? Did he know of the dangers a young man ran when he slept with one of these women? If only he could talk to him, Armstrong thought. . . . But even if he could screw up the courage to broach the subject, his son would send him to the devil.

It began to drizzle and Armstrong kept to the shop frontages, hurrying his steps between the awnings. His thoughts turned to the acquaintance whom he had just offended. The manner in which the man had gone away reminded him of B.A.'s temperamental behaviour. Had he become as touchy as B.A., so that he was tempted to make remarks calculated to drive his friends away? In fact why had he wanted to see the acquaintance at all, whose deliberately broken English and childish recollections about his father irked him to an intolerable degree? This puzzle exercised Armstrong's mind for several hundred yards and even when the street in which he lived came into sight he was still thinking of the man.

Nowadays he forgot so quickly! He could fetch up from the recesses of his mind all the details of his life in Agricola and even far back into his boyhood; but events of recent weeks never seemed to imprint themselves on his memory any more. If he were honest he would admit that life in the past few years involved a continuing loss. He no longer saw Doc, whose friendship had once been a cornerstone of his life. Armstrong's status in the home had been challenged successfully by his growing son, a mere boy. His possessions had dwindled substantially and, for lack of money, he lived in perpetual fear of hospitalisation. His doctor had warned him that if he continued drinking the condition of his liver would deteriorate and he would eventually die. Yet, some irresistible force drew him to the rum shop and the dingy eating places. When his daughter Genetha asked why he could not buy the rum, bring it home and drink it in the house he told her that she was a fool and did not know what she was talking about.

One night he went out on the jetty at Fort and looked into the grey swell of the spring tide. As the tide rose, the spray made the stone slippery and instinctively he bent down on his haunches lest he slip into the dark waters. This precaution disgusted him. He was afraid to the point of making certain that he would not slip into the water. The same cowardice that prevented him from asserting his authority in his own home held him back from standing boldly beside the heaving sea. The life of the aboriginal Indians, whom everyone despised, was one of action, a coming to grips with nature in an effort to survive. In contrast to them, the bread had been taken out of his mouth by the stroke of a pen when he had been made redundant, and he could only reply with a gallop down the slope of perdition.

The beaches were covered with mud. People said that the sand would never reappear. Someone had stayed on after dark to fly his kite which soared above, solitary against the ravaged sky, its ribboned tail wagging lazily in the wind. The sound of singing came from the sea-wall, now faintly, now loud, as the wind rose or fell.

There was this longing in Armstrong's chest, this emptiness in his chest that slept and woke like a living thing. Sometimes he tried to remember what Gladys, his dead wife, looked like, but he could only recall black hair, which he used to sit and plait while they were courting. He took to looking at her photograph to refresh his memory. If only he had his life to live over again! If only he could speak to his son and pass on to him the experience he had acquired at the expense of his happiness. The singing voice was joined by another, and at the end the two voices burst out into a fit of laughter. Then they struck up a more boisterous song:

> "An' I had it a'ready,
> An' it sweet like honey,
> An' I had it a'ready,
> An' it soft like a jelly,
> An' de mule said to de donkey,
> 'Saga Boy, don't you molest me,'
> Donkey-ho!
> Don' bother me now I tell you. . . ."

2

Dissension

Genetha had taken on the responsibilities her mother used to exercise before her death. She got up early in the morning and prepared the morning meal, dusted and swept the house, made the beds, went to the market every day, cooked the midday meal; and at night, when her father and Rohan were out, Genetha read and taught herself shorthand. After Rohan began to work at the Commissary Office he paid for her to attend shorthand and typing classes and in four months she knew enough to apply for and secure her first job. She repaid him with a fanatical concern for his welfare. Her father was quick to notice the special attentions, the waiting up at nights until her brother came home, so that he would have something warm to eat. The first time Rohan — his fond-name was Boyie — came back drunk she concealed her revulsion and made him drink a cup of bush tea, and the next morning she took care to say nothing about his condition of the night before.

"Who is the master of this house?" Armstrong once asked her, incapable of concealing his chagrin. "Well, answer: who is the master of this house?"

"Don't talk like that, Father. You get everything you want."

"I don't want the rags I'm wearing. Well, come on! Do I want the rags I'm wearing? Would you want to wear them?"

"You spend all your money on drink, that's why you haven't any clothes. I don't buy Boyie any clothes."

"It's about the only thing you don't buy him," her father retorted.

"If only you'd stop drinking, everything'll be all right."

There were innumerable conversations along these lines and one day Genetha lost her patience and shouted back at him.

"Take everything I've got! Take my bank book too and draw out everything, but stop telling me what I don't do for you!"

"It's not so much what you don't do for me, but what you do for Boyie," said Armstrong.

"Well, don't tell me any more what I do for Boyie either, d'you understand? I'm fed up of hearing the same thing over and over!"

"The best thing I can do in this house is to shut up and let the two of you run things as you like."

"Yes! But just leave me alone!" exclaimed Genetha.

Armstrong was ashamed and hurt. He vowed that he would never raise the subject of his treatment in his own house any more. But inevitably the rankling burst out into bitter reproaches. The fearful row that followed one of his strictures convinced him that he would have to abide by his decision not to accuse his two children of neglecting him.

One day Armstrong said something about his dead wife, their mother.

"You killed her," Rohan declared.

"You should be the last one to talk, you ungrateful louse! Since you were a baby she had nothing but trouble with you. She used to run out of the house and leave you with the servants. Yes! And don't you point a finger at me in my own house!"

Rohan invariably adopted an aggressive attitude in an attempt to hide his shame whenever his father conjured up recollections of his dead mother. Armstrong sensed his son's unease and redoubled his accusations.

"Once the neighbours took hold of you and beat you with a sewing-machine cord because you vexed your mother so much she was sitting at the window crying. Yes, you used to scream and stamp till she gave in to you."

Rohan angrily went inside, but his father shouted over the partition.

"And this sister of yours who can't do too much for you couldn't stand the sight of you. Go on!" he shouted, pointing to Genetha. "Tell him! You couldn't stand the sight of him. You used to beat her up mercilessly. Once you cuffed her so badly her whole face was black and blue. The only people who liked you were the old women. Yes! You young cock! You used to go round on a Saturday collecting your eight cent pieces from your old lady friends. Then you'd go off to the pictures and stuff yourself with black pudding—"

"Stop it, ne," Genetha pleaded.

172

He, too, was overcome with shame, but could not admit it. He picked up the *Daily Chronicle*, which was lying folded on the radio, and went to the gallery, where he sat down and read the paper for the second time.

After such quarrels Rohan was afflicted with a deep guilt about his mother's death. Sometimes he would sit alone and beat his chest softly with his fists on remembering the trouble he had caused her. His father did not suspect how vulnerable his son was to the kind of reproaches he, Armstrong, had just made.

Another time, the desire to measure Genetha's attachment to him led Armstrong to say to her, "I'm thinking of getting married again."

"Oh?" she asked. "To whom?"

"You don't know her," Armstrong replied. "She's a decent woman, a widow."

"Well, you won't be able to go round looking like that," Genetha admonished him.

"I suppose not," he said sadly.

"When you're getting married?" she enquired.

"How d'you expect me to get married on a pension, you fool!" he exclaimed.

She looked at him in astonishment.

Sometimes, filled with remorse at the recollection of his conduct towards his dead wife, Armstrong went out of his way to be good to Genetha. But no sooner had she recovered from her surprise than he yielded to the temptation to criticise her cooking or the way she dressed or the length of time she spent in the kitchen. Convinced that, at bottom, Genetha was as antagonistic towards him as was Rohan, he frequently reduced her to tears and then taunted her that she could always go out and find a man to protect her.

Rohan told his sister that more than once he caught their father talking to himself. Genetha, though worried by this discovery, pretended to dismiss it as normal.

"A lot of people talk to themselves when they're alone," she remarked.

Indeed, Armstrong had for long been in the habit of delivering extensive monologues to himself, usually accompanying them with the most grotesque mimicry, like outbursts of

173

soundless laughter and the clapping of his hands. Sometimes he would interrupt himself by exclaiming, "Ay! Ay! Ay!" several times, as if to emphasise that he was not prepared to share his secret with anyone.

One Monday morning, after a whole weekend of self-restraint during which he kept out of his children's way, he broke out in a veritable orgy of mimicry and declamation.

"I've got something up my sleeve you'll never find out!" he exclaimed, baring his teeth and pretending to laugh. "Yes, my devoted children, up my sleeve! Up! Understand? Up my very wide sleeve. Like Wu-li-Wong the Chinese magician. Your mother had a secret and so've I! What would we be without our secrets, eh? We take them out like playthings and fondle them when we're alone. You're nothing but forced-ripe children trying to be grown-ups, playing a game you don't even understand. You think I've lived all these years for nothing? Eh? Answer me! You dare not answer. Oh, yes, my children, your father's far from dead. I've got every passion there is, but I know to control them. Self-control. I invented it! It's my motto. When I lose my temper I'm only play-acting, pretending, to throw you off-balance. But you, you young cock, I'll nail you to the wall and make you render account for every slight, every injustice, every moment of unease you caused me."

Armstrong clapped his hands vigorously, pursed his lips and pretended to be urging someone on to attack him. He made a wide circle round the room, occasionally dodging an imagined blow.

"You're frightened, eh?" he burst out. "Not so easy, eh? These muscles aren't on me for nothing." He rolled up the sleeve of his right arm and measured his tensed biceps.

"Easier said than done, young cock. I'll tell you what! Let's put it off until you see what I've got up my sleeve. I know you; you'd like to see me under six feet of earth, prostrate and alone, conversing with all those worms. But I'll outlive you, my boy, and your sister, who trails in your wake, idolising you as if you were God."

Eventually, he went and lay down, exhausted by the role he had played. Soon Rohan would be home for the midday meal, and then Genetha, and he would be obliged to pretend

174

that he was calm under his mask and the clouded look of his stale-drunk eyes.

Sometimes, out of spite, Armstrong deliberately absented himself before Genetha came home to cook breakfast. He would then go to the Promenade Gardens and sit on one of the white-painted cast-iron benches by the gates and watch the occasional pair of lovers who met furtively after a quick snack, before returning to their respective offices. They reminded him of his courting days, when his dead wife was not allowed out of the house unchaperoned and he was obliged to face her arrogant sisters, who had no suitors, whose envy at their sister's good fortune was translated into an ill-concealed hostility towards him. Now recollections of his youthful love brought a sensation of longing, amplified by the idealised vision of his dead wife.

Now, in middle age, the days seemed longer. Besides, he began to value the things others appreciated, incomprehensibly, he once thought. To old photographs, an act of generosity and recollections of encounters were attributed an exaggerated importance that made them seem extraordinary, like those signals from departing ships which children believe to be alarms from another world. He had spoken of his disgust at the changing relations with the people and things around to Genetha, who listened indulgently, but did not seem to understand. He had lost his sense of humour, he confessed, and found himself unable to laugh at jokes that would once have all but given him a seizure.

"I heard a man telling a woman that he went to a shop and bought four bottles of rum, because, according to their advertisement, for every four bought the customer would receive one free bottle. The man paid his money and received as his bonus an empty rum bottle. 'But it empty!' he protested. 'The advert din' say you'd get a bottle with rum,' the shopkeeper told him. The woman laughed at the joke and I could see nothing to laugh about; *nothing*. I still don't see anything to laugh at."

Armstrong always felt at ease after nightfall, when Genetha was invariably home to keep him company. And he felt at ease because of the darkness that transformed the world, that brought the barking of dogs and the incessant whirring of

175

the crickets. And on those days when he sat on the Promenade Gardens in the shade of an ornamental tree he looked forward to night encroaching on the edge of day and the sun vanishing below the horizon and the white clouds shedding their light, and the enveloping shadows bringing a kind of peace to his destitution. He had long forgotten that in the past each night was like a desert to be crossed, the very image of his marriage.

3

Doc

Armstrong, it seemed to Doc, must have taken offence at a remark he had once made about the way he dressed. At the time he seemed to take it in good part, but when Doc came round to his house to find out why he had not looked him up Armstrong was out. A number of subsequent visits proved just as fruitless and Doc realised that his friend would see him in his own good time. Both men missed each other a great deal and neither could find anyone in whom he could confide so readily, nor with whom he could recall events in which they had shared. When Doc learned that the son of their mutual friend B.A. had become a successful boxer he lost no time in paying Armstrong a visit; but, as in the past, there was no answer to his knocking. While in the act of mounting his bicycle, he thought he saw the laths of a venetian blind being adjusted, but was not certain.

The acquisition of a car provided the occasion for dropping in to see his friend once more; but again the house seemed empty. Doc was angry and vowed that he would not go to see him again. He kept his promise to himself and even when, late at night, there was light in Armstrong's gallery, he drove on, unwilling to risk being faced with the evidence of his own eyes and ears. Like Armstrong, he sought refuge from boredom in drink; unlike Armstrong, he frequented the lounges of the elegant Main Street hotels, where he struck up acquaintances as plants take root in a shallow soil.

As his work as a teacher became less interesting, as life became less purposeful, he fell in love with Baby, his mistress. With love came jealousy and the manifold torments an older man suffers in a liaison with an attractive young woman. He began to watch her comings and goings, checked on her appointments, questioned her, set traps for her, pretended to be happy when he was suspicious, in short, became his own tormentor. She, in turn, sensed that he was losing his grip, so that the respect she had felt for him became slightly

177

tarnished. Doc, who prided himself on his realism, knew that he was making a fool of himself, but was nevertheless powerless to act in the way he knew a mature man ought.

One afternoon Doc spotted Armstrong as he was about to enter his barber shop and in his excitement nearly ran down a cyclist. Parking his car in the nearest side street he walked back hurriedly to the glass-fronted shop and peered over the swing doors. Tufts of hair lay on the floor around the three swivel chairs where the barbers were clipping their clients' heads. Armstrong, who was sitting in a corner, his legs crossed and his arms folded, did not notice Doc, even when he stood before him.

"You can't run now," Doc said; and Armstrong looked up, irritated at the intrusion.

"Well, well! What're you doing in this part of town?" he asked, on recognising Doc. And involuntarily he looked down at his soiled trousers and dirty shoes.

In his confusion he allowed Doc to drag him outside to the car around the corner. As they drove to his new Garden Street house Doc talked without a break, impelled by the anxiety that any silence between them might cause his erstwhile drinking companion to demand that he be taken home. He told him how he moved Baby and the old woman from the East Coast, first to live with him in Kitty and then to their present home. Baby had become an excellent dressmaker. If in Plaisance she was an ignorant country girl, during her apprenticeship with Mrs Ashurst she had learned fast. She was one of those people whose talent and ambition it is impossible to gauge until they are placed in a certain environment. Transplanted, they flourish abundantly, so that those who knew them before the change recognise them only with difficulty afterwards. Her imagination left something to be desired, but she learned avidly and remembered everything she learned. Mrs Ashurst found her progress embarrassing. When, finally, she was taught how to cut, the girl showed such flair for that most difficult of exercises that Mrs Ashurst offered to double her wages if she would undertake to work with her for two more years. In the two years Mrs Ashurst enlarged her clientele considerably and was able to buy more machines. Baby's insatiable capacity for work allowed her to take on new customers and get the work finished on time.

At the end of the two years, rather than lose Baby, who wanted to establish her own business, Mrs Ashurst offered her a partnership, duly drawn up and signed. But the two women, who had got on exceedingly well when one was the employee and the other the mistress, continually quarrelled once they were on an equal footing. They agreed to dissolve their partnership and did so with some ill feeling on both sides.

Doc, who had about nine hundred dollars saved, had invested all of it in setting Baby up. In less than two years, she had three girls working for her and was making so much that Doc was able to buy the house in New Garden Street. They lived in the handsome rooms upstairs and used the two rooms downstairs for business.

His colleagues envied him his success and some of them wished secretly that Baby would leave him for someone else. But Baby, acutely conscious of her inability to write or even read adequately, saw in Doc a buffer between herself and the smart world of Georgetown.

He always harboured the wish to be so well off that he could insult all those people he disliked intensely at the school where he taught. Now that he was in a position to do so the desire seemed to have left him. Furthermore, the occasions that roused him to anger seemed to present themselves much less frequently than before his good fortune. He himself noticed this and put it down to the fact that others, aware of his independence, no longer tried to take advantage of him. His colleagues, on the other hand, claimed that he was not as sensitive as he used to be, and was therefore easier to get on with. All in all he probably missed the days when he was at grips with the whole world, just as he missed his clandestine Sunday trips to visit Baby in Plaisance, since now he was obliged to endure the boredom of Sundays like everyone else.

Doc brought the car to a halt in front of his house, but Armstrong protested. At once Doc drove off, turning off in the direction of his friend's home. Once there, Armstrong could not suppress the feeling that Doc was gloating and quietly making comparisons between their respective lots. He would have left him, but felt that this might be interpreted as a confession of his decline. The insensitive flow of words, the boasting, so oppressed Armstrong that he was obliged to turn away.

"You're all right?" asked Doc.

Armstrong nodded, and his friend was encouraged to continue his interrupted monologue. How could he have tolerated him in the past? wondered Armstrong. His egotism, his dismissal of other people's problems as of little importance were like deformities that marred the frame of his character. And Armstrong forgot all of Doc's virtues, his unfailing good humour, his warmth and generosity; and that it was precisely this flow of words he once admired and which complemented his own reticence outside his home.

"Your children must be big now," Doc remarked.

All of a sudden he was seized with the urge to speak of Rohan.

"Children?" said Armstrong bitterly. "Children? If I had children I wouldn't look like this. Look at you! Anyone can see you don't have children. If you ask me, the function of a child is to destroy its parents. My son's working and what he gives me can't feed a parrot. But it doesn't stop him from complaining to all and sundry that I'm a disgrace. Not to me! But to every Tom, Dick and Harry. Children're a curse. Sometimes — sometimes I feel that my son's trampling over my chest and I wake up in a cold sweat. . . . When my father died I wasn't living in his house, but you'll never imagine the effect it had on me. I felt free, like a song bird that's got out of its cage. Yet I was a grown man and there was more than a hundred miles' distance between us. But _I_ had cause to hate him. What did I do my son? I can count the number of times I laid my hands on him. You think of the number of people you know who knock about their children. But it doesn't stop him from abusing me."

Doc listened in disbelief. Armstrong had only once before complained of his family life and then he had been drinking for hours. In fact, no sooner had he uttered a few words than he shut up like a clam. Doc remembered the occasion well. Was he now going mad? Doc had known of other men who were also victims of the slump and who went off their head. Armstrong's enforced retirement from his post office at an early age could not have left him untouched. And this talk of

180

his son trampling on his chest was so unlike him!

Doc really did not know his friend well. He had no idea of his behaviour at home, of the way he had driven his wife to distraction and of the hallucinations that afflicted him since her death.

Avoiding Armstrong's eyes he said, "This damned depression's got a lot to answer for."

And then, after another embarrassing silence, he went on, "You remember Lesney?"

Armstrong smiled, warming to the memory of the epileptic whore with whom he was once in love.

"Those were the days!" exclaimed Doc. "Ageing whores and fornicating government officers. . . . Somebody saw you stroking her breast under the street lamp. Could've told your wife, y'know. Ah! Those were the days! We took risks, just like schoolboys. And on Monday morning I lectured the children at school on morality."

"And that Sunday I came up to Plaisance? Or was it a Saturday?" Armstrong asked.

"A Sunday, a Sunday," Doc corrected him. "And you kept pinching Baby's backside."

Armstrong, sensing that he was not keen on pursuing the subject, put an abrupt end to the reminiscence.

His right arm on the wheel of his car, Doc surveyed the road ahead, this time unwilling to save the conversation. Armstrong was content to sit by him, buffeted by the wind that came through the car windows. Darkness had fallen and the street lamps came on simultaneously, like giant stars.

A young man went through the gate and began to climb the stairs, without bothering to greet them.

Doc guessed that he was Armstrong's son, and the sight of the youth aroused in him a longing for the children he never had. Intrigued by Rohan's apparent arrogance, he followed his progress up the stairs, until he opened the door and disappeared inside.

"You want me to go and get a bottle of rum?" asked Doc, out of the blue.

"What? What?" started Armstrong, choking with anger. "What does get my blood up is the way he behaves, as if he's a man."

181

"Most of them behave like that, y'know," observed Doc. "Young people of today . . . it's the war. Even in primary school you can't control them as you used to. Your son isn't different from the rest."

It was this attitude that infuriated Armstrong.

"You're talking about what you don't damn well understand. You don't have children of your own, yet you know that my son's behaving like other. . . . You couldn't put your own house in order, but you can tell me all about bringing up children."

"I wasn't talking about bringing up children."

"No! Because you damn well can't."

Armstrong's oblique reference to Doc's broken marriage hurt him deeply. Uncharacteristically, he did not answer, but waited for his friend to apologise.

"Anyway," said Armstrong, opening the car door on his side, "you and I don't have a damn thing in common."

"We're older, that's all," replied Doc coolly. "I came round here several times to see you, but you didn't have the character to show yourself like a man. I'm not responsible for your looking like an inmate of the alms house."

He had paid Armstrong back in kind, and when the latter stepped out of the car without a word, he closed the door which had been left open and drove off.

Armstrong realised that it was the last meeting with Doc, the last of so many that had spanned the years from their days as young men. He sat down on the lowest step of the staircase, wedged, as it were, between a recalcitrant son and a lost friend.

4

A Family of Women

Rohan, after a month at head office in Georgetown, was transferred to the Vreed-en-Hoop Commissary Office. There he assisted in the issuing of licences of all kinds and carried out general clerical duties. Still under the illusion that talent and hard work were advantages that distinguished a young man in the ranks of the Civil Service, Rohan devoted himself to his work. He was well liked by his colleagues, who were all much older than he. In turn, he admired the skill with which they carried out tasks that appeared to him excessively difficult.

But there was one among them he consciously tried to emulate, a grave, witty scholar by the name of Mr Mohammed. Never had he met anyone with such a command of English. His mastery of the language was such that he appeared to be able to display it on the slightest pretext.

A certain incident in particular left a strong impression on Rohan. One Monday morning the messenger spilt black ink on the concrete floor. All the poor youth could do was to blot it up and leave it to dry. Mr Mohammed, on entering the office, noticed the unseemly stain and remarked, "Who is responsible for this atramentous discoloration?" his eyes gleaming roguishly. Everyone laughed, more at Mr Mohammed's command of mime than at his language. But it was the immediate flow of words that took Rohan's breath away.

There was also something mysterious about Mr Mohammed, or so Rohan thought. His humour entertained, but his moodiness kept those eager to know him at bay. Every Monday he held court on the ground floor of the Commissary Office. East Indians from the West Coast and West Bank came to have their problems settled by him. He was constantly complaining that the allowance the government paid him for his duties as a mediator in family and other matters was too small. In truth, his ability to pour oil on troubled waters, his skill at finding solutions to apparently insoluble problems, had earned him a wide reputation. So much so that many East

Indians involved in a dispute agreed among themselves to consult him as a step in a legal process which might eventually take them to court. The poor East Indians idolised him and on consulting days often brought him gifts as a mark of gratitude for some dispute settled years before.

In these sessions Mr Mohammed spoke Hindi to the older Indians, who, unlike their children and grandchildren, felt more at home in their mother tongue than in English. Rohan, accustomed to the urban world of Georgetown, was fascinated by what he heard and saw in Vreed-en-Hoop, just across the river from town. Until he had witnessed these sessions he would not have believed that there were illiterate people in the country or that drainage of the land played such an important part in people's lives, or that Uitvlugt was as well known on the West Coast as Buxton was on the East Coast.

When Rohan was first invited to Mr Mohammed's home he went eagerly. He was not disappointed. The cottage stood about fifteen feet back from the Public Road and seemed to represent in some curious way Mr Mohammed himself, with its quaint jalousies and ample porch. They were welcomed not by his wife but by an attractive young woman in her early twenties. Two young girls, hearing that there was a visitor, came out to peep, glad at an occurrence they could speak about for days. Their giggling broke out and subsided at irregular intervals. Mr Mohammed watched Rohan from the corner of his eye and could not suppress a smile.

"They've got empty heads," he said, as if he had divined Rohan's interest. "Except Indrani."

Beckoning his eldest daughter over he introduced her in a way that left no doubt that she was his favourite. Rohan was to remember later how soft her hand was. He looked her boldly in the eyes and saw the highlights in her pupils and the long eyelashes that gleamed darkly. On learning, a little later, that Indrani was married, he felt a pang of disappointment.

When they were alone Mr Mohammed told Rohan how, four years ago, a young man asked for her hand in marriage. He agreed and tried to persuade him to contract a marriage by rites that were recognised by law. The suitor protested that Mr Mohammed did not trust him. His brother had been married under bamboo, he said, and he would not break with

184

tradition. Mr Mohammed pointed out that the marriage under bamboo could take place, but the added formalities would satisfy the requirements that would give his daughter protection in the event of a separation. The young man, unconcerned with legal requirements, insisted on having his own way. In the end Mr Mohammed gave in and the couple were married under bamboo. Two years later Indrani's husband sent her home, claiming that he was not satisfied with her as a wife. It was common knowledge that he had taken up with another woman, but he refused to admit that this relationship had had anything to do with his decision. Mr Mohammed pleaded with him to take his daughter back, but he taunted him with the observation that he had no legal obligation to support her.

Indrani came in carrying a tray with drinks on it. Rohan tried to avoid looking at her, but as she turned to go her dress grazed him arm, almost imperceptibly. Rohan felt a rush of blood to his head.

That night he lay on his bed and tried to recall everything that happened at the Mohammeds' that day. Once he had caught Indrani looking at him. There was never a hint of encouragement, but yet he was smitten by her, even though she was a married woman and older than he was. If there had been a late ferry he would have taken it, just so that he could walk past the Mohammed house and look up at the windows and conjure up her form, lying on a bed. Did she sleep on her side or on her back, as he did? How long did it take for her to fall asleep? Suppose he had done something absurd, like putting out his hand and touching her arm, what would have been her reaction, or her father's? How near he had come to doing what was absurd they would never know. He could not guarantee that in future he would behave. Even a simple act, like taking the glass from the tray she had brought, became a complicated operation, needing skill and great presence of mind to accomplish without spilling its contents. He wondered if she had noticed his confusion. Nonsense! He was a boy to her, not even capable of making the most elementary conversation; and besides, she must have noticed his scraggly arms and awkward way of smiling. His father was right: it would be years before he became a man.

This thought so depressed Rohan that he despaired of ever

attracting so much as a glance from Indrani. In any case she was married and he would be a fool to get involved with a married woman. Even if she let him know in no uncertain terms that she liked him he would not respond.

Rohan fell asleep, reassured that Indrani did not care for him. The next morning he found himself at the stelling a half-hour before the boat was due to leave. He went into Stabroek Market and bought two bananas, which he ate on the edge of the river while he watched Vreed-en-Hoop on the other side. The ferry boat seemed to be tied up an inordinately long time there. When, finally, it left its moorings Rohan's heart skipped a beat and he knew that there was no doubt that, married or not married, he was in love with Indrani Mohammed.

In the months that followed Rohan Armstrong became a regular visitor to the Mohammed home. The only one who seemed to resent his visits was Mohammed's son, a youth who took no trouble to hide his dislike for Rohan. But he was hardly ever at home.

As for Mr Mohammed's wife, Rohan only met her on his fourth or fifth visit, and thereafter he saw her from time to time. No one offered any explanation for her absences. Whenever she was at home the children acknowledged her presence as natural and looked to her for direction in household matters, but when she was absent they were equally able to manage without her. Mohammed and his wife were affectionate to each other, in an undemonstrative way. She was attentive to his needs and he was tolerant of her outbursts of temper. He never corrected her frequent grammatical mistakes and listened with apparent interest to whatever she had to say. He had only introduced her perfunctorily to Rohan, as if eager to get over the formality.

For Rohan, their house was a place of laughter and music. Although East Indian music did not appeal to him he was intrigued by the dancing of the two younger girls, Betty and Dada. Mohammed himself played the sitar and violin and accompanied the girls in the drawing-room, with its rug-bedecked walls and framed pictures with Persian captions. Sometimes Mrs Mohammed refused to be left out of the dancing and then Mohammed, with great tolerance, allowed her to

186

take part. When she danced the room was transformed into a setting for an incomparable display of the art and her daughters, suffering by comparison, invariably sat down and watched their mother.

The house, with its cherry-tree hedge, became familiar to him, and whenever he was seen approaching, there was no longer a scurrying of feet and giggling. His status as friend of the family was so established that, often, no one even bothered to greet him. Indrani treated him like a brother and listened to him when he spoke about his school days and his memories of Agricola. She told him what clothes suited him and advised him on what he should eat when he wanted to put on weight.

Rohan never mentioned the Mohammeds to his family, but Genetha and his father soon learned of his visits, by that strange telegraph that afflicts small towns. Genetha watched her brother closely and soon detected Indrani's influence in his dress and behaviour. Unlike her father, who bluntly asked his son what he thought he was doing, Genetha tried to hide her jealousy from Rohan. She was puzzled by his preoccupation with these country people.

One day she took the ferry to Vreed-en-Hoop and walked up the East Coast road and past the Mohammeds' home, which a passer-by pointed out to her. The house was quiet and no member of the family was about. Next door, prayer flags were flying in the yard and a group of young men were playing cards under the house. She dared not stop in the boiling sun, lest she attracted attention. On the way back, about fifteen minutes later, she saw two girls playing litty on the Mohammeds' porch. One of them looked at Genetha, who pretended that she had no interest in the house. Instead, she changed her parasol from the right shoulder to the left and hurried on to the stelling.

As she sat waiting for the boat she reflected that she knew no more than she had known the day before. Besides, what if Rohan had seen her from the house? Suppose the girl who had looked back at her had recognised her as Rohan's sister. . . . She knew nothing about the family, but it was more than likely that they knew a good deal about her. Was Rohan there when she passed? What could he be doing there a whole Saturday afternoon? The girls playing on the porch were too young to attract his interest. *She* must be a good deal older. But Rohan was so young! The relationship with the mysterious woman appeared to Genetha something obscene and unpardonable.

Genetha looked down into the river, which was in slack tide, and watched the shimmering water lapping against the greenheart piles. Across the river were the wharves and warehouses of Georgetown, which formed one grey mass under the brilliant sky. The worlds of Vreed-en-Hoop and Georgetown, separated only by the expanse of a river, were far removed from one another in Genetha's eyes. Where in Georgetown could Rohan ingratiate himself into a family of strangers in such a short time? The prayer flags, the hedges, the dusty roads, represented a vaguely romantic but wretched world. Genetha knew that her brother had fallen into bad company. Despite his excessive praise of Mr Mohammed as a cultured man when Armstrong accused him of mixing with ruffians, she knew that no good could come of such a relationship. She must do all she could to bring it to an end.

At first Mohammed was not keen on Rohan's frequent visits to his home. He was young, well-mannered and physically attractive, but he knew the risk of introducing a young man into a house of girls who had always led a sheltered life. Yet, the longer he worked with Rohan the stronger his affection for him grew, so much so that he felt the need for his company. For years he had denied himself the society of would-be friends, finding social intercourse exclusively with his colleagues at work. Married to a scatterbrained woman, he had awaited the birth of his boy eagerly. When the child arrived — after his eldest daughter — he lavished affection on him; but the longed-for son was lazy and self-indulgent. Encouraged by his mother, who kept him at home whenever he complained of an ache, he spent most of his time catching birds and, later, playing cards. Mr Mohammed's bitter disappointment was fortified by the birth of girls after the boy.

Though the reasons which made it unwise for Rohan to visit him were still valid, Mohammed told himself that the young man was an influence for the good on the girls and, for that, approved of his position as a close friend of the family.

Genetha saw the mounting evidence for Rohan's involve-

ment with the people over the river with dismay. Not only was
Rohan hardly ever at home, but he was having some of his
shirts laundered by them. It was galling to see him wearing
shirts that were not gleaming with excessive starch. She herself washed his underclothes and one Sunday morning when
she put the pile of garments on the chair next to his bed she
could not resist remarking, "I suppose you'll be having these
washed over the river soon."

He looked at her, but made no reply. Genetha had been
determined, until then, to say nothing which might betray
resentment at losing some control over his laundering, but his
expression caused her to lose her temper.

"Why you don't go and live there and done with?"

"What's wrong with you lately?" asked Rohan. "You're
going round as if you've got a bad smell under your nose."

"I'm the same," said Genetha. "You imagine that I'm different because you've probably got something to hide. Don't
let's make a big thing out of something simple; but you must
admit that you're eating less at home—"

He interrupted her brutally: "You should be glad! I give
you the same amount of money."

"It's nothing to do with money," said Genetha, doing her
best to contain her rage. Then, bursting into tears she shrieked,
"It's nothing to do with money!"

She held on to the chair and gritted her teeth. Rohan, tortured by the thought that he had caused his sister pain, wanted
to say something conciliatory but did not know what words
to use. At the same time he considered the intrusion in his
private life intolerable.

"Years ago you were always shouting and getting into
trouble. Nowadays you hardly ever talk," she said softly. She
wanted to add that she was sure that he talked a lot when he
was at the Mohammeds'.

"I don't know when it'll dawn on you and Father that I'm
not at school. What've the two of you got against these people
anyway? You've ever seen them? If I invited one of them home
you'd find an excuse to go out."

"You notice you don't even call their name?" Genetha said.

Rohan was vexed that she had pointed it out to him. He
himself had felt that he was unwilling to pronounce the

189

Mohammed name in the presence of his father and wondered why. He admired them, enjoyed being at their home, and could see himself married to Indrani, yet something prevented him from uttering their name in his home. Was he ashamed of them? Rohan rejected the idea violently.

"Their name is Mohammed. Would you like to hear their other names too? The eldest girl is Indrani and other two are Betty and Dada. Are you satisfied?"

"If we can't even talk as we used to," Genetha said coolly, "there's no point going on."

Later Rohan reflected that he had said what he did not want to say and had neglected to say the things he really wanted to say. For a long time now he wanted to tell her that he did not smoke because he knew she disapproved; that he only put up with her interference in his life because he respected her so much; that he wanted to speak to her about his friendship with the Mohammeds, but felt embarrassed at broaching the subject to her. That even now he had made up his mind to break with them because she disapproved of the friendship. There were a number of activities he could fall back on, like gambling in the billiard saloons, where he had made a name for himself.

All of a sudden her concern for him seemed reasonable. After all, if any man messed about with her he would kill him. Then Rohan thought back to the time before he knew the Mohammeds, the nights when he rode about Georgetown aimlessly, hoping to meet some exciting girl or get to know someone who would help him to fulfil his need for action. When he had attained that standard in billiards where he could not easily find partners he began to lose interest in the game. If he deserted the Mohammeds he would probably find himself in a wasteland of loneliness, he told himself. He had to admit that he could not give up Indrani. She did not love him. He was certain of that now; but the knowledge that he would see her the next day filled him with pleasure. The architecture of her house was as well known to him as that of his own, and in his day-dreams he saw himself rocking in a hammock on her back porch, staring at the smoke-blackened eaves. She would look down at him with a smile, holding in her outstretched hand an iced sorrel drink. The nipples of her unbrassièred chest would arouse in him a feeling of indescribable ecstacy. He dreamed often of her and her sisters and once, when he confessed to Indrani that he did, she was not pleased.

One afternoon while he and Indrani were playing draughts on the porch the two younger girls were whispering in a corner. Suddenly Dada came over to him and kissed him full on his lips. She rushed back to her sister and the two of them ran down the stairs as fast as they could. At the end of the game Indrani put her hand on his arm and said she was unwell and would go and lie down. Long after she had gone Rohan felt the warmth of her hand where she had touched him. The breeze blew gently across the yard, ruffling the beads that hung at the entrance to the kitchen, and the laughter of the two girls could be heard from behind the trees in the back yard. He could touch the leaves of the Ceylon mango tree from where he sat. Behind the porch Mr Mohammed was repairing the paling which separated his property from the adjoining one and from where salipentas crossed to attack his chickens. Rohan decided that he would go downstairs and help him.

5

Indrani

Mr Mohammed did not ask Rohan why he no longer came back to the house. He thought at first that he had had a quarrel with one of the girls, but all three denied having fallen out with him. Rohan admired the older man for his tact in not pressing him to give an explanation. If only he knew how he was suffering! In the afternoons, after work, it was all he could do not to accompany Mohammed home. And one night he watched the ferry boat make its last trip to Vreed-en-Hoop after he had bought a ticket to travel on it. What if he had turned up at the house at that hour, especially after staying away for two weeks? He was determined to abide by his decision not to go back. For Genetha's sake he would break with the Mohammed family for good. In Rohan's eyes his sister possessed those magical qualities which very young children attribute to their parents. For that reason one did not offend them with impunity. Now that he knew that Genetha was aware of his visits and that she disapproved, he could not lie in the Mohammeds' hammock without imagining that she was watching him; he could not eat their food without seeing his own food getting cold on the table at home. If he enjoyed crossing his father, he could not bear to hurt his sister.

It was on a brilliant morning, three weeks after Rohan's self-imposed exile from the Mohammed house, that Dada walked into the office. Through her simple shift dress her immature breasts swelled softly from her chest. Her long, slender, brown arms were bare and her fingers restlessly fondled a parcel she was holding in her hands. Rohan was just disposing of a man who had applied for two gallons of gasoline for his wedding. He tore out the single two-gallon rationing coupon and wrote "Container" on it, then entered the man's name and the purpose for which he was issued the coupon in his ledger.

"Is it for me?" he asked Dada as she handed him the parcel.

"No, for Pa," she said curtly.

"All right. I'll give him it."

But instead of going she stood at the counter, looking at him.

"I can't talk here, Dada."

"Why? There's nobody waiting on you."

He glanced at the chief clerk, who was making up the cash book.

"What did we do you?" she continued.

"Nothing. Why?" he asked foolishly.

"Why? What kind of a person you are? You know how Pa's worried about you?"

"He didn't say anything to me," Rohan retorted.

"You know you stupid!" she exclaimed. "Like those cows in the rice field."

Rohan glanced at the chief clerk again. He seemed engrossed in his work.

"Go out. I'll come in a minute," he told her.

Dada went out of the office, but remained by the door, looking straight at him, as though she were threatening to go back in if he did not keep his promise to come out. Rohan left the office by the back door and met Dada out front. Just as she began to talk he caught sight of Indrani standing at the gate. He did not hear a word of what the younger sister was saying, until she raised her voice.

"You wouldn't even come for her? Eh?" Dada asked.

Rohan looked at Dada's angry face and realised for the first time how incredibly beautiful she was. Even Indrani, with her woman's figure and dark eyes, was no match for her younger sister.

"You didn't do anything. . . . I'll come this afternoon, then," he said, in order to appease her.

She turned on her heels and as she walked away he waved to Indrani, who waved back as if nothing were wrong.

Rohan told himself that he was obliged to say he would come in order to avoid a scene. For the rest of the day he went about the office dropping things and made mistakes in his ledger. And at the end of the day he forgot to lock a cupboard for which he was responsible and in which the gasoline coupons were kept.

That afternoon, straight after work, he went up to the

193

house. Dada was standing on the bridge, unashamedly waiting. She came down the road to meet him, swinging a stick like a schoolboy. In contrast to her anger earlier in the day her eyes were bright and the corners of her mouth were drawn up in a fetching smile. Betty, who was sitting at the window, called out to him. She was just finishing a mango and as he came up the stairs she threw the seed at him. Dada shrieked at her and for a moment there was the threat of a squabble between the two girls. But Betty retreated inside to wash her hands.

Rohan walked through the house in search of Indrani, who had evidently gone out. Dada made him sit down and went to make him a lime drink. Soon after that Mohammed arrived home.

"You been sulking, eh?" he said mischievously to Rohan, who smiled back at him.

"I wanted to tell you about Indrani, but I thought you weren't interested any more," Mohammed added.

"Isn't she there?" Rohan asked, not attempting to conceal his unease.

"She and her mother've gone to her grandmother in Suddie. The old lady's frightened to stay alone with her husband, who's sick. According to her, ghosts're pestering the old man. She went to the office to see you this morning, didn't she?"

"She and Dada came, but she stayed by the bridge."

"She told me she was coming to see you. Funny!"

Rohan regretted that he had not gone out to meet her. Obviously, that was what she had expected him to do. What a fool he had been to miss an opportunity like that!

"Don't bother," Mr Mohammed reassured him. "She'll probably be back in a couple of days' time."

"When did she leave?"

Mohammed shouted out to the girls, "What train did Indrani take?"

"Twelve o'clock," a voice chimed out from inside.

Mohammed got up and filled a glass with water, which he put on the window ledge; then he sat down and looked out on the street. A woman was hectoring her son, who kept walking too near the middle of the road.

"You've ever been to the rice fields?" Mohammed asked him.

194

He shook his head, without replying.

"You should go and see how our women work and get old before their time. For about three months of the year their children don't go to school. They have to work in the fields with their parents. The sun at nine in the morning is hotter than at any other time of the day and by then they've been working for hours. It would break my heart if Dada and Betty had to spend hours in the sun, bending over the young rice. Yet why should they be spared and not the others? The land belongs to all of us, or so they say."

He drank from the glass of water and looked out on to the road again.

"The children's grandmother used to work in the rice fields and she's bent nearly double. Her husband's got the worst form of malaria; and the thing is they accept their lot as natural. Did you know that the country is the only one in the world with a falling population? Makes you think, eh?"

His voice dropped as he realised that his young friend was not interested. He emptied his glass and at that moment the mother with the son who would not walk at the edge of the roadway passed by again, going in the opposite direction.

"You gwine get lick down if you don' look whey you goin'. Get by de grass, I tell you. I gon' jook you in de back if you don' hear me," said the mother, her voice fading as she and the boy disappeared down the Public Road. A little later two children ran by, rolling their hoops. The afternoon was sunny, but cool from the wind that blew in from the sea.

"She's going to miss you. As a matter of fact she went partly because of you," Mohammed said to Rohan.

"Of me?"

"She had the idea you thought she was interfering."

"But—" Rohan began to protest.

"I know, I know," Mr Mohammed put in, with a wave of the hand. "Women are like that. They're not rational. And besides, who knows what her real reason for going away was? I gave up trying to understand women long ago. Indrani's not happy; and to make things worse she hasn't got anybody to turn to. You see what education does? It only separates people from the stock they come from. When I was a boy you could wander into a stranger's house and talk to him as if you'd

195

been life-long friends. Now everyone's on his guard, looking over his shoulder as if his shadow might pounce on him. Today people argue about the existence of God. Long ago it never entered your head to question it. Everything's changing. Look at Lilly," he said, referring to his wife, "what sort of mother is she to these children? She wanders off like a bird without a nest. If my father was alive he'd think I was raving mad to allow her to leave home whenever she took it into her head to go to her mother. But what'm I to do? Chain her to the house?"

She'd never given me a sign, thought Rohan. *How could I say anything to her first?* A wrong word, a gesture, would have spoiled everything.

He longed to have again the opportunities he missed. He recalled an incident which, in the light of what Mohammed had told him, showed without a doubt that she had wanted to encourage him. In retrospect everything was clear. How could he have hesitated when a schoolboy would have discerned the meaning of certain signs that at the time seemed ambiguous? The Saturday afternoons when she used to read to him and stop in the middle of a sentence to look up brazenly at his face; the nights when she, Dada and Betty accompanied him to the ferry to see him off and when, as they walked side by side, her arm would constantly brush his. . . . She was older than he and for this he loved her all the more and put her on a pedestal, above all women. She was married and inaccessible; and he saw her as a superior being, pure and incorruptible.

"Boyie! I'm talking to you, Boyie!" Betty's voice burst in upon his reflections, calling him by the name his sister and father used.

"He's dreaming of Indrani," Dada said with a nasty intonation in her voice.

Rohan followed Mr Mohammed to the table, which was laid for the afternoon meal. Beside his plate was the lime drink his young friend had made for him. No one was disposed to talk, except Betty, who soon gave up trying to rouse the others to conversation. The four sat, buttering their bread and drinking tea. Dada silently passed Rohan the cheese. He glared at her and pushed it away without thanking her.

Night fell and the crickets began to sing. In the perfect

196

evening there was a little sadness in the house; and when Mohammed got up to light the gas lamp Dada left the table and went to look for her sister's guitar. She came back, sat down and sang two Indian songs composed by her father. Then she began to improvise and hum in her thin, girlish voice. Her father had gone out to sit on the back porch, where he liked to rock in his rocking-chair when everything was well. Betty sat listening to her sister, her elbows on the table and her chin cupped in her hands, while Rohan, sick at heart, listened to the incessant pounding of his own regrets.

One Friday morning when Mohammed arrived at work he greeted Rohan with a twinkle in his eye. The first opportunity he got to speak to him on his own he whispered, "Indrani's back."

Rohan turned round and looked at the older man.

"You heard?" Mr Mohammed asked.

"Yes," he replied softly.

His tongue stuck to his palate, and when he was alone he considered what best to do. If he went to see her at midday Dada and Betty would be home from school. After work it would be even worse. He decided that he must go home to her during the morning. But when? Friday was the busiest day of the week. The bus-men, the launch-drivers, the taxi-owners would all be coming to collect their weekly ration of coupons. And if Ramnaraine, the office-helper, was left in charge, he would only get the books wrong and there would be the devil to pay afterwards. But it was the only way. He signalled to Ramnaraine to see him at the back of the office and offered him a shilling to keep things going while he went to the drugstore to get a prescription filled.

When no other officer was around Rohan slipped out and was soon on his way up West Coast Public Road. The walk seemed long in the hot morning sun. A stray dog sniffed at his heels and decided to follow him until he turned on it threateningly. The sound of women beating their clothes by the trench rang through the air. Rohan wondered what she would look like. Would she be working in the yard, or in the house? Then it suddenly occurred to him that her mother might have returned with her.

197

"Damn it!" he thought, hurrying his step.

He went up the stairs and knocked on the door. In his impatience he left like banging on the door and kicking it open; but the unmistakable steps of Indrani could be heard approaching.

"How you got off from work?" she asked, and in her voice was that sweetness he had known in no other woman.

He shrugged his shoulders. "I just came when I heard you were back," he said.

She smiled and looked at him without a word. The two were standing in the doorway when a voice from inside called out.

"Is who?"

"Boyie!" Indrani called back.

"Who?"

"Boyie!" she repeated.

Then he appeared, a full-faced man clad only in trousers and sandals.

"Eh, eh. That's the famous Boyie. Si' down, si' down, man. I don't got to say make you'self at home. From what I hear you do that long ago."

Indrani sat down on the couch, while the two men sat opposite each other by the window.

Rohan felt that the stranger had the advantage of him. He wanted to look him straight in the face, but could not sustain his gaze.

"Is which one o' the women in the house you interested in, eh?" he asked, showing his white teeth in a broad smile.

"Boyie—" Indrani began to speak.

"Get up and make some lemonade for the guest," the man interrupted peremptorily. Indrani got up at once and went off.

"Eh, eh, is where me manners gone? I'm Sidique, the husband. Well, I mean, not legal, but it don't matter."

He then turned and looked towards the back of the house. Something was making him impatient.

"What the hell you doing, growing the limes?" he shouted after Indrani. Then in a smooth, ingratiating way he turned back to Rohan.

"You in't say a word yet."

"I'm glad to see Indrani back," Rohan said.

"Back? For how long you back, 'Drani?" Sidique shouted.

"I don't know, a week?" she hazarded.

"She say a week. I say three days," he said, scratching his hairy torso, "so it's three days."

Indrani's husband started tapping on his chair as if he were reflecting on something.

"I suppose you t'ink I'm a nasty — you know. I'm not educated like you. Well, a nasty fella. . . . You're right. You see I hardly do any work so I got time to be nasty."

He smacked his lips, deliberately to irritate Rohan, it appeared.

Indrani came in with the tray. Rohan and Sidique took their glasses with ice floating on the top of the lemonade. Sidique began to hum and as he did so he looked unflinchingly at Rohan, who in turn looked at Indrani.

"You know Indrani can read Arabic?" Sidique told Rohan.

"He's not interested in Arabic," Indrani remarked.

"Hi hi hiiiii!" he giggled, "I kian' even write a letter good. An' I bet you can write one with you eyes close, Mr Boyie."

He burst out laughing as if Boyie's literacy was a great joke.

"But," he continued, "you got to go into a office at eight o'clock and lef' at four. You got to do what you boss say or you know damn well that you in' going to get promotion. An' you see me? If I go into you office and I say I'm Mr Ali son from the Essequibo, the man would jump up as if a pistol go off in his ass."

His eyes twinkled wickedly. "That's right, in' it, 'Drani?" he asked, turning towards her for approval. "That's right, Mr Boyie."

Indrani winced at the way he was talking.

"Take the glasses away," Sidique said curtly. She obeyed.

He began drumming with his fingers again and humming to himself in the high-pitched tone of the Indian singer.

"You see what they educate you for? To make you a slave. One day you might even be workin' for me," he grimaced exaggeratedly. "But I tell you, if you ever work in we rice mill I gwine pay you good. There's a chap name Johnny. You remember Johnny, 'Drani? Johnny from Leguan. Anyway, this Johnny does talk like you, Mr Boyie. Jus' like you. Good like, you know. I always say to Johnny, 'I wish I could talk like you,' and whenever I say that to Johnny I always laugh. I kian' help it. But Johnny don't laugh. I wonder why. I never see that man laugh yet. An' I say to you now, Mr Boyie, 'I wish I could talk like you.' "

And Sidique laughed heartily. Indrani's lips were pursed. She looked from her husband to Rohan, but said nothing.

Rohan got up to go.

"Don' go. I not as bad as I sound."

His tone was friendly and Rohan sat down again, ashamed of his desire to remain and be humiliated by a man he did not know.

"Come, 'Drani gal, sit 'pon me lap."

He put his arm round her waist as she sat down on his lap, her face turned in the direction of Rohan. Then, without warning, she got up and went off into the kitchen.

"She like that. I in' train she good yet. The faimly don' really like me, you know. I suppose is 'cause we in' got education. But my father always say you can buy education and if you kian' buy it for youself you can buy it for you children. But you kian' buy money. Anyway, I don' like them neither. All this singing and dancing in' good for women. That's why I tell 'Drani not to dance in my house."

Indrani emerged from the back of the house and took her place once more in the chair.

"'Drani, we goin' home tomorrow," he said to her, but looked provocatively at Rohan.

"Why?" Indrani asked him.

He shook his head and made an impatient sound with his tongue, which did not go with the calm of his voice.

"You know why I kian' love my wife, Mr Boyie? 'Cause she don' talk the English I talk. Is not nat'ral for a country woman to talk like a town woman. Besides, is too hot to talk."

Sidique wiped his sweating face with the back of his hand.

"O God! This heat! My father in rice. He don' plant it, mind you. Oh, no! Mills. Rice mills. The little fellas plant it and bring it to 'im for milling. Stupid, really. No risk in milling. All the risk's in plantin'. But that's why they're poor and my father rich, see? 'Cause he in' stupid. Anyway, last year was so good, he buy a motor boat. The latest t'ing from the

States. Wasted, mind you, on the Essequibo coast, wasted. If this year crop as good as last year I wonder what he gon' buy? 'Cause he got everyt'ing a'ready."

Then his tone changed all of a sudden.

"All I got to do is whistle an' she come runnin' like a dog!" he said maliciously.

Rohan got up in protest.

"It hurt you to hear it, eh, Mr Boyie? What's the good of you education if you run every time the truth hit you?"

As he was talking Rohan said goodbye to Indrani and moved towards the door.

"She father beg me to marry she. He even tell me he'd give me a interest in the house. But I tell him to keep he tumble-down house. I'd take she for she body. An' I did. But when—"

Rohan seized Sidique by the throat. The two men fell to the ground.

"Stop it!" Indrani shrieked.

Rohan managed to wrench himself free, his chest heaving and a streak of blood and spittle dripping from his lip. Sidique in turn got up with an expression of hate on his face. When he recovered sufficiently to speak he said, "Get out, you beggar!"

Indrani made a sign to Rohan to go. He passed his hand over his dishevelled hair and left. At the foot of the stairs he turned and looked at the house he had once loved and vowed that he would never return, nor even have anything to do with those who lived there. Was his sister not always right? Overwhelmed with shame that he had defended them so vigorously before her and his father, he was seized with the desire for revenge, which passed almost at once when he thought of Dada. What would she say now, when he failed to turn up? She could not possibly learn of the incident.

"To the devil with her and her family," he said, banishing the reflection from his mind.

As Rohan walked down the road Sidique put his head out of the window and shouted after him.

"Don' come back here, you sponger!"

The last word wounded especially. It kept ringing in Rohan's ears all the way back to the office.

Sponger! Sponger!

An approaching cyclist looked at him intently and, after riding past, turned and continued to look at him. The sun was more hostile than ever and he regretted not having borrowed someone's hat. He could feel the heat of the road penetrating his shoe soles. A chauffeur greeted him from a car, but before he could recognise him the vehicle was hidden in a cloud of dust. The incessant pounding of the washerwomen oppressed his ears and, in his mind, he confused it with the heat of the day, which made every solid object shimmer and gleam.

What of all the afternoons and evenings suffused in the light of sundown? What of the nights, lying in bed and lingering over incidents full of meaning? The bread and reproaches? The doubts. . . .

Rohan broke into a trot to get away from the sun and when he arrived in the Commissary yard, exhausted from running, he turned and went back to the bridge, where he vomited into the trench, standing on the very spot where Indrani had stood not so long ago. Opening his eyes he saw Ramnaraine standing near to him.

"Is wha' wrong, man? You all right?"

He nodded his head in assent.

"You want a drink?"

"No, I'm all right."

"A lemonade? I gwine run down to the shop an' buy a lemonade."

On returning he made Rohan sit at the back of the office where he poured half the contents of the lemonade bottle over his head and made him drink the rest.

The ice-cold liquid coursed slowly down Rohan's throat and into his thirsty stomach, reviving him slowly.

"You could'a fall in. It in' deep, but you could'a hurt yourself," Ramnaraine told him.

Rohan wanted to ask for the afternoon off, but dreaded making the journey through the sun to the stelling and from the Georgetown wharf home.

He could hear the typewriter upstairs and imagined his friend pounding away with two fingers. Tomorrow the secretaries of the District Councils would encumber the office and force him to move upstairs, where he would be unable to avoid the penetrating look of Mohammed, who would by then have heard the whole story from Indrani. He could no longer endure this clerking, he thought. Soon he would have to make up his mind about what his aim in life was. The futility of writing down numbers on a coloured coupon and giving them to others was never more apparent than now.

6

An Interrupted Meal

The following Sunday morning, at about eleven o'clock, there
was a knock on the door of the Armstrongs' house. Genetha
had come back from church and was cooking the midday meal.
Her father, at his accustomed place by a window, had completely ignored the visitor. Genetha wiped her hand and came
to the door. Although she had never seen the young woman
before she knew her at once.

"Is Boyie in?"

"Yes, come in," Genetha said coolly, but politely.

Indrani greeted Armstrong, who still gave no sign of life.
She was surprised that Rohan's home was so poor. Genetha
was as much ashamed of the appearance of the house and her
father's dirty clothes as she was dismayed by Indrani's visit.
The family would be eating in a quarter of an hour or so, but
she would be damned if she set a place for her. An hour ago
she had been taking Holy Communion, drinking what her
minister told her was the blood of Christ and eating His body
in a solemn ceremony.

When Rohan heard that Indrani was outside he got up from
bed, took a quick shower and dressed. He was ready to come
out at the same time as Genetha was putting the steaming
dishes on the table. She knew that her attitude would annoy
her brother, but deliberately went ahead, so that he would
be obliged to choose between offending Indrani or her.

Rohan came out to meet his friend, ignoring Genetha's
ultimatum. Armstrong had already sat down at table, with
his back to the drawing-room and apparently oblivious of the
diversion behind him. Although Indrani and Rohan were in
the gallery the silence at the table did not permit them to
talk without being heard. He therefore invited her to go
under the house, where they could speak freely. When Indrani
rose and Rohan followed her through the door Genetha
could have choked with anger. She put down her knife and
fork.

"Why you don't mind your business, girl?" Armstrong asked disdainfully.

"What I've got to put up with in this house!" she exclaimed, surveying her father with ill-concealed contempt.

"If you don't want that beef I'll eat it," he suggested.

Receiving no reply he transferred the two large lumps of meat from his daughter's plate to his own, with two vigorous jabs of his fork.

"Why you don't go inside and put your ear down to the floorboards? You'll probably hear everything they're saying. I bet you would! Go on! You know you're dying to do it."

Genetha made a feeble attempt to get some food into her mouth, but gave up and got up from the table.

"Go on, I tell you. It's the sensible thing to do. I wouldn't tell him anything, I promise. And you'd get satisfaction from doing it. You Christians make me laugh! They don't teach you about that in church, do they? But it's real, and does hurt bad, though, like a belly-ache."

She was determined not to be baited.

"If you had a boy friend you'd feel better, you know. Oh, well, you too stupid to know what I'm talking about."

There was not a sound in the house and only the faint murmur of voices from downstairs.

"Come to think of it, she doesn't look loose at all," Armstrong remarked.

"She's common!" said Genetha, who could no longer remain silent. "What sort of a woman would come to see a boy on a Sunday morning when he's in bed?"

"How you think you did come into the world? You think we found you under a sapodilla tree? There's a name for people like you, you know. You'd better go to church tonight and take another communion to calm you down. Isn't that why you go to church, to calm yourself down?"

Under the house Rohan and Indrani stood by a work-bench set up by carpenters years previously and which no one had ever bothered to take down since.

"How you managed to get away?" he asked.

"He's gone home. . . . I'm following him tomorrow."

Rohan involuntarily drew away from her. "You follow him like a puppy."

205

She did not answer right away.

"He's my husband. He's not like the way you saw him, showing off to impress you. I don't know why he hates you. When I used to talk about you in the Essequibo he never said anything."

"Your father said you were going to stay at your grandmother's, because her husband was sick."

"I did. Sidique came to see me there."

"You love him?"

"Yes."

"You like the way he orders you about like a servant?"

"I tell you he isn't like that," she protested.

"You say he isn't like that, but he left you soon after you got married, didn't he?"

"I looked up to you like . . . but you're weak and ordinary like everybody else."

"Well, I'm what I am," Rohan replied.

"I mean what I say. D'you know that people in Vreed-en-Hoop were saying that I was luring you to the house, that although I was older than you and married, I was seducing you? I let you continue to come because you were superior to the others, and I felt strong and could face their vindictive looks. But now, because you can't have your own way, you become nasty. I love Sidique because he's the only man I've known . . ." and then, continuing almost in a whisper, "and I love you because I need you. You're the only friend I've got. You could've had me weeks ago if you'd wanted. I never thought it was possible to—" she turned her head and looked away, as if ashamed.

Rohan stood next to her, dumbfounded at her confession. A feeling of elation overcame him and when, as he put his arm round her shoulder, she leaned her head on his chest he was beside himself with excitement. The desolation he had felt when she declared that she loved her husband had gone without a trace. This moment made up for all his thwarted desires and provided the proof of what he had never been certain: that between them there was a bond shared by no one else, forged in those long hours together, when their boat rocked like a cradle on a boundless lake of golden days. Even if he never saw her again this long moment was enough. He stroked her hair and pressed his lips against her forehead. When she drew out of her bag a handkerchief to wipe her eyes he felt that something had passed between them that could never be forgotten. They went and sat on the back stairs, in the shade.

Finally Indrani got up to leave. She forbade him to come with her and did not turn to wave to him.

Upstairs, no one was at table where his father's empty plate lay, conspicuously free of food. Genetha's unfinished meal had attracted a number of flies, which buzzed around or settled on the food she had left. His own plate had been covered with another and Rohan felt the reproach, but did not care. *She* had dared to come and she had dared to be honest with him. He loved her and would always love her. If she loved her husband that was as it should be. And him? He was the chosen, the admired one. He would miss her, but he was consoled by the fact that she had been prepared to give him that precious thing. He had not believed until then that a relationship could be so clean, so wholesome.

It was late afternoon. Armstrong wanted to talk, while Genetha, harbouring her bitterness at the way she was slighted, sat tight-lipped at the window. He was even prepared to tell her of the night, years before, when he, Doc and B.A. went up to an opium den in the Chinese quarter just off Water Street and stayed to watch the addicts half-reclining on reed mats, eyes riveted on their long pipes.

"You see that man passing," he ventured, pointing to a bald-headed man walking by, "I used to know him when he had hair."

But she gave him a withering look for his pains. And in disgust he turned on the radio so loudly she was obliged for a time to listen to the story being broadcast of the blind girl who fell in love with a man's voice.

Rohan was out and Genetha was certain he had gone after the young woman who had visited him. She sat watching the street, aware of nothing else except her offended pride. From now on, she thought, she would go out more often, rather than cultivate the bland acceptance of her lot as house-keeper to her father and brother. The idea of freedom filled her with uncertainty, even dread. To go to her dressmaker and say, "Make me such and such a frock," was certain to call forth an "Oh, so you painting the town red!" And she would find herself searching for some acceptable excuse while standing among the half-finished dresses strewn about the floor around the woman's oversized sewing-machine. Was she not her closest woman acquaintance? And did she not have to put up with her jibes? She had never confided in her dressmaker simply because the latter was never alone; and her helpers, unattached girls who came and went at all hours, did not inspire confidence. She must take the bull by the horns, however much the girls grinned while pretending to ply their needles. The intrusion of that shameless woman from Vreed-en-hoop into the household, like the irruption of a dormant idea, forced her to follow a course of action she had not, in normal circumstances, the courage to take. All the bells that once proclaimed her loyalty to her father and brother had fallen silent in her head and she sat in the broken light of afternoon inwardly cursing her past devotion.

"Did I tell you about the man and his dog?" she heard her father ask. And the decision she had just made disposed her to listen.

"The man said to the dog, 'Sit!' But the animal just went on rushing about. 'Sit! I tell you, sit!' You think that own-way dog would listen to him? He just went on ignoring his master. 'You wait,' the man said. 'Wait till your mistress come. She going fix you!' Just then the man's wife turned the corner. 'You see, she's coming.' The woman, seeing that her husband couldn't control the dog shouted out. . . . I must tell you, the woman couldn't pronounce the letter 's'. She shouted at the dog, 'Shit!' And the dog, frightened to death of the woman, started trembling from head to tail; and when the woman repeated, 'Shit!'—"

But she interrupted him.

"It's this vulgarity I can't stand," she said firmly, turning to face the street.

"Tch!" he exclaimed with a gesture of impatience.

But, in no mood for quarrelling, Armstrong fetched a pack of cards from inside and began disposing them on the oil-cloth which covered the dining-table, thinking all the while that it was not in Genetha's character to harbour a grudge, and failing to grasp the depth of the hurt Rohan had inflicted on her. He played alone until the night was silent, long after Genetha went to bed, and the ticking of the clock standing against the wall was the only sound in the house. Occasionally the weak light from the bulb over the table seemed to flare up as a car passed swiftly, crackling like burning wood as it disappeared up the road. Finally, Rohan came home, took a late bath before retiring for the night, leaving his father to bolt the doors and windows and turn off the light and the radio, which was still playing softly.

Offensive Smells

Armstrong became stricken with filaria, but with careful attention managed to keep down the swelling in his right leg. As the disease progressed, the cochineal cactus was no longer effective in driving the water from his legs. In time, despite his trousers, it was plain for all to see that the leg was swollen. Gradually he cut down on his outings to the rum shop until, weary and sensitive at his appearance, he stopped going out altogether. He became a prisoner in his own home. In fact, it is not quite correct to say that Armstrong never went out. Occasionally, between midnight and five o'clock in the morning, he stole out of the house and went, no one knew where. What is more, these sorties might take place in pouring rain or on a dry, moonlit night.

In addition to the irreversible swelling Armstrong had another cause for concern: he stank. The doctor was of the opinion that there was nothing in his bodily condition to justify the odours that emanated from his bed and his person. Genetha was in no way to be reproached with regard to the bedclothes, which were given out regularly for laundering. Armstrong himself swore that he bathed twice a day and, on the occasion of his midnight flits, a third time.

Rohan, unaccustomed to sparing his father's feelings, held his nostrils whenever he had to go into his room and opened his mouth only as much as was necessary for elementary speech. Genetha, on the other hand, thought it her duty to bear the stench and be as tactful as possible about it. Indeed, she often spent long periods in Armstrong's room, reading to him from the Bible. His favourite book was Ecclesiastes and the Book of Job, which he held up to her as models for the behaviour of young people. The readings invariably ended with Armstrong becoming depressed and talking of joining his dead wife. Genetha dreaded his attacks of filaria, which confined him to bed for days and forced her to spend hours with him in the dim chamber.

Armstrong took up the suggestion, made by the widow next door, that he should consult an old woman named Miriam about his illness. Miriam informed him that he was stricken because as a child he had not worn a guard round his waist. Impatient with her superstitions at first, he came in time to accept and believe them. He drank the concoctions she gave him and shunned the foods she considered harmful. Not content to fall under the woman's spell himself, he urged Genetha to get to know Miriam, but she refused and rejoined that one dupe was enough in the family.

"Well, what about your bread and wine? The body and blood of Jesus? That's pure cannibalism," taunted Armstrong.

"It's a symbol. What Miriam's teaching you's an absurdity," declared Genetha.

"My absurdity is as good as yours. At least it's not an alien myth."

"I feel sorry for you," Genetha replied. "One day I'm reading you from the Bible and another you're sprinkling the house with salt."

"Honour thy father and thy mother that thy days may be long in the land the Lord thy God giveth thee!" retorted Armstrong.

"You see what I mean? You quote from the Bible when it suits you."

"Don't let's quarrel, girl. Hand me the mirror."

She passed him a fairly large, free-standing mirror from the dressing-table.

"You see these lines?" he said to her, drawing his index finger downwards from his eyes. "I got them in the last few months. It's the pains at night and the thinking by day. A man shouldn't have to suffer like this. My father lived to be sixty-eight. When he did die his forehead was smooth and his skin tight."

He made a gesture with his fist to indicate how firm his father's skin had been and passed his fingers over his own forehead.

"They're like gutters in the dry season. My face does sicken me! I know the two of you waiting for me to die to get the house . . . and because I smell like a corpse. You see? You

211

don't deny it. I know you come and watch me when I'm sleeping and listen for my breathing."

"God'll punish you, you know," Genetha told him.

"The other day I did catch Boyie bending over me and listening with his hand to his ear. I pretended I was sleeping, but I was watching him through the slits of my eyes. You too! I'm watching you, wheeling round me like a carrion crow and sniffing at me. But this is my house! Miriam said I'll live for years. That's why you and your brother hate her."

He put down the mirror on the bed, beside him.

"Only your mother knew what I was really like underneath," he continued.

"Underneath what?" Genetha asked.

"Go on, go on. I can sense you want to get out of the room and pick up some stupid book," Armstrong said irritably.

"I didn't say I wanted to go."

"Why you don't get a man, eh?"

"One day I will," replied Genetha. "And he will take me away from this house so that you and Boyie can tear one another to pieces. Far, far away from the strife and your accusations . . . and Boyie's ingratitude."

She got up from the foot of the bed, where she had been sitting with her hands in her lap. She enjoyed her father's company most when they were outside in the drawing-room, listening to the radio together. Then, there was no astringent conversation, no heavy silence. He often fell asleep in the Berbice chair with his leg on the outstretched extension arm. The ample breeze through the windows and jalousies wafted away any offensive smells from his direction and they were able to remain in each other's company for hours on end.

"I gone," she said hesitantly.

"Go, go, I say. I want to sleep. Last night I had a bad night and I feel that tonight I'm in for it again."

"I'll be in the gallery," she said, as she went through the door.

He could feel the newly-applied cochineal drawing the heat away from the offending leg, and reflected that if he had had the disease when he met Gladys he would not have been allowed to go and see her at home. What would be his own attitude to a young man Genetha loved if he discovered that the

212

suitor had filaria? "God forbid!" he muttered. He thought of the attractive young women who were doomed to a life of spinsterhood only because their feet were swollen. When he was young he used to admire a girl who lived in Kitty. Every day he passed her house on his cycle he looked up to see if she was at the window. Once she even smiled back at him. He remembered well how he shuddered when he learned that her legs were swollen with filaria.

Armstrong lay back, waiting for the arrival of Miriam, who had a way with her hands. When her hands touched him the heat from his leg seemed to be dissipated through his whole body, leaving him with a sense of well-being he had not experienced for a long time. It seemed that a man needed a woman in his life right up to the moment of his death. There was something no one understood, some powerful force that kept men and women in orbit round one another, that lingered on even after the fires of copulation had gone out. You could not talk to people of such matters, for a man's impulse was to deny something that did not flatter his vanity. Suggest to him that he did not experience at thirty the erection he knew at eighteen and he would lie and cheat to prove that the opposite was true. No, these things one knew and did not bother to discuss. Like the dreams about one's mother that frightened and ravaged the conscience. Life was private as books were public. But it seemed to Armstrong that women knew far more about men than men about women. Those who knew said little, while those who knew little were presumptuous enough to write books. In bed he had had time to reflect on many things — on his boyhood, his life with his wife Gladys, and his present life — and there was no doubt that time and distance brought a sharper vision, illuminating the secret corners of one's yesterdays. He would now forgive her anything, even the dismissal of Esther, who had served them so faithfully for so many years. Her dismissal did not seem now the enormity it had then appeared. He understood his wife better, now that she was dead, than during her lifetime, and wished that he could fetch her up once again for a day or a week. in order to show how much he valued her presence.

Miriam came dressed in a blue robe; and with bare acknow-

213

ledgement of Genetha's greeting she asked to be shown to Armstrong's bedroom.

He was sitting up in bed, dressed in a clean pair of pyjamas and with his hair neatly parted on the side.

"What did *she* say to you?" he asked.

"Your daughter?"

"Yes."

"Nothing," Miriam answered severely.

"She doesn't approve of your treating me. She'd prefer a doctor."

"So would you, Mr Armstrong. I don't charge——"

"You're wrong," he protested with a great show of sincerity. "No doctor's got your hands, Miriam. And I *believe* what you're doing. I come from the country. I know what the hands can do and the. . . ."

"Please take off your pyjamas," Miriam said, untouched by his words.

Armstrong shed his pyjama trousers, which he left on the bed next to him. Miriam took the garment and folded it, then laid it on the straight-backed chair standing in the dimmest corner of the room. She pulled back the blanket, which he had drawn up over his naked body more out of modesty than fear of the chill. Miriam passed her hands over the swollen leg several times without touching it; and when finally she laid them gently on him he gave a slight start.

"Oh, Miriam, your hands!" Armstrong said, almost pleading.

"You should rather stop drinking than flattering me."

But he continued to groan until she stopped stroking his leg and set about cutting the cochineal in sections. She made him hold the cold, slimy cactus halves against the leg while she bound them against his skin with clean bandages. Armstrong winced to show the healer the effect of the cold cochineal on his body.

"God punishing you for all your sins," said Miriam, "for the nights in Sodom and your self-indulgence. You're a leaf in the wind, Mr Armstrong, but you still believe you're a strong tree."

"Tell me one thing, Miriam. What're people saying about me? I can't talk to my children, at least not to my son."

"Why not ask your girl the question then?"

214

Armstrong delayed answering until he had found the right words.

"I'm too proud to ask her," he declared, slipping on his trousers, which Miriam had handed him.

"If you had pride you wouldn't go about looking like a beggar and shaming your children."

"What're people saying about me?"

"They saying you corrupt, like your swell-up foot. They saying your wife better off dead than alive, that one day a strong wind going sweep through the house and blow you away."

"You think it's too late to start going to church again?" he asked, speaking urgently so as to postpone Miriam's departure.

"Some people go to church with they body, Mr Armstrong, and some people go with their heart. I don't see a Bible in this room—"

"Oh, I've got one! Wait."

He dug down in the space between the bed and partition and came up with his large, black-bound Bible.

"And why you hiding it?"

"I'm not hiding it. It fell down. Now I'm fifty I'm beginning to be afraid. Sometimes I wake up sweating so much I find the sheet soaking wet. If only *she* was alive she'd know what to do. People don't understand. I loved the dirt she walked on and was frightened that I depended on her for everything. I treated her like a dog."

Miriam, unable to tell whether he was play-acting, listened in silence, her head turned away from him. Armstrong was afraid to speak lest he lost her sympathy, but was equally worried that she might go if he stopped talking.

"Stay a bit longer, ne?" he begged, seeing that she was putting away the things she had brought, the soft-grease, camphorated oil and the cactus she had been using.

She sat down on the bed, but kept her head turned resolutely from him.

"Listen, Mr Armstrong," and her voice was filled with emotion. A woman in early middle age, she gave Armstrong the impression that she was in possession of great secrets. "I did come because I'm a Christian. After all, I come to the house although you daughter don't approve of me, and you

215

don't believe in what I doing. . . ."

"I do!" protested Armstrong, all but leaping at Miriam, who continued as if he had not interrupted her. She said she did not like him, that she felt uncomfortable in his house, and that people who did not go to church had a lot to answer for, all because she believed that Armstrong considered her to be beneath him and inferior to his family. He in turn wished he could reveal his fear of death, his sombre dreams, recalled in the passage of luminous mornings, of boats shuddering in port like live animals, and of sounds that wavered, fled away and returned to die on his fingers.

So Miriam went, persuaded that she had been snubbed. And after the door was closed behind her Armstrong was certain that Genetha was watching her walk away down the street.

8

Little Gifts

Rohan had long ago found out that his father visited a tenement house in Henry Street, but said nothing to his sister, telling himself that he cared little what he did, as long as the family was not personally affected.

Armstrong had been on nodding terms with the family in Henry Street for many years, indeed long before his wife's death, and even after the husband had mysteriously disappeared. He used to stop to talk to the wife, simply because she was attractive and treated him with considerable respect. When he began to neglect himself her esteem was as much in evidence as in the old days, feeding on Armstrong's exaggerated courtesy and her old blind regard for the remnants of what she believed to be his status.

On the verge of destitution she decided to make the rounds of the people she knew; she felt she had not underestimated Armstrong when he gave her fifteen dollars and swore he would have given her much more if times were not hard and he was not out of work.

Armstrong did not think he was overstepping the mark when he dressed, cleaned his shoes to a shine and went to look her up a few days after making her the gift. She welcomed him with a warm smile and he was soon talking about himself.

"She sleeps in my blood," he told her, referring to his dead wife.

He was put out by the sounds coming from the adjoining room, the only other in the small flat.

"Do you understand that?" he pursued. "Not many people would understand that."

"I understand," she said, with great dignity, Armstrong thought. "Excuse me for a minute."

She went inside and the noises ceased at once.

The flat was on the ground floor, behind that occupied by a plumber, his wife and four small children. Every five minutes or so the plumber would begin hammering away at a strip of metal, blasting the silence with resounding blows. The inhabitants of the district were accustomed to the disturbance, but Armstrong felt affronted, especially as the man worked by the light of a brilliant, unshaded bulb, which penetrated obtrusively into the room.

The couch on which he was sitting had lost a leg and tilted alarmingly away from Armstrong's end. The other pieces of furniture, two armchairs with gutted upholstery, were also past any pretensions to hospitality, while the remnants of a carpet, folded several times over, served as a prop for one of the three-and-a-half-legged chairs.

"She's making the children say their prayers," Armstrong thought, for no sound came from the room.

Eventually she came back and sat on the edge of one of the two chairs. About thirty-two years old, she had short, pressed hair and wore a brown dress trimmed with lace, which must have once been reserved for special occasions. There was about her the scent of a dimmed splendour, a relic of well-appointed drawing-rooms. She too had come down in the world, reflected Armstrong, "driftwood from the twenties".

Although she hardly spoke, Armstrong felt at ease, certain that she had made him a tacit promise and depended on his gentlemanly restraint. He could not know that she had been expecting him, having seen through his generosity. She had expected him the day after he had given her the money, for she was aware of his reputation, of his association with his former servant Marion, and his whoring companions. Expecting him, she had disposed the evidence of her poverty as effectively as she was able, in the way a photographer would arrange his lights round his client the better to model his features: the main light in front at a forty-five degree angle — the couch; and the fill-in lights softening the shadows.

When her husband disappeared — out of shame, she believed, because he no longer had the means to support his family — she made a list of those capable of helping her, mostly his men friends. Armstrong had given her the money, while dismissing her professions of gratitude. He had shown no interest in her as a woman, as others had; but she knew he would be back none the less, for he was betrayed, not only

218

by his reputation, but by his excessive courtesy, which he hung out like a banner on a special occasion.

"How well-behaved your children are," Armstrong said, nodding towards the bedroom.

"Only when there're strangers," she replied.

It was in the first weeks of an August — the dog season, when dogs mated furiously and the sun strode relentlessly towards the horizon. It was then that she saw him for the first time in his rags and concluded that his dress was a kind of mourning for his wife. But as the years went by and his rags grew on him and became as rigid as a mask, it occurred to her that he was not capable of that kind of grief. Her husband was the first to suggest that Armstrong was saving his money, and she made a note of that, against the day when she might need his help.

Now he sat opposite her, pretending to be comfortable on the sloping couch, while the plumber's light caused him to blink continually and the noise from his hammering disturbed his concentration.

"She sleeps in my blood. Do you understand that?" And once more Armstrong's hostess professed to understand, while deploring his vanity.

"You must learn to forget," she advised him. "Remembering can be—"

"Oh, yes. For a woman . . . I mean, for someone so young you're very wise."

"No, I'm not young," she said, surprised at his lack of discretion.

"I bet you're not a day over twenty-five," Armstrong put in hurriedly, seizing the chance to flatter her. "I wonder how your children can sleep with the light and the noise."

"Is the light bothering you? I can put a cloth over the window if you want. I do that when one of the children gets sick."

"It doesn't really bother me," he told her, and felt better for having got it off his chest. "The children are already sleeping?"

"Yes," she answered.

And Lesney came to mind, the prostitute whose livelihood was threatened by her bouts of epilepsy. He had stood by her window for the better part of half an hour because he had been more shy in his intentions than with his servant, for her reticence was as daunting as a sharp tongue. This lady's disinclination to speak was made bearable by a willingness to be pleasant to him.

"Have you ever seen the Kaiteur Falls?" he asked.

"No; only in pictures. Have you?"

"The nearest I've got to it was Bartica."

He told her of his trip there on a Saturday excursion. The soil was so fertile that people used limes and oranges to play ball. Bartica was the gateway to the vast hinterland, he remarked earnestly, the hinterland which made Guyanese such odd people.

"The ocean on one side and the forest on the other, threatening to crush us between them."

She again smiled as though she understood; and he was encouraged to tell her things he had only told Genetha. He spoke of the dream he had had thrice in his life, the last time about a year ago. Someone sent a message that he was going to visit him. On none of the three occasions was it clear who had dispatched the letter. He welcomed the man when he came; but before he could offer him a seat the stranger showed him a box he had brought; it resembled a small hat-box, widely used as late as the thirties and elaborately wrapped with several layers of paper. "It's for you," the stranger said to him. "You want me to open it?" Armstrong nodded, too affected to answer the man, who was shrouded in a long garment that came down to his feet. After struggling with the wrapping he hesitated when only the lid remained to be taken off. Then carefully he lowered his hands into the box and lifted out a man's head, from which grains of sand were falling, like granulated sugar from a punctured bag.

Armstrong's hostess was so perturbed by the dream she asked him not to go on. Her husband was a dreamer as well and a great-uncle, both of whom were collectors of misfortunes, like the rubbish squares at the edge of the road, where people without dustbins were allowed to deposit their trash.

Suddenly the woman was afraid of Armstrong, of his stilted courtesy, of his bizarre conversation, of his way of watching her breasts and of the contrast presented by his present get-up and his rags. Armstrong, in turn, interpreted her silence as discretion. He had expected his telling of the dream to arouse her sympathy and as she failed to respond could not believe that it had distressed her.

When, around ten o'clock, the plumber's light suddenly went out — a few minutes after the banging had stopped — Armstrong and his hostess sat in the dark.

"I'm sorry there's no oil in the lamp," she said. "Usually I'm in bed by this time."

"Don't bother," Armstrong declared, put out by the very situation he had desired and by her hint that she ought to be in bed. "In any case I think I ought to be going." And since she did not object he got up and waited for her to do the same.

"Thanks for coming," she said affably, "you can come again if you wish."

"May I?" he asked, somewhat too hurriedly.

"Any time."

"Are you sure?" he asked again, taking her hand in his.

He bent down to kiss her, but she turned her head away. Pretending not to be offended by the gesture, he said, "I'll come another time."

He left by the door, which opened on to the passage between the tenement and the palings of the house next door, a small well-maintained cottage with a garden of oleander and hibiscus at the front. There was no sign of the plumber's bulb, which he must have taken away into his room; but strips of galvanised metal laid against the paling fence that divided the passage from the house next door shone in the dark, allowing him to negotiate his way over the coconut husks laid unequally on the ground.

Once out in the street he considered his chances with the woman and decided he would try again. He had treated her like Lesney and she was offended. But at least she had allowed him to take her hand, a warm hand, but unlike his dead wife's before she fell ill, a working hand, leathery and calloused.

In the walk to his home on the other side of the town Armstrong was struck by the fact that little had changed since he was a young man; yet much had changed. In the daytime, the morning and afternoon stillness used to be continually interrupted by the cries of the fish-sellers, hucksters, umbrellamenders and the repairers of iron pots who, armed with their soldering irons, shouted incomprehensibly to attract the attention of housewives. The iron pot repairers had once been a great source of anxiety to him, for his father often threatened that if he did not do well at school he would apprentice him to one of these lugubrious individuals, with their soldering irons wrapped in dirty cloth, and their long faces marred by the expression of total failure. They had vanished from the face of the earth, swept away by the introduction of aluminium pans, which their owners did not expect to last forever. And the smoking iron pots had died with them, leaving the reek of progress and another kind of misery. Armstrong went by a shop where a young woman had once called him in from the street. That had been his easiest conquest and it was only his stubborn idea of a mistress dressed in finery that had prevented him from maintaining one in the back streets, as his friend Doc had done. He was certain now that such an arrangement would have saved his marriage.

Armstrong looked back on the time of ageing whores and fornicating priests with nostalgia, regarding progress as being responsible for his son's conduct. If the architecture of the town had hardly changed, everything else had, bringing with the transformation a depression that forced the current of time backwards into the past of his early manhood and youth. And with the dawn of every day he would become more preoccupied with the past and less interested in present problems.

One Sunday night when singing came from the many churches and the streets were empty, save for beggars and lottery-ticket sellers, Armstrong went back to see the woman in Henry Street. He was haunted by the idea of his failure, remembering only that she had turned her head away. And, oddly, the image of a sailor sprawled in a sitting position against the wall of the opium den in the Chinese quarter occurred to him. Armstrong remembered the metal buttons on his shirt and the total abandon in his stupor. Was not the depravity of a stupor similar to his own condition of enslavement to the image of hair and bared skin? He was taken with the idea that he would be punished for his depravity and die like his father, who had expired while vomiting blood through the window after coming home from a dinner at his Freemansons' lodge.

He stopped in front of a parlour from which the music of a popular record was issuing, to compete with the hymn-singing that appeared to come from every direction. He entered the empty shop and ordered a soft drink. There was no other customer, and he thought that the proprietor must have activated the juke-box on his own account; for, being an East Indian, he probably had no time for hymns.

Armstrong had left Genetha preparing the rice for the next day's meal. Why should she complain? he reflected. She went out to work and met people, a privilege her mother never enjoyed. Thus he set off again, as if the discovery of his daughter's independence was sufficient reason to pursue the woman he was going to visit.

She was surprised to see him, believing that he would not come calling on a Sunday.

"I'm sorry there isn't any light," she said, stepping back to allow him to pass. "The plumber doesn't work on Sundays."

"It doesn't matter," Armstrong reassured her, half-closing his eyes in order to find his way about the room.

"Sit down, please," the woman offered, indicating the couch.

On the other side of the room, between the two chairs, a little boy of about two years was sitting on the floor pushing and dragging a toy car back and forth. His back was to Armstrong and he turned from time to time to see if the visitor was still there.

It occurred to Armstrong that the length of time the woman took to put her son to bed would be an indication of his chances of success with her.

"Would you like a cup of chocolate?" she asked.

"Yes, thanks."

She went inside, leaving him with the little boy, who was making a noise with his mouth simulating the sound of a car driving along the road.

"What's your name, sonny?" Armstrong asked the boy, who did not answer, but a few seconds later turned around to look at him.

By now Armstrong could distinguish the chairs clearly and the boy leaning forward on his haunches and the broom

223

standing against the wall, the mortar and pestle next to it and a little wooden box by the door, inlaid with mahogany and purple heart.

When his mother came back and began talking, the boy's imitation of a car became louder, until it all but drowned their conversation.

"Come on, it's time for bed," she told him.

"I did know so," observed the boy without looking round.

"Say goodnight to the gentleman," she urged firmly.

"Good night," came the sullen greeting, to which Armstrong replied by squeezing his hand, only because the gesture would make a good impression on the mother.

He was left alone for a considerable time and wondered that there was no sign of the other child.

"She's at my mother's," the woman explained when she came out and he asked.

"Why not sit next to me?"

"I'm not sure the couch can take it," she replied, but did as she was asked none the less.

Armstrong took her hand in his.

"I was going to make you another little gift," he told her. "But I didn't know whether you'd mind."

"Since the children's father went I can use any little help I can get."

Armstrong drew her to him and kissed her on the mouth, and her lack of resistance, indeed her apparent indifference to what he was doing, astonished him. He opened the buttons down the front of her bodice to find that she was not wearing a brassière. Then he pulled her gently to the floor, where he lay on her. And he kept looking up, expecting to find her son watching them. For a moment he even believed he could see the child pushing his toy along the floor between the chairs. The boy's mother lay beneath him, motionless, as if she were drugged, like the woman neighbour who used to sing all night when sated with ganja, without moving from the chair on which she sat. She lay under him as if her soul had been stolen and left Armstrong to devour her.

When he finished, the woman did not make an effort to get up. Her hair was dishevelled, her skirt was still up and her bare breasts seemed flattened below her shoulder blades. Armstrong did not even resent her inactivity, concerned only that she was prepared to give in to him and permit him to leave his seed in her. He had learned from experience to savour every moment before and after the act, and out of habit ran his eyes over her body, the better to recall, later on, her manner of lying.

Finally both got up and sat in silence in each other's company while Armstrong watched the stars through the sash-window, unblinking in the immensity of the sky, gathered in constellations like jewels on an expanse of shadowed sand.

"My daughter reads me from the Bible," he told her.

"Would you like me to read you something?"

And he desired the affection of this simple woman, who had slept with him because he had promised her money.

"Please."

She fetched her Bible from inside, placed it on the window-sill to catch the little light that fell there from the street lamp, and began to read for him as she was in the habit of doing for herself every night.

Later, as Armstrong went out into the night, he would have given anything to learn whether she hated him or not.

The churches he passed on his way home were dark and the parlours that were still open, dim and forlorn, presented the only sign of life apart from the cottages with their drawn blinds and closed shutters.

Only a few weeks of the old year remained and would die to the singing of carols and the long dances that went on late into New Year's morning.

Armstrong could not get the little boy out of his mind, as though he were capable of being the agent of a terrible act. As a child he himself had known far more than his parents imagined. From the expression on his mother's face he knew when she was about to lie on the bed with his father in the adjoining bedroom and could not fall asleep because of it. He knew of his father's wish to have him die, because he suspected that he was not his son. And his wisdom led him not to ask questions about these things.

The only way to avoid the boy whenever he went to see the mother was to arrive late, after he had been put to bed and was bound to be asleep. Armstrong was certain that he could

225

not grow to like him, for he believed him to be as malicious as he himself had been as a child, when he wished ill on anyone who offended him.

9

A Rotting Structure

It was a sultry afternoon. There was an unwonted silence in the air, as if all the children had conspired to be quiet and all the stray dogs to stop barking. Rohan arrived with a stranger, who had in his hand an extension rule and a tape measure. The latter, seeing that Rohan had said nothing to the man at the window, did not greet him either, and the two began to examine the gate post. When Armstrong saw them measuring and jotting down figures he shouted out to Rohan, "Is what you're doing there?"

"Don't take any notice of him," the stranger was told. The two walked backwards and forwards from the gate to the front stairs.

"Ten," Rohan said aloud to the man who was holding the end of the tape measure. He jotted down the figure in his notebook.

Armstrong, who, by this time, was beside himself, got up from his seat and came over to join the two.

"I want to know what's going on! I'm the owner of this house."

The carpenter stooped and looked at Rohan, who ignored his father and touched the man on the elbow, indicating that he should follow him. Rohan took out a penknife and thrust it into the wood of the back staircase.

"Rotten, see?"

The carpenter sounded it with his knuckles and nodded agreement.

"Look. Who's going to pay for this?" Armstrong asked. He had followed them to the back.

"You," Rohan retorted curtly.

His father looked at him open-mouthed. "You're mad!"

"And I think you'll have to jack it up here and put in a new support," Rohan said to the carpenter, pointing to the house where a pillar met a cross-beam.

The man took a few paces backwards until he was able to

227

judge with his eye whether the support was needed or not. Armstrong planted himself between the man and the house.

"You're getting off my land or not? Just let me know before I take action."

Rohan drew out from his trouser pocket a bank pass-book, opened it and thrust it under his father's nose. Armstrong, fuming with rage, snatched it from him while Rohan turned to the carpenter and pointed to a beam.

"That's got to be renewed too."

The man made more notes. Suddenly Armstrong flew at the carpenter.

"You can't come on to my property and discuss repairs without my consent. If you don't go off now I'm going to call the police."

"All the while we thought you were drinking out your money you had it put away in the bank," Rohan told him. "You go round with holes in your shoes and your clothes in rags so that you can put aside money. And we kept feeding you. . . ."

He stopped, making a gesture of contempt, as if it were beneath him to continue speaking to his father.

"Go on! Tell all our business in front of a stranger. Let everybody know what a snake you are," said Armstrong.

"That's my father," Rohan said to the carpenter. "He isn't well." And then to his father, "We're going to repair this place and you'll foot the bill."

"So you go searching my things, eh? It's the police for you this time, my boy. I tell you, it's the police for you."

Rohan wished that the carpenter was not there, so that he could lay hands on his father. The desire to belabour him had never been so strong and the will to resist his impulse so weak. Nevertheless, he turned his back and started to walk back to the front gate.

"The police, you hear!" Armstrong insisted.

Rohan spun round and rushed up to him, hesitated for a moment and then turned away. Astonished by the suddenness of the charge, his father looked at him, wide-eyed and speechless.

"It's your father!" the carpenter remarked.

"T— tell him, tell him. He hasn't got any respect for me.

228

You tell him. You haven't seen anything yet. This boy makes my life a misery. Soon he'll be a man, according to the law, and I won't be able to touch him; you can imagine how he's going to behave then."

Armstrong took the carpenter by the arm, earnestly.

"What else can I do but send for the police? One day he'll really lay his hand on me and God will punish him."

"You're coming or not?" Rohan asked the carpenter.

"I—"

"You're coming or not? If you don't want the job, say so."

The carpenter went with him upstairs, where they examined the window ledges. Armstrong, shaken by his encounter with Rohan, went up by the back stairs and locked himself in his bedroom, determined to defend that part of the house at least with his life, if need be. He decided that he would call the police the following day if the boy did not apologise.

"I'll guarantee that you're paid. I'll put it in writing if you want," Rohan told the carpenter.

"Ah, don't bother with that," said the carpenter. "All I need is an advance for the materials."

That night, before Rohan went off to the billiard saloon he knocked on the door of his father's bedroom, but received no answer. He knocked again and just then Genetha came in from work. Armstrong heard her footsteps and opened up.

"It's a good thing you just came home," he said, almost throwing himself at her. "Boyie want to beat me up."

She looked at Rohan who, instead of answering, ordered his father, "Show her the bank book."

"Which bank book?" Genetha asked.

"He's got a bank book with eight hundred dollars in it," Rohan told her.

"Eight hundred!" Genetha exclaimed.

"Yes, I found it in his trunk."

"Where did you get all that money from?" asked Genetha.

"He's been banking his pension money," Rohan interjected.

"He's lying, girl, he's lying. It's not my money, it's the society's."

"Then how is it that the deposits've been made regularly at the end of the month in your name?" asked Rohan. "At the end of the month when you draw your pension? Anyway,

229

I'm not going to argue. But if you don't pay for the repairs I'm leaving this house for good."

"Which repairs?" Genetha asked.

"He's got some young fellow to come and measure up the house so that he can charge us a lot of money for repairing the gate. The chap looks like a thief in the *Daily Chronicle* who beat up the Chinee man and empty the till."

"Let's discuss this thing now," declared Genetha. "So that we know just how we stand." With this she put her handbag on the dining-table.

"Discuss? There's nothing to discuss," Rohan said sharply. "We pay for his upkeep. He's going to pay for the repairs or I go. I'm not discussing anything."

"Well, why you don't leave and get it over with?" Genetha said, offended by her brother's ultimatum.

"You keep out of this,' Rohan said. "He's not going to take me in."

"I'll pay half of it," Genetha offered.

"Don't you see? That's just what he wanted!" Rohan exclaimed, alarmed that the problem could be so easily solved.

"How much does the job cost?" demanded Genetha.

"About two hundred. But he's going to—"

"Two hundred dollars? To put in a gate?" Armstrong asked.

"I'll pay some of it I said," Genetha offered.

"Well, I don't know," Armstrong hedged.

"You better know!" Rohan said angrily. "He wants twenty dollars right away for materials."

"You see? What did I tell you?" his father shouted.

"You're a liar and a thief!" Rohan said, deliberately, so that the words might have their maximum effect.

"Boyie!" Genetha exclaimed, and looked at her father as if she expected him to do something.

"You know who he had in here?" Rohan asked. "Last night he brought Esther here. I saw her leaving as I came round the corner."

Armstrong shook his head and sneered at his son.

"I feel sorry for you, boy. You got a mind like a cesspool. She came here to tell me how she was getting on since she left. You don't expect me to stand at the street corner talking to someone who used to work as a servant for me. What would you say to that?"

"Nothing, knowing you, 'cause Esther's a whore!"

"What you saying?" Genetha asked.

"I've seen her in Mamus," Rohan replied.

"Ah-ha! What were you doing there?" Armstrong jumped up, pointing an accusing finger at his son.

"Don't try to wriggle out of it. I'm saying you picked Esther up, brought her here and paid her," Rohan accused him.

Genetha crossed herself.

"It's not true, Gen, I swear it. I'll swear it on the Bible," protested Armstrong. He turned abruptly, went inside and came out almost at once with a large, black Bible, which he raised solemnly to his lips and kissed.

"I swear before God I never did anything bad with Esther," he declared. Facing Rohan, he said to him: "You're foul-mouthed and can't stand there to be peace in the house for one day. If there's peace it does hurt you."

Then he addressed his daughter. "Ask him when last he's been to church. Ask him!"

Genetha stared at her brother as if she were trying to read something written on his face.

"Esther told me herself," Rohan said quietly. "And she told me how much he paid her, and that it wasn't the first time."

Armstrong hung his head for a moment, then jumped up.

"Lies! Lies! He's lying." He turned his back on them and went into the bedroom, where he locked himself in.

Rohan felt uneasy at being left alone with his sister.

"You think that by protecting him you're doing him any good? He's rotten."

"And what about you?" Genetha asked.

"What d'you mean?"

"If you had your way he'd only try to get it back on us and we'd be at one another's throats all the time."

"Don't talk about what you don't know," Rohan told her, searching for a way to break off the conversation.

"Then what were you doing at this Mamus place?" she asked.

"And you think," he replied, "that if I went to church and

231

listened to a minister stumble his way through a sermon I won't go to Mamus? And when you talk about Mother being a saint why don't you ask yourself why? If she'd left Father, where could she have gone? Eh? What work would she've done? She went to church because she was bored—"

"I didn't mention Mother. Why're you talking about Mother? Stick to what we're talking about."

In answer Rohan left the house, slamming the door after him. A few months before it had been her father who was continually disturbing the tranquillity of the house, but of late Rohan was even worse, Genetha thought. He would leave the house in good humour in the morning and return drawn and irritable, as if he had stayed up all night. Only this morning he was joking about people who admired her in the street. "They watch you down the street and admire you from their windows," he had said. She had pretended not to be interested, but when she was alone she found herself going over the names of her possible admirers, and yielded to the feeling of pleasure when she thought of one particular young man who lived in Albert Street and whose eyes she took care to avoid.

Rohan had slammed the door without a word, leaving her bewildered and confused at what she had heard of her father and what her father had said about him.

Wearily she set about preparing the evening meal and called to her father to come to table when she had finished. He came out and even waited before beginning while she said grace silently.

"It was true about Esther, you know; I mean about bringing her here, not about the rest. I can't admit anything to your brother. He's so violent."

Armstrong had forgotten that he had already confessed to bringing Esther to the house. He eyed his daughter, in the expectation of some word of approval.

"She's having a hard time, you know. God! If she told you the things she goes through. . . ."

"I don't want to hear them," Genetha told him.

The noise of the knives and forks against the plates broke the silence that blighted their conversation.

"Esther asked about you."

He had just finished and sat looking straight ahead of him,

wishing that she would say something that would show that she did not suspect him of any lechery.

"Do you believe what Boyie said about me?"

She continued eating without answering him.

"If Boyie went away would you stay?" he asked her.

"Why should I go?"

"I just thought."

Genetha finished her meal and was about to get up from the table.

"A Christian would take Esther in, you know. She took care of you two like a mother for years."

"So that you can carry on with her in the house?" Genetha asked.

"So you do believe what your brother said, eh? Everything I do he twists, so that even I think I'm rotten, as he says. I repeat, a Christian would take Esther in."

"No one is going to take Esther in here, least of all Boyie or me. How in the name of God could we take in a street woman? You wouldn't, if it came to it."

"If I died would you take her in? I wouldn't be there to do anything. Well, would you take her in? Answer, ne? You frightened to give me an answer? Would you take her in?" He shouted the last question at her.

"No!" she shouted back at him.

"That's all I wanted to know," he said quietly, and got up from the table.

"The next time you go to church," he sneered, "pray for yourself."

"When I go to church I pray for you," she retorted.

"I'll tell you something. Boyie would have Esther back in the house; he's got more compassion than you. And, besides, he doesn't care what people say."

By now they were talking in the dark and the only light came from the cottage next door, a dull, broken patch relayed through a closed shutter.

"So I don't have any compassion," said Genetha, converting the question into a statement. "Sometimes I wonder if you say things just to hurt me. I only wish you'd sit back and think about the sacrifices I make for you and Boyie. And the only thanks I get is to hear you say I don't have any compassion."

He would not have known that she had begun to cry had it not been for her refusal to face him.

"All right, all right," he said, "you make sacrifices for us all the time. But you don't seem to be able to do anything for anybody outside the house. In fact all you women are the same; your sacrifices stop at your front door."

"Do you think Boyie would move a finger to help you if you were lying drunk in the road?"

"No," he answered.

"Well, then."

"Turn the light on," he ordered.

Genetha went and turned on the light, which cast a bright glow over the centre of the room, but left the corners in shadow.

"When I was small I used to idolise my father," said Armstrong, "until I found out something about him. After that I couldn't forgive him for what I knew, Now I know it's not what he'd done I couldn't forgive him for, but what I knew."

Genetha ceased to hear what her father was saying and became wrapped in the mantle of her own reflections.

She had often thought of Esther. Since the servant's going away she could not think of her without a feeling of guilt and the belief that the family was bound to suffer for dismissing someone who, until then, had been an integral part of it. Her mother must have been right, but was she, Genetha, expected to forget Esther just because she no longer lived there? The disclosure of the servant's relations with her father stirred conflicts in her she was not prepared to face.

One day, on the way to Mahaicony, she heard two men talking. One of them was recounting with relish how his father had sired three sets of children with three different women. Every Christmas the twenty-three children were fêted by their father in two adjoining houses, since one was not large enough to accommodate them all. The man spoke with such admiration of his father that Genetha could not help comparing his attitude with that of herself and Boyie, who never mentioned his mother and spoke of his father only to belittle him. Even when the man told of hard times he had gone through as a boy, when apprenticed to a blacksmith who paid him a pittance, there was no resentment. Why could things not be so

234

in their family? Present and past deeds conspired to corrupt their relations and their words, to rise up and threaten even in the midst of brief periods of contentment.

Armstrong sent for Miriam when he thought he might be seriously ill. She came and confirmed his fears with the stern expression of someone whose predictions are proved correct. Fearing that he might not be long for the world she promised to send for his sister and to pray for him.

The next evening Genetha and Rohan were sitting in the drawing-room in the company of their grandfather who had come when he heard the news. From inside could be heard the indistinct voices of women, one voice in particular rising from time to time in an admonishing tone.

Armstrong's father-in-law stayed until he was assured by Miriam, who came out every half-hour or so to report on the patient's condition, that he was not getting worse. He then bade the children goodbye, after deploring Armstrong's rejection of his offer to send his doctor and the influence Miriam was evidently exercising over him.

"D'you think Father's pretending?" Rohan asked when his grandfather had gone.

"Why should he pretend?"

"Why? So that he can surround himself with his women! Look the fuss Miriam and this other woman are making of him. And Auntie, when last's she been here?"

"If he died then?"

Rohan did not reply.

"So—" Genetha began, but was interrupted by him.

"If you believe he's so sick, why you're not in with the other women?"

"With that fraud?" Genetha said indignantly. "Grandad's right. It's not healthy the way he does what she tells him to do. She preaches at street corners and hardly anyone ever stops to listen to her. It's a disgrace. She comes into the house as if she owns it, cleans everything I've already cleaned and doesn't ask my advice about anything."

"You want me to talk to her?" Rohan offered.

"No. What for? We'd never hear the end of it from Father if she never came back."

The sound of raised voices came to their ears, as if people were quarrelling.

"My God!" muttered Genetha, consumed with rage.

"No!" one of the women shouted.

Genetha jumped up, hesitated for a moment before deciding what she ought to do. Then, as the confused sounds did not abate, she went inside, where Miriam was haranguing her father.

". . . You're depraved!" shouted Miriam. "You want to enter the Kingdom of Heaven. . . . Admit you've been intimate with her!"

Armstrong would admit no such thing, fearing that if he did and recovered afterwards, the door of the woman from Henry Street would be closed to him forever.

"I'm not responsible for the condition of your soul."

Armstrong's head, the only part of his body not covered by the blanket, was sweating profusely, and his eyes stared, now at Miriam now at his woman friend.

"I love you all," he said, with a humility that sickened Genetha. "I can't slander you. She's a good woman and our relations are that of brother and sister. She came to me when I was down and out and behaved like a lady. She's a lady like you, Miriam. Why should I slander either of you? There's my daughter, ask her. She knows me even better than my sister."

Yet Genetha was in no position to speak of what had transpired between her father and the woman, whom she had seen for the first time.

Armstrong's sister looked at him sternly. She did not want to become involved in her brother's sordid relationships, she was thinking, and intended to communicate her wish to him by her expression.

But Armstrong ignored her and went on: "There're times when you frighten me, Miriam. You're so absolute. Life's not absolute."

"You should stop talking," his friend from Henry Street said gently.

"Very well," put in Miriam, afraid that she might lose control of the situation. "I think your sister should lead the prayer."

Armstrong's sister said a simple prayer, in which she asked

God to make him well, for he was not an old man. She prayed without a trace of emotion in her voice and at the end opened her eyes and looked at her niece, encouraging her to follow suit. But Miriam spoke to Armstrong's woman friend: "Will you say a prayer?"

And she as well prayed that Armstrong would get better. He was a friend in need and had come to her assistance when she was on the point of begging on the streets.

Then Miriam began her prayer, speaking at first in a soft voice.

"Some prayed for his body," she declared, "but I am praying for the salvation of his soul."

She began speaking more loudly and with an incisive tone that was out of keeping with a prayer.

"Take him! Take him, Lord! Take him to your bosom and show him your boundless mercy. . . ."

At that point Genetha slipped out of the room, where Rohan was waiting for her. With a desperate look in her eye she went past him and into her own bedroom, the door of which she closed behind her. Rohan remained there, by the door, his anxieties aroused on his sister's account rather than on his father's.

Back in the room Miriam continued her appeal to God, when, at the height of her passion, she stopped suddenly, like someone who has sat up with a start from a dream. She was standing under the bulb, which was capped with a white corrugated shade, the sort found in the old churches, associated in the mind of many worshippers with prayers, the music of worship and the dank smell of caked dust.

". . . Jehovah, look down on this house and bless it," she continued more calmly, "and bless those living in it. Guide them through the doors they must pass in order to reach you, the doors of pride, vanity and ambition."

She broke off to open her cloth bag, which was propped up on the floor against a leg of the bed. Then, while Armstrong's sister and his woman friend stood with bowed heads at the side of the bed, she took out a bottle of rum, a bag of rice and two crushed hibiscuses.

"For Jehovah the blood of Africa," she continued in a grave voice, pouring a libation of rum on to the floor. "For Jehovah

237

the body of the Nation," and she scattered a handful of the rice round her. "For Jehovah, flowers strewn on his paths, his paths without number throughout the world."

Then Miriam intoned a hymn banned by the official churches; and one by one Armstrong, his sister and his woman friend took up the words, until the soft music of their voices was heard throughout the house.

Rohan took his aunt aside as she left the room.

"You know that woman?" he enquired.

"Who?" she asked in turn, knowing full well he was speaking about Miriam.

"Miriam."

"I've seen her about. Why?"

"You approve of her brand of religion?"

"I'm surprised you ask a question like that," she observed. "Do you subscribe to any religion?"

His boisterousness as a child had never endeared him to her and she was not going to indulge him now that he was a man.

"No, I don't subscribe to a religion."

"Goodbye, Boyie."

Dutifully he saw her to the gate and came back upstairs. She was right. He was a follower of no sect, yet he saw fit to criticise Miriam; and the contradiction in his conduct made him feel deeply ashamed. If he cursed the established churches why was he incensed by the rituals of Miriam's religion? His anger was as inexplicable as his aunt's dislike of him.

Armstrong's lady friend came out soon afterwards and left the house through the back, although the front door was open. Rohan rushed down the front staircase to cut her off.

"Why did you use the back door?" he asked.

"It doesn't matter. I didn't want to offend you."

"I'd like you to know," he said, standing between her and the gate, "I'd like you to know I haven't got anything against you."

"You're a nice young man," she declared, her voice faltering. "Try and be good to your father. Try at least."

Rohan nodded without answering. Then she went off with careful steps towards Albert Street, away from the house she had visited with trepidation, because she believed it was her duty to see her seducer before he died.

238

And just three nights later, when the streets in Werk-en-Rust were resounding to the sounds of the plumber's hammer, Armstrong was again standing before her door with a little gift of chocolate sticks and cinnamon.

10

Noises in the House

Rohan arrived at the saloon on the corner of Ketley and Broad Streets. He had arranged to meet a young man with a big reputation in the clubs. The stake was five dollars and he was thirsting to get at his opponent. He had brought his cue with him but, on arriving, discovered that he had forgotten to bring the key to the case in which is was kept. Irritated by this lapse he was on the point of going back home for the key when his opponent arrived, accompanied by two friends. He borrowed a cue from the barman, found it too heavy, tried a few others, but settled for the one he was given originally.

He won the toss and brought the cue ball to rest in the D. From the young man's first shot it was clear that Rohan would have his hands full. The stranger played softly, as if he were afraid to offend the balls, but when he had to make a hard pot it was done with an incisive violence that brought gasps of admiration from the onlookers. Although Rohan made the highest break of the match, he lost. Afterwards the young man asked him why he had not played with his own cue, but he just shrugged his shoulders.

Rohan, the young man and his friends left to eat in a Chinese restaurant in Regent Street.

The young man was called Fingers by his friends, who treated him like a hero. Born in the slums of Kingston, he and his talent at snooker had attracted a number of admirers and hangers-on. On learning that Rohan was a Civil Servant he laughed, not knowing what the term meant. On the way to the restaurant they passed a horse-drawn cab — one of the few still plying — in which an American airman was unashamedly fondling a harlot.

"You son of a bitch, why you don' tek she under a bridge?" shouted out Fingers. They all laughed. All this was heady stuff to Rohan, who felt that he was taking a long look at a world to which he would have liked to belong and had always missed without realising it. Extravagantly, he suggested that after

240

the meal he should hire a cab and take them all up the East Bank. Everyone agreed readily.

When they stormed into the restaurant the Chinese proprietor looked at them anxiously.

"Upstairs, man; dat's where they got the rooms," one of the young men said.

They climbed the staircase and Fingers pretended he was an elegant woman. He placed his right hand at the back of his neck and his left on his hip, then swayed upstairs to the accompaniment of suppressed laughter and much face-making.

They all ordered steak rarely done and chips, just as Rohan had.

"Mek mine very raaaare!" ordered Fingers, with a prim expression.

When the waitress had gone he enquired, "What's dis rare? Is beef?"

"No, man, is roas' cat," Fingers's smaller friend Cut-up replied.

"Meeow!" exclaimed Giant, the other friend.

"We forget to order the rum," Fingers observed.

On the arrival of the meal they called for the rum. Everyone drank his straight, but Cut-up complained that he liked his mixed with coconut water.

"Is where you go'n get coconut water at this time of the night?" Giant asked.

Cut-up knocked on the table to attract the attention of the waitress, who came over timidly.

"We don't got coconut water," she explained.

"You kian' get some?"

"Don' tek no notice of he, miss," Fingers said.

The waitress smiled, relieved. As she went off Fingers smirked, "Mmm!" and curled an imaginary moustache.

"She likes you," Rohan observed, not suppressing a smile of admiration.

"Man," said Fingers, "dat's a cat dat can jump."

"Gie we one o' you speeches, Fingers," Giant urged.

Fingers obliged.

"Well, young lady," he began, pretending to be addressing someone in front of him. "Ah sorry Ah stepped on you toes! Ah mean to say you should not come dancing without shoes!"

They all laughed, while Fingers remained grave.

"But," he continued, "as you dance so divine, Ah'll let dat lil matter drop. Bang!" he shouted, pretending that the little matter had been dropped. There was another uproar.

"Look here, gal," went on Fingers, encouraged by their appreciation, "Ah had my eyes on you a long time; in fact, since you bend down to pick up dat hairpin. . . . Actually my eyes wasn't on you at all, but on your lace drawers."

The company was laughing loudly, but when they heard footsteps they all fell on their steak and assumed serious expressions, like a Sunday school party of young ladies nibbling their buns.

"Is you making this noise?" the proprietor asked.

"Noise?" enquired Fingers, picking up the folded napkin and wiping his mouth with care.

"'Cause if you kian' behave I'll get the police."

"The only noise," Fingers declared, "was the belching of my friend here," as he pointed to Giant, who was crouched on his chair as if about to spring at someone.

"All right, I warned you," threatened the proprietor, turning to go.

When he left they closed the door of the room and laughed themselves silly.

After the meal Rohan hired a cab at Stabroek Market and they drove in the direction of La Penitence. On the way up the East Bank Road, Giant wanted them to get out and have a pissing competition. The one who peed the farthest would win the stakes put up by them all, but Fingers was against the idea because it was too windy. Cut-up took it into his head to ask the cab man if he could drive, but was refused. They then started singing tuneless, ribald songs whose words flew up to the stars like birds.

On they drove, past Agricola, the village of Rohan's birth. He looked down the village street, with its dim lamps, then at the brightly lit rum-shop at the corner. Mr Grimshaw's house was partly hidden behind the guava tree, its palings neat and painted whiter than ever — or so it seemed in the dark. When they turned the corner on to the road leading to Providence he could see the drainage canal, like a pale streak in the moonlight, where he had made his biggest haul of shrimps in the floods of the late twenties. He remembered how Esther had looked at the basket, wide-eyed with disbelief. On their way past the mansion where Reverend Griffith used to live, memories of his first ride in a motor car came flooding back. The jalousies and windows were all closed as if the house was deserted.

The coachman sat on his perch, impassive and silent, while the cab drove on into the night, heading for Providence. At last they came to Diamond where the local cinema was just emptying. The people did not even bother to get out of the way of the cab as they ambled home and the vehicle drove slowly through the crowd until the way was free.

Suddenly Fingers called out to the cabbie, "Stop!" He made him turn round and head back for Georgetown, for the others shared his desire to get back to town, where their drive was likely to be more eventful.

They got out at Arujo's rum shop in Robb Street and drank till closing time, then Giant invited them to sleep at his house, but Fingers declined.

"I know you sister. She kian' stand anybody drunk. If we go home wit' you she gwine tell the whole street 'bout we condition."

Fingers decided to return with Cut-up, while Giant and Rohan took their separate ways home, their shirts flapping in the wind.

That night Rohan fell into a deep, peaceful sleep. It was the first night for months that he had gone to bed feeling content. He had drunk and eaten heartily; the night wind had blown through his open shirt and soothed his body, while the drive through Agricola had shown him how deep the memories of his childhood ran.

His sleep was untroubled until he was awakened by a shriek. Jumping out of bed he turned on the light and hurried over to his father's bedroom.

"What's wrong, Father? You're all right?"

Armstrong blinked. "Why? What happened?"

"You screamed in your sleep."

Genetha came rushing into the room. "You heard a scream?" she asked.

"Yes, it was him," Rohan replied.

243

"You're all right, Father?" she asked in turn.

"Was it loud?" Armstrong asked.

"It sounded as if someone was being murdered," Genetha said.

Armstrong looked furtively round him, then said, "I had a bad dream. I was — you know . . . well, I was a bit high and I tried to cross the road. Suddenly it did begin to rain . . . I mean all of a sudden, without warning, from a clear sky. And the rain was like a sheet of water. I didn't know that rain could frighten you. . . ."

He was shamefaced at the incident. Rohan did not believe him, thinking he had invented the story to save face; but Genetha took him at his word and went to make him a cup of chocolate. Rohan went back to bed and turned his head to the wall for he was vexed and disgusted on recalling that he had addressed him as "Father".

He soon fell asleep again, groggy from drinking.

The following evening when Rohan came home he found strangers on the stairs and the porch. Inside the house Genetha was sitting on a chair in the middle of the drawing-room and three women were sitting near to her in front of the long mirror over which a cloth was draped. He knew that his father was dead.

"What's wrong, Gen?" he asked.

"It's Father. . . ."

"What's wrong?" he pursued urgently.

"He fell from the porch," she answered; and with these words she put the handkerchief she was holding in her hand to her eyes.

"Where's he?" Rohan asked.

She pointed to his bedroom.

Rohan went inside and saw the body of his father stretched out full length on the bed, next to which a woman was sitting on a straight-backed chair, mumbling to herself.

"You 'e son?" she asked.

Rohan nodded.

"He din' suffer, they say. He mus'a been a good man," she told him.

"You know when it happened?"

244

"Dis morning."

He stood some time over his father's body, all sorts of thoughts whirring round in his head. When he went out of the room he saw the faces of neighbours and strangers peering through the gallery windows. It was about seven o'clock. There was a stirring among the people on the stairs and a burly, middle-aged man came up to Rohan and asked if he would come outside. At the foot of the stairs two men were deep in conversation. Rohan recognised Doc, who was wearing a worsted jacket and a felt hat.

"Ah, boy. I'm grieved, deeply grieved," said Doc when he saw Rohan. "I've taken care of everything, the funeral, everything. Two women're coming to wash the body and do all the necessary. I've seen your sister; she's in a state, but tell her she doesn't have to worry about a thing. Not a thing. My God, what a business! Ah, that must be the funeral people."

A hearse stopped at the door and Doc took Rohan's arm.

Rohan, Doc, the man he had been in conversation with and the burly man went out to the hearse. As the four pulled the coffin out of the back of the hearse, the horse defecated copiously.

The coffin was hoisted up the stairs, which had been cleared of people, and into the house. It had to be put on the floor, since no one had thought of bringing a stand for it. Genetha was still sitting motionless on the chair, and even the sight of the coffin seemed to have no effect on her. Finally stands were found for it and the men, with great care, lifted the coffin on to them, as if there was a body in it.

"I know you don't feel like it," said Doc, "but you'll have to have a sort of get-together, not exactly a wake; it's too late for that."

Rohan nodded assent. "I'll go and get some rum," he suggested but Doc stopped him.

"All that's been arranged. No, not a word. Your father and I were as close as two friends could get," he said, knitting his brows for a while, but quickly reverting to his busy, preoccupied expression.

There was something about Doc that irked Rohan. His generosity, his facility with words, everything about him which others might have found admirable told against him in the young man's eyes.

Rohan went off to inform those who knew the family well. He also telephoned the radio station, on the advice of Doc, who wanted to pay for the cost of broadcasting the announcement; but Rohan insisted that he would.

An hour later the house was full of people. Many of them were disappointed that there was no one with whom they could sympathise at length. Genetha just sat on the bed and stared in front of her. She had hoped that no one would intrude, but no sooner was it discovered where she was than the bedroom door opened and she was the object of the women's sympathy. It was only when her mother's father arrived that she felt comforted. He sat by her and answered all the questions that were asked about Armstrong.

"Is how he fall off the stairs?"

"I don't know."

"He was . . . in a state?"

"Of what?" the old man asked in turn.

"Was 'e drunk, she mean?"

"I don't know."

The same questions were put by many of the women, who all left Genetha with elaborate professions of sympathy. As there was no one for the women to gather round they huddled in the gallery. Soon a certain Mrs Yearwood was monopolising the conversation.

"Since the Americans got their base here everybody making money. If there in't work in town there's some in McKenzie or at the air base or in the interior. But he," she said, pointing to the coffin, "din' got no more appetite for work. They say that since his wife dead he gone to the dogs. She come from good family, you know. Her father inside now. I'll never know how she marry he!"

"They say she had to," another woman chimed in.

Interest flared up among the women at this remark. One of them who was dozing off caught the electric discharge in the atmosphere and woke up with a start.

"Had to? Well, I never! You live and learn," said another woman.

Mrs Yearwood leaned forward and whispered.

"I wouldn't be surprised if a lot din' used to go on in this house," she added. "They say he and the servant used to carry on."

"And she used to stand for it?" asked the third woman in surprise.

Mrs Yearwood nodded meaningfully.

"He was low," remarked another, and to this a chorus of women's voices said: "You right. Low!"

"And that one over there with the expensive clothes, he was one of his cronies. They used to prowl round Water Street on a Saturday night."

All eyes turned towards Doc, who was sitting next to Rohan, a rum glass in his hand.

"He *look* like one of them," observed Mrs Yearwood.

"De mills of God grind fine!" exclaimed a woman who had not yet spoken. She had banished sleep forever.

"You don't know him?" asked Mrs Yearwood. "He's the one with the dress business, you know, the teacher with that woman — she did make Inez' wedding dress."

Their eyes opened wide, for everyone knew of Doc's good fortune and his liaison with Baby.

The men were filling up their glasses as fast as they could and Rohan felt like a stranger in his own home. Had it not been for Doc he would have shut the door to everybody except his grandfather. He was resentful that neither of his mother's sisters had come, nor his father's for that matter. Unable to find her address she was, in all likelihood, unaware of her brother's death. Nevertheless, the absence of his aunts disposed him to believe all the malicious things his father used to say about them.

More especially Rohan felt a stranger among all those middle-aged men who talked a different language from his own, and went on about Lodges and their children. He waited a while, then excused himself, intending to go to the shops for a packet of cigarettes. He did not normally smoke, but for the first time he felt the lack of something to do while in these men's company.

At the shop he struck up a conversation with the shopkeeper, who sympathised with him when he learned of his father's death.

247

Rohan felt guilty that he did not experience his sister's anguish. He remembered how, at the time of his mother's death, all the wiles of his aunts to interest him in eating had failed. Was it because he was younger, then, that his mother's death seemed to be the end of the world? After his mother the only person who could have comforted him was Esther. But Esther was gone, far away, they had told him; perhaps to Grenada. Esther, who had combed his hair, put him to bed, played with him, beaten him with the belt. If, secretly, he had worshipped his mother, he had worshipped Esther only a little less. He had wanted to write like Esther, to sing like Esther when she sang. Esther, picking up men in the rain. *O Christ! You've got a lot to answer for!*

"You hear what I saying?" the shopkeeper repeated.

"Yes, I gone," he replied, and left the shop.

"What a funny family," she shopkeeper said aloud.

On getting back, Rohan saw a young woman he had passed on the stairs and Doc waiting for him at the gate.

"Where've you been?" asked Doc.

"Just to the shop."

"We've been waiting for you. This is my wife."

He shook hands with her.

"Look, your father doesn't have any decent suit to wear and he's got to be dressed properly. He can have one of mine. It's good serge, but I don't have any chance to wear it. Baby'll drop you and bring you back. All right?"

"I can pay for the suit, you know. I'm not a pauper." Rohan felt humiliated in front of Doc's attractive wife.

"Armstrong was my best friend. If you don't take it you'll be robbing me of a pleasure."

Rohan shrugged his shoulders and went off to the car, followed by Doc's wife. They headed for Main Street. Before driving off she had leaned across his lap, opened the car door and closed it firmly. Her full breasts had pressed hard against his right arm. When they arrived at the house, she again leaned across in the same manner to open the door for him; he looked at her, but she gave no sign of having meant to convey a meaning by her action. On the way upstairs she walked some distance ahead of him until they got to the door.

"Come and help me choose a suit," she suggested. "I in'

248

know anything about men's clothes."

He followed her into the bedroom. In the wardrobe Doc's suits were ranged on hangers along an iron rod.

"While you're at it I'll get changed," she told him. "I in' come home since morning time."

Rohan pretended to be examining the suits in the wardrobe while listening to the swish of her garments. Unable to resist the temptation to turn round he did so, saying, "I don't know what'll fit."

She continued dressing without answering. Her petticoat covered her head and was about to fall over her near naked body. He recalled Indrani's confession that he could have had her and his self-reproach about his immaturity. Stepping closer to her he took her hand in his.

"No!" she exclaimed. "Not here. I'll come to your house tomorrow."

"You can't," he rejoined hurriedly.

"Oh . . ." she said, apparently hurt.

She continued dressing, and when she had put on her shoes and brushed her hair went across to the wardrobe in a business-like manner to select a suit.

"This should fit," she declared, a note of annoyance in her voice.

She left the room without a word, returning in a few minutes with a cloth bag in which she had placed the suit.

"Please," pleaded Rohan softly.

"I'm not a loose woman, you know."

Rohan could only look at her apologetically.

"You can kiss me once, little boy."

Rohan kissed her and out of fear that he might be over-doing it was about to draw away, but she would not let him go. And there happened what he had long desired, that intimate contact with a woman, first experienced in his dreams of Miss Bourne, his primary school teacher.

When it was all over he felt like running as fast as he could. She, however, continued to kiss him on his cheek. He sat up in the bed and said to her, "Won't he suspect?"

"It don't matter. In the beginning he threaten to kill me, but now he take it like that."

"You disgust me!" Rohan said feelingly.

"And what about you? On the night you father dead and all."

"All you middle-aged people. . . ."

"I'm twenty-nine," she said, with some resentment.

He glanced at her, naked under the centre light. She looked even younger than twenty-nine, but he associated her with Doc in his mind and consequently thought of her as a much older woman.

"Why d'you do this sort of thing?" he asked.

"You don't start on me now. Why? The next thing you'll be asking is if I love him. Everybody ask me that. One thing I must say about you, you don't talk much."

She crawled over to him on the other side of the bed, where he had taken refuge, sat by him and kissed him in her clinging manner. Rohan found her style irresistible and allowed himself to be seduced. No doubt, at the end of the second bout he would again feel disgusted, but she would have him again and again if she wanted him.

When the rain began to fall Rohan was at peace, as if he had discharged a mighty burden from his shoulders. His body was at peace and his mind was at peace. The moth that circled the bulb confirmed the tranquillity of the night and the gurgling of the water down the drains gave depth to the silence that surrounded them. She was the banquet of the flesh he had dreamed of when alone on a Sunday morning. Her wanton limbs had plagued him in his sleep when he was still at school and secreted lecherous desires in the corners of his imagination.

"We've got to go . . . the suit," she said, nudging him into action.

When they got back, the women in the gallery had gone and only a handful of people were on the stairs. The men were drunk and the women who were attending to the body were glad to see Rohan back. One of them came up to him and said, "At last!" and took the suit from him without enquiring if it was indeed for the dead man.

Doc, on seeing his wife, shouted out, "I told them you were kept back by the rain."

He laughed at his own joke and then suddenly went grave. A while later, after Rohan had taken a seat next to his,

Doc said, "Your father wasn't always the way he was at the end, you know. His job used to be everything to him. When he lost it he went to pieces. Everybody thought highly of him."

Doc got up and went to the door of the bedroom where the coffin was, but the two women barred his way. He lifted the glass in his hand and said, "I wish I was with you, old, old friend. I wish I could take a crate of rum with us, to hell or Heaven, wherever we were bound, 'cause I know they don't make rum anywhere like our rum. Rest in peace, old, old, old friend, among the whores, the pepper-pot and rum."

His wife was looking at him, a faint smile on her face. Two of his Lodge mates tried to quieten him, but he shook them off violently.

"When Armstrong went to the dogs I avoided him, but I tell you I used to cry with shame inside me."

He put the glass down.

"I cried inside because I was going to the dogs too, in serge and worsted and tropical suiting. None of you know what I'm talking about, you band of sh— shrivelled up . . . so-and-so. . . . The next time you see a man without vanity, kneel down in front of him and cover his hands and feet with kisses."

He fell against the wall and his left arm hung, limp at his side, still holding the glass while the right arm served as a cushion for his head. A man went up to him and put his arm round his waist.

"Don't touch me, you leper!"

A late-comer relieved him of the glass. The rain which had begun to fall again had driven away the remainder of the onlookers on the stairs. Genetha came out to see what was happening. She had fallen asleep in her day clothes, which were crumpled. For a moment she was unable to take in the scene, like someone who, waking up on his first trip abroad, is bewildered by the sight of the strange furniture. She saw the faces and the coffin in the middle of the room and the two women bending over her dead father and put her hand to her mouth, as if to stop the wave of despair which threatened to overcome her. When she reached the door and found that everything was in order, she slipped back into the bedroom before closing the door.

Doc's wife got up and went over to him, and whispered

something into his ear, then smiled. Then she went to Rohan and shook his hand. Doc accompanied her to the door, saw her out and came back to join the company. Others followed her example, until only the two women, Rohan and Doc remained in the drawing-room.

"I'll stay with you if you want," he offered Rohan, who felt sorry for him so agreed.

"We had our disagreements, your father and I. He claimed that no one was capable of maturing while his parents were alive. So he couldn't understand how I felt about my ancestors. . . . And he had a habit of taking off his shoes before he entered somebody's house, like a real countryman. He thought it was the gentlemanly thing to do. . . ." Then Doc came out with the thing that was pressing most on his thoughts:

"D'you know, she isn't my real wife. My real wife's in Essequibo. When I made a lot of money she got to hear about it. A year or so ago she came to see me. She had become fat. I mean, to span all these years in a minute was a shock, eh? I asked if she wanted money, but she said no, she just wanted to see me. After all these years! She just wanted to see me. After all these years! She wasn't even bitter that I'd left her. We sat trying to make conversation. When I found out she didn't want money from me I felt disappointed. I saw before me the girl I used to court and her arms round my shoulder and her fingers against my face. And then she said something about her mother and I was suddenly furious that she'd allowed her mother to come between us . . . I never had luck with women. Tell me, did my wife make any advances to you tonight?"

"No," Rohan replied without flinching.

"Up to a year ago she was the most thoughtful, hard-working woman you could imagine. Then all of a sudden she took it into her head to go out to parties and dances. She was seized with a kind of frenzy. I hoped it was a phase, but it's lasted a whole year now, and she is more worked up than ever. . . . I love that woman so much I lie awake at nights, happy at the thought that she's in the same room as me."

It seemed to Rohan that, like his father, Doc spent much of his time whining. The man whom his father used to talk of in such glowing terms was a snivelling fellow, who closed

252

his eyes to his mistress's escapades and spoke of his failed marriage without any shame.

"The fact is." Doc continued, "I don't have any choice. I know you must despise me, but . . . I once read in a book about an American who couldn't satisfy his wife. He used to go out in the street and invite any stranger inside to have a go. . . . With your father you never had to bother about keeping the conversation going. When I'd talked and talked there used to be a feast of silence and the smoke would spiral up from my cigarette and you could hear the cars passing outside or the black pudding man calling out to someone. . . . Let me tell you something, boy — you're young, but you listen to me, Never let the lack of money stop you from having children."

These last words were the first to touch a chord of sympathy in Rohan, who thought of his father, lifeless and alone. Suddenly he was prepared to listen to Doc talking, but he had fallen asleep. He himself could not drop off and in his reflections Doc's mistress came back to him. His experience with her revolted him.

The next afternoon the house was full of people attending the funeral. A woman pushed her way through the crowd towards Genetha, bent down and kissed her on the cheek.

"You don't know me. I'm your father's cousin."

Genetha instinctively got up from her chair beside the coffin.

"Don't get up, chile. At least I glad to see he had a decent girl like you."

Her eyes blazed with a curious fire as she looked at the dead man in the coffin.

"He ruin his own sister," she said softly, "his own sister."

Genetha had heard her and, afraid that she might be the cause of a commotion, looked up at her with pleading eyes.

"You should know, chile," she said aloud, "he ruin his own sister."

Before anyone could protest she was making her way through the crowd, towards the door. Some of those present were acutely embarrassed, but others, though pretending to be scandalised, regarded the funeral as a great success. It only needed a relative to throw herself into the grave to provide the crowning moment of an unforgettable afternoon.

253

The cortège drove through the broad gates of Le Repentir Burial Ground. Behind the hearse came the mourners' carriage; and behind that about forty cars. Gradually the pace slowed down until the procession came to a halt under the eucalyptus trees. The warm afternoon shed a yellow, diffused light on everything. It was only when the coffin was pulled through the doors at the rear of the hearse that Rohan felt an access of emotion. He grasped a handle manfully and swallowed his saliva. *O God,* he thought, *I'm not going to make a fool of myself now.*

Doc, on the other side, looked at him reassuringly. He, Rohan and two post office employees bore the coffin to the edge of the grave, at one side of which the earth had been piled up. And then came the minister's voice,

"Man born of woman . . . he cometh up and is cut down like a flower."

Rohan would have liked to turn his back on the ceremony. Every word uttered by the minister seemed an affront. Every face around him resembled a mask; and even Doc with his excessive air of concern and his black serge suit appeared to be an intruder in a private affair.

The sound of clods of earth thudding on the polished wood awakened Rohan from his reflections; and as he looked into the pit and watched it filling, the picture on the drawing-room wall came to mind, with its shadowed corners, its vermilion and faintly decipherable caption: "Embrace me! Embrace me still!"

Genetha thrust her arm under his without a word and they walked slowly back to the carriage.

That night a fearful storm descended on the town. Rohan stood before the window and watched the lightning ripping the sky apart, while Genetha lay huddled between the sheets in her room. Both of them felt the absence of their father and Rohan especially missed him. The sulking figure had become a part of his daily experience, a warp in the pattern of things and events between sleeping and waking. For the first time in his life he thought he heard noises in the house and recalled the night they moved in, when he was still a boy. He remembered his love for his mother, a vast affection that had made him leap for joy when he saw her coming home at night, after sitting by the window waiting for her. And he thought of Esther who never lay down before reading from her black, soft-covered Bible; and more than once she told him that his unruliness would be punished by death; that the whirring sounds of the six o'clock bee were the voices of dead children.

He did not know that at that moment his sister was standing outside his room. Frightened by the violence of the storm and by her awareness of the covered mirrors hanging in the darkness, she had left her bed, wandered to the back of the house and now stood at his door. She remained there for several minutes, struggling against the desire to knock and ask if she could come in.

Rohan intended to look for Esther the next day and bring her back into the house; it never occurred to him that Esther might not want to come back. The man of twenty-one had changed little from the boy of ten, who distressed his mother and tormented his sister.

And yet, in the months ahead, when Genetha no longer scattered flowers on her father's grave, Rohan could never pass the burial ground without hurrying his pace.

11

The Bridge of Kisses

He had always wondered why his sister was never pursued by young men, nor seemed to have ever formed any romantic attachment. She was attractive and well-mannered. Yet something repelled would-be suitors, as Rohan himself observed when occasionally they met at the same dance. While girls far less attractive than Genetha were invited to dance even before the piece was struck up, she was left, leaning against the wall, watching the others. Rohan was therefore surprised when she began to receive visits from a tall, slim and downright ugly young man. In every way the pair seemed ill-matched. Rohan, on first meeting him, did his best to put him at ease but succeeded in extracting only monosyllables from him. With pursed lips and unblinking eyes, the impassive suitor gave the impression of posing for an artist. Later Rohan discovered that Michael and Genetha went to religious meetings together.

Genetha, apparently self-possessed, in fact suffered the most acute anxieties in the presence of young men and had found herself unable to establish any but the most tenuous relationships with them. Whenever she summoned up enough courage to go to a party she always left disappointed. Her anxiety turned to panic if a youth invited her to dance, so that she either refused or danced so badly that her partner shepherded her back to her place with a curious alacrity. Michael, after dancing with her once, came back and back again.

Since her father's death she had felt strangely alone. She had promised herself, after Rohan gave up his connections with that family over the river, to be happy. She would devote herself to him as their mother had devoted herself to them. But now Genetha realised that their father had meant more to them than they had imagined. He was the catalyst that had drawn Rohan closer to her, so much so that his death had left an emptiness neither had foreseen. Small wonder that Rohan

256

wanted to have Esther back with them, instinctively seeking out the one link with the past.

Genetha was aware of the apparent absurdity of friendship with Michael and was grateful to her brother for saying nothing disparaging about him. Had Rohan overheard a sample of their conversation he would have been even more perplexed that the relationship could have got off the ground at all.

"Someone said your father used to have hallucinations," Michael once remarked.

"Hallucinations? Sometimes he had bad dreams, but not hallucinations. Who told you so?"

"My mother told me."

"Oh?"

"You know, hallucinations're a bad sign," Michael pursued.

"Of what?" Genetha asked.

"Well, it's like . . . it's got that sort of . . . you know what I mean."

"No."

And the conversation came to an abrupt end. After one of these little quarrels she told him angrily that she could no longer go out with him, because they had little in common. But the very next day she rang and apologised. When she saw him again his lips were pursed ever more tightly and his nose was even higher in the air. Then, as if to emphasise his view of their relationship, Michael brought up the subject of her father's hallucinations once more, developing it at considerable length. He then allowed her time to defend her dead father, but she kept a proper silence. And as a reward he took her hand in his and pressed it.

One night on their way home from the cinema they took shelter from the rain under a shop front in Vlissingen Road. Michael's nearness to her in the dark made Genetha tremble and she felt a new sensation course through her body; but Michael noticed nothing, so that when the rain stopped the couple emerged as pure as when they had run for cover a half-hour before.

Genetha, before going to bed, prayed to be forgiven for her wicked impulses. On seeking the advice of the minister whose church she and Michael attended, she was told that she ought to obey her friend implicitly and follow his guidance. He-

257

knew from then on that God had meant her destiny to be bound up with Michael's and that any question as to their suitability as partners was irrelevant. His virtue and austerity provided a model acceptable to Christ and the Church. Henceforth she would shun even the cinema as Michael had repeatedly urged her to do.

As their friendship developed Genetha identified Michael in a curious way with her father, associating him with dark rooms favoured by the aged, and unmatched shoes. She had been the first to know of her father's hallucinations, believing that they were brought on by her mother's death and the loss of his self-esteem, and was deeply offended that Michael was prepared to trample on her pride by recalling them. But she all too readily forgot Michael's offensive behaviour and clung to him, his silences and his conviction of superiority. If her father's pretensions had disintegrated on her mother's death, Michael's rigidity, she was certain, would undoubtedly survive the rudest of shocks.

And yet there were moments when he touched her, as when he talked about his mother, whom he idolised, and his deformed brother. Encouraged that he had aroused Genetha's interest, he spoke at greater length than he had ever done. Then he put his arm around her waist and said, "Look! Only yesterday the sky was covered with stars and now there are shadows round the moon!"

But her daydreams, in which she danced the tango in the arms of a passionate young man who followed her home at a distance and stood looking up at her house long after the lights in the street went out, did not involve Michael, who looked on disapprovingly from some lofty perch. She fancied that he pitied her for the bright red dress she wore and the flowers in her hair, and the rings on all the fingers of her left hand; for her moist, parted lips, the sweat-bloom on her cheeks and exposed shoulders, and for her half-closed eyes, which looked past her partner's face, assured of his devotion.

Genetha did not ask herself why Rohan's approval of Michael irritated her to the point of distraction. Once when her brother addressed him kindly she trembled with resentment and, on his return home later that night, ordered him not to meddle in her affairs. She never enquired about his dealings with women and was entitled to the same degree of privacy. Rohan, from then on, treated Michael with the minimum of civility, only to find that his sister's irritation, on the occasions when the two found themselves face to face, was no less intense.

In the night, after Michael's departure, she would lie down, waiting for Rohan to come home and lock up. She listened to the ripe fruit falling and the inaudible squeaking of the bats, which disturbed the neighbours' dogs.

One evening Michael, in his most malicious vein, told her of a man who had spent years abroad and came back home with a great reputation as a musician. In the end everyone tired of fêting him and he was relegated to the status of a national monument, which people passed by without even turning their heads. He now lived alone and carried around with him a faded, dog-eared programme of a recital he once gave in Germany, dog-earder programme of a recital he once gave in Germany, was hurt, as if she were the victim of the story and of her companion's malice. So she professed to be unwell and he left, promising to come again the following night. She retired, undressed and stood by the back window, through which the plants in the back yard were barely visible and the clustered stars of red exora trembled under the window-sill; and she could not help wondering whether hatred and indifference were not the residue of love.

Looking across the back yards of the houses she imagined it was bright daylight and that women were tramping through the smart shops up-town, which sold clothes and trinkets to satisfy the illusions of customers, dimly perceived, like the clouded outlines of flowers in the smoke.

The war had come to an end some months previously. The closest connection the country had had with the conflict had been the presence of the American airmen. The rumours that the air base would be closed down had proved well founded. Already the amount of money in circulation had fallen and shopkeepers complained that their takings were considerably lower. A number of people who had been employed at the base were now out of work and others whose employment indirectly depended on the American money in circulation were also thrown on to the labour market. Many people felt that the sooner Europeans started fighting among themselves again the better it would be for the country.

Although Rohan belonged to the privileged few who had a permanent, well-paid job in the Civil Service he saw himself drifting, careless, pilotless, like a boat whose destiny was to end on some mud-flat up-river.

"You're lucky," he was told. "I'd give anything for your job."

But he was unable to escape the nagging feeling that he was wasting his days. He was afraid of becoming too involved with Fingers. The outings with him provided the only excitement in Rohan's life. Just as his father had known the location of all the brothels in Georgetown, Rohan and Fingers knew where all the billiard saloons were. The pair went from dive to dive, from cake-shop to cake-shop and occasionally were even invited to give exhibitions in the more decent establishments like the YMCA and the Catholic Guild Club. They attended dances at which Rohan got to know Fingers's friends and became familiar with their uninhibited pleasures. He remembered well the first night he went to Fingers's house. He arrived in the middle of a tirade by his friend's grandmother, who was venting her anger on her son, Finger's father, who had been out of work for a month.

"You lie in de hammock all day looking outside to watch de women pass! You in' got not'ing else in you head?"

While she was talking he was lying, following her with an indulgent grin. His two front teeth were missing and his greying hair was thinning on his forehead.

"You always quarrelling wit' de foreman or somebody and lossin' you job. Is wha' we gwine live 'pon? Air?"

Fingers, his three sisters and four brothers were eating from their tin plates, which were on the floor in front of them. No one seemed to be put out by the storm about them. From time to time Fingers looked up to wink at Rohan. He dipped his hand in the mountain of rice with relish, making sure that every handful was flecked with the little curry at the top of the mountain. Rohan wondered how his friend could be satisfied with curry, ungarnished with meat or fish or vegetables. As he was to learn later, it was Fingers who was usually the victim of his grandmother's sharp tongue.

"Talk, talk!" she continued. "I tell you to act humble, but you don't hear, you do de firs' t'ing dat come in you fat head!"

Almost bursting with fury she went up to him and slapped him on the head. He looked at her even more lovingly. Throwing up her hands in despair she unleashed a flood of imprecations on him.

"I could coungkse 'pon you, you so stupid!" she raged, lifting up her skirt and flouncing her backside in his direction, in the manner of a girl putting out her tongue as a final gesture during a quarrel with a friend. Fingers winked at Rohan and continued devouring his rice. His father lowered his head and disappeared behind the raised side of the hammock.

Fingers, since he began to work, was allowed to eat at home and had in fact become the main provider for the family. In the eyes of his grandmother, this had not increased his status and he, believing that his turn might come at any moment, hurried through his meal and left with Rohan.

Another time the two came back to Fingers's house at about midnight. By the light of Fingers's torch Rohan could see the members of the family scattered over the floor of the single room in which they lived. Fingers's grandmother, his youngest brother of nine months and two other children were sleeping in the bed. The others, except for the father, who was in his hammock, all slept on the floor on bedding put down for that purpose.

Rohan instinctively sought out the figure of Fingers's fifteen-year-old sister, who was lying by the partition, face down and legs covered with bedclothes. Fingers's grandmother shrieked out for quiet and the two young men retreated hastily, closing the door as they left the room.

But it was a certain incident that moved Rohan to think seriously of going away. On returning home from the pictures one night he thought he heard a scuffling sound. When he got upstairs everything seemed normal. He took a shower and then went to bed, but had difficulty in falling asleep. The creaking of the floorboards and the closing of the front door took his mind back to the scuffling sound he had heard on arriving home.

"Who'd ever've thought that Michael had it in him?" he mused, sitting up in bed.

261

The next morning, at table, it was Genetha who confessed that she had been entertaining a friend the night before.

"You're corrupting Michael," he said jokingly.

"It wasn't Michael . . . it was your friend Alec."

"Alec? You mean Fingers?" he asked, his expression changing suddenly.

"Yes."

Rohan looked at her, dumb and unbelieving.

Finally, after a long hostile stare, he asked, "You had Fingers in your bedroom?"

"Would you've preferred it to be Michael?"

"Yes! " he answered indignantly. "Isn't Michael your friend? What're you, a slut that doesn't care who she goes with?"

She said nothing for a few moments and then retorted, "Alec was the first."

"Christ, Fingers of all people! " he exclaimed, thinking of his coarseness and the poverty of his home.

"You might as well know, it's been going on for some time."

Rohan did not want to hear any more.

He had offered him the hospitality of his home, introduced him to his sister and that was the way he repaid him. The thought of what had happened seemed to him so sordid that he tried to shut it out of his mind. He could think of nothing else, but refused to allow his train of thought to lead him to any act of intimacy between his young friend and his sister.

She had stopped eating and was watching him anxiously, but he avoided her eyes and left the table as soon as he had finished.

Soon thereafter Rohan decided to leave Georgetown. He had lost all interest in billiards, dismissing it as a game fit for morons. And whenever Michael came to the house Rohan went out of his way to insult him and taunt him with his inability to make advances to his sister.

He thought of ringing Doc's mistress, but on the point of telephoning, he changed his mind. After the night of the wake she kept pestering him, till Rohan ended by brutally telling her to leave him alone. One afternoon, however, as he was riding about aimlessly, he went boldly up to the house and knocked. The servant who answered the door invited him in, saying that the mistress was at home. When she saw him standing in the gallery she hurried towards him, attempting in no way to conceal her pleasure at his visit. Rohan unceremoniously made her take him to her bedroom and, without the slightest preparation, possessed her. The facility of his success, her lack of pride combined to arouse in him a contempt she did not fail to notice and he left immediately, declining her invitation to go for a car ride.

Finding himself in Vlissingen Road he went into the Botanic Gardens, where he dismounted and sat on a bench by the Bridge of Kisses. As he looked into the water he thought of his wasted life, that at twenty-two he had achieved nothing. His parents were dead and his sister had committed an unforgivable act. The sun gleamed through a palm, covering a patch of grass in light. If only his mother were alive, he thought — just as his father was wont to do — and the memory of the way he had treated her filled his eyes with tears. Why should he be so plagued with remorse? He was young at the time. He had to get away from Georgetown. He need only wait until information as to posts in the country and the interior were circularised.

Some months later, as Rohan was talking to Mr Mohammed, his eyes fell on a circular which lay on the latter's desk. He turned the pages in a desultory fashion and was just about to close it when the name "Suddie" caught his attention. Suddie! Indrani must still be there. Although neither men in their conversations ever mentioned her name, Rohan felt that if she was back home Mr Mohammed would have said so.

Bowed over his revenue classification sheet, Mohammed did not notice his young friend's agitation.

"How's Indrani?" Rohan asked casually.

Mohammed looked up, surprised.

"She's all right. Got a child, you know. Nice little boy."

"That's good," he said, and felt like cursing the world. "Still up at Suddie?"

"Mhm," Mohammed muttered absently between his calculations.

Rohan lost no time in applying for the vacant post. The waiting was intolerable. Often, in the past, he had seen such posts appearing and re-appearing in the circulars, for want of applicants; but he was sure that, because he was after it, someone else would be preferred to him. When a letter offering him the post arrived he showed it at once to Mr Mohammed.

"Pity!" he exclaimed.

"I won't even try to see her."

"And why d'you want to go then?"

Rohan knew that it was foolish to try and answer.

"I promise I won't try to see her," he said.

"You think Suddie's Georgetown or Vreed-en-Hoop with its straight roads and palings and its street lamps and cake-shops? Night after night you'll sit watching the beetles circle the kerosene lamp and count the days to your leave in George-town. You'll pray that somebody'll write to you and save you from talking to yourself. Besides, people will watch your every move. If you so much as look at Indrani they'll start gossiping; and when that happens, God help her! Remember she's a Mohammedan. If his parents get to know of her association with you in Vreed-en-Hoop they'll carve her up!"

"You think her husband will tell them?" Rohan asked.

"He won't be such a fool. My advice to you is to withdraw the application, in everybody's interest."

The two men were silent. Mohammed, annoyed that Rohan would not comply, made a last effort.

"Listen. Her father-in-law's a big man in Suddie. You'll be just another Civil Servant with good manners and town talk." His hostility took Rohan by surprise.

If what the older man had said was true, it was equally true that he could not stand the thought that Rohan would no longer be working beside him. He had seen him develop into a man. The youth who had arrived a few years ago, diffident, impressionable, had become his close friend; he was the only person in the office who cared about books and politics, whose ambitions went further than driving to the Carib every night to impress women.

Mohammed often wondered whether Rohan's real motive for not coming back to his house was that they were East Indians. Probably his family had got wind of his visits. Non-sense! He was always independent and wouldn't have allowed his family to influence him, Mohammed thought. After him, the office would be a wilderness again.

264

12

Essequibo

The morning of his departure Genetha accompanied him over the river. Neither wanted to look at the other as he leaned out of the Parika train. He had not forgotten the incident with Fingers, and she, in a revulsion of feeling, felt all the shame Rohan thought she ought to feel. Suddenly there was a gulf between them, as if the years of their childhood together had meant nothing. On purpose she had dressed with a modesty that almost amounted to drabness.

Without warning, the train began to move. The lump in Rohan's throat prevented him from waving and Genetha in turn could only stare at the receding carriages. She turned and walked back to the stelling. So many years! If he knew how much she loved him. . . . She loved him for their dead mother and feckless father, for Esther, who had doted on him when he was a boy; for his friend who had seduced her — him, who could just spread his wings and fly away and leave her behind as if she were not entitled to say anything. Every man she had known was selfish. He, Michael, her dead father. . . . Their selfishness was like a force that swept everything out of their way. She could never marry. Never!

The landscape sped past in a confusion of hovels and prayer flags, houses on their high pillars, an occasional glimpse of the mangrove that rose out of the water on a tangle of roots. At one stop, perhaps at Uitvlugt, an East Indian priest was standing on the station platform, his lota in his left hand and a stick in his right. The bizarre thought occurred to Rohan that he might be waiting for the end of the world. As the train pulled out of the station he was still standing there, his gaze fixed on some point in the distance. Trenches crisscrossed the countryside and occasionally a bateau, hardly disturbing the water, would make its leisurely way up one of these narrow waterways. The train pulled into Parika and the sun was ablaze from a cloudless sky.

Rohan had never come so far up the West Coast, and for the

first time since he set out he felt a certain excitement. He got out his suitcase and trunk and had them transferred to the *Basra*, then went back down on to the stelling to look at the ancient paddle-steamer which was to take him from Parika to Suddie. A man who was fishing from the stelling had just caught a large, odd-looking fish which he was holding up for everyone to see. The *Basra* seemed small, compared to the boat that plied the Georgetown to Vreed-en-Hoop ferry.

"You're young Armstrong, aren't you?"

Rohan turned round to see a man in an unidentifiable uniform. He nodded, disappointed by this intrusion into his annonymity.

"Your father and I used to play whist together. Wonderful man," he said, putting out his hand.

Rohan shook his hand.

"Who? Him?" said a middle-aged man who was passing. Rohan had noticed this man watching him as he was leaving the train. He felt that he had seen him before.

"Who? Him? He's a wharf rat. Know every billiard hall in Water Street," the stranger said, laughing, before he passed on.

The man in uniform shook hands again and left Rohan with a warm smile. Disturbed by the incident, Rohan went upstairs into the saloon and sat down. A few feet away a European priest was talking about his mission among the aboriginal Indians up-river, saying that some of them understood him when he read from the Bible. At these words Rohan felt an urge to insult the priest, who suddenly stopped talking and looked at him, irritated that the young man should take such an unabashed interest in what he was saying. When Rohan did not look away he turned and continued to harangue his companion.

Everything now appeared to Rohan in an absurd light, his trip, the people round him, the exaggerated reflections of the sun on the placid water. The resolve awakened in him that, once he was in Suddie, he would spare no pains to see Indrani. What did he owe society, which had foisted on him the participation in a daily ritual, devoid of meaning, a society that was unmindful of his own private aspirations?

Once the first wave of bitterness had passed, Rohan asked

himself what his aspirations really were and he had to confess that they amounted to a vague desire for adventure and change.

The Essequibo river with its farther shore lost in the distance lacked the intimacy of the Demerara. Rohan, finding nothing to interest him on the water, went downstairs to the second-class deck, which was packed with people. At the foot of the stairs a woman with a string of crabs dangling at her side was sleeping with her mouth open. Despite the rocking of the boat she remained anchored on her seat, like a pillar in its fundament while the chugging sound of the engine caused everything to vibrate. He caught bits of conversation, which floated about like stalks in the wind.

"Dat in' he sister — dat's 'e wife!"

"You in' know what you talkin'. Shut you mout'."

Two women further on were talking about food.

"He tek de foo-foo and eat it straightaway. 'E couldn't wait for de cook-up rice. You ever hear o' anybody eatin' foo-foo without nothin' else? So I look at 'e and 'e look at me. After all dat trouble I tek wit' de rice. I couldn't stan' it no mo' and I say, 'Is why you don't eat de mortar too, you good-for-nothin' glutton?'"

When Suddie came into sight, passengers went to line the side of the boat. A crowd was on the stelling, waiting with heads raised. Some children among them were waving vigorously, although it was impossible to recognise anyone from such a distance. Passengers were getting their things together or straining their eyes to spot those who were expecting them. Rohan had no idea who was going to meet him, and after the gang-plank was placed against the boat and people began disembarking he remained watching from the first-class deck. Slowly, the boat emptied and the bustle on the boat became the bustle on the stelling. He did not notice the man who approached him from behind.

"Mr Armstrong?"

Rohan turned and saw a thin East Indian smiling at him. "Yes?"

"The District Commissioner send me to meet you."

Rohan was taken to his predecessor's cottage. He was burning to enquire where Mr Ali lived and if his wife was in Suddie with him.

He could no longer resist the temptation.

"Mr Ali? Which one?" his thin companion asked.

"It doesn't matter."

"They all live about a mile, mile and a half from here."

Ramjohn, Rohan's guide, had smelt a rat. "They soaking in money. It running out their ear-holes and nose-holes and—"

"All right," Rohan hastened to stop him. Then he asked, "What do people do round here when they get bored?"

"They get married," came the reply.

Rohan smiled. He liked Ramjohn. Everything about him was comical, his gestures, his speech and even his appearance. On top of a head shaped like a long mango, three hairs were stretched carefully across a shining bald crown. Occasionally Ramjohn put his hand on his crown to ensure that the three hairs were still in place.

After he had introduced Rohan to the old servant, he showed him over the cottage, the pride of which was its arsenal of rifles; one of them was kept loaded since a burglar attacked his predecessor. Downstairs, beside the house, was the pump, used to raise water to the tank in the roof. It had never needed to be repaired since it was installed, Ramjohn told him, although it was as old as the housekeeper. The two men walked over the gravel, which cracked under their feet and stopped abruptly where the tamarind tree rose towards the shadowed evening sky, across which clouds were suspended like white schooners on a windless sea.

Finally, he took Rohan over to the Commissary Office where he worked and of which Rohan was to be the acting chief clerk. The only other employees were the forest ranger, who had been out on his rounds for more than a week, and another clerk by the name of Downes. The latter was, according to Ramjohn, "a glutton for work". All Rohan needed to do was to tell him what work there was and then leave everything to him.

Night had fallen and Downes, who had kept the office open in anticipation of Rohan's visit, was anxious for him to leave, so that he might lock up and go home.

"We'd better go," urged Rohan. "Mr Downes ought to be getting home."

"Oh, he won't mind," Ramjohn said confidently, "I know him."

They bade Downes good night and he immediately began to lock up.

It was unjust, Rohan thought, that he should be the superior of a man older than himself, who knew far more than he about the district and the routine of the office. Besides, he was disappointed by the size of the office which, by Demerara standards, looked like a seedy back shop.

When they got back to the cottage the gas lamp was lit, and the light, brighter than any domestic light bulb, attracted a host of insects. The sight of the lamp in the strange room and the perfect quiet of the night compounded Rohan's loneliness until, desperate lest Ramjohn should leave him with his taciturn servant, he offered to buy him a drink. Ramjohn stroked his three hairs and tactfully explained that a man of Rohan's position could not be seen in the local rum shop. He could drown himself in liquor at home if he liked. In fact, nearly all his predecessors had been heavy drinkers and the last one frequently came to work in the mornings shamelessly stale-drunk.

"D'you play draughts, Mr Armstrong?"

"Yes."

"Good! I'm a champion!"

Rohan could have wept for joy. He gave Ramjohn a five-dollar note to buy a bottle of rum.

"I not going t'be long. Got to go home and tell my wife and get the set."

He disappeared into the night, muttering cheerfully, "Hand wash hand make hand come clean," past the forbidding tamarind tree which seemed to grow out of the water of the trench that ran ten yards or so in front of the house.

Rohan went to the office every morning at eight and returned at four in the afternoon, after a break of an hour and a half for his midday meal, which he ate at home. Far from leaving the work to Downes he welcomed any file, letter or memo that gave him the opportunity to kill time. Never before had he taken such a pleasure in office work. Ramjohn compared him with his predecessor and thought him odd to drive himself like that.

The nature of Rohan's work brought him into contact with

a large number of people, some of whom invited him to their homes. Away from Georgetown, and among people he did not know, he introduced himself as Rohan; from the age of seventeen or eighteen the name "Boyie" had begun to prove an embarrassment, though it was difficult to persuade friends to call him any other.

Since his first invitation to the home of one Mr Friduncle — whom Ramjohn called Mr Carbuncle — as a guest at his brother's wedding, Rohan was swamped with others, so that he became anxious lest people interpreted his disinclination to go to their house as disapproval of themselves.

One of the homes he frequented was that of a widow and her daughter. It was said they both wanted to marry him, a rumour which was encouraged by the fact that on each occasion when he visited them the windows on either side of the house were closed against the prying eyes of their neighbours. Ramjohn saw no reason why he should not continue his visits.

"Nothing like a scandal to make the women toss in bed at night. In truth, in truth. If I was chief clerk here, I wouldn't bother with what people say." He got up and began gesticulating. "I'd create havoc among the women, run them through like a knife through butter. Husbands would come and plead for me to leave the Essequibo, but I'd refuse. Then they'd appeal to the District Commissioner. There'd be a petition, 'Ramjohn must go!' "

He felt his bald crown and stroked his three hairs.

"If shit had wings it'd fly," he said sadly.

"You're a degenerate," Rohan said smiling. "Have you ever been unfaithful?"

"No, I love my wife. That's my trouble. She's like Lakshmi, the Hindu goddess. She look so young you'd think she's my daughter."

After being lost in thought for a while, he then continued: "When my father-in-law complain about how I lef' her alone so much I say that she's never alone — she got seven children. One day he tell her it's unnatural to take care of me as she do. Her own father! I complain to the priest 'bout him, but instead of cursing him the priest curse me for not coming to the temple for so long. I so vexed I tell him I was going

270

to change my religion. Guess what he tell me! He say it's the best thing I could do."

Ramjohn then started talking to no purpose and the old servant inside kept sucking her teeth in annoyance, but he paid not a bit of attention to her, except when he was about to go. He then said, loudly:

"Not because you had a hard life you got to think everybody must be miserable like you." Then to Rohan he muttered, "Get her to talk about her father; is a story to beat all stories."

Rohan's coming was a blessing to Ramjohn. All the chief clerks he had hitherto dealt with snubbed him as soon as they could fend for themselves. As he had once remarked bitterly to his wife, he was good enough to show them the ropes but not good enough for company. He worshipped the dirt Rohan walked on and, in spite of the fact that they had become friends, always treated him with the greatest deference. A life of boot-licking had left its mark on him.

Rohan, generous and broad-minded, nevertheless suffered from the limitations of all his class. Ramjohn was thrust into the background whenever there were guests, and although he found this only proper, Rohan was conscience-stricken over his own cowardice.

His way of life settled into a pattern he himself had professed to despise before he came to the Essequibo, and people came to associate him with expensive suits, copious liquor and the company of attractive women.

13

An Offer of Marriage

Sidique Ali learned of Rohan's arrival the day after the *Basra* moored at Suddie stelling. He had never managed to lay the suspicion that there had been something between Rohan and his wife. In his opinion a married woman's smile was a gift to her husband. If ever it were directed to anyone outside the family circle, she had committed adultery. What offended him most of all was the apparent ease with which Rohan spoke to Indrani. That day in Vreed-en-Hoop when he deliberately remained in the bedroom in order to hear how Rohan would speak to her his tone of voice might have been that of a husband who had not seen his wife for several weeks.

Indrani, by custom, went out only with other members of the family. Her life had become almost intolerable, so that she could no longer decide whether the yoke of her mother-in-law's authority was worse than the boredom of her confinement. Sometimes one of her sisters came to visit her for a few weeks, and she made her remain until it was clear that she was overstaying her welcome in Sidique's eyes. The presence of her sisters was like a sudden wind on a close, humid afternoon. But when they went they left an emptiness greater than the emptiness their arrival had relieved. Once Sidique found her looking out on the river and he remarked, "He's miles away; stop dreaming."

Then a quarrel followed, in which he said the harshest things to her.

On learning of Rohan's arrival Sidique offered Indrani to go through the kind of marriage ceremony recognised by law and after which her father so hankered. Her lukewarm approval of the idea wounded him deeply.

Sidique, fancying that his wife no longer loved him, went out of his way to humiliate her. Indrani reacted by withdrawing even further into herself, and this was the beginning of the long period of bitterness that was to afflict the couple. They did their best to hide their unhappiness from others; and in this they were successful, save for Sidique's mother, who watched her son and daughter-in-law like a hawk, taking a malicious delight in any evidence of strife between them.

"I did always say so," she kept telling herself. "Education don' make a good wife. What she want is the whip."

It was by accident that Indrani found out that Rohan was in Suddie.

One afternoon Sidique's brother Jai took the family for a drive in the car while Sidique and his father were at the rice mill. On the way back Jai stopped to help a taxi driver whose car had stalled. The driver and his young passenger were peering under the raised hood at their engine. Indrani, her husband's brother's wife and his mother were looking out impatiently when Indrani, for a moment, caught sight of the young man's face. She was not sure and had to wait until he turned again in their direction. There was no doubt. It was Rohan. Leaning back, she hoped that the two women had not noticed her agitation, and put her hand to her chest in an effort to still the furious pounding of her heart. Almost involuntarily her eyes were drawn to the window on the left through which the other two women were also looking. He had put on weight and looked taller. She closed her eyes and opened them again, in order to test the genuineness of the apparition. Her mother-in-law spoke and Indrani drew back behind her to avoid his gaze.

"Jai, hurry up, ne!"

He made an impatient gesture and continued to help the man.

"I going to tell his father," his mother said softly.

At the mention of her father-in-law Indrani suddenly felt cold. If Rohan recognised her what would he do? She would speak naturally to him as to someone she once knew in Vreeden-Hoop. Why not? But she knew that fear of her father-in-law and of her mother-in-law would strike her dumb. They would ply her with questions as to their acquaintanceship. And what could she do when her own husband would not stand up for her? These thoughts flew through her mind pell-mell.

"You're sweating like a horse, Indra," her mother-in-law remarked. She opened the car door to let more air in and began to fan herself with her hand.

"It'll be a long time before I allow Jai to take me out again, I can tell you," the old Mrs Ali observed.

Jai's wife noticed that Indrani was watching Rohan from the corner of her eye. "It's natural," she thought, "but I don't find him good-looking."

A passing car left a whirlpool of dust in its wake, and Indrani's mother-in-law shut the door and wound up the window to avoid the swirling dust. At that moment Jai closed the hood of the taxi, while the chauffeur got in and started it up, whereupon Rohan took his seat and closed the door. Jai waved after them and returned to his car, smirking with satisfaction. At least there was an incident to talk about that night.

"Wonder is who?" he mused aloud as he pressed on the accelerator. "Probably a new lawyer, as if the country din' have enough of them. Imagine wanting to practise in the Essequibo."

"You do it on purpose," complained his mother. "You always do things on purpose. If you move something from here to there you got a reason. But I goin' tell your father."

Indrani and her sister-in-law exchanged glances and smiled. Through the window which was lowered once again a cooling gust of wind blew in. The trees sped by along the dusty road and the setting sun coloured the horizon lavishly. A flock of parrots which had settled on a tree resumed their flight home as the vehicle went by, making a darker pattern against the sky. Indrani wished, after all, that he had recognised her and had said something to her. She would have been proud to acknowledge that she knew him, and would have smiled at him as in the old days when she was virtuous. Never more! Now she was filled with thoughts of deception. If the incident were to recur she would contrive to write him a note and pass it to him, so that they could arrange a secret assignation somewhere by the river. She would give herself to him and suffer the consequences gladly. God! she thought. *What is this pain, this racking pain?* It was the same pain she often felt when she was seventeen or eighteen, when, as she lay in bed in the morning, her body dissolved in some immeasurable longing.

As the car turned into the large garden she saw her son through the windscreen, sitting on the lowest stair, waiting for

274

her. She went up to him and lifted him as high as she could. Although he was not yet two he could say quite a lot. Had she brought any "tweets" for him? Did she see Masacurraman on the way? Was the steam "woler" out on the "woad"? The light went on in the drawing-room as the women went up the long front staircase. The old Mrs Ali still bore her son a grudge for his conduct on the road and the young Mrs Ali, Indrani's sister-in-law, nursed her inscrutable thoughts.

Indrani fed and put Abdul to bed. She then took a shower and joined the family at table where the old Mrs Ali complained to her husband about Jai. He shook his head in sympathy, but said nothing to his son.

14

Dada

Rohan and Ramjohn hurried up to the stelling as quickly as their dignity would allow. The boat was only a few yards away and no doubt the fellow from Georgetown would be looking out for them from the rail. Relieved that he had arrived in time, Rohan took a handkerchief from his hip pocket and mopped his face. It was four o'clock on a sweltering August afternoon and the stelling was packed with people. Ramjohn wanted to make his way to the front of the crowd, but was content to wait at the back and so avoid the jostling crowd. Two men were standing by the gang-planks, ready to shove them on to the second-class deck, from where most of the passengers would emerge.

"Boyie! Boyie!" he heard someone shouting behind him. He turned round involuntarily and stood face to face with Dada.

"Dada!" he exclaimed. "What're you doing here?"

"That's what I wanted to ask you. Father told me you'd left, but he said he didn't know where you'd gone."

Suddenly Rohan was aware that Dada was not alone. Three women stood in a group behind her and among them was Indrani, her lips parted and holding a parasol against her shoulder. He tried to conceal his surprise and nodded a greeting.

"You're not going to go and say hello?" Dada asked him.

At that moment Sidique, who had just arrived with Jai, came up to them and said to Dada, "You in't in Vreed-en-Hoop, y'know."

"I'm talking to a friend," she said, whereupon he turned on his heels. Muttering something to Jai and the women — the other two were Jai's wife and his mother — the group moved ahead of Dada and Rohan.

"Where're you living?" Dada asked him.

Rohan told her.

"I'm going to come and see you. I bet you're just as untidy as you used to be."

"Come soon," he said.

In reply, she took his right hand and squeezed it. She then rejoined the others.

The passengers had begun to disembark. One of the first was Sidique's father. The group surrounded him and went off in the direction of the Public Road, and Dada smiled as she passed by. There was no sign of recognition from Indrani, who had closed her parasol and was deep in conversation with Jai's wife.

"That's him!" exclaimed Ramjohn, as he spotted the man he and Rohan had come to meet.

That night Rohan lay in his bed under the electric fan. He had been invited out to a crab party to which, until that afternoon, he had been looking forward. It was the crab season and scores could be picked up on the beach at that time of the year. The Nassen boys were taking a few of their friends over to Tiger Island where they would gather them from the beach there. Mrs Nassen entertained great hopes for a marriage between Rohan and her daughter and was planning to manoeuvre him into a position which might lead to an indiscretion between the two. After that, he would have to become engaged to Lucille, if he was a gentleman. If he did not, there were ways of fixing him.

Dada had grown from an attractive girl into a beautiful woman. She had always been the prettiest in the family, but womanhood had endowed her with its most extravagant gifts. Her large, dark eyes and full lips were matched by a finely proportioned figure, with firm breasts. But Rohan could only think of Indrani. If only she had called his name or even smiled at him on the way from the stelling. She had completely ignored him! If it were not so, how could she have been engrossed in a conversation with the other woman as she walked past him?

The night was silent, except for the humming of the gas lamp. Angrily, he rose from his bed and began dressing for the party.

She might have made him a secret sign in passing by. Did she not appear to smile when he greeted her? The uncertainty

277

about her attitude routed him. To hell with Indrani!

He took great care over his appearance, having made up his mind to seduce Lucille Nassen.

The next day, a Saturday, Dada came to see him. He was swimming in the river, about a hundred and fifty yards behind the house. When he caught sight of her she had already been sitting in the stern of a boat on the beach for about two minutes.

"Hi! Who told you where I was?"

"The old woman."

She thought how different he looked with his hair flattened by the water. His chest was gleaming in the sun.

"You're very subdued," Rohan observed. "Weren't like that at Vreed-en-Hoop."

She smiled at him and only replied as an afterthought. "I was a girl then."

"Weren't subdued yesterday."

She did not answer him.

"In any case, you'll always be a girl to me," he said. "Want me to come out now?"

"No. I like watching."

"I'm no professional, girl. Anyhow, you make me embarrassed."

"Then come out," she suggested.

"No, I'll stay in," he replied.

"Then stay in."

He turned over on his back and began floating, while Dada watched him.

She felt like taking off her clothes and joining him in the water. But who would understand? With him everything was so simple. Sitting in silence and watching him was so simple. "When he comes out of the water," she thought, "we'll walk back to the house and my sleeve will get wet from his arm and I wouldn't need to pretend." And yet he was like all other men. If she said, "Let's get married," he wouldn't understand. He was still in love with Indrani. Well, it was all in the family. . . .

Rohan lay motionless in the water, rejoicing in Dada's presence. It was like the old days, the happiest days of his life. He loved her family unlike the way he had loved the members of his own family, without the hate and dismay. Besides, her uncommon beauty flattered him.

"They didn't want me to come," she shouted out to him, "but I said they couldn't stop me."

"You mean you defied them?" he asked, standing up in the water and looking at her admiringly.

"Yes."

"Was the old man there?" asked Rohan.

"Yes. Listen; someone's shouting."

"It's food, girl, food," he said, laughing.

"You eat so early?"

"I eat when the housekeeper tells me it's time," came his reply.

"That's what you call her? A housekeeper?"

"That's what she is, officially. Tobesides, what else can I call her? She keeps the house, doesn't she?" And he laughed.

Rohan came out of the water and felt her eyes on him. While she examined his naked trunk he examined her legs and bare arms. He remembered her leaving the Commissary Office at Vreed-en-Hoop. Her figure was attractive then, but in a fragile, girlish way. Rohan remembered her father and was ashamed of his thoughts, for how could he ever face Mr Mohammed if the latter knew that he coveted his daughter? When all was said and done it was indiscreet of her to come against the wishes of Indrani's in-laws. They would never forgive her.

The two sat down to a meal of rice, eddoes and curried snapper and after that they shared a small soursop with milk and brown sugar. The east side of the house was completely open, so that there was a view of the river from where they ate.

"Never see you eat like that. Wha' come over you?" said his housekeeper mockingly.

"It's the swim, I suppose," Rohan answered.

"Only day before yesterday," she continued, "you was cussing the Essequibo, the food, the people. I know is not me cooking. Is what, I wonder?"

"I never hear you talk so much either," he taunted her in return.

279

"I don' talk 'cause you don' eat my food, that's why."

She brought a tray to table with two glasses on it, one with iced mauby and the other with rum and sorrel.

"You wait till Ramjohn get here," said the housekeeper, "I gwine tell he how you stuff youself wit' all that food." She laughed hilariously, as if what she had said was vastly amusing.

"Never heard her like that before," Rohan said, turning to Dada. "Well, I never!"

Dada got up and began fondling the objects round the house. She thumbed through the books and stroked the jaguar skin on the floor.

"Pa doesn't speak about you any more, you know," she said.

"He didn't think I should bury myself here. I should go away and study medicine or something."

"He told me that too."

"I thought he didn't talk about me," Rohan remarked.

"Well, from time to time. He said if you didn't go away you'll end up by doing something bad. He said you're unstable."

A shadow crossed Rohan's forehead, but he made no reply.

"I know what you need," she said, after hesitating.

"What?"

"You ought to get married," she replied.

"That's all women can think of. You all hanker after marriage. I don't think any man wants to get married."

Dada was annoyed at his remark. "You mean women force them into it?"

"I wouldn't say force. What're you getting vexed for?"

"I'm not vexed."

They said nothing for a while.

"I don't know," said Rohan. "Somehow I feel as if I'll never go back to Georgetown. Not that I want to go back, but—"

"Oh," she interrupted him, "you just want to be near Indrani."

"How's Betty?" enquired Rohan.

"She's all right. Pa said you're selfish. You know you'll only cause trouble for Indra by coming here, yet you came."

None of the things Dada claimed her father had said were true.

"I haven't tried to see her," said Rohan, "so how can I cause trouble?"

"You can't help seeing everybody in Suddie," remarked Dada. "Sooner or later they all go down to the stelling when the boat comes in."

There was a pause in their conversation and she looked at him to see if he was annoyed. A car passed outside and a dog gave a short bark.

"In the old days I was madly in love with you," she said.

"I know."

"You're the most conceited. . . . You wanted to do something big, then. Like Pa. He wanted to do something big when he was young, he said. People say — people say if you've got a good relationship with your father you'll be a good wife. I've got a good relationship with Pa."

"Stop talking nonsense," he said sharply, pretending that he did not understand the significance of what she had told him.

"What'd your father say if. . . ." Rohan began.

"He'd be glad. He isn't very religious, so your not being a Mohammedan. . . ."

"He'd be against it. You don't know your father. Deep down he believes in everything Sidique and his father stand for."

"Then why doesn't he go to the mosque?" she rejoined. "Tell me that."

"That's the religious side," Rohan pointed out.

"But that's just what I was saying! "

"All right, all right. But the other side," went on Rohan, "the social side is different."

"Then why does he allow Mother to wander off to Grandma whenever she likes?"

"Don't ask me," replied Rohan irritably. "Probably it's the most sensible thing he can do."

"But everything you say supports my argument," Dada insisted.

Rohan began to get annoyed. He knew instinctively that he was right, but could find no convincing way of putting his point of view.

"I bet," said Rohan, "he'd have nothing against Sidique if he married Indrani officially. In fact. . . ."

"Sidique wants to marry her properly."

"What? Who told you so?" asked Rohan, giving himself away.

"Indra herself."

"When're they?" asked Rohan.

"She doesn't want to."

He got up and went into the kitchen where he poured himself another rum and mixed it with sorrel from one of the jars. When he came back he impulsively handed her the drink he had made for himself.

"D'you want me to?" she asked.

"Yes. . . ."

She sipped it and felt even closer to him. At a party or even at home he would never have approved of her touching rum. They talked until late afternoon, when he took her to the bridge and saw her set off for Sidique's house. A donkey cart laden with coconuts was approaching, a kerosene lamp swinging from the underside of it, and he waited until it had passed before going in. Ramjohn would arrive after dark for a game of draughts.

15

A Streak of Spittle

It was about seven o'clock, some time after Ramjohn had come, that there was a knocking. The housekeeper, who was reading an old copy of the *Daily Argosy* newspaper, got up and made her way slowly to the front of the house.

"Wonder who that is?" Rohan said, half turned in the direction of the door.

Dada entered with a suitcase in her hand.

"What's happened?"

She looked at Ramjohn. Rohan led her out on to the porch where she told him that Sidique's father had put her out for coming to see him alone. She was a bad influence on Indrani and would only give the family a bad name.

"I won't be able to go and see Indra anymore."

"You can stay here tonight and travel by boat in the morning to Parika."

She stood next to him, picking her nails and not knowing what to say.

"You want me to go and see them?" Rohan asked.

"What? They'd set the dogs on you."

A scarf was tied round her head, so that her hair was hidden. The light wind blew up her dress to expose her knees and the lower part of her thighs. From the road they could hear donkey carts passing on the way to the cinema, where an East Indian film was being shown. Rohan put his arm round her shoulders and she did not look up lest she saw his eyes.

"You want me to send Ramjohn home?" he offered.

"No. I'll come out and sit here alone. I like to hear you talking with other people."

She took off her head scarf while Rohan carried her suitcase into the empty bedroom, next to the housekeeper's. He then came back to her and asked if she wanted anything. In answer she held his arm.

"I'll speak to her later," he said, nodding in the direction of the housekeeper.

Rohan went back to Ramjohn and continued his game of draughts.

"Let's go and see the Indian film," Rohan suggested.

"You? You don't understand Hindi."

"Let's go," he insisted.

He felt unaccountably happy. Dada had tempted him too far. Ever since he watched her from the water that morning he realised that he desired her and if he pretended to be indifferent it was because he knew that she was his for the asking. At Vreed-en-Hoop it was not the same, for the realisation that her father was not far away would have made the enormity of his behaviour more apparent.

Tomorrow afternoon he would walk with her to the stelling arm in arm, in full view of everyone in Suddie. They would walk together in the hot sun like man and wife. He savoured the scandal in advance.

Back from the cinema he drank a glass of milk and ate the sweetbread the housekeeper had left for him; he then opened Dada's door and watched her lying on the bed. When he kissed her face and she said nothing he knew that she was pretending to be asleep. This discovery sent a wave of passion through his body and he kissed her lips and her breast through her bodice and found that she was naked underneath. She pressed her lips against his and as he caressed her between her thighs she whimpered.

"O God, Boyie, leave me alone! Leave me alone!" she groaned, crushing her lips against his mouth, whereupon he lay on her gently. "Don't hurt me too much, darling," she whispered.

The tamarind tree whispered softly, like a mother who knows everything. That night, like some indefatigable steer, he mounted her, and by the morning he had robbed her of her innocence. She was his wife and he her husband, strong, domineering, invincible.

On hearing Rohan go into the room the housekeeper pressed her ears against the wall, while a streak of spittle coursed down her chin from her open mouth and she lay like that until she dropped off, a smile on her wrinkled face.

Ramjohn sniffed the air on his way home, not knowing what to make of the situation at the cottage.

"Wonder if it's trouble," he mused. "Y'never know. Wonder

284

it Armstrong know what he letting himself in for. Men get
break for less than that. Tomorrow morning everybody going
know she been here. The Commissioner in' no help 'cause he
does close his eyes to everything that don't concern the office.
Not like Commissioner Garret. He would've had Armstrong
transferred before you could scratch you tail. If . . . if . . . yes,
if shit had wings it would fly."

Two afternoons later Rohan was preparing to go and visit
Ramjohn. Dada had persuaded him to allow her to stay until
the following Wednesday, since he father was not expecting
her before then. She was sitting in a wicker chair in the
drawing-room, fanning herself slowly with a large, plaited fan.
  "Why don't you come too?" he asked her.
  Her swift reaction to the suggestion contrasted with the
picture of indolence she presented the moment before. She put
on the same dress she had worn the previous day, but changed
her shoes, preferring to wear modest sandals.
  The couple left the house just as the sun was setting and
by the time they arrived it was pitch dark. At their approach a
mangy little dog started barking fiercely at them. So pathetic
was its appearance that neither of them took any notice of
it. In front of the tiny cottage ochro and cassava were growing.
A girl of about nine came to the front door and when she saw
the couple approaching disappeared inside. In a trice Ramjohn
himself appeared and came downstairs to welcome them.
  "Ah, you bring the *Mistress!*" exclaimed Ramjohn in his
confusion. "Good, good. Come up, come up. Asha, get the
chairs ready," he then said, addressing his daughter. "Deen,
the guests arriving. Come right up, come right up. Careful
how you walk. That's one of my offspring. Yes, yes, there're
seven Ramjohns, all girls. We like girls, don't we, Deen? Yes,
we like girls. This is Deen," he said, pointing to his wife, who
was dressed in white and carried an infant on her hip.
  "Asha, the chairs," he said to his daughter.
  Asha brought two boxes from the back of the house and
placed them on the floor.
  "I don't know why 'e invite you," said Deen. "We kian'
give you anything to eat and we kian' even give you a chair to
sit down 'pon."

285

Before Rohan could reassure her she was off behind another baby, who was creeping on the floor.

"Is what wrong to you?" Ramjohn said to the eldest.

Asha took over from her mother who went down into the yard and came back soon afterwards. By this time the other children had made a semi-circle round Rohan and Dada, who were sitting gingerly on the boxes provided for them.

Deen was twenty-six and had had her first child at the age of fifteen. Her father had arranged her marriage with Ramjohn when she was only fouteen. She was glad, as marriage to him provided a means of escape from the rice fields, where she had helped the family since she was able to hold a cutlass. Ramjohn's position in the Commissary Office meant that the days of back-breaking toil in the fierce sun were over. Her husband-to-be, who had always been neatly dressed and whose shoes shone like lacquered wood, walked upright and could talk like a city man. Sometimes, when the official chauffeur was sick, Ramjohn even drove the car for the Commissioner. The first weeks of her marriage were blissful. The tiny cottage was exclusively in her charge and no one could tell her what to do, when to do it, how to cook or what to cook. When she picked up the coconut broom it was to sweep her own house and to swell with pride at the way it looked afterwards. At night when she woke up and felt the warm body of this strange man next to her she desired him for the pleasures he had brought her and for the new life he represented. She worshipped him.

But Deen's illusions were punctured one by one with the passing years. Ramjohn's well-groomed appearance was the result of extreme diligence on his part. The one suit and one pair of shoes that provided the glistening exterior were taken off as soon as he came home from work and exchanged for an old pair of trousers, a garment resembling a shirt and a pair of sandals beyond repair. His salary of fifteen dollars per month could pay for little more than the food and when the landlord raised the rent the couple were forced to reduce their food budget. After the third child Deen complained of being constantly tired, but with every succeeding year she bore Ramjohn another. He could no longer face his family after work and took to visiting the rum shop before going home in the afternoons. Rohan was the first chief clerk who

286

welcomed him into his house, saving him the expense of a couple of daily schnapp glasses of rum; and for this reason Deen was grateful to him.

"The lan'lord see we growing the ochro an' want half what we get," Deen confided in Rohan. "He say is the law."

"There's no law saying you have to give the landlord anything you grow. Can't you move?" asked Rohan.

"I keep telling her," replied Ramjohn, "we can go to my mother house; but she don't want to go."

Deen, meanwhile, had put the infant on her lap where it was adjusting its toothless mouth to the nipple of her breast. Asha came inside with a can of rain water she had drawn from the barrel in the yard. She and her mother constantly quarrelled because the latter felt that the girl did not help enough.

"If I had a boy," said Deen, "'e would help more an' I could sit down and res' me back."

Sometimes, if none of the children were sick, Deen helped Asha with her reading at night, when the others were sleeping and Ramjohn was out. At other times she would fall upon her with a brutality that was out of keeping with her gentle nature. Intimidated by this aggression, Asha would pull her weight for two or three days then lapse into her old ways, confident in her mother's long-suffering nature. Deen dreamed of having a son one day, who would excel at school and go to the college. He would grow up to be a doctor and earn her and her husband the respect of the people round them. Her fantasies had even conjured up a room in the mansion where her son would permit her to live, where she would end her days, shielded by the security of his wealth and generosity.

The child nodded off to sleep against Deen's full breast which was in stark contrast to her thin, almost emaciated body. She got up to lay it down among the bedclothes in the other corner of the room, but hardly was her back turned than the baby began to scream. She took it up again and began rocking it in her arms. The child screamed at the top of its voice and a few moments later was joined by the other baby, whereupon Ramjohn suggested that he and his guests go on the steps, out into the moonlight.

"Yes, go," Deen agreed eagerly with her husband.

Rohan and Dada left the house with relief.

Ramjohn was ashamed. Things had not turned out as he had intended. He had imagined his wife impressing the visitors with her gentleness and concern for his children. Still regarding her as the buxom young woman he married, he was convinced that she was capable of turning the heads of the men in the district.

As there was no letting up in the screaming Ramjohn offered to take them down to the river.

"You don't do any work in the house?" Dada asked him.

"Sometimes."

"Suppose anything happens to her," Dada pursued.

"I don't know, Miss," came the reply. "She's goodness itself. I don't know what I would do without her."

Dada despised him. None of his talk amused her and when, late that night, Rohan said, "You'll like him when you get to know him," she replied: "I'll never get on with him. How can you get on with a man like that?"

"Don't be naïve," Rohan told her. "You know how many hundreds of women there are like her on the Essequibo coast, with husbands far worse than Ramjohn? You think you can change the world by going round feeling sorry for people?"

They quarrelled for the first time, and Dada refused to be reconciled, unable to drive out of her mind the image of Deen clad in white, the colour of death.

Dada put off the day of her departure until it was no longer possible to hide her whereabouts from her father. After writing to him to say that everything was all right she wrote him a further letter, explaining that she was living with Rohan and would marry him as soon as she could. She begged him to trust her and pray for her. When she came home she would explain in detail what had happened.

The weeks Dada was with Rohan seemed to transform him. He threw his first party in October and invited the young people he had got to know at the parties to which he had been invited. In the next few months he became the centre of a group of acquaintances to whom he held open house. They knew that at Rohan's home they would be assured of being offered the best rum and occasionally meet a girl on holiday from Georgetown. At all events there were the Saturday night parties and the excursions across the river to Tiger Island where, if people were to be believed, Rohan and his friends indulged in the wildest orgies.

Mrs Nassen, attempting to carry out her plan, according to which Lucille would be compromised by Rohan, saw her daughter drawn into the vortex of this society of Sodom. Her husband would have stopped the unsavoury business, as he put it, but Mrs Nassen preferred to err on the side of boldness. If Lucille failed to land Rohan, there were the others, Civil Servants, lawyers and other desirable matches. She only had to be careful, that was all. In truth, Mrs Nassen found a vicarious pleasure in her daughter's carryings on. When she herself had been young the place was dead and a girl had no chance to meet a decent young man, unless he was fool enough to walk into her parents' home.

Lucille did not even get near enough to Rohan to find out what her chances were. Dada made no bones about her own claim to him and her obvious superiority to the women who came there, coupled with her position as hostess, made it relatively easy to keep off anyone who might be interested in him. When it was clear to everyone what the relationship between Rohan and Dada was, Mr Nassen considered his wife's plan hopeless, but the good woman refused to believe that "a coolie woman could land him".

Ramjohn was in his element. Besides having access to Rohan's rum he often received the odd sixpence for securing the cheap hire of a boat. Yet whenever he took this extra money home to his wife she would make a derogatory remark.

"That's all you get for wearing out you shoes runnin' up an' down the coast for these people?"

He thought she was unjust. Did he not have to run about for the last chief clerk, who never gave him a cent for it?

Ramjohn would have liked to confide in Deen about the goings on at the cottage, but she greeted these disclosures either with a stony silence or downright hostility. Instead, he had to fall back on the forest ranger, who was often out on his rounds for weeks on end. Ramjohn stored up his observations, to discharge them whenever the ranger spent a day or two in the office. The latter received all this information with little apparent interest, and once, after they had both been drinking and the ranger had been listening to Ramjohn, he grabbed him by the collar. "Listen, Ramjohn, you dog! Don't tell nobody a word o' what you been tellin' me, understand."

Ramjohn's face screwed up in an expression of mixed pleasure and terror. Delighted that the ranger had shown interest, but frightened by the outburst, he smiled like a half-wit, while uttering profuse promises to keep his silence.

The lack of direction in Rohan's life, of which he had complained so bitterly to his sister, seemed of late to have been replaced by a feeling of being anchored to Suddie. The want of intellectual content in his social and working life was no longer important to him. Despite Indrani's apparent indifference to his presence in Suddie and his own agitation at the thought that she might be irretrievably in love with her husband, there was some inextricable link with her.

Rohan was now able to consider Genetha's position. Until then, the thought of her physical relationship with Fingers so disgusted him that any desire to write or even think of her was rejected out of hand.

The fact was that Rohan had desired his sister. And it was in the aftermath of resisting the impulse to touch her in a forbidden way that he was assailed by the intention to do violence to his father. On his death, when every obstacle to their intimacy was removed, he became terrified of the consequences that were bound to follow their exclusive occupation of the house. Perhaps, he reflected, it was this fear that impelled him to seize the opportunity of going to Suddie. The revulsion at Genetha's intimacy with Fingers, an habitué of Tiger Bay, and the well-nigh irresistible call of Indrani, provided the triggering mechanisms to a background cause that, in the beginning, was too terrible to admit. His flight, in his sister's eyes a callous abandonment, represented, for him, an act of the utmost necessity.

But, as time went by, he was plagued by premonitions of an impending disaster centred on Genetha, As a salve to his conscience he told himself that she was capable of looking after herself, what with her job and hed good sense. In any case, he would write and offer to send money if she needed it; and during his fortnightly leave he would go and see her.

16

A Well in the Yard

Dada's explanation to Rohan about the manner in which she had left the Ali house the day she appeared with her suitcase had been inaccurate. When she had returned from the stelling Mr Ali had made it plain that while she was at Suddie she was expected to behave like the other women. But when she said, after visiting Rohan at his house, that she had actually gone to see him he shouted at her.

"My father doesn't shout at me," she told him quietly, while marvelling at her own courage.

Trembling with rage, he declared, "I don't know what you can do at home, but here you got to behave like the other women. You go to see a man at his house! And he live alone! People'll be bandying we name all about the place, jus' 'cause of you. You get this in you head: from now on you go out wit' the women and not any other time, you understand?"

"I'm not staying," she answered.

"You do what you bleddy well like," replied Mr Ali, "but while you here. . . ."

"I'm leaving now."

"Now?" he asked, taken aback. "There's no boat goin' before tomorrow."

At that point Mrs Ali walked into the room. "If she goin' don' stop she!" she said sharply.

"Where you going?" Mr Ali asked anxiously.

"I've got a lot of friends in Suddie."

Mr Ali was not sure what he ought to do. He felt responsible for her, but was too proud to ask her to stay. Short of keeping her by force he felt powerless.

"Do what you like," he enjoined, turning on his heels and leaving Dada and Mrs Ali facing each other.

"Sidique was a fool," said Mrs Ali. "There was a hundred girls on the Essequibo coast who would've give anything to marry a boy like him. But he had to go to Vreed-en-Hoop!" she said contemptuously.

If she thought that Dada would not have retaliated she would have spat at her, but she, in turn, left the room. Dada at once began getting her things together, while reflecting that her insolence had achieved the very purpose she had desired.

She said goodbye to Indrani before she left and told her that she was going to stay with Rohan for the night. In fact, she had not intended to let her sister know, but the remark slipped out of its own accord. Indrani said nothing, neither did she betray the way she felt about Dada's decision by her expression.

The idea that she would remain in Rohan's house had come all of a sudden, while she was being harangued by Mr Ali. She did not really believe that Rohan would really take her in, for, convinced that he was still in love with Indrani, she reckoned that he would not risk offending her. Furthermore, Rohan still considered her a girl and would hesitate to do what would cause her father much distress.

Bah! she thought. She had been in love with him since her schooldays and she had suffered from his indifference and his attachment to Indrani.

It was not long before the Alis heard that Dada was staying with Rohan. When it was evident that she was not going home Mr Ali wrote Mr Mohammed a letter, asking him to send for her, but received no reply. Interpreting Mohammed's silence as a snub he approached the District Commissioner, who told him curtly that he always made it a point of minding his own business and advised Mr Ali to mind his as well.

The latter was more than ever determined to get Dada home. His family would look like fools if his daughter-in-law's sister were known to be living with a man under his own nose. It was probably common knowledge already.

Mr Ali announced to his family that he was going to see Rohan. He got Jai to drive him to the cottage, where Rohan himself opened the door.

"I'm Mr Ali."

"Ah?"

Mr Ali smiled and asked if he could come in and sit down.

"Sure," replied Rohan, pointing to an easy chair in a corner of the gallery.

"You got a nice place here," said Mr Ali, trying to overcome the embarrassment this young man caused him to feel.

"Yes, it's not bad," replied Rohan.

"Commissioner's office, eh?" pursued Mr Ali.

Rohan said nothing.

Mr Ali was a small man, unlike his son. Neatly but unostentatiously dressed, he gave the impression of being the businessman he was. If his son appeared likeable but turned out — at least in Rohan's eyes — to be unpleasant, Mr Ali on the other hand projected a warm, fetching personality as the conversation progressed. People who met him found it difficult to credit his reputation for ruthlessness.

Rohan knew immediately why Mr Ali had come and, though he concealed his resentment under a show of courtesy, was prepared to allow him little leeway in the contest he anticipated. Dada's account of how she was shown the door, the experience with Sidique at Vreed-en-Hoop, and Mr Mohammed's story of Indrani's marriage, had all contributed to the unfavourable picture he had built up in his mind of the Ali family.

Rohan and Dada had just finished their evening meal, and she still lingered at table, while the housekeeper cleared away the plates, cutlery and glasses. Mr Ali, evidently embarrassed by Dada's presence, kept looking over at the table, which stood in the dining area, about twenty feet away, towards the back of the house.

"You don't know me, Mr Armstrong," said Mr Ali. "It's a pleasure to come visiting somebody like you. On the Essequibo coast you can count the people like you 'pon the hands; and they wouldn't hob-nob with me, I can tell you. I understand, mind you. Like to like! We Mohammedans don't go round hob-nobbing weself. Anyway, anyway. . . ."

"Can I help you in some way, Mr Ali?" enquired Rohan.

"Oh, yes, yes, Mr Armstrong. As I was saying. I'm a Mohammedan and it's a little matter — not a little matter at all, but a matter. . . . First I mus' say sorry for the incident in Vreed-en-Hoop wit' Sidique."

Rohan dismissed his apology with a smile.

"Oh, it was a misunderstanding. I had no right to be there."

"You say so you-self? You see, Mr Armstrong, I din' misjudge you. My son say you unreasonable, but I tell him you not educated for nothing. In fact that's why I come, 'cause I know you're a reasonable man. Sidique's character is not exactly what it should be. Of course he was spoiled bad by his mother. That boy was so spoiled! And then is his own character, too. Come to think of it, is not that is his character, or that he spoiled. I think it's the times. Oh, is no joke, Mr Armstrong. The times isn't a joke at all. . . . But if you look at the thing close you'll see it's not his mother or his character or the times. It's the fourth element. A terrible thing, the fourth element, you know. It does work like yeast on the molasses, slow, slow, slow, and before you realise what happening, bam! the thing change before you eyes. But le' me ask you something. You really think they in' got another element *lurking* in the background, watching and saying, 'Hee, hee, hee, hee!' Mr Armstrong, we're like grass in the fields. We lie down and stan' up and don't know why. . . ."

"Mr Ali—" Rohan interrupted him.

"I forgetting myself, Mr Armstong. You such a interesting man an'. . . . You got to admit I not a fool, though. You got to admit that there's something in what I say."

"You're no fool, Mr Ali. Decidedly not. What I want to know is why you come to see me?."

Mr Ali smiled in an embarrassing way and looked rapidly at Dada.

"You know," he began again, "there was a man who dead from embarrassment? When I tell people that, they laugh. But I understan' it. At this very moment I feel so embarrassed about telling you what I come to tell you I feel like rushing outside and jumping down the well in your yard."

"There's no need," said Rohan encouragingly, by now close to falling under Mr Ali's spell.

"A umbrella!" exclaimed Mr Ali, catching sight of a parasol belonging to Dada. "You know in nearly every house on the Essequibo coast the umbrella is the preciousest possession. You steal a man umbrella an' you drive him crazy. This little thing," and here he fondled the fabric of the parasol, "belong to somebody who could go out an' buy one tomorrow if she los' it. Life, eh? People don't appreciate what they got. . . . No, no, I comin' to the point, Mr Armstrong," Mr Ali hastened to say these last words. "I *so* embarrassed!" he exclaimed, hanging his head. "I dying of embarrassment!"

And here he stole another glance at Dada, who had got up and was apparently preparing to leave the table. When, finally, she went inside, Mr Ali sprang to life.

"See! See! I can't talk in front of a girl. With Mohammedans a girl is a girl. Now we're alone, two men, as it should be."

He cleared his throat. "Mr Armstrong, I'm so pained to talk about this matter, this thing ... this element. ..."

"Come to the point," Rohan said, more sharply than before.

"Dada is a girl. I think she's seventeen. I can't understand why her father allow her to stay in your house. I know, Mr Armstrong, you're the sort of man who wouldn't take advantage of a girl. I *know* that. But a fact is a fact. On the Essequibo coast everybody know everybody. And you know what?"

Mr Ali bent over and whispered into Rohan's ear.

"The Mohammedans watching you like a chicken hawk."

He waited for the effect of the remark to sink in, but Rohan continued staring at him without flinching.

Put out by his lack of success Mr Ali seemed at a loss for words.

"I can't see you worrying about what Mohammedans think," he said at last. "But I know you're a intelligent man an' that you not going ignore somet'ing as *serious* as this. You see, you can't bother with Mr Mohammed. He's only a Mohammedan in name. Look at the name he give his daughter! 'Indrani'. That's a Hindu name. Wha' kind of Mohammedan would give his daughter a Hindu name?"

"So, what you expect me to do, Mr Ali?" asked Rohan.

"You want to kill me, Mr Armstrong? The embarrassment gettin' too much for me."

"Damn it!" exclaimed Rohan, losing his temper. "What you want me to do?"

"To send Dada away," Mr Ali answered at once, as if he was expecting the outburst. "Away to Vreed-en-Hoop. She's a girl and you don't want her to stay. I *know* so. You're a intelligent man. And you're a man o' principle, else you wouldn't be working in the Civil Service. The District Commissioner think his officers're men of principle. I'm a personal frien' of the Commissioner and he tell me hisself the onliest time he ever

295

had a man working for him who din' have principles was . . . anyway, that's beside the point. You *know* what I driving at, Mr Armstrong."

Rohan got up. "You told me what you came to tell me, Mr Ali. So, goodbye."

Ali frowned threateningly and pursed his lips. After searching for his words he said, "You in't say nothing yet, Mr Armstrong."

"You came to talk. I didn't invite you. You said it was a social visit, but it didn't stop you from threatening me."

"Threaten?" Mr Ali asked, getting up slowly from his chair and standing before Rohan. "I don't threaten people, Mr Armstrong. You offend our customs in full view of everybody; you harbour a minor in your house although she's got a family; an' when I come in a friendly way an' want to discuss it you accuse me of threatening you? That's not the talk of a intelligent man, Mr Armstrong. You, who go flitting from one house to the other—"

"All right," Rohan broke in, "you said what you wanted to say and I have nothing to say to you." He detected in Ali's silence a more menacing threat than the veiled hints contained.

Suddenly Mr Ali thrust out his hand and smiled broadly. "Goodbye, Mr Armstrong. After all it *was* a social visit. Don't let's quarrel when we hardly know one another."

He made for the door, but, his hand already on the knob, turned round and said, "I did forget, Mr Armstrong. How I could forget like that?" He struck his forehead with the palm of his hand and looked up at Rohan with a fetching smile.

"My son's in a state. He's jealous of you 'cause you did know he wife. Now he think you come to Suddie to follow her. He's suffering. That's between you and me. Don't take no notice of that. But when he did know that Dada staying here he won't eat, he won't sleep. He in' brainy, but he's a man, after all. Now I appealing to you as a man with a lot of sympathy. The fact that you listen to me talk all this nonsense *prove* you's a man with a lot of sympathy. I bet you been good to your mother!"

Rohan frowned.

"I begging you, do it for Sidique. Send Dada away. You not mindful of our customs, but do it for him."

Rohan, despite Mr Ali's transparent tactics, was moved by his appeal.

"Mr Ali, Dada's father knows she's here. She wrote him."

"But you think he want her to stay here?" Ali asked, seeing the weakness in Rohan's protestation.

Rohan saw that the only way he could be honest was to confess his relationship with Dada, and this he was not prepared to do.

"I understand your standpoint," he declared, "but I can't do anything to help."

Meanwhile Mr Ali had taken something out of his pocket and was holding it out. "Look inside, Mr Armstrong," he urged. "Look inside."

Rohan took out a wad of notes from the envelope and looked at Mr Ali with such an expression of contempt that the latter was obliged to lower his gaze.

"There's one thousand dollars there, Mr Armstrong. That's not chickenfeed."

Handing the envelope back to him, Rohan observed, "At least I know you're determined to have your own way."

Mr Ali, his hand on the knob once more, kept shaking his head. "To think that two grown men can't come to a under-standing about a woman! A girl. . . . At least you can't say I din' warn you, eh? A intelligent man like you must know you not going win. Even your own people not going stand by you in the end, mark my word. Think it over. Think of Indrani."

He left the house and Rohan heard his steps disappear at the foot of the stairs. Suddenly he had an idea. He rushed out of the door and down the path, where he caught Mr Ali, who was halfway to the bridge.

"About Indrani, Mr Ali. I've got. . . . If you touch a hair of her head I'll—"

"You threatening me?" asked the older man.

"Yes," replied Rohan bluntly.

He watched Ali's car drive off and thought anxiously of Indrani. Perhaps it would have been better to agree to send Dada away.

When he returned to the house Dada asked, "What d'you say to him?"

"Leave me alone!" he retorted, and went into his room, closing the door violently behind him.

Dada remained standing where she was. She had no secrets from him. What could Mr Ali have said to put Rohan in this frame of mind? She could never bear it when he sulked and would have preferred him to hit her, so long as he did not shut himself away. She sat down, but immediately got up again, and went back to his room when she hesitated at the door. Unable to contain her agitation she changed her shoes and went out for a walk.

On the road she met Asha, who was carrying an empty basket.

"Where're you going?" Dada asked her.

"I going to Mr Armstrong to get some water from the well," Asha drawled. "The barrel run out."

Dada accompanied her and lowered the bucket into the dark, narrow-holed well for her. Asha was afraid of the spiders, which scurried down the hole when the cast-iron lid was taken off. Dada then went with her down the road along which the black sage rustled in the warm breeze.

"Is you married?" Asha asked, without looking up.

"Why d'you ask?"

"'Cause Ma and Pa was talking 'bout you."

"What'd they say?"

"I kian' remember," replied Asha.

"You must come over to the house when you've got time. Ask Ma."

"I don't got nice clothes to wear," said Asha.

"Doesn't matter. Do you want to come?"

"Yes. But I don't know if Ma gwine let me."

"Ask her and see what she says," Dada suggested.

"A'right."

Dada stood at the roadside watching Asha walk up to her house, and for a moment thought of following her; but she knew that her parents would have been put out. Smoke was coming from the chimneys of many of the houses. When Dada returned she found Rohan talking to the housekeeper.

"Where've you been?" he asked Dada. She went and put her hand round his waist, then took his right hand and kissed it.

"Where've you been?"

"I just went out to help Asha with the water. I invited her round if her mother'll let her."

The housekeeper, who had just brought in a pot full of hot chocolate, sucked her teeth. "If you don't look out you gwine have the lot of them crawling round the place."

"Can't you get any ice?" Rohan asked the old woman.

"What? At this time of day? You should get the government to give you a Frigidaire."

In truth, hardly a breath of air seemed to be stirring. From the house the river was like a sheet of glass and the trees appeared limp. After their light meal Rohan and Dada went out on the veranda, where they sat in the dark. Rohan wondered at her poise and maturity. Placed before the choice of having her with him or living alone with the assurance that Indrani would not be persecuted in the Ali's house, he had not consciously decided one way or the other. He could not go back to "flitting from one house to the other", as Mr Ali put it, and he could not give up Dada. Yet he knew that he loved Indrani more than ever, and each time that her name was pronounced by Mr Ali he resented it as an impertinence. *Indrani, Indra, beloved one. Once the scent of sweet-broom, the fluttering of prayer-flags, the lettering on the clock face, the silence across a littered table, the swell of flood-tide, the neon lights in the houses of Vreed-en-Hoop, the circling fans, like chained birds, the long dreams we travelled together, all these things united you to me. The perfect days are gone forever, but my heart is full of memories. To touch you would have been profane; but I loved you as I will never love again, and look on your sister for what might have been.*

He bent down and kissed Dada and she wondered why.

When the housekeeper came out and joined them she placed her chair close to Dada, who urged her to speak of her life on the sugar estates. She recounted her youth and childhood, telling them that she was the illegitimate daughter of an overseer and was conceived in the bushes at Land of Canaan. She told them of a teacher at the secondary school she attended, whose zeal in imparting information to his girl pupils attracted the attention of their mothers. She spoke of her father's housekeeper who loved her with a special affection and made

299

her work from morning to sundown without respite. Of her painless monthly periods, all because the self-same housekeeper had taken care to scrub her from head to foot when she became a woman and make her suck a teaspoonful of salt until it dissolved on her tongue. And of the thirteen-year-old twin sisters who arrived and left school, arms round each other's waist. When one died of blackwater fever the other pined away and floated off into the void on a pitch-black night. She explained why she got up at five o'clock every morning: on her father's estate everyone was awakened by the watchman at five, and the habit had never left her, for she could still hear the five resounding thuds he made on the door with his wamara stick. She sighed when she told how her father tried to despatch her to America on a ship that waited for the flood-tide in order to get across the bar. But inexplicably, the tide never came and she lived on the becalmed boat, where her father came daily to bid her farewell. People believed the ocean was draining away to the other side of the world, and her father was obliged to come to terms with the fact that the presence of his illegitimate daughter was decreed by God. Finally, they went to live in McKenzie on the old man's retirement and there he died from the bauxite dust that settled on the trees and turned them a luminous grey.

After recounting her life Rohan's housekeeper began humming softly, as though she were alone in the world. A breeze had sprung up and the innumerable leaves of the tamarind tree shivered, making the sound of foam expiring slowly on wet sand. And those were the only voices of the night.

17

Pleasures Past

The longer Dada stayed with Rohan the less frequently Ramjohn was invited to his house. For weeks they had not had a game of draughts and their drinking bouts had stopped altogether. He knew that Dada could not stand the sight of him and he kept out of her way as much as possible; but he felt betrayed by Rohan who, he had told his wife, was a real friend.

"They're all the same," he once told her when, stripped to the waist after a day's work, he sat looking through the door into his yard.

"You don't know nothing," she replied. "You don't know nothing."

She had just recovered from an attack of malaria and looked even more emaciated than ever.

"You got you pain again?" he enquired.

"Don't bother 'bout my pain," she answered curtly.

Reflecting that she had become sour and was incapable of engaging in any pleasant conversation, he got up to go and sit under the house, when he noticed that she was shivering.

"Is the ague again?" he enquired, but she did not reply. "I tell you not to get out o' bed so quick, but you wouldn't hear."

He helped his wife to the corner of the room where she lay down on the bedclothes on the floor.

"You feel bad?" he asked and was frightened that she did not answer him. He made a resolution to come home early every afternoon to help her with her work.

The children had been put to bed without any food and the peas she was preparing were meant for Ramjohn.

For days Deen lay on the bedclothes in the corner, her body racked with malaria. Ramjohn wanted to ask Rohan for money to pay the doctor to come and see her, but he was so bitter about the way Rohan had let him down that he could not bear to ask him a favour. At the office he avoided Rohan's eyes and spoke to him in as formal a manner as he dared.

"All that money they spend on rum alone could feed my family for weeks," Ramjohn thought, as he sat in the dark one night, listening to the breathing of the eight members of his family. "What can all these District Commissioners and chief clerks do that I can't do? This man come from miles away to vex me and fob me off with tips."

He sat on the low stool for the greater part of the night, grubbing in the deepest recesses of his mind in search of reasons for his hatred of Rohan, remembering that from early on his wife had warned him about getting too friendly with him.

"He in' no different from the others," she used to say. And now she was not even prepared to listen to his complaints about the chief clerk.

"You playing great," she once told him. "You got shiny boots, but they don't give you the money to go with it. You in' no better than the people round here who work in the rice fields."

She had said some harsh things to him, and yet he loved her so. Still, Ramjohn was worried at the increasing frequency with which Deen beat Asha. Nothing would induce her to touch any of the others, nor would she permit her husband to do so; but her application to the task of punishing Asha bordered on frenzy. What was more, there was never, afterwards, any sign of remorse on her part. Usually, he went downstairs to avoid having to witness these scenes, but one day, unable to bear his daughter's shrieking, he hurried upstairs and dragged the belt from his wife's hand.

"Go on!" Deen shrieked. "Beat me instead o' she! Go on!" She held his arm and tried to make him strike her with the belt. Meanwhile the children were screaming round them.

"Beat me, I tell you. Beat me!" Deen kept shrieking.

She pulled the belt from Ramjohn's hand and began belabouring him. Asha seized her mother's skirt in an effort to distract her attention, while Ramjohn attempted to catch her arm and defend himself at the same time. Suddenly Deen dropped her arm.

"Is what allyou trying to do to me?" she asked weakly, while her husband took the belt from her. "You know nothing," she said, and sank wearily to the floor, "nothing. You never even see one o' your children born; and whenever I in labour you go under the house with a bottle of rum and cry like a child. If I go an' dead you'd buy a bottle o' rum an' do the same thing. An' the nex' day you'd make Asha do all the work an' say how good she is."

She bent double, her head almost touching the floor and her teeth chattering.

"I don't know what you all want with me. You all trample me from morning to night and then *you* say I don't sing no more. . . . I feel so cold. . . ."

Ramjohn took up some bedclothes from the corner, covered his wife with them and made her lie down.

The next morning she remained on the floor only sitting up to drink some soup. The malaria had come back, as bad as ever.

One afternoon two policemen came to see Ramjohn at the office. He was out, making enquiries about a launch, the owner of which had applied for a licence. Mrs Ramjohn's body had been found in the well behind Rohan's house. Rohan left the office in charge of the clerk and accompanied the police home. They believed that Deen had thrown herself down the well, since her bucket was found some distance from it.

When Rohan and the police arrived at the house they found Ramjohn weeping. On his way back to the office someone had called out to him that his wife was drowned and that her body was at Mr Armstrong's house. He was wringing his hands and staring at the thin body lying on a couple of greenheart planks. The wet hair made her head seem even smaller and her painfully meagre thighs showed through the soaking dress.

Rohan put his hand on Ramjohn's shoulder and whispered to him, "The police want to ask you some questions. Come on, stand up and be brave."

Ramjohn got up and Rohan went over to Dada, who was standing at the foot of the stairs.

"Get him a shot of rum," he told her.

She went upstairs then came back with a glass and a big bottle of rum.

"How you so sure she kill herself, eh?" asked Ramjohn. "How you know somebody didn't push her in?"

"Pull yourself together, Ramjohn," the constable told him. "It was in broad daylight and nobody hear any shouting."

"Why, Deen? Why? Why you do this thing?" he addressed his dead wife.

The older of the two policemen put his pocket book away and mopped his brow under the peak of his cap.

"You better think of the burial. In this heat the body don't take long to stink, y'know," said the constable.

Ramjohn watched the two policemen walk down the path, then sat down on the earth next to Deen and began wringing his hands once more. He took the glass Dada held out to him automatically and emptied it in one gulp, then started talking to Deen.

"What I going do without you, Deen? You kian' leave me all alone like this. I going to kill myself if you lie there all the time like that. O me God!" he began to wail.

Rohan sent home the crowd that had gathered gradually. One man who was reluctant to go away offered to fetch Egbert, the coffin-maker, who was probably in the field looking after his vegetables. He ran off on his errand when Rohan agreed.

"We've got to get her home, Ramjohn," Rohan said. "The police doctor'll be coming soon."

Rohan undertook to go down to the Public Works to see if he could get hold of a van, while Ramjohn remained with Deen and Dada went upstairs to discuss the whole affair with the housekeeper.

"Nobody goin' use water from that well no more," she told Dada. "They might as well block it up for good."

And Dada was treated to tales of various unusual and mysterious deaths in and around Suddie since the old woman came to live there.

Rohan returned a couple of hours later with a lorry, on to which he and the driver managed to lift the dead woman. They helped Ramjohn into the back and helped him down again on arriving at his house where Asha was sitting at the top of the stairs, red-eyed and bewildered. When she saw her mother's corpse she got up slowly, as if she were in a trance.

"Ma!" she suddenly screamed out, and rushed forward to the men. Rohan held her back.

"Take these in for me, like a good girl," Rohan said giving

304

her the bottle of rum and her father's hat. She obeyed, preceding the men up the stairs.

It was not until night that the doctor came. He had no difficulty in establishing that death had been caused by drowning after he had been informed that Deen had fallen down the well.

"Bad business," he muttered, as he wrote out the death certificate. Rohan paid him and he drove away in his limousine.

It seemed that there was not going to be an inquest, for the police had said nothing; but Rohan did not want to worry Ramjohn unnecessarily as to the wisdom of arranging for a funeral the next day.

Asha, when Rohan gave her a note for Dada, looked at the ground and shook her head, unwilling to leave her father. So Rohan went home and got Mrs Helega the housekeeper to pack a basket of provisions and take them to Ramjohn's house. When he himself returned there he found Ramjohn's brother and a handful of relations standing about. Egbert the coffin-maker had apparently come and gone away for wood to make the coffin. A woman was sitting in a corner all alone, her head in her hand, and Rohan reflected that it might be Asha's ajee, Ramjohn's mother. The children were remarkably quiet, and Asha, half lying on the mattress with the baby, was watching a relation unpack provisions.

The kerosene lamp, smoking faintly, gave off a sickly odour. Rohan knew none of the new arrivals and felt like a stranger intruding into a family circle at meal-time. He wanted to console Ramjohn, but thought it out of place to do so. Slipping out by the back way he cut across the next yard and went down to the river, where he turned left and walked along the beach until he came to his own back yard. Someone had left a boat anchored a few feet out on the river, now the colour of cinnamon in the evening half-light, and the craft was rolling gently on the swell.

The death of Ramjohn's wife affected Rohan greatly, for he had never heard her complain; yet she seemed to be crying out incessantly for help.

"What the hell's it got to do with me?" he said angrily, taking a decisive step towards the house.

Rohan seemed to live only for the weekend carousals at his home. He no longer went out, but made up for it by the near frenzy of his way of life. When Mrs Helega urged Dada to persuade him not to poison himself, as she termed it, Dada laughed at her.

"Why not?"

"Look at me an' tell me you in't worried," the old woman challenged her.

For a moment Dada was silent. "If I can't have him nobody else will, I'll tell you that," she said defiantly.

"What he need is a family," the old woman said, shaking her head.

Dada laughed without humour. "I'm pregnant."

"You in't tell him?"

"No."

"Why not?"

"'Cause I'm frightened," Dada said for an answer.

"Tell 'im, miss," the housekeeper exhorted her. "Deep down I t'ink is what he want. When he hear, he goin' stop all these people comin' in and out of the house lookin' for free rum. An' let me tell you one t'ing. If he don't talk about marriage, don't say not'ing, 'cause the chile gwine bind him to you more than a thousand rings."

That night Dada announced to Rohan that she was pregnant.

"A child?" he asked involuntarily. "You're getting a child? You sure?"

She nodded.

"You want it?" he asked.

"Why? What about you?"

"It's up to you," Rohan replied. "If you want it we'll have it. I've got to have children some time."

"It's you I want, Boyie. I want the baby because it's a part of you."

"When we first met you said you'll go whenever I wanted you to. D'you still feel so now?" Rohan asked.

"You're trying to hurt me."

"Do you still feel the same?" he persisted.

"You want to send me away."

He did not answer for a while.

"No, no. Whatever I do I'll be dissatisfied," Rohan remarked.

"If I ask you a question will you answer me?" Dada asked him.

"What?"

"Promise you'll answer."

"Yes," he said impatiently.

"Do you love me?"

"Yes," he said readily.

"Then why don't you ever say it? I love you and I've told you so a hundred times, but if I try to stroke your head you turn away."

They talked on late into the night and when Dada finally dropped off, Rohan stayed awake thinking. He felt more like an animal in a cage than at any other time in his life. The fear that Dada might become pregnant had always been at the back of his mind, but because it had not yet happened he somehow believed that it would not happen. He had suggested to her a way out, but she chose to ignore it. Why should she want a child? *"A part of you,"* she had said.

"She even wants my soul," he said, half aloud. "And all I want is her body." With no complications, he thought.

"Bleddy well yes," he said aloud again, and watched her stir in her sleep. "Probably nine out of ten children in the country are a result of chance. I don't want any complications."

No doubt every time she slept with him she hoped he would fertilise her. Very well, he thought, and turned towards the sleeping form of Dada: "It's already done, and now you take the consequences." His knee touched her soft, warm form and he remembered the pleasures past and to come that were locked up in her smooth flesh. In the beginning they had slept in separate rooms, but, without either of them knowing when, they began to sleep as man and wife, in one bed. He knew that sending her away was out of the question, for he would never stop wanting her, even when she had a swollen belly and a stranger waxing in it. He felt like a man who had built his own prison and locked himself in it.

307

18

A Disturbing Suggestion

The next day Mr Ali summoned his wife, Jai and Sidique to the dining-room and ordered one of the servants not to let anyone in. For the first minute or so he did nothing else but rant and rave about Rohan's impertinence.

"All right, all right," his wife interrupted him. "We got to t'ink of a way to get rid of this whore. The whole Essequibo Coast talking 'bout she and this whoever-he-is, I sure."

"Why not let Indrani go and talk to him?" Jai suggested, trying to look earnest.

In fact he was earnest, if somewhat easygoing; but the permanent smile that played over his face and his nonchalant attitude gave others the impression that he was never serious. His suggestion that Indrani should go and see Rohan was followed by a menacing hush. Sidique did not dare speak before his father.

"You gone out of your mind?" Mr Ali asked, breaking the silence.

"You making fun o' me," said Sidique.

"There's only one person he'd listen to," continued Jai, "and that's Indrani."

"You think I'd allow my wife to go in that . . . house? Why not send you own?" asked Sidique.

"Well, nobody's after her," answered Jai.

Sidique jumped up.

"Stop it!" ordered Mr Ali, waving his fist.

"Why you can't talk sense?" Mrs Ali put in, exasperated by Jai's suggestion.

"He's talking a lot of sense," Mr Ali answered for Jai.

"She's my wife," said Sidique, "and she in' going nowhere."

"He's talking a lot of sense," repeated Mr Ali, "when you come to think of it; but we can't do it."

Then turning to Sidique he said, "You just remember she got a home in Vreed-en-Hoop to go to and stop piassing. You can start by treating she better. She's no fool, you know."

"She's got everyt'ing she need in this house," Mrs Ali took him up. "She don't move a finger, and she and Abdul got everyt'ing she want."

Mr Ali looked up in exasperation.

"Let we keep to the business. Well, what you got to say, woman?"

His wife shrugged her shoulders. "Why not go and see she father?" she suggested half-heartedly.

"I write already, you know that," Mr Ali replied. If only Sidique had Jai's brains, he thought.

After Rohan's last party, which became the talk of the coast, the Alis all agreed that they could no longer delay taking action. And who knew what they might do next?

The more Mr Ali thought of Jai's suggestion the more obvious it became that it was good sense. The difficulty was getting Sidique to consider it without becoming hysterical. After all, he had the most to gain from Dada's departure, especially as Armstrong was likely to follow her.

When he and Sidique were on their own, Ali offered his son the same envelope with money he had offered Rohan.

"What you take me for? I love my wife," declared Sidique.

"Then why you desert her after you married?"

"Well, I been back for her, didn't I?"

"You young people soft like soursops," said his father. "We had blood in we veins when I was young. You goin' just sit down and watch this Armstrong chap ruin your life? I know you! Six months from now you goin' come to me and say you should've take my advice. But it's goin' to be too late! 'Cause the longer Dada stay with him the harder it'll be to prise them apart."

When Sidique said nothing he knew that his son was wavering.

"And I know women," the older man pursued. "You notice that since this Armstrong been in Essequibo Indrani's changed. She more . . . more difficult . . . more defiant."

"But," replied Sidique, a note of alarm in his voice, "she din' know he was in the Essequibo till Dada meet him 'pon the stelling."

"How you know? In truth how you know she in't meet him in secret? Eh?" His face was thrust forward, as near to his

309

son's as possible, as if to emphasise his last words, which had been whispered.

There were beads of sweat on Sidique's brow. On the veranda he could see the parakeet's cage dancing in the wind. "Is impossible," he whispered back at his father.

"Impossible?" asked Mr Ali, pressing home his advantage. "Boy, when you aunt Farah was sixteen she become pregnant under my mother nose, when she did never go out by sheself. The only place she ever go was to the latrine in the yard to empty the po. One night, in the three or four minutes it take to empty the po and come back upstairs she pull up her frock behind a tree and that was it! She belly start for swell and later she say she din' even know what the boy was doing!"

Mr Ali realised he was overplaying his part. He only wanted to arouse his son's jealousy sufficiently to make him act.

"Mind you," he added, "Indrani not that sort of woman. If anybody faithful, is she."

"You think so?" Sidique asked eagerly.

"I know so! But you got to be realistic."

"Suppose we get rid of Dada, Armstrong'll still remain here," objected Sidique.

"Ah, ah-ah! That's where you're wrong. Now from what I hear he's run after Dada like a dog in heat. If she leave the Essequibo it won't be long before Armstrong follow after her."

"Who say so?" asked Sidique.

"Why not get about and listen to people talk? His house-keeper say he's always trotting after her."

"But I in't sure that he'll do what Indrani ask him," said Sidique.

"What you mean is you frightened to send she there. You don't trust she?"

"Course I trust she. Is you who don't trust she," replied Sidique.

"Well, why not do it?" pressed Mr Ali.

"Give me till tomorrow," Sidique said eventually.

"And what I goin' get if I send she?" he asked, after a long pause.

His father reflected for a while and then said, "A quarter share in the Leguan rice mill."

Sidique stared at him disbelievingly.

After this conversation Sidique told his wife that he wanted to talk with her in private and they went to their bedroom. He intended to ask her if she had ever seen Armstrong. Not wishing to vex her lest she refuse to do as the family wanted, he resolved to be calm.

"Something's wrong?" she asked him when he had closed the door behind them.

Her clearly ennunciated words offended him. "What you always reading books for? Whenever I want to talk you got a book in you hand."

"Your mother doesn't want me to do any work in the house. I've got to do something."

Whenever he wanted to ask her if she had ever met Rohan since his arrival in Suddie his pride would not permit him.

"Is nothing," he said abruptly, and opened the door.

"What you wanted me for?" she asked. "Tell me."

"Is nothing," he said angrily. "Get back to you books."

He strode out of the room with thunder on his brow and as he passed the bird cage on the veranda he was seized with an almost irresistible impulse to grab the parakeet and strangle it. He felt like cursing and lashing out violently at anyone within striking distance.

When he was not with her he knew exactly what he would say, but no sooner had the time come than he either allowed himself to get angry or completely forgot what he intended saying. He wanted nothing more passionately than to revive the relationship they had enjoyed in the beginning, and indeed even after he had sent her away. Then, she was compliant and warm. Now, she still did as he said, but there was lacking in her attitude that willingness to please which used to mark her behaviour towards him. The more he tried to accommodate her the less she responded until, anxious and ashamed, he lost his temper and abused her. She, in turn, saw his outbursts as proof of his contempt for her. If only he were himself they might make a go of it. But one day he was obsequious, showering gifts on her, and the next he would accuse her of slighting him or of disloyalty. The only thing that seemed to unite them was their love for their son. With him Sidique was a boy again, the greatest of bird-catchers, the most feared

311

of paper-boat captains, crab-catcher extraordinary, whose Bunduri crab traps were models of craftsmanship. The boy adored his parents. If his father was a god who could bring about any result he desired, his mother was always at hand when he woke up at night; whose breath on his face was warm and familiar. When he wanted to suck his finger he had to go under the bed to hide from his father, but in his mother's presence he could suck to his heart's content.

Sidique felt that the only chance of rehabilitating his marriage lay in getting rid of Rohan. But though he could see no alternative to Jai's plan, he also believed that it was risky to send Indrani to Rohan's home alone.

"Why can't she go with Ma?" he thought. But immediately the absurdity of this course was clear to him. Armstrong could hardly be expected to accede to her request if it were put in his mother's presence.

But why not? he pursued his train of thought, "If he'll do it for Indrani it don't matter who's with her."

His father dismissed this suggestion contemptuously. How could Indrani play on Armstrong's sweetness for her if Ma was with them? When Sidique asked what Indrani was expected to do his father lost his temper and told him that he was going to wash his hands of the whole business if he were not allowed to do things his own way.

"All right, all right. But I wonder why everybody so interested in helping me," rejoined Sidique.

"Is not you," his father replied, "is us. You want to see our women end up smoking and going out to work? Is not you!"

"Just tell me exactly what she got to do."

Mr Ali put his arm round his son's shoulders reassuringly. Already he was planning to hint very broadly to Indrani that she must use all her charm on Rohan. "God!" he thought. "Sidique always give me trouble, ever since a lil boy, If he'd only stay out of this business and let me handle it!"

Although he did his best to persuade Sidique to broach the plan to his wife, his son objected. Mr Ali did not press the matter, but now that he was faced with the task of doing the job himself he hesitated. The girl gave herself airs and whenever he spoke to her he always had the feeling that she

was not taking him seriously. How could he make such a proposition to her? What if she refused point blank?

"We'll see about that," he reflected.

Mr Ali went to the back yard where Indrani was hanging
out some garments she had been washing.

"Indrani? You have a minute?" he asked.

"Yes," she mumbled, a clothes-pin between her teeth, as
she put the first pin on a corner of a sari she was hanging up
with some difficulty.

"I don't know how you do it with my grandson," said Mr
Ali ingratiatingly. "The things that boy know! He'll be able
to turn cents into dollars, I can tell you."

"I been calling him," Indrani said, "you didn't see him?"

Her father-in-law shook his head. He then smiled at her
and said, "You know your sister still in Suddie with that
Armstrong chap?"

"Sidique told me."

"People talking and giving you a bad name. Sidique's
mother and me was discussing it and it hurt us to know that
people talking 'bout you like that."

"I know they're talking," said Indrani, annoyed at his
hypocrisy.

"You in't the sort of person to. . . . Anyway I want you to
do something for me. Is no use trying to talk to Dada. I think
she doin' it to spite the family. You know Mr Armstrong, so
we . . . I think that if a upstanding person like youself go and
ask him to send Dada home he might . . . well, you never
know."

"No, I can't do that," Indrani replied, wiping her hand on
the side of the dress she was wearing.

"You didn't even let me finish," he said. In fact he had
finished what he had been saying, but her brusque dismissal of
the suggestion forced him to pretend that he had not.

"You won't go alone," Mr Ali continued. "Jai can drive
you there."

"I'm not going," replied Indrani, trying to master her
irritation. "I can't even go for a walk with Sis without you
giving me a nasty look, and now you want me to go on my
own to this man's house." Sis was the name of Jai's wife.

"But you talking as if he's a stranger," remarked Mr Ali.

"For me he is."

"And I was the one," said Mr Ali, "who tell Ma we can rely on you."

"I'm sorry. You've got to tell Ma I won't do it," she said firmly.

"Indrani, do this for me, ne?" he pleaded. "I know what I'm really like. You don't got to tell me. Sometimes I glance at meself in the looking-glass and start to think. I say to meself, 'Is why you so greedy, man? What you do with all that money from you rice mills? With the rents from the rice fields? You won't even spend some to educate you sons. When the cow dung lying on the ground you won't even let the poor woman from next door take it up for she fire.' I look at meself in the glass and I feel sick in here," he said, thumping his chest. His voice faltered. "I tell you this: I never tell anybody this before, but is true. I hate meself, but I kian't change. You think if you give a beggar a new hat he'd put it on? No. He'll stay in his rags and put all the new clothes you give him away. You know why? 'Cause the rags become part of him. I kian' change. I won't know what to do. I can tell you lies, 'bout how I do a lot of good things, but — I never tell anybody this."

He looked at her with a hang-dog expression.

"Look, look!" he said urgently. "You know me to do anything really bad? Course not! I in't got it in me. Is just that in trying to do the right thing I do some bad things, that's all. You think that with all this money I feel secure? You wait till Sidique get hold of some real money. You'll see how you'll husband it and try to make it grow. Is natural. You doing it for the people who depend on you. Is this feeling of insecurity that make me behave like a animal. Do you know I never been to Georgetown once to have a good time? Is not that I didn't want to go. But the thought of spending the money on something that is all in my mind is so stupid to me. I know that deep down you understand what I trying to say. After all, what it bring me? The only one who really care for me is my wife; and is because she come up the hard way. She know why I behave like this."

This outpouring was intended to impress Indrani with its sincerity. In fact Mr Ali was saying what he often thought, just

314

as many people who choose to impress frequently speak the truth, and later, on reflection, are astonished to discover that they had not lied. Indrani was touched. He had always been hard on her. He had humiliated her, ignored her, turned his son against her with insistent whisperings in his ear. Besides, some of the things he had told him were patently untrue. By the standards of his friends he was anything but miserly; and as for the story about the woman next door, it was Mrs Ali who had prevented her from collecting the dung of their cows. Nevertheless, his confession touched her.

"I'm sorry, I can't do it, Pa."

"Don't you want Dada to go home?" he asked.

"Yes. But if I go I'll only make things worse. People'll see me and then you'll blame me when they begin to talk."

"You can go at night," he suggested.

"And the car?" she asked.

"Jai'll be in the car. When you arrive you needn't go in unless the road is clear. And I can put up a black cloth 'pon the windows, so that anybody passing won't know is you."

Indrani reflected for a while.

"All right," she said in a low voice.

Mr Ali could hardly contain his glee. He wanted to kiss her, but managed to restrain himself.

"From now on everything'll be different. And Ma will be different. And I'll be different. And you'll teach me how to read them contracts I does get and how to write some of them letters. You'll be my daughter, 'cause I always wanted a girl."

Rain began to fall, first a drizzle and then a downpour. The drought was over and the smell of damp earth rose to the windows. Indrani and Mr Ali, who had meanwhile gone upstairs, went to the window to look next door at a group of boys and girls who were dancing in the downpour, opening their mouths to drink the warm, filtered water. The earth, strewn with playthings and debris, drank up the rain greedily through its deep lacerations and two dogs chased each other in turn across the dampening grass, drawing their excitement from the children's shrieking.

Mr Ali left the room and went in search of his wife, who then informed Sidique of Indrani's agreement.

315

"You tell the fool," Mr Ali had said. "I bet he'll burst out in tears and say he change his mind."

Later, when he looked back on his discussion with Indrani he mused, "She din' put up much of a fight, did she?" and he smiled to himself.

Jai was delighted that Indrani had agreed to go. He looked forward to the escapade like a boy whose father promised to take him to a test match. Besides, he enjoyed Sidique's discomfiture.

The latter went round the house like a jaguar in a cage. No sooner had he heard of Indrani's acceptance than he was convinced that the whole family had mounted a conspiracy against him. Most of all he was vexed with Indrani, who had accepted so readily.

Had he not been afraid of his father he would have refused to allow Indrani to go through with the arrangement. He dared not even have it out with her, lest she changed her mind and roused his father's wrath. Jai would only sneer at him if he attempted to discuss the matter with him. Only his mother was left. She noticed that he had hardly been eating anything and enquired if he was not well.

"I'm all right. Is you who's gone out of your mind."

"What? You mean about Indrani going to see this chap? Bah! What you got to worry about. Jai going with she."

"But is a stupid idea, I tell you."

"I know what eating you, boy," she said. "Is cause she say yes. But you don't think she got sense too?"

"You in't better than the rest of them."

"No, Sidique. I never hide nothing from you. I tell you is a good idea."

"When I get enough money," Sidique declared, "I going clear out of this house."

"Son. . . ."

"Don't 'son' me! When I send she away the first time you was glad. You tell me she wan' no good. You scheme and scheme till you had me believing you lies. Pa tell me that you suggest that he get me a girl from the village to keep me quiet. I did want Indrani back. When I look back and see how you and Pa use me I feel sick."

"I always act in you interest, Sidique. If you did marry she lawful you would've regret it. She play so great she think she above all of we. Well, you meet she father. He's the same, isn't he? These people think that 'cause we live in Suddie we stupid."

"Well, I tell you something now. I goin' marry she legal, whatever you think."

"Don't say I din' warn you, boy. You tell you father?"

"Is nobody business but me own," replied Sidique angrily. "No man ever touch she except me."

"You sure o' that?" asked his mother.

Sidique raised his fist and brought it down with a thump on his mother's back. She winced in pain as he struck her again and again, but uttered not a sound. When he had finished he stood over her with an ugly expression.

"Yes, I sure of that!" he hissed, "An' you jus' remember she's my wife."

His mother got up from the floor and, without a tear in her eye, sat down in a wicker chair. She had much to say, but was afraid to say it. Adjusting her saffron-coloured sari, she looked at him furtively, feeling desperately sorry for him. If only he would allow her to come near to him she would soothe him, just as long ago, when, a little boy, he had received a beating from his father. She would console him with words and with her fingers as he cried his eyes out on her breast. She knew that he needed her now more than ever, even if he was unwilling to admit it, for all he required was patience, unending patience, which she had in abundance.

She waited until he left the room before she went to the mirror to look at her face. One of his blows had caught her on her temple and another on her left cheek. If there was a swelling or bruise she would have to account for it to her husband. But apart from a slight redness on her cheek there seemed no injury. These men — Sidique, Jai and even her husband — were weak and impatient. There were ways of dealing with this Armstrong fellow, of wearing him down and forcing him to go in the end, but they would all shrink from the methods she might suggest. In the effort to protect themselves why should they hesitate to use any way? She could see weaknesses in the plan that had been proposed. What of it? If it did not work, they would turn to her. They always did.

19

The Forest Ranger

Since his wife's death Ramjohn's attitude towards Rohan changed. He no longer came to his house, except on office business; and he made it quite clear to Rohan and his friends that he would no longer run their errands. Rohan was offended at Ramjohn's behaviour and sought to discover what he had done to displease him. Ramjohn would not be drawn out and simply insisted that it was only because he missed his wife that he had become less talkative. But one night when he was obliged to return a batch of unissued bicycle licences to Rohan — the office being closed — he began to talk.

"I mean, 'twas your well, Mr Armstrong; and is not every day that somebody fall down a well. She was always warning me 'gainst your house. She say, 'Keep away from that house, Ramjohn. Bad things going to happen there.' You look at me and I know what you thinking, Mr Armstrong, but you're not in a position to judge me. You've got too much to answer for."

"I haven't got anything to answer for, Ramjohn. I wasn't even there when it happened."

"I din' say you was, Mr Armstrong. It was your well, that's all I'm saying."

Rohan lost his temper. "Don't be a damn fool, man. Deen killed herself."

"My wife lived for her children, Mr Armstrong. She would never kill herself. I've got young children that need a mother and my wife did know all about duty. What she going to kill herself for?"

"Get to hell out of here, Ramjohn! Get to hell out of here!" Rohan exclaimed.

"As soon as you great people klan' get your way," said Ramjohn, "you start cursing. I wonder if she made a noise when she fall? You wouldn't kill a dog like that, let alone a woman with children — so many children with their mouth open every night. . . ."

While he was talking Rohan was thinking that Ramjohn was

right. "As soon as you great people kian' get you way you start cursing," he had said. Rohan was quite prepared to put up with him, provided he showed the kind of respect proper to his station in life.

"Asha is a little mother, you know," said Ramjohn. "She cook and wash and clean the children, and mend their clothes. The girl change overnight. She was lazy and my wife couldn't get a hour work out of her; but now she works from morning to night-time. Last night I did take her hand and look at it. 'Girl, is what you been doing to your hand?' I ask. She just been working."

Rohan was about to interrupt, but changed his mind.

"It's uncomfortable to hear about poor people, eh, Mr Armstrong? You don't complain. You don't tell anybody anything; but then you don't got anything to complain about."

Rohan summoned up all his powers of self-restraint to thwart his desire to put Ramjohn out of the house.

"Why you don't hit me, Mr Armstrong? You wouldn't hit a poor widower with seven children, would you? I mean you might fracture my jaw or make me fall on something hard. And you'd have that on your conscience, Mr Armstrong, just as you got Deen on your conscience."

Rohan leapt on him like a tiger. With a wild expression in his eyes he shouted, "I don't have anybody on my conscience, d'you hear? Nobody! I've got a clear conscience! My conscience is clear!"

Dada and Mrs Helega rushed out at the same time. They both tried to pull Rohan away from the struggling Ramjohn.

"Boyie!" shouted Dada. "Let him go! You'll kill him!"

Rohan let go, breathing heavily, while the hapless Ramjohn took to his heels, and his footsteps could be heard in the yard and then over the bridge, as he made for his house.

"You gone mad?" Dada asked.

"He's crazy! He keeps blaming me for Deen's death."

"I tell you long ago," said the housekeeper, "to keep him far from the house. Either he's avoid you or when he come he take a hour over complaints that in't got nothing to do with you."

"I still can't understand what I've done him," Rohan said with a perplexed gesture.

When Mrs Helega had gone inside he said to Dada, "You know, the same thing happened at Vreed-en-Hoop."

"What?" asked Dada.

"I grabbed hold of you brother-in-law in the same way."

"Sidique?"

"Yes."

"In front of Indrani?"

"Does it matter?" he asked irritably. "I wonder if. . . ."

"If what?" Dada enquired, but received no reply.

Rohan only spoke of his fight with Sidique out of embarrassment, knowing perfectly well that Ramjohn's remark that he had Deen and other things on his conscience had struck a deeper chord. He was to discover later that Ramjohn knew very well why Deen had killed herself. He had confided in the forest ranger, who, in turn, told Rohan. Deen had been expecting her eighth child and had told Ramjohn that she did not want it. He promised to get a larger house, but Deen said she could not have another child anyhow, because she was always so tired. According to the forest ranger Ramjohn blamed himself for Deen's death and went to her grave every afternoon to beg her forgiveness.

It turned out, in fact, that Ramjohn's guilt feelings about Deen's death were common knowledge in the area. Rohan was dismayed that Ramjohn, who accused him of being involved in some way in his wife's death, should nevertheless inform every Tom, Dick and Harry in the district that his wife had been pregnant.

One day when Rohan was out on his rounds checking weights and measures the forest ranger went over to where Ramjohn was writing. The office was empty, except for an old woman sitting in the doorway, who had come to collect her old-age pension on the wrong day and was too tired to go home.

"Is what?" Ramjohn asked, looking up.

"You stupid or what?"

"Is what wrong?" Ramjohn repeated.

"You think Mr Armstrong don't notice how you behaving? You want to lose you job or what?"

Ramjohn wiped the nib of his pen on the blotting paper and put it down.

"I can't help it. He did tell you to talk to me?" Ramjohn asked.

"Don't be a damn fool. He in't gwine tell you nothing. He goin' just sack you, then you'll be in the shit."

"Is that blasted woman. . . ."

The forest ranger drew up a chair and looked at him solicitously. He had always despised Ramjohn and would call him all sorts of names whenever he crossed him; but Deen's death seemed to dispel his contempt for him.

"Since that woman living with him," observed Ramjohn, "he never had any time for me. He don't like playing draughts any more."

"The trouble with you is you kian' stand people without education. If you want friends all you got to do is to go down to the rum shop."

Ramjohn picked up the clean pen and wiped it again. He looked out of the window to avoid replying.

"We did become friends, you understand," he could not resist saying. "It wasn't like playing draughts or going to the pictures with just anybody. We used to drink together. And then that woman come along."

"I don't understand," said the forest ranger, perplexed.

"No, you don't understand. You're a loner. You don't need anybody excepting yourself. You think it's everybody can go off on his own in the bush like you?"

"You better pull yourself together. If everybody do like you half the world would hang themselves."

"Well, what you want me to do? Act as if nothing happen?" asked Ramjohn.

"You have to!" rejoined the ranger emphatically.

Ramjohn dipped his pen into the ink-well, then held it over the sheet of paper.

"I never do that woman anything," he observed, "but from the time she set eyes on me she hate me. I never see anything like it in my life. You think we did know one another a long time ago and she got something against me. From the time she set eyes on me, I tell you."

"You know what eating you up?" asked the ranger. "What eating you is that Mr Armstrong been more friendly to you than the other chief clerks. Yes! The others did treat you like a dog and you did prefer that. You coolie people, if you not cutting somebody throat you licking their boots."

"Tell me something," Ramjohn said to him. "When last you had a woman?"

The ranger drew back in surprise at the unexepected question.

"Night before the last. Why?"

"Ah," said Ramjohn. "Since Deen dead . . . is not only sex, you know. A man needs a woman in the house."

"And what you going to do?"

"Dunno. What woman's going to want to take care of a man with seven children?"

"I don't know. You just got to keep searching."

Ramjohn looked at him, already ashamed at having spoken about such a private matter.

"A lot o' men would give you their daughter," said the ranger, "if you only ask. I mean, you got a roof over you head and a steady job. You're the funniest chap. I mean, I see funny people, but you're the funniest I meet."

Ramjohn was annoyed and dipped his pen in the ink-well once more.

"Le' we go to the rum shop tonight," suggested the ranger. "I got lots o' money."

Ramjohn nodded and began writing. Then, a few seconds later he said, "There's things you keep to yourself because nobody would understand, you see. I can't get accustomed to my wife being dead. She comes and talks to me at night. The other night she did sit down on the bed, and when I put out my hand to touch her she go over to the dressing-table and start combing her hair. . . . I know Mr Armstrong responsible for her death."

And as the forest ranger tried to interrupt him he said sharply, "I know it! And I can't get it out of my mind."

The two men sat staring at each other.

20

A Mission

Indrani and Jai had just left in the car. Mr and Mrs Ali went
outside on the lower porch, where they could talk without
being heard by Sis — Jai's wife — who had taken her place
by the radio. She was as keyed up as anyone else about the
trip, but knew that any display of interest would be unbecom-
ing.

"Sidique in't come home to eat," Mrs Ali said to her husband.

"Is the first sensible t'ing he do in weeks," he answered.

"Is what he doing at the mill, then?" she asked.

"Probably sitting 'pon a rice bag and broodin'.'"

"I don' like it when he like that."

"I tell you, is better that way," he reassured her.

"You t'ink Indrani going get this Armstrong to send Dada
away?"

"I don' know. To tell the truth I don' know. If she kian'
manage it we got to take some drastic action."

"Like what?" she asked.

"We could always offer he five thousand dollars," he said
calmly. Then after a pause he continued ruefully, "I wish this
business would come to a end. In the old days we'd call he
outside the house and set a couple o' cross dogs 'pon he an'
teach he a lesson. He would a been gone by morning. But nowadays the police poke they nose in everyt'ing, as if they in't got
criminals to catch."

They sat in silence, surrounded by the night sounds.

"You in' look so good lately," she observed, as if she could
see him well enough in the dark.

"I kian' sleep at night for this damn trouble."

"Sidique too, he don' sleep."

"How you know?" he enquired.

"I can tell. And I hear he walking 'bout the house at two
in the morning. That boy usually sleep like a mule after working."

323

"You always worrying 'bout Sidique," he said reproachfully. "One day he going have to solve he own problems and he won't know what to do if you always worrying for him."

A car flashed by and momentarily caught their attention. For a second they had thought that Jai and Indrani could be back so early.

"The men at the mill want more money," Mr Ali said.

"Sack them! The lot!" she advised. "If they don't know how lucky they is."

"You kian' pick up good men jus' like that. Tobesides, some of them gone already. Since these Yankee people come during the war and pay high wages at the base they make all the work people dissatisfied. Everybody t'ink they entitle to a radio. They t'ink they got a right to it."

"You take what I tell you," his wife said. "Sack the lot of them and close down the mill. They'll come back with they tails between they legs."

Mr Ali fell silent, as if he were lost in thought. In fact, he was turning over his wife's suggestion in his mind. He could even pretend that the closure had nothing to do with the workers' demands for more wages.

Over the years he had come to listen attentively to her opinions. At first he used to pay little heed to what she said but, as time went by, the soundness of her suggestions was demonstrated often enough for him to show his grudging respect. In the end he had to confess that she possessed an uncommon instinct for the right solution. But this was a matter less for instinct than for experience and common sense. His wife had not had the opportunity to rub shoulders with all sorts of people.

Another car passed by, more slowly this time. Both of them lifted their heads and looked expectantly in the direction of the Public Road.

A figure appeared in the drive. It was Sidique, who was walking slowly, his hands deep in his trouser pockets. He had hoped that his parents would be in the house so that he could take the back stairs.

"She back yet?" he asked.

"Is only eight o'clock," his father replied impatiently. The very presence of Sidique seemed to unsettle him.

"You mus' be hungry," his mother said, getting up.

"Naw, I eat somet'ing jus' now."

She knew that he was not speaking the truth.

"What about Abdul?" Sidique asked.

"Indrani put he to bed before she go. He in we room. Don' change he over till Indrani come back," his mother advised.

"Anybody upstairs?"

"Only Sis," his mother replied, unnerved by his questioning.

Sidique mounted the stairs ponderously.

Mrs Ali felt for her son. She knew that the urge to go to Armstrong's house was so strong in him that, once in his room, he would walk up and down, torturing himself with questions and self-reproach. The day before he had told her, "I don' know why he don' give me the money he putting aside for me. I could go away with my wife and Abdul and run my own life."

"I goin' up and see if he want anything to eat," she said, rising with effort from the stair.

"Lef' he, ne," Mr Ali said, sucking his teeth.

A few seconds later a fearful shouting came from inside the house.

"Leave me! All of you leave me! What I do allyou that you don't leave me alone? Take you food and stuff it up you batty!"

There was a crash of smashed crockery. Mr Ali rushed upstairs, taking two steps at a time. He surveyed the scene in the dining-room. Broken crockery, cutlery and enamel cups lay all over the room. Roused to anger by his son's intemperate behaviour Mr Ali crossed the dining-room to go down to the room where he, Indrani and the child slept.

"Lef' him!" his wife urged. "He probably lock heself up. It in' goin' do no good if you bring he out."

Mr Ali ignored her and was already on the other side of the room.

"Do what I tell you," she begged, running after him and taking hold of his shoulder. Beside himself with rage, he stood where he was.

"Sis!" Mrs Ali called out to her daughter-in-law, who had got up and was looking on from a distance. "Call John and ask he to come clear up these t'ings."

325

Jai's wife went downstairs to fetch the man who looked after the house and garden. Meanwhile, Abdul, Sidique's son, had been awakened by the noise. His grandmother had put him to bed again and explained why his mother was not there to do it.

"Ma gone to see a friend," she reassured him.

"She coming back soon?"

"Jus' now."

"Can I wait up to see her?"

"No, 'cause she in't comin' right away."

"O.K.," he said, easing his thumb into his mouth, and fell asleep almost at once.

Mr Ali did not want to go outside again, nor did he want to remain in his wife's company. In ordinary circumstances he might have gone over to see his brother, who lived a stone's throw from the stelling; but all he wanted now was to think over all the problems that seemed to have arisen in so short a space of time. He went for a walk alone on the Public Road, beating the bushes with the stick he carried.

"These damn children!" he thought. "When I did want to arrange his marriage he wouldn't do what I say. He did want to marry for love. Well, look where love get he. Look where it get all of we. An' look at Jai! He din' marry for love, but he and Sis does understand one another as if they was made to live together."

Indrani, as she sat in the car, wondered how she could let herself in for such an arrangement. She knew Dada as none of them did. Nothing would induce her sister to leave Boyie. Ever since the Vreed-en-Hoop days Dada had not concealed the fact that she was in love with him, for unlike herself and Betty, Dada never bothered to dissemble. If ever she wanted to give him a present she saved, bought it and presented it to him. When she was impatient at his lateness, she went and waited for him on the bridge and, on catching sight of him, ran down the Public Road to meet him. Furthermore, despite her youth, Dada had a will of iron. If she believed that she and Boyie were destined to spend the rest of their days together she would do whatever was necessary to attain that end.

"Why then," Indrani asked herself, "did I agree to go and see Boyie?"

She kept repeating this question to herself. It would be foolish to pretend that she wanted Dada to leave. Rohan would almost certainly follow her, as Sidique and his family intended. If Dada went and he remained, Dada would never forgive her, and her in-laws would be odious towards her. Why then was she ensnaring herself like this? Did she want to see Boyie so badly? Only a fool would. He had flaunted Dada at her and at every decent person in Suddie; they strolled about arm in arm in the hot sun, and whenever he was expected back from a trip she went to meet him on the stelling with her yellow parasol. He embraced her in full view of everyone, full on the lips, according to some.

Deep down, she thought to herself, she was on the Alis' side. If people wanted to behave like that they should go and live in some isolated place. This depravity was like a drug, the more you took it the more you needed it. When all was said and done Boyie and Dada were insulting not only the Alis, but her as well.

By the time the car stopped in front of Rohan's house Indrani knew that she must persuade him to send her sister away.

The barking of the dogs brought Dada to the window.

"Indra! Don't stand there. Come up."

The sisters kissed each other, then Dada made Indrani sit down.

"How you got away?" she asked.

"Well, you know. . . ."

"But how?" Dada insisted.

Indrani tried to avoid her sister's eyes. "Boyie there?" she asked diffidently.

"Why you come to see Boyie?" Dada's face fell.

"Don't get vexed. I don't want to see him; but I've got a message from Sidique's father."

"Him? He was round here offering Boyie money to go away. What does he want now?"

"More or less the same thing," said Indrani.

After a pause Dada said, "So they sent you?"

It was difficult to adopt the big sister attitude. Indrani

327

did not know why. Perhaps she recognised Dada as a woman.

"Boyie's out," said Dada.

"Oh?"

"He'll be back soon, don't worry."

"I'm not worried," said Indrani, and at once regretted that the words had slipped out.

Dada, who was sitting by the window, turned and looked outside, for when Indrani said that she had come to see Boyie, her delight at seeing her sister drained away.

"Does Boyie stay in Suddie because of you?" asked Dada.

"Of course not!"

"You can't know, can you? When he comes I'll ask him."

"Jai must be wondering why I'm so long. I'll go and tell him," said Indrani.

She got up and opened the door, but, just then, her sister said, "That's Boyie now."

Indrani knocked over the straight-backed chair as she was going back to her seat. Dada was watching her and she tried to sustain her gaze. This was an impossible situation, reflected Indrani. She would look like a fool when she tried to say what she came to say.

Rohan was whistling and again Indrani felt her sister's gaze on her. As he came in through the open door Dada went to meet him and kissed him on the mouth before he caught sight of Indrani behind the door.

He stood stock still, as if mesmerised.

"Hello," he managed.

"Hello, Boyie," Indrani said. "I — I . . . it's nice to see you."

The silence that ensued was broken by Dada. "Aren't you going to kiss her?" she asked.

Rohan looked at Dada, then at Indrani. He hesitated for a while then kissed Indrani on one cheek, then on the other.

Indrani looked at her sister, whose gaze was on Rohan, a hateful, vindictive gaze.

"I suppose you want to be alone," Dada said. Then addressing Indrani she said, "I see him all the time." With that she left the room and went inside.

"They sent me," Indrani said. "They sent me to. . . ."

She was unable to continue. That day on the stelling when

328

she pretended to ignore him came back to her in all its clarity.

"You didn't even bother to speak to me that day on the stelling," she said.

"I? Why d'you think I'm in Suddie?"

"And living with Dada," she replied, raising her voice a little.

Then adopting a businesslike expression she said, "They sent to ask you to send Dada away. And I came because I couldn't miss the opportunity of seeing you."

Rohan came towards her, but she stopped him. "Stay away from me. I don't want anybody's leavings."

She looked him straight in the eye, brazenly, hoping that he would protest that he loved her. But he said nothing.

"I've heard about your women and your orgies. Why d'you pretend you stayed here because of me when the whole coast knows how you spend your weekends?" she asked, apparently angry.

Without warning she came over to Rohan and kissed him on his mouth. She held him in a long embrace, not caring that Dada was only a few yards away in the next room. She sat down in the chair next to his and hid her face in her hands.

"O God! What am I going to do?" she said.

Rohan put out his hand and stroked her neck under her hair. "Come again," he said. "Tell them I haven't made up my mind yet."

"I can't," she replied, "Sidique would kill me."

"He let you come today."

"Yes. But twice? He'll never let me come again."

"Come next Tuesday. I'll see that Dada is out," Rohan suggested.

"All this time," said Indrani, "knowing you were here and knowing where you were living. Sidique used to taunt me and say, 'That's where your boy friend living,' when we passed the house. Once I saw Dada sitting at the window. I nearly turned in and left the others. If it weren't for my son I would've come."

"You're coming?" Rohan asked.

"You want to ruin me?" asked Indrani.

"You're coming?"

"Don't you care what happens to me?" she enquired weakly.

329

"Yes," she answered in the end and thereupon took his right hand and covered it with kisses.

They sat without talking, side by side. Finally she said, "I'd better go, or Dada'll become suspicious. Careful!" she exclaimed as they stood up. "Jai can see us from the road," forgetting that she had not minded when she kissed him.

"Dada! Indra's going," Rohan called out.

Dada took some time to come out and when she did, approached her sister coolly and kissed her once. She and Rohan watched her walking down the path and heard the car driving off in the darkness.

"What's wrong?" asked Rohan.

"Nothing," Dada replied.

"Have I done you anything?"

"Why? Is your conscience bothering you?"

"You're not jealous of your sister, are you?"

"No. So why were you whispering?"

"I?" asked Rohan.

"You! Both or you!"

"What. . . ." started Rohan.

"Stop! You'll only lie, lie and lie!"

He went into the drawing-room and half lay in a Berbice chair. Immediately, his thoughts turned to Indrani. Her aloofness and the discovery that she was not indifferent to him fired his affection. He dreamed of the day she would come, alone. His plan to get Dada away had not yet been worked out, but he was certain that she could be persuaded to go and see her father in Vreed-en-Hoop, or even to spend the night helping Ramjohn's daughter, Asha.

"I'll come," she had said. The words rang in his ears like the notes on a bugle. *I'll come*.

Afterwards, he thought, let anything happen. Once he had tasted the food she set before him life was complete.

At that moment he felt the presence of Dada, turned round and saw her standing a few feet from him. He pulled her towards him and she put her arm round his neck.

"We're happy, aren't we?" she asked.

"Yes," he replied, stroking her hair.

"D'you love me?" she asked.

"Yes," he answered, realising that nothing less would do.

"I forgot to close the window this afternoon. The rain came in."

"You cold?" he asked.

"No," she replied, snuggling up to him. "The dog's expecting."

"Again?"

"I'll bring it up into the house," she said, "out of the wet. Want anything?"

He shook his head.

"When last've you been over to help Asha?" he asked her.

"Day before yesterday. Why?"

"Nothing. I was only thinking."

"Why don't you go over?" Dada said.

"Ramjohn can't stand the sight of me."

"He can't stop talking about you," she observed.

"I don't trust him any more."

"I think he admires you, else he wouldn't talk about you all the time."

"At the office," said Rohan, "he only talks when he has to. And when I corner him alone he gets embarrassed and talks a lot of nonsense. The other day he was telling me how some man down the road had a bakoo that had escaped and that I had to be careful."

"I heard the same story from the housekeeper," said Dada.

"It's a lot of nonsense," he remarked.

"I don't know. You won't let me going out alone after dark."

"Is that why you don't want to go and see Asha?"

"That's just across the way," she said with a deprecating gesture. "Why're you in such a bad mood all of a sudden?"

"I'm not in a bad mood. It's just that Ramjohn's hypocrisy annoys me. He didn't know what to say, so he told me that Bakoo story."

Dada got off his lap and sat down opposite him. She watched him attentively.

"Come to think of it, I'll go and see Asha. Ramjohn's out tomorrow?"

"No," said Rohan. "But he'll be out on Tuesday."

Dada closed her eyes and began stroking her belly. And later on, on thinking over their conversation Rohan wondered why she had agreed so suddenly to go and see Asha on Tuesday.

21

As a Seal Upon Thine Heart

When Jai and Indrani arrived home, his mother and father were waiting in the gallery for them. Sidique, as if sensing his wife's arrival, came out into the gallery. There was an air of expectancy in the house as Jai entered, his hands in his pocket.

Indrani resented the fact that she was expected to give an account of her mission in front of everyone. Her father-in-law got up and unceremoniously announced, "I want to talk to Indrani alone," whereupon Mrs Ali and Jai left the room. Sidique remained seated.

"I say I want—" repeated Mr Ali, but Indrani interrupted him.

"Leave him!" she said firmly.

"All right. What happened?"

"Nothing," replied Indrani. "He can't give an answer before Tuesday."

Sidique jumped up.

"You're not going there again," he intervened. "I'll go."

"I don't mind," said Indrani, "but you won't expect him to say yes if—"

"If he decide to leave why should he say no just because I go?" remarked Sidique.

"Because people don't like you, boy," his father said.

"She's not going again!" exclaimed Sidique.

"Just as you like," she complied.

"No!" Mr Ali put in. "He in' goin' spoil everything at the last moment."

"How you know he'll say yes?" Sidique asked.

"But he *might* say yes, you fool!" Mr Ali shouted at his son.

"My wife in't going! She in' going, you old fool!" screamed Sidique at the top of his voice.

Mr Ali gazed up at his son with an expression of such astonishment that the latter drew back. Indrani came between father and son, looking now at one and then at the other.

Mrs Ali came rushing in. "Is what wrong? You din' hit the boy?"

Her husband did not answer, but pointed to the door, unable to speak for anger.

"Boy, is wha' happen?" Mrs Ali asked, holding her son before he got to the door.

"I cursed him," he said, and opened the door. His mother watched him leave and then turned to her husband.

"God! Why I let you alone? I did tell you I should stay."

"Don't feed him. I'll decide tonight what to do 'bout him. I goin' leave everyt'ing to Jai. He won't get a cent," Mr Ali told her.

Indrani left the drawing-room and went down the back stairs to the part of the house occupied by herself and Sidique and their son. She knew that her father-in-law would have to relent, if only because he believed that she was the only one who could persuade Boyie to leave Suddie.

She found Sidique slumped in a chair near his son's bed. Abdul had been taken downstairs by his grandmother, who had put him to bed again and stayed with him for a while. The boy was lying on his back, one leg hanging from the bed and the other flung across it. She drew the blanket over him and sat on the edge of the bed.

"He won't do anything, don't worry," Indrani tried to reassure her husband.

"I get trapped between a dodderin' old fool and a slut," he retorted.

Indrani's back straightened.

"Say something, you rotten stray dog!" he ordered. "I bet you wasn't silent in his house. I bet you talk your head off! From now on everything going change down here. You'll go when I say go and come when I say come. You mightn't talk, but you goin' obey! If you t'ink life was hard before, you'll see what it can be like. And understand, you'll go upstairs only with my permission. You may be his daughter-in-law, but you're my wife. And pray that he don't put us out, 'cause we'll have to go and live in the bush."

"I'm not leaving Suddie," said Indrani.

"Ha! You're damn funny," he said, with a deadly serious face. "You go where I go!"

He articulated his last words carefully, as if speaking to a child.

"Where I go!" he shouted at the top of his voice. The boy stirred. Indrani tried to cover him up, but he sat erect and began to look round him.

Sidique got up and started pacing up and down the room. When Indrani had succeeded in calming the boy Sidique was still pacing the room, his brow knitted. Indrani did not realise that Sidique was aware of the damage he had caused by his outburst. He knew from experience that kind words would achieve nothing at this stage. His impotence to remedy the situation enraged him. Like a man who is standing at the edge of a precipice and feels an irresistible urge to jump, so he stood before Indrani. Suddenly he began to rain abuse on her. Her mother was a vagrant and her father a thief. The latter remark hurt particularly, since there was an old story connecting her father with the disappearance of some money which had never turned up. On a number of occasions she had discussed the matter with Sidique, who appeared as convinced as everyone else of her father's innocence. Apparently unable to rouse her, Sidique went on heaping insult upon insult on his wife. Finally he lost control of himself and fell on her. Putting her hands over her face and crouching low she took his blows without a whimper until, drained of his resentment, he stepped back, panting and uneasy. Never was her superiority over him more evident than at that moment. He wanted to confess this to her, but what difference would it have made? She was better educated, more intelligent and knowledgeable. With her help he might have outwitted his father, but alone he was like a sloth in the path of a jaguar. Overcome by a measureless despair he sought the door knob and stumbled out of the room. He sat on the white painted garden bench and contemplated the spring flowers growing at the foot of the new pavilion, encouraged by recent rainfalls, and the lattice-work shadow of the willow tree. How could a young man of twenty-seven face the fact that his marriage had failed? No, no, it must all be a nightmare. He was a good Mohammedan. His mother had always said so. Not once had he ever touched spirits or tobacco, nor violated the laws of the Qur'an. This searing distress must have an end, since it had a beginning. Once, last month, when he tried to take the priest into his confidence the latter had told him, "You're young. You've got good prospects, a fine wife and son. What're you complaining about?"

Perhaps he should go back and explain. No. That wouldn't do. Hearing footsteps on the path, he looked up and saw his mother.

"What you doin' here, boy?" she asked solicitously.

He did not answer.

"You father won't do nothin'. That's between us. He say is the first time and. . . . Listen, boy," she continued, "you don't see there'll never be peace in the house till Dada and she friend leave Suddie? If I was you I'd be jus' as jealous as you, but I'd be practical. We kian' help how we feel, but we can control how we behave."

Sidique looked up uncertainly.

"I make him promise," she continued, "not to say nothin' 'bout what happen."

She sat down next to him.

"If you want to go far in life," she said, "you got to learn to be patient. Men don't know how to wait. I respect Indrani 'cause she know how to wait. When we women get married we go and live with the man parents and suffers for years till his mother dead. I was lucky. You father mother was a good woman. But my mother suffer and my sisters too. My mother dead at sixty-two and she mother-in-law was still alive. I did know my grandparents like my own parents. It was like having two father and mother. But you're spoiled, boy. You got ambition and you want everyt'ing now. You t'ink that it's the end of the world to got a wife who don't love you."

"You talk like that 'cause you forget," he told her.

"You'll see if what I say in' true," Mrs Ali said in turn. "I want you to do somet'ing fo' me. You don't have to . . . I'll tell you straight. You father ready to give you five thousand dollas if you let Indrani go and hear what Dada boy friend got to say. No, no. Jus' say yes or no."

Sidique was caught off his guard. His mother pretended not to see the light in his eyes. She got up and began to walk away.

"Don't go!" he said. "How I know he goin' keep his promise?"

"I tell 'im he'll have to get the money tomorrow."

"Tomorrow?" he whispered.

"Tomorrow," she replied.

"How he could give me five thousand dollars after I curse him?" Sidique enquired suspiciously.

"You don't worry 'bout that. When the money in you hand you won't be asking no questions. You in' tell me if you say yes."

"Yes," he muttered after a moment.

"You do right, boy," she said, got up and patted her son affectionately on his back.

'Don't say nothing to Indrani 'bout the money," he told his mother. "She won't understand."

Sidique felt a glow in his innards. Already the idea of his wife's visit to Rohan seemed less offensive. Jai would be going with her. Dada would be there and the housekeeper. In fact, he wondered what had got into him before, when he made such a fool of himself in front of Indrani. He had to admit that his mother had never given him bad advice. One thing was certain, though: he would not be patient enough to wait until his father's death in order to put his hands on a substantial sum of money. Only success in some business venture could win back Indrani's respect for him, there was no doubt about that. Breathing deeply, he filled his lungs with air but the smile disappeared from his face when he remembered how he had fallen on Indrani a short while ago.

She was lying on the bed, on her side. He stroked her face with his hand, but when he came to her breast she turned over on her belly. In a trice Sidique felt in himself the rage he dreaded so much. He then turned and left the room.

Tuesday came, as inexorably as the day before, or the day before that. In the Alis' house there was a palpable tension. Sidique, who had come to accept the inevitability, even the desirability, of his wife's visit to Rohan, became more irritable as the day wore on. Mr Ali avoided his son, not only because he was embarrassed at having threatened and not carried out his threat, but also because any exchange of words between the two might result in him changing his mind and thwarting the family plan.

At meal time Mr Ali was found to be away on business. In the morning when the rest of the family were getting up he had already left the house for the mill, and Sidique soon realised that his father was avoiding him and was pleased. He had kept his promise about the money, which he received from his mother the day before.

In the afternoon Indrani asked him whether she was permitted to go to see Rohan or not and he asked why she was so interested in going. She replied that it was impossible for her to do what she was not aware had to be done.

Later that day Sidique met his father in the drawing-room and thought he detected a sneer on his face as he passed him. When he tried to speak to his mother on her own she was engaged with someone else or was on the point of going out, so, in the end, he left for the mill to supervise some work.

That night he watched Indrani and Jai leave the house in the company of his parents, who walked with them to the car. Before they drove off Mr Ali bent down and said something to Indrani, who was sitting beside Jai. Both Mr and Mrs Ali were smiling as they climbed the stairs.

22

Broken Glass

Rohan tried to relax by reading a book, but in the end he went and lay down on the bed. He had sent the housekeeper to visit her friend, a servant who worked for the District Commissioner and Dada had gone over to see Asha as she had been urged to do. On hearing the knock he was expecting, he got up calmly and went to the door. It was Ramjohn.

"Can I come in?"

"Well, I was just about to turn in early tonight. I thought Dada was over at your place."

"Yes," replied Ramjohn. "She send me to get some spoons. She's helping out with a little cook-up we got."

"How many?" asked Rohan.

"About eight or so."

Rohan went in and fetched ten table spoons.

"They're ten," Ramjohn observed, and started counting them again.

"Take them, man, take them," Rohan said impatiently.

"I goin' bring them back as soon as we finished."

"For Heaven's sake," said Rohan, "Dada can bring them back."

But Ramjohn hesitated at the door. Rohan, unable to endure his delayed departure, was about to speak severely to him, but reflected that Ramjohn might retaliate by sulking at home and causing Dada to come back.

"What's wrong now?" Rohan asked, as calmly as he could.

"Nothing, is nothing," came the reply, and he set off down the stairs. He seemed to take an age walking down the path.

After his visit Rohan could no longer relax. He sat in a chair, got up soon afterwards, went downstairs, came back up almost at once and finally mixed himself a rum and soda. He fondled the glass while he looked down at the path that led to the road, which Ramjohn had just taken. Suddenly, for some unaccountable reason, Ramjohn's visit had spoiled everything. Only that morning Mrs Helega had been telling him the story of the escaped bakoo. There was no apparent reason why this bit of news should be connected with Ramjohn's visit, but to Rohan both occurrences filled him with foreboding. The thought came to him that the frogs were silent and that there was not a breath of wind. The road was deserted and the overcast sky seemed to brush the old tamarind tree by the bridge. When the car stopped and he saw Indrani getting out he found that he had not finished his drink, so he quickly swallowed it in one gulp and went to the door to let her in.

"You can see right to the back of the house from the outside," she told him on entering.

He set about closing a window, but she quickly advised him not to. It might appear suspicious.

They went into the unlit kitchen, at the back, where he took her trembling hands.

"I shouldn't have come," she whispered.

"I'll keep my promise not to touch you. I promised myself not to touch you."

"Just tell me I'm not just one of your women," Indrani pleaded with him.

He pulled her towards him and kissed her passionately. Indrani yielded with her mouth, with her loins, with her legs. The world rocked like a vast cradle of half-remembered pleasures, when the mouth was the first source of satisfaction and the warmth of another body. Suddenly she broke loose from his embrace and went to sit down at the kitchen table.

"I'm so happy," she said. "No, don't come close."

"I've offended you?"

"No, my darling, you haven't offended me," she said, smiling. "I'm so happy I'm trembling. I can't even stand up any more. O God! I only wanted one minute. Now I want to spend a whole night with you, a week. . . . I love you. I adore you. . . . Touch me . . . softly. . . ."

She closed her eyes while he stroked her breast, and her breathing became audible, like wind in the trees. Her lips brushed against his hand, following it in its slow, circular motion. She pressed his hand against her breast cruelly and drank her depravity with relish.

Outside, there was the sound of a sharp explosion and Indrani's body became limp in his arms. But before Rohan realised what had happened, another shot broke the night stillness. He involuntarily put his hand to his neck, succumbed to the feeling of weakness that had overtaken him and fell to the floor, dragging Indrani's inert body with him.

And as his life gushed away Rohan saw the idiot who lived by the stelling performing the trick that was his only source of income; he saw him crush a sheet of paper between his fingers, and with a flourish open them again to reveal a handful of broken glass. Then the image of the idiot face faded, leaving the sound of crumpled paper resounding in his ears. And briefly he saw her sitting in the centre of a room under a blaze of light, Genetha, his sister, her waxen face rigid, as in death.

At first the police were of the opinion that Rohan had murdered Indrani and had gone into hiding; but tests on the blood stains on the kitchen floor showed that two persons had lost blood as a result of the rifle shots. They turned their attention to the theory that Rohan had been murdered at the same time as Indrani and his body disposed of in a manner they had not yet discovered.

The result of this new interpretation was that Sidique was asked to go to the station to help the police with their enquiry. Two days later he was released and the police confessed that they were as perplexed as ever. They intensified their enquiries in the district, but to no purpose, since neither Rohan nor Indrani had any enemies. Sidique was the obvious suspect, if, indeed, Rohan was dead, but all the evidence pointed to the fact that Sidique had not left the house the night of the murder. Both of his parents confirmed his alibi. To the insistent questioning on the reason for his wife's visit to Rohan's home, Sidique told the police that she had gone to see her sister. Sidique confessed that the two saw little of each other, but on that occasion Indrani wanted to invite Dada to come and live in the family house, since no one relished the idea of her living with a man to whom she was not married. Was Sidique's father capable of killing the couple? Sidique was scandalised at the suggestion.

It was Jai who had found Indrani's body. In his statement to the police he said that he had been waiting for about an

340

hour in the car when he went up to the house and knocked several times. In the end he opened the unlocked door and found his sister-in-law lying on her side in the kitchen. The police reasoned that if Indrani had been killed shortly before Jai went up to the house, Sidique would have had enough time to make the journey from the house to Rohan's home. Nevertheless, Sidique and his parents stuck to their story that he had not left the house until he learned of his wife's death. Further, the sincerity of his grief could hardly be doubted. For days he stayed in his room, dishevelled and unshaven. Whenever the police came to speak to him he received them in his pyjamas and answered their enquiries without seeming to care how long they stayed or how many questions they asked. And on their leaving he immediately went back to his room. His mother took him his meals on a tray, but he hardly ate anything, so that she was obliged to take away most of what she had brought.

Indrani's death disrupted the way of life of the Ali family to such an extent that when night fell only Jai and his wife remained up listening to the radio and talking in a low voice. Indrani's son, who during the daytime hung on to his grandmother's sari with a pathetic tenacity, went to bed at sunset in the hope that on waking the following morning he would see his mother lying at his father's side. His grandmother had told him that she had met with an accident and was in hospital far away; in a few weeks she would come back and they would all be happy again.

"Is that why Pa won't shave?" he asked.

"Yes," his grandmother replied.

Mr Ali was convinced that Sidique had murdered the couple. His suspicions were reinforced when, the morning after the crime, one of his employees told him that he had seen Sidique in the yard next to Rohan's house around the time when the deed was done. His disappearance for more than an hour, the mud on his shoes — which Mr Ali himself had thrown into the river when the news of the tragedy came to the family's ears — and his reticence when he arrived back home, all left no doubt in Mr Ali's mind that his son was guilty. He gave the employee fifty dollars and threatened to dismiss him if he breathed a word of what he had seen. When the whole thing had blown over he would be made a foreman, Mr Ali promised him.

"Why not now, Mr Ali?" the employee asked.

"Because people'd be suspicious, you fool. After all, you're the worst worker in the mill."

Mr Ali could get nothing out of Sidique, even when, in exasperation, his father threatened to put him out of the house.

"Is better he shut up than talk somet'ing stupid," his wife told him.

It was five days after the murders that events took a remarkable turn. Some distance from Rohan's house, three stray dogs kept going back to a bush, although a group of boys pelted them with sticks and pebbles. Their curiosity aroused, they went after the dogs and drove them from the spot. There, glaring out of the thicket, were the staring eyes of a dead man, whose face was covered with a mass of flies and whose body was gored in places where the dogs had torn his flesh away. Only the profusion of growth had prevented the carrion crows from discovering the body. One boy ran to the field where his father was working and told him of his discovery, and the man, frightened out of his wits, hurried to the police station to report what his son had told him. The boy then led his father and two policemen to the spot.

The body was identified by Dada, who looked at it unflinchingly. She was accompanied by Asha, large-eyed and serious, who remained outside while she entered the makeshift morgue. The two had become very close over the last few months and Asha accompanied Dada wherever she went.

Dada wore dark glasses and as she and the diminutive Asha were getting into the car to go back home, one of the onlookers said, "Is what she wearing them t'ings for? She bring bad luck to the distric' ever since she come. These people from town does always bring trouble an' vexation."

"First suicide an' now murder," remarked another. "Is obeah business, I tell you!"

The car drove off in a cloud of dust.

Dada looked at Asha to see if the reference to her mother's suicide had had any effect on her, but the girl was as placid as ever.

"You want a soft drink?" Dada asked her.

342

"Yes. But they'll all stare at me if I get out the car," said Asha.

"I'll ask the driver to get it."

The car stopped and the driver went into the cake shop for the sweet drinks. Two passing women recognised Dada, stopped and stared unabashed into the car.

The chauffeur dropped Asha off first. When Dada arrived she paid him and walked away, up the path, up the front stairs and into the lonely house. She had given the housekeeper two weeks' holiday, fearing that the woman might give in her notice if she were compelled to work in the house before Rohan was buried. She could not bear to look at his things.

At the time she had laid her plans to have him watched she had been transported on the crest of a wave of hatred for him and her sister. Now she thought that it would have been a thousand times preferable to have an unfaithful Boyie than be without him. Often, in quarrelling with him, she had shouted, "I'll kill you!" without intending any harm. She had come to know him well, and through him Genetha, his sister, to whom he had signed away all rights to the property they owned jointly. She had learned of his dead parents, about their life in Agricola, before they went to Georgetown, and all this she had shared with him, to the exclusion of Indrani.

That night, about six months ago, she recalled his interest at her confession of jealousy for Indrani, which began soon before her marriage. Still only a girl, Dada had felt an inexplicable envy that could be traced to nothing in her sister's behaviour, nor in her father's attitude to Indrani. It was just an unseemly emotion that had taken hold of her without warning and possessed her throughout the preparations for the marriage and the celebrations that followed the ceremony. Afterwards, the emotion disappeared without a trace, like some seven-day wonder that, years later, needed an effort to recall.

23

Suspicion

When the news of the murders was broadcast, Ramjohn experienced a feeling of elation. It then occurred to him that he might be under suspicion. Rohan must have told Dada how they had fallen out; and the forest ranger as well knew of Ramjohn's bitterness towards the young Armstrong. He must be careful to go about with a suitably grave expression.

The night Dada had come over to visit Asha, Ramjohn had sensed that something was wrong. Dada had sat on a box, her hands clasped and her eyes empty. Certain that something was amiss he had gone over to see what was happening at Rohan's house and concocted the story of the spoons. The latter's impatience to see him off deepened his suspicions and for the first time suggested that Rohan was expecting a woman. After all, there was talk in Suddie that Mrs Nassen's daughter was in love with him.

Ramjohn had to gain entrance to Rohan's house while the woman and he were on the premises in order to secure the rifle he kept in his bedroom. He could do this from the back stairs, provided that they went out on the porch, or at least in the gallery. He kept watch and when he caught sight of a woman coming up the path, saw her hesitate at the foot of the stairs and look round, he knew that he was right. He could hardly believe that Rohan and the woman friend had played right into his hands by going into the kitchen. If he entered the house by the front door he would not be heard at the back of the house.

Ramjohn stopped, on remembering that from the kitchen he might be seen if the couple were in the doorway. He changed his plans and tried to get into the house by climbing on the concrete pillar below Rohan's bedroom. It was only after several attempts that he managed to reach the bedroom window ledge once he had hoisted himself up on to the pillar.

After firing the two shots from Rohan's loaded rifle Ramjohn ran down the back stairs and waited to see what effect they would have on the neighbours. Several minutes later he came out of his hiding place. He dragged Rohan's body down the stairs, but once it was in the wheelbarrow he only had to cut across one lot of land and make for the path behind the property, where he was able to dispose of the body in the bushes, clean up the wheelbarrow and take it back to Rohan's yard. When the alarm was raised he was already back in his hammock under the house. Asha had had no idea that he was out for any part of the night and his main concern was the way Dada might feel.

When the police arrived to tell her what had happened she appeared to be so distraught, he was afraid lest she might point him out as a suspect. But evidently she suspected nothing. Gradually he was invaded with a feeling of immense satisfaction at the sight of her suffering.

After she went back home and Asha was in bed, Ramjohn lay down on the floor and went over his evening's work at leisure, the humiliation that had been ripening in his heart for months and was to grow into a cancerous hatred for Rohan and his mistress.

"Why didn't I want to get rid of Mrs Ali's body?" he thought. This problem intrigued him. "In fact, why did I want to take *his* body down to the bushes?"

He turned over several possible explanations, but none was plausible.

Shooting Mrs Ali, he mused, had also given him pleasure. His own wife had died before her time, why should someone else's be spared? But it was the shooting of Rohan that brought the blood rushing to his head.

Life without his wife was not worth living, and in killing Rohan he committed himself to a form of suicide.

A dog in the neighbourhood began howling.

"Is probably his," Ramjohn said to himself.

That night, between the peals of thunder the darkness was filled with the noise of the wind and the long drawn-out howling of the dog. Never had Ramjohn experienced such a feeling of power, just as in the first months of his marriage. He turned and looked at his children, lying about the floor. The baby was nestling against Asha, who had been the last to go to bed.

The morning after the murder Ramjohn felt uneasy, but at the office he played his part in the general amazement at what had happened. When, soon after the District Commissioner's arrival, he was sent for, his knees almost buckled under him. He knocked on the door feebly and heard a voice inviting him to come in.

"Ramjohn, this is Sergeant Gaskin," the Commissioner said.

The two men stared at him as he sat down heavily. Taking off his glasses, the District Commissioner rubbed them with his handkerchief.

"I know how you feel, Ramjohn, about your friend."

Ramjohn hung his head. Then the sergeant spoke.

"Just tell me the last time you saw him alive," the sergeant asked in a booming voice.

The two men mistook Ramjohn's confusion for grief and looked at each other.

"When he left the office, that's when I see him last."

"You're sure?" pressed the sergeant.

"Yes."

The District Commissioner shrugged his shoulders when the sergeant questioned him with his eyes.

"Thanks, Ramjohn; you can go now," the District Commissioner told him.

"One more thing, Mr Ramjohn," said the Sergeant. "Were you on good terms with the dead man?"

"Yes. We were friends."

"Thanks."

Ramjohn left, shaking uncontrollably.

That night he was unable to fall asleep, and when, far into the night, he heard a noise on the stairs, he sat up, trembling like a leaf. After a long spell of silence he got up and bolted the top and bottom of the door, a precaution he had never taken until then.

Just before dawn, as he was on the point of falling asleep, his youngest child began to cry, but by the time Asha had quietened him the gaps under the window were pierced with light and the cocks were crowing fitfully.

"Pa, is time," Asha called out to him, to remind him that he had to cut the wood before he took a bath and went to work.

He got up from the floor, stepped over the children, opened the door and went out into the cool, dawn air. A flight of parrots passed silently overhead, but he took no notice. He fetched the axe from under the house, and almost mechanically split each portion of wood with one blow. The chore over, he went to the latrine, which stood some distance behind the house, as much to relieve himself as to reflect on his fears. The noises of the unfolding morning, the voices, the barking dogs, the chattering birds, filled the air. If he had not slept that night, he shit long enough that morning, long and copiously, so that on stepping out of the latrine he felt weak, and sat down for a time on the lowest stair in order to recover. Asha had to remind him again that it was getting late and that the sun would soon be above the tamarind tree.

Ramjohn pulled himself together, got washed and dressed, and without taking any tea left for the office.

A few days after Rohan's body was found Sidique was arrested. Ramjohn returned from work with sweets for the children. He made his eldest son collect all his friends and organised a game of cricket for them. That night he went to the rum shop and drank until it closed; then, instead of going straight home, he went to Dada's house and knocked on the door.

She let him in, annoyed and surprised that he should think of coming to see her in that state.

"What d'you want, Ramjohn?" she asked.

"You hear the news?" he asked, grinning from ear to ear.

"Yes, but why d'you come here?"

"I just did want to pay you a visit. I in't got any friends, you know."

Dada turned her head to avoid his breath. "Come back when you're sober," she ordered.

Still grasping his bottle of rum he fell on his knees in front of Dada.

"Just let me touch you. Please, Miss Dada," he pleaded.

"Get up!" she ordered him.

He fumbled in his trouser pocket and pulled out a five-dollar note.

"I'll give you this if you let me touch you. I beg you . . . touch you and go away."

"Please get up and go, Ramjohn. Don't let me have to call for help."

Ramjohn, unsteady on his feet, put out his right hand and touched her dress. Dada recoiled.

Suddenly his pleading expression was replaced by a look of hatred.

"Who the hell you think you are, eh?" he cried out. "You wasn't even married to him. Playin' so damn great! You—"

"Get out!" she exclaimed in a low voice, although the nearest neighbours lived a good thirty yards away.

Ramjohn spat at her.

"That's what I think of you and your big belly! People don't know you expecting, but I know. And let me tell you something, *Miss* Dada," he said. "Your sister *Mrs* Ali no better than you. I come and find them doing it on the floor, with their clothes off. Yes, in the kitchen, there," he said, pointing to the back of the house, "on the floor, like animals, glued together like stray dogs at your gate. You call yourselves decent people. Decent people? I wouldn't touch you with a barge pole!"

Dada stared at him, motionless.

"And you should hear," continued Ramjohn, "how they been talking to one another! As if they was man and wife. And the people round here think you all are the salt of the earth. And I'll tell you another thing: my Asha'll know that you're not good enough to come within a hundred yards of her. Poor little mother, she talk about you as if you're purity itself. But *I* know and *you* know what you and your sister really like. Yes, 'pon the floor! And he lie 'pon top of her and bare her legs. And it was he and she, and you were over at my house thinking they were talking. You ever watch two people doing it, Miss Dada? It as sweet as the thing itself. But on the floor! That's like nothing else, watching and hearing them groaning as if he and she were alone. Your sister like a wild animal. Oh, yes! That lady who walk with her head high up in the air's like a wild animal once she's lying down."

"Get out," Dada said absently. "Get out."

348

In answer Ramjohn sniggered, pointedly looking below Dada's waist, then left the house.

Dada sat down on the nearest chair, her hands on her lap. Involuntarily, her right hand was raised to her belly.

"I hate life! I hate life! And the deceit!"

Everything was unbearable, the chairs, the blinds, the painted walls. And where could she go? To Vreed-en-Hoop? And embarrass her father? And even if he were prepared to have her in spite of the murder, what about her swelling form? Boyie used to stroke her there and kiss the taut skin on her belly. They planned for many things; he would build her a house with a tall flight of stairs, white jalousies and sliding doors.

Dada went and lay down. When she woke up, a wan moonlight was filtering through the window panes. Two minutes later she was back in bed. She pulled the blanket over her shoulders and fell asleep soon afterwards. The next morning she opened the back doors to allow more air to circulate through the house, then went back to bed at once, where she spent the rest of the day.

Unable to sleep, she recalled the days of her youth, the time at Vreed-en-Hoop, when she loved Boyie, without ever dreaming that one day they would share the same bed. Those interminable days when she often pretended to be ill so that she could stay in bed and think of him. In her imagination he held her hand or combed her hair, or ran with her among the flowering shrubs. Despite stories she heard from the older girls at school, love was a touch and a dumb look, and above all the silence of unspoken words. The painful sweetness of her first experience with Rohan provided the pith of another passion, the blinding sunlight as against the moon-glow.

Then came the doubts and the suspicions and finally the almost certainty that that Tuesday he was expecting Indrani, when she agreed to go over to Asha to leave the field clear for him. If he must deceive her, she must make things as easy for him as possible. If he loved her he would be faithful to her, however great the temptation. She had stubbornly told herself that the fact that Indrani came to visit him the second time did not necessarily mean that there was anything between them; now Ramjohn's disclosures robbed her of the will to go on living.

24

The Arrest

The first day Sidique went back to the mill — before his arrest — the employee to whom his father had given money, in order to keep him quiet, was insolent to him. Sidique fired him on the spot, and when he continued arguing with him in front of the other workers Sidique took off his belt and drove the man from the mill. Smarting under the humiliation he went straight to the police and gave them the information he had already disclosed to old Mr Ali. That was all the police needed. His information confirmed their suspicions of Sidique's guilt and he was taken to the station to be formally charged with the murder of his wife.

Sidique was conscience-stricken after his wife's death, feeling in some way responsible for what had happened. All his former suspicions seemed absurd and unjust. Indrani had been a good mother and wife, had suffered in his father's house and had not complained. Was it surprising that she became withdrawn? All he need have done was to show her that he understood.

The night of the murder he had slipped out of the house soon after she had left to visit Rohan, and walked along the Public Road as quickly as he could until he saw the car waiting outside the house. There was only one thing for it; he had to cut across the back yards of several houses until he got to Rohan's cottake. Turning into the Lot 46 — Rohan's was Lot 38 — he skirted the yards along the river. But at Lot 41 a new fence stood in his way. He had no hesitation in deciding to smash two staves in order to get through. When, however, he gave the fence a blow with his elbow, the noise roused a dog which rushed towards the spot, barking furiously. Sidique withdrew hastily and made his way back to the Public Road. Bitterly disappointed, he walked back along the road, reflecting on the possibility of getting a boat and approaching the cottage by way of the river.

"Stupid," he thought. "By the time I get there she'll be gone."

He walked slowly, ignoring the risk of being overtaken by the car which Indrani and Jai had taken. Back home, his mother came to meet him at the foot of the stairs.

"Where you been, boy?" she asked.

"Jus' for a walk."

"Is wha' wrong wit' you shoes?"

"They jus' muddy; why?"

"I want to know where you go to get shoes like that," his mother remarked.

Upstairs he took off his shoes and gave them to his mother. He reproached himself for not borrowing a boat after all. The uncertainty was unbearable.

Then came the news about the murder. At first he was filled with shame at the thought that people would assume that Indrani and Rohan were lovers, but in the end his grief overcame his shame and, to his parents' dismay, he seemed less upset at the possibility of being charged than at the memory of his dead wife.

When he went back to the mill he could not bear the inquisitive glances of the employees for more than a few hours, especially the one with the close-cropped hair, who seemed to smile every time their eyes met. His manner became more familiar and the tone of his voice more insolent.

Mr Ali, on learning that his son had fired the man he had paid to keep quiet, hastened to his house, only to find that he had already informed the police.

"I goin' to break you. You an' your family," Mr Ali told him. "You won't work anywhere along the coast if I can help it."

The poor man's satisfaction at cutting down Sidique had long been replaced by dread of being unable to find work. He told his wife what he had done and she began cursing him. He had to go to the police and retract his statement. Terrified at the prospect, he nevertheless went to the police station and declared that he had been lying, but the sergeant chased him away, telling him not to come back until he had been sent for. He had started off a train of events he could no longer control and when Mr Ali arrived he was lying on the floor.

The man's wife came into the room where the two men were.

"Mr Ali, I hear what you say, but gi' we a chance. We got the children. Me husban' stupid, Mr Ali. You kian' le' we starve after all these years he work for you."

"Now listen to me," Mr Ali said, "he mus' keep tellin' the police it was lies, that he only did want to get he in trouble. Understand? Keep tellin' them that. If he say so at the trial they kian' hang he. I goin' see you later."

"What about the job?" the woman asked.

"When my son free he goin' get he job, not before. Not before."

The woman ran after him. "Please, Mr Ali."

He wrenched her arm away and left while she looked after him and watched the car drive off.

Her voice, a moment ago pleading and tearful, broke out into another spate of abuse, directed at her husband.

The light was failing and the sun abruptly disappeared. The sound of bicycle bells, voices of passers-by and cars indicated that the last ferry of the day had come in.

Mr Ali went to see his son in prison and the two dollars he slipped the warder was enough to secure a private meeting with Sidique.

He placed the parcel he had brought him on the camp bed. It had been opened by the warder and the contents, carefully wrapped by Mrs Ali, lay in disorder in the deep cardboard box.

"We get the best lawyer, the best," he said, in an effort to rouse Sidique to conversation.

All day Sidique had been reproaching himself for allowing Indrani to go and see Rohan against his better judgement. The sight of his father was more than enough to rekindle these reflections.

"You sit down on my bed without asking."

Promptly, Mr Ali got up.

"If I hadn't listened to you Indrani would've been alive," Sidique continued. "You-all wouldn't take no for a answer."

"But if you din'—" Mr Ali began, but was peremptorily interrupted by his son.

"I din' kill her!" Sidique said emphatically.

The contrast between his torpor before he went to prison

and his present attitude did not escape his father's notice. He still firmly believed that his son had murdered Indrani and did not take his denial seriously.

"Here, in prison," said Sidique, "is the first time I in' frightened of you."

Mr Ali could only speak to his son in one way, and now faced with a bolder Sidique, he was perplexed and lost for words.

"Well, what you come for?" Sidique asked.

"I talk to Harry and tell him he got to deny he see you near the house that night. Is the only good evidence the police got. And the lawyer say when he finish with him the judge wouldn't believe him."

"Why?"

"'Cause you sack him. He make up the story out of revenge."

"But he say he see me before I sack him."

"That don't matter. He say it *after* he get sack, that's the important thing."

Sidique was silent.

"A lot o' things goin' change when you get out o' here," his father said, trying to be pleasant.

"You kian' bring Indrani back, though."

"She dead," said his father. "But isn't that what you did want?"

"No!" Sidique reacted violently. "I did love my wife!"

"You don't look as if you in pain now. At least not like soon after she dead."

Sidique looked at him angrily. It did not seem possible that father and son could have a conversation which did not end in one of them losing his temper.

"Boy, you is a real fool, you know," Mr Ali said.

Sidique grabbed him by the collar and began shouting at him. The door opened from the outside and the warder rushed in. He asked Ali to go, begging him not to mention the incident.

This time Mr Ali did not experience the sense of outrage that he had on the previous occasion when Sidique had cursed him. On the other hand there was no feeling of guilt in Sidique either. A new life was germinating in him, he felt, for within the four walls of his confinement he dared to do more than he

353

did when he was free; to challenge what was accepted in his father's house. Here he dreamed and he dared. He dreamed of Indrani's belly and the sweat beads on her forehead. Between these walls, with bent head, he played his guitar at noon-time, now, when the young rice was emerging from the water. His greatest injustice to Indrani had been forcing her to live in his parents' house. Should he ever leave this hole he would marry again and set up house among the sand hills and bring up his son as he wanted, even at the risk of being a pariah in the Mohammedan community.

Sidique went and lay down on his bed to reflect on how he ought to fight for his life. Who could have killed Indrani? Was it his brother? At the thought he sat up on his bed; he felt the blood draining from his face, for, looking back, he imagined he recalled bits of evidence to support his belief, a look, a remark. And Jai had the opportunity to do it. Sidique had found a new way of torturing himself.

Dada surveyed the suitcase on the floor, while the housekeeper stood next to her, wearing a black arm-band. Ramjohn had just been to tell her how sorry he was for the things he said, and invited her to come and see Asha whenever she wanted.

The donkey-cart man was coming up the path, apparently impervious to the downpour. The gallery was empty of its furniture and had an air of desolation, despite the bird cage which still hung from the wall.

Both women were reluctant to open when the knocking on the door came, but finally the housekeeper let the cartman in. When all the luggage was in his cart he got up on the front and waited for the women. Dada fought back the tears and, without looking at the housekeeper, went out by the open door.

The raised planks in the yard were already covered with water, and runnels of water made their way from the high ground on the edge of the yard to the centre, and the trees, flailing their branches in the wind, scattered raindrops along the path. The bridge was just a few inches over the flooded gutter. No doubt a flood was due that year, and there would be death and untold sorrow, and when the waters subsided the coast would carry its scars for years.

354

On the boat Dada sat among her belongings, looking out at the grey sky and a flight of birds sculling their way back to the mainland. A middle-aged man began to sing, "Is what you waiting for, me gal, is what you waiting for?"

Came the disembarkation at Parika and before boarding the train Dada bought a glass of cane-juice to slake her thirst. She drank the sweet, undiluted cane to the dregs and joined the crowd hurrying to secure a seat on the waiting train.

The countryside went by as on an interminable slide, and women with baskets on their heads waved to the passing train without looking up at it. Cattle stood motionless in the rain and unpainted houses were closed against the wind and water. Then at Uitvlugt the train stopped longer than at any other station and hucksters flocked to the windows to sell their wares. There was laughter as a party of people said goodbye to a youth who was apparently going to Georgetown. Dada stared out of the train at the beaming faces and could not help admiring the appealing face of one of the girls, who caught sight of her, but looked away at once, unconcerned at her interest.

Dada found herself looking for pregnant women everywhere. She scrutinised every woman who might be in her second or third month and thought that she detected among them some who were in her condition. She began thinking of Vreed-en-Hoop and as the train pulled in she saw that nothing had changed.

A forest of expectant faces were looking up to see if friends could be recognised, or relatives, while the train came to a clanging, jerking halt, and those standing up were thrown forward. Dada was in no hurry to leave and allowed the other passengers to vacate the compartment before she got up. When she appeared in the doorway her father took her in a long, silent embrace, but as soon as he tried to speak the words choked in his throat. He left her on the pretext that he was going to see to her luggage.

The rain had stopped and as Dada and her father came out of the hired car faces appeared at the windows of the houses opposite. She crossed the bridge under which the water shone with a pale light. The exora and crotons were still dripping from the rain and their once blood-veined leaves were now almost colourless. The Ceylon mango tree, its scrawny arms

355

stretched out, had lost most of its foliage, throttled by the bird-vine encircling it.

The dog bounced from the back of the yard to greet her, jumping almost to the height of her face. No one else except the servant seemed to be in the house and as her father offered no explanation she waited for him to tell her.

The servant at once brought in a bowl of hot soup.

"You're not eating, Pa?"

"I've eaten," he said. "After all, I didn't even know whether you'd come."

In fact, apart from a cup of coffee and two slices of bread and butter early that morning he had not eaten all day since. The excitement and anticipation had been too much for him. While waiting at the station he had bought a soft drink, but it was left undrunk, with its straw rising from the bottle mouth at an angle. No sooner had he sat down to drink it than he looked at his watch and got up again, afraid that the train might appear before he had finished.

"Your mother's gone again," he told her. "She said she'll be back next Wednesday. Betty's working in Georgetown and only comes home on Saturdays for the weekend. She's engaged."

Dada rose from the table and went to sit by the window. Her father watched her anxiously, wanting to speak, but not knowing the words to console her. He watched the light fading behind her and her full belly under the frock she had put on for the first time. Despite the evidence of womanhood Dada was still a child to him, an innocent victim of bad company. If Indrani had been his favourite, Dada was the purest and most guileless of his daughters, for in the manner of her mother she wore her heart on her sleeve, like some trusting animal. All alone on a night when couples laughed under the windows and music crept up the road from the rum shop, he often sat in the dark and watched the chairs where his wife and children sat when they were at home. He expected nothing from life now. The thought that Dada would remain with him and bring up the child in Vreed-en-Hoop was too desirable to be capable of fulfilment.

That night when the wind was howling Dada came to his room and asked him if she could sleep there.

"You frightened?"

She nodded.

The next morning was as dull as the day before. Dada was at table, but could hardly eat and when her father joined her he asked why she had eaten so little.

"You say everything except what you want to say," she remarked.

He put down his cup with a clattering noise.

"Sometimes it's the best way," he said.

"Not in this case."

"Very well. Did Boyie have anything to do with Indrani?"

"No!" she answered defiantly.

"That's all I wanted to know. You know, I used to have the idea that when I grew old my children would look after me."

"People always see things from their side," replied Dada. "I loved Boyie, but not enough."

"There's an after-life," he said softly.

"I'm clinging to this one," she said, "because I was once happy."

"That's a good sign. . . . You know, when you come to think of it, Man's the only suicidal animal."

Dada smiled. If only he knew how her words said nothing of what was really in her heart. If only she could forgive Boyie this fog would lift. This incoherent conversation, with each following his own line of thought, went on for a while until Dada became lost in her thoughts.

"The world is changing too fast for me," said Mr Mohammed. "Some worm is eating at the family. My father's family was like my grandfather's and probably like his father's. Not so now. It's like having to learn a new language when you're old. The best people—"

"Ah!" exclaimed Dada. "I wondered when you'd come to that. Who told you that Indrani was one of the best people?"

"What're you driving at? Out with it!"

"I'm simply asking you how you know Indrani was one of the best? Sidique didn't think so."

Her father made a deprecating gesture.

"I didn't think so either," she persisted.

"Well, why?" he asked again.

"She wanted Boyie to get rid of me."

357

Her father's silence was irritating.

"Why? Because you weren't married?" he finally asked.

"She loved Boyie."

"No. That's a lie!"

"She loved him, your Indrani. She loved him and went to him behind her husband's back."

Mr Mohammed stood up. "Is that why she was killed?"

"I don't know," she answered.

"But it's probable."

"Yes," Dada answered.

"The police didn't know that, from what I heard on the radio."

"They don't know," said Dada.

"Then you're not to repeat a word of it to anyone."

At that moment there was the sound of someone coming up the back stairs. It was the servant. Dada pushed her breakfast away from her and got up. She felt the need to continue the conversation with her father, but saw that it was impossible. She now wanted to tell him everything, while yesterday she dreaded the thought of being questioned by him. If only he were not so pig-headed about Indrani! She knew that he did not believe a word of what she had told him about Indrani's feelings for Boyie. What did he know of women? What did men know of women, who behaved in a certain way because men expect it of them? It was a man's world and men never allowed women to forget it. When Indrani's respect for Sidique had gone, the constraint it had imposed upon her must have weakened in a way few men would understand. All Suddie knew that Indrani had been cool to Sidique towards the end. If the police had had any sense they would have suspected him long ago.

But what was the significance of Ramjohn's remarks about seeing Boyie and Indrani together? When did he see them together? Had they been seeing each other at times she had not been aware of? Or did he see them the night of the murder? Was it he who . . . ? That was impossible. Ramjohn lacked the courage to kill a rat. Besides, the person who had committed the murders must have been exceptionally cool. Ramjohn was nervous and excitable.

Strikingly evident was the fact that Mr Mohammed understood far less about Indrani and Dada than he imagined. He had known them in the home, where children are good or bad, compliant or recalcitrant, bearing little resemblance to the complex, devious figures that people the stage of adult life. It had always struck Dada that her teachers knew nothing about her; about the way she felt or thought or suffered. And it was the same for the other children. They knew little about one another, but far more than teachers knew about them. To a certain extent it was true of parents. The very people who spent a good part of their life looking after, teaching, guiding children, knew practically nothing about them.

Dada looked out of the window as she had done a thousand times in her girlhood and she was filled with an infinite sadness. Then, love was simple, and even death. When her grandmother died they buried her at Poudroyen. The children cried, since everyone else was crying. Then when it was all over she and her sisters ate a hearty meal because the funeral had lasted so long. They had wondered why their parents were so silent and ate nothing. Love and death wore masks when they were young, no doubt, to hide their fearful countenance.

She looked down into the garden.

"The crotons will recover in December and the oleander bloom again," she thought.

That night Mr Mohammed woke up and saw his daughter wandering about the room, apparently looking for something.

"What's it, Dada?" he asked.

"He's here somewhere."

"Who?"

"Boyie. Didn't you see him? He touched me and moved off. I *know* he's in the house."

"You've been dreaming."

"No, no, he touched me here," she insisted, indicating her left arm. "I can still feel where his cold hand held me."

"Girl, you're dreaming."

He led her to the bed and sat her down on it. She still seemed dazed. "I'll make you some chocolate," he offered.

"All right."

He left her sitting on the edge of the bed and when he came back she said to him, as she took the cup, "I must go back."

359

"But they won't let you have the house, Dada."

"I know a family . . . a girl and her father. He said I could come whenever I liked."

The stillness of the night was broken by the whirring of an engine on the river.

"What about the child?" her father asked.

"I don't know, Pa."

After a long silence her father said, "You've always got a home here, whatever happens. I've never seen my first grandchild. I hope I'll see the second."

The next morning Dada left by train for Parika.

25

Echoes of Fulfilment

The prosecutor made much of the fact that Sidique was known to be on bad terms with his wife, that he must have been suspicious of her visit to Rohan and that the employee saw him approaching his house at or about the time of the murder.

Defence counsel based his case on two facts; namely, the employee's retraction of his statement before he returned to his original story; and Sidique's summary dismissal of the employee before the latter made his statement to the police, which was clearly, in his view, motivated by the desire for revenge.

The judge, in his summing-up, drew attention to the distinction between the degree of proof required in a civil case on the one hand, and in a criminal one on the other. The criterion in the former was a balance of probabilities. In the latter, proof was only satisfied when the prosecution could show that the matter was beyond all reasonable doubt. The judge also pointed out the significance of the employee's statement to the police. It was the hub of the prosecution's case. Was the employee lying? Did his dismissal cause him to fabricate his account of Sidique lurking in the vicinity of Rohan's house? And even if his story were true it did not necessarily follow that Sidique went into the house, or that he shot his wife and Armstrong.

The jury saw fit to deliberate for three hours, before bringing in a verdict of "Not Guilty".

Outside, Sidique met his mother, who had been waiting in the car with Sis. She left the car, placed a garland of flowers round his neck — as if he were a bridegroom — and embraced him.

Sidique's father lingered in the courtyard to talk to the newspaper reporters, but in the end he took his place beside Jai in the front seat of the car, maintaining his stony silence throughout the journey.

The older Mrs Ali thought to herself, "Indrani gone, like we did want. Armstrong and Dada gone, like we did want. And the family together again. All they got to do is listen to me and nothing'd ever go wrong."

"At least Jai isn't a fool," the old Mr Ali thought. "And Sis is obedient. And there's my wife, who got more brains than the rest o' them put together."

Sidique was thinking of his son, who must be looking out of the window, or licking patterns on the pane for want of something better to do. He must marry again and have children so that his son might have playmates to romp with.

Jai wished he could hum a tune which kept running through his head, but he did not dare; and the inscrutable Sis was examining the back of her husband's neck.

When they arrived home, Abdul ran down the stairs to meet his father. He delved into his pockets to look for sweets, and reproached him for not bringing anything home.

"I did tell you I'd be back," Sidique said to his son.

"Come and play a game of okari with me. Uncle Jai got two bi-iig okari seeds and they round, round, round."

The child tripped along next to his father and never left his side until bedtime.

Dada came back to Suddie and put up with Ramjohn's family, but did not stay long. There was talk about her being responsible for the tragic deaths and that she would corrupt Ramjohn and his children, just as she and her sister had bewitched Rohan Armstrong. If she did not want to end up like her sister she would do well to leave and never return. When her condition began to show, things got worse. One night a stone came hurtling through the window of Ramjohn's house and landed a few feet from the baby, who was crawling on the floor.

Dada felt, in any case, that she could not remain since, unable to work, she was yet one more mouth to feed; and coming back was not like being there before, in spite of Asha and the house, a short distance away; in spite of the house-keeper's friendliness, in spite of the impassive tamarind tree guarding the entrance of the house she had shared with Rohan; and the river with Tiger Island in the distance, and the chugging of phantom boats at night. Every time she heard the grinding cart-wheels on the road, when the East Indians went in droves to the late cinema show, she became frightened, believing them to be vehicles of vengeance. One morning she looked up at the clouds overhead, endlessly changing shape like garments drying, and she decided to go home to Vreed-en-Hoop.

Three months later she gave birth to a daughter in her father's house. Exhausted, she watched the midwife put the child on the table and leave it there, as if it were a bundle of provisions. Dada had known the woman since she was a little girl, and had seen her entering and leaving various houses in Vreed-en-Hoop and Poudroyen, dressed in her uniform.

It seemed an age until she was allowed to take her daughter in her arms. The midwife went to fetch Mr Mohammed, who was kicking his heels in the dining-room, and he, in turn, took up his grandchild and held her close to his body. This was the proof that his daughter was not a girl anymore.

When Mrs Mohammed came home again she made much of the infant, sang it songs from her childhood and marvelled that its eyes moved rapidly whenever she sang. And when Betty came to stay for the weekend and brought the baby a shak-shak she tried to attract its attention by holding it up and shaking it. Her mother suggested that she sing instead, and it was only then that the child's pupils moved from side to side.

One day as Dada was sitting with the child under the house, her father went into her room to borrow her pen. On the dressing-table was the draft of a letter addressed to Rohan, which began by telling him that he was the father of a girl. She had wanted a boy, but knew that he had always wanted a daughter. She was glad for him. The letter continued:

"I know that you come and stand by my bed when I am asleep. I'm not afraid, but please don't touch the child, lest you frighten her. Time is spent, and love; and the echoes of fulfilment sound more faintly than the sorrowing heart laid, like thine, to rest where lilacs grow beside the shallow water. The child has given me the will to live, but no man will ever touch me. When I saw its head emerge I knew that our love was eternal. You forgot that, and paid with your life. I cannot bear to think I did not trust you with

Indrani and I am constantly punishing myself for it. But I know you will forgive me. Sleep well, beloved, and think of me among the shadows.

Your loving
Dada."

Mr Mohammed at once saw the contradiction between her reproach to Rohan for his unfaithfulness and the statement that he must forgive her for suspecting him of unfaithfulness. It was like Dada, who acted and spoke without reflection. Through the window he could see the bent figure of a man cutting the grass with long sweeps of his scythe, and he saw the heat rise from the corrugated iron of the outhouse in a shimmering, transparent wall. He went downstairs to see whether his daughter and granddaughter had fallen asleep.

Dada was rocking her child slowly, looking upward at the floorboards of her father's house.

There was another day, another way of life beyond the cast skin. And the eye of Day closed and the voice of Night was heard in tremulous bubblings of frogs from the pools, Krrrrrrrrrrrrrr. And Dada recalled other days, a journey from Parika to Vreed-en-Hoop, the rhythmic sound of carriage rails, a blurred landscape rushing by through diagonal lines of dirt on the panes where the wind fled.

Genetha

I return to the edge
Where the sea gnaws always

– Christopher Aird (Guyanese poet)

"Shall my heart go
As flowers that wither?
Some day shall my name be nothing?
At least let us have flowers!
At least let us have singing!"

– Poem from the Aztecs

I

1. Recollections

Genetha was left to brood in the house when her brother Rohan
went away, driven by the fear of incest after their father's death.
Night after night, on coming home from work, she went over
the events since her family had come from Agricola to settle in
the north of Georgetown, back to the area of her mother's birth:
the dismissal of Esther, the servant who had done all but suckle
them; her father's reproach that she lacked compassion because
she would not entertain the idea of taking Esther back to live
with them; the discovery that he had brought the former
servant to the house and paid her as other men did. . . . And
every night the recollections brought the same panic fed by
some demonic energy.

Rohan had told Genetha that he could not remain when he
found out that she had become intimate with Fingers, a young
man from one of the deep yards that spread like scabs over parts
of the town. She had believed that his poverty was no impediment to their association since Fingers was Rohan's best friend,
so she was not prepared for her brother's fury. She was never to
discover the true reason for his departure.

Rohan had gone away as if he had the right to. And she, in
the same way as her mother had been until death, was tied to
the house like a dog to a post.

The war between Genetha's loneliness and her vague fear of
allowing an intrusion in the family home reduced her to tears on
her waking up in the empty house. She came to dread the
morning with its clamour of bells interspersed with the pounding of dray wheels, and the muffled sounds of night-time.

She became furtive, if her neighbour was to be believed.

"You're getting like my son. Secretive, like my son," the
woman once said when she caught Genetha scurrying to the
back of the yard to avoid her. "But you don't have any reason.
He's got debts."

Genetha talked to her for a while through the walaba paling
staves and even forced a smile when the neighbour asked her to
laugh a little.

"You've been through a lot," she told Genetha, in an effort to console her. "But I had a hard life too! When your father died it was a sort of deliverance, wasn't it? It *was* a deliverance."

"No," retorted Genetha sharply.

Undismayed, the neighbour persisted. "You can entertain now, at least. You didn't have a chance to live your own life."

Genetha bowed her head. If the neighbour were younger she might have told her of the morning dray-carts and the evenings when shadows kept thronging at the doorway, like the visitors on the stairs after news of her father's death had spread.

"You need friends, Miss Armstrong. You give your life for your father and he went and died. And for your brother and he gone away. They wouldn't let you have friends and look how they left you in the lurch!"

Genetha was no longer offended. She would not have dared speak to the neighbour like that, and God knows her son did enough to be gossiped about. But she was not offended, for the neighbour was older and had no malice.

When Genetha left the neighbour she locked herself in, switched off the light and took off her clothes. Then she wandered about the house for a few minutes in her nightdress before delivering herself up to her secret vice, which consisted of taking a poisonous concoction that went to her head, left her arms heavy and numb and in the end vouchsafed her visions filled with purple clouds. Marion, one of their servants of long ago, had taught her brother the secret of visions and he, in turn, had passed it on to Genetha, who remembered well the forbidden euphoria of that late morning when they were on school holidays and going from house to yard and from yard to house, frantic with boredom, and the break in the monotony that came with the new-found indulgence. After that long August the secret lay dormant, for Rohan had discovered cricket and left Genetha to the insipid games of girlhood. Now, as in that far-off August, she indulged herself endlessly, having summoned up her brother's presence with copious tears.

As always she sank on to the floor after standing defiantly before the looking-glass, weighed down by her numbed arms and visions of blood-stained beds. But the short period of nausea was soon followed by a feeling of contentment and then by an indescribable sadness as she rediscovered her whereabouts, the long sky-light through which filtered the gently bleeding night and the feeble rays of a handful of stars.

There came an unexpected respite for Genetha when the neighbour's misfortunes were made public in a distraint by the bailiffs, who "levied" on her late one Friday morning. Her furniture was piled high on the pavement and tallied carefully by one of them, dressed meticulously in jacket and well-pressed trousers. Her son, no doubt the cause of his mother's shame, was seen by the curious – who had gathered in front of the house in spite of the sun – to be smoking nonchalantly at the window, looking on as if it were someone else's disgrace. In the end he was obliged to give up his seat at the instance of the second bailiff, who remained in the house.

Genetha, home for the midday meal, went over to offer her neighbour tea and had to endure a flood of invective, directed ostensibly at her but meant for the ne'er-do-well son.

The experience, unforeseen despite the son's trail of past misdeeds and his notorious skill at persuading those who dealt with him to part with their money, had a salutary effect on Genetha. She resolved to stop taking the mild poison and to renounce the favourite recollections of her brother and the time when her parents were alive and a destitute aunt lived in the room under the house.

On Sundays she went to church and took a Sunday-school class of children between the ages of seven and eleven; and once during the weekend ventured over the river on a taxi ride past the house of girls on New Road where her brother used to visit. She got out at some nameless village on the coast and walked along the ploughed fields above which wheeling gulls squawked endlessly.

Time and time again she came back to take the taxi ride until the villagers began waving to her, believing that she was looking for a plot of land to buy. Two of them even took her to the dye-pits which were about to be uncovered now that the sun was low and invited her into their houses afterwards where their wives admired her bodice all covered in braid. She in turn wondered at the soles of their feet, which had the tapir-like thickness of those who had never worn shoes.

There was soon an end to her excursions after she had explored the length and breadth of the village; but at least they had exorcized her panic; and now boredom had settled in its place, a healthy boredom that afflicted most of her class.

Genetha found herself watching the young men go by as her

mother had done even after she was married. Unabashed, she gazed at the odd passer-by who stopped to urinate against the corrugated fence at the corner, uninhibited by the presence of a father or brother. And now that she was alone it dawned upon her to what extent her behaviour used to be regulated by them. The mask she had worn on their account she still wore, but only when she was out of the house and her behaviour was subjected to the examination of others. Yet all around her she saw the way other women had changed, how they smoked and drank, how they took advantage of their status as working women to go out with more than one man or to leave their men if they were married; how they flew in the face of convention with that aplomb of a youth who had drunk for the first time. But some unseen hand guided her conduct outside, and even her father would have approved of the show of propriety and the proper opinion those who knew her held of her.

Then came February, when the window panes melted in their frames, and the brilliant nights. And once more her recollections pressed upon her, the childlike obsession with pictures, the afternoon when in a fit of jealousy she had deliberately left the gate open and Rohan, then only two years old, had wandered into the road and was nearly run down by a horse and carriage. She recalled the castor-oil doctor who always gave a word-for-word commentary of a one-horse race he had witnessed on the race-course when he was a youth and then cleaned up on the gambler's spinning-wheel by putting a five-dollar note on the ace of spades. She recalled the woman who lived on the edge of Agricola, in a house overlooking the back-dam, who, according to her father, shaved in secret. And her story book with a blue, pellucid sea, and her disappointment at the first encounter with the curling waves that died on the sand; her father's anger when he found that a new pair of trousers had been destroyed by the moths, in spite of the precaution of naphthalene balls which gave to the wardrobe a scent that came to characterize for her the better side of domesticity; and the long stay in her mother's parents' home, after her mother's death, when her father grudgingly gave his consent for her to be taken away, even though he was overcome with grief and wanted nothing better; and her grandparents' house where there was constant talk of superior things, like saffron and potted orchids.

At the back of her grandparents' yard was a swing on which

she used to spend much of the afternoons after the ritual of the main meal, which everyone called *breakfast*, at eleven in the morning. She could not believe that such a wondrous toy remained unused, that the neighbourhood children did not flock into the yard to gaze at one another soaring up to the roof-top and falling back in an arc.

And then came the loss of her father on that afternoon when dust spun in the late sunlight. A single accident achieved what a long illness did not, when the sick-room smelled of bay-rum and damp from the yard. Everything threatened: the coming dusk, the indistinct voices. A single accident that prevailed over the long months when sickness hammered on the walls. In that night filled with people Rohan had remained calm and the old women who came to tend the corpse never tired of caressing the weathered head while outside the wind scattered leaves like monstrous insects. Genetha had been warned about death and had covered the mirrors, as was the custom. So many things she had learned about death since her childhood, but it had been different. All she could remember was the sense of loss and the leaves scattering as if dealt by mysterious fingers.

February passed; then came April and early May with much rain and grey days. Genetha felt less oppressed, and the routine established after the neighbour's misfortune was elaborated by regular visits to her father's sister and her grandparents' house.

After a time people no longer enquired about Rohan, just as they stopped asking after Esther a year or so after she was dismissed. The shopkeepers, like the neighbour, grew accustomed to the fact that there was a house in the street with one occupant, as they had grown accustomed to the sight of Genetha shopping for the household when for years Esther had haggled with them with the assurance of one who controlled the family's purse-strings.

Every Saturday afternoon she looked up her grandparents in Queenstown, in the house where her father had courted her mother and learned of the gulf that separated him from her family. Genetha's mother's two sisters never failed to remind him of his origins in a hundred and one little humiliations. And for that reason he did everything he could to keep their family and his apart after his marriage. Rohan hardly knew them and Genetha's tenuous connection with the household really began with that stay in the wake of their mother's death. After that she did not dare speak of those relations in her father's presence and only dropped in to visit them on occasion, when she found herself riding past on her bicycle.

Now, with the Saturday afternoon visits established as a routine, she got to know them better, even though she remained on her guard, carrying deep within her a residue of her dead father's resentment.

"When are you getting married?" her elder aunt was in the habit of asking, for the sake of conversation.

"No one's proposed yet, Aunt," she always replied.

"I can't believe that, dear," her younger aunt would put in. She was like her father, Genetha's grandfather, gentle and warm.

And sometimes her grandmother, kindly but distant, would smile at her as if she were still a child. She and her husband seemed to be one in their decrepitude, with their backs stooped in the same way. They had aged together, and so suddenly that now her father's monstrous curses seemed charged with absurdity.

Her two aunts were preoccupied with marriage.

"Has Rohan written lately?" asked the younger aunt once.

"Not lately, Aunt," replied Genetha.

"I suppose he'll at least write when he gets married," observed Deborah, the elder aunt, always the more officious.

"I hope so," said Genetha dryly, seeking to quash a subject that never failed to pain her.

"The family before everything else," went on Deborah. "The individual is nothing. The family's everything."

"Yes, Aunt," said Genetha dutifully, not certain what she meant by "family". The word was widely used to include even cousins far removed, to the sixth and seventh degree, because they were "blood".

Whenever Genetha happened to speak of her father she was met with a frigid silence. And once her other aunt, her father's sister, who used to live in the room under their house, told Genetha that those two fine aunts of hers in Queenstown had once remarked that their sister, Genetha's mother, *tolerated* Armstrong, her own husband.

Genetha recalled this remark when her older aunt said, "Your mother was a fine musician before she got married, Genetha. Did you know that your mother was a fine musician before her marriage?"

"We knew. We all knew," replied Genetha. "Father knew, too," she added deliberately, with unwonted boldness.

"You must miss him, dear," said Alice, her younger aunt, in a conciliatory voice.

Genetha looked at her, astonished that she should be required to respond to a remark like that so many months after her father's death. Her younger aunt mistook her silence for grief and started smoothing her dress.

And yet Genetha was drawn to these two ageing women, whose hair was streaked with silver since, disdaining the new style, they could not bring themselves to dye it. The same tranquillity that had fired her mother's nostalgia for the house long after she was married had begun to infect Genetha. Had she been able to visit without being obliged to make formal conversation, she would have come when the spirit took her and lingered as long as it suited her.

If the Queenstown relations did not approve of Genetha's father they would not have approved of his sister either, because she used expressions like "take out your photograph" for "take your photograph" and "keep noise" for "make noise", and for all the other reasons they never approved of him.

Genetha found her father's sister pleasant enough, but there was something lacking in their relationship, that something which distinguished maternal aunts and uncles from paternal ones and placed the former on a higher plane in the scale of affections. Genetha's visits to her paternal aunt were made out of duty, while the visits to the Queenstown house, even when they were casual, were the result of a deep need.

"You can't keep away from your grandparents' house," her father's sister once told her, and in an effort to compete with her dead brother's in-laws had a bracelet made for Genetha of eighteen-carat gold. But the niece's exaggerated delight on receiving the present only increased her bitterness. Though she had occupied a room under the family's house for years, in contrast to their mother's sisters who had never even condescended to visit them since they came to live in Georgetown, that had brought her no closer to them.

Her paternal aunt's obsessive conversation, consisting of little else save her opinion of the Queenstown aunts and her dead brother's injustice towards her, had the effect of reducing the frequency of Genetha's visits. And as these visits became rarer so her aunt concentrated even more on the subject of the ageing women in Queenstown and on her brother who once robbed her of two houses, the remnants of a fortune. In the end Genetha stopped going altogether, daunted by her aunt's resentment.

All this happened within a year of Rohan's going away to take up a new post in the Essequibo. And in that year Genetha had learned to live alone.

2. A Dog in Heat

Before Genetha had taken up with Rohan's friend she had gone out for a while with Michael, and it was to him that she now turned for male companionship. Their relationship before, up to the moment when it was interrupted, had not been happy. They used to go to religious meetings together, continuing a tradition in his family that went back two generations. The fervour he displayed at these gatherings surprised Genetha, who was always acutely embarassed by his silences. But, as he explained, his was a deeply religious family which practised what the Church preached.

Michael did not approve of her clothes, by most standards conservative, nor of her love of the cinema, an incipient vice he denied her after they had gone out together for a few weeks. Convinced that she was unattractive, Genetha did her best to please him. Mistrusting the model of marriage her parents had presented her, she relied on her own ideas of what her role as a potential wife ought to be. When Michael boasted of the number of professional people among his relations she concealed her revulsion and listened dutifully.

Against her expectations she grew to like him, but noticed that as he became certain of her affection and loyalty he set about imposing his will on her with unexpected ruthlessness. She was to go here, could not go there; she ought not to eat this and should drink that or that bush tea because it cleaned you out. And the one shortcoming he was unable to forgive was her inability to show enthusiasm at religious meetings. Her Methodist background had inculcated in her the habit of restraint, and at best she managed to sing hymns that were not to be found in the Methodist hymnal.

Genetha would not give Michael up, despite all this, believing that his uprightness was the uprightness of her dead parents.

Her brief association with Fingers, Rohan's best friend, had been partly responsible for her brother going away: if she had learned anything she had learned that the flesh was not to be trusted, that the spirit must maintain its ascendancy above all. On a visit to the Courantyne when still a little girl she had accompanied an East Indian woman to a Kali Mai Poojah ceremony and was mesmerized by the disc of burning camphor in the priest's hand; to her the dazzling flame at one and the same time promised warmth and threatened disfigurement, a chastening fire that nevertheless aroused in her for the first time a longing for an unknown contact. Michael was sobriety, the mid-point between two fires that spun as one in the priest's hand.

Michael's refusal to countenance any experience that he deemed improper made Genetha suspicious of confiding in him. The guilt she felt at possessing the secret of visions and at indulging in the euphoric poison had to be borne alone.

But Michael was not entirely without experience; more than once he had, in his peremptory way, made one of his mother's servant girls take down her drawers when everyone else was out, and he had contemplated her featureless body for several minutes on end like the traveller who, for the first time, casts his eyes on a stunning landscape of desert and brush. Yet despite Genetha's vulnerability he had remained aloof, seeming to want nothing from her in that way. In the past when she had suffered from Michael's virtuousness she turned to Rohan's friend; but now she would not make the same mistake again. After all, there were women who had been courted for as long as ten years before they married.

He always came after dark, like a rider in the mist, hardly making a noise as he pushed his cycle over the bridge. People in the street would not have credited the innocence of their association and Genetha's neighbour remarked to her son that since her father's death she had gone to the dogs. Could he remember the daughter of the sea captain, who lived in Light Street? While he was away for months on his schooner she behaved correctly, never giving tongues a reason to wag. But soon after his death she began to carry on like a dog in heat and any newcomer was welcome.

Genetha's doctor urged her to wear glasses and Michael strongly advised her to follow his counsel. When she declared herself willing to risk further deterioration of her eyesight, Michael's fury was incomprehensible. He accused her of never following advice, even though Genetha hardly dared to ignore his. She gave in and for a few weeks took on the habit, which she firmly believed disfigured her. But Michael's repeated assurances to the contrary made her suspicious of his motives in condoning the doctor's views. She abandoned the habit abruptly, and, in what was until then her only act of revolt, refused to discuss the matter any further with him.

So they grew to know each other and she went to meet him with hurried steps when he came visiting at night with his ponderous observations as to the state of the world and his mask well adjusted like the revellers of the twenties on the eve of a new year. She loved him and opened her heart to him; and he in turn told her of his resolution not to take advantage of her.

One Sunday as Genetha and Michael were listening to the service on the radio she saw Rohan's friend strolling by in the presence of a young woman and involuntarily gave a start and rose from her chair to look at them until they went out of sight.

Michael must have seen the despair in her eyes for, uncharacteristically, he interrupted the voice on the radio to ask:

"What's wrong? You're not listening."

"No . . . it's someone I saw passing."

Michael represented the genteel side of her upbringing. Rohan's friend, on the other hand, was the forbidden face of Georgetown and Agricola which surged up out of the alleyways and cook-shops and blew down the necks of decent women who walked the pavements alone.

The mole on Michael's chin suddenly seemed offensive, like a floor strewn with toenails, and the conviction that she loved him was suddenly intolerable.

"What's wrong with you?" he persisted.

"Nothing," she said sadly, ashamed at the things swarming so close to the surface of her composure.

"Listen to the service, then," he declared impatiently.

Genetha was overcome by that same despair that overtook her when Rohan went away to live on the Essequibo and from which the neighbour's distress had wrenched her. Rohan's friend had pricked her flesh and opened a wound she thought had healed, but for the sight of him in the company of a woman.

At the end of the service Genetha could not bear the silence, that void that could last all night because Michael was sparing

376

with words. She found herself saying whatever came into her head, unable to stop although she knew he was judging her.

". . . and d'you know that in Barbados there's such a shortage of wood that the coffin-makers go to the cemetery the night after the funeral to steal their own coffins?"

"What's the matter with you?" Michael asked. "What's got into you?"

She could not answer. Then, after a short while she said, "You tell me something for a change, Michael. We're together so much and we don't have much to say to one another."

"What do you want me to say? I'm happy. Nothing's happened, so what can I say? Aren't you happy?"

"No, Michael."

And from that night their relationship began to wither. He came and went as before, but they grew impatient with each other. He accused her of being less compliant than before and believed that she really took his silences to heart. So each night he came armed with a tale to tell, about his home or work, or about something he had heard during the interminable hours he listened to the radio.

One night just before he was about to go home she said, "I'm not coming to the meeting tomorrow night, Michael."

"Don't be foolish; of course you're coming."

"I'm not coming to the meeting. I don't want to come. I don't want to come any more. Not tomorrow night, anyway." The last few words were spoken in a murmur, for she was still uncertain about standing up to him.

Michael was nonplussed. "Very well," he said. "Goodbye."

He got up, took his hat from the hat stand and was about to go out. At the door he turned and with trembling voice said, "You're no Christian! I can't marry a woman that blows hot and cold like you."

It was the first time he had ever mentioned marriage, as far as Genetha could recall. She did not answer him. Michael thwarted his urge to do something positive. If only *she* would say something. He had never felt so humiliated and remained rooted to the spot, twirling his hat in his hands.

"Say something, damn it!" he exclaimed, half-imploring, half-dictating.

"Michael, I . . . I thought I loved you; but now I . . ."

He stared at her, unbelieving. "Since when?"

She remained silent.

"I can't stand here all night. Since when, I asked?" he repeated.

She was loath to answer him. "I don't think I ever loved you, Michael."

Michael sat down in a chair opposite her, never taking his eyes off her. "I don't believe you."

She leaned forward and put a hand on his arm.

"I want to be alone, Michael. Since Boyie went away I don't know where I am."

Her use of Rohan's fond name increased Michael's dismay.

"I don't want to be alone," he declared. "It's not natural to want to be alone. Only yesterday my mother said she wanted to see you. You don't understand: I can't stop seeing you now."

Overcome by a strange sense of power Genetha put her hand on his arm once more, but he drew away with a violent gesture and got up.

"You're one of these women who lure a man then imprison him for months, even years; and when at last he's got peace of mind you slam the door in his face. What d'you expect me to do? Knock on somebody's door and say, 'Have you got a daughter who I can see and be friends with?' This isn't a village where you know everybody. I've never been so lonely in my life as since I've come to town."

He sat down once more.

"People say you're eccentric," he continued, twisting the hat energetically in his hands, "because you don't make friends easily. Only God knows what I've been through. When I started going out with you I told myself how lucky I was to meet someone clean, someone decent who doesn't only think of men. At home I don't speak of anything but you. My mother and my aunts are tired of hearing what you wear and what you say. . . . O my God!" He bit his lips and closed his eyes.

"Don't touch me!" he cried in despair, as Genetha came towards him.

A few moments later he got up and with great dignity held out his right hand.

"Goodbye," he said in a firm voice.

"Goodbye, Michael," Genetha said in turn, shaking his hand weakly.

He left, closing the door quietly behind him.

378

Genetha went out to eat. The night was warm and couples were walking arm in arm. She took it into her head to go past the house where her aunts and grandparents lived. It was in need of painting. Someone was at the window and as Genetha looked up the person stared back but did not recognize her. It was several weeks since she had gone to visit them and on an impulse she nearly went in, but changed her mind and walked past slowly. She found herself walking in New Town, Kitty. Why? she reflected. Only once had she been there before and the impression then was of wretched houses and poorly lit streets. It was odd that Georgetown should stop at Vlissingen Road with its smooth asphalt and massive trees, and that a different world should lie beyond.

She turned back to go down Lamaha Street and walked on without knowing where she was going; and when at last she found herself in front of the Astor cinema where a queue had formed for the night show – the "theatre" as it was called – she joined it. There was a certain excitement in rubbing shoulders with the crowd that slowly gathered, and as the queue started moving she was impatient with anticipation. She was going at night-time to see a film! And she would get home after eleven, like hundreds of others.

3. A Humble Mortal

The next time Genetha saw Rohan's friend she smiled at him warmly. As she had anticipated, he came back to the house, to see Rohan on business, he declared. She offered to make him a meal and he was so tongue-tied he answered her questions awkwardly. When she complained that the tap was dripping he jumped up and came to her assistance. In no time he had dismantled it and made a makeshift washer from a piece of rubber he found lying about the house. As she watched him working and admired his body he looked round and saw her staring. From then on he was more at ease, his words came more readily and he no longer avoided her eyes. In fact she began to avoid his, which were frank and smiling.

When the meal was ready the two sat down at table. From force of habit Genetha joined hands to say a prayer which she shortened on his account. He ate like a stevedore and at the end got up to pour himself a glass of water from the clay goblet in the kitchen. He then came back to the table where he stood watching Genetha, who was chewing the last mouthful carefully. Then pretending that he had to go to the kitchen once more he excused himself, but on coming back remained standing behind Genetha's chair.

She neither looked round nor said anything, but continued chewing her last mouthful. He eased his hand into her bodice and began stroking her left breast, while she went on chewing, bent over her plate. Unbuttoning her bodice and letting down the straps of her brassière he lifted out her breasts with both hands. Genetha continued chewing, from time to time looking down at her bare shoulders and exposed breasts, cupped in his hands; and when she was naked to her hips she raised herself slightly from her seat so that he could pull off her dress and petticoat. Sitting on the chair, clothed in nothing but her panties, she felt like weeping and fell to thinking of the night before her father's accident, when she sat reading to him from Ecclesiastes, a passage she knew by heart:

"For the living know that they shall die; but the dead know not anything, neither have they any more a reward; for the memory of them is forgotten. Also their love, and their hatred, and their envy, is now perished; neither have they any more portion for ever in anything that is done under the sun. Go thy way, eat they bread with joy, and drink thy wine with a merry heart. . . ."

Genetha opened her mouth wide and accepted her lover's mouth. His left hand was on her breast and his right hand was on her leg. She yielded with her mouth and with her arms and with her shuddering loins. They copulated on the floor, by the dining table; and the cat at the foot of the chair blinked once before falling asleep again.

Long after he went, she lay naked under the blanket listening to the crapauds croaking, to the hum of a distant traffic and the voice of her reflections.

Her father and brother's conduct had goaded her into setting out on the road to freedom; but soon afterwards her father had died and Rohan went away, precisely because of her show of independence. Then came the discovery that she had not yet learned to use her freedom, that her belief in the strength of men was so deeply rooted – a conviction confirmed by Michael's single-minded egoism – she needed the resentment of the men in her family to impel her towards her goal. "Men are so strong!" she had once heard her mother say; and the seed of that remark had grown into a massive trunk which towered above the trees of her illusions. She remembered how Michael had nearly broken down when she confessed to having no love for him; how she looked on, refusing to accept the reality of his weakness, and how, as his vulnerability was exposed by the fear in his eyes and the way he twirled his hat in his fingers, she quivered with elation. Then Fingers came with the brutal affirmation of her father's and brother's egoism. But she persuaded herself that so long as she was certain of his loyalty she would accept him for what he was.

However willingly Genetha gave herself to Fingers he believed her to be aloof. He did not realize that she had never been so happy, that the people she worked with noticed the transformation, as did the neighbours and the shopkeepers.

"She getting it, dat's why," one of them said to a customer who remarked how well she was looking.

"Since the men gone away the chile don't got to work so hard," was the opinion of another, who went on to say how she remembered well the night the family moved into the district.

"Is 'cause she getting it, I tell you. Is 'bout time too," insisted the first.

"Funny, funny family."

"You din' know she mother? Is she husband send she to she grave."

"An' the son. I only know he when he grow up, but I hear that when he was a boy they couldn't control he. Between he an' he father they drag that poor woman to the grave. She had rings under she eyes like that; big, big like that, bigger than the rings under Quashie eyes."

The customer made a gesture denoting the size of the rings, to which her companion replied, screwing her face in a gesture of pity and shaking her head eloquently, "Tut, tut, tut. Like that, eh?"

"Rings like that?" asked another customer, who had moved into the district after the death of Genetha's parents. "Death was a deliverance then. I hear she family only live up the road, y'know. Yes, in Queenstown. Somebody tell me that since she marry she husband she sisters din' have nothing more to do with she. So I hear. I in' know if is true."

"My Eversley say it's in the blood," said the woman acquainted with the size of the rings under Mrs Armstrong's eyes.

"What's in the blood?" asked the second speaker.

"Women."

"Well, I know 'bout the father. . . ."

"The son is the same."

"Oh?"

"I mean he's more discreet, but is the same."

Fingers tried to teach Genetha how to dance and paid her compliments about the clothes she wore and went with her to the shops to help her choose her shoes. If he was not enthusiastic about anything she bought, she gave it away or exchanged it.

He was again out of a job and Genetha helped him to look for one, but employers were not encouraged to take on a man skilled at nothing except billiards. In the end Fingers was offered work at the ice factory; six weeks later, however, he gave notice because the factory was too cold. Genetha found him his next job at Sprostons foundry, where the foreman was a slave driver, according to Fingers. Eight weeks under a man like that was enough.

Genetha instinctively knew that he would tolerate no serious interference in his way of life. Her strategy was a long-term one; she would strengthen their relationship and accustom him first to the bondage of domestic life. Then she would set about changing him. There was time.

One night the minister of the A.M.E. Zionist Church which she used to attend with Michael paid her a visit. Fingers was out playing billiards and Genetha was sitting near the radio, picking the rice for the next day's midday meal.

"Let me put you at ease about my visit, Miss Armstrong," he began. "I've come to find out why you don't go to church any more, that's all."

Taken aback by his bluntness, she replied, "I don't have the time."

"Would it be too presumptuous to ask what takes up the time you would otherwise devote to the church?" asked the minister.

"I don't know," she stuttered.

"God still exists," he said, with a slight, supercilious smile. After a pause, he went on: "Michael. . . ."

"Yes?"

"Let me hasten to add that he didn't ask me to come. It's just that he's such a fine young man. I wondered why he comes to church alone."

She looked at him, but made no answer. His impertinence, his arrival at the wrong time, irked her. Above all she was ashamed that she had not been attending church.

"He looks bad," continued the minister, speaking of Michael. "If, if I'm . . . perhaps I'm broaching a subject that — that, um. . . ."

"Yes," said Genetha.

"I see."

And silence fell between them, the minister fearing to pursue a thorny subject and Genetha determined to do nothing that would encourage him.

"What shall I say to him then?" he asked in the end, taking out his handkerchief to give his hands something to do.

"There can't be anything between us," Genetha said slowly and deliberately.

"You're a headstrong young woman; but as I said I won't interfere," he declared regretfully.

After another embarrassing pause in the conversation he looked up abruptly, as if something had suddenly occurred to him.

"Do you believe in God, Miss Armstrong?"

"Yes."

"Miss Armstrong, after all I'm only a humble mortal, trying to make something of a new church. I'll be frank with you. You're a young and attractive person. Someone like you draws others to the church. It's only natural. They see you and say, 'Well, if she goes then there must be something in it.' I know this sounds vulgar and — well, you know, but it's true. . . . I mean I'd be surprised if Michael comes much longer now that we've lost you."

"Do you mind if I attend to the rice?" Genetha asked. "I'm sorry, I've got to get things ready for tomorrow."

She went and fetched the bowl, but it was impossible to find the unwanted bits in a light which suddenly seemed too dim. She returned to the kitchen with the bowl and came back once more to join the minister.

"I know what you must think of me," said Genetha, "but I need a few months to consider things. Besides, I'm a member of the Methodist Church, you know. If I start going to church again it won't be —"

"Oh," he said, crestfallen.

Had Genetha treated this humble representative of the A.M.E. Zionist Church so shabbily because he had no big church behind him? This, at least, was what the minister himself thought.

"Do you want something to eat?" enquired Genetha, wishing to make amends.

"Thank you," he said eagerly.

The cocoa and sweet bread he had just had at the Braithwaites' could make way for anything offered here, he thought.

"Fried plantain and rice! My favourite," he said with a broad smile, as he sat down at the table.

Genetha's evening was ruined. She had to put off washing her underclothes until the following day. And as for the midday meal, she would have to eat at a restaurant. But what about Fingers?

While the minister talked she kept turning these things over in her head. Whatever happened she had to get something cooked for Fingers that very night and in that case she might as well cook for both of them, she decided. Anyway it would have been foolish to let the shrimps go bad.

"I'm sorry, Reverend," she interrupted him, "but I've got to push you out. It's just that I've got a lot of things to do before I go to bed."

God's servant had settled in his chair and was looking forward to a long, uninterrupted digestion. Like many people who had never had to raise a finger in a home he could not conceive of work that could not wait, and only left reluctantly.

A few minutes later, Genetha heard someone coming up the front stairs. She went to the window even before the knock came. It was the minister, who must have left something behind.

"Listen, Miss Armstrong," he said to her when she faced him with a puzzled expression. "Is there another young man living here with you? I mean beside your brother — I know he's in the Essequibo and I just wondered. . . . If Michael asks me about his chances of a reconciliation I'd like. . . . I mean, I want to know what to tell him."

"No, Reverend," answered Genetha, incensed by his officiousness. "But he practically does. You can tell Michael that his name is Fingers."

She looked at the man of God unblinkingly and he turned tail and fled, as if he was being pursued by the devil himself. Genetha cleaned the ashtray in which two of Fingers's stubs lay among the grey and white ash. She made up her mind there and then that she would never cross the church door again.

Genetha was convinced that the minister's conduct lay behind her decision. In fact from the moment when she became intimate with Fingers she had begun to feel guilty about taking the Sunday school classes and instructing little children in morality and the Bible.

Now, without the slightest twinge of conscience, she put away her Bible in the bottom drawer of the chest of drawers, beneath the old dresses and worn-out underwear which she tore up and used as old cloth, as her mother used to do. In the middle of the Bible was a sprig of hyacinth which an admirer had given her when she was seventeen and had no thought of entering into a serious liaison. Pressed and faded, it lay between two pages of the Book that had been her father's favourite reading.

An hour or so later Fingers came in. He had lost an important match against a sailor and was in no mood for chit-chat.

"You're not talking?" she asked him.

"No."

"Why not?"

"Cause I in't got nothing to talk about."

"You want something to eat?"

"Well, course I want somet'ing to eat," he replied brutally. "Y'tink I been to a banquet?"

It was the first unpleasantness between them. She made him an omelette and a bowl of boiling chocolate with fat swimming on top and beside the plate and bowl placed four two-cent loaves of bread.

Genetha went and sat by the window, filled with contentment. She remembered that her father used to sit there, mumbling about the rattling street lamp; and her mother sat there when her father was out. Why, she wondered, had no one ever come to visit her mother?

A gentle rain began to fall. It soon became a downpour and wind blew in from the sea, shaking the paling staves of the house in the yard across the road. She could hear the talking of a man and a woman who had run in from the street to shelter under the house. Although she strained her ears the rain prevented her from hearing what they said. Were they happy? Was the man in love with her? Did they fall asleep as soon as they lay down at night? Or were they plagued by sleeplessness? Was she ever sick? Did she dread dying? Did he ever strike her or was he gentle? Was she afraid of letting herself go when she made love or was she. . . . Was she, Genetha Armstrong, the peer of this girl who ran in from the rain to shelter with her sweet man under the house? She, Genetha Armstrong, who called to mind her father whenever she saw a drunkard go by or heard a voice that bore the slightest resemblance to his. Her father, a depraved, good-for-nothing who had lied, cheated and frequented the houses of prostitutes when he was alive. He had taken no interest in his family, except to revile them.

"God forgive me," she reflected. "I've tasted the fruit of depravity and enjoyed it."

Her love was strong and beautiful. If it was sinful then she would embrace this sin and be glad of her happiness. If Fingers left her after a week or a month she would thank God that she had known a week, a month of joy. He had given her flowers of wickedness in handfuls, black orchids that gleamed like pearls. Every morning when she woke up she believed that she had been the victim of some dream; and every night when she said goodbye to her lover she saw him leave, uncertain whether he would ever come back. Were it not for the shadow of her brother she would give him everything she possessed.

When Rohan was a child her mother said to him, "Why don't you be as good as your sister?" Yet no one knew how desperately she, Genetha, wanted to be as bad as her brother. But she dared not face the consequences. She had been good out of fear, as she had worked at school from fear. Whenever a teacher had occasion to speak to her she used to tremble inwardly lest she had made herself conspicuous. For her this silent suffering had become part of the fabric of her behaviour and, in fact, she had ceased to suffer, and moved about in the world of grown-ups like a ghost in a peopled room. Something had exploded in her first experience with Fingers. She had given herself to him because she was in her twenties and could not wait any longer. She had frequently pictured herself in the grip of remorse if ever it happened before she was married but the remorse had been an illusion, like so many fears. Rohan's favourite rhyme flashed through her mind:

> My grandmother was a leper
> My grandmother died
> But never once
> Has my grandmother cried.

> Her face was like parchment
> Her hands were like wood
> But no one could sin
> As my grandmother could.

Genetha began to laugh softly. Then her happiness was marred by a sudden uncertainty, an unexpected doubt. Did people not say that lust had killed her father? And was it not she herself who accused Rohan of lusting after that woman in Vreed-en-Hoop? Would people not say that her lust had driven her to take up with Fingers? What she was doing was a thousand times worse than what Rohan had done. Besides, she was a woman. She closed her eyes and listened to the rain drumming on the roof. Voices started whispering incoherently and as they became louder the sound of the rain grew softer. In the end the voices were thundering at her: "Lust! Slut! Lust! Slut!" Bright lights began to appear on all sides while the voices kept up their thundering, and as they came nearer and she could see the faces behind them they turned out to be all women with bared teeth and hateful faces. She searched them diligently for someone she might recognize, but they were all strangers. She opened her eyes. The rain continued to thunder on the roof and the voices, a moment ago so clear, had gone. The faces had disappeared, like chalk from a slate over which a damp cloth had been passed.

When Fingers came and put his hand on her shoulder she shuddered and resisted his embraces, complaining of a headache.

4. A Knock on the Door

Genetha woke up from a dream of Esther, sweating. All her family had, at one time or another, dreamed of the servant, filled with guilt at her out-of-hand dismissal. She looked around, expecting to find Esther in the room with her. But there was only the furniture in the bedroom lit by an unusually bright moon. The dressing-table, the foot of the bed and the chair

387

were covered with that wan sheen whose paleness had given rise to the prohibition against allowing moonlight to shine on one while sleeping. She threw the blanket over the lower part of her body and tried to fall asleep again.

The next morning Genetha tried to recall her dream, but remembered only the anxious awakening. All day at work she was dogged by the image of Esther's face, so much so that her closest associates noticed how preoccupied she was. At the time of the servant's dismissal she did not understand why she was leaving, for her parents pretended that it was Esther's decision. But later, after her father lost his job as a result of widespread retrenchment in the government service, he became less discreet and reproached his wife openly for choosing to send away the more loyal of the two maids. Side by side with the fond memories of Esther grew a fear of her because she had been wronged. And after that night when she heard her father thundering at her mother on the same theme and accusing her of "throwing the servant into the cauldron of Georgetown" although she was from the country and knew no one in town, she found herself spontaneously calling to mind Esther's dilemma.

It was a few weeks later that Esther came to see her. Her face was grey and gaunt, as if she were ill. Genetha did not recognize her at first, but when she spoke her soft deep voice was the same as in the days of Agricola. The dress she wore fitted badly, as if it had been made for someone else, while the lipstick did not follow the curves of her lips accurately and gave her the bizarre appearance of an actor's mask. Her eyes, set in hollow sockets, seemed more gentle than ever.

"This is for Master Boyie," said Esther, who always called her brother by his fond name.

She handed Genetha a small tin of Milo, Rohan's favourite beverage.

"He's in the Essequibo," Genetha told her. "It's been a few months now."

Esther looked surprised. "You keep it then."

"Esther, what's happened to you?" Genetha enquired of the servant.

"I've been sick."

"You've been to see the doctor?"

"I know what's wrong with me," replied Esther. "Look . . . I came to borrow some money."

388

"How much?" asked Genetha, eager to be of service to her.

"Ten dollars."

"Is that all?"

"Some people've got so much and others so little," Esther said bitterly.

"I'm glad to see you," Genetha said.

"Miss Genetha, the women in your family never liked me. And I can see from your eyes. . . . You don't need to pretend, you know."

Genetha felt the same disturbance. If she gave her the money at once she might take it as a hint to go. If she waited she would have to endure her reproaches.

"I'll make you a cup of Milo and some bread and butter," offered Genetha.

"Yes," she said hurriedly, "thank you."

Genetha was also afraid that Esther might have some terrible infectious disease. Maybe she came to give it to her on purpose. There were people like that, she reflected. She must remember to smash the cup when she went, or throw it away.

Instead of inviting her to the table Genetha brought the things on a tray which Esther placed on her lap.

After the snack Esther seemed to be in a better mood, smiling whenever she caught Genetha's eye.

"You'll feel alone in this house, Miss Genetha. You need a man with you. But be careful not to give him anything. He'll only hate you for it." She paused for breath before she continued eating.

Genetha was certain she could not conceal her feeling of oppression. She got up, went inside, and came back out with three five-dollar bills in her hand.

"It's a gift, for all you did for me and Boyie . . . and the rest of the family."

Esther took it and looked at her with what seemed to Genetha like hatred.

"You think that fifteen dollars can pay me for all I did for your family? After I worked myself to the bone for you, your mother put me out on the street. Your Christian mother. You don't know how I lived these last few years. But I prayed for your mother and God answered my prayer. She died before me."

Genetha hung her head and pretended not to see how the

former servant was gasping for breath.

"I can't answer for what my mother did, Esther. She suffered too."

"We all suffer, Miss. If I was healthy I would come back and do for you. But the doctor said I'll be all right in two months or so. I have to take care of myself until then. Any exertion makes me break out in a cold sweat. The doctor said months ago he couldn't do anything for me. But I knew he was talking nonsense. Now he's changed his mind and told me it's because I've got a strong constitution."

She paused again for breath.

"The only thing I regret," she continued, "is that I didn't have any children."

Genetha put out her hand to touch the servant, but she had vanished. She jumped up from the chair by the window. Had she been sleeping? She rushed outside and once on the road looked back at the house. Fingers was not home and she was obliged to go back and wait under the house until he came.

That night she invited him to come and live with her. He was delighted and wanted to get his things at once, but she was unwilling to remain in the house alone.

"Why? Been seeing ghosts?" he asked.

The couple made their nest in Genetha's parents' room. The four-poster bed that had been in the family since her parents' marriage had not been slept in since her father's death, but a few weeks later they felt as if they had been sleeping there all their lives.

She did not install Fingers in the family house with impunity, for she often heard the whispering of her dead parents about her, even in broad daylight, and their squabbling at night-time just as when they had been alive and believed that she and Rohan were asleep. The intrusion could not have failed to offend them, as it had offended her brother. Yet she hoped that the voices would weaken with the coming months; and if they did not she intended to move and take her resolutions elsewhere.

One afternoon when she came home from work Fingers told her that a woman had been to see her.

"Kian' remember she name, but she look as if she jus' come out of the Best," he informed her, evoking the woman's appearance by comparing her with inmates of the dreaded hospital for patients with consumption.

She forgot about what Fingers had said until, in the middle of their meal, he snapped his fingers and declared:

"She name Esther!"

Genetha's cup fell to the table. The coffee spilled over the edge on to the unpolished floor, where it made an ever-widening puddle.

"Is wha' wrong?" asked Fingers, alarmed.

"I don't want to see her," declared Genetha. "Tell her if she comes again I don't want to see her."

"Why? You know she?" he interrupted.

"Yes, she was our servant."

"Oh, but she does talk good, like you."

Fingers went into the kitchen and brought back a cloth with which he wiped up the coffee.

"You want another cup?" he asked solicitously.

"No."

"You feeling cold?"

"No, it's all right."

She was unable to shake off a fit of trembling. Fingers wanted to go out to play billiards, but was reluctant to leave her in the condition she was. He went and made the coffee, although she had declined his offer to make another one, and forced her to drink it before telling her that he was going out.

"No! Don't leave me alone," she pleaded.

He sat down, got up again and then came back to sit down once more.

"Let's go to the pictures," she suggested. "I'll treat you."

Fingers liked the idea. So she cleared the table and began washing the cups and saucers. But when she was on the point of finishing there was a knock on the front door. Genetha grew faint as Fingers opened and exchanged a few words with the stranger. Then he came into the kitchen and said:

"Is the woman."

"I told you not to let her in!" Genetha whispered.

"Come an' get rid of she. I goin' stay by you," Fingers suggested with an encouraging smile.

Esther had the same gaunt face and hollow-set eyes as in her apparition. "Miss Genetha," she said smiling.

"Hello, Esther."

The servant rummaged in her bag for something.

"This is for Master Boyie."

It was a tin of Milo and at the sight of the green container Genetha drew back.

"You know he always did like Milo," Esther reminded her.

"He's in the Essequibo."

"Oh?"

"Yes."

"I won't beat about the bush, Miss. I came because I'm in trouble. Can you lend me some money?"

"How much?" Genetha asked, clenching her fists in agitation.

"How much can you afford?" Esther asked.

"Ten dollars?" Genetha suggested.

"Yes," Esther said hurriedly.

"Wha' wrong?" Fingers asked Genetha, who was staring at her.

"It's just that I feel giddy," she replied, grasping for his arm.

"You're not well, Miss Genetha? She isn't well?" Esther asked, turning to Fingers.

He shrugged his shoulders.

"Get ten dollars from inside and give her quick," Genetha ordered Fingers, who did as he was asked.

"I'll never forget this, Miss."

"That's not what you said the other night!" exclaimed Genetha, more agitated than ever.

"The other night?" asked Esther. "I came in the morning."

"You were here?" Genetha asked urgently.

"Yes. You don't remember? You acted so funny."

"Yes . . . well, I don't know. I'm not well. All right, good-bye," Genetha said, nodding and looking at her askance.

Esther stepped forward.

"No! Go! For God's sake, go."

"All right, Miss, I just wanted to say thank you." She nodded to Fingers and left.

"God's punishing me," wailed Genetha. "But there're people worse than me. Promise you won't leave me."

"What give you the idea I goin' lef' you? If you go on like that I'll slap some sense into you."

"She always liked Boyie . . . and Boyie would do anything for her. That's not right either. She was all smiles tonight, to impress you; but the other night it was different, and when she bared her teeth. . . . She hated me and my mother and my mother got rid of her because she was afraid of her; and my father could never understand. Right up until she died he used

392

to blame my mother for getting rid of her. You see, if you weren't here tonight she'd have dragged up the whole story again."

Fingers slapped her face and she burst into tears and was soon in the grip of an uncontrollable sobbing. Impatiently he started pacing up and down the room, more perplexed than annoyed.

Later Genetha confided in Fingers about Esther's relations with her household. On no account would her brother have done so, she reflected; but she did not possess his iron will. Fingers, bearing a latent hostility to Genetha's class deep within him, listened without comment. Taking his silence for sympathy with her and the family, Genetha stretched her confession back to the time of Agricola when the servant girl was still uneducated. She repeated everything she had heard her mother say, even the remark that Esther did not have drawers when she first came to the house in Third Street. And Fingers stored up all these remarks as if they were directed against him, for one of his sisters was also a servant and spoke ill of the household in which she worked.

But the longer they lived together the more her confidence grew. And she began to tyrannize him in little ways: through his food, to which was added colallo, something he did not care for; through his clothes, since he was made to wear flannelette vests to avoid catching a chill after his billiard matches in the stuffy dockside halls; and in countless little rules she inflicted on him in order to foster the illusion of her mastery over the household. Fingers yielded with a docility that was not in his character.

5. Sweet Cakes

Genetha sat at table, alone after a day's work. Fingers had given up coming home to have his dinner with her. She had not been feeling well lately and had seen the doctor on a number of occasions. He had advised her to eat a lot of cheese and join the YWCA and above all to take the muddy-looking liquid he was fond of prescribing.

Apart from the advice to join the YWCA Genetha followed his instructions carefully, but felt no relief from the headaches that plagued her at night. The best hours of her day were at work, when the colourless routine which others found irksome acted like a balm on her. The dark half-moon depressions under her eyes, more prominent to others than to herself, prompted Fingers to tell her that she was getting ugly. He suggested that she take a holiday abroad; and to please him she went to Barbados.

On her return her cheeks were full and her headaches were gone. Yet, a few weeks later, she was as ill as before her trip, her cheeks were as sunken, while a faint line appeared between her nose and the corner of her mouth; and she ceased complaining of her headaches, which had returned.

Occasionally Fingers was his old charming self. One afternoon when she returned from work he offered to take her to the pictures. He made her put her feet up and rest while he made coffee and an omelette, beamed at her across the table and talked incessantly about billiards and snooker.

"I'm in great form," he told her. "I potting bad, bad! I tell you. I just got to look at a ball and it going down. Last night I was playing a chap from the Guild Club. 'You got cramp, Guild Club man?' I say to him. He had four shots in the whole game. I din' miss one free shot, I tell you. One time the white did standing nearly on the cushion and I take it as a free shot out of bravado. The ball sink with a plop. I tell you the Guild Club man look at me as if I was a jumbee. He couldn't even stand up any more."

Fingers laughed and added, "But the best part of it was, at the end of the game he put down another five dollars and say he did want to play again. He really did think that I fluke all them shots. I wrap he up in fifteen minutes. He leave the club as if he was going to murder somebody."

Genetha understood nothing about snooker, but she shared his satisfaction. They talked for an hour or so, and when she went into the kitchen to wash up he followed her to keep her company until she had finished. They then sat on the stairs and continued talking in the dark until eight o'clock when they locked up and set off to the cinema, arm in arm. Once in their seats he took her hand.

On the way home they went to a new shop called "The Patisserie", a stone's throw from the Metropole, where they drank coffee served in a pot and ate sweet cakes coloured like tinsel on Christmas decorations.

At other times he encouraged her to talk about herself and she did so at length, becoming drunk with the opportunity to let herself go.

"When I went for the interview to get this job I was made to wait in the outside office where a man was typing slowly, picking at the keys. Before I left home my father said, 'Oh, you'll get the job, don't bother.' These words kept drumming in my ears and my head and with every clak clak of the typewriter I said a word to myself, 'Clak . . . O . . . clak . . . you'll . . . clak . . . get . . . clak . . . the . . . clak . . . job . . . clak . . . don't . . . clak . . . bother.' And you could hear the voices of the interviewer and the other applicant through the closed door whenever there was a pause in the typing. It was my first interview for my first job and I could hardly bear the waiting and the clak-clak of the typewriter and the sound of the voices from inside. I crossed my legs and started pressing. I don't know what made me do it because it had never entered my mind before to do anything like that before. I pressed, pressed, until. . . ."

And then, for no apparent reason she stopped, ashamed of her confession. Fingers, who had only been half listening, asked, "What happened? You did get the job or not?"

"Yes, I got the job," she said.

She never again came so near to discussing such private matters with him again.

But the occasional access of kindness did not make up for Fingers's temperamental behaviour and his interminable silences. Genetha began to fear his outbursts, especially when he was drunk.

One night she screwed up her courage and told him that she did not want him to live with her any more.

"I coming home early tonight," he said, disarmingly.

"Don't come back in the house, please," she repeated. "I don't know whether I'm coming or going with you, that's all. One day you're considerate and the next you behave as if you don't even know me. In the mornings I wake up wondering what you'll be like and at night I go to bed racking my brains to find out what I did you. You've got something against me. I can tell."

"I in' got nothing 'gainst you," he protested.

"It looks so to me. Anyway, I can't stand your moods."

"Listen," he said in a conciliatory voice.

"No!" she cut him short. "Apart from my mother's death I've suffered. . . everything I've suffered was through men. And in any case you don't intend to work. I can't keep a man: it's not in my nature."

"I'll get a job, Genetha. Look, by year end I'll be working —".

"Don't lie! Even if you get a job you'll look out for the first opportunity to give it up. Why can't you face up to what you're like?"

Fingers was not accustomed to seeing her in this mood and did not know what to say next.

"You always talking 'bout the past," he said, hoping to make an impression. "If you not going on 'bout tram cars that use to run as late as the thirties you telling me 'bout some blue dress you did wear when you was a little girl. That's why I does get fed up with you. That's the only reason for my moods."

Genetha, though she realized how transparent this excuse was, hated him for belittling these memories of her girlhood. For her, the recollection of that single trip, the return in the creaking, grinding tram, the image of the conductor going from one carriage to the other along the running-board, the descent at Agricola in the company of her mother and Boyie and the whining of the tram as it gathered speed and disappeared round the bend on its way to the terminus at Bagotstown, was sacrosanct. Believing that their intimacy had made him sensitive she had disclosed her most secret preoccupations to him only to hear them treated with scorn. Thank God she had held back in time before telling him about what happened at the interview!

Revolted by his insensitivity Genetha fell silent.

"Is what I do you?" he asked, fearing her silence.

"You didn't do anything. My mother and father wouldn't have wanted anybody else to live here, that's all."

"Your mother and father? Your father used to —"

"That's enough!" she jumped up angrily. "You've insulted me over and over, but leave my parents out of it."

"Don't come looking for me, understand?" he said, stifling his rage, " 'cause I in' crossing the door-mouth of this house again. You understand?"

He then went inside to collect his belongings, apparently master of himself.

That night Genetha went to look up her grandparents, whom she had not visited since she took up with Fingers. But as before she hesitated and turned back in front of the gate. On returning home she switched on the radio and listened to a concert on the short wave. Twenty minutes later when it was over she began to rack her brains to recall whom she might visit, but no one suitable came to mind. She got up and closed the jalousies and windows out front, secured the door and turned in, after dosing herself with bush tea. She could hear the animated whirring of the night insects and the sound of talking from next door and see the lights of the occasional passing car reflected on her bedroom wall in muted illuminations. She wished she had a dog to sleep at the foot of the bed. Her aunts once kept two dogs, ugly, ingratiating animals. At that point her thoughts wandered to the work she did and her colleagues, but then she fell into a deep, remote sleep.

A few days later, unable to bear her loneliness, Genetha went round to Fingers's place. She had to go back the next day, as he was on the coast.

Fingers packed his things and accompanied her home as naturally as if they had agreed that he should return on that day and in that manner.

But no sooner had he moved back in with her than she regretted having exposed herself to his ridicule; and for a few days afterwards she remained guarded in her dealings with him, answering only after a pause whenever he asked the most innocent question. If he came home after she had eaten she did not rise promptly to warm up his meal. On waking at night she would draw away from him lest he mistook her proximity for an attempt to worm herself into his favour.

Incessantly she asked herself, "What would other women do? What *do* other women do? How is it that some manage to hold their men with such ease?" Before, she had been content to let him serve her, as hired bulls mounted their cows, for a season, while now she thought of holding him forever, until they grew old together in that unhappy house. Yet she foresaw the outcome: she would relax her vigilance, inevitably, and he, predator that he was, would be soon digging his claws into her, reducing her to a proper state of subservience.

For Fingers's part, he was as anxious as Genetha to promote harmony between them. The brusque manner of his dismissal had impressed him, for what she did once she was capable of doing again. He understood when she rejected his invitation to go to the cinema; but he would wait, he told himself, having gauged the strength of her will.

When Genetha was herself again, displaying the same weaknesses, the same over-concern for his welfare, he went along with her, resisting the temptation to take without asking.

She remembered the time she first met him, when he was in steady employment and the mainstay of his sisters, grandmother and father. If only he went to work every morning like all *decent* men, he would add dignity to their relationship and she would disregard the fact that his family were the only beneficiaries of his labour. What did it matter?

She would have liked to stroke his head, to smother him with her indulgence, for she knew no other way. And was that not the very essence of love? At times she sat watching him, unabashed, while he muttered over a newspaper, reading aloud as many half-literate people do. She followed the curving line of his biceps until she came to his hands. Her mother had been incapable of describing a person without referring to his or her hands: "long fingers", "affectionate hands", "knuckles like a workman's", "untended nails" were expressions she had fashioned out of the curious preoccupation. Fingers's hands were of a piece with his body, neither arresting nor insignificant, no open book that gave him away. And if she loved him it was not because of his hands. She was certain she had chosen him because she believed she would know how to keep him and to change him to her liking; unlike Michael, who had taken charge of her as if she were an employee, who saw courtship as the long, sterile season before marriage.

It mattered not what Fingers looked like. Indeed, the very mediocrity of that physical appearance – a matter of great concern to her on contemplating her own reflection in the mirror when she first became aware of her body – was his most powerful attraction. Her own disabilities were the infallible indicators of a woman's unsuccessful journey through life; and the absurd exaggeration of every such lack fed upon itself to the point where she made unflattering comparisons between her behaviour and that of other women in the most trivial matters. The typists at work chose their brassières by the size on the label. She, on the other hand, astonished shop assistants – so she believed – by insisting that she tried on hers before paying for them. What better proof was there that she was odd, she asked herself.

When the period of caution inevitably came to an end Fingers's behaviour improved beyond all expectation. His undoubted kindness was no longer cancelled out by the wilful insistence on doing as he pleased, on going out simply because his spirit gave him to do so. And after several weeks in which Genetha was able to judge the consistency of Fingers's conduct she settled down to enjoying the most satisfying period of her life since she emerged from girlhood and learned to assume responsibility for her actions.

It was just then that an unusual occurrence took place, which was to reinforce her hold on Fingers, as if Fate had been watching closely and had decided to reward her. Ulric, the feckless neighbour who had been distrained upon because of his unpaid debts, called over the paling fence one Saturday afternoon. Fingers was repairing Genetha's bicycle, which was lying on its saddle with its wheels in the air.

"Give me a hand here, man," Ulric asked, waving a saw in his right hand.

Fingers dropped his spanner and went over to the neighbour's assistance.

And so began their association. Fingers would not have dreamed of addressing Ulric first, for the latter spoke to no one except his mother and appeared impervious to all overtures of friendship. He never attended any of the functions to which neighbours were usually invited, like christenings or funerals, and emphasized his contempt for those living in the vicinity by burning rubbish when a strong wind was blowing.

Ulric's mother was "getting on" and had all but lost the power in her right arm. Needing assistance in the construction of a crabwood wardrobe to replace the one taken away by the bailiffs he had called on Fingers, who was brought up to believe that it was not for him to question a neighbour's appeal for assistance. All he expected in return was a schnapp-glass of rum and a couple of grunts by way of conversation.

Fingers did not come back until the street lights went on. He spoke with enthusiasm about Ulric, who knew everything there was to know about wood. Genetha asked the question that her parents and all Ulric's neighbours had asked themselves at one time or another: "How does he earn his living?"

"He does do jobs for people. He can do anything."

Fingers reported that the house was bare, except for the beds and Ulric's tools, which the bailiffs had left.

"He say he goin' learn me how to polish furniture with bee wax, and other things too."

"Is he going to pay you?" Genetha asked.

"I suppose so."

"So you're going to work for him, then?" she asked, at once glad at the opportunity thrown Fingers's way and sceptical about his enthusiasm for working with Ulric.

But Fingers went over the following day, a Sunday, to continue work on the wardrobe; and when Genetha called out to inform him that the midday meal was ready he shouted back, "Gi'e me ten minutes."

She went downstairs and saw the two men under Ulric's house. Fingers was sweating over a half-finished wardrobe, his shirt cast aside and dressed in his short pants and singlet.

"You're coming?"

"I comin'. Gi'e me a couple of minutes."

The twinge of jealousy she felt on seeing him so devoted to what he was doing, standing in the sawdust, while Ulric's fowls pecked the ground around him for the remains of a snack his mother had brought down, was tempered by her satisfaction at seeing him sweat to some purpose.

Genetha stood at the paling fence, staring at the two men, who exchanged a few words from time to time without looking up at each other. And when at last Fingers, unable to ignore her any longer, shook off the sawdust and put on his shirt she went to the gate to meet him.

"You'd think I been gone miles away," he reproached her.

"You should be glad," she told him, "you've got a woman who comes to meet you at the gate."

Fingers took a shower before sitting down at table, where Genetha was told in detail what he had learnt.

"I can do a dovetail, now," he declared. It was all very easy, and was really nothing but common sense. "You know what you look for in furniture wood?" he went on.

"No."

"It got to be nice lookin', like a woman. An' easy to work, just like a woman. And it got to be stable; like a woman."

"What you mean by stable?" Genetha asked.

"It mustn't twist up or crack."

"Ah," said Genetha, "how do you know?"

"Some woods naturally like that, like huberballi and crab-wood. All you got to do is cure it."

She wondered if Ulric was responsible for his satisfaction or whether it was the work. What did it matter? she told herself. She would keep him as long as he was happy.

She rejected from her reflections everything that might embarrass her. Whenever she sat watching Fingers her eyes never descended further than his hands, so that she could truth-fully say that no forbidden reflections had crossed her mind. And even now she had banished the fleeting thought that she would wish to see him maimed so that she might have every reason to care for him, while he would have none for straying beyond the boundaries of her yard.

Yet at certain times she never spared herself an indulgence and threw herself into love-making with an almost morbid exuberance. And at such times she felt she belonged to the earth and understood the despair of those girls who discover a passionate belief in Christ that transcends the adherence to a religion, and those women on the threshold of middle age who rant and rave about Christ's coming, knowing full well that their bodies no longer respond to their husband's embrace. Yes, those were moments of oneness with every single living thing and with every human experience, when her skin blew hot and cold, panting for some eternal affection.

Fingers became apprenticed to Ulric, who undertook to teach him everything he knew. They went around to old customers whose furniture they varnished, for it was only a couple of weeks before Christmas time and people were busy stripping and varnishing the chairs and tables in their drawing-rooms and galleries. After Christmas they took to painting partitions, never the outside of houses, which were left to professional painters. Then, when the searing hot days of February came, Ulric and Fingers remained under the house, doing any work that was offered them, provided it was connected with wood. They made cupboards, wardrobes, chests-of-drawers, bookcases and all manner of wooden contraptions Ulric could make at home now that he had Fingers's assistance. And only the turned work in very hard wood, like lidded purple-heart jars, was undertaken by Ulric alone. Nothing seemed to be beyond him, once he had committed the client's specifications to a drawing. The wonder, according to Genetha, was that such virtuosity was allied to a complete lack of ambition and the need to borrow money he could not repay within the specified period. He had already relieved Fingers of his first weekly wages and, unabashed by his apprentice's presence as a constant reminder of his indebtedness, he boldly approached Genetha to ask for ten dollars, which he would pay unfailingly the next weekend. Genetha lent him the money, believing that Fingers's apprenticeship might be endangered if she refused. And Ulric, without so much as a blink of embarrassment, paid off his apprentice with the money he borrowed from the latter's lady friend.

But as things turned out the matter was not serious, for Ulric appeared never to borrow from the same person twice, unless he was a shopkeeper. Having exhausted his credit with the South Georgetown merchants he was well into Kingston and the area north of Murray Street, where his sincere manner and deadpan expression encouraged all but the most cautious to trust him.

As for Fingers, his enthusiasm for joining and polishing was equal to his passion for billiards. He played only on specified evenings, so that Genetha could arrange meal times with some certainty. She occasionally accompanied him on his outings when he was playing in a decent hall, like the Guild Club or the Tower Hotel. Then she was wont to keep her eye on the green baize cloth as though she enjoyed the game. Sometimes they arrived when the barman was brushing the table with his long soft brush, a useless precaution, she thought, since it never looked less than immaculate to her. On these occasions she sipped her soft drink slowly and to such good purpose that the straw through which she drank disintegrated, so that she had to take the rest from the bottle itself.

At times, infected by the excitement around the large table when a match was close, she would look at Fingers proudly, encouraging him with a glance he never answered. Just her presence was bad luck, which he dared not compound by catching her eye.

After these matches they would walk along the Main Street avenue, under trees with grey, knobbled trunks, where the road surface, transformed by the sodium street lamps, shone like water beneath a spectral moon. He would not allow her to put her arm through his, for fear that one of his friends might see them. But she walked close to him and took side-streets

402

oppressed in daytime by heat that rose from the burning asphalt, coming out again into the broader thoroughfares of young trees protected by rings of flattened iron staves. They had learned to be together without the benefit of conversation, and fell into listening to their footsteps on the gravel, while slipping deftly between the baluster-shaped bollards that marked the end of each stretch of road. Many of the trees were adorned with metal strips bearing the names of their species and genera in Latin, just as a number of mansions off the road carried enamel plaques no less mysteriously inscribed.

Genetha dared not measure the extent of her happiness lest it evaporate like those translucent bubbles of pale blue foam that vanish at the approach of warm fingers. How strange that her contentment had been mediated by a neighbour who had spoken no more than a few words to her in all the years she had lived in Albertown.

Genetha took down the large photograph of her dead father from the partition where it had hung as long as she remembered. While she felt uneasy about those eyes that followed her all the way from the dining area to the gallery and from the gallery to the back of the house, she could not bring herself to touch the framed portrait. Thinking it proper that he should look down on her comings and goings while she harboured a stranger in the family house she kept the glass over his face polished to a shine. But as satisfaction with her treatment at Fingers's hands grew and her guilt concerning her morality diminished, she ceased to be aware of the vigilant eyes; and that day when, during her routine dusting, she climbed on to a chair in order to pass the buff cloth over the frame and glass she hesitated, then with a sudden resolution she raised the picture from the nail. Curiously, it was as light as the lightest thing she had ever lifted, like the most insubstantial cloth or a handful of fluff from a silk-cotton pod. She recalled his wantonness, his palpable anxiety at being challenged by Rohan, her brother, his shameless lying to secure his ends, all of which had not prevented her from accepting the moral strictures and the judgments he passed and, deep down, even his infallibility.

Fingers enquired of the photograph, which he found lying on the dressing-table: "Is what you take it down for?"

"Do you want me to leave it up?"

"It don't matter to me," he declared.

He was unable to understand why Genetha was perplexed at his indifference and she was just as surprised that he had never resented the photograph.

At times Genetha, on turning the corner from Albert Street, would hear the humming of Ulric's new lathe above the sound of traffic. The almost sensuous undertones of that voice imbued her with a kind of strength, a powerful, almost sinister conviction that nothing was beyond her, provided Fingers was happy. He was her rock, and she, his mainstay. After putting away her bicycle under the house she would stand at the window for a few minutes listening for a snatch of conversation between the two men.

One afternoon, when she took them tea on a tray, Fingers was put out at the intrusion and from then on she left them alone, having finally understood that theirs was a man's world and that her lover set great store by his manliness as it appeared to the eyes of other men.

She had taught him to respect time and he came over promptly at sundown when the shadows lengthened and the whirring of six o'clock bees filled the brief twilight. But even she did not need the clock, which she nevertheless kept wound up, only because her father had acquired an obsession for clocks and keys from his post office. He believed that it was a sign of good breeding to display a working clock prominently in his home and to fit even his back door with a lock, although he hardly ever used it, the bolts being sufficient for locking up at night.

So time gave rise to an accumulation of new gestures, repeated over and over again like hammer-blows on hot metal, out of which emerged shapes at first tentative and ever changing until the final pattern was revealed, recognizable in form, but distinct as one flower resembles no other. Genetha could now claim to be married: she was the "reputed wife" of her brother's friend and their life together was particular to them.

6. Ulric

Ulric resisted all efforts to persuade him to cross Genetha's bridge and converse with Fingers in the same way as he did under his house. He did not go visiting, he declared. He had his principles and would not depart from them. He did not go visiting and did not lend money. At his age he had no intention of compromising himself. And so, one warm evening, when all was peace and, as it seemed, all wickedness was suspended in deference to the awesome beauty of an equatorial night, Fingers got to talking with his friend at the open window. From his own window opposite, Ulric grunted in his usual incoherent manner, as placid as the night itself, even while discussing the political issues of the day, which never failed to reduce stout men to a state of helpless excitement.

Genetha was wondering what to cook the next day, while sewing two buttons on to one of Fingers's shirts.

"You coming?" Fingers asked her, suspending his conversation with Ulric.

"Where?"

"To Morawhanna."

"Who's going to Morawhanna?" Genetha asked.

"Me and Ulric. You coming?"

"When?"

"Saturday."

"But I don't have anything to wear," she protested, more because she was taken by surprise than because she had nothing suitable to put on.

"Is not Georgetown, y'know," Fingers said.

"Come, Miss Armstrong," she heard Ulric call out in an uncharacteristically resonant voice.

"All right," she agreed, thinking that if Ulric was capable of making himself heard across the space between their houses it must be worthwhile to go to Morawhanna.

"Ulric say is no use goin' to Morawhanna," Fingers said, "if you don' stay for two weeks." He made this declaration after a brief consultation with his friend.

"I can't stay away from work," Genetha told him.

"She say she don' want stay away from work," Fingers relayed the message across the gap.

Then a few seconds later he looked round once more and said that it was settled. They would make the trip during her annual fortnightly holiday. Ulric was able to go at any time.

And so their intended visit to the North-West, of which she had only heard stories, and Fingers knew next to nothing, was settled in a few brief exchanges. Her holiday, starting shortly, and which she counted on using to scour the house and run up a few things on the sewing-machine, was to be frittered away in the North-West.

Had she been offered the opportunity of going away with Fingers alone she would have seized it with both hands. But she knew what to expect: the two men would engage in interminable rounds of conversation or play interminable games of Chinese checkers while she languished just within earshot. Why did she say yes? Whatever got into Fingers's head to ask her anyway?

She had no idea how much Fingers had changed. What was at the start an intolerable constraint for him, the time-keeping, the renunciation of three billiard evenings and the innumerable restrictions she had imposed on him, proved to be bearable, even pleasant, provided he could spend all day with Ulric. Whenever she called out to him over the fence, Fingers, believing Ulric to be envious of his good fortune, used to pretend not to hear, while telling himself that he was the most fortunate of men. When he came back to Genetha he was thirsting for revenge because of his injured manhood. Although the males in his home were ruled with an iron hand by his grandmother, who often struck her son – Fingers's father – in front of his own children, his humiliation at having suffered at the hands of a woman was no less great for that. His grandmother was *blood* and two generations removed from him, and had acquired the status of a revered ascendant. He had planned to rob Genetha in some way and then leave her, after a period, during which he would play a false role, so that she would come to rely heavily on him. Things had not turned out that way. The first weeks of uncertainty and caution were followed not by any deliberate attempt to cultivate her confidence but by the slow realization that his independence was like that strange sweet fruit which women in Mara are reputed to use to dispatch their unfaithful men. It was in his interests to resist its temptations. Not only must he put aside thoughts of vengeance, but he would make every effort to accept Genetha's constraints. Should she go too far he need only rear up and snarl at her.

At times her talk of servants and her past was so irksome that he was taken by the desire to injure her in some way. But as the months went by she spoke less and less of these things, and the day she took down her father's photograph was like the end of one way of life, a kind of death, to which he affected indifference, but which in reality had soothed him much.

Fingers was not certain whether he loved Genetha or not, but he liked being with her. Even if he were to fall in love with another woman he did not intend to abandon the charted course of a fertile association in order to embark on a voyage into the unknown and perhaps dangerous waters of self-indulgence. "Better cornmeal pap dat don't got taste dan pepperpot dat in' cook yet."

Genetha was sick on the boat. She began to throw up soon after the *Tarpon* left the muddy waters of the Demerara estuary and started to rock violently. Fingers took her astern, where a wide tarpaulin awning provided shelter from the morning sun and there was space to lie down.

The *Tarpon* had spent most of its life on the ferry from Georgetown to Vreed-en-Hoop, but was pressed into service on the fortnightly North-West run when the old steamer started to break down regularly and travellers claimed that she was no longer suited for the open sea and would rock on a lake.

When Genetha had brought up everything there was to bring up from her inside an ageing man with luxuriant grey hair presented himself to the couple.

"Quashie Uba. I come to help the distressed lady."

He took two phials from his jacket pocket.

"Dis one it has aromatic vinegar and dis one it contains spirits of ammonia. If the lady put one to the right nostril and the other a little way from the left I guarantee she will be better in ten minutes. If I come back and she not up and *laughing* I going to throw my body overboard."

When Mr Uba came back as he promised, Genetha was sitting up and managed to smile at him.

"Thank you," she told him. "I'm feeling a lot better."

Fingers gave him back his phials.

Mr Uba told them that he was a New Brethren preacher and was on his way from Kwakwani to Morawhanna "in haste", because his reputed wife had published their banns of marriage without his consent. She was a practised forger – her father was a calligrapher and her brother a clerk, and writing was in the blood. She must have written out a consent and forged his signature on it.

"She is a very enterprising woman," he added.

The preacher then launched into a sermon on the merits of the New Brethren doctrine and urged Fingers to join the sect.

"The first man was black, I tell you," declared Mr Uba.

When Fingers expressed surprise at the confident assertion the preacher used arguments in justification of his view as curious as those used by others to prove their fancied superiority.

"Is like dis," said Mr Uba, sitting down next to Genetha. "You hear 'bout Cain? Right! Is he did kill Abel. Well, Cain fader and moder and broder was black people. Cain was jealous of Abel 'cause Abel had rich clay soil land and he only had pegasse. So one afternoon Cain he hide behind a moka-moka bush and swipe Abel 'pon he head when he was coming from his clay-soil land. Den he bury the body quick and trample down the earth flat flat. Eh-eh! Who tell he to do a t'ing like dat? A took-ah, a took-ah, a took-ah, he walk walk a few yards when he hear a voice, 'Cain! Cain! Is why you sneaking away like dat? Cain, is where your broder Abel dere?' 'Broder? I in' got no broder!' Cain say, lying like horse trotting. 'I say is where you broder Abel dere?' God he ask again. 'I in' got no broder,' we black ancestor say, getting more and more vex all the while. 'You getting ignorant like policeman. The power we give you going to you head!' 'Den is who lying in dat grave?' God ask. And Cain turn *pale*! And all Cain children he had after he get married was born pale. Dat's how white people come into this world."

Mr Uba went on to relate the history of his sect and took out a newspaper clipping from his pocket.

"Read it," he said, handing Fingers the soiled paper.

"Sect's numbers growing", said the caption in heavier print than the rest of the article.

"I believe you," said Fingers, anxious about Genetha's condition and wishing to be left alone with her.

Mr Uba sat down and began telling Fingers about his travels up and down the rivers in an effort to convert people, and about the failure of other established Christian denominations whose only hold on their members was that they were backed by the colonial administration.

But in the end, perhaps despairing of Fingers's lack of enthusiasm for his infant church, the preacher said, "I would give you more proof, but I can see you not a church-thinking man. But if ever you change you mind remember my name, 'Quashie

Uba, in care of Brother Ebenezer who does sell late beef 'pon the front road at No 2 Canal'. Any time, brother, any time."

With a flourish of his hand he bowed deeply to Genetha, but gave Fingers a look of the utmost contempt.

"Goodbye, mistress. Sit up straight and don't watch the water."

Around midday the steamer arrived at the mouth of the Waini river. Stilt-rooted mangrove trees gave way to the uniform green of riverside vegetation and the silt-laden water from the Orinoco met the ocean surge in shifting unequal lines that stretched across the river mouth. Those who were making the journey for the first time stood up to watch the shore, believing that Morawhanna was not far away. But they were soon back in their places, tired of waiting for their destination to come into view.

Ulric and Fingers were playing checkers, while Genetha leaned against the rail staring at the moving water. The sight of the river and the steamer's smooth passage had encouraged her to get up. Like everyone else she was praying for the journey to come to an end, but having already asked Fingers to enquire of the purser how much further they had to travel she kept her questions to herself, preferring to stare blankly at the narrow strip of foam that stretched behind the boat.

Now that she was away from her home she realized how much she depended on Fingers and how much she cared for him. Deep down he had not changed, she believed. Not having mixed a great deal, her view of men had been conditioned by what she knew of Rohan and her father and the terrible suffering inflicted on her mother by the latter's conduct. If her grandfather did not conform to her view of men as the embodiment of selfishness he was exceptional. Besides, there was something unusually pure about her grandparents' love for each other. Genetha's need for a certain degree of independence precluded that kind of relationship. The stablility of the family had always been bought at the expense of women, her mother had once remarked to her paternal aunt. Yet her mother, having acted as a doormat all her married life, had not attained any worthwhile stability, either for herself or for the rest of the family. And indeed, Fingers had only become tolerable when she showed she could be firm.

Not all the thinking in the world could lay her mistrust for Fingers. She needed him desperately, but was convinced that one day he would leave her. Of that she was as certain as that the river had a source and that it gained in breadth in its search for the vast mausoleum of the sea.

"Look at it!" someone shouted.

There was a general stir, but this time fewer passengers got up to witness the approach of Morawhanna. People were lining the river bank in the distance and further on the houses, which were drawing closer together, seemed to be coming down to the riverside as the people were.

Ulric and Fingers joined her, one on each side, to see the ropes being thrown and caught by two Transport and Harbour employees.

Ulric led them off the boat. He was wearing short pants and his long, hairless legs seemed to say, "I know exactly where I'm going." Fingers was carrying the suitcase, in which were his and Genetha's clothes, soap and other toilet goods.

Genetha had completely recovered and as she followed the men opened her large handbag to check that she had brought her make-up.

It was the two men who were thinking of resting for a while. Genetha, like a girl on her first outing, was determined to drag Fingers out after the sun went down. In the distance the hills rose behind Mabaruma, the new township established ostensibly to attract the inhabitants of Morawhanna away from their malarial swamp-land.

In less than five minutes they were standing on the bridge of a tiny cottage, no larger than the drawing-room in Genetha's house.

"Quickey!" Ulric shouted, then waited without the slightest trace of impatience.

A good minute went by, but no one came.

"Call the man again," Fingers suggested.

"Give him time," Ulric said quietly without turning round.

The sunlight, broken up by the fan-like ite palms behind the house, made patterns on the low, rusted corrugated-iron roof. From a pen under the house came the grunts of an unseen family of pigs, an unhurried snorting, as if the languid afternoon had done to them what it had done to Quickey.

"Is you?" a voice questioned from a head that eased itself through the window.

"Quickey, man," said Ulric, "is how long it does take for you to get up?"

"Come up, ne? You write you was comin' tomorrow and you come today."

"I wrote *today*," protested Ulric. "You in' change a bit."

Genetha marvelled at the ease with which Ulric slipped into Creolese.

"This is Genetha," Ulric introduced her. "And this worthless man is Fingers."

"All you come up," Quickey said, stretching out his hands in order to open the door.

Fingers sat down in a Berbice chair while Ulric, disregarding Genetha's presence, lay down full length on the floor.

"All you mus'e thirsty. I goin' get some coconut. You comin'?"

"No, man," said Ulric. "After that journey?"

Quickey eased himself up with the help of his hands and went through the back door.

"How old d'you think he is?" Ulric asked.

"Late fifties?" Fingers suggested.

"That man is seventy-two."

"What?" Genetha exclaimed with surprise.

"Seventy-two," continued Ulric. "And he still goes hunting in the bush. In fact he's the best hunter round here, except for the aboriginees. And don't think he's slow because he's old. He's always been like that. The only time he hurries is to get out of the rain. He hates getting his head wet."

It had not escaped the notice of Genetha and Fingers that Ulric's tongue was loosened, as if he had been drinking. The way he had thrown himself on to the floor and had begun to speak Creolese told them that he knew Quickey well; but the quickened tempo of his speech was an indication of a stronger connection with the North-West than he had led them to believe he possessed.

Quickey came back with a cutlass and half a dozen coconuts strung together. One by one he cut off their heads with a single stroke and gave them to each of his guests in turn, beginning with Genetha. Then he split each spent fruit into two to allow them to get at the jelly, which they ate with a slice of husk left dangling from the coconut after another deft stroke of the cutlass.

"The lady better take the bedroom, eh?" Quickey said. "Right? I goin' carry the grip inside, then."

He took hold of the grip and hoisted it into the adjoining

411

room, which could hardly have been wider than the suitcase itself, judging from the amount of space taken up by the drawing-room.

"You in' got ambition?" Ulric said to Quickey. "You still living in this fowl-coop?"

"Is me own," answered Ulric. "If I get a bigger house is more cleanin' and repairin', and I'd only end up with me relations moving in and tellin' me what to do. I in' right? Eh? An' what about you? You in' even married yet. You in' shame?"

"That's a long story, man," answered Ulric.

Fingers felt certain that Genetha's presence prevented him from disclosing the reasons for his single state.

"I better cook now," Quickey said, "seein' as how all you come so far. If you want eat before the food ready I got banana and cashew and t'ing at the back. The trees them full o'fruit."

He left them to finish their coconuts.

"What you want us to do with the shell?" Ulric called out.

"Throw them in the front yard," he said from the back. "A man does come to collect them."

When the three had finished scraping their coconuts they took them out and laid them in a heap at the foot of the front stairs. Ulric then went out on to the road.

"You like it here?" Fingers asked Genetha.

"I like it, yes. You?"

"How you mean? Is mag-ni-fi-cent!"

"How much will we have to give them, you think?" Genetha asked.

"I don' know."

"I brought thirty dollars."

"You hold on to your money, girl," Fingers advised. "Country people generous. Ulric say Quickey would sell the shirt off his back to entertain him."

"Anyway, I can't leave without giving him something."

Ulric came back and joined them on the stairs, where they talked of country people's generosity, of the inhabitants of Morawhanna, many of whom were half aboriginal Indian, of the tiring journey up from Georgetown and of anything that came into their heads. They talked until the sun began to set and flocks of birds came flying up-river. Then the terns appeared as if from nowhere, wheeling like gulls and shrieking like children in a school playground. The noise of the pigs under the house

412

had given way to the humming of mosquitoes, a slow persistent whine that filled the cool night air and reminded the visitors that they were in the country.

When the stars came out and voices from the riverside fell silent, Quickey joined them. He had spent hours preparing their meal, now almost ready but for the rice, which was boiling.

"You got a nice life here, Mister," said Fingers enviously.

"An' we in Morawhanna," answered Quickey, "think all you got a nice life in Georgetown. Is we who does leave here to go there. Is only government people does come down, 'cause they got to do as they're told. Else nobody would come."

"What about your sister?" Ulric asked.

"You in' hear? No, how you going hear? She take in sudden and dead. She was younger than me, only sixty-seven. That woman never had a day sickness. You know she used to go creek-side to bleed she own balata? Yes. She uses to make cricket balls with it and sell them to people from Georgetown who did come up here on holiday and did want a lil game o' bat and ball. Well, one afternoon she come home and say, 'Is who you think I see?' 'I in' know,' I say. 'I see Charlene.' Charlene was she best friend from school days, but she did go an' get drowned years ago during a storm. 'Bout twenty years ago. Well, she say she see Charlene collecting firewood across the creek. She says, 'Is you, Charlene?' Charlene turned round, and was she in truth. She din' say a word, but just stretch out she hand and make as if to call she. My sister was so frighten she say, 'Le' me go home and take this balata, then I going come back.' Of course she din' go back! But that same night she dead in she sleep. Is a nice way to go, though, you in' think so?"

Quickey smiled. He then went on to speak of his family, nieces, nephews, cousins up to the seventh degree, and of frequent reunions when one of them earned enough money.

"They does all come here, though the house is small," he said with satisfaction. "And my second great-granddaughter start to talk a'ready. She does try to ride the pigs them. And I don' like that 'cause you can't trust pigs."

The barking of a dog came from the riverside.

"Is the men setting out to put down they cadell," Quickey told them. "Le' we go and eat."

While the men washed their hands in a basin of water Genetha stood at the window watching the fishermen laying out

413

their calabash floats on the water. Cadell fishing was still widely practised in the North-West, despite the heavy losses caused by sharks. Very often the largest fish on the hooks were eaten up to their heads. The fishermen refused to change their methods, despite attractive inducements by way of loans to pay for nets.

"They put out their hooks every night?" Genetha asked.

"Yes, Mistress," Quickey answered. "They uses to sell they fish in Venezuela, but they not allowed to no more. I in' know what they going do 'cause by the time the fish get down to Georgetown it all stink up and nobody want buy it."

Genetha washed her hands and sat down with the men at table, which was so laden with food that it might have been laid for six rather than four. And through the open window nothing was visible save the stars and the ceaselessly shifting lights of the fishermen's boats.

7. A Season in Morawhanna

There began for Genetha a season of ineffable contentment. She could not believe that she had, at first, regretted accepting the invitation, being uncertain of the role Ulric would play and just as uncertain of the strength of her tenuous relationship with Fingers.

The morning after their late meal she awoke last of all and found a note on the dining-table saying that the three men had gone to see some friends of Quickey's and would be back before midday. There were eggs and bread in the box under her bed and the coffee was in a tin on the kitchen table.

After tea, the morning meal, she put on her white frock and went down to the riverside. Little boats were scattered on the water, in which children, some as young as eight years, were making their way to the school house on the opposite bank. Hardly anything was as in Georgetown. Here the absence of cars, the numerous boats, the generous build of the people, the willingness to talk of death, the candid pleasure the men took in going off alone persuaded her that she was at the start of an experience that could not fail to leave a permanent impression on her.

When the last boat tied up in front of the school and the glare of the sun on the ebbing water became intolerable Genetha set off for a walk on what appeared to be the main east-west road, running parallel with the river. She bought a soft drink at a roadside shop with a display of half a dozen bottles and a tray of sweet cakes. A hand's breadth away was the pharmacy on the front of which was painted "Jesus is coming". Some anarchist who must have travelled had written beneath it "Jesus gone".

There were no other shops in the vicinity and Genetha, after slaking her thirst with a second drink – a purchase that seemed to alarm the lady behind the counter – went back to the house to await the men's arrival. She promptly dozed off and slept until she was awakened by the squealing of the pigs, which were being tortured by Ulric.

"You in' die of loneliness?" Fingers mocked her.

"Where did you go?" she asked.

"To see a man who going hunt with Quickey and us. You coming? He say you can come as long as you know how to walk quiet."

"I'll see."

Ulric asked if she had slept well and actually looked her straight in the eye.

Genetha helped Quickey to prepare the main meal, breakfast, which was not ready before two in the afternoon.

And for the first time everyone spoke freely. After the meal Genetha, emboldened by the new sense of well-being, followed Fingers's suggestion to take off her dress and walk around in her petticoat, as so many of the women of Morawhanna did, he said. She lay on the floor, her head on his lap, and listened to him talk and felt the vibration of his voice through his thighs.

"This is the main street, Quickey?" she asked.

"No. Is two streets away," he replied.

She told him of her trip to the shop.

"The woman does own the pharmacy next door, too," he said eagerly. "If you go to buy cascara she does got to run over and leave she customers in the cake shop to sell you in the pharmacy. On Saturday night when people come from up river to sport she does sweat like pig, runnin' from one shop to the other."

Ulric spoke of one of the periods he was in steady employment during the war. He was then a member of the militia and often had to do guard duty on one of the cargo ships in harbour. Once when he had been relieved and was descending the rope ladder to the launch which was to take him back to land he dropped his rifle in the space between the launch and the ship. To his surprise the incident caused such consternation among

415

his superiors that he began to tremble for his life. He was made to write several reports, fill out forms specially printed for the occasion and finally recite and sign an oath of loyalty to people and institutions he had only read about in the papers. As if that were not enough he was brought to trial before a specially constituted court which, after lengthy deliberations, decided that as he had not thrown away his rifle, and as it was unlikely to fall into the hands of the crew of a German submarine, he would be absolved of blame. But since such negligence could not go unpunished he was to be discharged from the militia in disgrace. Ulric hung his head in a suitable display of grief and disappointment.

Quickey spoke of Sibyl, his spirit-child, who came to visit him every Friday. She was one of the two teachers who worked in the school across the river. The first Friday after arriving to take up her post she came and sat on his doorstep as if she had known him all her life.

"She come an' go, just like that," said Quickey. "Always on Friday afternoon. Then one Friday she come through the door and sit in that very chair Ulric sitting 'pon. And is so I get to know she."

"How you mean she's a spirit-child?" Fingers asked.

"Oh, you can tell," Quickey answered. "First you suspect, then things happen that make you know. They don't get malaria like we. And they does hear the faintest noise. She going come this afternoon."

Quickey went on to tell them that before Sibyl started working at the school the aboriginal Indian children used to go off in their boats during recreation. No one had succeeded in pinning them down to a pattern of behaviour alien to their way of life. But Sibyl had no difficulty whatsoever in keeping them within the school precincts. People began talking about her; and when she increased the practical side of the curriculum at the expense of Arithmetic and English she was dismissed. But even more children began treating recreation as the end of the school day, so that at mid-morning the river stretching away on both sides of the school was dotted with boats heading in every direction, as if the children were fleeing some kind of pest. In the end the authorities were obliged to climb down and Sibyl was reinstated.

"People don't talk 'bout she no more," Quickey said. "They

just accept she."

"And where your family live?" enquired Fingers.

"All over the place. They in balata bleeding mostly, so they spend a lot o' time in the bush."

Quickey fell asleep during one of Ulric's stories. Genetha went inside and was followed by Fingers, who lay down beside her and began fondling her breasts lazily. Hanging from the window ledge above their heads was a line of pupae strung out like dried fruit. Genetha was thinking of the swarming insect life in Morawhanna as her lover stretched out his strong fingers over her breast, of the covered walks through which termites marched to attack the woodwork of houses, of the protection afforded them by Morawhanna's inhabitants, as though they were bringers of good fortune rather than destruction. When Fingers mounted her he found her weeping from contentment and rode her gently, understanding at last the extent of her dependence, that she was wearing her petticoat as a bridal gown and her impenetrable expression like the veil behind which teemed a hundred gestures of welcome and despair.

As they lay beside each other they heard Ulric's snoring and the half-hearted chattering of squabbling birds. Then Fingers fell asleep and was awakened briefly by the monkeys of the monkey-woman who sold her captives at exorbitant prices to people from town. And in the wake of their screaming and hissing Genetha herself dropped off, her body moist with sweat.

Genetha, who awoke with the scent of herbs in her nostrils, heard muffled voices coming from the adjoining room. When she put out her hand she found that Fingers was no longer on the bed.

From the tone of the men's voices and the quality of their laughter she knew that there was someone else in the house. She knelt down on the bed, through the mattress of which she could feel the bed-boards. Cupping her chin in her hands she looked down into the yard, where the only cock was treading the hens. They ran in a frenzy along the narrow space between the house and fence, releasing feathers in a vain flight from persecution, then submitting to the cock's attentions with tails spread out like fans.

"There'll be more eggs," she thought, lazily trying to work out at the back of her mind whether the visitor was a man or woman and how she would manage to go down to the yard and get washed without being seen. Craning her neck she only managed to see a patch of the river reflecting the sun on its surface sheen. The latrine and bath-house in the back yard stood side by side like companions, unpainted structures under a coconut tree that went curving away over the neighbour's yard. The sun was sinking on a horizon of rainbows where God the mist-maker sat and judged men's deeds, according to a Macusi hymn. One fatal day he would decide that the accumulation of wickedness had overwhelmed his compassion and then he would hold back the wheel on which the sun climbed to its ascendancy in the east.

Genetha decided to leave by the window. She put on her frock and panties and eased herself down into the yard. With a calabash standing on the rainwater barrel and a bucket she washed herself from head to foot in the bath-house before going back into the house through the front door.

"Mistress," said Quickey, standing out of respect for Genetha. "This is Sibyl."

Genetha shook the young woman's hand and could not conceal her surprise that it was this frail, ethereal creature who had such influence on the children she taught.

"If you hungry it got food on the table," Quickey offered.

"No, I'm not hungry, thanks."

So well had Genetha settled into her new way of life that she had forgotten to put on her shoes. She went and sat down on the floor next to Fingers who, she saw right away, was embarrassed in Sibyl's presence.

"Sibyl was just starting to tell we 'bout school," Quickey said, pointing with considerable pride at the young woman.

When Sibyl rested her eyes on her Genetha felt that she had come under a powerful scrutiny, and even after Sibyl turned away and began to talk, Genetha believed that she was being gazed at.

Speaking softly Sibyl said, "No, Uncle. They told me old stories, some of which were false because they know I like listening to old stories."

"And what 'bout you?" asked Quickey. "All your stories true?"

"No. I mean false because they made them up just for me. The Warraus can tell stories all night about the Carib-Warrau wars."

418

"Are there any Caribs left?" Ulric enquired in a carefully enunciated English.

"They got some up this very river," Quickey informed the company. "And I hear they got a lot in Surinam. Long, long ago they was much more than the Arawaks. This river self got a Carib name: Waini. It was up this river and the Orinoco that they come into South America. To this day the Arawaks and Warraus frighten of them even though only a handful left."

They talked until Quickey said that he, Ulric and Fingers were going to drink rum.

"When you going, niece?" Quickey asked Sibyl.

She looked at Genetha then answered that she would be leaving soon, but would come the next morning.

"Saturday!" exclaimed Quickey. "Good. Careful how you go cross the river. They in' got moon tonight."

The men left the two women alone. Only the crickets and tree-frogs could be heard and the murderous humming of the mosquitoes.

"I wonder how the Indians can go about naked with all the mosquitoes," remarked Genetha, put out by Sibyl's presence.

"In the bush where they go about naked the same dye they use to paint themselves with keeps away insects. And the wood from which they get the dye is like cocoa wood: they make fire with it. They plant whole fields with it."

"Truly?" asked Genetha, her embarrassment growing with every word the young woman spoke.

When the men were there her presence was bearable, but alone there was something curiously oppressive about her frail body. Was it because of what Quickey had told them? Or would she have felt the same otherwise? Genetha was certain that there was little between them in their education.

"Why you don't like me?" Genetha asked, preferring to make a fool of herself rather than to endure a long silence.

"You only ask that because you don't know what to say."

And this retort only increased her malaise.

"Look how I'm trembling," Genetha said. "A half-hour ago I was sleeping and now I'm trembling like a leaf."

"You're sure you're well?" Sibyl asked.

"Of course I'm well! I've got more weight than you."

Sibyl got up. "I'll go then," she offered.

"Right!"

419

"Look," Sibyl said, hesitating by her chair. "This only happened once before. I can't help it. Come with me across the river, ne?"

Genetha recoiled at the suggestion that she should hazard her life on the river with Sibyl in a frail craft when she could not even swim and had no confidence in her.

"All right. I'm gone," Sibyl said softly.

She went through the back door, down to the riverside where her boat was moored. Genetha followed, realizing that the stranger was hurt. Standing in front of the bath-house she waited until Sibyl was in her corial then she called out.

"I don't know how to sit in that thing."

"Try it."

Genetha went down to the bark canoe and sat down as carefully as she could, but as she had anticipated, the craft nearly capsized.

"I'll come tomorrow and you can practise sitting in it," said Sibyl, when Genetha was standing once more on the bank.

"All right."

Sibyl headed for the open river and was soon lost in the gloom on the water.

Genetha went back to the house, ashamed at her loss of control. She reflected on the opinion others had of her, of an unruffled character, which she herself had come to believe, in her habitual way of looking in other people's mirrors.

"I like this mirror," her mother used to say about the looking-glass on the dressing-table, "because it fills me out."

She had come to believe in a serene presence that dwelt in her, now exposed as a figment by a school teacher Quickey and the other two men treated as a sage.

The next morning Sibyl came when the sun was hardly over the horizon and the men were preparing to go hunting. The actual hunt was to take place the coming night, but they had to paddle some distance up-river.

Sibyl sat down on the back stairs without announcing her arrival and it was Ulric who first saw her.

"Howdye," he said.

"Howdye."

"You always use that small boat?"

"It's easy to handle," Sibyl explained. "How far are you

going?"

"A few miles up the creek."

Quickey came out on hearing them talk.

"Howdye, niece. You want to come?"

"No. If it was cooler," she declined.

"Miss Genetha don't want come either. She think she going get snake bite."

"So she's staying?" asked Sibyl.

"Yes. First she say she coming," said Quickey, affecting exasperation, "then she say she staying. Take she round to Miss Gordyck, ne."

"I'll see."

Genetha had heard every word. She was sitting at the dining-table, watching Fingers unravel a length of knotted string. The talk of hunting, the day before, had posed one problem for her: should she or should she not go? Now, however, as she witnessed the actual preparations for the trip, she began to imagine that Fingers might be exposed to all kinds of perils. He might be bitten by a labaria, a snake quite common in the surrounding bush. Quickey had talked the night before of the ineptitude of townspeople during a hunt, yet denied the possibility of her lover being in any danger. She sat following him with her eyes, but on hearing Sibyl's voice she rejected the idea of asking him to stay behind with her. Although he did not stop what he was doing when Sibyl came he nevertheless kept looking towards the back door.

A good half-hour later the men left amid much laughter and ribaldry. Genetha kissed Fingers in front of everyone. The latter, acutely embarrassed, wiped his lips in jest, so that Ulric and Quickey laughed out loud. She went down to the gate while Sibyl stood at the window watching, waving once in answer to Quickey's rapid gesture of farewell.

Genetha, on returning to the house, was overcome with the same hostility towards the visitor as she felt yesterday until the moment she said she was going home. The desire to meet her again that Genetha had felt, watching her boat move away towards the opposite shore, had vanished some time that morning, perhaps when she heard her voice.

Sibyl spoke first: "I was to teach you to sit in the corial. You're coming?"

"Teach?" asked Genetha. "I'm not one of your pupils." No

421

sooner had the words escaped than she was ashamed.

"You're coming or not?" Sibyl persisted.

"What have you got that makes men run after you?" Genetha demanded, knowing that she would be unable to keep up the pretence of being friendly.

Sibyl did not answer.

"I mean, you're not even good-looking," Genetha continued. "And you're small. Men don't like small women."

Genetha listened to herself talking, and as in a dream could not help behaving in a way contrary to her real nature.

"I got up early," said Sibyl, "just to come and see you, and you're chasing me away again, like yesterday."

Genetha did not reply at once. She stood in the centre of the room, helpless in face of the young woman's calm.

"You want some ginger tea?" she said at length, without turning to the visitor.

"Yes, thanks."

When she came back again from the cubicle at the foot of the stairs – in which there was a clay stove and the most rudimentary kitchen furnishings – she was carrying two large enamel mugs, both of which were badly chipped around the rim.

Genetha sat down at the dining-table, where Sibyl joined her.

Then, partly to atone for her rudeness, partly on account of a desperate need to share her secrets with someone, Genetha began to talk of her past, of her parents and brother, of her Queenstown aunts and her paternal aunt and of her grand-parents. She spoke of the former servants of the family, Marion and Esther, who had left a legacy of guilt to them all, like lead embedded in the flesh, that caused pain when all seemed well.

"I want my freedom from Fingers, yet I can't do without him. I've never been so happy in my life as since I've been here in Morawhanna. But I know it can't last."

"What if it doesn't last?" Sibyl asked.

"You don't think it matters," said Genetha. "For me it is of the utmost importance . . . the utmost importance."

"Why?"

"Why does Quickey call you a spirit-child?" Genetha asked.

It was the first time that Sibyl appeared to be less than mistress of herself.

"The aboriginal Indians are all spirit-children. Because I'm not an Indian people think it odd that I can do certain things, that's all."

"Like what?"

Sibyl turned to look her in the eye, and once more she was afflicted with that feeling of oppression.

"What people can't do always looks extraordinary. The Indians can see fish under water when you couldn't see them. They can call birds towards them and make monkeys come down from the trees. They can harm people in strange ways. And they know the bush: they know that jaguars never move about during a full moon, and that vampire bats avoid places with dogs."

"Can you do all the things they can do?" Genetha asked.

"Not all."

"I see."

"You talk about your family," Sibyl said. "The Caribs are all but extinct. I can show you a group of Caribs without children. Their women are terrified of conceiving because they feel they're doomed. They're afraid of the bush, of darkness, of strangers, even of their own dogs."

"So I shouldn't complain," Genetha remarked.

"When you don't *want* to complain, that's freedom," said Sibyl.

"Resignation," retorted Genetha quietly.

"People who struggle don't complain."

"Neither do people who're resigned," Genetha returned hotly, thinking of her martyred mother.

Then, after a long pause, Genetha said, "You make me feel ashamed. . . ."

"Why not stay here? Your friend could buy a piece of land and farm it."

"Fingers wouldn't stay, because Ulric wouldn't."

"You can still ask him. He looks as if he's having a good time."

"I'll ask," Genetha agreed, knowing full well that *she* could not stay away from Georgetown.

Once more she had talked too much, Genetha thought. One day she had confided in Fingers, with the result that he began taking advantage of her. Heaven knows what Sibyl must think, for *she* had confided nothing in return and had even failed to answer directly when asked what those powers were that had earned her the reputation of being a spirit-child.

"I'll take a swim while you learn to sit in the corial," Sibyl suggested with a smile so warm that once more Genetha experienced the extraordinary effect of her personality.

The guest went down to the river, Genetha remaining behind to change her dress and put on a pair of sandals.

From the top of the back stairs she could see Sibyl's corial, its stern moving from side to side on the water, and, beyond, the flight of marsh birds straying from the reed banks. Then, just as she decided to fetch a hat against the sun, she saw Sibyl come out of the bath-hut and run down to the river, stark naked. Genetha knew that outside Georgetown nude swimming was commonly practised, yet the sight of a woman unclothed in the open was the witnessing of something unforgivably immoral. She took down Fingers's panama hat from the nail, telling herself that her astonishment was yet another proof of her ignorance of the world around her.

"When you can balance," Sibyl called out, "try and paddle a bit. It's shallow for about ten feet out. Don't be afraid."

Balancing was far easier than it had been the previous day and almost at once Genetha tried her hand at paddling.

"Don't scrape the paddle against the boat," advised Sibyl. "Hold it a little away from the boat. That's it. . . . Now paddle on the other side, softly . . . like that. When you want to come back, keep paddling on the left side and the corial will turn gradually."

A feeling of elation overcame Genetha, who forgot that her companion was swimming naked, that she herself could not swim and that her jealousy had burgeoned like a mysterious cloud. She paddled, propelling the corial now in one direction now in the other, like a child discovering a new world of sensations through walking. Sibyl, who was treading water as expertly as the aboriginal Indian children she taught, now swam away from the shallows, certain that Genetha knew what she was about.

Beneath the morning sun the two women moved in the solitude of a derelict civilization which, hundreds of years ago, pushed up the great rivers into the hinterland of a continent of profoundly disturbing echoes, a solitude of buried potsherds, of once ruthless conflicts and bleached bones, of cowering remnants of a proud nation that had lost the instinct to bear children.

The marsh birds shrieked over the mud-banks, and far above in an endless circling, a pair of vultures scanned the islands of a waterlogged landscape.

Genetha paddled towards the open river, towards the place where the sun dazzled and the deep water was still in slack tide, and the births and deaths of a million small creatures were neither celebrated nor mourned.

8. The Spirit-Child

Night fell and with it a plague of hard-backed beetles and yellow moths with diaphanous wings. The beetles were everywhere, on the table, the floor, crawling up the walls and occasionally penetrating the women's hair. Quickey, Ulric and Fingers were playing cards in the corner, huddled under a pale kerosene lamp, from time to time interrupting their game to curse a beetle that crawled up an exposed leg or into an ear.

The guests were leaving the following day and the grip stood on the floor by the door with a leper-wood bow lying next to it.

Twice the men had gone hunting without success and on each occasion Sibyl kept Genetha company, the second time staying overnight at her request. Genetha came to consider her a close friend, though she would have admitted that to no one. Sibyl's influence on her was undeniable and after her initial resistance to the young woman's criticism of her tendency to brood she set about systematically putting into practice some of her advice. Her first aim was to overcome the senseless jealousy of Sibyl herself, and now that she was all but successful it was time to go back to Georgetown.

While the men played cards the women could only talk, Genetha reflected. Men talked, went hunting and played games. Only for little girls was it seemly to play games. When the family moved to Georgetown she remembered well how difficult it was to join a group in her new primary school. Her mother had asked, "Did you make a friend, Gen?" And not, "Did you manage to get in with a group?" Boyie simply took up a fielding position in the playground cricket match, while she stood by the girls with their skipping rope, waiting to be *called*. Now, she had no recollection of how she managed to get in with the girls, it just happened, just as, after a painful start, her friendship with Sibyl just happened. Sibyl had shown her that she need not be at the mercy of the past or of other people's actions, a lesson so momentous to her that she was disposed to tell Finge about it, and even Quickey, who was goodness itself.

The rains had come, hence the plague of beetles, which would vanish by morning, as if they never existed.

"How do the fishermen manage in the rain?" she asked Quickey.

Everyone laughed, and Genetha was at a loss to know why. No one except her was thinking of the following day, it seemed. The rain clouds would burst then, according to Quickey, and all the passengers would huddle under the awnings and throng the saloon, so that the purser would give up trying to sort out the first-class ones from the second-class, who belonged downstairs.

Genetha and Sibyl were unable to make conversation, their talk being unsuitable for men's ears, so they watched the candle flies that kept invading the window spaces at the front of the house, their lights vanishing and reappearing a few feet away.

"The hard backs going put out the light," Quickey warned when two beetles fell down the kerosene lamp chimney at the same time.

"Good," said Fingers. "Is more nice in the dark when the dies around."

"Hunting in the dark didn't do you much good," Genetha sed him, recalling the men's elaborate preparations for two tless expeditions.

You right, girl," he said, shaking his head.

know a man who caught deer on the sea wall," Ulric joked.

sooner had he spoken the last word than the lamp went Quickey said it would.

you hold on," he told the company. "I got to clean out d backs. They worse than last year, I in' telling lie."

ew minutes light was restored and the men went on with ne while Genetha and Sibyl discussed the forthcoming to Georgetown. The last time they were alone they en at length about marriage and Sibyl's man friend, a dispenser on the island of Wakenaam.

lling asleep again," Fingers complained.

lling asleep?" Quickey protested. And with that he ard at random and played it confidently.

could play forever," Genetha told Sibyl, to whom scent of vanilla from the cake she had baked that for the departing guests.

When Sibyl got up to go, everyone rose with her.

"Careful with the cassava near the bottom step," Quickey warned.

They picked their way through the newly harvested cassava piled in two heaps by the foot of the stairs.

"You gone then," Fingers said to Sibyl as she took the paddle, ready to dig it into the mud and shove towards the open river, now shadowy under a starless night.

"Next time you come this side," she told them, "stop off at Wakenaam. Ask for the dispenser. The young dispenser. And you all can stay as long as you like."

Quickey and the guests stood watching Sibyl and the boat and her paddle dripping whenever it was raised out of the water.

"She forget to take the fat-pork," Quickey said. "I going give her next Friday."

With that the men went back to their card game, leaving Genetha standing by the river's edge.

Her thoughts wandered from her travelling friend to the street with two shops and she deemed it strange that in the past fortnight she had gone nowhere yet had been happier than ever before, that she had stored up memories in the way her mother used to keep her girl's hair and other momentoes of her life in Queenstown, in little carved boxes scented with naphthalene balls. She had also learned to guard against the tortures of jealousy, for when Fingers said, "You gone then," she had schooled herself to pay no heed. If she had not understood why her friend was regarded as a spirit-child she nevertheless discovered what in the past she had missed by way of friendship, and that her exaggerated regard for Sibyl was perhaps the shadow of a childhood lack.

The next morning Quickey would not come with them to the boat. Goodbyes were for women. He tied up the bag of vegetables and fruit and strung it from a cord, so that Genetha, who was carrying little else, could hang it over her shoulder.

"Ulric, man," he said, "I know you in' going come back 'cause I cut you ass at cards."

"I goin' come back," Ulric replied, "if you promise not to chase away all the animals in the bush with your ugly face."

Their laughter attracted the attention of an old man sitting on the porch of the house opposite.

"Neighbour," he called out to Quickey, "you goin' away?"

427

"No! Is where I goin' go at my age? Is me friends from Georgetown. They goin' home."

"From where?" the neighbour enquired.

"Georgetown!"

"Yes, well," he grumbled.

"I goin' come with you to the corner," Quickey declared.

And he ended up on the stelling where the gangway rose steeply to the boat, which was riding on a high tide.

Ulric, Genetha and Fingers toiled up the gangplank, over-burdened with their luggage and presents from Quickey, only to find that all the good seats in the saloon had been taken.

Placing their things together in a corner they went out to wave to Quickey who, meanwhile, had got into conversation with another old man; and it was only when the shouting of the Transport and Harbour employees took his attention that he turned and waved as the boat drifted away from the stelling and the mooring ropes were hauled aboard.

Back in Georgetown they took a hired car home. The streets were teeming with people as though some fête were being celebrated.

"Political meeting," Ulric said knowingly.

Since the Enmore sugar-estate riots when several people were killed or hurt by police bullets political meetings had become a commonplace.

Now the hired car slowed down almost to a halt in order to negotiate a passage through a crowd, many of whom bent down to look into the vehicle, whose occupants were too tired to take an interest in the reason for the gathering.

Finally they arrived and Fingers jumped out in order to pay before Ulric could do so. Not having been asked to contribute to the cost of the stay in Morawhanna he was determined to show that he, too, could be generous.

Having said goodbye to Ulric the two lovers laboured up the stairs, Fingers carrying the grip while Genetha struggled with Quickey's presents.

Fingers picked up a piece of folded paper lying on the floor just beyond the doorway.

"My grandmother want see me," he said, after reading it.

"Go tomorrow, ne," Genetha told him.

"Suppose so. If it urgent she'll come sheself."

428

Genetha sat down in an easy chair, but Fingers got undressed and went straight to bed. She picked the paper out of the kitchen bin she knew he was asleep, but learned nothing more from it than she had been told. Until then she had never enquired as to his relations with his grandmother, his father and sisters, and he had told her nothing. After the holidays when she had him to herself the sudden realization that he was bound to others came as a jolt. Instead of retiring as Ulric had done, she remained in the gallery turning the matter over in her mind.

Already Morawhanna was a dream, a garden where flowers were memories, deep-hued or yellow, blood-red roses and lady-of-the-night. That table where they ate together, the base of its legs wrapped in silver paper and standing in old tobacco tins half-filled with disinfectant as a protection against marauding ants, always laden with fruit on those glittering mornings, was as vivid in her imagination as the children paddling to school or Sibyl running down naked to the river's edge. She and Quickey were of Morawhanna as Ulric and Fingers were of Georgetown, all shadows of a particular place. Was not Ulric *levied* upon by the bailiffs? Not many people in Morawhanna knew the meaning of the word; of that she was certain.

9. Strangers in the Kitchen

Fingers went to see his grandmother the next afternoon and the following day as well. Then he assured Genetha that when he went out the night after that he was going to play billiards and not to visit his people. He became secretive and resented Genetha's ceaseless questioning as if he were a child. In the end he was obliged to admit that his grandmother was demanding that he continue to support the family; for his father, in his late forties, was unable to find work.

"Support them!" said Genetha angrily, failing to understand why he was making such a song and dance of a simple matter.

"If you don' mind."

"Of course I don't mind," Genetha said, peering into that gulf between them which she always knew had never been bridged.

They began quarrelling frequently. Fingers had changed and she could not bear the uncertainty of her position.

One afternoon she came home to find Fingers's father, his

three sisters and grandmother in the kitchen. The oldest girl, in her late teens, had taken off her shoes and was sitting with her legs sprawled and her plate on one knee for the world as if she were mistress in the kitchen. The two other girls, about eight and nine years old, were eating with spoons rice heaped on their plate, while Fingers's father and grandmother kept an eye on them.

"He gone downstairs," the father told Genetha, who had as yet said nothing.

She went into the bedroom, placed her handbag on the bed, then left in search of her lover, who came to Ulric's front window when she called out for him.

"Is you?" he asked sheepishly. "Wha' you doin' home so early?"

"Please come over. I want to talk to you."

He took his time and even when on her bridge he found it necessary to strike up a conversation with a passer-by. She met him at the foot of the stairs.

"Can you tell me what your family are doing in my kitchen?" Genetha asked him, filled with rage at his apparent indifference to the urgency of her summons.

"Is my food," he lied. "Truly."

"So that's why —"

"Look, Gen. Is this once. The ol' man not working. It not goin' happen again."

Genetha pressed her thumb deep into the back of her hand, determined not to lose her temper with him.

"You will never change," she said, "and I can't go on like this."

"Listen, Gen. Listen! I goin' get rid of them now!"

"No. . . ."

But he did not wait for her to finish. Genetha heard the clamour of raised voices and stamping in the kitchen; and soon afterwards someone's legs appeared on the back stairs, only to disappear promptly. Then Fingers's grandmother began descending the steps with great dignity, followed by the girls and her fifty-year-old son. And none of the group addressed Genetha as they filed by.

Fingers did not come down and Genetha on going upstairs found him in a dejected pose by the kitchen sink.

She was the one who was wronged, Genetha told herself, resisting the urge to climb down. Besides, she did not know

430

how long Fingers had been entertaining his family behind her back, perhaps as long as the time they came back from Morawhanna, when he claimed that his appetite had grown. His eldest sister could not have looked more relaxed in her own house; and his father's unsolicited advice to seek his son downstairs confirmed the impression that the family had had some practice in making themselves at home.

Through all the contradictory thoughts that raced through her mind flowed the strong, persistent current of a single emotion, her anger at being used.

"I know how you feel," Fingers said. "But is my family. I can't see them starve."

"You'll have to choose between me and them," Genetha said.

If only she was certain of him she could bring herself to stomach this invasion of her home. How solid and healthy the girls looked, in spite of the family's privations. And this observation only served to fire her resentment all the more. If Fingers's grandmother had got up deferentially, as Esther and Marion had been trained to do, the impertinence might have been softened and she might have dismissed her lover's boldness as a lack of breeding.

Fingers, at a loss for words, and terrified lest he had gone too far, came and put his arms round her waist.

"I care for you a lot, Gen," he declared, in that honeyed tone that might denote either sincerity or hypocrisy.

"Do you?" she said with a flat voice.

"You don't know that? Look how much you do for me."

She felt his arm round her and recalled that his hands had brought her a measure of peace, that she took pride in watching them grip the tools of his new trade, which, after all, promised to earn them years of tranquillity. It was through her that he had learned to love and respect work.

Genetha turned and looked at him.

"The trouble is," she said, "you know you can twist me round your finger. But if you want us to go on living together don't bring your family to eat here."

"You make me forget," said Fingers. "I had something to show you. Wait, I goin' bring it."

He went inside and came out again with her father's framed photograph in one hand and a small sepia print in the other.

"This one drop out of the back of you father photo," he said,

431

while handing her the two.

The small photograph was that of Esther, Boyie and herself. On the back of it was written: "Rohan, Genetha and servant."

"You an' you brother small, eh?" Fingers nudged Genetha, delighted that he had found an excuse to take her mind off his family's intrusion.

Genetha waited until he had gone back over to Ulric's before picking up the old print again. Boyie was standing on a wicker chair, one hand clasped in hers, while Esther stared at the camera with that proprietary expression that so irritated her mother. What, indeed, was family? Marion, with her flamboyant dress, her men friends, her independence, had been, as a servant, as much a part of the family as Esther. But no one would have described her as *family*. Esther, never as close to her mother, had an essential place in that web of relationships that bind groups together, and if her parents would never have included her in the term "family" Genetha and Boyie had had no doubt as to her position. Ah, those days of long ago, those gentle hours, the things one loved, the strange, absurd attachments! Genetha had never come to terms with the knowledge that her father did not perform miracles, with the altered landscape of adulthood. So passionate were its embraces, yet how much would she not give for her mother's gentler touch, or Esther's, before she was shown the door.

Fingers began complaining that his own conduct was due to his feeling of insecurity, for he had nothing while she had a steady job and the ability to find another if she lost her present one. She even had a house. He harped on this theme so consistently and sulked so often that she agreed to see a lawyer with a view to transferring her share in the property to him. When everything seemed settled she changed her mind at the last moment. Fingers packed his things and said that he was going abroad to get away from her.

Genetha, although she had changed her mind, went to see a lawyer nevertheless, who explained that to deal with the property she would have to secure Letters of Administration from the Deeds Registry. She would not be granted them unless Rohan gave his consent.

Glad at the opportunity to contact her brother she wrote that she wanted to raise a mortgage on the property but was unable

432

to do so without Letters of Administration. Rohan answered in an affectionate letter granting her what she sought.

"That he can hold it against me for so long," she thought, dismayed that he did not invite her up to Suddie.

Fingers left her once more, saying that the length of time the business was taking showed how insincere she was; and when, once again, she went to fetch him back, he showed her his passport. He had definitely made up his mind to go away. Genetha pleaded with him, promising to be his slave; for all the conversations with Sibyl had come to nothing, and the resolution to be independent at all costs. He demanded that she make over to him the property, without including in the transport that a half share belonged to Rohan. It was as if the spirit had departed from her body, leaving it powerless to resist her lover's demands. She agreed and Fingers went back with her. When finally the court proceedings were over, transport was passed and the property was in his name, Fingers jokingly threatened her with eviction if she did not behave.

He disappeared for a fortnight and on returning disclosed to her his plans for the house. He intended to have all the outstanding repairs done. In addition he would paint it blue, the colour of the dress she was always recalling.

He and Genetha talked about his plans for a long time and agreed that she would have to find temporary accommodation until the work was over. She put a brave face on things when she read the carpenter's report: crumbling pillars, rusted guttering, ant-infested wood and a host of other defects that brought home to her the necessity of urgent action. It was surprising that the house was still standing. The gate was hardly doing that at all.

Genetha went to stay with her father's sister, who upbraided her for not having visited her. And, as if out of revenge, she dragged out Genetha's father's misdeeds every day of her stay, and the arrogance of her Queenstown aunts. Obliged to put up with this implacable hatred Genetha learned not to be offended; but this was not enough for her aunt, who took to seeking her approval for the opinions she expressed.

In the end Genetha, exasperated by her insistence, declared, "Can't you see how you're offending me, Aunt?"

"So I'm offending you! And what did your father do to me? The whole world knows what he did me. But it didn't stop him ending up a pauper, the pauper he made me."

"I know, Aunt," Genetha replied. "But can't you forget?"

"Never!" came the reply, like the recoil of a weapon. "I had gold and tables made of mahogany. People used to come to my house to admire my furniture, and the brass was cleaned every week by a girl from the village. Every Sunday she used to sit in the middle of the brass pots and the lamps and bed-knobs and she left the drawing-room and gallery glistening. Go to Anandale and ask them about Miss Armstrong. Even now they remember my house. But your father respected nothing! I went to him for advice and he robbed me as if I was a stranger. That day he treated me like a dog while your mother tried to console me. Then suddenly he was all smiles. He took my hand, saying that he would help me because we were brother and sister and we should stick together. And in a few weeks I was destitute and was glad to take a room under his house later when he offered it. It was like that, God is my witness. It was like that."

Her voice fell to a whisper.

"That man used to pass me on the stairs," she continued in a whisper, "even after he robbed me. Yes . . . and he had friends, believe it or not. He had friends who did stick to him through thick and thin as if he was a good man. . . ."

Genetha, for the first time, felt sorry for her, until the hysteria came back into her voice and she began to behave as if she was at war.

"But the sins of the father will be visited on the children. You and your no-good brother will come to a bad end. I'll pray for you and you will go under wishing you were never born! Look round you and see what I'm left with. I use enamel plates, like a range-yard woman, and have to empty my own po! And I was once respected in Anandale. Who respects me now? Who can respect a woman who does empty her own po? God is my witness that I've never had a moment's peace since he stripped me of everything I had."

Then, losing her temper completely, she stamped violently on the ground like a small child in a rage, so that a piece of furniture in which she kept a few glasses shook alarmingly. And Genetha sat opposite her, her head hanging as if she had been the cause of the disasters that had befallen her aunt all those years ago.

For weeks afterwards she never saw Fingers who, according to his sisters, was in the islands on business. The workmen who were painting the house knew nothing of his whereabouts. One night when she knocked on the door, from the front of which all the debris had been cleared, it was opened by a young girl of about ten.

"Ma! Is a lady!"

The girl's mother came out and asked what Genetha wanted.

"This is my house. I live here," Genetha said helplessly.

"Stanley! Come, ne?" the woman called out to someone in the back of the house.

"Is what?" came the answer in a booming voice.

"A lady say she live here. Come, ne?"

"Is what you talking 'bout? Live where?"

"I say come!" his wife called back, raising her voice in a show of irritation.

The booming voice appeared, followed by two younger children, a boy of about seven and a girl a year younger, both of whose faces were smeared in what they had been eating.

"Is what wrong?" the man enquired, evidently angry at being called away from his meal.

"I live here," declared Genetha. "I live in this house. It was under repair. . . ." She was lost for words. A wild look came into her eyes at the sight of the strange furniture.

"You must be mad, lady. We rent this house from Mr Bellamy."

She looked beyond the man's stocky figure towards the dining-room. Little was recognizable and the painted walls gleamed, and the place where the hatstand used to be was empty. She would write Boyie and ask him to come and settle things for her. He would evict these strangers, who were eating and sleeping in their home.

Genetha went away, but on turning the corner it occurred to her that Ulric's mother could help her. She could convince the strangers that she was not lying.

Ulric's mother was glad to see her and agreed readily to support her story.

"You should see how their children does climb over the paling! Of course I'll come, child. Of course."

She shuffled round the house in search of her hat.

It was Ulric's mother who knocked on Genetha's door with

her walking-stick. A child came to the window and shouted out:

"Is same lady! She come back with another lady, Ma. And a stick!"

Following the sound of hurried steps the door opened and the man of the house stood before them, hands akimbo and a terrible expression on his face.

"Is what you come back for?" he demanded. "You think I can spend the whole day opening and closing my door? This in' a hotel."

"This young lady lives here," said Genetha's neighbour. "I've been her neighbour for years."

"I don' doubt you, lady. But I living here now," the man retorted indignantly.

"You want me to call the police?" asked the widow, brandishing her stick.

"An' you want me to throw you off my stairs? Eh, eh! Some people wrong and strong!"

"Right! Come, girl," the widow said to Genetha.

The two women retreated down the stairs, accompanied by a torrent of obscenities from the man.

"That's what the district is coming to now," said the widow, when they reached her gate. "You go straight to the police! This minute!"

Genetha lost no time in going to the nearest station, the large Albertown Police Station.

"From what you tell me it's got nothing to do with us. See a lawyer. He'll tell you how to recover possession."

"But the neighbours can tell you I lived there," protested Genetha.

"People're always moving out and in, lady. According to what you tell me yourself you did make over your house to the Fingers chap of your own free will. Didn't you? Isn't that what you did say?"

She left the station and went back to the house. As she stood in the street looking at her former home the lights went out. Genetha could not resist the impulse any longer. She opened the street gate and went up the stairs. Timidly, she knocked at the door. There was no answer. She knocked again, more loudly this time, but no one came to the door. She knocked again and again, no longer fearing what the man might do. At last she abandoned her efforts and went to the back door which appar-

436

ently was only bolted, for it rattled under Genetha's fist and threatened to yield at any moment.

In the end she gave up and sat on the back stairs, still unable to comprehend her misfortune.

"He thief he own sister house," somebody had remarked at her father's funeral, referring to her dead father.

She was now sitting on a staircase her family had gone up and down all these years, the approach to a door now bolted against her. And all was silent now under a forest of stars.

10. My Father Stole a House

A doctor was holding Genetha's wrist with his left hand. She was lying on a hospital bed and had been talking intermittently, sometimes with a feverish urgency and at other times in mono-syllables, as if she could only speak with difficulty.

"The candles are wet," she said decisively, and tried to wipe her hands on the sheet on which she was lying.

"I have it here in my bag. Here . . . I told you, you're like a little boy."

The nurse wiped her forehead.

"I've always got to bring something home for you," Genetha continued in her delirium, "but when you. . . . Why're you looking at me like that? The trouble is you're too sure of me. I can't pretend. My eyes give me away. I wish I could pretend; it makes things so much easier. . . Can't you love me? Can't you try? When I was a girl in Agricola a man who played the 'cello used to live opposite us. You look like him, but what's in your hand is uglier. You've caused me more pain than my mother and father; and the 'cello screamed one night because it was alone. . . . With you everything is pain. My brother said you were always laughing and joking. But with me you hardly laugh at all. As soon as you come into my house, my house. . . . My father stole a house. . . . No! No! Father! It isn't true!" she screamed the last words, sobbing.

"Why did you wear rags?" Genetha continued. "If you only didn't wear rags! Father, why don't we go back to Agricola? All you've got to do is follow the pitch road and turn off by the rum shop."

She fell silent for a few minutes.

"Once," she began again, "Boyie pulled a hair from the police

437

horse's tail. I promised not to tell, but it doesn't matter now . . .
I used to stay awake until you came home and then when I
heard you cross the bridge my heart used to beat as if a hammer
was in my chest. There was always pain, pain . . . and then this
man, all because Boyie went away. If I had a daughter I'd teach
her to. . . . Snuff out the candles, please . . . then I'll say all the
unsaid things. . . ."

"Nurse," the doctor called, "pull the blinds, please."

The nurse complied and then returned to the bedside.

"She'll have to go to New Amsterdam."

The nurse stared at him.

"We need the bed for patients, nurse," he said irritably.

Genetha was transferred to the Berbice Hospital for the
mentally ill, where she spent six weeks before she was then discharged. Her condition had been diagnosed as a form of
hysteria, occasioned by acute distress, which did not amount to
a mental illness.

Many years later, the hateful stay in the mental home was
erased from her memory, except for a certain incident. Once
she and a score of patients were taken on a bus trip to East
Canje where they got out and were allowed to roam about at
will. She went a couple of hundred yards up the drainage canal
with a young woman and they both sat on the koker, the only
place that provided shade from the fierce morning sun. The air
was filled with a terrible stench they were obliged to endure
because they were not permitted to go back to the bus. In the
end her companion discovered the source of the smell, a dead,
bloated alligator which lay upturned in the canal at the base of
the koker.

Genetha's only memory of New Amsterdam was an abiding
stench and the slack water of the canal.

11. Tiger Bay

Genetha rented a room in Albouystown while she looked for a
job and tried, through her lawyer, to regain possession of her
house. Her former employers made her an ex-gratia payment of
sixty dollars, but declined to re-employ her. In the end she had
to take a job selling sweets and cigarettes at the Empire Cinema,
where she earned just enough to pay the rent and buy a little
food. Her one concern was to spend as little as possible until she

438

found satisfactory work before her savings gave out.

Rohan had remained ignorant of Genetha's stay in the mental hospital; but, convinced that he wanted nothing more to do with her, she did not get in touch with him.

She sold her bicycle and a few weeks later pawned her gold ring. But, inevitably, she began to draw money from the bank in order to pay for food, shoe repairs and a hundred and one other expenses. In the end she was forced to give up her efforts to re-occupy her house, for lack of money to pay her lawyer.

Some weeks later, despairing of ever finding work, she was taken on as a cashier at a Chinese wholesale grocer shop in a side street off Water Street. The twenty-five dollars she earned a month barely saw her through, provided she cut down on food and clothing; and when her umbrella was damaged she could not afford to repair it. But after facing the fierce midday sun for a week, she could bear it no longer and drew on her dwindling savings to have it mended. And so it went with the passing months until there was no more money left in the bank.

One morning she found she could not get out of bed. The sun was streaming through a chink in the wall and she heard the voices of children on their way to school. Her shivering was so bad that she plucked up the courage to hammer on the wall in order to attract the attention of her neighbour, whom she hardly knew. Moments later there was a knocking on her door and only then she realized that her neighbour could not get in. Summoning up all her strength she eased herself on to the floor and crawled over to the door, which she managed to open.

"Is wha' wrong, chile?" her neighbour muttered when she pushed the door and found her, face down on the floor.

She dragged Genetha to the bed and hoisted her bodily on to it, and on feeling her burning forehead covered her with the blanket. Later in the morning she brought her soup and bandaged her head with cochineal.

At midday Genetha heard the neighbour talking with her husband, but was unable to make out what he was saying. Later that afternoon when she came back to bring Genetha more soup she told her that her husband had been annoyed on account of the soup which, he claimed, they could not afford.

"Don't worry," she assured her, "he heart so soft he stupid sometimes. I tell you he'd give you he shirt if he take to you."

Genetha could only try to keep her teeth from chattering. She drank her soup greedily, but the dryness in her mouth remained and she asked her neighbour to leave a cup of water on the table beside her.

The afternoon stillness was broken by the school children returning home. The neighbour came back to open the door and window, in order to air the room, and the wind brought the scents from the streets with it and the cool air; and Genetha felt that the fever had fallen.

When her neighbour's husband appeared at the door she wished she could muster a smile. He placed an orange on the table and left without a word; only afterwards did it occur to Genetha that he could have let the owner of the grocery know why she was away.

Towards midnight, after she had given up all hope of her neighbour coming, there was a knock on her door. The good woman had gone to the pictures with her husband and was dropping in for the last time that day to see if she needed anything. Genetha asked if her husband might tell her employer why she was away and was assured that he would go early in the morning before he went to work.

"You're sure he'll do it?" Genetha asked.

"Oh, he like you. He say you look so thin and weak."

The next morning she came back unexpectedly, before the street had become noisy. Somebody, a woman in her thirties, was enquiring after Genetha.

"Tall?" Genetha asked.

"Yes."

Genetha knew at once that it was Esther and nearly wept with relief.

"Y'know she?" asked the neighbour.

"Yes. Her name's Esther."

Esther was already standing in the doorway. She was well dressed and had an attractive wicker basket in her hand, while on her left wrist she wore a gold bangle and a watch.

"I go'n see you," the neighbour said as she left Genetha, nodding a silent goodbye to Esther.

"You see?" Esther said, spreading out her hands. "I didn't forget."

She opened her handbag and took out a wad of notes from which she pulled the amount Genetha had lent her.

Genetha had never before seen Esther smile so readily. There

440

was a certain verve in her bearing, a certain confidence in her speech. Her even white teeth gleamed and her arms, plump and dimpled, gestured while she spoke. Yet there was a shrillness in her manner that was equally puzzling.

"How you knew where I was living?" Genetha asked.

"I live near where you working and I've seen you a lot of times."

"They told you I was living here?"

"Yes."

"So you live near there?" Genetha asked, for want of something to say.

"Yes. Well, you can't pick and choose, can you?" She sat down on the bed, beside Genetha.

"You know . . . they've got a new girl," Esther told her, hesitating a little to soften the blow.

"Where?"

"In the grocery."

She fumbled in her handbag and brought out a packet.

"They asked me to give you this," she said, handing her the sealed, lined envelope.

Genetha looked up at Esther.

"Don't bother," the older woman reassured her, "they know me in the area. He trusts me."

Genetha opened the packet and found a week's money with a dismissal notice. She said nothing, but sank back on to her pillow.

"What happened to your house?" Esther asked her, after allowing her time to recover.

Genetha, whose face was turned to the wall, did not answer. The noise of bicycle bells stood out among the assorted sounds of Albouystown.

"That's life, isn't it?" Esther observed. "I asked him if he had to do it, but he said he couldn't afford to have you off sick. He said you're sickly in any case and he didn't think you could last." She took out a cigarette and lit it, then got up, went to the window and leaned out.

Genetha could not believe that Esther's presence had terrified her when they last met.

"You didn't seem surprised to find me sick," Genetha remarked.

"I knew. I came yesterday and your neighbour told me. She's nice."

441

Then, after a long pause, Esther said, "The same thing happened the last time. I came twice before I could see you."

"Why didn't you come in, then?" asked Genetha.

"I don't know."

"You should've come in. The lady next door's been helping me, but I'm not sure if her husband likes me. He doesn't talk much."

"Probably he hasn't got anything to say," observed Esther flippantly.

For the first time Genetha looked Esther up and down.

"You look well."

"You notice," she said, with an expression of feigned indifference.

"I went back to Diamond, you know," Esther began again, as if she were confiding something she wanted to get off her chest. "A few years ago I couldn't stand it in Georgetown any more. Ha!" she laughed dryly. "I was soon back. I missed the noise and the pictures . . . and everything, you see."

She put out her cigarette and began tidying the place up, and when she had finished she asked Genetha if she wanted her to make the midday meal.

"Yes. You'll have to get ground provisions from the market, though."

"You know you look bad. I suppose you know," Esther said.

"Very bad?"

"Terrible. . . . You still like cook-up rice?"

Genetha nodded.

As Esther was getting ready to go Genetha said to her, "Go and tell the lady next door you're doing the shopping. Probably she intends to bring something for me. And, listen . . . say thanks for what she's been doing."

Esther slipped out of the door without saying goodbye.

Genetha was overcome with a wave of bitterness. The firm in which she had worked for years dismissed her because she had been in the mental asylum, even though she had not been mentally ill; and now a short illness was sufficient to cause her dismissal from the grocer shop where, she thought, she was liked and appreciated by the owners.

She had gone so far as to work late in order to help with the backlog of work. Besides, she had been ill only once in all that time. She pulled the blanket more closely round her and turned

442

over on her side to face the wall. The old wood had been recently given a single, inadequate coat of white paint which made it look even shabbier and the damp, musty smell that came from beneath the bed caused her to long for the soup the neighbour had been feeding her.

Genetha was incapable of fixing her thoughts on any single thing. Above all, if she attempted to dwell on Esther and the significance of her visit, some other less important train of thought interrupted the main theme of her reflections. She remembered that she had not given Esther any money for the shopping and almost at the same time she became aware of the extent of the change in her.

As soon as she returned, Esther asked:

"You want to come and live with me?"

Genetha propped herself up on her elbows and said:

"If you really want me to."

"I can get a taxi," declared Esther, "and the driver and I'll lift you out. I can't very well walk over here every day." Her last words were uttered as if she needed the utmost self-control in order to speak patiently.

"All right," Genetha said, trying not to show relief.

"Good. I'll cook and then order the taxi. We'll move this afternoon."

Esther unpacked the provisions and set to work picking the rice, while Genetha soon fell into a deep sleep, during which she perspired profusely.

That afternoon the two women got ready to make the journey by taxi to Esther's place.

Genetha had never recovered her clothes and furniture from Fingers. She had gone to his house several times, but in the end his sisters became so hostile she decided to keep away. When Esther asked where her belongings were Genetha told her that the man whom she had paid to move them had stolen everything.

"You don't have to lie to me. I know all about you and that Fingers that thief you out. Anyway, you must be a fool to give a man your house! Starting with property like that I would've owned a whole block in Georgetown by now," said Esther with as much feeling as if she had been Fingers's victim as well.

"You know where I live," said Genetha reproachfully, "and you know about me and Fingers."

"But everybody knows how you lost your house and that

443

you've been up to spend time in New Amsterdam."

"Oh," was all Genetha could reply.

"You should be accustomed to it. People've been talking about your family ever since the Agricola days."

"Why?" asked Genetha, out of annoyance rather than curiosity.

"Don't ask me. Some families attract attention. Besides, a lot of things happened when you were young that you don't know about."

"Well, tell me."

"You won't like me for it," warned Esther.

"Why did you mention it then?"

Esther was vexed by the younger woman's attitude and, partly out of spite, partly out of the need to communicate a secret that fascinated her, told of an incident at her father's funeral which at the time caused a considerable stir in the neighbourhood.

"At your father's funeral they had to stop a woman from coming upstairs. They had to turn her away by force. And you know what she did? She got a crowd of people outside the gate and told them that she had a child by your father. If they had let her in she would've caused confusion, she said. She came to make it a funeral people would never forget. When your grandfather went out and asked her to go away she went to the car that was waiting for her and came back with a little boy. He was the spitting image of your father."

Genetha bowed her head.

"You said you wanted to know, didn't you?" taunted Esther. "You're a big girl now. . . . You know that your father was at home in Tiger Bay? He knew every house, every rum shop. It's true. Your family wasn't ordinary. They were never happy if they weren't suffering. Admit that you like hearing about your parents, ne? You like it, don't you? Go on, admit it. You're no different from them. If you're not torturing yourself you fall sick and only get well again when you're sure that there's confusion. I've never seen people like you. To God I've never seen people like you. Your mother —"

"Don't talk about my mother, please," Genetha pleaded, afraid of any further revelations.

Esther lit another cigarette on the one she had just finished smoking and, satisfied with the revenge she had sought, fell silent.

"What did Father do around there?" enquired Genetha in an

444

almost inaudible voice.

"The same as all the other men," replied Esther, "the men from 'good homes', as your mother liked reminding me."

"You don't hear from Boyie?" Esther asked after a while, yielding to a feeling of pity for her erstwhile mistress's daughter.

"From time to time," Genetha lied.

"Boyie isn't like any of you."

"How do you mean?" Genetha asked, suspicious at the sudden shift in the conversation.

"He's just different, that's all . . . I bet women like him. But he won't make a woman happy. He's got the Armstrong cross. It's marked all over him. When he was a boy if anybody touched him I used to suffer, but I never showed it, because your mother didn't approve of the way I used to pet him and fondle him. She used to watch me whenever I took him on my lap and began kissing him on his neck and face. 'Put him down, Esther,' she used to say quietly; but I did know that inwardly she was boiling and wanted to scream at me."

Esther got up and went to the door.

"When's this man coming?" she said, with an irritable expression. "Did I tell you why I went back to Diamond? Yes, I told you; didn't I? I wanted to get married. I couldn't take the life here any more. . . . But there the smell of the sugar factory was the same and people were as poor as ever. My brother didn't get the dray-cart he wanted and my father still complains of his drinking. So I came back, back, back. Why do people always want to go somewhere and do something? And do this and do that? As if just living isn't enough."

As she spoke there was the blast of a horn outside. Esther took a battered suitcase filled with Genetha's few belongings out to the waiting chauffeur, then came back to fetch Genetha, who winced in the sunshine and gathered all her strength to descend the few stairs. The chauffeur glanced at them, then at his watch and no sooner were the two woman installed than the hired car shot away up the street.

Genetha closed her eyes and fought back the tears. She did not know why she wanted to cry; the sun, her weakness and the sensation of abandonment were all too much for her. Esther was about to speak, but shrugged her shoulders and said nothing when she saw her closed eyes and trembling lips. As the taxi swerved into High Street Genetha's shoulders were forced against Esther's body.

"These damned chauffeurs!" exclaimed Esther, making a grimace.

The sun streamed mercilessly into the vehicle, where Genetha leaned back on the worn leather seat. The whole street seemed to be on fire. There were a few pedestrians on the tree-lined walk between the two arms of Main Street, where flowers shuddered amid the foliage of the hundred-year flamboyant trees. The two-storeyed houses with their flying staircases slept behind closed shutters, indolent and aloof.

On opening her eyes Genetha noticed that the car was driving more slowly in the Tiger Bay area. It came to a halt in front of a low cottage, typical of those houses behind which festered a range of rooms for the desperately poor.

Esther got out, paid the chauffeur and then helped Genetha to come down. This time the man hoisted the grip on his shoulder and followed the women. He placed his burden on the lowest stair, smiled and waited to be paid. He then went off without a word.

Once in the room Esther helped Genetha off with her dress and made her lie on a bed with a thick mattress. From a chest of drawers she took out a blanket with which she covered her sick companion.

Through the single window the steely, implacable sky stared and Genetha closed her eyes to shut out the fear of the sky and the strange dim room. A few minutes later she heard Esther calling her, but pretended to be asleep.

When she awoke it was dark, and for a long while she was unable to tell where she was. The fact that the window was on the opposite wall instead of on the wall beside the bed confused her.

Suddenly she heard a man's voice; a moment later Esther appeared in the doorway and then a man, much taller than she.

"Don't make any noise. Shhh! I say. You not in a rum-shop, you know," Esther said sharply.

The bed on the other side of the room began to creak noisily.

"Well, tek it off, ne?" came the man's voice.

"God! You want everything."

"You t'ink I pay me money to —"

"Shut your mouth and get on with it," came Esther's angry voice.

446

Then there was heavy breathing, followed a few minutes later by a long drawn-out groan and then silence.

"Christ be praised!" Esther said mockingly.

After some shuffling and bumping Esther said with intense irritation, "Is what you waiting for, Christmas?"

"Well, gi' me a chance; le' me get me breath back," said the man.

Genetha saw Esther get up and pull her skirt on, while her client stood by, surveying the room.

"Is who that?" he suddenly asked, pointing at Genetha when he noticed her for the first time.

"Is my grandmother!" Esther exclaimed, beside herself with exasperation.

"You grandmoder? I din' know you was living wit' you grandmoder."

Esther sucked her teeth for a reply.

"She don' mind you carryin' on?" he ventured once more.

"Put your two dollars down and get out! I'll tell you about her another time."

"All right, all right," he said, slipping on his trousers and looking at Genetha from time to time as if he were afraid of what she might do.

When he had gone Esther lit a candle so as not to wake Genetha, and placed it on the dressing-table, where she adjusted her hair and put on fresh lipstick. Before she left she went over to see if Genetha was sleeping, then returned to the dressing-table, blew out the candle and went out again.

Genetha got up and hurried to the window, through which she could see Esther pass under the feeble lamplight and stop some distance beyond to light a cigarette. Her unusual gait gave the impression that she was walking on inordinately high shoes.

Once she had disappeared into the darkness Genetha looked more closely at what she could see of the street from the window. Opposite was a dingy little eating place, lit by bright bulbs, where two men could be seen just inside the doorway. They were engaged in an animated conversation and one of them was gesticulating violently. Next to the shop was another range-yard, wrapped in gloom. Next to that was a cottage, the porch of which was faintly lit by the street lamp. Although the area was as poor as Albouystown the latter was noisy and alive; the scene Genetha was looking at was like the section of a street leading up to a cemetery, sharing nothing with the bustling part of Tiger Bay where she had worked. It seemed to her strange that, though the men in the shop were obviously talking in a loud voice, she could hear nothing. Someone who must have been the proprietor appeared beside their table and said something to them. After that the man who had been gesticulating appeared more calm.

Genetha began to feel tired and went back to bed where she soon fell asleep.

12. Anandale

When Genetha was well again she began talking about looking for a job.

"Where?" Esther asked her. "When you been up to New Amsterdam people don't forget. Try getting a job without a reference; you won't get far, unless you want to sell in a cake-shop and get next to nothing."

"I can't go on living off you," Genetha protested.

"Anyway," said Esther, ignoring the younger woman's objection, "tonight we'll go out and eat somewhere nice, somewhere you'll like."

"You've got your work."

"You needn't say it like that. I've got a bank balance to show for it."

Esther jumped up, stung by what she fancied to be the derogatory tone in Genetha's voice. She drew out the lower drawer of her dressing-table, pulled a post office pass book from under a pile of clothes and opened it at the last entry, where Genetha could see the total of four hundred and fifty dollars.

"You think I'll end up like those rats at Mamus?" she asked heatedly. She was prompted to curse Genetha and her family, but restrained herself, fearing that she might only end up by driving her away.

"Anyway," she continued, "it's nothing to crow about. I could've had more if it wasn't for some money I lent a friend. I could kick myself. Men! They suck your blood. It's like an instinct with them. If I ever see him hanging round here I'll put the police on his tail before he knows what hit him."

Genetha was curious about Esther's acquaintances, but dared not ask.

448

Esther tried to find a way of proposing to Genetha that they should dine out with two of her men friends, but felt almost certain that she would not approve of the company she kept. If only she knew that Genetha had witnessed the love-making between her and her client the night when Genetha arrived, and the effect it had produced! Her body, drained of its energy by the bout of sickness had caught fire like a parched stubble field. The vicarious experience had left her exhausted. She had wanted to put out her hand at the departing client and ask him to lift up her petticoat and molest her and brutalize her as Fingers used to. She had wanted to drag him down on to the bed on top of her and partake in the act. When the torrent had subsided she felt ashamed and said a prayer, just as a child who, replete after a forbidden meal, allows itself the luxury of a short and silent penance.

"A friend'll be waiting for us tonight," said Esther, trying to be casual. "He might be bringing someone. You don't mind?"

"No," answered Genetha.

"He's decent. You won't mind him. A Trinidadian. They're nice, Trinidadians. Talk well. He's been to the States and all. A bit crazy, but he's got good manners. He's a gentleman. The first thing he said to me was that I'm the best spoken – well, you know what I mean – he's ever been out with. And he liked my teeth. Sometimes he says, 'Let me see your teeth,' as if I was a horse or something. I got your mother to thank for the way I talk."

"When you were with us you never talked much," observed Genetha.

"I didn't have anybody to talk with, except your mother. And you couldn't say the things you really wanted to say when you were talking to her."

"You were telling me about this Trinidadian," Genetha reminded her.

"Oh, Daley. He's a character. He always likes to see my teeth. . . . Oh, I've told you that. Let me see. Oh, yes. He says he likes ugly women. He says a lot of men like ugly women. No! It's true."

Esther burst out laughing and slapped her legs.

"He likes ugly women. So I said to him, 'You mean I'm ugly?' 'No,' he said, but I was an exception. We killed ourselves laughing. He said that ugly women drive him mad in bed. Once in Trinidad – this is what he says – he had a girl friend. She was good-looking, because he couldn't *marry* an ugly girl, you see. It's just for screwing, you see. Anyway, this girl wore glasses. So one day they were climbing a hill near Port-of-Spain and he threw her down in the grass and began kissing her. Eh, eh! This girl took off her glasses and put them down in the grass. So he told her to put them on again because she drove him wild with her glasses on. And she said she hated them, so she told him. She hated them and wasn't going to put them on. But he insisted. Anyway she was stubborn about them and told him to make up his mind if he wanted to or not."

"And what happened?" Genetha asked.

"I suppose they made love in the grass with her glasses on. But I don't see how she could've enjoyed it if she hated wearing them," Esther said thoughtfully. "When you hear him talk you'll break your sides laughing, 'cause he's like that."

"What's his name?" Genetha asked.

"Daley. I told you. . . . Oh, yes. I said to him . . . what was it I said? Oh, yes, I said, 'What you really need is an ugly woman with glasses.' We killed ourselves laughing. He said he couldn't stand it, going out with an ugly woman who wore glasses."

Esther was in high spirits. She lit a cigarette and prepared to continue her monologue. Genetha's father used to say, "People don't change," but in her eyes Esther had changed. The only thing that was left of the old Esther was the capable way she organized her life and the lives of others.

"Go on, try one," she said, tending Genetha a cigarette, but the younger woman declined.

"This business is hard work," continued Esther. "But you meet some characters. Now Daley, he said I'm useless in bed . . . I was really lying when I said that he never made a pass at me. Anyway, he said I'm useless in bed. Now, if anybody else said that to me I'd be up the wall! But we laughed at it, just as we laugh at everything else. And it must be true, because all he wants to do when he's with me is talk. One day I told him that instead of talking to him I could be making money, so he pulled out a five-dollar note and gave it to me. Just like that. Well, I felt so . . . so . . . well, embarrassed! I gave it back to him; and it was the first time I was ever vexed with him. He looked at me in a funny way. . . . Another time a German sailor came back

450

with me to my place. I wasn't living here, was I? No, it's true. I wasn't living here at the time. He had a stick with him. I mean he wasn't lame or anything. Anyway. . . ."

Esther talked on and Genetha felt that she was expected to take her into her confidence by disclosing some secret about her private life. But she was unable to make any confessions, restrained by that feeling of superiority that lingers even after a person ceases to occupy the position that, in the beginning, gave rise to it.

She looked up at Esther, who smiled; and for a moment that warmth and repose she once knew so well while still a little girl appeared in the older woman's eyes.

That night Esther and Genetha went to meet Daley in front of a club in Water Street. He was waiting with another man, whom he introduced as Cecil. Daley suggested that they should walk to the restaurant, as it was such a warm night.

At first an embarrassed silence fell on the company, but Daley then launched into an exaggerated account of his friend's prowess on the saxophone, which he played in a local band. His gestures and manner of talking soon had the two women laughing.

Cecil was just as retiring as Genetha, who found herself walking next to him. Daley had promised his friend that she would be beautiful. Her sunken cheeks revealed the unprepossessing bone-structure of her face; and the lack-lustre eyes gazed wanly beyond the company as if she were looking for someone.

Indeed, a marked change had overtaken Genetha's features. Like many people whose attractiveness appears to depend in no small degree upon how gaunt or well-covered their faces are, she had progressively lost her good looks as she grew thinner.

The eating house into which they went stood opposite the one where Rohan and Fingers had taken their first meal together. The proprietor brought the pepperpot in a deep bowl, which he placed on the table. He then went back to the kitchen and returned with four enamel plates, spoons and a bottle of cheap rum. Daley poured an excessive amount of pepper sauce on his food, partly to impress the company. Everyone agreed that the food was excellent.

Genetha declined the rum Daley had poured for her; but,

451

pressed by the others, she took a sip and made such a painful face that they laughed.

The sound of conversation, the reek of curry, the muted jazz from the radio and the dim lights created an atmosphere at once intimate and public. People kept coming through the open door and leaving, without attracting any attention, and occasionally a light breeze blew in a piece of paper from the pavement.

The meal and the surroundings had the effect of a heady wine on Genetha, who immersed herself in it like a swimmer in a warm sea. Even those who were sitting alone seemed to belong there, to be part of the fabric of the life of the district. Some came to be alone, others came to meet an acquaintance, while others came simply to be surrounded by people.

Esther watched Genetha obliquely. She noticed that the younger woman was sweating and kept wiping the palms of her hands. As a girl she often came to have her small hands wiped and Esther, jealous of the child's awareness of her needs, felt slighted if she went to her mother instead. She resisted the impulse to offer her a handkerchief.

During the meal Genetha felt Cecil's leg against her own, but the sense of well-being induced by the meal prevented her from doing anything. If she took her leg away she might offend him.

Towards the end of the meal a beggar came in from outside and started making the round of the tables. When the proprietor caught sight of him he shouted, "Get out!" waving a cloth after the beggar, who fled with little dignity. But a few minutes later, the proprietor having gone into the back-shop, the beggar reappeared to complete his round. On arriving at Genetha's table, instead of putting his cap out he stood staring at her, and as she looked up at him his eyes widened.

Esther delved into her purse for a coin.

"I know you. . . . You in't shame?" he said to Genetha, his face twisted into a grimace.

He looked at Esther and at the two men in turn and crossed himself slowly, almost theatrically. Then he turned round and left without accepting Esther's money, which she was holding in her outstretched hand.

A gloom seemed to fall on the table and Esther, impatient at the silence, testily put out a half-smoked cigarette.

"I hate beggars," she said.

Daley was annoyed with the beggar for having spoiled their

meal, while Cecil, uncomfortable because he was unable to contribute much to the table conversation, felt even more ill at ease, now that everyone else at the table was.

Genetha racked her brains to remember who the stranger was. There was something familiar in his appearance, though the appalling condition of his clothes seemed to exclude all possibility of a previous acquaintance.

"Do you know him?" Cecil asked.

"Mind your own business!" Esther snapped with unusual vehemence, and both Genetha and Daley turned to look at her.

"Come on, let's go," Daley suggested.

The company got up and Daley went to the counter to pay the bill.

Outside, grey clouds had massed over the sky. The air was close and humid and the hoardings on an adjoining building site were damp.

"Rain going fall," Daley said as he joined them outside and stopped to look up at the sky.

"Le' we take a taxi," Cecil said, in an effort to placate Esther. "I going to pay."

They waited on the pavement until a taxi came into sight.

On the way to Esther's place it began to rain heavily and all along the way people were sheltering under the awnings and the overhanging sections of shop fronts. Cars flashed by without dipping their headlights, while the four stared outside at the driving rain, preoccupied with their own thoughts.

Daley and Esther began a whispered conversation in the back of the car.

Then Esther announced, "I'm going dancing with Daley. You coming?"

"No," Genetha answered.

Esther guessed that Genetha did not dance well. "You can take her home, Cecil," she urged.

"Sure," Cecil said hesitantly.

Shortly afterwards it stopped raining, though the clouds remained thick and dark. Esther leaned forward and spoke to the chauffeur. A few minutes later the car stopped somewhere in Water Street and Esther and Daley both got out by the door on the left.

"I'll see you later, Gen," Esther said.

It was the first time she had addressed her by her fond name

453

since they had begun living together.

Cecil got out of the front seat and joined Genetha in the back.

"All the bounce gone out of Daley," he said, trying to stifle his excitement.

Genetha smiled.

"I've just been thinking," she said, "I've not been to church for weeks."

"Me neither; but I should."

"Aren't you ever afraid of the consequences?" Genetha asked earnestly.

"How d'you mean?"

"I mean what would happen to you if you didn't go?" Genetha retorted, curious as to why he had not understood her.

"Could anything happen?"

Genetha turned and watched him in the darkness. Suddenly she felt a tugging sensation in her belly. Just as she closed her eyes the car stopped in front of Esther's room.

Cecil got out and paid the driver, then went round to open the door for Genetha, who hesitated a moment before stepping from the car, which drove off, leaving the couple standing in front of the range yard.

"Good night," she said, giving Cecil her hand.

"I goin' see you in," he declared. "You never know; booboo man might get you."

He laughed and followed her, then when they were inside, said, "I don' want to give you the wrong idea, so I goin' go."

"You can stay if you want," Genetha said.

Cecil, taking her offer as an invitation to intimacy, was emboldened to take hold of her arm; but Genetha shook herself free. Cecil grabbed her and tried to kiss her forcibly, but she insisted, "No!" and freed herself once more.

"I thought . . ." he began.

"I'm sorry. I can't give myself to somebody I don't love."

"You make me look like a fool, then. I mean you ask me to stay."

She did not answer right away.

"Tch! I don't know what I want. Couldn't you just keep me company?" she asked.

"You must take me for a damn fool or something," Cecil said.

The long months of abstinence had stored in her a fiery hunger for a man's embrace, but when it came to it there was no desire to give in to this man.

"I gone," Cecil said finally, taking a step towards the door, but hoping that Genetha would change her mind.

"You're not coming back?"

"No. Unless. . . ."

"Can't you wait?" she asked. "I hardly even know you, and. . . ."

"I gone," he said, and left, closing the door behind him.

Genetha could not bear to be left alone. She put on an extra blouse and went out into the chilly night.

She found herself walking in the direction of the sea wall, past the dingy shop-fronts of Upper Water Street. Her life was in a haze, she reflected. Before, there were landmarks by which her thoughts could pause: mother, father, a steady job, Boyie, even Fingers, who had treated her like dirt. Esther was only a shadow from the past, matching in no way the memories she had of her while still a small girl. The uncertainty of the future gnawed at her inside. If her mother had been alive she might have pulled the "strings" she and her father always talked about as being indispensable in securing a job. Alone, and dogged by her confinement at the mental hospital, she felt helpless and frightened. The area she now lived in was as alien as the people she was now forced to associate with. Late at night and in the early hours of the morning there was often shouting and hammering on doors, and sometimes there was fighting among customers of the rum shops, who left at closing time, besotted with rum. It was the quarter of the damned, silent in the day-time and rowdy late at night.

Genetha approached the sea wall, which was deserted although it was no later than ten o'clock. She sat down on the wall and watched the flamboyant trees that rose from the edge of the road. The lights of Georgetown were hard and cold and the houses roused in her a fierce jealousy of those who lived in them. Couples were entertaining in their drawing-rooms or looking out of the window, and in the morning husbands would go off to work while their wives would send their children off to school and laze around or go back to bed, relying on servants to cook and do the housework. The shutters and painted wood of the palings embracing the yards spoke of security and ease.

Boyie must be living like that in the Essequibo. Why should she not write him and tell him everything? The thought came to her that he must have heard about her being put away. In a small area like the Guyana coastlands no one went to New Amsterdam without the news being bruited about even in the remote Essequibo. Boyie was unable to forgive her for her friendship with Fingers, to the point of pretending not to know of her confinement in the mental asylum. She must write and ask him if he knew. No! If he had cut her off she would not be the first to ask him to forgive her. What was Boyie's attitude to her in truth? But why was she afraid to write him or go to him? After all, he was the only person she had in the world, so that once and for all she wanted to know where she stood with him. Had she disapproved of one of his associations it would never have come to this. Her parents had always expected her to observe a higher standard of behaviour than he, to be careful about what she did and said, about the way she sat and the way she walked.

All this thinking gave her a headache. Sometimes she wanted to make love all night and perform all the depraved acts that had so often beset her erotic fantasies.

"You alone, lady?"

She looked up into the face of a young, handsome youth. Deliberately she stood up and walked away without answering.

When she arrived back at Esther's place the latter was in. Sitting on the bed in her slip she was putting varnish on her toenails.

"Thought you were with Cecil," Esther said to her.

"No, I went out alone."

"Where?"

"On the sea wall."

"Alone?"

"Why not?"

"Anything happened?"

"What?" asked Genetha, irritated at the suggestion that she might have picked up someone.

"Don't bother. There's bread on the dresser and some peas in the pot. Eat as much as you like, because I'm not hungry."

"Where're you going?" Genetha asked.

"To work."

"Can I come?"

Esther looked up at her. "No, you're not better yet. There're some American magazines on the bed."

When Esther left, Genetha lay on the bed, an open magazine by her side. Music could be heard coming from another street, the potent music of Tiger Bay where sailors, prostitutes and drifters make a festive season of every Saturday night.

Genetha lay on her bed, her hands serving as a pillow. She called to mind the asylum and the new doctor who took up his post the week after she arrived. He asked to see all the patients and soon afterwards there was a rumour that he considered many of them were perfectly sane and ought to go home. Indeed, some began leaving at the end of the month, while others, encouraged to believe that they would be sent home, waited in vain for the word.

She remembered the day she left vividly. On the ferry from New Amsterdam to Rossignol a man was performing magic. She recalled his good-naturedness and the wonder of his audience; she had felt so lonely in the midst of it all that she went aft to be on her own.

The journey from Rossignol to Georgetown she had made by bus. It was the first time she had seen the coast at close quarters, so to speak, and the swampy land and the lonely houses appealed to her. If she could raise the money she would buy a house in one of those villages: Mahaicony, perhaps, or Union or Anandale. Places with such names must be harbours, with stellings for the tired souls. Anandale, Anandale, Anannnnn-dale. On the steps of one house, which was leaning heavily to one side, about a dozen persons were sitting, ranging in age from about two or three to about seventy; and the harmony of the group had had such a profound effect on her that she looked back and watched the house until it went out of sight behind a clump of trees.

Two women, bent double in a large field, were collecting cow dung in baskets, while a herd of cows grazed placidly on the sparse grass. Then came the coconut plantation, an endless succession of palms along the border of which ran a trench overgrown with weeds and water hyacinth. Occasionally the road came close to the sea defence wall, so that the expanse of mud and sand could be seen, broken here and there by shimmering puddles or long stretches of courida bushes. Every now and then a koker rose from the flat, featureless landscape, its sluice gate raised to let out the drainage water. This was her country, this sprawling, sea-beleaguered land; the roar of the sea by night, the heat of the sun by day would follow her wherever she went, as would the trenches, the wild eddoes, the dark folk and the tamarind.

For the rest of the journey everything seemed unclear. It was only at La Bonne Intention that she was awakened from her half-dream, for there had been an accident on the Public Road. Two men were trying to right an overturned car, but Genetha looked away and stared in the direction of the sea wall. She wished that the driver of the bus, who had stopped to give the two men a hand, would get back in and drive them home. Were there not enough people to help? And was the business of the people in the bus not as urgent?

"Anandale," she thought. "I love night and the silence of night time, and the cocks flapping their wings long before dawn . . . . One day I'll go to Anandale and build a house. I'll find someone who would teach me to dance and treat me like a woman."

13. Veil and Gloves

Genetha felt that she was on the threshold of a new life that would overwhelm her. Too weak to struggle she saw the only possibility of escape in a confession of her plight to her maternal aunts, who would without doubt invite her to move in and share their house at Irving and Laluni Streets. But the thought of disclosing her association with Fingers, in order to explain how she lost possession of her house, and the certainty of humiliation at their hands, was intolerable.

She decided to go and see them at least once before it was too late; so one Saturday afternoon when Esther had gone out on her business – "picking fair" as she bluntly described it – Genetha put on her best frock, took care to use as little make-up as possible and walked all the way to Queenstown.

Her elder aunt, Deborah, on catching sight of her, promptly gave her a piece of her mind.

"You're anaemic. Go and see Doctor Bailey. Every Tom, Dick and Harry can eat well nowadays and you have to be anaemic. Aren't you ashamed? What're you doing? Saving money?"

Genetha had to endure a lecture on the dangers of anaemia and constipation, conditions that should never be tolerated in a decent family.

"Do you know that your grandmother went to St Rose's school? In those days you had to be somebody to go there, I can tell you. Money alone couldn't get you in. Your parents had to be somebody. She had to wear ribbed black stockings to school and gloves and a panamá hat with a veil to hide her face from men's eyes. And every week she and the other girls had to submit their boxes – with veil and gloves – for inspection by the nuns. And look at her," she declared, nodding towards the back of the house where her parents were, "she'll outlive us all. Discipline doesn't kill. When discipline goes everything else goes. . . . You'd better sit further back in the gallery, so that Mama doesn't see you in this condition when she comes out."

Genetha listened without interrupting, near the window where her mother used to sit for hours as a girl, watching the drifting clouds.

"You favour your mother so!" her younger aunt, Alice, once said, and was at once chided by her elder sister for using the word "favour" instead of "resemble", as the common people did.

No, Genetha thought, she could never come back to this house after she set off on the same road as Esther had been travelling.

They were joined by their father, Genetha's grandfather.

"Genetha! How well you look!" exclaimed the old man.

She got up and embraced him before he sat down to take part in the conversation.

"You must come more often," he said. "Things're changing so fast! You know the picture-house opposite has got a new name; and they've begun showing Indian films. East Indians used to have to go to the country to see films in Hindi. And now, just on the edge of Queenstown, you see them thronging to see a film in a language they no longer speak. Change, change, nothing but change. The other day I saw a funeral procession passing and there wasn't a carriage in sight! Even the hearse was motorized. What're things coming to when you're driven to your long home by an internal combustion engine? But some things remain the same," he added with a sigh, at the same time glancing meaningfully at his two unmarried daughters.

The older aunt, out of respect for her father, did not venture an observation, although she had strong opinions on the subject.

The old man sighed, tried to cross his legs, but failed, then

459

sighed again.

"Since I was fifty I began preparing for death," he declared. "But here I am, dragging along, witnessing all these changes round me." He sighed again and went off in a reverie. Then, without warning, without taking leave of Genetha, he got up and left the women, seemingly irritated.

"His chocolate," Deborah, whispered urgently, whereupon the younger aunt got up to prepare her father's afternoon drink.

"Have you heard from Boyie? Is he yet married?" came the inevitable question.

"He hasn't written yet, Aunt, but I don't think so. He would have written if he had – or so I imagine."

"And your job? How's your job? Are you climbing ladders?" Deborah pursued.

Genetha stammered, unable to find a ready answer. "No ladders, Aunt. I'm managing."

"No disgrace in working, especially in your circumstances. I myself started giving piano lessons. Your grandfather's pension doesn't go up, although the cost of living does . . . . But my heart's not in it. If you do intend to work you must start young."

"Nowadays most women work, Aunt," Genetha declared, as tactfully as she could.

The younger aunt came back and joined them and Genetha got the impression that she would have made some remark had she not been there.

Deborah went inside for a while, leaving her alone with Alice who, no sooner was her sister out of sight, put her hand on Genetha's arm without a word. And Genetha, touched by the gesture, had difficulty in restraining herself from confessing everything she sought to keep from them at all costs. She started groping in her handbag for a handkerchief, only to look up and see her older aunt standing before her.

"Now what's this?" Deborah asked severely. "Tears? From a working girl?"

"I'm so tired, Aunt," Genetha said.

"Go and lie down then."

"No, I have to leave now. I just dropped in for a minute," Genetha said decisively.

"As you please, child," Deborah retorted, with a slight gesture of the hand.

"Stay, Genetha, like a good girl," urged her aunt Alice.

460

Genetha stayed, and saw evening fall. She clung to the silence in the house and the repose of her two aunts, who were content to do nothing but sit and exchange at intervals brief remarks that might just as well have been left unsaid, but which in the gathering dusk seemed apt, like the bands of embroidery adorning their window blinds.

The potted cochineal cactus on the Demerara window ledge melted into the shadows made by the fading light, until Alice, the younger aunt, put on the gallery bulb which brought it to life again.

"He was only fifty-one," said the younger aunt.

"Heavens," came her sister's retort, "in the 'thirties many people died in their forties and fifties. People're spoiled now. Everybody wants to live on into their seventies."

Silence fell again, broken only by the noise of a moth vainly charging against a window pane.

They were in their late fifties, Genetha's two aunts, and dressed in the fashion of the early 1930s, as if time had been suspended and the clothes other women wore were the result of some collective aberration. Deborah was dressed in a bodice that gripped her neck in a vice, while Alice wore a pleated skirt of great length.

"Do you know," said the older aunt, "that there used to be a pomegranate tree in the garden before you were born?"

"And red flowers no one could identify," added Aunt Alice eagerly.

"They were blue," Deborah corrected.

"No, I'm sure they were red."

"Then there were blue ones and red ones. In the end a very knowledgeable young man came to visit your grandfather. He identified them."

"Did he?" asked the younger aunt incredulously.

Their exchange was followed by an even longer silence. In the hours she had visited, in the weeks of her stay in this house, Genetha had never once heard a quarrel. There had been a pact to banish dissent and confusion; and any threat to harmony was quashed before it could grow. Genetha recalled the violent scenes in her parents' home, all caused by her father, as she remembered. How her mother must have suffered!

Yet, she reflected, there must have been some purpose in this turbulence, for in the end the thought of living the sterile life of

461

her aunts revolted her. Thinking of the way Fingers had revealed her own body to her always sent a warm sensation coursing through her. She recalled the slow hardening of her breasts under his palms, the heat generated by his embrace. When she became a practised lover he needed only to leave his manliness at the door of her body and her vulva engulfed it in a series of rapid contractions, so that Fingers never stopped wondering at her prowess.

"You don't know where we can find a carpenter, do you, Genetha?" asked Alice, breaking in on her reflections of a sudden.

"We can't get hold of one for love or money," added Deborah.

Genetha knew no one she could recommend and in any case the thought of a carpenter brought back distressing memories about the home of which she was robbed.

"Do you, Genetha?" asked her aunt Alice once more.

"No, Aunt, I don't."

"Never mind," she reassured her.

One of the new big buses passed by, its yellow erased by the gloom. Above New Town the first stars sprinkled the sky to the rim of the horizon.

Genetha now knew that if her older aunt had been like the younger she would have confessed that she had no decent place to live in and could not, at least for the moment, find a job; that a haven for a few months would be sufficient for her to find her feet again. But she was never certain where she was with Aunt Deborah; whether she was pleased or displeased, whether she looked down on her on account of her father, or accepted her wholeheartedly because she was the daughter of her mother. Genetha could never cut through the undergrowth of dissembling that surrounded the things this aunt said and the things she did. She now knew that it was her younger aunt who brought her back to the house with her few words and youthful smiles.

Genetha was suddenly overwhelmed with grief, as though someone close to her had died. And this readiness to weep took hold of her and fought with her until she could bear it no longer.

"I don't know," she apologized. "It's so foolish. There's no reason for it. It's so these last few days. I must be anaemic, as you say, Aunt."

She wiped her eyes, now more put out by the scrutiny of her

aunts than by her pain. From the look in their eyes they must be imagining the worst.

"You're not . . . expecting?" Deborah enquired, with panic in her eye.

"Certainly not, Aunt," Genetha said, thinking that that would be infinitely preferable.

And her aunts' eyes were unashamedly examining Genetha's belly for evidence of the disaster.

"There's no retching?" Aunt Deborah pursued, evidently unconvinced by Genetha's denial.

"Aunt, I'm not pregnant! In any case it's not possible," Genetha protested, looking her senior aunt straight in the eye.

Deborah raised her head in a non-committal gesture, but said nothing, while her sister, pained by the turn the conversation had taken, was looking at her niece sympathetically.

Genetha got up and went inside to say goodbye to her grandparents.

That night she struggled with sleep as if her life depended on it; for it seemed that the last chance of maintaining her status as a decent person lay in keeping awake. But in the end she fell asleep and dreamed of raindrops scattered in the dust, of dripping candles and soiled hands. And she stared in the candle flame as if it were impossible to look away, as if in it lay all the memories of childhood and the antidote to the condition that kept draining her will. Then she relived the night when she went out with Esther and her two friends and met the beggar with his peremptory manner and wagging finger. The paper that blew in from the pavement alighted on her table, a paper smeared with filth which the others did not seem to mind. She turned away to avoid looking at it, but Genetha's companion picked up the paper and deliberately thrust it in her face, to the amusement of everyone in the restaurant. Then her younger aunt, Alice, appeared and led her out of the eating place, away from her companions.

Occasionally Genetha awoke, but kept still so as not to embarrass Esther's clients who came and went like shadows, leaving Esther to tidy herself up and prepare for the next.

II

14. Reflection from a Hand-Mirror

Genetha lay on the floor, drunk and half-naked. The customer outside was clamouring for a Portuguese girl.

"I want a Putagee, I tell you. I gwine pay too! I gwine pay. Me pockets full of money. I got money an' money does talk, although it only whisperin' now. . . . Is who does run this place at all? Come on, I ask is who does run this place?"

Esther came out, dressed in a silk dressing-gown.

"Why're you keeping all this noise? You don't have what you want?" she asked the drunk.

"I want a Potagee an' dat in't no Potagee there," he said, pointing to Genetha on the floor.

Esther closed the door and shouted out, "Vera!"

The girl appeared almost immediately at the top of the stairs.

"Where's Irene?"

"She's got someone with her."

"You hear that?" Esther said to the drunk. "You can wait or come back another time. But whatever you do, don't come in here keeping that noise, you understand? Or we'll have to bar you from the house."

"Hey, hey, who . . .?" the drunk began.

"Bigfoot!" Esther shouted.

A few moments later a strapping man in his middle twenties came out of the room opposite the one in which Genetha was.

"Well, you don't got to get rough wit' me," the client protested. "I know me place wit' a customer like dat," he continued, nodding in Bigfoot's direction, "I can tell you."

He measured the giant from head to foot, showing his teeth in a wide grin as he did so.

"Allow me to feel them spectacular muscles, mister."

He put both hands around Bigfoot's biceps, then went towards the street door. Without warning, he shouted, "Kiss me ass!", turned tail and ran down the stairs, leaving Bigfoot and Esther staring at the door.

"Genetha's drunk again," Esther said to Bigfoot, "Since her brother died I can't get any work from her."

"But that's four months ago. You goin' keep she?" Bigfoot asked.

"Course; but I can't allow her to work. Go and take her to my room."

Bigfoot went to Genetha's room and emerged soon afterwards with her over his shoulder. He took her bodily up the stairs to Esther's room, where he placed her flat on the bed. It was a job he enjoyed doing. He had conceived an extraordinary respect for her and might even have fallen in love with her if he were not convinced that she was above his station in life. The fact that she was a prostitute now seemed to make little difference to him.

Bigfoot was undemonstrative, but Genetha sensed his interest and treated him with deference.

There were five girls in the establishment. Besides Vera and Irene there were Salome, Shola and Netta, the last two being new arrivals from the country. Both Shola, who came from a village on the East Bank, Berbice, and Netta, who was from Wismar, were much sought after by the clients for their fresh, innocent appearance.

From the very beginning Esther was firm with the girls and they respected her for it. Should one of them infringe the rules of the house she was to be warned once, while the second occasion meant the door. But the condition of service that attracted the girls was the one which provided them with a bonus of two hundred dollars if they decided to leave Esther's employment, provided they had worked with her for at least two years. She was the first to admit that at the end of two years she would have made a good deal of money out of them. The condition guaranteed the girls' loyalty and clients liked to know that if they went away and came back again they were likely to find the same girls working for her. Esther gave them seventy-five cents for every client they entertained, keeping four dollars and twenty-five cents for herself. She made a handsome profit on each girl after paying rent for the house, feeding them, putting aside a cut for the police and defraying other expenses. She herself did the cooking and ran up dresses for the girls on her Pfaff foot-machine.

In fact, only half of the profit belonged to Esther, for she had been set up in business by a man who lived abroad and had established a number of such houses in other parts of the world. This one had been going for two years. Esther had bought the house in her name, as a nominee of the stranger, who had been impressed by her the night they met at a party in Tiger Bay. When he found out that she had seventeen hundred dollars of her own he did not hesitate to put the proposition to her. She saw it as a chance of a lifetime and set to work to make the concern a profitable one.

She was now worried by Genetha's inability to work, for any reduction in the profits would make a bad impression on her employer. Boyie's death had come at the worst possible moment, when Genetha was at last finding her feet in the profession. After a bad beginning, when her unco-operative attitude had led to violent quarrels between them, Genetha gradually became accustomed to the company Esther was keeping. But it was Esther's disinclination to threaten her that finally brought Genetha round. However badly they quarrelled Esther fed her as before and gave her money.

At first Genetha chose one young man to sleep with, and thereby prompted Esther's taunts about making a fortune with one client. When, eventually, she tried a second, she complained that it was physically impossible for her to satisfy two men on the same day.

"Then thousands of women throughout the world are performing the physically impossible every day, eh?" Esther rejoined.

Esther taught her how to manipulate the men and showed her the tricks of the profession and, in time, she was able to work as the other women did.

Just before Rohan's death Esther had come home to hear her singing a song to the accompaniment of music from the radio. The next day, the news of his death was published in the newspapers and since then she spent most of the day listening to the radio and drinking cheap wine. Esther had left her alone, in the hope that she would snap out of her condition and begin working again.

"You know you costing me over twenty-five dollars a day," Esther told her.

"You're lying," Genetha retorted. "You're lying, Esther. There you go, lying again."

"I'm not lying, you little idiot. If it wasn't for me you'd really be on the road, picking up men at the corner for fifty cents."

"Leave me alone. You've changed. You're coarse and you think of nothing but money all the time."

"I was always coarse —" said Esther.

"When we were in Agricola you weren't coarse," Genetha interrupted her.

"I was coarse in Agricola when your mother wasn't looking, I can tell you. And your father was coarse when your mother wasn't looking, too. And I bet your mother was coarse when no one was looking. Huh!"

"You see how coarse you are, Esther. I've just been telling you so and you go and prove it to me."

Esther stalked off in a rage, leaving Genetha with her wine and her radio.

She decided to take on another girl and give Genetha a couple of weeks to leave. When, however, two days later, an applicant presented herself, Esther found all sorts of objections to hiring the girl. She was sickly; she lacked experience; she looked like the type who would attract trouble from clients. Bigfoot thought that the girl was attractive and men would like her, but Esther told him to mind his own business. In fact, he had no idea that the girl was to replace Genetha.

Esther sent her away and at the same time gave orders that Genetha was to have no food or drink. At midday, when everyone sat down at the big table to eat, no one called Genetha, who was sleeping. In the middle of the meal she appeared at the door of the dining-room and there was a sudden hush as the others became aware of her presence. Esther, who hesitated momentarily, continued eating, pretending not to notice Genetha, until finally, unable to contain her anger any longer, she exploded.

"What's happened at all? You all gone dumb?" Then, turning towards Genetha she asked: "Who the hell invited you anyway?"

Genetha turned away and went back to her room.

The girls, resentful of Genetha's independence, were glad that Esther was standing no more nonsense from her, though their silence was interpreted by Esther as support for Genetha.

After a while the company began talking and laughing again and Esther made a show of enjoying herself, determined not to give in on this occasion. Rohan's death had shaken her as well, but the last years had drained her of all sentimentality. Life had to go on. Genetha could have begun to work, if only out of gratitude.

That evening Genetha went to Esther and asked her if she

was to have anything to eat.

"If you work, yes. If you don't work you can go to hell," came Esther's reply.

There were deep, indelible rings around Genetha's eyes, and the furrows in her face appeared more pronounced than ever.

"I'm not begging, you know," said Genetha, "I'm just asking."

"I don't care what you're doing. You're not eating unless you work."

"Can I have a bottle of wine?"

"No."

"I won't beg you. I won't lower myself to beg you!" exclaimed Genetha.

Esther looked up from the table in the drawing-room, pretending to be amused. Genetha went to the chair by the window, which overlooked South Road and Croal Street, divided by a wide trench. As it was getting dark Esther turned on the light and then went back to sit at her table.

"Money is everything to you, isn't it?" Genetha suddenly asked Esther.

"You'll soon find out if it's not everything," declared Esther, maintaining her show of indifference.

"No, but it's everything to you, isn't it?"

"Yes, you —" replied Esther losing her composure. "And if your sweet man didn't rob you, would you be waiting now for me to put bread in your mouth?"

"You're right, you know. Money is everything," said Genetha.

"You needn't be sarcastic. It's your parents that taught me that first. I worked my fingers to the bone for your mother and she kicked me out. Then I realized how important money was. More important than loyalty and trust and such . . . . When people like your mother talk about loyalty and trust they meant my loyalty and my trust, not theirs. It's she, when all is said and done, who taught me to sell my body for sixpence on the race course. You remember how people used to say what a good Christian woman your mother was and how your father didn't deserve her? And she did give you the same education she got herself, that makes you hate housework. I mean, did you learn from anybody how to satisfy a man in bed? You just lie down like a piece of wood . . . ."

"You know," said Genetha, "when you talk like that it goes

468

through one ear and comes out of the other. I've heard it so often before."

Esther went inside and came back with a hand mirror, which she held under Genetha's nose.

"I don't want to look," declared Genetha, turning away abruptly, "I don't care. In any case I'm too ugly to be vain."

These last words touched Esther, who put the mirror down on the table.

"You're going to work?" she asked Genetha.

"No!" she exclaimed with violence. "I'm going to join the Catholic Church so that I can confess to someone. These Methodists don't do anything except sing and pray. I don't like singing anymore. Things die, just like people."

Esther took up her newspaper and continued to read, for she had already relented, but did not want to appear soft in the younger woman's eyes.

"You know," she said, without looking up from her paper, "if you worked we could have good times together."

There was no answer for a while and then, as if giving expression to an afterthought, Genetha declared:

"I notice that you don't work since you got this place."

How exasperating she could be, this blasted woman, Esther thought. When she recalled the years of hard work, the foul men she had to put up with, the back streets and alleyways she frequented, the encounters with the police, the constant fear of disease or being assaulted by a client. The ignorant fool!

"No, I'm the boss now, you see," Esther answered in a measured voice.

From one of the rooms came the voice of a man singing the tune "Trees" with improvised words:

"And when I'm feeling very dry
I point my cock up to the skyyyyyyyyy;
And if it then begins to rain
I put it ba-a-ack againnnnnnnnnnnn,
Poeeeeeems are maaaade by fools like me,
But only Gooooood can make a tree."

When he emerged, followed by Netta, Esther could not conceal her irritation. She had secretly hankered after an establishment of a higher tone and was disappointed that the clientele was similar to the one she had while she was still practising. The well-maintained exterior of the house, the painted jalousies and

469

chintz blinds had failed to attract the select types who would pay more, speak quietly and occasionally come to play dominoes or bridge in the back room. The refuge away from their wives turned out to be a convenient drop-in, like a dog's favourite tree.

"You sing loud like that and the police'll close the place, you understand! Just keep your voice down in future," she said peremptorily.

When he reached the foot of the stairs Netta burst out:

"He smell o' fish! Next time tell him I out."

She then handed over her money and Esther opened a canister with a key she kept round her neck. Having placed the notes inside and locked it she put the canister back into the desk drawer.

A few minutes later Shola saw off her client, a well-groomed middle-aged man, who kept his lips pursed so as to conceal his embarrassment. She, too, handed over her money to Esther, who secreted it in the canister as before, leaving the change on the table.

Bigfoot, who had been sitting on the veranda, came in and whispered something in Esther's ear. She got up and disappeared with him through the front door.

"You in' working today, Genetha?" Shola asked, taking advantage of Esther's absence to pick a row.

"No."

"Why? You too great?"

"Yes," replied Genetha.

Shola said something to Netta and the two girls burst out laughing.

Genetha got up and went over to Shola, asking her: "You've got any wine?"

Shola placed her right hand on her chest and said:

"I don' drink, I don' smoke an' I don' talk to strange men."

Shola and Netta exploded in fits of laughter, at the same time hugging each other for support.

"You in' a lil old for this work?" Netta ventured. She herself was only seventeen.

Genetha went back to her seat.

"You're young, with soft skin and dimples," said Genetha, "but it'll all go, and then you'll find yourself alone, just when you need someone more than ever."

"Is what she talking 'bout?" Shola asked, turning to Netta,

who shrugged her shoulders.

"I had my first experience with a man . . ." Genetha began.

"That must a been twenty years ago," Netta interrupted her, in an attempt to make Shola laugh.

But Esther came back into the room and all laughter was stifled.

"Go and warm something up for her," she ordered, nodding towards Netta.

"She goin' eat?" the girl asked naively.

"Yes, 'she goin' eat'," Esther mimicked her.

Netta went inside, wearing a surly expression.

"You'd better come over," Esther beckoned to Genetha, who got up, went over to the table and sat down opposite Esther.

"Bring the Correia wine," Esther ordered Shola, who went off unwillingly and came back a few moments later with the bottle of cheap wine. The girl was still in her slip and her full breasts danced about, threatening to burst out of their confinement with every step she made.

"The trial's beginning tomorrow," Esther told Genetha.

"Which trial?"

"The Ali chap . . . about Boyie's death."

"Oh."

Genetha took a mouthful of the wine Esther had poured out for her and when Netta brought in the food she fell on it like a dog fed only on rice for months.

Vera came downstairs and looked in disapprovingly. She was dressed to kill. Pulling up her dress slightly she sat down at the head of the table.

"Look who coming! Is Teeth!" Vera warned the girls, as she saw Teeth's head bobbing up through the window.

Teeth, a man in his thirties with an array of gold teeth, was the establishment's most mysterious client. He was always impeccably dressed, had excellent manners, but managed to give the impression of the utmost severity behind the façade of concern and attentiveness. The girls were afraid of him and complained that he was brutal in bed, so that there arose a tacit agreement that they should take it in turns to entertain him.

"Is Irene turn," Shola whispered.

"Get her quick," Netta urged, nodding in the direction of the stairs.

Shola came back with Irene, who welcomed Teeth with a

471

broad smile and shepherded him upstairs to her room.

"At least he don' beat about the bush like some of the rest," Netta said.

Indeed, less than fifteen minutes later, Teeth reappeared at the top of the stairs with that superior manner which might have misled strangers into thinking that he owned the place. As he left he bowed slightly and went out through the front door.

"You got the itch or what?" Esther asked Vera, who sat fidgeting at the head of the table. "Why don't you go for a walk and get it over with?"

Vera had been going to the window at frequent intervals as if she were expecting somebody. At Esther's suggestion she sprang up and went out through the front door. She was going "to take a little air", she said.

And so the girls spent the days and nights, unable to leave the house except with Esther's express permission. The money that came into their hands was just enough to keep them in clothes, make-up and cigarettes.

In proportion as the money came and a regular clientele was built up, so Esther became stricter. She came to discover a severity in herself that was never apparent before. The girls grew to fear her and began whispering among themselves that she needed a man. Salome had already made up her mind to leave with her two hundred dollars when her two years were up.

One morning at about two o'clock the girls were awakened by screaming and the sound of breaking glass. From the top of the staircase they saw Bigfoot belabouring Shola with a strap while Esther stood looking on a few paces away. At a signal from her Bigfoot stopped and Shola was ordered to her room.

The next day Bigfoot told the girls that Shola was caught trying to open Esther's canister, in which the girls' earnings were kept. Then a pall fell on the house. But within a few days the girls had recovered their gaiety and the incident was forgotten. They needed only to be careful, to abide by the rules and to keep in Bigfoot's good books, and all would be well.

In time, too, the girls accepted Genetha's special status as hanger-on. Indeed, she did work from time to time, when the spirit moved her. And despite the state of continual warfare that existed between her and Esther they recognized the peculiar relationship that seemed to bind them together.

472

15. Sunday in the Red House

It was Sunday evening. Some of the girls were sitting at the windows and on the veranda. The street lamps had just gone on and the church bells of St Andrews were ringing to remind the faithful of evening service. From the house could be seen the shadowy figures of people hanging about the Law Courts. The men kept away on Sundays, either as a form of tribute to their conscience or because they were immobilized by the general apathy that infected everyone on the Lord's day. The empty street of day-time had given way to the empty street of night-time where, occasionally, a car rolled past, filled with young people who were bent, no doubt, on defying convention by enjoying themselves. The rum-shop at the corner, a source of loud music on weekdays, was curiously quiet.

The girls sat, enveloped in a complicity of silence, weaving their own thoughts. Shola was recalling the village she came from, while Netta reflected on her neglect of the Bible. Her mother would never forgive her if she knew what she was doing. In her letters home she wrote that she was getting on well with her typing and English.

Vera had caught sight of the young man whom she had once invited in when no one else was there. He was lurking in the shadows of a nearby house.

"He's too young," she thought, "I going have to brush him off."

Irene was not thinking anything, or rather she was incapable of dwelling on any one subject sufficiently long to be certain of what she had been thinking.

Esther was the only one in the house to remain in her room, lying on her bed, mentally revising the accounts she had made up that day. Salome was not well and would not be working for a few days. The doctor had repeatedly warned her against leading the "life", but Esther was leaving the decision to her, with the remark that she was old enough to make up her mind. Esther's partner, in his last letter, had written sarcastically about the profit the establishment was making, reminding her that none of the girls was indispensable. What would he say if he knew about Genetha? she thought.

"To hell with him," she said to herself, but could not dismiss the nagging anxieties. She was looking forward to his next visit

473

to the country and would have it out with him, though there was no doubt that Genetha would have to pull her weight.

One of the clients had offered Bigfoot a job with higher wages than she paid him. She was especially reluctant to let him go for he could turn his hand to nearly every type of repair.

There was a knock on the door.

"It's who?" she asked irritably.

"Me, Vera."

"Come in, ne?"

Vera came in. "I want to go out for ten minutes," she told Esther, avoiding her eyes.

"Where?"

"It's private."

Esther waved her consent and as the girl turned to go she looked at her suspiciously.

Vera went up to the youth who had been hoping she would come out. He seemed less good-looking than she remembered, and very thin.

"Is what you want?" she asked.

On seeing her coming down the stairs he had felt the excitement welling up in him and imagined that they would just walk off to another part of town where they would be able to be alone.

"You coming for a walk?" he asked her.

"No!" she replied.

"Why?"

"What you come hanging 'bout the house for?" she demanded. "You want to get me in trouble? You can't just come an' wait. . . ."

"How else I could see you again?"

"Who said I want to see you again?" she asked him, emphasizing the first word cruelly.

Her irritation puzzled the youth, who could not believe that she had dressed up to tell him that she did not want to see him again.

"Well, if you don' want to —" he began saying, only to be interrupted without ceremony.

"No, I don' want to." Thereupon she turned away brusquely and went back to the house.

"You got typee, girl," Shola teased, as Vera came through the door.

474

"If looks could kill," Netta said, noticing the way Vera looked at her friend.

Shola and Netta watched the youth disappearing up the road, in the direction of the Law Courts.

The service had begun in St Andrews and the congregation were singing "For those in peril on the sea". Two women in their Sunday best were hurrying down the road towards the church.

When a client pushed the gate open the girls cursed him inwardly and Shola withdrew from the window, while Netta got up and went inside.

"Esther!" Shola called out.

Esther came out to see the man, who was standing by the big table, arms akimbo. After a short conversation with him she pointed to Shola, who looked up to the roof in exasperation, but got up and went to her room, followed by the client.

Esther went out on the porch and asked Genetha to come inside. The two women sat down at the table.

"You got to work like the other girls, starting tonight if we get sufficient people, you understand?"

Genetha did not reply.

The next morning Genetha's grip stood by the front door. She sat with the others, eating her breakfast, and they looked at her furtively. Esther, conspicuously absent from the table, was sewing on her machine, and when there was a knock on the door she knew what it was for.

Esther went to say goodbye to Genetha, who was standing next to Bigfoot. He took up her grip and carried it to the waiting taxi.

"Is where she going?" asked Netta, to which Shola sucked her teeth and said, "Is why you always asking such stupidness? 'Is where she going'! "

"I wonder where she going to go?" Vera asked in turn, to spite Shola for the remark she made the previous evening after she had seen the youth.

"I in' know," replied Netta, "probably to family. I hear she got family."

They all watched the taxi drive off, and Bigfoot standing on the bridge long after the vehicle had left, his gaze fixed in the distance. The girls avoided him for the rest of that day.

Their attention turned to Genetha's replacement. Would she be tall, short, ugly? Anyone would be an improvement on Genetha, one of them observed, a remark with which they all agreed.

Shola wanted her room, and since no one else dared object the matter seemed to be settled. Apart from Esther, Genetha was the only one who had had a room to herself. Shola went at once to see Esther who had no hesitation in agreeing.

Not concealing her delight, Shola set about transferring her things at once. From now on she could furnish her quarters as she wanted, read as late as she liked, choose her own radio programmes without the eternal wrangling with Netta.

Netta kept looking at the door of Shola's new room, and seeing this Vera nudged Irene, who nodded and smiled. The others did not fail to notice Netta's interest either.

"You looking for something?" Salome asked.

"What?" Netta replied absentmindedly.

"You loss something?" the young woman repeated, with a vindictive smile on her lips.

"Oh, lef' me alone!" she burst out. "Mind you own kiss-me-ass business, you whore."

"Who you calling a whore?" Salome asked, jumping up from her seat.

"You!" declared Netta defiantly.

Salome sprang at her and the two women rolled on the ground, scratching and slapping each other. Salome, tall and strapping, had no difficulty in overcoming the younger women, while Netta, hands pinned to the ground, burst into tears and showed no more resistance.

"All right, all right," Salome said, consoling her opponent, "take a cigarette. She got her own room, but that don't mean she going stop being friends with you."

Salome got up, reached for her packet from the window ledge where she had left it, and gave a cigarette to Netta, who took it with an unsteady hand.

The new girl came two days later. She was from Wakenaam, but had been in Georgetown for two years. Her aunt, with whom she had been living, had just died and rather than go back home to Wakenaam she tried working as a waitress in a restaurant. But she was unable to earn enough money to keep herself, so she supplemented her income by going out with customers who bought her things. Esther persuaded her that she could earn more living in her establishment, and would not need to pay for food or lodging. If she did not like it she could always leave.

All the girls watched her from head to foot when she stood in the doorway, holding her ancient grip in her right hand.

"Madame dere?" she asked in her Essequibo lilt.

"Esther!" Shola shouted out, not bothering to greet the girl.

"Girl, you must've been born shouting," Esther said to Shola as she came from the kitchen.

The new girl's face beamed when she caught sight of Esther and she put her grip down on the floor.

"Netta, show her to upstairs, ne?" Then, to the girl she smiled and said, "You can then come out and get to know the girls."

"Is where she come from?" Vera remarked. "Look at them clothes!" She opened her eyes wide in feigned astonishment.

"You just jealous," Salome joked. "Wait till Esther fit she out, she going take all you men away. You hear what I telling you."

"Her name is Clem," Esther told the girls. "Try and be nice; she's from the country."

"You don't say!" Shola mocked. "And we din' even guess!"

Esther tried to get the girls on her side.

"You remind me of my father," she said. "He was always making fun of people. Once when somebody asked him why he painted his house with ordinary paint, but painted the latrine with whitewash he said, 'Well, the latrine's almost as big as the house and so that people would know which is which I paint the house and whitewash the latrine.' "

The girls laughed. She promised chocolates after lunch, but as soon as she went back to the kitchen they began running down the girl again.

Once in the kitchen Esther brooded over Genetha's going away and the emptiness which was bound to follow her absence. She detested Shola, not for her thieving habits, nor for the hold she had over the other girls, nor even for her impudence; she hated her because she had never shown Genetha the deference she deserved. Now that Genetha had finally gone she harboured a deep feeling of vengeance in regard to Shola and on that account decided that she would forbid the girls to call Genetha's name in the house.

477

16. Zara

Genetha once more hired a room in a hovel in Albouystown and immediately looked around for work as a waitress. Her speech made an impression and she was taken on in a dive near the Stabroek Market, but her wages were too low to live on, so she decided to get another job. She was paid a dollar a week more and had to work four hours a day longer. At nights she could only wash and go straight to bed where, exhausted, she fell asleep at once.

One Saturday night she went to the pictures and hardly fifteen minutes of film had gone when she dozed off and slept all through the show. She found a peculiar satisfaction in this lonely existence, for her soul was her own at least.

Another evening when she was passing the Brickdam Church she felt an urge to go in and sit in a pew, and on an impulse she took her place behind a line of women who were waiting to confess to the priest. It was not uncommon for people to change their religion. Indeed some belonged to two faiths, practising one in the day and the other at night.

When her turn came she sat in the cubicle and waited.

"I'm not a Catholic," Genetha began, and waited for the effect of her words.

"Why have you come then, my child?" the priest asked with exaggerated indulgence.

Genetha hesitated. She could not answer, in fact.

"Well, why did you come, my child?"

"I don't know . . . . I don't go to church any more. But I feel that something's gone out of my life."

"Do you then want to become a Catholic?" enquired the priest.

"I don't know, Father."

"Well, go on, my child," said the priest softly.

Genetha started to tell him of the life she had been leading and of her need for forgiveness.

"God is generous, my child. He bears no grudge. What God and the Church are interested in is the kind of life you're leading now. Do you think you have the courage to face your new existence and the character to resist the temptation to return to your old ways?"

"It was not temptation that led me into it, Father," she said, suddenly irritated. "I was sick."

"These are excuses, my child. Christ suffered on the cross to redeem our sins. You could not suffer a few weeks of hunger. Besides, you spoke of relations. Couldn't you have seen them and asked them to take you in?"

"It was pride, Father," Genetha declared, suppressing her mounting annoyance.

He uttered an exclamation and said harshly, but quietly, "There is no pride in the true Christian, my child. Look what your pride has done for you! You have sold your body and soiled your soul. Do you think that your pride was worth it?"

Genetha bowed her head.

"What will you do now?" pursued the priest.

"I'm working, Father."

"Come to see me whenever you can, my child," said the priest. "And think of what I said about joining the Catholic Church."

Genetha left the cubicle and went to sit in one of the pews. Throughout the building were scattered figures in various poses of meditation, mostly old women. The fiery candles hypnotized her. They seemed to have a significance that was important to unravel and burned with a steady flame that occasionally swayed like the muslin cloth of a Chinese dancer. From time to time an old woman would take a new candle and light it with the flame of another after depositing a coin in the collection box. People were continually entering and leaving the church, taking care to make their genuflections and signs of the cross. Genetha resolved to come to church whenever she could.

The sense of peace the visit gave her lasted until the following day, when the demands of work cancelled its effect.

Genetha became friendly with a young workmate named Zara, who invited her home. The girl lived beyond the trench and after putting off the visit for a few weeks she finally went.

She worked to support her parents, who lived on her father's meagre pension. The tiny drawing-room was dominated by a large picture of Christ wearing a crown of thorns and exposing his bleeding heart. Zara's brother sat in a corner of the dining-room, eating a plate of rice and salt fish, but Zara did not think it necessary to introduce Genetha to him.

Zara would have invited Genetha long ago, but felt ashamed of her home. However, when Genetha invited her friend in turn to her room, Zara thought rather less of her, and from then on she became more communicative and started to confide in Genetha. Her brother had spent six months in prison. He used to go out at night and come home early in the morning, and when his father demanded to know where he had been he would reply, "Nowhere." Her parents did not bother any more and the young man was allowed to go and come as he wished.

Zara, as she and Genetha drew closer to each other, turned out to be quite different from the person her friend had imagined her to be. On warm nights they used to go walking up the East Bank as far as Meadowbank, exchanging in their long conversations their ambitions and anxieties, and it was on these walks that Genetha discovered that Zara's apparent self-confidence masked a surprising vulnerability. She confided that she was afraid of going out with boys because she did not know what was expected of her. When she was eighteen, a year ago, she went out with a young man with whom she had fallen in love. At night she waited for his knock with an expectancy that was physically oppressive. When, however, he began making demands on her, she took fright and broke off. Genetha found out later that the young man lived in Meadowbank. The mere sight of his house, the blue door, the broken jalousie, the porch and stairs filled her with vague yearnings.

Zara complained that Genetha never told her much about herself, except that her people were dead; but Genetha objected that her past was painful and she hated recalling her family, with whom she had been close.

"Everybody's close to their people," remarked Zara once.

"But mine are dead!"

Zara explained how she and her brother wanted to give their parents a comfortable old age and how difficult it was.

Genetha tried to teach Zara shorthand, but her English was so poor that she gave up. Besides, Zara had no ambition to improve her situation.

Once the two friends went to a fair at the Chinese Cricket Club. Having spent their shillings in the first few minutes they wandered round the ground watching others ride on the merry-go-round or lose their money on the gambling games. When they were tired they sat down on the grass, closed their eyes and listened to the shouting and the music that came from the pavilion, where couples were dancing to a quartet. The

480

coloured lights shook with the flailing bodies and made swiftly changing patterns in the dark. The wooden horses of the round-about rose and sank like porpoises in a calm sea, presenting their expressionless faces with every revolution. It was one of those rich nights that tell the gentle hours beneath a profusion of stars, when humans catch a fleeting glimpse of a redemption beyond their grasp.

Genetha took her young friend's hand and held it while she watched the fair. Soon they began to recognize people they had seen earlier, who had made a tour and, unwilling to leave, were making a second round of the fairground. Snatches of conversation came down to them.

"Every time he throw up and he still going 'pon the round-about." Or "Is what Nancy doing? She hanging 'bout that dance hall and she know she kian' pay to get in."

Two young women sat down near to them and one began talking about her mother whom she never succeeded in pleasing, and then about her husband who spent a large amount on gambling on horse races run abroad.

"Everything is horses, horses, horses. Yesterday I say to he, 'I don' know why you didn' get married to a horse'!"

Both Genetha and Zara listened intently, to save up stories to giggle at when there were together.

Others, tired from the incessant walking and standing around, sat down on the grass as well, couples, groups of boys and individuals. The boys seemed more curious than others as to what was going on around them and spent their time devouring with their eyes every young woman who passed by.

Momentarily, a threatening cloud passed overhead, but it was soon gone and the stars re-emerged, as bright and splendid as ever. A number of people were now gathered round the dance hall and at the end of a piece clapped to show their approval. The vendors and those in charge of the gambling stalls had ceased shouting, while the roundabout was now carrying only half its complement of passengers. Genetha and Zara got up and went over to the dance hall, pushing their way through the four-deep crowd until they stood against the railing.

"Genetha!" someone called.

She looked round and saw a man gesticulating in her direction. It was Daley, the young man to whom Esther had introduced her some time before. He was in the company of

481

another man and was pushing his way towards her.

Genetha took Zara's hand and thrust herself through the crowd in the opposite direction.

"Is what? You know him?" Zara asked.

Genetha, without answering, shoved and nudged her way through the crowd and, once free, she ran across the field with her friend in tow.

"Stop, Gen, I out of breath," Zara pleaded.

But Genetha kept on running and only stopped when they reached the gate. She leaned against it for a few seconds to catch her breath. On looking back she could see no sign of Daley.

"Let's go," she said to Zara.

"He's still coming?"

"I don't know," Genetha replied.

The two set off down the road at a brisk pace, only slowing down on reaching Regent Street.

Zara wanted to stop and buy a mauby to slake her thirst, but Genetha insisted that they should go on, upon which the younger woman became annoyed and stopped in the middle of the pavement. She refused to continue unless Genetha told her what they were running from.

"It's an old friend, if you want to know. My brother used to know him, but I don't like him. You satisfied now?"

"You should've say so," Zara said, content with Genetha's explanation.

They walked on without talking.

"Why you don't talk?" Zara asked.

But Genetha answered nothing.

17. White Corners

It was late December and the big stores in Water Street were overflowing with people buying presents or admiring what they could not afford to buy. Everywhere in the town the sound of carol-singing came from houses, creating the mood that justified a name for the time of year. It was now less a religious festival than an excuse to dance, to eat and drink excessively. Bottles of sorrel, fly and ginger-beer ripened in cupboards and under beds, to be opened on Christmas Eve or offered to acquaintances who dropped in during the season. Rich, black Christmas cake, jealously guarded until the festive lunch, appeared on the dining-table in plates with gilded rims, while a leg of York ham spiked with cloves was served at night and strictly rationed until the New Year, to prolong the nostalgia of the succulent fare of Christmas Day.

Genetha looked in the mirror and saw the white corners of her mouth, the unmistakable signs of malnutrition. She and Zara had decided to attend one of the public dances, impelled by a desire to take part in the general merry-making. Zara, thin and haggard-looking, and Genetha, her white corners clearly visible, looked like candidates for a "before" advertisement of a fattening diet. There is an indomitable streak in human nature, which permits vanity to grow in the meanest of soils.

Both girls were working on Christmas Eve until midnight, but they planned to go home to Zara's and ask her parents for permission to go out again. Genetha thought that it was a better idea to ask a few days before, but Zara knew her parents. They would agree and change their minds afterwards. Whenever they had a chance the girls talked of the dance that night, Genetha confessing that she had already laid out her dress on the bed at home. She would wear a flower in her hair and her silver earrings. Zara had bought a new pair of shoes with a decorative buckle at the front.

By midday Genetha was already tired and had to exchange her breakfast hour with Zara, who should have eaten first. When the proprietor was not looking she took a piece of mutton out of the pot and put it on her plate, which was filled with rice and sauce. She ate the meat quickly and then proceeded to consume the rest of the food at a more leisurely pace. Of late, she had experienced difficulty in focusing and objects often appeared blurred.

"Oh, to hell with it," she thought, "tonight I'll dance my legs off."

Zara was primed for any adventure. If only a man knew how to handle her he could have his way with her that night.

At midnight the two women left the restaurant arm in arm. They turned into Princess Street by the timber yards, then right into Russell Street, crossing the Sussex Street trench with its stagnant water. The dances had long begun and no sooner had they left the music of one dance hall behind than the strains of a pick-up came to them from a private party. They quickened their steps until they reached the back streets of Albouystown.

The door of Zara's house was unlocked and she pushed it, followed by her friend. She lit the kerosene lamp, placed it on the little table, hesitated for a moment and then went over to her mother, who was lying on a low bed beside her husband. It had slipped her mind that she would have to wake her parents in order to speak to them about the dance.

"Is you, Zara? Is what?" her mother asked, turning over to look at her.

"Is me," her daughter answered. "I want to go to a dance."

"A what?"

"A dance," Zara said, summoning up all her patience.

"You mad?"

Zara's mother, about fifteen years younger than her husband, shook the sleeping form.

"Is your daughter. She want to go to a dance. She crazy."

"She crazy!" he echoed, then turned his back to the wall and began to snore almost immediately.

"You big old fool!" Zara shouted, stamping her feet.

The snoring stopped abruptly.

"Is what she say?" he asked his wife.

"She call you a big old fool," his wife declared, repeating the invective with unconcealed satisfaction.

He got up, climbed over his fat wife and, taking no notice of Genetha, cuffed his daughter on the side of her head. Thereupon he climbed back over his fat wife and lay down again. In a few moments he was snoring more loudly than ever.

Zara's mother turned her head away from her daughter, who stood motionless next to her friend. She was consumed with chagrin and humiliation. Her brother was out, enjoying himself, caring little about anyone's feelings and she, concerned to please them, could not once in a year go out and do what everyone else was doing. When Zara's anger subsided she looked up at Genetha and raised her head apologetically.

"You couldn't help it," Genetha said, in an effort to console her.

"What you going do?"

"Go home."

"At this time?" asked Zara.

"I've got to."

"Sleep here, ne?"

Genetha was tempted to accept the invitation, but was not

484

certain that Zara's parents would have approved.

"No, I gone."

Zara stood in the doorway and saw her walk away into the darkness.

Back in the street alone, Genetha was afraid of every shadow and every rustling, and, turning back incessantly, she kept to the middle of the road. She pushed her own door and, without bothering to take off her clothes, fell on the bed, fatigued and disappointed. Her body was aching so badly she felt like vomiting, and the thought came to her that the disappointment was a deliverance. No one could have danced in that condition.

She got up and went to the mirror to examine the whites at the corners of her mouth, which were more pronounced than ever. Dismayed, she took off her shoes and went back to bed. Here in Albouystown the sound of Christmas seemed to have been banished to less forlorn quarters. An almost irresistible urge to pass by Esther's establishment seized her, for she imagined the girls dancing in fancy dress, wearing masks and coloured paper hats. At least Zara had a home, she thought, where she could talk to someone and even quarrel.

Genetha fell asleep suddenly, like a candle blown out by a gust of wind.

When she was off on the same day as Zara, Genetha was in the habit of going to her home after finishing her washing and other household work. One night Zara's brother came in, swaying unsteadily. His father looked at him suspiciously. The youth, who hardly ever looked Genetha straight in the eye, offered to take her out for a drink.

"Thanks, I don't drink," she said.

He flung his head back and laughed.

"Don't tell me that! That's for them," he said, indicating with a sweeping gesture the others. "I know all 'bout you," he sneered. He then sat down on a chair in the corner of the room and fell into a surly silence.

In the end he got up and demanded of his mother, "Any food?"

She pointed to the enamel plate on the table.

"That's all?" he asked.

"When last you bring money in the house?" his father asked the youth, who did not answer.

He ate his food quickly and left, slamming the door.

Everyone was relieved. Zara's mother, who was in the habit of saying to Genetha, "We's decent people. Is only that we in' got education," went in dread of her son behaving in such as way as to prove that they were not decent people. They were Portuguese, their grandparents having come from Madeira to work on the sugar estates as indentured labourers. They had tried hard to give their children a good education, but both had got into bad company, which ruined their chances at school. Besides, their teachers had had no particular liking for them. All this both parents firmly believed.

Genetha was waiting for an opportunity to leave and when she announced her intention to go Zara's father would have none of it.

"Stay an' eat," he told her.

Zara's parents considered her a good influence on their daughter and hoped that Zara would emulate her "superior talk". Genetha had become fond of the couple, especially of the old man, who spoke little, but had the gift of instilling confidence in others. He spent half of his life at the window, only going out for walks in the burial ground and to collect his pension. He used to be a carpenter and went about shaking his head at the work of the younger generation of carpenters. His ambition was to own a house in Camp Street, where he would really have something to see from his window. If he had his time to live over again he would pay attention to his own "heducation". It would give meaning to his happiness. Although whenever Genetha came he did not return her greeting, nor by his expression show that he was pleased to see her, he felt, in truth, a kind of inward glow and followed her with his eyes, fearing that she had only come to see Zara home or to stay a short while.

Genetha stayed as she was asked and went home at about eleven that night.

The following day she thought she detected a coolness in Zara's manner and feared the worst. When, however, at lunch she laughed louder than ever and put her arm round her, her fears were allayed.

That afternoon, on the way home Genetha said; "I'll go home with you."

"No," her friend answered hastily. Then she stammered,

"Mother sick, you see."

Genetha's feet suddenly felt heavy.

"I gone," she said abruptly to Zara and turned into a street that could not possibly take her home.

"Where you going?" Zara called out.

Genetha just waved her hand and hurried away.

She thought of the priest to whom she had confessed and cursed him. Seized by a kind of elated hatred for the rest of the world, she told herself that there was no one she could trust and was glad of it. All those she loved had died and all those she trusted had spurned her trust. From then on she intended to make her way through life alone and resist anyone's attempt at forming an association with her.

Zara's brother had come back after Genetha's departure the night before. In fact, he had waited at the street corner, watching for her to leave. No sooner had he seen her turn the corner than he left his hiding place and went back home. He immediately picked a quarrel with Zara, reproaching her with bringing her friend home too often. His mother objected that it was none of his business and his father accused him of being jealous. It was this last remark that caused the youth to lose his temper and declare, "She's a whore!"

He was standing in the middle of the room, under the gaze of his family. His father got up and came over to him.

"Genetha's like me own daughter, you understand. She can come when she like an' go when she like. If you got any respect lef' in you, you'll respect she as I does respect she."

"You don't believe me, eh? You know what they does call she in Tiger Bay? They does call she 'Nora lie down'."

"Liar!" Zara exclaimed.

"Why you don't ask she then? Ask she when she come back."

"You in' got nothing to do but make mischief, boy?" his mother asked, already half-believing what her son had said. "Is what you trying to do? Just 'cause you don't like the girl."

"I trying to tell you," pursued the youth, "that some-one eating you foot and in' fit to come in the house. You always saying how I don't bring money home. This woman never bring nothing in this house, but she does sit down and eat we food. . . ."

"We food?" Zara asked mockingly. "Is me bringing in the

487

money, not you."

"Well," her brother said, "if we couldn't eat fish or beef before she used to come here how we can manage now, eh?"

"You're the only one in the house objecting," his father interjected. The old man sat down again. A cloud had come over his face.

Zara's brother left the house muttering under his breath and no one spoke after he left. Night had fallen but the lamp remained unlit. Zara's father was staring out of the window, while her mother had gone into the kitchen to prepare the evening meal. Zara had picked up a magazine which she was pretending to read in the dark.

The frogs filled the early night with their ghostly concert and the breeze, penetrating the half-open doorway, was moist and cool. Someone in the street was practising on a saxophone, repeating a phrase several times before moving on to a new one.

Zara's father got up to close the door as the breeze was now chilly, then lit a lamp and adjusted the wick to prevent it smoking. Zara closed her book and prepared to go to bed.

If Zara had been asked whether she believed her brother she would have denied that she did. Yet the incident at the fair, offhand remarks vaguely remembered now, implanted in her mind a nagging doubt. Whatever anyone said about Genetha her father would never believe and if he were faced with proof he would still shake his head stubbornly. But her mother was not capable of such faith. Had it not been for her father her mother would have questioned her brother further and would have asked Genetha round to question her about what her son had told them.

When Zara met Genetha the following day she was incapable of formulating the question on the tip of her tongue. If it were a matter of dealing with her father and her brother she could let the matter pass; but Genetha would notice the change in her mother's attitude. The latter would not rest until she had come right out and broached the subject.

It could not be possible, reflected Zara. Tiger Bay? Those painted women! She was determined to find out more on her own account. In the meantime Genetha would have to stay away for a few days, even though her father would miss her and ask after her.

Genetha, offended by her friend's unwillingness to take her home, went looking for another job the next day. She could not face Zara again and decided to forego her three days' pay.

That afternoon while she was sitting on her bed mending a dress there was a knock on the door. It could only be Zara. Genetha's hand shook as she plied the needle. She wanted to open and apologize for her behaviour the night before, but the thought of being hurt again gave her the determination to ignore the rapping, which was loud and insistent. The only other sound was the water simmering on the coal-pot.

18. Parade

Weeks after she started working at her new job in the Lombard Street cake shop she recieved a message by hand. Delivered by a small boy it said that S. was coming to see her when she had time. The boy did not know the lady who had given him the message, or her address.

The following Sunday when Genetha was sitting on a stool behind the glass cases, looking out on the pavement, Salome walked in. Genetha was not sure if she was glad to see her or not. They had not been on friendly terms at Esther's and she was the last person Genetha would have expected to pay her a visit. She had sent the note the day she caught sight of her from a taxi as she was driving away from Medici's cloth store. A client had taken her out to buy some cloth.

"But you looking bad!" Salome said, surveying Genetha with staring eyes.

"I know, I don't feel so well."

"That white corner! You going get sick," she continued, not realizing how deeply the observation affected the older woman.

"I feel better now that I can sit down," Genetha said. "In the last job I had to stand up all the time."

"God! Anyway, I going bring Netta to see you soon."

"No," protested Genetha at once. "You must come alone."

Genetha took a pine tart from the glass case and gave it to Salome.

"Thanks. I better don't tell the girls or they'll all come round. You should see Shola! She gone fat. And the new girl name Clem. Clem! Imagine a name like that. Anyway, I got to go now."

489

She bent forward and kissed Genetha on the cheek and was gone before the latter could say goodbye.

Genetha decided to change her job again. The last thing she wanted was the girls finding out where she was and what she was doing. Her decision was forestalled by an unexpected rise of a dollar a week given her by the proprietor, who came himself to see her. His wife ran the shop and had reported favourably on Genetha. The rise was no great inducement to remain, but it did persuade her to change her mind about leaving. However it did not take her long to notice that the proprietor's wife spent less time in the shop, leaving her to do most of the work.

One morning, while on her way to work, Genetha noticed Zara's brother coming from the opposite direction, but on seeing her he quickly ducked into a doorway. Genetha had to steel herself against looking back. If she had, she would have seen him standing in the middle of the pavement with his hands in his pockets, staring after her. On reflection, she realized that he had never looked her straight in the eyes, and his shifty manner was the lasting impression he had left on her.

After work, instead of going home, Genetha found herself walking up Lombard Street into Water Street. It was eleven o'clock at night. In front of the vast wrought-iron structure of the Starbroek Market the pavement was empty, apart from a few carts strewn with rotten fruit, pieces of paper and vegetable peel. A solitary old woman sat behind a cart on which were a smoking carbide lamp and the remains of her load of nuts. She had nodded off, but looked up at the sound of Genetha's footsteps.

Down Regent Street she walked and back through a side street until she found herself in South Road; and from where she stood she could see the lights of Esther's establishment. She walked towards it and, as if drawn by some magnet, she mounted the stairs.

When she stood in the doorway she heard someone say, "Is Gen!"

It was Salome, who was sitting at the large table with Netta and Vera. The latter looked at her as if she were a ghost.

"You look terrible!" Netta exclaimed. "Is what happen to you at all?"

"Who's it?" a voice came from inside, followed almost immediately by the figure of Esther.

She was wearing heavy golden earrings and on her right arm were several gold bangles, which made a clinking sound whenever she moved her arm. An elaborately embroidered bodice joined a blue skirt at her waist. Her face seemed smoother and her eyes reflected more light, while the rings round her eyes had all but gone and her once lack-lustre hair was tied in a molee above her neck.

Esther could not conceal her astonishment at Genetha's appearance. The greyish white corners on her mouth, the thin, whip-like body and the slightly bent shoulders caused her to hesitate, as when, after an absence of several years, a man sees his mother again, ravaged by age, and draws back momentarily, believing that he is mistaken, but on closer scrutiny discovers the features he knows and loves so well.

"It's you?" she asked.

She was about to embrace her, but put out her hand to shake Genetha's instead. And for a few seconds neither of them spoke.

"Where's Shola?" Genetha asked.

The girls looked at one another.

Then Esther said, after hesitating, "She had to go. She wasn't too good. Besides, she got so uppity, she wanted to run the place."

"Go and get Genetha something, ne?" Esther asked, speaking to no one in particular.

"What?" enquired Netta.

"Black cake and wine. Not the Correia. Get out the French wine." Then, turning to Genetha, she said: "A chap from the boats brings me wine and perfume from Guadeloupe."

Genetha fell on the black cake and consumed it without touching the wine. Esther made Netta fetch some more cake from the kitchen.

"I want a piece, too," Netta pleaded.

"No!" came the firm reply.

The young woman went off and soon came back with another piece of cake.

"Salome told me she saw you in the cake shop," said Esther.

Genetha looked reproachfully at Salome.

"Don't bother with her," declared Esther, understanding what had happened and nodding in Salome's direction. "She's as bad as Netta."

"What've you been doing all this time?" asked Esther, trying

491

her best not to look embarrassed.

Genetha resented her composure and when she caught Esther looking at her shoes she drew her feet in under the bench and took a handkerchief out of her handbag to give herself something to do. She had a pain in her stomach and the room began to spin. Thinking that she had to get away as quickly as possible she made an effort to stand up.

On recovering consciousness Genetha found herself in a room through the window of which the air was making billowing patterns in the blind. The night outside was dark, but a bulb shed its light over the low partition from the adjoining room. She could hear Netta talking to a man. It seemed that he wanted to go back to her room with her again but she refused.

Then there was silence, followed soon afterwards by the sound of a radio being tuned, picking up successively a number of stations in Spanish, and finally a programme of Flamenco music. The sound of the guitar in the late night hour filled the house with, as it were, a wave of reassurance. Occasionally the music died away but came back in greater volume, punctuated by cries of "Alla! Alla!"

Genetha cast her eyes round the room and could tell by the furniture and the upholstery that Esther was doing well. She was overwhelmed by the soft bedding, the night air and the seductive music. She remembered her first night in Tiger Bay in Esther's room, with its unpainted walls and hard bed. The blinds were dirty and tattered and did not yield with the gentleness of this diaphanous cloth.

Then she could hear voices again, and the sound of soft laughter.

"You wicked," a woman's voice said.

"You vex wit' me?" a man asked.

"I kian' vex with you."

"Well, let me feel you bubby, then."

Another fit of softly repressed laughter came over the partition.

"But you feel it already."

"But it so small and hard!"

"All right, but jus' quick."

Then silence fell once more.

Genetha fell asleep again and when she awoke the walls of the room were transfigured by a bright, almost white light, like the screen of the cinema she used to attend after she broke with Michael. The rest of the room was in darkness and Genetha could hardly make out the upholstered chairs. So she was not dreaming!

She closed her eyes, and when she opened them once more the walls were just as bright as before. Far from being afraid Genetha marvelled at the steady phosphorescence that had transformed the wood. She sat up and looked round her as if she were expecting a companion.

Suddenly the wall ahead of her became animated with indistinct shapes which gradually became clearer. And as the forms became more distinct, music could be heard coming as it were out of the wall. The scene might have been taking place on the street under the sunlight of noonday and she might have been watching it through an open window. A brass band was playing a rousing march of such transcendental beauty that the windows of other houses, which could be seen at the top of the wall, were soon filled with people. Louder and louder the music grew until it seemed to fill the whole world.

Her attention was drawn to the wall on the right of her bed, which represented a street, smaller than the one in which the march-past was featured. A group of little children were running towards the main street shouting, "Parade! Parade!" and when they reached the point where the two streets joined they stood to watch the uniformed men in awe, marching in unison to a music that gripped the heart. A few boys, caught up in the occasion, started to accompany the procession down the road, but the fast-growing crowd soon reduced their progress and they were obliged to remain in one place. Then out of the side street emerged the well-dressed figure of a woman who, with dignified gestures, was trying to restrain two young children from breaking away and joining the others. And as the young woman, wearing a maid's cap and long white dress, grew larger on the screen Genetha recognized Esther. The little boy unmistakably resembled Boyie, her dead brother, while the girl, who must have been herself, she could not recognize. On the photograph Fingers had found her face was blurred and she had forgotten what she looked like as a child.

Genetha gazed intently at the little girl on the wall whose face and ancient dress drew her like a magnet. Her wonderfully dark eyelashes looked as if they were covered with layers of mascara.

493

Genetha studied every pleading look, every wide-eyed expression of the well-fed, smooth-skinned little girl. And finally, like all the children who had come out of the side street, Genetha, Boyie and Esther were lost among the crowds.

Genetha tried to retain the tune the band was playing, feeling certain that it was connected with some forgotten incident from her childhood. But soon the band itself had passed and the wall was now filled with marching, uniformed men with chins raised under severe expressions like those on the faces of the free-masons as they marched down the Public Road at Agricola, their silver-painted wooden swords glistening in the sunlight. And just as the band and their playing had roused her these men turned her blood cold. But they were soon gone and the only sound they left behind was the tramp, tramp of their steps when the music died away. Long after the street was empty, except for its steady phosphorescence, there could be heard that tramp, tramp of absent feet which, like the music a few moments earlier, filled the room with its pervasive sound and, seemingly, the whole world.

Genetha tried desperately to recall the tune that she had heard repeated several times, but could not. She knew that the second note rose from the first, but she was unable to remember the interval and in the end gave up.

But the wall ahead of her was already coming to life once more. On the western corner of it, black clouds intruded, darkening the edge of the screen, along the middle of which ran a thick wall of sugar cane, while at the bottom stood a small cake-shop next to which was a vegetable patch planted with cassava and pumpkin. Genetha knew she was in East Canje, for that one visit with the patients from New Amsterdam had left an indelible impression on her mind. There was no one in sight and the dusty, pot-holed road stretched along the cane field out of the picture. Then the first drops of rain began to fall while the wind whipped the ribbon-like leaves of the tall cane this way and that, so that the tiny cake-shop seemed threatened. The raindrops in the dust became magnified before Genetha's eyes, leaving tiny craters in the road which, however, soon disappeared in the deluge of rain that all but blotted out the landscape. The wooden shop became darker and the cane fields presented the appearance of a mass of growth, waving about like giant sea-weed in a translucent stretch of ocean. She had come to East

Canje in bright sunshine and only the cake-shop, the cane fields and the dusty road were recognizable. This forlorn scene, the complete absence of people, made her wonder whether she might be somewhere else. But on turning to the wall on her right she recognized the koker, rising out of the landscape above the drainage canal, and the spot where she had taken shelter from the threatening sun.

A sudden longing for this landscape gripped Genetha, an absurd desire to be in a place whose air, at the time of her visit, was filled with an almost unbearable stench; a sun-drenched, flat landscape, criss-crossed with ribbons of stagnant water, accessible only by means of the infrequent bus or taxi. Perhaps because the rain had obscured it, or perhaps because the air was now clean again, she saw it as the primeval landscape of her childhood, filled out by the curiously large figures of her mother, Esther and her shadowy father.

The rain came down, endlessly, monotonously, with a deep, hollow sound, joining sky and earth with innumerable threads. The dust of the road was gradually changed into slime and mud and ran away into the gutters and low-lying cane fields. Genetha looked for the bus that had brought her there, for a moment enchanted into the belief that she was in that gloomy landscape. With relief she saw that there was no bus in sight, that the only man-made structure was the diminutive shop battered by the downpour.

Increasing in intensity the rain now sounded like the con-certed lowing of a herd of cattle; and when, as if from nowhere, the hardly discernible figure of a man materialized in front of the koker, Genetha sat up, afraid. Cutlass in hand, he walked hurriedly along the dam and turned into the shop, out of view, leaving Genetha more astounded by the apparition than by the ferocity of the rain and wind and by the veiled landscape.

And as the landscape faded on the wall, so the sound of the falling rain diminished, until the room was once more silent.

Hardly had Genetha begun wondering about the significance of what she had seen than the wall of a sudden presented another different scene. She immediately recognized the drawing-room of the family home, which appeared so desolate after her father's death. There was the familiar furniture, the familiar door opening on to the porch. But everything was covered in a layer of dust and the roof of the porch, seen through the open front door, was in such a state of disrepair that it was threatened with collapse. The bedroom door was closed and as the scene shifted to the back of the house she saw that the other bedroom doors were closed as well. The kitchen was dark, for the window above the back stairs was closed.

Genetha knew, somehow, that her father had only recently died. There was no evidence of this from what she saw, but she was convinced that it was so.

As the scene shifted back to the drawing-room the conviction grew that, despite the apparently empty house and the dilapidation of the scene, someone was there, either in a locked room or even in the drawing-room which at that moment lay before her on the wall. Back and forth the scene shifted, now to the dining-room then back to the drawing-room with the gallery door open out on to the derelict porch.

Then, as though to dispel any doubts she might still have, the scene narrowed to take in two upholstered chairs which were pressed near to each other and behind which grunting sounds could be heard. The scene then took in the narrow passage between the chairs and the wall and there, in a kind of twilight, two figures were making love on the floor. The woman's face was turned towards the space under the chair while the man was lying down, making imperceptible movements over the woman in his embrace. And the light sought out the two figures, exposing first Genetha's still young features and then, as he collapsed on her at the moment of climax, Boyie.

Genetha shuddered at what she beheld. It was not possible, she told herself. Yet it was indeed her face and her arms clasping Boyie's and urging him to go on. And the features were unmistakably his. Even his shirt and trousers were familiar. Had she not washed the shirt herself, fearing that he might have them washed at that woman's house in Vreed-en-Hoop?

She saw him get up, ponderously, for there was just enough room behind the chairs to accommodate one person. He left her alone behind the chair and went inside, opening and closing the door of the bedroom which adjoined the drawing-room. And she lay on the floor, one leg resting against the wall and the other against the upholstered chair and the black recesses of her legs exposed to the light that spared nothing.

It was not possible, she kept telling herself. And she could not know that it was precisely the fear of incest that had driven her brother away to live in Suddie. She kept denying the possibility of what she saw and the uninhibited way in which he rode her and then walked off. Yet she made no attempt to look away. She had made no attempt to look away.

Then she recalled the two previous scenes that had unfolded before her on the wall and remembered that neither the procession nor the downpour at East Canje were real. This reflection calmed her somewhat, but there still lingered the feeling of having been exposed, that it might be commonly believed that Boyie had seduced her, that whatever she said would not dispel the cloud of guilt which had surrounded her.

What were these visions anyway? she asked herself, looking round the room to ensure that she was alone. She was not asleep, that was certain. It was equally certain, she told herself, that she was not having hallucinations.

Jumping out of bed she left the room in search of one of the girls. She did not wish to meet Esther, but she did not know who slept in the special room. It was almost certain to be one of the girls who had been there from the opening of the establishment. Perhaps Netta or Salome.

Then Genetha changed her mind and decided to leave the house without telling anyone. She opened the door quietly, slipped out and closed the door again with the utmost care.

But as she approached the gate a voice from under the house called out.

"You kian' go home at this time o'night, Miss Genetha." It was Bigfoot, who was sitting alone, watching the road.

"Why're you up so late?" Genetha asked him.

"Is in the day I does sleep most, mistress," came the deferential reply. "I does watch the place by night."

"Oh."

"You kian' walk the streets alone now," he warned her again. "If you want I can take you home. That's if you want."

"I'd be glad," Genetha said.

"All right." He got up eagerly and joined her. "You living far?" he asked.

"Albouystown."

They walked for some distance without speaking.

"I did miss you, y'know, mistress," said Bigfoot, without turning towards her, and using the term of respect country people use when addressing their wives or women for whom they have great respect.

"Ha," was all Genetha could reply, to hide her confusion.

"Why you don't come back?" he asked. "Everybody know how Madame does like you."

"She said so?" Genetha enquired, more at ease now that the conversation was on firmer ground.

"Yes, she say so. Is true she been a servant in your mother house?" Bigfoot asked, slowing his pace.

"Yes, but that was years and years ago," Genetha told him.

"Years and years?" said Bigfoot. "You talkin' as if you old."

Why did he have to mention her age if he did not know that she was no longer young? He knew and felt sorry for her, she reflected. She had never met such consideration from the men in her house. Even Fingers at his most tender never spoke to her like that.

"What happened to Shola?" asked Genetha, curious as to the fate of her chief persecutor at the brothel.

"Madame put her out 'cause she did get too big for she boots. And she find out she been takin' more money from the clients than the other girls. It was a big thing: the other girls threaten to stop work if Shola go. But Madame give them all twenty-four hours to leave the house. The nex' morning even Netta wouldn't show she face to Madame. An' when Shola leave Madame start taunting them an' asking them why they wouldn't go. She refuse to cook for them and at midday she alone sit at the dining-table an' eat. It wasn't till the nex' day they get food. You never see such a thing in you life, but it happen."

"So Shola's gone," Genetha said in a soft voice.

"Is it 'cause of she you go?" Bigfoot asked hopefully.

"No, I wanted to go anyway."

"Madame say you goin' come back again," Bigfoot remarked. "She say she know you too good, an' that you goin' come back."

"Oh, yes?" said Genetha angrily.

"Why you vexed? I thought she did know something we din' know . . . . So you not comin' back then?"

"No, definitely not."

Bigfoot would say no more, fearing that he had offended her.

What Esther had actually said was, "She'll come back and kiss my feet and repay me for everything her mother did do me."

"I can't come back, you see," explained Genetha. "I wasn't cut out for that sort of life. I knew one man before I started. I can't explain what I mean. It's not only that I knew just one man. It's the guilt and the feeling that one day I'd have to pay for everything."

Bigfoot gave Genetha time then began to speak.

"I uses to own a launch you know, mistress. I uses to be a decent man. Then in 1946, when the yankee air base close down and nobody had money no more, I had was to sell my launch for what I could get and come to town to look for work. When I meet Madame and she tell me she would like me to work for she I grab the opportunity. I tell you, if you come back I would look after you good."

"I'm not what I look like, Bigfoot. And if you got to know me you would take what you could from me and let me down. . . ."

"I wouldn't, mistress," Bigfoot hastened to assure her.

"No, you wouldn't," said Genetha. "I haven't got anything left for you to take."

"All right. That's what I did mean. I don't want nothing."

They walked at a leisurely pace, neither wishing to hurry. But Bigfoot believed that he had offended her and longed to make amends, while Genetha, unaware of his concern, was glad of his company and the discretion of his words. She wanted to ask him whether Esther had a man friend. And Bigfoot himself had never shown an interest in any of the other women in the brothel. Did he have a woman friend outside? Being married and having a wife in one place while working in another was a common condition. The men often started another family in the district where they worked. Bigfoot almost certainly had a woman in Georgetown, but was successful in hiding her existence from the others.

"You vex with me, mistress?" asked Bigfoot, without turning to look at her.

"Me? No, Bigfoot. I was just thinking how I enjoy walking when everybody else's asleep." Then, to reassure him, she went on. "I'm going to go and live with my aunts."

"Where they living, mistress?"

"Near Vlissingen Road." Then, after a while, "I haven't told them yet, but they won't say no."

"I think that would be good," he said simply, imagining that his words bore the weight of his sincerity.

If Bigfoot had put his arm round Genetha she would have done nothing to repulse him, for the need to be protected by someone was now strong, as if her abortive visit to the brothel had robbed her of the little confidence she had left.

What did women need men for? she reflected. If she worked and lived at her aunts' would she not have the security and protection of a home? Her body had no more need for a man's embrace. In the end was she not free now? Were not her father's death and her brother's going away a deliverance?

Finally she and Bigfoot stood in front of the near derelict building where she lived. Connecting it to the street lamp-post were two wires from which an abandoned kite hung, quivering with every gust of wind. The two solitary figures faced each other under the lamplight with no idea of the remarkable picture they made standing on top of their round shadows.

"Well, thanks," said Genetha.

"Remember what I did tell you," said Bigfoot.

She nodded to show that she understood, although she was not certain what he had said to her.

"Goodnight, mistress. I goin' stand here till you go inside. Just in case."

Genetha crossed the bridge and disappeared into the shadows of the house.

19. Aunts of the Blood

Genetha moved in with her aunts who, appalled at her appearance, granted her request to come and live with them. She gave up her job at the cake-shop, knowing that if she left for work every morning they would eventually enquire where she was working and, on finding out, demand that she stopped.

She recovered her strength quickly, her face filled out, her breasts and hips grew round and firm again. During this period she was encouraged by her aunts to do as little as possible around the house. But as she grew well again she relieved them of the sweeping and dusting, then of the ironing until she was taking her full share of the household work. Genetha did not mind, for she now felt stronger than she had ever done.

She came back to find that her grandfather had become senile and spent the greater part of the day in his bedroom, emerging in the afternoon to look out of the window across the trench to Vlissingen Road and at the crowds waiting to get into the cinema. From time to time he would say out loud, "Oh, my!"

500

Oh, my!" This occurred with greater frequency as the weeks went by, until no one took any notice of him any more, even when he accompanied these outbursts with cupping his head in his hands.

In his periods of lucidity, when he saw and recognized Genetha he would make her sit down and tell her how his brother died while still in his thirties, "wrenched away after stepping on a rusty nail and contracting tetanus". Otherwise he ignored everyone, although frequently calling for their help, and spent the mornings contemplating the vast desert of blue beyond the eaves of the back-house, and the evenings out front.

His wife, Genetha's maternal grandmother, fell into a long silence as her husband became more confirmed in his senility. She had long ceased going to church, after the foreign minister went away and was replaced by a local man, and had also stopped taking her evening walks, as her husband was no longer fit to go out. His senility was the final blow and, fearing that her daughters could not grasp the seriousness of her plight, she withdrew into her implacable silence.

Genetha's elder aunt, Deborah, stubbornly refused to believe that her father was permanently afflicted and kept saying that he would soon pull out of it. She reproached him for his table manners, once impeccable, she often reminded him. And the morning she caught him urinating out of the back window it was all she could do not to raise her voice. She had noticed the stain on the painted white-pine boards beneath the window and was mystified as to its origin. He denied knowing anything about it, claiming that bats often left stains from their droppings. And the more he tried her patience the more she insisted that he would get well again.

As Genetha gained in strength, the old desires came back to plague her body. She decided that it would be best to work again and set about looking for a job in an office. But her first interview was disastrous for no sooner had she been called in to be questioned than she was recognized by one of the men.

"Excuse me," he charged bluntly, "weren't you working at a certain place in South Road?"

Genetha fled rather than deny the accusation, cursing the need to live in a town where anonymity was impossible. She had not told her aunts about her application, partly because she felt

501

they might be displeased at the prospect of her working again and being unable to help in the house as before.

Embittered by her experience Genetha thought that she ought to go and see her paternal aunt and confess everything. But as the weeks went by she was overcome by a sort of torpor. Her only problem was that of renewing her wardrobe which, with care, would last another two or three years, she told herself. Until then, she would live as she had lived, sharing the food and shelter of her relations.

Genetha was now careful to go out only at night. She insisted that, though she was prepared to do all the work given her in the house, she would go out whenever she wanted. Her aunts gave in, seeing in her defiance a quirk that harmed no one. After all, the cook did the main part of the shopping in the morning, while the East Indian woman came round every day with her tray of greens. Only the bread had to be fetched and that had been the younger aunt's duty for a long time.

One night while Genetha and her younger aunt were out walking on a moonlit night, chatting like two young girls who had escaped the constraints of a supervising adult, Genetha saw a young man approaching them. She could not understand why her attention should be drawn to him because, at that distance, she was unable to make out his features. As he went by she smiled at him and he smiled back, an exchange that passed unnoticed by her aunt. Then on reaching home she said she was going out again, offering as an excuse that she did not get enough exercise.

She saw the man waiting in Anira Street and went boldly up to him, smiling but saying nothing.

"I didn't think you'd come," he told her, and they walked off together.

The young man was unable to make conversation, so taken aback was he by his unexpected success. He walked her along Albert Street and along the old highways, until they came to Palpree Dam, a haven for lovers.

When he saw that Genetha did not object to being taken to this road of shadows, where the light of the moon was shut out by the canopy of massive tamarind and saman trees, he became more confident. He put his arm round her waist, drawing her closer to him. Then, unopposed, he fondled her small breasts. Encouraged by her passive manner he bent down to pull off her panties. She lifted one foot then the other and saw him put her undergarment in his pocket as he would a handkerchief with which he had just wiped his face. Half-naked, bathed in a cool film of moisture, she walked with him, sometimes trampling wild flowers on the parapet, sometimes exposed to the gaze of the moon where the canopies did not meet.

The young man laid her down in the grass and her skirt became covered with pollen and the clinging seeds of the sweetheart plant. She did not even know the stranger's name or if he was . . . . What did it matter when all her woes melted in the wonder of creation? Did anything matter? Who was she and her self, struggling against the perpetuity of things? Her transitory longings, her vain words? Then her body shuddered for the third time and the light of a fourth candle began to burn before her eyes, as if he had just lit it. When she was at secondary school a friend once explained to her how these soft tapers could be used to provide the most delicious of forbidden sensations. So struck had Genetha been by what she heard that the sight of those countless candles in Brickdam Cathedral and their shuddering flames never failed to intimidate her. Yet on Old Year's night she always accompanied her best school friend to Midnight Mass, where they met other acquaintances, Catholics and non-Catholics, who used the mass as a pretext to get away from home and mingle with the crowd of worshippers.

At last the young man collapsed on her with the same long gasp Fingers used to utter, like the panting of a dog. Then she would have preferred him to leave her there; but she knew he would be calling on her to follow him and that he would lay claim to her affection, as if by giving him something she owed him something more.

On the way back she asked him if his name was Glen, one of Fingers's formal Christian names.

"Why should my name be Glen?" he asked.

"Nothing."

"But why?"

"I tell you, nothing," she replied, irritated by his interest.

"You did know somebody name Glen?" he asked.

"Don't take me all the way," she said, anxious to see him go. "Why?"

"Because my people don't like me having men friends."

He left her two corners away from Laluni Street.

503

But every night after that he came walking or riding by in the moonlight like a dog in dog season, when the whole family save Genetha's grandmother were assembled at the front of the house, on the porch and at the windows. One night she turned and followed him with her eyes as a sign of her interest.

When she went out on her own about ten minutes later he was waiting as she expected, round the corner in Anira Street in front of the church.

Genetha recalled the admirer who used to prowl round the brothel in South Road until one of the girls chased him away.

"What you want with me?" she threw at him.

"Don't you want to see me again?" he enquired.

"No. I thought you understood!"

"Aren't you in love with me?" he asked.

"No, I'm not."

"But you let me . . . the first time," he almost pleaded.

"How could I explain?" she thought.

"You're so decent," he said. "Decent women don't carry on like that. I *know* women." He came round, on the other side of his bicycle, to be nearer her.

Genetha stared at him indignantly, exasperated at his persistence. "Please leave me alone," she said. "You don't know me. If I'd passed you on the road that night you wouldn't have come here. Leave me alone, please. I don't know you."

He made a gesture of bewilderment, but could answer nothing.

As he started to move off Genetha held the handlebar of his cycle. But instead of saying what she had to say she turned away abruptly and made for the house. One day, she thought, she would take her younger aunt into her confidence.

Genetha walked away, impelled by an unreasoning fury, and when she reached the house she did not go upstairs right away, but remained under it.

"He knows women!" she said to herself. "He knows women. The same arrogance as Boyie and Father."

She recalled the conversation of one of her father's acquaintances, an assistant to a land surveyor, whose job it was to cut survey lines in the jungle. He often talked of his experiences in the forest, of being unable to see further than a few yards above his head into the upper reaches where most of the army of animals lived and, even farther above, where eagles soared.

That represented for her the state of her self-knowledge; only in her dreams did she glimpse that swarming world within her and a partial understanding of her nature that the men she knew claimed to have. Only Fingers seemed free of this masculine conceit and it was he who had brought her to this pass!

Gradually Genetha's anger subsided and her thoughts turned to her conduct on Palpree Dam. Had her life in the brothel made her depraved? Or did the brothel uncover what was already there? She felt no shame at her conduct, only curiosity that it was in contrast to the behaviour of the women from her social class. She remembered her disgust for her work at Esther's establishment, which, even now, made her head grow to think on it. But in retrospect there was something heady about the depravity, the wanton disregard for the regulated life of the family. Some of the girls openly admitted this, especially the East Indians from the country.

It was curious that everything she did seemed to be in relation to men. The problems of her freedom, of her depravity as well, were all reflections of her life with men. Even her rejection of male companionship was an admission of her preoccupation with them. Had she not been maltreated by Fingers she would not have treated the young man so harshly tonight. What was certain, however, was her resolve never to be hurt again. Every month she would seek out a stranger and entice him to Palpree Dam to assuage her own longings and then return to the house of women, where the once all-powerful male was dying a slow death and the elder aunt was becoming more authoritarian every day.

That night Genetha's grandfather took a turn for the worse and everyone sat up late, lit by the rays of two night-lights, watching and waiting. Genetha's elder aunt was staring straight ahead, while Alice's chin had fallen on to her breast.

The next day they took it in turns to watch, through the slow afternoon hours and throughout the night. When her turn came to relieve Alice, Genetha sat down at her grandfather's bedside, not daring to look at the old man lest he were already dead. At her father's wake she had sought refuge in sleep. This was the first time she had stayed up long after midnight and known the silence of those hours, broken only by an incessant chirping of crickets. The Old Year's night when she and Zara were on the way to her house came back, with its dance-hall sounds, the strident call of trumpets and the thud of stamping feet.

What was Death, in truth? She had heard so many stories of its coming. According to some, it arrived accompanied by a demon animal, while others said it came alone, invisible to all except the dying person and small children. Her mother, as it seemed, had been wrenched away; her father just went, discreetly, when she and Rohan were out at work, yet with the same effect, a terrible emptiness or an accumulation of some special misery. But on neither occasion did she see anything to confirm the hundred tales about death. Perhaps Death was silence, encompassed by night and its dark winds. Long ago, she believed that anyone who survived beyond the age of sixty was indestructible. Long ago, long, long, long ago, in the time of mask-makers and jumbee-band dancers of great reputation, when old things were revered and therefore indestructible.

Genetha turned to look at her grandfather, stretched full-length, with hands placed across each other at the wrists, like a corpse laid out. He was wearing his slippers, though uncovered by a blanket, an eccentricity her aunts allowed him on the grounds that his feet were perpetually cold, only to explain away an indulgence which had grown out of their respect for him. He wore his slippers even on the warmest and most humid nights, when sweat blinded the eyes.

Alice had said it was bad luck to interrupt the watch, and here, because the advice had been repeated when she arrived to take her place, she felt the urge to urinate. That was a portent, too, as was the inordinate silence. If only she had company she would listen to any trifling conversation. Words that seemed arid in Georgetown had been, in Morawhanna, like ripe-bursting fruit. "Who with you?" "Is me one." Or, "Where he is?" "Some place." And Ulric – who surely withdrew again after Fingers abandoned her – with his stories of keeping watch during war, and his halting way of speaking.

The old man made an unexpected movement, which gave Genetha such a fright she almost fell off her chair. At all costs she must concentrate and pray for him, she told herself, not only because it was her duty, but because the love he bore her shone even in his decrepitude. "Dear Genetha, no one is ever alone . . . everyone must love you, dear child." He was all her own father had not been, who never sighed nor wasted terms of

506

endearment.

Death was the end. And Time was its vahana, the drive to decrepitude, new leaf, old leaf, the precondition of perpetual renewal. Or an old East Indian man crying the hours on a sugar estate, "One bhaja, ohhhhhh!" "Two bhaja, ohhhhhhh!" Or simply a mathematical rate of ageing and decay.

"Almighty God," she prayed inwardly, so as not to disturb her grandfather, whose hands had become separated from one another when he moved. Genetha prayed for his recovery, using all the formulae she had learned since her church-going days and her childhood Sunday-school classes and the night services on the radio.

It must have been during her prayer that she dropped off with that abruptness that defies recollection.

Suddenly the shrill cry of an owl caused the younger aunt, Alice, to wake up with a start and the elder to make the sign of the cross on her chest, for there were no owls in the area.

Genetha's grandmother came out of the bedroom where she was sleeping.

"Was that an owl?" she asked. "I heard an owl."

"Yes, Mamma," answered Aunt Deborah, speaking over the partition. "It was an owl. It probably just flew over."

"Yes," said the old lady. "But why here?" She went back inside without an explanation.

"Genetha," said Deborah, who came to join them, "make us some chocolate. It's turned chilly. We're all imagining things."

"Yes, Aunt," Genetha said, getting up to go into the kitchen.

They watched for nine nights, Genetha and her two aunts, taking turns to stay up until dawn broke. But despite the omens, the dark dreams and their conviction that death had installed itself at his bedside, the old man recovered. And in the days that followed Genetha's elder aunt's irritation with him increased. The scent of bay-rum from the sick room, his constant demands made in a surprisingly loud voice, disturbed her music students' lessons, she claimed. Even when he could walk about again he behaved as if he required attention and, what was worse, wandered about the house in his pyjamas, to the amusement of the students doing their theory of music at the large table in the drawing-room. Genetha then detected for the first time flaws in Aunt Deborah's exterior.

In one of the old man's lucid periods she suggested to him

507

that he go to a lawyer and have all his possessions made over to those who were likely to survive him, so that they would have access to his bank account and government bonds after he died. He agreed, on condition that Genetha came with them. Genetha could not refuse, even though all the lawyers' chambers were in or near Croal Street, a stone's throw from Esther's establishment. Besides, she reflected, they would be going in broad daylight, and she would have to linger by the car while her aunt shepherded him from the vehicle to the office, an operation that was bound to attract the attention of passers-by.

The morning planned for the visit arrived. It was eight months since Genetha had been living with her aunts and this sortie was to be her first in daytime for nearly a month. With trepidation she stood on the porch while Aunt Deborah accompanied the old man down the stairs. He was dressed in a suit more than thirty years old which, though eccentric in cut, might have been made no more than a few months ago, so well-kept it was.

"Come on, Genetha," her aunt urged, with that new irritation that soured the atmosphere in the house.

"I'm coming, Aunt," she called out, deliberately going inside to fetch something imaginary.

Genetha came out when she was certain that her grandfather and aunt were already in the car.

"Why you don't want to go?" enquired Aunt Alice, who was leaning out of the window to watch the departure.

"I don't mind," Genetha protested, hurrying down the stairs.

Not a word was spoken in the car, and when it stopped in front of the Lawyer G's chambers Genetha's elder aunt helped her father out and beckoned Genetha to take his arm on the other side. Here, in the bustle of town, amidst the honking of cars and the continuous roar of traffic, she felt as if she were being observed. Fighting the impulse to rush back to the car in which they came she turned round to look at the passers-by.

A woman came out of the lawyer's chambers, staring at the threesome as she went by, much to Genetha's dismay. And so it was throughout the time of waiting in the chambers, in the company of three clients whom they met there, and of others who came in after them.

At last Genetha's aunt and the old man went through the open doors and disappeared into the room where the lawyer saw his clients, leaving Genetha in the company of four others.

Though her chances of being recognized as a prostitute were small, in the confines of the office, Genetha sat rigid on her chair, imagining the worst and not daring to look round her. Then the typist addressed her and she started from her seat. "Me?" she asked. "No, I'm with the two people inside. Remember? I came in with them."

The young woman did not look away at once.

After what seemed an interminable period of waiting, Genetha's aunt and grandfather came out, accompanied by the lawyer, who followed them solicitously as if they were his own relations. The old man looked exhausted, while Deborah, relaxed and triumphant, patiently walked with him back to the waiting car.

"What a nice day," she said, to no one in particular, as the car drove off. She then lowered the window glass, so that the wind came in.

"He's a pleasant man, isn't he?" Deborah said to her father, hunched in his seat. But either he did not understand her or he did not care to answer.

For her, Genetha was still a girl, to be ignored or ordered about. She had no idea that the niece was sizing up the aunt, that for the first time since her return she was seriously asking herself whether the increasingly authoritarian régime in the house was worth bearing with, in return for three square meals a day and a roof over her head. Had she been able to earn a living, matters would have come to a head before. Now that her aunt was in charge of the source of the household income – apart from the old man's pension – things would certainly not improve. The prospect of a more severe régime, the anticipation of what might not even come to pass, set up Genetha's defences and disposed her to a hostility that, in the light of her older aunt's character, could only be to her disadvantage.

Genetha edged away from her and pressed herself against the side of the car. It occurred to her that, although the car followed a route that took them past Esther's establishment, she had not even noticed the place, so preoccupied she had been with reflections about her aunt's growing power in the house.

Now they were rushing past the cottages in upper South Road in the reckless manner that distinguished Guyanese drivers from those elsewhere. Almost thwarted in his headlong rush by

509

a car emerging from a side street, the driver pressed his horn in a long, angry reminder that his vehicle had right of way.

Aunt Alice came to the front to meet them with a smile which seemed to ask if everything went as was planned. Genetha and Aunt Deborah helped the old man up the stairs and into the house and he made for the back, to spend the rest of the day with his wife.

20. The Hinterland

Almost a month had passed since Genetha's encounter with the stranger and their walk to Palpree Dam. She had taken to going out in the daytime again. Since the trip to the lawyer's chambers she felt that, if she took great care in leaving the house, no one who recognized her on the road would be able to connect her with her aunts. It was on one of these morning outings to the bakery that she came face to face with Michael in the company of a woman and three small girls the image of him. In utter confusion at the unexpected encounter Michael made as if to go by, but Genetha stepped in his way and greeted him.

"Michael?"

"Good Heavens!" he exclaimed. "Genetha!"

He introduced her to his wife while the three children looked on, left out of the formalities.

"Joyce, this is Genetha . . . Genetha, my wife. I used to know Genetha at the church."

Michael's wife was a small, nervous-looking woman, who listened to her husband as if she expected to be beaten when they got home. She smiled, but said nothing, only occasionally turning to look at her brood anxiously.

"Look, I've still got the hymn book you lent me so long ago. Why not come and get it? I live in Irving Street with my aunts. . . ." She gave him the lot number and said that she would have the book ready for him.

Michael said goodbye, enjoined on his wife and each of the children to do as much, and took leave of Genetha with even more confusion than he had shown in acknowledging their acquaintanceship.

"Michael . . ." thought Genetha. "Well, well, well."

But he did not come, as she expected he would. Then the night when Genetha planned to go out alone, in the expectation

510

of a new passing encounter, after she had spent three-quarters of an hour in front of the looking-glass following a shower and wash with her aunts' bath salts, she was taken aback to see him at the gate as she opened the front door to leave the house.

Michael was his old self, composed and priggish, professing to have the right to call her Genetha after all that time.

She hurried down to meet him before one of her aunts could come out, and in a flash saw him as her husband and his three children as her own. She was about to go down to meet her husband who had taken her visiting and had now come to accompany her back home. She was clean and honourable, had known only him intimately, as her mother must have known only her father. Genetha experienced such an access of joy at his coming that she completely forgot herself and shouted, "Michael!" And he stood at the foot of the stairs, surprised by her extravagant greeting, having no idea that she was transported by her own anxiety to a time that never existed, to a place that was neither her old home nor her present abode in her mother's father's house; that the cry of his name was a call for help, and the laughter in her cheeks the banner of her desperate need.

"Hello, Genetha," Michael answered soberly.

The tone of his voice brought her back to her senses more sharply than an unexpected blow with his hand could, so that her laughter became a smile.

They went off in the direction of the sea and crossed the wall that ran along the beach. They talked of old times, while kicking the seaweed underfoot, and thought of what the next hour would bring.

"When I saw you with the children I had a wrench," she told him.

"So you didn't get married after all?" he asked.

"No," she replied.

"And what about that man living in the house?"

"We broke up," she said simply.

Michael fell silent, relishing the discovery that she had been abandoned by a man and that she had remained unmarried.

Genetha took his arm.

"Things weren't easy after we broke up," he told her, unwilling to let her off so lightly.

"I want you to kiss me," she declared, stopping abruptly.

After he had kissed her she led him towards the pavilion with the long staircase and seduced him there, enveloped in darkness, with the sea sounding far away.

He wanted to rush off, but she would not let him go.

"No, stay and talk to me!"

Thereupon Michael took out two five-dollar notes and gave them to her, "For old times' sake," he declared.

Genetha began to laugh softly.

"What's wrong?" he enquired.

"Nothing."

"Don't laugh like that. Someone might pass and hear you."

Genetha stopped laughing as he ordered. "I suppose you see this as a kind of revenge," she told him.

"I . . . it gave me a certain satisfaction," he admitted.

"You got your revenge on me a long time ago. But why you should need revenge I don't know. . . . Never try to avenge yourself on your wife or your daughters. Wait till you get sons. You all men lurk behind trees for one another with knives and guns and sticks and hit one another with all your might, even though you're avenging things done years ago. . . . And to think I still feel attached to you for old times' sake, as you say."

"I didn't wrong you," he declared. "It was you who did me wrong. But I don't want revenge at all. I just felt that you owed me something. We were all but engaged, weren't we? I can't stay here talking. I've got to go."

"You don't have to go right away, Michael."

Believing that he detected a threat in her voice he decided to remain. But being too embarrassed to speak first he allowed silence to settle between them.

"You wouldn't have me when I was pure," Genetha said at last. "Now I'm a slut you behave like an animal —"

"I . . ." he broke in.

She allowed him time to continue, but he had nothing to add.

"I'll tell you two stories, Michael. My younger aunt is nice. She's always telling me family stories. A few days ago she told me about their brother. I didn't even know I had an uncle; but they're not supposed to talk about him. When he was still at school he was always saying, 'All I want is a gun and a dog.' My grandfather doted on him and wouldn't shut him up when he talked like that, although Grandmother and my aunts were frightened at his threats to run away as soon as he could afford to buy a gun and a dog. He passed all his exams with distinction, and at eighteen left school to go abroad to study medicine. But during the holidays he went off into the bush – just as he said he would do – with an old hunting gun he bought from the vet who lived next door, Mr Bruce. The last my grandparents and aunts heard of him was that he had married an aboriginal Indian. It's not an exciting story, but it keeps haunting me: a gun and a dog. Do you know Georgetown has more stray dogs. . ."

". . . than any other town of similar size in the world?" Michael mocked her.

". . . and the biggest cemetery in the world?" she went on as if he had not interrupted. "And best of all, the country's got a huge mental hospital and the biggest wooden church in the world. Yes, Michael, while your priggish wife and your priggish children walk about with their noses in the air we are —"

Michael broke into her monologue, protesting. But Genetha replied sharply:

"We are a distressed people, but we know all about pleasure, don't we, Michael? Half the population dance through Old Year's night into New Year's morning, until they all but drop from exhaustion."

Michael made as if to go, but Genetha, with a short, malicious laugh, ordered him to remain with her.

"If you go now I'll follow you home, Michael, and tell your wife what we've been up to."

He stared at her, terrified at the implication of her words. Inwardly he began to go over different plans to slip away if she did carry out her threat.

"What was the second story you were going to tell me?" he asked, in order to appease her.

"Oh . . . the gun and the dog didn't appeal to you. Yet that's what most of you men want. When all is said and done that's what my father wanted, and Boyie. . . . Anyway, you'll like the second story, Michael. My aunt said that a man went abroad and returned with a European wife. Every day she came out with him to his work-place by cab. She then took him home again the same way. And you know what she did while he was at work?"

"What?"

"She waited in the cab all those hours while he was at work,

513

with only the cabbie for company."

"I don't believe it," Michael said. Though his protest was prompted by a need to placate Genetha there was genuine interest in his voice.

"I knew you'd like that one," she told him. "You find that kind of sacrifice exciting. But it doesn't appeal to me. It's the gun and the dog I like in a way I can't explain. Hundreds of porknockers take to the bush in search of gold, yet those who make a fortune hardly ever come back to town. They don't get further than Issano, where they spend their money on the whores. And they go in search of the very gold and diamonds they squandered at Issano. You know why they don't return to town? My aunt thinks that once they've tasted the freedom of the bush there's nothing to come back to. The hinterland, she calls it. To me the question is not why they remain in the bush but why they go at all. What draws them to that wilderness of trees and all the dangers? There's never been a single woman porknocker. Have you ever heard of a woman porknocker?"

Michael shook his head.

"You understand, Michael, for me that's the problem. Freedom and the secret of a settled mind. Because I was 'up there' for six weeks, I can't get a reference and have to take whatever job I'm offered. When I took up with Fingers, Boyie went away. And you wouldn't be content with my friendship: I had to love you. I'm not up to all these rules."

"I didn't abandon you," put in Michael, who did not care to find out what she meant by "up there". "It was you who showed me the door."

"My young aunt," said Genetha, "tells stories, kisses my hand to show how much she cares. But she'd never put herself out to help me. . . . Do you know I used to be a whore, Michael?"

Michael, despite his resolution not to offend, changed his expression involuntarily.

"I used to pick fair in doorways and worked in a whore-shop, undressing for men I'd never seen in my life. After a time I noticed nothing about them, except their teeth. And I'll tell you something. Some of the girls I worked with enjoyed fairing. Like the porknockers they'd never give up the life for the security of marriage. You think if your priggish wife came into a fortune she'd be so docile? My younger aunt is quiet and affectionate, but dangerous. She'd kiss the inside and outside of

514

your hand but she wouldn't lift a finger to help you."

"You were always rebellious," Michael said softly, sensing that her resentment had drained away.

"One day," she said, turning to face him, "I'll discover my hinterland, Michael. And all the wild demons rushing by in their phantom carts wouldn't stop me from travelling there."

They went down the stairs of the pavilion together, she a little behind him, dwarfed by his stature.

Two streets away from the house she asked him, "Why did you offer me the money? Is it because you knew?"

"Knew what?" he asked, even now pretending to be puzzled.

"Oh, nothing. You needn't feel sorry for me. I'm happy with my people."

"Yes," he observed, "you're not as thin as you used to be."

"You see?" she said with a smile.

They took leave of each other, and despite the need she had for him Genetha had no intention of seeing Michael again, while he had already calculated how often he could afford to meet her in future, notwithstanding her threat.

As she skirted the grass verges the most unlikely thoughts passed through her mind. She must hoard the empty jars of night-cream she used to keep the furrows on her face at bay. There was a secret of great importance lying in those jars of soft, cool cream, something that chased away old age and remained in the thin film that lined them when empty.

The first thing she noticed on approaching the house was that the light in the gallery was on. Usually it was left off in order to save money. On coming closer she saw her elder aunt sitting at the window. As soon as Genetha opened the door the aunt said:

"I want to talk to you, Genetha."

Genetha hated being left alone with her older aunt and asked, "Where's Aunt Alice?"

"She's inside. Earlier she got hysterical when she saw the cat trying to deal with a centipede which had come out of the corner and was running across the floor. She's so squeamish! Listen to me, Genetha. It is not seemly for a young woman of your background to go out so heavily made up. And those long earrings! They —"

"I'm sorry, Aunt. I'm a grown woman," Genetha declared.

"If as your aunt I'm not permitted to tell you my feelings about the way you dress then who is?"

"Aunt, I'm a grown woman. I don't need advice on my clothes any more."

"So you're defying me!"

Genetha did not answer, and her aunt, enraged at her unexpected opposition, decided to bide her time.

"Very well, Genetha, I've done what I consider to be my duty." And she spoke with an ominous detachment.

"I'm sorry, Aunt . . . ."

But her aunt got up with a false smile and excused herself.

Genetha waited for the first opportunity to confess to her younger aunt what she had done on Palpree Down and in the pavilion by the sea, and when she did she was surprised at her horrified reaction. She had overestimated her Aunt Alice's broadmindedness and thanked God she stopped short of telling her about her way of life in Tiger Bay and at Esther's establishment.

The estrangement from her Aunt Deborah had brought with it the need to get closer to the younger aunt, who herself was suffering from her sister's growing power mania. Although according to the old man's recently made will their father's property would belong to the two sisters jointly after his death, Deborah had managed to persuade him since to sign a power of attorney in her favour, as he was incapable of going out to draw his pension or cash the coupons on his debentures when interest fell due. The possession of that piece of paper had accelerated the process of the growing authoritarian manner in which she managed the house.

Genetha did not again make the mistake of confiding in Alice, and whenever she went out to still the hunger of her flesh she pretended that she was going to visit her paternal aunt. And as time went by she and Aunt Alice grew even closer, to the chagrin of her Aunt Deborah, whose dislike for her niece, aroused by her defiance, waxed into hatred.

Genetha learned a good deal from Aunt Alice about her sister. Soon after Genetha's mother got married she took up with a gentleman who, like Genetha's father, came to visit her at the house. But Genetha's grandfather found fault with him, especially with the shoes he usually wore.

"Who ever heard of a decent young man wearing two-toned shoes?" he used to say.

She gave up the young man, only to take up with another

who was promptly criticized by her father as being too small in stature for her. The elder aunt decided to have it out with her father, but he declared that she could marry "who she damned well pleased". Yet when a third young man came visiting, he ignored him completely, causing Deborah the most acute embarrassment. No man ever came to see her after that and she, out of pride perhaps, never broached the subject with her father again.

Genetha, in time, learned many things from her Aunt Alice, only because she too was suffering at Deborah's hands, and gained satisfaction from reducing her sister in the niece's estimation. In her opinion, it was a good thing that her sister had never married, because she had been as demanding with young men as she was with everyone else. It was possible that she was afraid of marrying, knowing that she could never yield to a man's authority. After all, she responded all too readily to their father's criticisms of the male visitors.

Genetha also learned things about her grandfather; that, for instance, he had been contributing to the Burial Society for twenty-five years, since he was fifty, so that when he died he would be given an expensive funeral.

And so things went, the rift between Genetha and her aunt Deborah widening while her relations with the younger aunt were being cemented with the passing months.

21. Gold Bangles

One evening when the scent of the last August rains was in the air, Genetha's elder aunt settled in a rocking-chair with her crochet basket a few feet from the piano, where Alice was playing a piece by Granados. So peaceful was the night and so apt the music that Deborah put down her work and lay back in the chair. Outside, the occasional thud of the coconut-seller's cutlass opening up a fruit came through the window, or the hum of a car engine from Vlissingen Road.

"I think someone's outside," Alice said, stopping in the middle of a phrase.

"I didn't hear anything," rejoined her sister, who nevertheless got up and went to the front.

"Can I come up?" a woman standing at the gate asked.

"You want to see someone?"

"Yes, Miss Genetha Armstrong," came the reply.

"I see . . . . She isn't here; she's gone out."

"Will she be long?"

"No, I suppose not," Deborah said, reluctantly.

"Can I wait?"

"Yes, of course."

The woman, dressed with a certain ostentatious elegance, came up the stairs and through the door opened for her.

It was Esther, who recognized Deborah at once, recalling her stay at the house in Agricola after Rohan's birth, when she and Genetha's father fell out.

Alice got up from the piano and excused herself, while Deborah offered Esther a chair in the gallery, after turning on the electric light.

Esther was wearing a ring on every finger of her left hand while on her right arm were several gold bangles; and Deborah, at once repelled and fascinated by her attire, could not resist asking who she was.

"You don't know me. I'm sure you don't."

"Do you mind excusing me?" Deborah asked. She got up to join her sister in the kitchen.

"She knows Genetha," said Deborah to her sister. "You see how she makes up lately when she goes out. I'm not surprised, if she consorts with women like that. She's wearing a fortune in jewellery . . . a woman like that."

Alice shrugged her shoulders. She was as intrigued as Deborah, but afraid that her interest in the visitor might be detrimental to Genetha.

The two sisters stood watching Esther from the kitchen; but if Deborah hoped that Genetha would come back soon so that she could hear them in conversation, Alice prayed that her niece would stay away until the stranger left.

"Go and keep her company," Alice suggested to her sister, who declined.

"You go, I'll make her something."

Dutifully, Alice joined Esther in the gallery and began talking to her, avoiding any mention of Genetha's name.

It was while making sweet chocolate for the visitor that Deborah hit upon the plan to follow her if she left before Genetha came home. After putting a pan of milk on the fire she came back and went into the bedroom she shared with her sister, where she took out a hat to wear as a disguise in case Esther saw her.

Deborah could not explain to herself the extraordinary effect the woman made on her, and even when the chocolate was ready she stood watching her from the kitchen, across the intervening space of the large drawing-room with its open piano and abandoned crochet basket.

On bringing Esther the drink Deborah said, "She should be back any time now," her normally supercilious manner replaced by a nervous uncertainty.

But an hour passed and Genetha had still not returned. Alice would have liked to go back to the piano, for the visitor, uncommunicative and even haughty, intimidated her. But she could not leave the gallery unless Deborah was prepared to take her turn with the stranger.

Another hour passed and when Alice repeated that she had no idea what had happened to her niece Esther got up and declared that she would not wait any longer.

"Tell her for me," Esther said, "that Netta's friend came to see her and invited her round to the house."

"Of course," Alice promised, and accompanied her to the gate, which was "not easy to close", she told the visitor.

Alice came upstairs to find her sister with her hat on and looking out of the window after the visitor, who had turned into Laluni Street.

"What's the matter with you?" asked Alice.

"I'll tell you when I come back," said Deborah, who hastily left the house to follow Esther.

The mild evening hour had given way to a gusty night and Deborah cursed herself for not securing her hat more firmly on her head. Her right hand holding down the incongruous-looking head-gear she swept down Laluni Street as quickly as she could, so as not to lose the stranger, who was walking more briskly than she anticipated and had already crossed the next road parallel to Irving Street.

Esther did not turn again until she came to Foreshaw Street and then Deborah had to increase her pace so as not to lose her. Finally, in Regent Street, she could follow at a much closer distance, protected from the possibility of detection by the large number of pedestrians on the pavement and the noise of the cars on the road.

Once in South Road Deborah allowed Esther to increase the distance between them, for the street was practically deserted; but as soon as the latter turned into a yard she hurried up, even at the risk of being seen.

To her surprise the house was large and well-kept, and its bottom-house enclosed by lattice work. But her suspicions about Esther were aroused once more when there was a burst of loud laughter, followed by the appearance at the window of a young woman with a cigarette in her hand. Deborah only had time to note the lot number on the gate before she went past the house.

She turned east at the corner and made for home, where she found that Genetha had not yet returned.

Deborah told Alice of her suspicions and of the house where the stranger appeared to live.

"The young woman at the window was definitely not her daughter," Deborah observed.

"Why you're so anxious to find out?" Alice asked her.

"Where does Genetha go at night? Why does she make up like that and put on those earrings?"

"But she does everything you tell her to," Alice protested, fearing for her niece.

"She is a disgrace! And what about this woman?" asked Deborah. "I'll ask cook to find out who lives in the house. We'll see," she added.

Genetha came back home at half past midnight, later than she had ever done before. No one, apparently, had been concerned about her absence and so she stayed up to listen to the mysterious sounds of night-time and wonder what strange processes were at work within her, driving her on to a state of such utter indifference that she cared nothing for the elder aunt's veiled allusions to her position in the house.

When it became evident that Deborah was pursuing a vendetta against her she no longer minded to appease her, and even Alice's sympathy and her grandfather's affectionate ways were not enough to make up for the other's hostility.

In any case, if her elder aunt had done nothing, she, Genetha, would be obliged to break away from the family. Whatever her needs were – and she herself was uncertain what they were – they could not be satisfied in that house. Neither her grandmother, withdrawn and aloof, nor her Aunt Deborah were the real cause of her feeling of estrangement. It was rather a desert-like bareness, on which their very lifestyle was grounded, an absence of joy, of quarrels and reconciliations. Her younger aunt's affectionate spirit quailed before her sister's sternness, while her grandfather's whimsical nature was never allowed to flourish.

Perhaps Esther had suspected all this when she told Bigfoot that Genetha would come back to the brothel. Or perhaps she knew that any woman who set out on that road would have to travel along it to the very end.

Whatever happened, though, Genetha was determined never to return to the brothel. Somehow she must travel another road and if this was not possible she now had the will to end her life; and the only impediment to this course was her belief that such an act would be sinful. She knew that there was an after-life and believed that in another world she would be reunited with her parents and Boyie. Turning her hand against herself might rob her of the chance of such a reunion.

It was hard to believe that her dear mother had grown up in that house, had endured the punishments meted out by a vindictive sister and learned to shape her gestures to a sterile tradition.

So silent was the night that Genetha could hear the sea pounding the shore nearly a mile away, a shore she imagined littered with debris brought down by the rivers from the great forests of the interior and from the Amazon river, a thousand miles away.

She got up and glanced on the gloom of Laluni Street, its parapet littered with the cast-aside shells of empty coconuts, its houses floating in the shadows like birds in a mist.

Early the next morning Genetha's younger aunt told her of Esther's visit and of her sister's anger; and for the rest of the day the two women waited for the storm to break. But Deborah said nothing and Genetha noticed no change in her behaviour.

Then, just before the evening meal, Genetha saw her carrying in her parents' fare on a tray, and, on glancing at the table, noticed that it was only set for three.

When she and her two aunts sat down to table the air of expectancy was almost palpable and Alice forgot to say grace.

"We haven't said grace yet," Deborah observed icily.

Grace was duly said, and then the sound of the knives and

forks against the plates was so loud – in the absence of conversation and the awareness of a tense atmosphere – it appeared to be deliberately made.

In the middle of the meal the elder aunt, with great ceremony, wiped her mouth with her napkin.

"You had a visitor yesterday, Genetha," she said, having judged the timing of the remark to achieve the greatest effect.

Genetha did not answer.

"A person who refused to give her name," she continued. "And, if my suspicions are justified, had every reason to be silent. Do you know an extravagantly dressed *person* who lives in South Road?"

"I do, Aunt. Her name is Esther and she is very close to me."

"Really? Close?"

"Yes, Aunt. In fact since Mamma died she is the person closest to me, apart f—"

"Never!" exclaimed Deborah. "Never you speak of that *person* in the same breath as your mother. *She* was a lady."

Genetha hung her head.

"I haven't yet found out," Deborah pursued, almost bursting with rage, "what goes on in that house in South Road. . . ."

"It's a brothel, Aunt," Genetha answered without defiance.

"A. . . ."

"Yes, Aunt. I used to work there, and it was my home for —"

"Be quiet! You . . . creature! You're no niece of mine. O Lord in Heaven! To think we're harbouring you. . . ."

"Aunt, I'm looking . . . ." But she, in turn, was not allowed to finish.

"Your mother —"

"My mother!" screamed Genetha. "You never even came to see her once. None of you!"

And Genetha broke off to look at her other aunt.

"It's you who mustn't call my mother's name," she continued. "My name is Armstrong and that was my mother's name!"

"I won't compete with you in shouting," Deborah said with a smile of triumph. "But I must correct you. Your mother was no Armstrong. That was your father's name. We are forced, when we get married, to bear the names of men a whole lifetime . . . . And I *did* come to take care of you when your brother was born and you were two years old and not yet so impertinent. But your father insulted me. That's why neither I nor your Aunt

Alice ever came again. But ingratitude is a vice that becomes you. . . ."

Genetha was looking past her aunt, vacantly staring at the wall behind her, as if she were alone and reflecting on a problem of incalculable weightiness. She began to weep, silently, crushed by the torrent of reproaches heaped upon her and the ignominy she had brought to her father's name. All the nights she had left the house to seek the company of strange men, enveloped in a kind of numbness that protected her from the enormity of her conduct, came back to her vividly: the moonlit night on Palpree Dam, the encounter with Michael, the fleeting, secret meetings with other men assaulted her memory, and the way they behaved afterwards. Some cursed her for not wishing to see them again; others offered her money, while others fled from her as if she was possessed of a score of devils. Genetha recalled how rapidly she had matured after leaving school and starting work, her preoccupation with the idea of marriage, and her desire to have girl children so that she could dress them up.

Suddenly her elder aunt's hectoring words broke in on her reflections and she heard that she was obliged to leave by the weekend. Genetha held it against Aunt Alice that she did not speak up for her. All her attentions, all her protestations of affection had come to nothing in the face of her sister's harshness. Her weakness had rendered her incapable of loyalty.

"As I've said," declared Genetha, "I've started looking for a place. At least that's what I wanted to say."

Deborah, as if that assurance had been the object of her tirade, got up and left the table to her sister and niece, who found nothing to say to each other, for all the affectionate exchanges of the long months Genetha had stayed in the house had been erased with the silent betrayal.

Genetha carefully placed her knife and fork together, as she had been taught to do, with that involuntary action that informs all acts inculcated in the minds of young children as the indispensable equipment of gentility.

Nothing was said between them, and, urged by an unspoken understanding, they got up simultaneously and started to clear the table.

Genetha's grandfather came out, as was his custom, when the heat of the day had settled and the trade winds blew in from the sea over the warmer land. Genetha helped him to his armchair;

but as she was about to go off he asked her to sit beside him.

"When my grandfather died," he said, "the pictures were turned to the wall and all the mirrors in the house were covered. We were sitting in the drawing-room, all of us except my younger sister. Suddenly there was a scream from inside. We rushed in and saw her – she was nine then – in hysterics on the floor; and when we asked her what had happened she couldn't answer. But the cloth that covered the mirror on the chest-of-drawers had fallen off and the mirror was left exposed. I don't know why, looking back now, but we stood staring at that mirror as if it was a gateway to somewhere. I'll never forget that. Oh! I could tell you scores of stories like that. . . . Do you know? Last night . . . I saw my death. It came out, emerged from a dense wall of smoke and started coming towards me. I shouted, 'Halt!' But it kept coming on until it was so near I couldn't see it any more . . . . I am dead and grateful for the respite, for the chance to look at familiar things for the last time. . . . One day you will marry and have children. He will marry you for your gentle eyes and make you happy. There's no doubt that *you* will make him happy."

He fell back into his usual silence, the same silence which his wife inhabited like a home. Genetha and he sat alone in the gallery, framed by the casement windows and walls. She felt that a part of her had never grown up; that some people were still capable of inspiring awe in her, an almost physical reverence that small children have for grown-ups, who tower like giants above them.

He nodded off and Genetha quietly got up and went to sit alone on the stairs.

22. Rats

At the end of the week Genetha moved out, taking her grip to her paternal aunt's flat. She had been promised her old Albouystown room when the man who now lived in it went home to Truly Island; and the landlord, who could not say whether he was to leave in a week's or a month's time, said he would let her know when she could move in.

Mercifully, she was able to move in less than a fortnight afterwards; for if life at her maternal aunts' house had its harsh side, here there was no pleasantness whatsoever. Apart from the eternal complaints of Genetha's neglect, there was little to eat.

The dilapidated condition of the house in which her aunt lived was accepted as a fact of life by the tenants, so that Genetha's aunt's objections to living in a building with a leaking sewage pipe and a yard infested with rats appeared excessive to them. Most of the tenants, with but a toehold in the capital, saw the quarter as a stepping-stone to a more desirable life.

But after moving out Genetha went back to see her regularly, whether in recognition of the fact that she was the last blood relative whose home was open to her or impelled by sympathy for her, she was unable to say. Yet from then on she went to see her aunt every Friday night until her death many years later, when all the goodness had been extracted from her by the pressures of her solitary existence and all that remained was a crabbed view of life and those around her. And Genetha never discovered the extent of her aunt's degeneracy, for she had learned to close an ear to everything she said about what she owned – knowing that they would end with her father's misconduct – even to the tales of her once magnificent house in the country.

When Genetha was back in the hovel in Albouystown she asked herself if she had not been hasty in crossing her Aunt Deborah, whose table overflowed with good things. The week before she left she and Alice had baked bread, and as a joke had spread it with the cheapest butter, a pink, salted fat that was used in cooking and making nut-butter. They had laughed while eating, as if the thought of cheap butter was a hilarious artless joke.

Genetha bought a second-hand lamp, trimmed the wick and set it up in the old place on the table. She disposed her meagre belongings in the room as before, reinforced the defective lock on the sash window with a piece of wood and swept out the room with her little hand broom. And bit by bit she settled into her old life, often thinking of Zara, whom the room called to mind.

The following day she tramped the town in search of work, but things seemed to be worse than ever. Even the jobs in cake-shops, which were once there for the choosing, were hard to come by, though no one could live solely on the income they brought in. More women than ever were moving from the country to seek work in town and competition for what was going had become fierce. And when night came and she had found nothing she went to lurk in the vicinity of the South Road brothel until Bigfoot came downstairs to act as watchman during the late hours.

"Eh, eh, mistress! Is you?"

"Hello, Bigfoot. I don't want anyone to know I'm here. I came to borrow some money until I get work."

"Of course. How much you want?"

"Ten dollars, if you've got it. I'm sure I'll find work this week."

"You stay here, mistress. I'll be back in a minute."

Genetha listened for the footsteps of anyone who might be coming down the back or front steps, ready to hide behind one of the brick pillars. Bigfoot seemed to be gone for five minutes or more, but there was no sound of anyone moving about upstairs. Then Genetha remembered that she needed much more than ten dollars, for by the end of the week she had to pay the rent and it was not certain that, even if she found work tomorrow, she would be paid at the end of the first week.

She heard the back door close and took refuge behind a pillar near the back stairs, where it was pitch black.

"Mistress!"

Genetha came out to find Bigfoot carrying a cloth bag. He gave her an envelope and explained that there were fruit in the bag, and bread with cold beef.

"I thought that after I hadn't got in touch with you you wouldn't want to help me," she said.

"But I told you, mistress."

"I thought. . . ."

"I can't come with you tonight. Madame in a bad mood. An' if she know I gone out is going to be the licks of Lisbon."

"I'll be all right," said Genetha. "It's the money I was worried about."

Bigfoot opened the gate for her after checking that no one was at the window. And as Genetha slipped through the half-opened gate he bowed slightly and whispered good-night.

On her way home Genetha recalled how Bigfoot was feared by the girls and his uncompromising attitude towards them. Esther had told her more than once that he was kind. The role he was forced to play in front of them suited his huge frame so well, as did his tone of voice, that Genetha had never really come to terms with his inordinate respect for her.

She recalled, too, the night she and Zara hurried to the latter's home in order to get her parents' consent to go to the Old Year's dance and their disappointment at her father's refusal. She had come back to her room and fallen asleep to the faint sounds of a closing year.

The next day when Genetha had begun to despair of ever finding work she went and sat down in a cake-shop in Werken-Rust, where she ordered a soft drink and a pine tart. The fierce heat of the midday sun had abated somewhat, but the interior of the poorly ventilated cake-shop, which was on the western side of the road and therefore exposed to the morning sun, was oppressively close. Genetha rolled the lump of ice from the drink round her mouth, then took it out to pass it over her lips before drinking the sweet liquid slowly. Afterwards, she felt as thirsty as before and, on an impulse, asked the young woman for a glass of water. She complained of the heat and like that the two got to talking, exchanging bits of information that told them little about each other. Their conversation was interrupted by a young boy who came in to buy a packet of cigarettes. When he went Genetha remarked in the most off-hand manner that she envied the young woman her job.

"You can have it if you want," she remarked with a wave of the hand, not taking Genetha's remark seriously.

It turned out that she lived over the shop and was only helping out her uncle, who had been looking for someone for more than a fortnight. Nobody wanted work like that now, she said, at least not for the money he was prepared to pay. He was stingy and, knowing that he could always count on her to stand in whenever a girl left, he sacked his employees on the slightest pretext.

"But I'm serious about the job," Genetha insisted.

The young woman looked at her in some surprise, but then shrugged her shoulders and suggested that she wait. Her uncle could be back at any time, in a few minutes or at midnight.

After that the young woman was reluctant to talk and Genetha could only sit and wait for her uncle to return. Clients came and went, until it began to rain; and then only the odd child ran in to buy cigarettes or a cake or a soft drink. Opposite there was a shop whose front was open along its entire length, and from the interior of which the faint click of pool balls came.

Opened only in recent months it had enticed the young men of the district, who had taken rapidly to the American game.

Soon after the rain began to fall a car drew up in front of the shop and a man stepped out, slamming the door behind him. It was the proprietor.

The salesgirl promptly introduced him to Genetha, who was hired with little ceremony for a derisory wage.

"You not goin' complain!" he exclaimed, anticipating a protest. "You'll eat my cakes and open the drinks when my back's turned anyway."

And with that the proprietor lifted up the flap of the counter and went into the back shop where he rummaged about among the boxes before coming out again to drive off in the rain.

"When am I to start?" Genetha asked the young woman, disconcerted by the rudeness of her new employer.

"Tomorrow!" she exclaimed in surprise.

"What time?"

"Seven. He does open at six o'clock, but you don't got to come before seven."

So Genetha came back to step on the treadmill from which she descended when she went to live with her maternal aunts.

Nearly all she earned the first week went to pay back Bigfoot, who would have refused to accept the money, had she let him. And this time she stayed to talk to him for more than an hour, no longer afflicted by the embarrassment she usually felt in his company. Esther had been ill and was now convalescing in her room on the top floor. Shola was now married and was living in Houston and came to Georgetown daily to follow a course in hairdressing, on completion of which she intended to set up the first hairdressing establishment in her husband's village. Bigfoot thought she was not really married, but the news did not fail to impress Netta, who had been sulking ever since she heard it.

Bigfoot wanted her to go up and see Esther, but Genetha decided against it.

"You don't understand," Genetha told him. "I want to cut myself off completely. In the end people'll forget I was in the business and I'll be able to work again. I can't take the chance."

And she told him what happened when she attended the interview for the office job.

Above her head she heard the windows being closed and bolted and the jalousies being secured with their metal pins, and the sound of footsteps crossing and re-crossing the spacious drawing-room. The ray of light that fell on the boards of the house opposite disappeared when the last drawing-room bulb went out, and after the girl who was responsible for locking up went upstairs to the top storey a long, homely silence fell on that area of night. In Vlissingen Road the cinema must long since have emptied, and the hoardings advertising their East Indian films under the street lamps must now dominate the entrance to New Town, with their fleshy heroes and voluptuous heroines.

In the end Genetha went home alone, refusing Bigfoot's offer to accompany her. There was a danger in his obligingness, the beginning of a sort of dependence that did not accord with her bid for self-sufficiency.

From the very beginning of her move back to the area Genetha knew that the itch that had taken her in her aunts' house – the irresistible urge to sleep with strange men, which somehow seemed connected with that house – had gone. In retrospect the episodes were incredible, and in them she no longer recognized herself. In any case the old feelings of impotence crept back with the lack of the diet she could not afford and the sweet cakes she ate at the shop.

Occasionally, after twelve hours at the shop and a meal cooked on a kerosene burner her aunts had allowed her to take away, Genetha would go down to one of the new eating places in Albouystown. There she felt less conspicuous among the new wave of East Indians arriving from the sugar estates than among her own people, one of whom sooner or later would point a finger at her; sometimes she even ate there, at a cost not much greater than her own meal.

After a time she gave up cooking for herself altogether and appeared in the cook-shop at about a quarter past seven, when her plate of rice and curry was promptly placed before her on the uncovered metal table with its plaques of rust.

And the old signs of malnutrition began to reappear: first the brittle nails, then the lack-lustre skin, and finally the white corners of her mouth, offensive-looking slits associated with the diseased and underprivileged.

In the old days there was Zara, and even after they became estranged, a memory of friendship and the belief, unprofessed though it was, that one day it would be repaired. Now she walked the street, head down, haggard and overcome with an indescribable fatigue. All her liaisons were strewn in the wake of the present like jetsam, becoming smaller and smaller with the increasing distance. Even Boyie, the most enduring memory, no longer crossed her thoughts or, if he did, only like the swift flight of a small bird.

Sometimes, overwhelmed by her loneliness, Genetha would think of joining the church, not the Methodist – her mother's religion and her own in the early days – but the Catholic, with its scent of incense, its mysteries and above all its weeping candles. But something held her back, a vision, as it were, of a kind of degradation, as irredeemable as her years as a prostitute. She would sometimes lurk in the shadows of the brothel, in search of something, some part of herself perhaps, or of her family, or even Michael, who once believed that without her life would be unbearable.

At other times she would take her Bible from her grip and read a part that she had been in the habit of reading to her father when he was ill and began to stink like a corpse:

"For that which befalleth the sons of men befalleth beasts; even one thing befalleth them: as the one dieth, so dieth the other; yea, they have all one breath; so that a man hath no pre-eminence above a beast: for all is vanity.

"All go into one place; all are of dust, and all turn to dust again.

"Who knoweth the spirit of man. . . ."

The first time she looked at herself naked in the mirror – she was thirteen – she had done, it seemed to her, a secretive thing, for which she ought to have asked her mother's permission. And the next time the minister spoke at church of sin she trembled with dread that he somehow knew what she had done and that she was the object of his sermon. Was she now alone because of her past? Was there the possibility of atonement?

One evening in the middle of her meal in the cook-shop Genetha made up her mind once and for all that she would go and see the priest at the Brickdam Cathedral, the same one who had irritated her so much. She would wait a full week and if at the end of that time she was oppressed by the same questions she would see him.

And with that decision came the sensation of excitement

experienced before a long journey to another country. She ordered a beer and then another, and to the proprietor's question about the state of her pocket she laughed and made a humorous reply.

"First time I see you laugh," a middle-aged man playing cards at another table observed.

Genetha laughed again without turning round.

"Gi'e the lady another beer, Josh," ordered the middle-aged man, when Genetha had emptied her glass.

"No, no. I'm not a drinker," she protested.

The proprietor took no notice and in a trice he had opened a bottle and was pouring it out into a glass over her shoulder.

Intrigued by Genetha's unexpected sociability the card-players plied her with beer, and after her fifth joined her at her table.

"We thought you was too great to talk to, lady," said the one who first ordered her a beer.

"I thought you didn't like women," she retorted, her remark raising a guffaw among the men.

Genetha dared not confess how overwhelmed she was by their attention. At first the effect of the alcohol was to make her drop her mask. But as she drank more she exaggerated her companions' kindness in a way that was all too apparent to the proprietor.

"A'right, a'right, ease up. She in' from the Punt Trench, you know," he said, referring to an East Indian settlement of tenements and hovels.

But Genetha, under the increasing influence of the beer, was laughing and talking with the men as if she had known them for years.

Protesting when the proprietor refused to serve them more beer she got up and fetched the bottle herself from the counter and brought it back to the men, who had ceased drinking. When she faltered at the table one of the men got up and pulled out her seat for her, winking at the others as he did so.

"Is who goin' take you home, eh?" the proprietor asked, concerned lest he offended her companions.

"I only live down the road," Genetha protested. "No one . . . ."

"I goin' see you home, missie," the middle-aged man said gravely. Sweat was pouring from his face and, as the proprietor saw it, he had only stopped drinking with one aim in mind.

The proprietor washed his hands of the matter and settled into his chair, his head disappearing behind the assorted bottles on the counter. His wife had retired when meals were no longer sold, leaving him to serve and shut up shop after the customers went home. Women hardly ever stayed so late, so that Genetha's presence disconcerted him, especially as he believed that the three men had planned to follow her home. The district was full of East Indian men without women, and for whom the prospect of marrying was remote.

More than an hour passed, during which time the footfalls of passers-by became rarer and finally ceased altogether. The proprietor stood up behind his counter, impatient to close his shop, but at the same time unwilling to offend his regular customers.

"I want shut me shop!" he burst out in the end, unable to impress them with his stares.

Genetha was sitting, head bent over her arms, which were stretched out on the table in the posture of someone engaging in exercises. The three men looked at her, exchanged glances and then got up.

"You t'ink we goin' interfere with she or somet'ing?" asked the boldest of the East Indians.

They filed out of the shop without another glance at Genetha.

"You better wait a lil bit, lady," said the shopkeeper. "They does live at Ramsaroop house, so you never know."

Ramsaroop was the owner of the Dar'm Saala, a doss-house in Albouystown where beggars and the homeless put up for the night. The proprietor had been told that one of the men had at some time in the past put up there, and it was on this information that he based his remark that they were all living there at the moment.

A little while later he went and peered out of the window, but saw no one in the mist which had descended in the last couple of hours, and through which an empty dray-cart and a row of palings could barely be seen.

"I think they gone," he said, without turning round, "but you better wait a lil bit more."

Genetha was now sitting up, just able to concentrate on the proprietor's words and the bearing they had on her short trip down the road.

A faint odour of damp came through the open front of the

shop, and the muffled yapping of stray dogs which broke the stillness from time to time sounded like echoes from another place. No one was about in this late hour of night and the lamp-light, usually visible as a yellow patch on the bridge, was sucked up by the dank mist, leaving the boards in darkness. At best a sombre quarter, this portion of Albouystown now presented the aspect of an entrance to an eerie land.

"I shutting up now," he reminded Genetha. "If you want me advice, don' mix with them people any more."

She got up with the assistance of the proprietor, who, before he could ask how she might manage was told, "I know the way home, thank you. I don't need any help."

Once out in the damp air, she shuddered and folded her arms, then looked around her to take stock of her position in relation to the street which she had to walk. She then set off in the gloom, guided more by her instinct to make for the street-lamp a hundred yards away then by the houses along the road.

With each step the mist rolled away before her, unveiling now an empty cart, now a garbage square littered with vegetable peel and paper, and continually the thick, uneven grass of the parapet. Genetha walked slowly in an effort to counteract the slight swaying of her body. About halfway to the house a light in a house on the other side of the road came on and almost at once was put out again.

"Missie?"

Thinking she could hear someone calling in the mist she looked about her, but could see nothing. The street lamp in front of her house was now only about thirty yards ahead and, nudged into action by a sudden fear, she took it into her head to run for it, only to find that she was not even in a condition to walk more quickly.

"Missie!" came the voice again, in an insistent, threatening tone.

This time she stopped.

"Where're you?" she said, just audibly enough to be heard by anyone within a few yards of her.

"Over here," the voice came again. "On the other side."

"I'm home now, thank you," Genetha called out, trying to be conciliatory.

"No, missie, you live further down there," came the voice again.

And with that the three men from the shop appeared to climb out of the gutter on the other side of the road.

Genetha set off again without answering.

"Me friend want fo' ask you somet'ing," the one who had said nothing to her all night now declared.

They surrounded her, preventing her from going any further.

Now that Genetha felt that she was capable of running, her way was barred by the burliest of the three.

"Hold she," one said aloud, "then I goin' hold she for you."

The one behind Genetha grabbed hold of her from the back, but then, without warning, she let out a shriek so terrible that within a few seconds lights began to go on in houses on both sides of the street.

Only the man in front of her reacted at once: he took to his heels in the direction of the shop, leaving the other two momentarily dazed by Genetha's reaction. Then they too made off almost immediately behind their friend.

"Is wha' happen?" the unseen head of a woman called from an open window.

But Genetha started off again for her house, trembling violently, yet anxious not to be found out as the cause of the disturbance. She only looked back as she turned into her yard and saw the shaft of light from a torch sweeping the road.

In her agitated state she went straight to bed without bothering to take off her clothes. Her head was throbbing violently. Had one of the men struck her? She got up, put on the electric light and looked in the mirror, then, feeling the back of her head, she examined her hand for any trace of blood; but there was nothing.

As she lay back and fell into a doze she heard a voice say:

"My child. . . ."

"I was coming to see you, Father."

"Only when you're alone you come," he said kindly. "How can I take you seriously if you only come when you're alone?"

"When I'm alone there's so much I would like to ask you, Father. But now you're here. . . ."

"I know what you want to know, my child. You want to know about purity, don't you? You soil yourself and the more you do so the stronger your interest in purity becomes. A roof cannot be repaired without much hammering. You must go back the same way you came, my child. You must travel the way of

534

suffering."

"Haven't I suffered enough, Father?"

"Can the measure of suffering ever be filled?" asked the priest.

"Can I be loved, Father?" enquired Genetha timidly.

"Loved?" exploded the priest, his benign expression disappearing under a terrible anger. "Did you not see what love was a moment ago, in the street? Only God's love is worthy of that name. You were sent that experience as a warning, but far from heeding it you still persist in your passion for the flesh, calling it by a name you do not understand."

"I can't go on living like this, Father," Genetha pleaded.

"No, child," he replied, adopting his kindly manner again. "That is why you must join the church, where you will know the unending mercy of Jesus and the example of his mother, the Virgin Mary. As you have known suffering you will know joy, the joy of fulfilment in the bosom of Jesus Christ."

And with that he turned to go.

"Don't go, Father. Don't leave me alone."

The priest spun round, and with an evil smile said:

"Why do you call me 'Father', eh?" And with that he made an obscene gesture with his hands.

"Father!" Genetha exclaimed. "I'm not accustomed to that kind —"

"What? Didn't you entice those poor men in the shop? Didn't you accept their beer, knowing perfectly well why they were offering you it?"

"I didn't —" she began to protest.

"If they had been caught you would have testified against them when in fact it was you who led them on."

"You're not a priest!" she exclaimed. "Are you the Devil?"

He smiled his benign smile again. "Do I look like the Devil, my child?"

"No, no, Father," Genetha hastened to assure him. "But just now — your hands. . . ."

"My hands, child?" he asked, raising both his hands with the palms turned towards her. "These hands are used to bless people, to baptize children and close the eyes of the dead. You were never kindly disposed towards me. Can you remember the first time you came to the cathedral? Your insolence? The Church demands utter subservience, nothing less. Didn't Christ submit to the will of God? How can *you* afford to be insolent?

535

All around me I see nothing but vanity, insolence and upheaval; impossible demands are made by working people, political parties challenge authority. . . . No, my child. The way to salvation is through subservience, not strength of will."

"There's another way, Father," Genetha declared.

"Which?" the priest snapped."

"I dare not say it, Father."

"Do you see how ensnared you are in your insolence?"

"You know, Father, when I was a girl my brother and I used to have identical dreams. . . ."

"Don't babble on like a heathen! Before you seek God you must rid yourself of all superstition."

Genetha burst out laughing in an uncontrollable way and was only brought to her senses again when the priest raised his hand to display the sexual sign.

"Listen to me, you heathen! I'm here to *teach* you, and it is I who should be laughing, not you with your ignorance."

Put out by his violent reaction to her laughter, Genetha suddenly thought she saw him facing and backing her at the same time, and rivulets of water running down the nape of his pale neck. Once she had witnessed a fight outside her parents' house in Albertown and now she remembered the white bubbles oozing from the cutlass-wound one man had received.

"Father, are you all right?" she asked involuntarily.

"Yes, my child. The first time you came to the cathedral . . . the first time. It's never the same again after the first time. . . . We are humans, you know, and no vows of chastity can ever change that. Your insolence that first time was like a whiff of some forbidden drug."

"I was not a Catholic, Father."

"You're still not one now, my child," he reminded her.

"But I *want* to be one, with all my heart," Genetha declared, roused by a strange yearning. "I want to serve God and be near to him . . . and touch him."

"Will you come to the cathedral then?" the priest asked, betraying his eagerness. "On Monday?"

"Yes, Father."

"Very well, my child. I will be expecting you."

And, with an ambiguous gesture, he vanished.

23. A Mountain of Food

The following evening, Genetha cooked for herself. So shaken had she been by the experience of the previous night that she made up her mind to avoid the cook-shop for a couple of weeks. After that she intended only to eat there and leave immediately after the meal.

It was Friday and the proprietor of the cake-shop where she worked did not pay her her full wage. She had to wait until Monday for the rest, he told her, Genetha was in the habit of taking a loaf of bread or a bottle of stout for her paternal aunt when she went visiting on Friday nights. But tonight she would have to go empty-handed, she thought. She recalled the mist of the night before and wondered whether it would be like that on her way back home.

It was a cool, starless n'ght, its silence broken by the occasional voices of passers-by or the clinking of harness as a late donkey cart was unhitched. Genetha looked out of the window for any sign of mist or rain, but the only indication of an unfriendly evening was a thin veil of cloud over the sky. The blind of the single window on the front of the house opposite was down to reveal the profile of the old woman who lived there, puffing away at a tiny clay pipe. A figure of a well-dressed woman appeared from the direction of town and slowed down to survey the houses on Genetha's side of the road. Genetha made up her mind to leave at once and come back as soon as her aunt would allow her.

Having changed into her only other decent skirt she was about to pick up her bag when there was a knock on the door. Immediately Genetha thought of Zara and she rushed to open the door. It was Esther, taller in appearance, with a tasselled shawl round her shoulders.

"Well, well," she said. "You don't come to see me, so I've come to see you."

"You're the last person I expected to see," Genetha told her.

She let the older woman in and cleared the bed so that she could sit on it.

"You were going out?"

"Yes." And Genetha explained how she was in the habit of looking up her paternal aunt every Friday night.

"I'll only stay a while, then I'll come with you to her gate.

537

You don't mind?"

"It's just that I. . . ."

"What?" asked Esther.

"Nothing."

Esther fingered the bed-covers, passed her hands over the table next to Genetha's bed and examined the wretched furniture with her eyes.

"You go to see Bigfoot, your aunts and everybody else, but not me," Esther complained.

"Who told you I was living here?" Genetha enquired.

"Your aunt."

"In Queenstown?"

"No. Them? They haven't changed. The one time I went to see you there they made me feel like a leper. They kept staring at me and asking all sorts of foolish questions. What do I care? I can buy them out. . . . It was your other aunt."

"So you came to seek me out, Esther, and flaunt your jewellery. You can buy me out, as you can see."

Genetha cast her eyes round the room.

"I came to see you, not to seek you out," Esther protested.

"My life," Genetha declared, sitting down on the bed next to Esther, "is nothing. Look!" she exclaimed, roused to anger by Esther's manner. "Don't misunderstand me. I have nothing, but I'm free. All I need is a full stomach. I've forgotten my family, and my aunts mean nothing to me. You'll never understand what I mean, Esther."

"I. . . ."

"You'll never understand! You spent your life serving other people. Even now your establishment's owned by a stranger living abroad."

"And how do you intend filling your stomach?" Esther asked sarcastically.

"I will. In a couple of months I'll be working again."

Esther contemplated the wasted, pathetic figure of her former mistress's daughter, the sunken eyes and premature lines in her dried-out face and made up her mind not to quarrel with her.

"Try getting a job looking like that and you'll see what'll happen to you!"

"I know why you came to see me," Genetha said resentfully.

"I came to see you for the same reason I came years ago . . . . I used to undress you when you were a girl. And even when you

538

were old enough to comb your hair I used to comb it for you. I'm not made of wood. I'm not your mother."

"You can never forget that, can you? You'll carry your resentment to your grave. I bet you take it out from time to time and examine it like a hoard of jewellery. . . . . It's the sign of a mean soul."

Esther remained silent, angry that the enormity of Genetha's mother's conduct should be dismissed in such a way. She, Esther, was mean in Genetha's eyes, while there were no harsh words for her mother. It was this arrogance in the Armstrong women that routed her. She recalled the visit of Deborah to Agricola, when Genetha was a little girl. Mrs Armstrong accused her sister of behaving arrogantly towards Mr Armstrong, failing to understand that it was a trait shared by her whole family. Deborah's contempt for her brother-in-law's words and her conviction that even in his own house he should know his place had angered her sister beyond measure.

Unable to quell the flood of resentment Esther said:

"One day you'll come to me after you've done the round of your good aunts, your blood relatives. And I'll take you in as if your mother had never misused me and. . . ."

"That's what Bigfoot said," Genetha broke in. "But you'll never have that satisfaction."

Genetha's anger gave her face the appearance of a grotesque mask and Esther, remembering the child's soft skin and affectionate nature, felt an immense sympathy for her.

"This is for you," she said, bending down to pick up a cloth bag at her feet.

Esther, seeing that Genetha did not intend opening the bag, got up and emptied it of its contents. Fruit, salt, tinned food and other foodstuffs were piled in a corner on the floor.

"Put it all back," said Genetha quietly. "I don't want it."

"No, it's food," objected Esther.

"Put it back. I don't want it."

"No!" exclaimed Esther. "It's food."

"Put it back!" Genetha burst out. "Food! Food! I'm not obsessed with food. Put it all back in your dirty bag and get out of here! Leave me in peace. I never came and sought you out. What do you want with me? My mother sent you away and you keep coming back like a dog. Get out of my room, you stray dog! Everything about you is vulgar. You dress like a whore;

539

you drink wine, even though you don't like it. You think that dressing me as a girl gives you the right to follow me around? Take your hatred and old resentments to the men you've gone with. Take them to Bigfoot, who'll do whatever you ask him because he's got to eat. I don't have to drink wine and eat brown bread!"

Esther waited until Genetha had finished, then began replacing the mountain of food in her bag, carefully and deliberately, to ensure that it should all fit. Meanwhile Genetha stood with her back turned to her, in an attitude which indicated that she would have her finish as quickly as possible, so that she could go out on her business.

In the end everything was put back. Esther picked up her bag and went out and as she closed the door Genetha started weeping in that undemonstrative, uncontrollable way which took her as a girl when, overcome by frustration, unable to assert herself as Boyie used to, she would succumb to the need for tears. Her humiliation at Esther's restraint in the face of her outburst, her intense loneliness and the belief that she was beyond redemption were too much for her.

As soon as she was certain that Esther was out of sight Genetha left to visit her aunt, without any thought of the weather she would encounter on her way home or the possibility of being molested.

Once out of Albouystown and she could feel the pavement underfoot and could see her own shadow lengthen and shorten between the street lamps, placed at more frequent intervals than in the quarter where she lived, she shed her depression as a garment that was unsuitable in a certain place, or on a certain occasion. Cars rushed past her, their headlamps like beacons, their engines roaring momentarily, only to fade in the distance. She turned down the street that would take her to her aunt's house, hidden behind two other, more presentable cottages. The city was growing not outwards, but in its back yards, in its bowels as it were, at the expense of fruit trees and yard space.

24. The Cathedral

The day came for Genetha to go to see the priest. She had informed her employer that she was feeling unwell and that if

540

she did not come to work on Monday he should understand. Genetha had set so much store by her "confession" on Monday that she was ready to run the risk of losing her job.

To make certain that there was no hitch she waited for the same hour as the last time she went to the cathedral.

As she walked by the eastern façade with its well-maintained flower-beds she brushed a finger lightly against the iron railings, wondering the while what would come out of her visit. If there were a number of women waiting to confess he would probably dismiss her with the minimum of conversation.

The pavement came to an end at the corner to give way to the pitch road, glistening from a recent shower and from which a vapour rose as from the vent of a laundry. Across the way the pillar-box stood like a strange red growth in the broad grass verge.

Genetha turned into the avenue of shade-trees, then into the grounds of the cathedral. An old woman was coming down the concrete steps, sideways, as if afraid that she might slip on the wet stairs. Apprehensive about her visit, Genetha asked the woman if the priest was there; and learning that he was she hesitated, filled with the urge to turn tail and flee.

"It's so hot outside," the old woman remarked. "But inside it in' warm up yet."

The woman went on her way, leaving Genetha standing on the stairs, looking backward for no reason at all.

The church was indeed cold and the few worshippers were almost all wearing raincoats. The music from the organ appeared to be rising from beneath the church, while the cubicle seemed smaller than the last time and smelt faintly of sweat.

"Do you remember me, Father?" asked Genetha.

"I do, I do. But you come only when you need us, my child."

And then, unaccountably, as if she had been directed to speak by someone whom she dared not disobey, Genetha became offensive.

"I don't need you," she declared.

"Pride does not suit you. You are not by nature a proud person. Why do you pretend to be what you're not?"

Genetha did not answer. She had no slip on and the thin material clung to her body.

"Can I ask you a question?" she said.

"You're here to confess your sins, not to ask questions," the priest answered sharply.

"Then why didn't you send me away the last time?"

"I felt sorry for you . . . and I hoped you would become a Catholic."

"Can I ask you the question?" Genetha persisted.

"Go on."

"Why are all Catholic priests foreigners?"

A long silence followed.

"There are local priests in some countries. But if there were local priests here would you respect them?" he answered finally.

"I respected my teachers, and my father and my mother," Genetha retorted truculently.

"A priest is not your father or even your teacher. He is God's representative."

"I'm sorry I came," Genetha told him. "The last time I left feeling you had given me something. I didn't want to admit it to myself then. . . . Last night I dreamed you were the Devil."

The priest stiffened, astonished at her hostility. His face was pink, marred, as it seemed, by a permanent blush.

"I feel sorry for you," he said.

"You can't feel sorry for me, Father. You don't know me."

"You are one of God's creatures," he said.

"When I'm alone," said Genetha, "I long for my mother and father and a man I once knew. He was handsome and strong. But I didn't know how to keep him. He walked all over me and took away everything I had. . . . If I had a child I'd teach it all about the pleasures of the flesh, and especially how to survive in your world."

"You measure survival by material standards," said the priest.

"I've got to eat or I'll get sick and die."

"And then?" he asked, his self-satisfied manner again beginning to come to the fore.

"And then I don't care."

"It's not food you need," he declared, shaking his head in sympathy for her.

Genetha noticed that his eyes were continually sinking.

"You see how thin my knees are?" she said, lifting her skirt two or three inches above the knees.

The priest closed his eyes and said, "You don't understand, my child. I'm beyond temptation."

Genetha pulled down her skirt.

"God sent you to test me," he observed. "There is something disturbing about your presence. I don't think ill of you, my child. You're sick and need help."

"I told you so, but you wouldn't believe me."

"Will you join the church?" he asked kindly. He was himself again.

"I don't know, Father. I want to, but something's holding me back."

"Confess that you didn't mean what you said about the way you'd bring up a child," he invited.

There was a long pause before Genetha answered.

"I meant it," she said.

"I don't believe you. It can't be true."

Genetha got up and left the cubicle, disgusted by her own behaviour and by her futile conversation with the priest.

Outside, in the street, a dray-cart pulled by two donkeys with their heads down made its way through the drizzle which had begun to fall while she was in the cathedral. Genetha, dogged by an overwhelming fatigue for the last few months, wanted to sit down but was not able to return to the empty pews. She would have been obliged to pretend that she was praying or meditating, and the thought that the priest might have caught her made her put the idea out of her mind. She leaned against the wall and watched the rain, overcome by a feeling of aloneness that she had often experienced as a girl when her parents went out and left her at home. A young woman standing on the other side of the doorway was also looking out on the street. She wanted to go over and speak to her, but did not know how to.

Did she come to church because she had troubles? Genetha wondered. Her dress was shabby, but well cut. What did it matter?

The young woman turned and caught Genetha staring at her, but she looked away just as the stranger smiled.

The organ stopped. Suddenly the rain began falling more heavily and gradually the porch began to fill with worshippers who could not get away.

Genetha, on a sudden impulse, stepped out into the rain and was drenched before she reached the corner. As she was crossing the road a passing car had to swerve to avoid her. She walked as in a dream, taking corners instinctively.

On reaching home she took off her wet clothes, changed into her nightdress, then drew the worn blanket over her and fell asleep soon afterwards.

At about two o'clock in the morning she was awakened by a knock on the door and when she got up and called out, "Who is it?" a voice answered, "It's me, my child."

It was the priest's voice.

Opening the door she saw him standing on the step. She hesitated a moment before letting him in, then sat down on the bed without a word. The priest, uninvited, sat on the only chair and looked at her as she instinctively arranged her hair.

"How did you get my address?"

"You gave it to me the first time you came, do you remember?"

"I didn't," Genetha replied.

"I never lie, my child."

"Why did you come?"

"I came to apologize," he said. "I didn't realize you were living like this."

Genetha did not answer. She made no attempt to button up the top of her nightdress.

"The women nowadays," he said, "have bold smiles and a partiality for indecent jokes."

"If you're staying, I'll light the lamp," Genetha offered. "The electricity's not working."

"No, it's all right. My child, will you let me help you?"

"How?" Genetha asked.

"In God there is security and salvation."

"I need money."

He took out a bank note, which she accepted without a word.

"You don't call me 'Father' any more," he protested.

Genetha did not answer.

"It's too late for you or anybody to help me," she said, unable to bear the way he stared at her.

"I know you have relations in Queenstown. Why don't you let. . . ."

"How d'you know so much?"

"You told me about them," he replied, as if he were talking to a forgetful child.

"I don't like asking my relations for anything. Even my brother."

544

"And your brother, what's he done for you?"

Genetha did not answer. As at the time of her last visit to the church he kept looking at her legs. Genetha pulled her nightdress down over her knees. The priest got up and sat beside her on the bed.

"My child, my child! Don't torture me!"

Then, trembling violently, he put his hand under her nightdress and placed it on her knee. He explored the upper reaches of her leg until he touched her pubic hair.

"You pig!" she exclaimed, yielding to the pressure between her thighs.

The bed creaked mercilessly. Outside, the night silence pressed upon the house, broken occasionally by the distant sound of a car in Sussex Street. She remembered her lover, the asylum and the things that had gone for ever. Even now, what she had desired most of all gave her no pleasure. Her chronic malnutrition prevented her body from responding.

Then there was silence in the room. Turning her face to the wall, Genetha heard the rustling of his garments. Then she heard the door knob turn and knew that he was leaving.

Jumping up from the bed, she called, "No! You've got what you wanted so you're slinking away."

"I . . ." he began.

"Stay and talk to me! Tomorrow I'm going to do something terrible. I want to talk to someone tonight."

"All right."

He sat on the edge of the bed, staring at the floor. There were no words, until, in the end, looking round him he asked her:

"Don't you eat?"

"There's nothing in the house," she replied.

"How can you live like that?"

"Hundreds of people've confessed to you, yet you don't know how to make conversation."

"Listen, my child. . . ."

"Don't 'my child' me!" Genetha exploded. "One day we'll run you all out of the country."

"When? In a hundred years? All these political speeches are going to you people's heads. In any case. . . ."

"Just sit there," Genetha said, "you don't have to talk. It's enough to have a human being in the room. I can't bear to be alone. I had a dog, a puppy. But he got run over the day after I got him."

"You said you were going to do something terrible tomorrow," the priest said.

"I was only talking," Genetha answered. "There must be talking . . . . Is it true that if you taught everyone to play at least two games well the crime rate would fall?"

"Hm," said the priest. "And where would you get the money and the facilities?"

"You could use the churches as games rooms. . . . I feel as if my life is drawing away from me. Here, you see, is my life . . . and here I am. They're attached like the engine and carriage of a train. And I feel as if my life is drawing away from me. It's odd. How different you are now from the figure of authority listening to my confession."

"I've got a confession to make. From the first I admired your defiance. It's a quality the early Christians had. . . ."

"I'm not defiant," said Genetha, as if all fight had gone out of her. "I'm submissive. I enjoyed being ruled. If I'm —"

"Then why don't you join the Catholic Church?" he asked.

She was silent for a long time before saying, "I don't know."

Suddenly a thumping from the floor above made them realize that they had been raising their voices.

"I'd better go," he whispered.

"If you want to. It doesn't matter after all."

"Promise — no, you'd better not. Do me a favour . . ." he said.

"No, I won't tell anyone."

"Thank you," he said, looking at her with an odd expression.

Genetha opened the door and he went out into the night. She looked up at the low, fast moving clouds and, feeling afraid, closed the door. Then she lit the kerosene lamp before lying down; but she could not fall asleep. She tossed from one side of the bed to the other and every time the bridge creaked she thought than an intruder might try to enter the house. Each outburst of barking announced a prowler. When, finally she fell into a fitful sleep a wind rose up and she awoke and drew the blanket over her scantily clad body. She could hear the branches of the coconut tree in the back yard and the wind rushing down the street.

Genetha was awakened by a knocking on the window. The

kerosene lamp had gone out and the wind had fallen.

She got up, cautiously drew the blind aside and saw the priest standing on the bridge, half-turned towards the road, but looking back at her room. He must have knocked and withdrawn to the bridge at once.

She was uncertain whether to go and open the door or pretend she had not got up. Raising the window she stood before it without a word, and the priest returned hesitantly.

"You weren't expecting it was me."

"No," Genetha said harshly.

The gutter in front of the house was overflowing and the street was empty under an ashen sky. Looking down at the priest's feet Genetha saw that he was wearing a pair of galoshes.

"Can I come in?" he asked.

"What for? If I stand here talking to you they'll hear upstairs."

"Well, can I come in for a few moments then? I promise I won't be long."

Without answering, Genetha went and opened the door. She followed him into the room. He sat down without being asked, as on the previous visit. Genetha slipped under the blanket, lay full length on the bed and looked up at the floorboards above her head. She had eaten nothing since the day before, but the pain of hunger had given way to a dull sensation in her stomach.

"You're still angry?" he asked.

"That's what you came to ask me?"

"Look," said the priest, his eyes blazing as if he had suddenly come to life, "I'm alone. It's just that I can't talk about myself. The last time I tried to talk to you, but you seemed to be mocking me. I know what annoys you about me, but I can't help it. You can't help what you are. This room – the dirty blinds, the floor, the wooden partition fascinate me. It's hard to explain, but I feel drawn to this room. Don't you want to know how I got your address? You know, I became. . . . You live in a country bursting with love. But instead of reaching out and grabbing it you cut yourself off from everybody. . . ."

"I'm going to do a terrible thing," she interrupted him.

"What? Tell me and perhaps I can help you. I respect you, you know, as I respect the Virgin Mary."

"My brother was murdered in the Essequibo," said Genetha.

"What are you saying? Are you trying to frighten me?" asked

547

the priest in a pleading voice.

"My brother was murdered in the Essequibo," she repeated.

"Why didn't you tell me?"

"What for? You don't listen."

"But you don't know what you're saying. I've spent my life listening."

Then, seeing that Genetha did not want to say anything more to him, he got up. Without warning he threw himself on her and began kissing her fervently on the lips. She struck him in the face with both fists and when he persisted scratched him with both hands. Drawing back he put his right hand to his face.

"Is there a mark?" he asked, alarmed at the thought that she might have left some evidence of their struggle on his face.

"If you don't go. . ." she began.

"All right, all right," he whispered, "I'll go. I'll go, my child."

Genetha turned her head away from him as he passed and then slammed the door after him. She went to the window to watch him walk down the road in the direction of Sussex Street, where the street lamps had already gone out and the morning glow brightened the ridges of the roofs. Someone came down the stairs and left by the front door, closing it gently so as not to disturb the occupants of the house.

She heard the noises of the awakening day, the carts, the stray dogs, the banga mary seller, the bicycle bells, the kiskadees; and the bustle of morning and the silence of afternoon and the falling of day and the gathering night succeeded one another.

She got up at about midnight, took a shower in the corrugated-iron bath in the back yard, dressed and packed her clothes into a cloth bag.

On approaching South Road there was a certain exhilaration in the air. She stopped under a street lamp, took the small mirror from her handbag and looked at herself. Then she patted her hair into place, put back the mirror into the bag and resumed her way. As she crossed the bridge she impulsively threw her cloth bag into the trench, looked down into the water and watched it float for a while, then sink slowly.

Esther's establishment was brightly lit. She could hear music, while shadows appeared and disappeared at the window.

When she opened the door it was Esther who saw her first.

The man to whom she was talking turned round to look at Genetha as well, while Esther came forward and embraced her friend.

"You've come back," Esther said, trying to sound detached.

"Yes."

"I'm glad."

"Eh, eh! Is where you come from?" Netta shouted out across the room. "Eh, eh! You come back!"

"I come back," replied Genetha.

The band was playing a popular tune and the girls were dancing. Salome, despite the violence of the rhythm, was dancing slowly with her partner who at the same time was kissing her on her neck.

There were new girls, who seemed more vulgar than the others. Everyone, apart from Salome, was caught in a frenzy induced by the music, the dancing and the alcohol.

Esther was dragged off by a middle-aged man and Genetha went to sit on a chair against the wall. She knew none of the men, but surveyed them one by one.

"Cigarette?"

The cigarette was offered by a man in his early thirties with a pock-marked face, whom Genetha hardly looked at while stretching her neck to accept his light. They smoked together without talking and when a slow piece was struck up Genetha put her cigarette out and fell on his shoulders. He led her through the crowd of dancers to the middle of the floor where they swayed gently.

The music stopped as the Stabroek Market clock struck one, and the cool air rushed in through the open window and the lattice-work.

Genetha and her friend sat down by the window, then she accepted another cigarette, before looking outside on the empty street and up at the stars. For the first time that day she felt the pain of hunger.

549

Epilogue

The years went by; and the only major event in Genetha's life
– apart from the racial riots that set East Indians against
Africans and Africans against Indians and spawned a breed of
fire-raisers who threatened universal conflagration – was her
grandfather's death, the news of which she heard over the radio.
It came eleven years after she went back to live in Esther's
establishment. She attended the funeral and saw the diminutive
coffin – he had shrunk – being lowered into the grave, and the
spadefuls of clay falling and obscuring the lid, and finally its
disappearance under the indifferent earth. She called to mind
her father's funeral and her ride back with Boyie in the
mourners' carriage. Her grandfather's remains had been transported in a motorized hearse, an abomination, Genetha reflected.

No one recognized her, although here and there she picked
out, apart from her aunts, well-known townspeople and others
she had known. The anonymity she had prayed for years ago
was now complete, for in her seclusion she now hardly saw anyone from the outside world.

Genetha brushed past her aunts, both dressed in black, both
incredibly gaunt, and between them, a frail, veiled old woman
with a pronounced stoop. The austerity of the three women set
them apart from the crowd, like the remnants of a singularly
striking species that was no longer capable of breeding and so
was doomed to extinction.

Genetha herself was grey, her hair yellowing in parts, like the
colour of dead leaves. The slight stoop of her back, although
pointed out by Esther, could not be detected by looking in the
mirror. Besides, she had lost her vanity and even the memory of
it. Making her way among the crowd to the hired car that was
waiting for her she gave no thought of her appearance, only to
the confirmation of her belief that she was indeed nothing in a
town where she had once had mother, father, brother and
grandparents.

Back at the brothel Esther, by way of an indulgence, invited
Genetha for a drive. She only accepted reluctantly and the two
women drove down to the ocean where Esther sat on the wall
looking out over the beach, while Genetha went walking on the
corrugated patterns of sand until she came to the retreating sea.
Here and there jellyfish bobbed up and down on the waves,

Portuguese men-of-war with indigo crests. The sea had left behind masses of seaweed, like the hair of drowned women, wet and limp. Above, gulls were wheeling over the empty expanse of beach and grey water, occasionally diving low to recover just before striking the waves. Genetha, far from reflecting on herself, was thinking of Bigfoot's cedarwood bird-cages, hung out from the back and side windows, on nails hammered into the boards. He had bought her a field canary and a blue saki, whose azure wings soon faded to a lustreless grey.

That night she ate with the household, after which she went up to her room to conjure up the past and the future, before her birth in Agricola and beyond her death in another time of streamlined hearses and small funerals with two cars and the indifferent faces of their occupants. And she heard the drunken voices of children crying out and saw a vast forest of pillars stretching like trees to the unanchored peaks of Akari.

Came July, the season of mangoes, and August, when the plums are ripe. The months passed like leaves from some ill-used picture book, glimpses of a dimly perceived time. And one December evening she sat on the ornate porch that looked out on Croal Street where barristers' chambers stretched in a row, her eyes fixed obsessively on a fine persistent rain that had been falling for most of the day, and which curled and folded in the distance like drifting wreaths of smoke.

The servant was now the mistress, the former mistress's daughter a dependent friend with a room on the upper floor and, for the succession of girls who came and went, an obscure connection with Esther's past.

Genetha woke up on the porch and saw the houses and offices opposite smeared with the colours of morning. She found a shawl round her shoulders, a tasselled, multi-coloured cloth she had never seen before. It must have been Bigfoot who had put it on her while she was sleeping; and she wondered at his devotion.

The sound of birdsong had awakened her, the warbling of canaries singing from their cages as if they were free. Observations floated around in her head, remarks unconnected to one another. "We'll never dance again in Wakenaam!" "What's your direction?" as a young woman once enquired of her address. She smiled and got up from her seat; and at the sight of a shutter of a cottage opposite being pushed open she recalled her own home that had been closed to her, and the woman and her son living next door, hardly ever seen, like polyps in an underwater garden.

Genetha saw the hues of the sun changing by the moment and felt that she had come to the end of a long journey, arriving at a place where she was to be cleansed, to be freed from all notions of happiness and unhappiness, pain or exhilaration. The sun and the smell of grass from the verge were like the broom that swept the house after a corpse had been taken away and the merriment of the wake had been forgotten. Here was the root of all awareness, the knowledge of death, the mystery of time and insights into the unexplored countries of the heart.